超完勝
新制多益
高分5回

黃金試題
1000題

解析版
試題本

U0033632

超完勝新制多益

高分5回 黃金試題 1000題

解析版
試題本 + 解析本

作 者	Ui-Geol Lee／Gi-Won Yun／Global21語學研究所
譯 者	劉嘉珮／蔡裴驊／關亭薇
編 輯	楊維芯
校 對	黃詩韻／申文怡
主 編	丁宥暄
內文排版	洪伊珊／蔡怡柔
封面設計	林書玉
製程管理	洪巧玲
發 行 人	黃朝萍
出 版 者	寂天文化事業股份有限公司
電 話	+886-(0)2-2365-9739
傳 真	+886-(0)2-2365-9835
網 址	www.icosmos.com.tw
讀者服務	onlineservice@icosmos.com.tw
出版日期	2024 年 7 月 二版一刷（寂天雲隨身聽APP版）

國家圖書館出版品預行編目(CIP)資料

超完勝新制多益高分5回：黃金試題1000
題(解析版雙書裝)(寂天雲隨身聽APP版)/
Ui-Geol Lee, Gi-Won Yun, Global21語學
研究所著. -- 二版. --
[臺北市] : 寂天文化事業股份有限公司,
2024.07
　面； 公分
ISBN 978-626-300-268-5(平裝)

1.CST: 多益測驗

805.1895　　　　　　　　113009567

Original Title: 완전절친 실전 토익 5회
Copyright © by Global21 LRIAll rights reserved.
Traditional Chinese Copyright © by Cosmos Culture Ltd.
This Traditional Chinese edition was published by arrangement with Global21co.,
Ltd. through Agency Liang.

CONTENTS

NEW TOEIC 新制多益簡介

多益為針對英語非母語人士所設計,將重點擺在語言原本的功能——溝通能力,評價考生在日常生活或國際業務上所具備的英語應用能力,為全球適用的英語能力測驗。新制多益自 2018 年 3 月起實施,各大題的題數有所更動,增加新的考題類型和文章。但是總題數和測驗時間與改制前相同,整體難易度也維持不變。

測驗內容

測驗項目	Part	題型說明			題數		分數
聽力測驗 45 分鐘	1	**照片描述**(照片印在題本上) 聽完四個短句後,選出最符合照片的描述			6	100	495
	2	**應答問題**(該大題僅有 3 個選項) 聽完題目句後,選出最適當的答句			25		
	3	**簡短對話**(題目和選項皆印在題本上) 聽完對話後,作答 3 個相關問題 新增考題類型 新增三人對話與來回次數超過 5 次以上的對話;新增「**詢問對話中的說話者意圖題**」和「**圖表整合題**」			39		
	4	**簡短獨白**(題目和選項皆印在題本上) 聽完獨白後,作答 3 個相關問題 新增考題類型 新增「**詢問獨白中的說話者意圖題**」和「**圖表整合題**」			30		
閱讀測驗 75 分鐘	5	**句子填空**(文法、詞彙) 從 4 個選項中,選出填入後能使句意最為完整的選項			30	100	495
	6	**段落填空** 從 4 個選項中,選出填入後最符合上下文意的選項 新增考題類型 新增「**句子插入題**」			16		
	7	**閱讀測驗** 閱讀單篇或有關聯性的多篇文章後,作答 2 至 5 個相關問題 新增考題類型 新增文字簡訊和線上聊天文章;新增「**詢問文章中的說話者意圖題**」和「**句子插入題**」	單篇閱讀	29	54		
			雙篇閱讀	10			
			新增考題類型 **多篇閱讀**	15			
總計		7 個大題			200 題		990 分

1 詢問說話者意圖題：題目考的是根據前後文，判斷說話者說出某句話的意圖、意涵或原因，題目會出現在聽力與閱讀測驗中。

→ What does the man mean when he says, ". . . ?"

→ Why does the woman say, ". . . ?"

→ At 2:34 PM, what does Ms. Marna mean when she writes, ". . . ?"

2 圖表整合題：Part 3 和 Part 4 中，題本上會印出圖示或表格，作答時需搭配圖表資訊進行解題。每大題會出現 2 至 3 題。

→ Look at the graphic. Where will the parade start?

3 Part 6 句子插入題：Part 6 的文章中會空出 4 個空格，需根據前後文意，將句子插入最適當的位置。每篇文章會出現 1 題。

4 Part 7 句子插入題：題目考的是將列出的句子插入文中適當的位置。

→ In which of the positions marked [1], [2], [3], and [4] does the following sentence best belong?

命題方向

- **一般商務｜**簽約、協商、行銷、銷售、商業企畫、會議
- **製造業｜**工廠管理、生產線、品管
- **金融與預算｜**銀行、投資、稅金、會計、帳單
- **研發｜**研究、產品開發
- **辦公室｜**董事會、委員會、信件、備忘錄、電話、傳真、電子郵件、辦公室設備與用具
- **人事｜**徵人、僱用、退休、薪資、升遷、應徵與自我介紹
- **住宅、企業房產｜**建築、設計圖、購屋、租賃、電力和瓦斯
- **旅遊｜**火車、飛機、計程車、公車、船隻、郵輪、票務、行程表、車站和機場廣播、租車、飯店、預訂、延期或取消

報名方式

請上官網 www.toeic.com.tw 確認測驗日期、報名時間等相關細節。報名時，請先查看定期場次和新增場次的時間，再選擇欲報考的測驗日期。完成報名後，請務必再次確認報考測驗日期和應試地點。

應試攜帶物品

- **指定身分證件：**國民身分證、有效期限內之護照等，詳細資訊請以多益官網公告為準（如未攜帶者，不得入場考試）
- **考試用具：**2B 鉛筆和橡皮擦（不可使用原子筆或簽字筆）
- **手錶：**指針式手錶（不可使用電子手錶）

成績查詢

通常會於測驗完的 3 周內開放網路查詢。成績單將於測驗結束後 16 個工作日（不含假日）寄發，一般郵局大宗郵件平信寄送作業約需 3-5 個工作天（不含假日）可寄達。多益成績效期為自測驗日起的兩年內。

聽力 & 閱讀高分戰略

聽力

第一大題	照片描述 （6 題）	本大題是測驗看圖作答的能力，可藉由以下方式來練習：找一些照片來看，並思索針對這些照片，可能會問哪些問題。
第二大題	應答問題 （25 題）	本大題是測驗對問句的理解，作答時請特別注意問句開頭的疑問詞（Who、What、Where、When、Why、How 為六大疑問詞），可提示需要什麼樣的答案。
第三大題	簡短對話 （39 題）	本大題會先播放簡短的對話，再測驗你對於對話的理解程度。本大題訣竅是先看問題、答案選項和圖表，然後再聽對話內容，這樣你在聽的時候會比較知道要注意哪方面的資訊。
第四大題	獨白 （30 題）	本大題是聽力測驗中最具挑戰性的部分，平時就需要多聽英文對話和廣播等來加強聽力。

聽力題目前的英文指示 & 高分戰略

In the Listening test, you will be asked to demonstrate how well you understand spoken English. The entire Listening test will last approximately 45 minutes. There are four parts, and directions are given for each part. You must mark your answers on the separate answer sheet. Do not write your answers in your test book.

聽力測驗在測驗考生聽懂英語的能力。整個聽力測驗的進行時間約 45 分鐘，共分四大題，每一大題皆有做答指示。請把答案寫在另一張答案卡上，而不要把答案寫在測驗本上。

I Photographs 第一大題：照片描述

Part 1

Directions: For each question in this part, you will hear four statements about a picture in your test book. When you hear the statements, you must select the one statement that best describes what you see in the picture. Then find the number of the question on your answer sheet and mark your answer. The statements will not be printed in your test book and will be spoken only one time.

Look at the example item below. Now listen to the four statements.

(A) They're pointing at the monitor.
(B) They're looking at the document.
(C) They're talking on the phone.
(D) They're sitting by the table.

Statement (B), "They're looking at the document," is the best description of the picture, so you should select answer (B) and mark it on your answer sheet.

第一大題

指示：本大題的每一小題，在測驗本上都會印有一張圖片，考生會聽到針對照片所做的四段描述，然後選出最符合照片內容的適當描述，接著在答案卡上找到題目編號，將對應的答案選項圓圈塗黑。描述的內容部會印在測驗本上，而且只會播放一次。

（A）他們正指著螢幕。
（B）他們正在看文件。
（C）他們正在講電話。
（D）他們正坐在桌子旁。

描述 (B)「他們正在看文件」是最符合本圖的描述，因此你應該選擇選項 (B)，並在答案卡上劃記。

高分戰略

❶ 如照片以**人物**為主，人物的**動作特徵**是答題關鍵。

照片題中有 7–8 成的題目是以人物為照片主角，這些照片時常會測驗人的動作特徵，因此要先預想相關的動作用語。舉例來說，如照片中有一個人在走路，就要立刻想到和走路有關的動詞，如 walking、strolling 等，聽題目的時候會更容易抓到線索。

❷ 如照片以**事物**為主，事物的**狀態或位置**是答題關鍵。

如照片以事物為中心，要特別注意其狀態或位置。準備方式為預先熟習表示「位置」時經常會用到的介系詞，還有表現「狀態」的片語。舉例來說，如要表達「在……旁邊」時，next to、by、beside、near 等用語可能會出現，最好整組一起背誦。另外，也須事先熟悉多益中常出現的事物名稱。

❸ 出人意料的問題時常出現。

與一般題型不同，題目的考點可能會靈活變化，這已成為一種出題趨勢。舉例來說，照片是一個小孩用手指著掛在牆上的畫，按照常理，會想到是要考人物的動作，要回答 pointing 之類的動詞。但有時正確答案會是掛在牆上的畫（The picture has been hung on the wall.）。所以出現人的照片時，除了注意人的動作，周邊事物也必須稍微觀察。一定要是照片中可看出的資訊才會是正確答案，且有時考點不會是第一眼看圖時想到的問題。

Let's at the example item below. Now listen to the four statements.

(A) They're painting of the medical
(B) They're looking at the documents.
(C) They're talking on the phone.
(D) They're sitting by the table

best answer (B) and mark it on your

Part 2

Directions: You will hear a question or statement and three responses spoken in English. They will be spoken only one time and will not be printed in your test book. Select the best response to the question or statement and mark the letter (A), (B), or (C) on your answer sheet.

第二大題

指示：考生會聽到一個問題句或敘述句，以及三句回應的英語。題目只會撥放一次，而且不會印在測驗本上。請選出最符合擺放內容的答案，在答案卡上將 (A)、(B)、(C) 或 (D) 的答案選項塗黑。

高分戰略

❶ 新制加考**推測語意**的考題。

PART 2 少了五題，但命題方式變得更靈活，難度也隨之提升。新制多了推測語意的考題，考生必須根據全文判斷語意才能找出答案。聽完此類題目後，須迅速推敲並挑出正確的答案，才不會錯失下一題的解題機會。請務必勤加練習，熟悉此類題型的模式。

❷ 題目最前面的**疑問詞**至關重要。

Part 2 經常出現以疑問詞（Who、What、Where、When、Why、How）開頭的疑問句，會出約 9–10 題。只要聽清楚句首的疑問詞，幾乎就能找到這類題型的正確答案，所以平常要培養對疑問詞的聽力敏銳度。

❸ 善用**消去法**縮小選擇範圍。

Part 2 是最多陷阱的大題，所以事先統整陷阱題可以事半功倍。舉例來說，若疑問句題目以疑問詞開頭，那幾乎可以判斷用 yes 或 no 回答的選項不可選，可以先將其刪除。另外，若題目出現的單字在選項中再次出現，或出現與題目中字彙發音類似的單字，如 copy 與 coffee，也是常見陷阱題。在準備時可將具代表性的陷阱題整理好，以提升本大題的答對率。

❹ 常考**片語**要熟背。

多益中常出現的用語或片語，最好整組背起來。舉例來說，疑問句「Why don't you . . . ?」是表達「做……好嗎？」的提議句型，而非詢問原因。這類用語時常會快速唸過，所以事先整個背起來，會增加理解聽力內容的速度。

III Conversations 第三大題：簡短對話

Part 3

Directions: You will hear some conversations between two or more people. You will be asked to answer three questions about what the speakers say in each conversation. Select the best response to each question and mark the letter (A), (B), (C), or (D) on your answer sheet. The conversations will not be printed in your test book and will be spoken only one time.

第三大題

指示：考生會聽到一些兩個人或多人的對話，並根據對話所聽到的內容，回答三個問題。請選出最符合播放內容的答案，在答案卡上將 (A)、(B)、(C) 或 (D) 的答案選項塗黑。這些對話只會播放一次，而且不會印在測驗本上。

高分戰略

❶ 有策略地聽比全部聽更高效。

Part 3 是兩到三人的對話，每組對話要回答三道題。本大題作答時並非十分吃力地記下全部內容，而是事先快速瀏覽題目和圖表，判斷須注意哪些線索，在聽對話時重點記下與題目對應的資訊。本大題擬出聽力策略才可奪高分。

❷ 聽對話與找答案要同步進行。

光是事先掃過題目，而沒有邊聽邊找答案，仍無法達到高答對率，因為有些細微訊息聽過後很容易忘記。邊聽邊作答的能力於新制多益中更為重要，因為新增了角色性別及彼此關係更為複雜的三人對話題，所以避免聽完後混淆的方式則是立刻作答。這項能力較難速成，須在平時就不斷積累。

❸ 對話開頭不可漏聽。

詢問職業、場所或主題的問題在 Part 3 中經常出現，這些問題的答案時常會出現在對話開頭。不僅如此，掌握對話開頭也可幫助推敲接下來會出現什麼內容，讓解其他題目更為順利。

IV Talks 第四大題：簡短獨白

Part 4

Directions: You will hear some talks given by a single speaker. You will be asked to answer three questions about what the speaker says in each talk. Select the best response to each question and mark the letter (A), (B), (C), or (D) on your answer sheet. The talks will not be printed in your test book and will be spoken only one time.

第四大題

指示： 考生會聽到好幾段單人獨白，並根據每一段話的內容，回答三個問題。請選出符合播放內容的答案，在答案卡上將 (A)、(B)、(C) 或 (D) 的答案選項塗黑。每一段話只會播放一次，而且不會印在測驗本上。

高分戰略

❶ 要事先整理好**常考的詢問內容**。

不同於 Part 3，本大題談話種類較固定，像是交通廣播、天氣預報、旅行導覽、電話留言等的題目經常出現，且內容大同小異。所以只需要按這些談話種類，整理出常考的問題類型即可。舉例來說，跟電話溝通相關的主題，時常都在開頭出現「I'm calling to . . .」，聽到這個敘述後，要找出正確答案就容易多了。

❷ 具備**背景知識**可加快答題速度。

Part 4 的談話種類是有固定模式，題目做多了會發現考法大同小異。舉例來說，若是機場的情境談話，飛機誤點或取消是最典型的情境，最可能的原因則是天候不佳，這就是多益的背景知識——不一定要全部聽懂，光看題目也能找出最接近正確答案的選項。平時多累積背景知識很重要。

❸ 訓練找出**重點線索**的能力。

Part 4 和 Part 3 一樣，每個題組有三個問題，所以同樣要養成先掃描過題目和表格的習慣。由於 Part 4 的談話內容更長，全部內容聽完後再答題很容易會有所遺漏。因此可以先找出題目的要點，利用背景知識，在試題本上推敲正確答案。不像 Part 3，Part 4 的答案通常會按照題目的順序，一一出現在對話中，答案逐題出現的機率很高。

閱讀 ··

第五大題	句子填空 （30 題）	本大題字彙和文法能力最重要。其所考的字彙大都跟職場或商業有關，平時就要多背誦單字。
第六大題	段落填空 （16 題）	除了單字，也需要將比較長的片語或子句，甚至是一整個句子填入空格中，掌握整篇文章來龍去脈才能找出答案。
第七大題	單篇文章理解 （29 題） 多篇文章理解 （25 題）	本大題比較困難，須熟習經常出現的商業文章，像是公告或備忘錄等。平時就要訓練自己能夠快速閱讀文章和圖表，並且能夠找出主要的內容。當然，在本大題字彙量越多，越可快速理解文意。

閱讀題目前的英文指示 & 高分戰略

In the Reading test, you will read a variety of texts and answer several different types of reading comprehension questions. The entire Reading test will last 75 minutes. There are three parts, and directions are given for each part. You are encouraged to answer as many questions as possible within the time allowed. You must mark your answers on the separate answer sheet. Do not write your answers in your test book.

在閱讀測驗中，考生會讀到各種文章，並回答各種型式的閱讀測驗題目。整個閱讀測驗的進行時間為 75 分鐘 。本測驗共分三大題，每一大題皆有做答指示。請在規定的時間內，盡可能地作答。請把答案寫在另一張答案卡上，而不要把答案寫在測驗本上。

Part 5

Directions: A word or phrase is missing in each of the sentences below. Four answer choices are given below each sentence. Select the best answer to complete the sentence. Then mark the letter (A), (B), (C), or (D) on your answer sheet.

第五大題

指示：本測驗中的每一個句子皆缺少一個單字或詞組，在句子下方會列出四個答案選項，請選出最適合的答案來完成句子，並在做答卡上將 (A)、(B)、(C) 或 (D) 的答案選項塗黑。

高分戰略

❶ 要先看**選項**。

試題主要考句型、字彙、文法以及慣用語。要先看選項，掌握是上述的哪一個，便能更快速解題。所以要練習判斷題型，並正確掌握各題型的解題技巧。

❷ 找出**意思最接近**的單字。

Part 5 是填空選擇題，若能找出和空格關係最密切的關鍵字彙，便能快速又正確地解題。所以要練習分析句子的結構，並找出和空格關係最密切的字彙作為答題線索。一般來說，空格前後的單字就是線索。舉例來說，如果空格後有名詞，此名詞就是空格的線索單字，以此名詞可以猜想出空格可能是個形容詞。

❸ 擴大**片語量**。

多益會拿來出題的字彙，通常以片語形式出現。最具代表的是：動詞和受詞、形容詞和名詞、介系詞和名詞、動詞和副詞等。有些詞組中每個單字都懂，但合起來就並非所猜想的中文意思。因此，平日要將這些片語視為一個單位整個背下來。舉例來說，中文說「打電話」，但英文是「make a phone call」；而付錢打電話不能用「pay a phone call」，要用「pay for the phone call」。但是多益中 Part 5 考「pay for the phone call」的可能性很低，因為多益大多出常見用語，而這句不是。所以，常考片語要直接背起來，不要直接用中文去猜想，才可在本大題奪得高分。

Part 6

Directions: Read the texts that follow. A word, phrase, or sentence is missing in parts of each text. Four answer choices for each question are given below the text. Select the best answer to complete the text. Then mark the letter (A), (B), (C), or (D) on your answer sheet.

第六大題

指示：閱讀本大題的文章，文章中的某些句子缺少單字、片語或句子，這些句子都會有四個答案選項，請選出最適合的答案來完成文章中的空格，並在做答卡上將 (A)、(B)、(C) 或 (D) 的答案選項塗黑。

高分戰略

❶ 掌握**空格前後**的文意。

Part 5 和 Part 6 不同的地方是，Part 5 只探究一個句子的結構，而 Part 6 要探究句子和句子間的關係，因此要練習觀察空格前後句子彼此的連結關係。如果有空格的句子是第一句，要看後一句來解題；如果有空格的句子是第二句，就要看前一句來解題。偶爾，也有要看整篇文章才能作答的題目。PART 6 最難處在於要從選項的四個句子中，選出適當的句子填入空格中。此為新制增加的題型，不僅要多費時解題，平時也得多花功夫訓練掌握上下文意。

❷ 掌握**動詞時態**

Part 5 的動詞時態問題，只要看該句子內的動詞是否符合時態即可，但 Part 6 的動詞時態，要看其他句子才能決定該句空格中的時態。大部分的時態題目都區分為：已發生的事或尚未發生的事。從上下文來看，已發生的事，要用現在完成式或過去式；尚未發生的事，就選包含 will 等與未來式相關的助動詞（will、shall、may 等）選項，或用「be going to . . .」。針對 Part 6 的時態問題，多練習區分已發生的事和尚未發生的事便能順利答題。

❸ 掌握**連接副詞**的功用

所謂的連接副詞，是指翻譯時要和前面的內容一起翻譯的副詞。一般來說，這不會出現在只考一句話的 Part 5，而會出現在有多個句子的 Part 6。舉例來說，副詞 therefore 是「因此」的意思，所以若前後句的內容有因果關係，多半會用它。若是轉折語氣，用有「然而」含意的 however。此外，連接副詞還有 otherwise（否則）、consequently（因此）、additionally（此外）、instead（反而）等。另外，連接詞用於連接句子，而連接副詞是單獨使用的，要將它們做清楚區分。

Part 7

Directions: In this part you will read a selection of texts, such as magazine and newspaper articles, emails, and instant messages. Each text or set of texts is followed by several questions. Select the best answer for each question and mark the letter (A), (B), (C), or (D) on your answer sheet.

第七大題

指示：這大題中會閱讀到不同題材的文章，如雜誌和新聞文章、電子郵件或通訊軟體的訊息等。每篇或每組文章之後會有數個題目，請選出最適合的答案，並在做答卡上將 (A)、(B)、(C) 或 (D) 的答案選項塗黑。

高分戰略

❶ **字彙量**是答題關鍵。

字彙能力是在 Part 7 奪取高分最重要的一環，它能幫助你正確且快速地理解整個篇章。平時就要將意思相似的字彙或用語一起熟記，以快速增加字彙量。

❷ 要將問題**分類**。

Part 7 的題目看似無規則可循，事實上可以分作幾種類型，如：

① 細節訊息類型：詢問文章細節。
② 主題類型：詢問文章主題。
③ NOT 類型：詢問哪個選項是錯誤資訊。
④ 邏輯推演類型：從文章提供的線索推知內容。
⑤ 文意填空類型：將題目中的句子填入文意通順的地方。

在解題前先將題目分類，解題會更有頭緒。

❸ 複合式文章題要注意彼此**關聯性**。

從 176 題開始是複合式文章類型，每題組由兩到三篇文章組成，有許多問題出自多篇文章內容的相關性。解題關鍵在於找出相關或相同的地方，並注意篇章之間是以何種方式連接。

❹ 培養耐力。

Part 7 是整個聽力閱讀測驗的尾聲，注意力是否在前面的奮戰後仍高度集中是勝負的關鍵。平常要訓練至少要持續一個小時不休息地解題，養成習慣才能在正式考試時不被疲勞打敗。

〔寂天編輯群整理製作〕

SELF CHECK 自我檢測表

請以參加實際測驗的心態作答每回試題，並於作答完畢後，紀錄測驗結果。此作法將有助於提升學習動力與專注力。

		作答日期	作答時間	答對題數	答對總題數	下個目標
Actual Test 1	聽力					寫完所有題目！
	閱讀					
Actual Test 2	聽力					要有更遠大的夢想！
	閱讀					
Actual Test 3	聽力					我做得很好！
	閱讀					
Actual Test 4	聽力					離目標越來越近了！
	閱讀					
Actual Test 5	聽力					我做得到！
	閱讀					

Actual Test

1

手機關機！
開啟聽力 MP3！
保持專注 2 小時！

Check

開始時間 ＿＿＿：＿＿＿

完成時間 ＿＿＿：＿＿＿

LISTENING TEST

In the Listening test, you will be asked to demonstrate how well you understand spoken English. The entire Listening test will last approximately 45 minutes. There are four parts, and directions are given for each part. You must mark your answers on the separate answer sheet. Do not write your answers in your test book.

PART 1 🎧01

Directions: For each question in this part, you will hear four statements about a picture in your test book. When you hear the statements, you must select the one statement that best describes what you see in the picture. Then find the number of the question on your answer sheet and mark your answer. The statements will not be printed in your test book and will be spoken only one time.

Statement (C), "They're sitting at the table," is the best description of the picture, so you should select answer (C) and mark it on your answer sheet.

1.

2.

GO ON TO THE NEXT PAGE

3.

4.

5.

6.

GO ON TO THE NEXT PAGE

PART 2 🎧02

Directions: You will hear a question or statement and three responses spoken in English. They will not be printed in your test book and will be spoken only one time. Select the best response to the question or statement and mark the letter (A), (B), or (C) on your answer sheet.

7. Mark your answer on your answer sheet.

8. Mark your answer on your answer sheet.

9. Mark your answer on your answer sheet.

10. Mark your answer on your answer sheet.

11. Mark your answer on your answer sheet.

12. Mark your answer on your answer sheet.

13. Mark your answer on your answer sheet.

14. Mark your answer on your answer sheet.

15. Mark your answer on your answer sheet.

16. Mark your answer on your answer sheet.

17. Mark your answer on your answer sheet.

18. Mark your answer on your answer sheet.

19. Mark your answer on your answer sheet.

20. Mark your answer on your answer sheet.

21. Mark your answer on your answer sheet.

22. Mark your answer on your answer sheet.

23. Mark your answer on your answer sheet.

24. Mark your answer on your answer sheet.

25. Mark your answer on your answer sheet.

26. Mark your answer on your answer sheet.

27. Mark your answer on your answer sheet.

28. Mark your answer on your answer sheet.

29. Mark your answer on your answer sheet.

30. Mark your answer on your answer sheet.

31. Mark your answer on your answer sheet.

PART 3 🎧 03

Directions: You will hear some conversations between two or more people. You will be asked to answer three questions about what the speakers say in each conversation. Select the best response to each question and mark the letter (A), (B), (C), or (D) on your answer sheet. The conversations will not be printed in your test book and will be spoken only one time.

32. Where is the man going?
(A) To a bus stop
(B) To a concert hall
(C) To a sports venue
(D) To a theater

33. What is mentioned about Satellite Avenue?
(A) It is a new street.
(B) It is being repaired.
(C) It is closed.
(D) It is near downtown.

34. What does the woman suggest the man do?
(A) Catch a taxi
(B) Go home
(C) Ride the Blue Line
(D) Wait for the next bus

35. Who most likely is the man?
(A) A branch manager
(B) A job candidate
(C) A job recruiter
(D) A reporter

36. How long has the man been working in his current job?
(A) 2 months
(B) 3 months
(C) Half a year
(D) A year

37. What is mentioned about the man's family?
(A) His wife is not happy with his job.
(B) His wife got a new position.
(C) They are from Oak City.
(D) They do not want to relocate.

38. Why does the woman apologize?
(A) Because she has to cancel the appointment.
(B) Because she is late for the meeting.
(C) Because she needs to reschedule the meeting.
(D) Because she refused the man's offer.

39. What does the man mean when he says, "Works for me"?
(A) He is agreeing with the place to meet.
(B) He is fine with a video chat.
(C) The suggested schedule is convenient for him.
(D) The woman works in his department.

40. What will the speakers discuss at their meeting?
(A) A collaboration plan
(B) A merger
(C) The man's budget ideas
(D) The woman's qualifications

41. What did the woman do on the weekend?
(A) She did home repair works.
(B) She did some gardening.
(C) She visited an amusement park.
(D) She visited her parents.

42. What did the man have trouble doing?
(A) Deciding where to go
(B) Finding his destination
(C) Getting a parking space
(D) Making a reservation

43. What will the woman probably do next?
(A) Call her children
(B) Look at some photos
(C) Take a break
(D) Talk about her holiday

GO ON TO THE NEXT PAGE

44. How many people will accompany the man to the restaurant?

(A) 3
(B) 4
(C) 5
(D) 6

45. What is mentioned about one of the man's party?

(A) She has a serious allergy.
(B) She is a vegetarian.
(C) She likes the table with a view.
(D) She will show up late.

46. Why does the man say, "That's a relief"?

(A) He is concerned his guests will not like the restaurant.
(B) He is glad the chef can do what he asks.
(C) He is happy to get a reservation at a busy time.
(D) He is worried that there will not be enough menu choices.

47. Where is the conversation taking place?

(A) In a community center
(B) In a hotel
(C) In a library
(D) In a retirement home

48. What problem does the woman mention?

(A) The building is old.
(B) The construction outside is noisy.
(C) The heater is not working properly.
(D) The rooms are too cold.

49. What will the man do next?

(A) Call the maintenance department
(B) Have his lunch
(C) Listen to a lecture
(D) Retrieve his tools

50. Why is the man congratulating the woman?

(A) She got married.
(B) She got promoted.
(C) She received an honor.
(D) She won a contract.

51. What does the woman say about her group?

(A) They have not worked with her before.
(B) They put in a lot of effort.
(C) They were not cooperative with her.
(D) They will get reassigned soon.

52. What kind of products does the woman's company sell?

(A) Clothes
(B) Digital devices
(C) Automobile
(D) Medicine

53. What is the man's problem?

(A) He cannot find a photographer for a project.
(B) He does not have enough pictures for a catalog.
(C) He does not have the right kind of pictures.
(D) His deadline is already past.

54. What will happen in two weeks?

(A) A photographer will be available.
(B) An update will be finished.
(C) The man will get a job.
(D) The woman will take over the project.

55. What does the woman offer to do for the man?

(A) Accompany him to a photo shoot
(B) Call a different photographer
(C) Find a new studio
(D) Review a previous catalog

56. What are the speakers mainly discussing?
    (A) A business trip
    (B) A new company policy
    (C) Their new branch
    (D) Their recent vacations

57. What does the man mention about Singapore?
    (A) It has a lot of good food.
    (B) It has many sightseeing spots.
    (C) It is a beautiful city.
    (D) It is easy to get around.

58. What does the speakers' boss want them to do?
    (A) Go over the inspection checklist
    (B) Save on costs
    (C) Stay in a specific hotel
    (D) Treat a facility manager to dinner

59. What is the woman's problem?
    (A) She cannot find her ID.
    (B) She forgot her purse.
    (C) She is lost.
    (D) She is missing some papers.

60. Who most likely is the man?
    (A) A building security officer
    (B) A taxi driver
    (C) A traffic reporter
    (D) Her colleague

61. What does the woman imply when she says, "I won't be long"?
    (A) She does not want to go to the meeting.
    (B) She does not want to turn right.
    (C) She prefers a short conversation.
    (D) She will come back soon.

62. What is the purpose of the meeting?
    (A) To conduct an employee evaluation
    (B) To discuss a new branch
    (C) To interview a job candidate
    (D) To offer a position

63. Who most likely is Mr. Evans?
    (A) The company president
    (B) The overseas branch head
    (C) The Personnel Department director
    (D) The woman's direct supervisor

64. What does the woman need to do by the end of the month?
    (A) Find a new job
    (B) Get a visa
    (C) Make a decision
    (D) Move to Shanghai

GO ON TO THE NEXT PAGE

Name	Monthly Fee	Songs available /month	Devices
Music Depot	$8.50	unlimited	phone
PlayNow	$5.00	2,000	phone
Smartsound	$3.99	1,000	phone, PC
X Hits	$9.50	unlimited	phone, PC

65. What does the woman say about the service?

    (A) It is convenient.

    (B) It is high-tech.

    (C) It is priced fairly.

    (D) It is very popular.

66. Where does the man like to listen to music in particular?

    (A) At home

    (B) At the gym

    (C) At work

    (D) On the train

67. Look at the graphic. Which service will the woman most likely choose?

    (A) Music Depot

    (B) PlayNow

    (C) Smartsound

    (D) X Hits

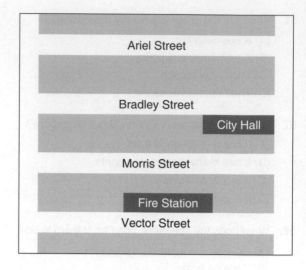

68. What can be said about the parade?

    (A) It was successful last year.

    (B) It will be canceled this year.

    (C) It will be held for the first time.

    (D) Its budget was increased.

69. Look at the graphic. Where will the parade start?

    (A) On Ariel Street

    (B) On Bradley Street

    (C) On Morris Street

    (D) On Vector Street

70. What does the woman say she will do?

    (A) Call City Hall

    (B) Fill out a job application

    (C) Help the man with the paperwork

    (D) Visit a government office

PART 4 🎧04

Directions: You will hear some talks given by a single speaker. You will be asked to answer three questions about what the speaker says in each talk. Select the best response to each question and mark the letter (A), (B), (C), or (D) on your answer sheet. The talks will not be printed in your test book and will be spoken only one time.

71. What is implied about Orangeton?
    (A) It is experiencing a lot of growth.
    (B) It is getting a professional sports team.
    (C) It is Mr. Jones' place of birth.
    (D) It is the speaker's favorite place.

72. How long was Mr. Jones a professional athlete?
    (A) For 5 years
    (B) For 8 years
    (C) For 10 years
    (D) For 20 years

73. What did Mr. Jones recently do?
    (A) Opened a store
    (B) Left a hospital
    (C) Played in a tournament
    (D) Traveled around

74. Who is the caller?
    (A) A business owner
    (B) The listener's friend
    (C) An engineer
    (D) A weather forecaster

75. What can the listener provide?
    (A) A catering service
    (B) Locally-grown food
    (C) A new window
    (D) A quotation

76. What does Mr. Conklin ask the listener to do?
    (A) Call back quickly
    (B) Contact his assistant
    (C) Reply by e-mail
    (D) Stop by his office

77. What kind of business is being advertised?
    (A) Childcare service
    (B) Cleaning service
    (C) Delivery service
    (D) Elderly care service

78. What does the speaker mean when she says, "It will give you a big lift"?
    (A) The service will make listeners save money.
    (B) The service will be used to make listeners feel lighter.
    (C) The service will make listeners happy.
    (D) The service will take listeners where they need to go.

79. Who can get a discount?
    (A) Those who give a discount code
    (B) Those who have a certain size house
    (C) Those who have not used the service before
    (D) Those who live in a certain area

80. What will the new bridge go over?
    (A) A lake
    (B) A river
    (C) A valley
    (D) Some train tracks

81. Why was the project delayed?
    (A) The citizens did not want to approve it.
    (B) The city could not decide on a builder.
    (C) The city did not have the money.
    (D) The construction company had problems.

82. What is the construction company expected to do?
    (A) Employ many people
    (B) Give a press conference
    (C) Start the bidding process
    (D) Underbid its rivals

GO ON TO THE NEXT PAGE

83. Where is the announcement taking place?

(A) At a bookstore

(B) At a clothing store

(C) At a grocery store

(D) At a shoe store

84. What does the speaker imply when she says, "business really picked up between 5:00 and 7:00 PM"?

(A) A lot of customers came during the evening.

(B) The customers used a shuttle bus to come to the store.

(C) A special discount was offered in the evening.

(D) Those who work in the evening were paid double.

85. What will listeners receive if they work longer this weekend?

(A) A bonus

(B) Free merchandise

(C) Higher salary

(D) A paid day off

86. What is being advertised?

(A) A drink

(B) A health food

(C) A medication

(D) A supplement

87. Who can use the advertised product?

(A) Anyone

(B) Hospital patients only

(C) Students only

(D) Those over 15

88. Where can the product be purchased?

(A) At a health exhibition

(B) At all health food stores

(C) At any drugstore

(D) On the Web

89. What is the talk mainly about?

(A) An expansion of the office

(B) A new employee's first day

(C) Parking location changes

(D) Public transportation fees

90. What are listeners encouraged to do?

(A) Keep their desks clean

(B) Participate in a survey

(C) Ride to work together

(D) Welcome a new employee

91. According to the speaker, what might some listeners experience next week?

(A) A long walk

(B) Loud construction noise

(C) Low temperatures in the office

(D) A new desk assignment

Fern Grove Department Store	
♪♪ Thank you for shopping with us today. ♪♪	
Women's blouse	$55.00
Tax (10%)	$5.50
Total	$60.50
We appreciate our customer's feedback: www.ferngrovedepart.com	

92. What discount can a customer get on a child's jacket at most?

(A) 30 percent

(B) 40 percent

(C) 50 percent

(D) 60 percent

93. When does the sale end?

(A) This afternoon at 5:00

(B) Tonight at 8:00

(C) Tomorrow at 12:00

(D) Tomorrow night at 8:00

94. Look at the graphic. What can the customer receive?

(A) An extra discount

(B) A free gift

(C) Free parking

(D) A refund

Platform	Time	Destination
1	15:30	Arendale
2	15:35	Hastings Cross
3	15:45	Gilmore Station
4	15:48	Green River

95. What industry does the speaker work in?

(A) Architecture
(B) Construction
(C) Medical
(D) Publishing

96. Look at the graphic. Which room will be smaller after the renovation?

(A) The meeting room
(B) The office area
(C) The storage room
(D) The studio

97. What most likely will the listeners do next?

(A) Discuss the office layout
(B) Have lunch together
(C) Plan a new product
(D) Speak with an architect

98. Who most likely is the speaker?

(A) A passenger
(B) A train conductor
(C) A train driver
(D) A train station staff

99. Look at the graphic. What time is the train to Gilmore Station going to leave?

(A) 15:35
(B) 15:45
(C) 15:48
(D) 15:55

100. Where should passengers with reserved tickets go?

(A) Car 1
(B) Car 2
(C) Car 4
(D) Car 8

This is the end of the Listening test. Turn to Part 5 in your test book.

READING TEST

In the Reading test, you will read a variety of texts and answer several different types of reading comprehension questions. The entire Reading test will last 75 minutes. There are three parts, and directions are given for each part. You are encouraged to answer as many questions as possible within the time allowed.

You must mark your answers on the separate answer sheet. Do not write your answers in your test book.

PART 5

Directions: A word or phrase is missing in each of the sentences below. Four answer choices are given below each sentence. Select the best answer to complete the sentence. Then mark the letter (A), (B), (C), or (D) on your answer sheet.

101. If you would like to book one of our meeting rooms, please let us know if you need any ------- such as a projector or a video camera.
(A) equipment
(B) amenities
(C) instruments
(D) materials

102. AtoZ Industry offers plenty of ------- office furniture and supplies suitable for your needs.
(A) rent
(B) rental
(C) renter
(D) rents

103. If you have a problem installing our software on your computer, you can call ------- send an e-mail to our customer service staff.
(A) and
(B) nor
(C) or
(D) to

104. The city council ------- receives architectural proposals created by a group of graduate students.
(A) recently
(B) similarly
(C) highly
(D) regularly

105. As the keynote speech was cancelled at the last minute, the event organizer had to find a -------.
(A) replace
(B) replaceable
(C) replacing
(D) replacement

106. The leader talked at length about how practical his project plan was ------- all of his team members agreed to proceed.
(A) in case
(B) given that
(C) until
(D) whether

107. Sarah Luther had to hurry back to her office to attend a ------- seminar for the new intranet system.
(A) numerous
(B) mandatory
(C) versatile
(D) voluntary

108. Because of a heating problem, the sales team had to hold their meeting in an ------- cold room.
(A) exceed
(B) exceeded
(C) exceeding
(D) exceedingly

109. All employees are required to acknowledge that ------- have been informed of the new company policy and agree to it in all respects.

(A) theirs
(B) them
(C) themselves
(D) they

110. Melba Logistics is a licensed carrier ------- rapid and safe transportation services all over the world.

(A) forwarding
(B) equipping
(C) providing
(D) receiving

111. More than 300 people ------- 50 different countries took part in the 15th International Conference on Environmental Science.

(A) among
(B) from
(C) over
(D) through

112. With the board members' -------, Mr. Henderson will assume the post of chairperson next month.

(A) endorsable
(B) endorse
(C) endorsement
(D) endorser

113. If you have any problems with or questions about the network access -------, please ask our IT department.

(A) selection
(B) advance
(C) protocol
(D) sequence

114. According to the financial advisor, conducting ------- research beforehand is crucial for buying stocks.

(A) detail
(B) detailed
(C) detailing
(D) details

115. The personnel chief considers that asking an unexpected question can be useful to judge candidates ------- interviewing them.

(A) as well as
(B) unless
(C) still
(D) when

116. Rather than partially modifying it, the team manager thought they should reconsider the ------- design of the new product.

(A) center
(B) extra
(C) main
(D) whole

117. As the contract is coming to an end, the company will have to remove all possessions and ------- the rented property by the end of the week.

(A) vacancies
(B) vacancy
(C) vacant
(D) vacate

118. The consumer trends report found that people have recently spent ------- money on vacations and have saved it instead.

(A) fewer
(B) less
(C) many
(D) more

119. The new laptop, TGX 800, received many good reviews as it has been ------- improved from its old model and is a lot easier to use.

(A) mostly
(B) drastically
(C) scarcely
(D) temporarily

120. The CEO is extremely concerned that the company's stock price ------- steadily over the past few weeks.

(A) has dropped
(B) has been dropping
(D) is dropping
(D) will drop

GO ON TO THE NEXT PAGE

121. -------, the product launch went quite smoothly even though several urgent changes were made.

(A) Surprise
(B) Surprised
(C) Surprising
(D) Surprisingly

122. Mason Engineering has ------- some major changes over the year to become more customer-focused.

(A) underestimated
(B) undergone
(C) undermined
(D) understood

123. An e-mail was sent to notify all the participants that the event would take place at Hamilton Hall ------- Celia Hall.

(A) prior to
(B) instead of
(C) though
(D) thus

124. There were nearly 1,000 people ------- at the protest against the discontinuation of free bus passes for seniors.

(A) present
(B) presentation
(C) presented
(D) presenter

125. The collected personal information will not be disclosed to third parties without prior -------, except under court order.

(A) analysis
(B) consent
(C) discussion
(D) engagement

126. Compromise does not always resolve the issues ------- contain underlying interpersonal conflicts.

(A) what
(B) that
(C) where
(D) whose

127. Jade Private Hospital has established an excellent reputation in the community for its high ------- to patient satisfaction.

(A) commit
(B) commitment
(C) committal
(D) committed

128. As the restaurant has been -------, the owner is considering expanding his business in the region.

(A) productive
(B) prosperous
(C) strategic
(D) struggling

129. At the lecture, the renowned chef told the audience ------- such an easy recipe could result in such a delicious dish.

(A) as if
(B) despite
(C) how
(D) then

130. Even after spending long hours trying to fix it, the IT worker could not iron ------- the problem with the network.

(A) down
(B) off
(C) out
(D) over

PART 6

Directions: Read the texts that follow. A word, phrase, or sentence is missing in parts of each text. Four answer choices for each question are given below the text. Select the best answer to complete the text. Then mark the letter (A), (B), (C), or (D) on your answer sheet.

Questions 131-134 refer to the following e-mail.

To: Amanda Green
From: Exciting Travel Co.
Subject: Visit Costa Rica
Date: March 19

Exciting Travel's Top Three Reasons You Should Visit Costa Rica

1. ------- you crave adventure, Costa Rica is definitely the place for you. You can go white-water
   131.

rafting, kayaking, scuba diving, cliff diving, sky diving… the list is endless.

2. -------. Both public and private beaches are sure to please lovers of sun and sand like -------.
   132.   **133.**

3. Costa Rica has been called the happiest country on Earth, and for good reason. The people are

peaceful, friendly and go out of their way to make every visitor feel at home.

For details about our travel ------- to Costa Rica, please visit our Website: www.excitingtravel.net.
                             134.

---

131. (A) If
(B) Probably
(C) Where
(D) Whether

132. (A) Costa Rica has a world-famous rainforest and many environmental organizations give tours of it.
(B) If you have kids, you'll definitely want to take advantage of our resort's six swimming pools.
(C) We have several great travel deals to Costa Rica, but they expire soon so don't put it off —call today.
(D) With almost 1,000 miles of coastline, Costa Rica is home to some of the world's loveliest beaches.

133. (A) ourselves
(B) them
(C) themselves
(D) yourself

134. (A) agency
(B) insurance
(C) package
(D) tips

GO ON TO THE NEXT PAGE

Media Company to Relocate to Stamford

STAMFORD—Blasted, a live-streaming media company ------- in Westville, plans to move within the
135.

next few months to an office park in Stamford's south end. The firm is set to make the move during the

second quarter of this year after ------- a long-term lease for 9,500 square feet at Brookbend Center.
136.

"Brookbend Center has been home to many high technology companies ------- its founding, and
137.

we're pleased Blasted is making Brookbend its future home," property manager Jonathan Turner said

in a statement. Situated next to the Norton River, Brookbend Center covers 40 acres. It features a

conference room that can hold up to 200 people, an auditorium, and six meeting rooms. -------.
138.

---

135. (A) base
(B) based
(C) is basing
(D) was based

136. (A) creating
(B) losing
(C) proposing
(D) signing

137. (A) by
(B) since
(C) until
(D) yet

138. (A) Mr. Turner is taking applications from other prospective tenants for an available office unit.
(B) The company will expand its domestic manufacturing capacity after the move, sources say.
(C) The office center also includes a cafeteria, 1,457 parking spaces, and several walking trails.
(D) Time will tell if the move by Blasted will result in higher earnings for their struggling products.

Questions 139-142 refer to the following memo.

MEMORANDUM

To: All Employees
From: Oscar Mendelson
Date: May 25
Subject: Welcoming our new employee

I'm happy to announce that Ms. Joanne Remnick is joining Medifast, Inc. to fill the open position

in customer service. Joanne ------- for more than five years in customer service at BioServe. She
                           139.

earned several employee-of-the-month awards while there and she comes ------- recommended by
                                                                         140.

her superiors.

Joanne's direct supervisor will be Robert Vesper, so if you have questions, you can ------- with Robert
                                                                                     141.

before she starts.

We are delighted to have Joanne join the Medifast team. Joanne's first day will be Tuesday, June 13.

142.

---

139. (A) is working
     (B) will have worked
     (C) worked
     (D) works

140. (A) highly
     (B) mainly
     (C) mostly
     (D) fairly

141. (A) share
     (B) solve
     (C) talk
     (D) think

142. (A) As we will have safety inspectors here next
         week, please don't be late to work.
     (B) If you see Joanne around the building, be
         sure to welcome her to the company.
     (C) Joanne was one of our best employees in
         customer service and we will miss her.
     (D) Please make sure to submit your suggestion
         for employee of the month by then.

GO ON TO THE NEXT PAGE

To: Atlas Property Management Agency
From: Rita Hanson, Buildmore Co.
Date: May 13
Subject: Necessary repairs

As a follow-up to our conversation on May 12, this is a ------- for repairs at our office located in the
                                                     143.

Bradford Building, Number 301. The office was in need of these repairs ------- we moved in, not
                                                                       144.

through any fault, abuse, or negligence on our part. These are the items in need of repair: one inner

office door (latch broken) and the heating unit on south side of office (doesn't turn on and off properly).

------- It regrettably interferes with our ability ------- business in this location. Please let me know
145.   **146.**

when you will be making the repairs.

Sincerely,

Rita

---

143. (A) bill
(B) quote
(C) reply
(D) request

144. (A) although
(B) because
(C) when
(D) whether

145. (A) Our firm has recently earned several awards for design and efficiency.
(B) This office has many great attributes like spaciousness and natural light.
(C) We look forward to hearing back from you about our collaboration proposal.
(D) We would like this matter to be taken care of as soon as possible, of course.

146. (A) conducting
(B) conducted
(C) conducts
(D) to conduct

PART 7

Directions: In this part you will read a selection of texts, such as magazine and newspaper articles, e-mails, and instant messages. Each text or set of texts is followed by several questions. Select the best answer for each question and mark the letter (A), (B), (C), or (D) on your answer sheet.

Questions 147-148 refer to the following product instructions.

TopSpeed

Thank you for purchasing the Trine Blender TopSpeed. We pride ourselves on easy-to use high-quality kitchen appliances and utensils.

To start using your new blender, first you will need to remove the pieces from the container and begin setup. The blender base is heavy, so please be aware it might fall out if the package is opened from the bottom.

The contents of the box will include: one base, two blade attachments, one pitcher attachment, and four serving cups. Before using, make sure to thoroughly clean all parts of the machine. Choose the blades needed (one large and one small blade; other sizes sold separately) and screw the blade attachment to the base. Once secured, it will be ready to use. Next, plug it in, add your ingredients, and make sure the pitcher is on tight. You will be then ready to use the Trine Blender TopSpeed.

147. What should customers pay attention to when removing the product?

(A) The installation instructions
(B) The sharpness of the blades
(C) The type of knife to open the box with
(D) The way the box is opened

148. How many types of blades are included in the box?

(A) 1
(B) 2
(C) 3
(D) 4

GO ON TO THE NEXT PAGE

Steve Bedrosian   9:34 AM
Hey Mark, sorry to bother you. I know it's almost time for your appointment with the new client, but I have a favor to ask.

Mark Fitz   9:37 AM
Sure, What's up?

Steve Bedrosian   9:39 AM
I'm stuck in meetings at the office all day, so I was wondering if you could swing by our westside office and grab the design documents for the Bunker Hill project on your way back here for the meeting this evening.

Mark Fitz   9:41 AM
No problem. I'm heading into my customers office now. It's not too far, so I can stop and get them after we finish here. Is the project back on the schedule?

Steve Bedrosian   9:43 AM
Thanks. I appreciate it. We are having discussions about using the designs either to restructure the original BH project or possibly using them to start the new Wilder project next spring.

Mark Fitz   9:48 AM
Wow, that's good to hear! I was hoping it would be picked up again for something. I really liked the way it was shaping up when it was pitched. I'll message you once I have them and am heading your way.

149. What is preventing Mr. Bedrosian from getting the meeting documents?

(A) He has to go to Bunker Hill.
(B) He has to stay at the company.
(C) His colleague took a day off.
(D) The documents are not ready yet.

150. At 9:48 AM, what does Mr. Fitz mean when he writes, "I really liked the way it was shaping up"?

(A) He thought that the design of the project was good.
(B) He thought that the meeting was well-organized.
(C) He thought that the project was losing unnecessary things.
(D) He thought that the schedule would work.

Questions 151-152 refer to the following notice.

Rosa's Italian Homestead is proud to announce that we will be reopening our 52nd Street location on Saturday, April 16, and we would like to invite everyone to come see our new look and menu. For over 30 years, we have served the area the finest dishes possible, but wanted to modernize and update our design and the meals for you.

To show our gratitude for your time in the Mariemont area, we will be offering a few special items that will only be available this month! Come and enjoy traditional Sicilian Pasta alla Norma, Manicotti, and a fresh seafood plate of Pesce spada alla ghiotta. During the first week, we will be offering a special three-course meal for the price of a large pizza. Come in and experience the fresh new tastes at Rosa's!

151. When will the special discount end?

(A) In a few days

(B) At the end of the week

(C) At the end of the month

(D) At the end of next month

152. Which kind of plate is Rosa's NOT offering in the special reopening menu?

(A) A large pizza

(B) Manicotti plate

(C) Seafood plate

(D) Sicilian pasta

GO ON TO THE NEXT PAGE

Questions 153-154 refer to the following e-mail.

```
┌──────────────────────────────────────────────────────────────────┐
│  ▦                         e-mail        ▦                         │
├──────────────────────────────────────────────────────────────────┤
│   To:      │ James McCullen                                        │
│   From:    │ Sebastian Bludd                                       │
│   Subject: │ The Winterholm Project                                │
│   Date:    │ April 20                                              │
└──────────────────────────────────────────────────────────────────┘
```

Dear Mr. McCullen,

The Winterholm Project has been given clearance to start, but I think I am going to need your help on a few things. This will be my first time as lead of a new construction site, but I know you've had a lot of experience in situations like this, so I would appreciate your input.

First, we only have 14 months to complete it, but we will have to start construction in November, so the winter air will make it more difficult for our construction team. Do you think we should start with the smaller construction crew and add more later? It will be a large structure, and we will need quite a bit of time for creating the best workspaces for all of our recruits. I understand that speed is as important as quality in this matter, but I want to do it right. Let me know what ideas you can come up with.

Sebastian Bludd

---

153. Why does Mr. Bludd ask Mr. McCullen for his advice?

(A) He does not want to be responsible for the project.
(B) He has no experience in construction.
(C) He thinks he needs approval to start it.
(D) He trusts his opinion about the project.

154. What problem does Mr. Bludd mention?

(A) The placement of the offices
(B) The price of the building
(C) The size of the land
(D) The weather during construction

Questions 155-157 refer to the following memo.

ATTENTION: ALL EMPLOYEES

The Annual Summer Warehouse Sale will begin on June 5! All employees can participate in the sale, which will offer merchandise for 60-80 percent off and includes anything currently housed in our warehouse located near the main office. That means televisions, ovens, radios, and more.

We have updated the Employee Sale section of the company intranet so that you can start searching the catalog now! Please note, once the sale begins, the Web page data may be incorrect, as it will take some time to update sales that week. All items will be sold on a first come first served basis, so don't wait if you see something you are interested in.

Make sure to bring your company badge with you for entry into the warehouse. The sale will only last two weeks, so take advantage of this once-a-year savings opportunity!

155. What kind of products will be available at the sale?

(A) Electronics
(B) Kitchen utensils
(C) Office equipment
(D) Summer clothing

156. When does the sale end?

(A) June 5
(B) June 19
(C) June 30
(D) July 1

157. How can people find out about sale items before the sale begins?

(A) By accessing a Website
(B) By asking for a list
(C) By contacting someone in the main office
(D) By visiting the warehouse

GO ON TO THE NEXT PAGE

JD Turk Cleaners will come to your office, store, or warehouse and create a safe clean working environment for your team. We have been in business for six years and have been the recipient of numerous awards for our thoroughness and work attitude. You can put your faith in us to take care of your office, wherever it may be. We have members of our staff ready at any time required by you. Our team leader Glen Matthews has over 20 years of experience in the field, and will be able to get the job done for you.

We don't want to interrupt your important work time, so we are available 24 hours a day and seven days a week, whenever you need us. To contact JD Turk, you can call our office number: 916-555-2342 or send us a message to jdturk@mailme.com or you can send forms to our address:

4023 Sacred Heart Boulevard,

San Difrangeles,

CA 94207

158. What is true about JD Turk Cleaners?

(A) They can finish the job quickly.

(B) They can work at any time.

(C) They only hire the top workers in the industry.

(D) They started their business 20 years ago.

159. What does Mr. Matthews do?

(A) He answers the phone at the office.

(B) He hires new employees for the company.

(C) He is the field manager for JD Turk.

(D) He responds to all e-mails directly.

160. How can a customer NOT contact JD Turk Cleaners?

(A) By mail

(B) By phone

(C) Via e-mail

(D) Via the Website

Questions 161-163 refer to the following article.

Garibaldi Security Services was celebrating today after receiving word that they had received the prized Londo Award for Internet protection and safeguarding of clients. GSS is responsible for over 235 customers, and had zero server failures of service during the time frame of the award. In recent years, GSS has overcome past mistakes and become a leader in security technology, as well as new security measures to prevent loss of corporate and consumer information.

This is the first time that GSS has won the award, and a spokesperson said, "This award recognizes all of the efforts our company has made in the last year to ensure that our clients can trust us with their privacy." The spokesperson continued to say that the reorganization of the company five years ago helped create a stronger commitment to staying on top of new hacking techniques and espionage from outside sources. GSS is also looking to expand their services in the next year, in an effort to maximize profits and name recognition.

161. What is the article mainly about?

(A) A company recognized for outstanding service

(B) A failure of a newly established company

(C) A major change in personnel at an IT company

(D) A recent trend in the information technology industry

162. Why did the company restructure five years ago?

(A) To expand their business overseas

(B) To get better ideas to support clients

(C) To purchase updated technology

(D) To replace older workers

163. What is the company NOT looking to do in the near future?

(A) Improve brand awareness

(B) Make their profits

(C) Expand their business

(D) Pursue government contracts

Do you want to spend your summer working as a mentor to children? If so, come join us for an exciting six-week program at Camp Crystal. — [1] —. We will spend two weeks working and training together at camp, doing all the fun things you remember from your own childhood.

We have three areas at Camp Crystal where children can learn and have fun. — [2] —. Sharing the duties and helping with chores set the example of teamwork. Campers will help create the decorations and meals in the cabins.

— [3] —. Next, in the forest that surrounds the camp, everyone will see wildlife up-close and personally, as many kinds of interesting animals live around Camp Crystal. In past treks, we've seen everything from insects to foxes and bears! Trained outdoor leaders supervise all nature walks, so there won't be any danger of getting hurt or lost.

Finally, in our most popular area, we have a large lake, where counselors and campers alike will enjoy swimming, boat rides and if they are lucky, they might see Old Jason, a large tortoise that has lived near the lake for 100 years!

We also offer music, cooking, and painting lessons at an additional cost. If you have a class that you can teach, please let us know. Come to Camp Crystal and see what everyone is screaming about! — [4] —.

164. What is the main purpose of the advertisement?
(A) To draw tourists to Camp Crystal
(B) To hire new camp counselors for the summer
(C) To inform people of changes in Camp Crystal
(D) To introduce outdoor summer activities

165. How long will employees train before the camp begins?
(A) A few days
(B) A week
(C) Half a month
(D) A month

166. Which additional lessons does Camp Crystal NOT offer?
(A) Cooking
(B) Horseback riding
(C) Music
(D) Painting

167. In which of the positions marked [1], [2], [3], and [4] does the following sentence best belong?

"First, in the lodging area, we live, cook, clean, and have fun as a group."
(A) [1]
(B) [2]
(C) [3]
(D) [4]

Questions 168-171 refer to the following e-mail.

To	Sarah McGinly
From	Frank Tyson
Subject	Our products
Date	April 14

Dear Ms. McGinly,

We recently received an e-mail from you about our lineup of educational products that you recently used and we appreciate your wonderful words about your experience with them. —[1]—. We always love hearing from those who are satisfied with our products and would be excited to offer you a chance to help decide what kinds of future apps, games, and software we will release.

In our customer beta program, you would be sent versions of apps or computer software that we are currently working on. You would be able to download and use them for free and all we need for you to do is answer short questionnaires and give feedback via our preferred customer Website.

—[2]—. If interested, please fill out the form attached, which includes sections such as preferences of what kind of apps and software you would most enjoy beta testing and how often you would want to be included in the test. —[3]—. Once we receive these forms and after we find products you are most interested in, we will contact you to start your first test period. —[4]—.

Thanks and have a wonderful day.

Frank Tyson, Product Manager
Brain Games Entertainment

168. What type of product would Brain Games NOT send to Ms. McGinly?

(A) Apps
(B) Books
(C) Games
(D) Software

169. What would Ms. McGinly have to do as part of the program?

(A) Come to the office to work
(B) Fill out reports for the manager
(C) Respond to questions about the products
(D) Speak to reporters about the new products

170. What should Ms. McGinly do to participate in the program?

(A) Call Mr. Tyson directly
(B) Download an application form
(C) Send back the attachment
(D) Visit Brain Games Entertainment

171. In which of the positions marked [1], [2], [3], and [4] does the following sentence best belong?

"We would also need you to sign a secrecy agreement to be included in the preferred customer program."

(A) [1]
(B) [2]
(C) [3]
(D) [4]

GO ON TO THE NEXT PAGE

Steve Banner 2:23 PM		Hi, Brand and Kate. Thanks for giving me a few minutes. I need to ask about the traffic on our Website. I have checked the data and it shows that customer traffic has been declining sharply for the last few days. Any ideas what's happening?
Brand Thompson 2:24 PM		There was a special report on the news a few days ago saying that one of our products caused an injury, which might have something to do with it.
Kate Marna 2:26 PM		What? I hadn't heard anything about this. What happened?
Steve Banner 2:27 PM		This is news to me as well. Can you fill us in, Brand?
Brand Thompson 2:30 PM		A local news channel interviewed a parent about learning to ride a bicycle with training wheels, the Cubby 200. The parent said that the wheels just popped off, which made the child fall and scrape up his legs and face a bit.
Steve Banner 2:32 PM		Why was this not brought to my attention? We need to contact this parent and extend our apologies, as well as we offer a replacement. Let's try to turn this around to show that we do care about our products and customers.
Kate Marna 2:34 PM		Brand, message me which news station it was, and I will get in touch with them so I can help straighten out the situation. Let's put out this fire before it's too late!
Brand Thompson 2:35 PM		OK. I'll have to find the information, but I will send it over today.
Steve Banner 2:37 PM		OK. Thanks for the update. Looks like concerned parents are hearing about this by word of mouth, causing the traffic drop, so you two need to work together to help get these customers back.

172. What caused a drop in Website traffic?

(A) A defective product

(B) A hike in prices

(C) A new company policy

(D) A piece of incorrect information

173. How will they try to solve the problem?

(A) By giving a new Cubby 200

(B) By sending an apology letter

(C) By using the media to promote their products

(D) By warning customers not to use a product

174. Who will contact certain news media?

(A) Mr. Banner

(B) Mr. Thompson

(C) Ms. Marna

(D) Their boss

175. At 2:34 PM, what does Ms. Marna mean when she writes, "Let's put out this fire before it's too late!"?

(A) They need to encourage other employees of the company to do better.

(B) They need to address the issue quickly before they lose more customers.

(C) They need to start offering more discounts to customers who are loyal to the company.

(D) They need to keep the customers updated.

Expanse Engineering has started an online board for employees who wish to rent, buy, sell, or trade housing, furniture, appliances, and more. There is a small fee for posting, but replying or trading in the employee lounge is always free. To post an ad, please fill out all of the required information on the application, pay the fee.

Price

Item listing (under 50 words)	$2.00
Item listing (50-99 words)	$3.00
Item listing (100 words or more)	$4.00
Pictures	$0.1 per picture

---

www.expanseengineering.com/board

Employee name: Mary Logan

Section: Sales/Furniture

Date: March 23

Item Description:

I am preparing to move after this fiscal year and want to sell some of my furniture. I have three things for sale. First is a large wooden dresser with four drawers. I've had it for four years and it is in excellent condition. I also have a small, white computer desk that is big enough for working, but won't get in the way inside a room. Finally is a small refrigerator that can hold several containers and up to around six drink cans. I would like to sell them together, but will sell piece by piece if needed. Check out the pictures for each piece included and contact me to make an offer!

Words: 114

Photos attached: 3

How many days posted: 30 days

176. What kind of services does the company board offer?

(A) Exchanging goods
(B) Collecting unwanted items
(C) Delivering appliances
(D) Translating documents

177. How is the price of the service determined?

(A) By the category
(B) By the number of items
(C) By the number of words
(D) By the posting period

178. Why is Ms. Logan selling the items?

(A) She is going to buy new ones.
(B) She is leaving the company.
(C) She needs the money.
(D) She will relocate.

179. How can a person know about the condition of the items?

(A) By contacting a Web administrator
(B) By looking at photos online
(C) By sending Ms. Logan an e-mail
(D) By visiting Ms. Logan's place

180. How much did Ms. Logan probably spend for the advertisement?

(A) $2.10
(B) $3.30
(C) $4.30
(D) $9.30

GO ON TO THE NEXT PAGE

New Hires – Orientation Schedule
April 3rd – 7th

Schedule	Times
Welcome Breakfast	8:00 AM – 10:00 AM
Introduction to Policies and Procedures	10:15 AM – 11:05 AM
System Training (Customer Service Reps Only) – Lana Carney	11:15 AM – 12:00 PM
System Training (Engineers) – Vince Turner	11:15 AM – 12:00 PM
Lunch	12:15 PM – 1:15 PM
System Training (Inside and Outside Sales) – Richard Bird	1:15 PM – 2:00 PM
System Training (Management Trainees) – Lori Stevens	1:15 PM – 2:00 PM
Breakout Session with Division Managers (Division Leads Only)	1:30 PM – 2:00 PM
Breakout Session into Department groups – Manager Introductions	2:15 PM – 3:00 PM
Team Breakout Session – All Groups	3:15 PM – 4:45 PM
End of Orientation Day	5:00 PM

	e-mail
To:	Richard Bird; Lori Stevens
From:	Vince Turner
Subject:	Orientation Schedule
Date:	March 31, 2:43 PM

Hello Rich and Lori,

I know that orientation for new employees is coming up next week, but a Towson manager asked me if I had time to work with them directly next week to assist with building their new database. They would need me to be at their offices in the morning to start the process. If possible, I would need to switch training times with one of you.

Normally I wouldn't ask, but this is a Top 10 client, so I didn't want to say no. Since I was the captain of the ship for our databases, they said they needed me to come in and guide them through it. I feel it is important for me to show loyalty to our customers for the installation.

It would only be from Monday to Wednesday, but I think it would be easier for all involved if we could reschedule the entire week. Can either of you switch times with me so I can work with Towson in the mornings?

Thank you,
Vince Turner

181. How long will the session take for the team?

(A) For half an hour

(B) For 45 minutes

(C) For an hour

(D) For one and a half hours

182. What is the purpose of the e-mail?

(A) To ask what will be discussed at the orientation

(B) To determine which managers are attending

(C) To find out who is running the training programs

(D) To request a change in schedule

183. In the e-mail, the word "building" in paragraph 1, line 2, is closest in meaning to

(A) adding

(B) creating

(C) enlarging

(D) revising

184. Why doesn't Mr. Turner want to turn down the customer's request?

(A) He promised to help them anytime.

(B) They are an important company.

(C) They cannot use the database without him.

(D) They paid for a tour.

185. When would Mr. Turner like to talk to new engineers?

(A) 11:15 AM

(B) 1:15 PM

(C) 1:30 PM

(D) 5:00 PM

Damaged Baggage

If your checked baggage arrives damaged, you'll need to report the damage within seven days of receiving your bag. You can contact one of our ground staff at the airport or send a message to our Customer Service section. cs@forwardair.com

Forward Airlines responsibility for damaged baggage is limited. Please see full details of our Baggage Policy here. Forward Airlines Baggage Policy

As a general rule, we do not assume responsibility for normal wear and tear to baggage. This includes:

* Cuts, scratches, scuffs, dents and marks that may occur despite careful handling
* Damage to, or loss of, protruding parts of the baggage including: straps, pockets, pull handles, hanger hooks, wheels, external locks, security straps, or zippers
* Unsuitably-packed luggage (e.g. over-packed)

To	Forward Airlines Customer Services <cs@forwardair.com>
From	Beverly Rodriguez <brodriguez@pronto.net>
Subject	Damaged luggage
Date	May 22

To whom it may concern,

I recently returned to Los Angeles from Hong Kong on Forward Airlines. I was dismayed to see that my checked suitcase had been damaged. I took it to a luggage repair shop the same day and got it fixed. I have attached the bill to this message. I expect to be reimbursed for the full amount of the repair. This is my first bad experience with Forward Airlines and I hope to have this problem resolved quickly.

Beverly Rodriguez

THREE STAR LUGGAGE REPAIR

Date received	May 17	Invoice number	5V803
Customer name	Beverly Rodriguez	Staff member	Yannick
Bag type	Large rolling bag, black	Date finished	May 21
Bag maker	Stenson, Inc.		

Description of repair:
Replacement of retracting handle mechanism

Note: All repairs completed according to manufacturer's standard using parts from original manufacturer.	**Subtotal**	$35.50
	Tax	$5.00
	Total	$40.50

186. What is true about the information?

(A) Customers should report the damage within a week.

(B) Damaged luggage is covered by insurance.

(C) Customers should bring their luggage to the office.

(D) Worn baggage is dealt separately.

187. When did Ms. Rodriguez arrive in Los Angeles?

(A) May 15

(B) May 17

(C) May 21

(D) May 22

188. What does Ms. Rodriguez imply in her e-mail?

(A) She has flown on Forward Airlines before.

(B) She has recently moved overseas.

(C) She repaired the luggage by herself.

(D) She flew to Hong Kong.

189. Why might Forward Airlines deny Ms. Rodriguez's claim?

(A) She did not report it to the proper staff.

(B) She had a damaged handle.

(C) She had over-packed her bag.

(D) She didn't make the claim.

190. What is mentioned about the repair?

(A) It cost less than expected.

(B) It was finished earlier than requested.

(C) The item was sent to the manufacturer.

(D) The replacement parts were from Stenson, Inc.

GO ON TO THE NEXT PAGE

Castle Clothing Order Summary

Customer: Eric Pratchett
5400 Hanover Rd.
Smith Village, Ca 94423

Order Date: May 14
Ship Date: May 17

Item #	Item name	Color	Qty.	Unit Price	Total
SW99	Sweater	Blue	1	$50.00	$50.00
CR67	Men's pants	Gray/Black	2	$80.00	$160.00
BL02	Light blazer	Brown	1	$150.00	$150.00
SH14	Shirt	White	2	$40.00	$80.00
				Subtotal	$440.00
				Total Order	$440.00

* For residents of CA, tax is included in unit price.
** No shipping charges for orders over $300

---

e-mail

To:	Eric Pratchett <ericpratchett@strongly.net>
From:	Castle Clothing Customer Care <cccc@castleclothing.com>
Subject:	Your order
Date:	May 29

Dear Mr. Pratchett,

Unfortunately, the following item that you ordered is now out of stock: #BL02. Although we try our best to maintain 100-percent accuracy with inventory, there are rare occasions where we experience an inventory error.

Attached is a description of an item that is similar to the one you purchased that we currently have in stock. This item is cheaper than the one you purchased, so the difference would be refunded. Please let us know if you would like this one as a replacement or if you would like to wait until your original item becomes available.

Sincerely,
Raleigh McIntosh
Castle Clothing Customer Care

Graveline Sports Jacket

This jacket for men is light enough to wear on a warm spring day or with a sweater underneath on a chilly day. Made of 100-percent breathable cotton, the jacket has five front buttons, two roomy side pockets, and one inner breast pocket. The wind-blocking stand-up collar is stylish and practical. Available in a variety of colors for $140 (incl. Tax).

191. What can be inferred in the order form?

(A) It was shipped on the day of the purchase.

(B) Additional tax has been charged.

(C) The items were shipped at no charge.

(D) The items can be returned.

192. Which item Mr. Pratchett ordered is NOT immediately available?

(A) Black pants

(B) Gray pants

(C) The blue sweater

(D) The brown blazer

193. What information does Mr. McIntosh want?

(A) A credit card number

(B) A customer's decision

(C) The delivery address

(D) The item number

194. How much can Mr. Pratchett get a refund on a new jacket?

(A) $10

(B) $40

(C) $50

(D) $80

195. What material is BL02 most likely made of?

(A) Silk

(B) Nylon

(C) Cotton

(D) Wool

GO ON TO THE NEXT PAGE

Questions 196-200 refer to following schedule, list and e-mail.

ITINERARY FOR SINGAPORE TRIP
May 10 – 13

Wednesday, May 10
- 4:00 PM   Arrive in Singapore
- 7:00 PM   Dinner with team (at your discretion)

Thursday, May 11
- 10:00 AM – 4:00 PM   Tour of manufacturing facility, led by Mr. Chang
- 7:00 PM   Dinner cruise with Mr. Chang

Friday, May 12
- 10:00 AM   Sightseeing around Singapore
- 2:00 PM   Presentation by product development team
- 6:30 PM   Dinner reservations at Waverly Point

Saturday, May 13
- 10:00 AM   Check out of hotel
- 12:00 noon   Flight departs for San Francisco

Where to Eat in Singapore

Pavilion
Located in the Western Hotel, Pavilion offers travelers a taste of home when away from home. We will pair your meal with a great glass of wine.

Open 7 days/week

Fortini
Don't ask for the menu. We don't have one. Allow our award-winning chef to choose for you. We promise you won't regret it.

Open 7 days/week

Aubergine
French chef Paul Desautel left his comfortable Parisian life to start Aubergine five years ago. One of Singapore's most delightful restaurants.

Closed Wednesdays

Chantilly
Located in the heart of Marina Bay, Chantilly takes fusion very seriously. Combines the best culinary tastes from around the world.

Closed Mondays

To	Jocelyn Woods
From	Brandon Ainsley
Subject	Recommendation
Date	April 28

Hi Jocelyn,

I heard you're going to Singapore. That's fantastic! You absolutely cannot miss this great restaurant called Fortini. It sounds Italian and they do have delicious Italian dishes, but they serve so much more. I've been there three times and each time I come away thinking that was the best meal I've ever had. And you don't need to worry about Megan either, since the chef always has something terrific for vegetarians. I guarantee you all will love it!

Safe travels,
Brandon Ainsley

196. According to the schedule, when will the team visit some tourist places?

(A) Wednesday

(B) Thursday

(C) Friday

(D) Saturday

197. Which restaurant will the team be unable to visit on the first day?

(A) Pavilion

(B) Fortini

(C) Aubergine

(D) Chantilly

198. In the list, the word "pair" in line 3, is the closest in meaning to

(A) combine

(B) double

(C) keep

(D) treat

199. What is mentioned about the restaurant Mr. Ainsley recommends?

(A) It has no menu.

(B) It has outdoor seating.

(C) It serves fusion food.

(D) It serves only vegetarian food.

200. What is implied about a member of the group?

(A) She went to the diner before.

(B) She doesn't like Italian food.

(C) She has a dietary restriction.

(D) She is not going on the trip.

Stop! This is the end of the test. If you finish before time is called, you may go back to Parts 5, 6, and 7 and check your work.

Actual Test

2

LISTENING TEST

In the Listening test, you will be asked to demonstrate how well you understand spoken English. The entire Listening test will last approximately 45 minutes. There are four parts, and directions are given for each part. You must mark your answers on the separate answer sheet. Do not write your answers in your test book.

PART 1 🎧05

Directions: For each question in this part, you will hear four statements about a picture in your test book. When you hear the statements, you must select the one statement that best describes what you see in the picture. Then find the number of the question on your answer sheet and mark your answer. The statements will not be printed in your test book and will be spoken only one time.

Statement (C), "They're sitting at the table," is the best description of the picture, so you should select answer (C) and mark it on your answer sheet.

1.

2.

3.

4.

5.

6.

GO ON TO THE NEXT PAGE

PART 2 🎧06

Directions: You will hear a question or statement and three responses spoken in English. They will not be printed in your test book and will be spoken only one time. Select the best response to the question or statement and mark the letter (A), (B), or (C) on your answer sheet.

7. Mark your answer on your answer sheet.

8. Mark your answer on your answer sheet.

9. Mark your answer on your answer sheet.

10. Mark your answer on your answer sheet.

11. Mark your answer on your answer sheet.

12. Mark your answer on your answer sheet.

13. Mark your answer on your answer sheet.

14. Mark your answer on your answer sheet.

15. Mark your answer on your answer sheet.

16. Mark your answer on your answer sheet.

17. Mark your answer on your answer sheet.

18. Mark your answer on your answer sheet.

19. Mark your answer on your answer sheet.

20. Mark your answer on your answer sheet.

21. Mark your answer on your answer sheet.

22. Mark your answer on your answer sheet.

23. Mark your answer on your answer sheet.

24. Mark your answer on your answer sheet.

25. Mark your answer on your answer sheet.

26. Mark your answer on your answer sheet.

27. Mark your answer on your answer sheet.

28. Mark your answer on your answer sheet.

29. Mark your answer on your answer sheet.

30. Mark your answer on your answer sheet.

31. Mark your answer on your answer sheet.

PART 3 🔊 07

Directions: You will hear some conversations between two or more people. You will be asked to answer three questions about what the speakers say in each conversation. Select the best response to each question and mark the letter (A), (B), (C), or (D) on your answer sheet. The conversations will not be printed in your test book and will be spoken only one time.

32. What will the woman do in October?
    (A) Attend a seminar
    (B) Go on vacation
    (C) Study abroad
    (D) Take a business trip

33. What does the man say about the suspension of service?
    (A) It cannot be done.
    (B) It has to be longer than a month.
    (C) The procedure needs to be done online.
    (D) There will be a charge.

34. What information will the woman give next?
    (A) Her account number
    (B) Her e-mail address
    (C) Her home address
    (D) Her phone number

35. Who most likely is Ms. Jackson?
    (A) A receptionist
    (B) A school owner
    (C) A student
    (D) An instructor

36. Why is the woman calling?
    (A) To book an appointment
    (B) To cancel an appointment
    (C) To confirm an appointment
    (D) To reschedule an appointment

37. What did the woman decide to do?
    (A) Call the man back later
    (B) Choose a different person
    (C) Make an appointment next week
    (D) Talk to Ms. Jackson

38. What are the speakers discussing?
    (A) A company symbol
    (B) A new building design
    (C) A painting
    (D) A photograph

39. What does the woman mean when she says, "That's it"?
    (A) She has said what she wants to say.
    (B) She is amused by his opinion.
    (C) She thinks the man made a good point.
    (D) She wants to end the conversation.

40. What does the woman say she will do?
    (A) Ask another coworker for help
    (B) Contact an artistic firm
    (C) Hire a different firm
    (D) Think of new slogans

41. What is the cause of the delay?
    (A) A mechanical problem
    (B) A staffing problem
    (C) A traffic jam
    (D) A car accident

42. Who most likely is the man?
    (A) A mechanic
    (B) A passenger
    (C) A station worker
    (D) A Website designer

43. What does the man give the woman?
    (A) A line map
    (B) A refund
    (C) A URL of his company
    (D) An update on the delay

GO ON TO THE NEXT PAGE ➡

44. What will the woman's family most likely do tomorrow?
    (A) Go fishing
    (B) Purchase mementos
    (C) Return home
    (D) See a friend

45. What does the man mention about the boat?
    (A) It is fast.
    (B) It is small.
    (C) It needs some repairs.
    (D) It runs only once a day.

46. How did the woman hear about the tour?
    (A) From a brochure
    (B) From a friend
    (C) From a TV show
    (D) From an online advertisement

47. What does the woman imply about the finances?
    (A) The speakers are in debt to the bank.
    (B) The speakers are making a lot of money.
    (C) The speakers have enough money for advertising.
    (D) The speakers do not have extra money.

48. Why does the woman say, "word of mouth doesn't cost us a thing"?
    (A) She believes there is a cheaper way.
    (B) She does not like what the man said.
    (C) She is not sure how much advertising costs.
    (D) She knows referrals are free.

49. What does the man say he will do?
    (A) Give free drinks out
    (B) Take a class in finance
    (C) Talk to some friends
    (D) Upload a photo online

50. Why is the man in a hurry?
    (A) He has a job interview.
    (B) He has an appointment.
    (C) He needs to catch a train.
    (D) He wants to get home quickly.

51. What is mentioned about the food at the restaurant?
    (A) It is all from local suppliers.
    (B) It is all organic.
    (C) It is prepared ahead of time.
    (D) It is prepared when ordered.

52. What will the woman bring the man first?
    (A) A hamburger
    (B) A salad
    (C) An iced tea
    (D) Potato soup

53. Where most likely are the speakers?
    (A) At a university
    (B) At an awards ceremony
    (C) In a radio station
    (D) In a TV studio

54. What is the man's research about?
    (A) Environmental concerns
    (B) Political issues
    (C) Private sector growth
    (D) World economy

55. What will the speakers do next?
    (A) Continue with an interview
    (B) Listen to audience questions
    (C) Look at some data
    (D) Watch a video

56. Who most likely is the man?

(A) A dentist

(B) A medical assistant

(C) A patient

(D) A receptionist

57. What is mentioned about Dr. McCloud?

(A) She is completely booked this week.

(B) She is leaving the office soon.

(C) She will go to a conference.

(D) She will take a break now.

58. When will Mr. Stuart's next appointment be?

(A) Next Thursday morning

(B) Next Thursday afternoon

(C) Next Friday morning

(D) Next Friday afternoon

---

59. What will the speakers do at the store tomorrow?

(A) Get ready for a sale

(B) Make a list of stock

(C) Pack items in boxes

(D) Put out new merchandise

60. Why is John unable to stay late tomorrow?

(A) He has a doctor's appointment.

(B) He has another job.

(C) He is going out of town.

(D) He is in school.

61. What can be said about the woman?

(A) She does not like to work overtime.

(B) She has some free time tomorrow.

(C) She is not sure of her schedule.

(D) She wants to get promoted.

> ## Lacy's October Sale
> ## 7th – 13th
>
> The earlier you shop, the more you SAVE!
>
> **25% OFF!**   Friday thru Sunday
> **20% OFF!**   Monday and Tuesday
> **15% OFF!**   Wednesday
> **10% OFF!**   Thursday

62. What does the man want to buy?

(A) A bag

(B) A jacket

(C) A pair of shoes

(D) A shirt

63. What will the woman do this weekend?

(A) Attend an event

(B) Buy some clothes

(C) Relax at home

(D) Take a business trip

64. Look at the graphic. What discount will the speakers most likely get?

(A) 10 percent

(B) 15 percent

(C) 20 percent

(D) 25 percent

Board Meeting Schedule
November 1

10:00	Ms. Erin Sinclair
10:30	Mr. Leo Anderson
11:30	Sales team
12:00	President Matt Moore

Products	Band Material	Band Color
Chater 400	Metal	Silver
Elling 2Z	Metal	Gold
Millseed CR	Leather	Brown
Vextron 7T	Leather	Black

65. What will the woman's boss do before 11:00 tomorrow?

(A) Attend the board meeting

(B) Interview candidates

(C) Prepare for the presentation

(D) See a client

66. Look at the graphic. What time will the sales team present their report?

(A) 10:00

(B) 10:30

(C) 11:30

(D) 12:00

67. What does the man say he will do?

(A) Edit a schedule

(B) Finish a report

(C) Send an invitation

(D) Talk to the sales team

68. What was wrong with the first watch the man tried?

(A) It was not the right color.

(B) It was too expensive.

(C) It was too heavy.

(D) It was uncomfortable.

69. Look at the graphic. Which watch will the man probably order?

(A) Charter 400

(B) Elling 2Z

(C) Millseed CR

(D) Vextron 7T

70. What does the woman offer the man for free?

(A) An extra band

(B) Delivery service

(C) Gift wrapping

(D) Parking

PART 4 (08)

Directions: You will hear some talks given by a single speaker. You will be asked to answer three questions about what the speaker says in each talk. Select the best response to each question and mark the letter (A), (B), (C), or (D) on your answer sheet. The talks will not be printed in your test book and will be spoken only one time.

71. Who most likely is the speaker?

(A) An IT employee

(B) A police officer

(C) A postal worker

(D) A store owner

72. According to the speaker, what is unique about her business?

(A) It is the cheapest.

(B) It is the fastest.

(C) It is the largest.

(D) It is the oldest.

73. What does the speaker say she will do soon?

(A) Move to a different location

(B) Open a new branch

(C) Post an advertisement

(D) Visit the listener's office

74. What is the broadcast mainly about?

(A) A new sports facility

(B) A new sports team

(C) A retiring player

(D) A sports tournament

75. What is mentioned about Stanleyville?

(A) It has a new mayor.

(B) It has an excellent ice rink.

(C) It has hosted sporting events before.

(D) It has more than one professional team.

76. What will listeners hear next?

(A) A city leader's speech

(B) A reporter's story

(C) A weather report

(D) Advertisements

77. What type of store is the announcement for?

(A) A deli

(B) A department store

(C) A grocery store

(D) A wine shop

78. When is the announcement most likely being made?

(A) On Monday

(B) On Wednesday

(C) On Friday

(D) On Sunday

79. What is mentioned about the online option?

(A) It offers more selection than the store.

(B) It has recently been redone.

(C) It is cheaper than the store.

(D) It is secure.

80. What is the speaker mainly discussing?

(A) A new government policy

(B) A new local facility

(C) Personnel changes at his work

(D) Recent economic news

81. Who most likely is Kevin Chang?

(A) A biotechnology expert

(B) A company owner

(C) A government spokesperson

(D) A news person

82. What will listeners hear next?

(A) An advertisement

(B) A biotechnology report

(C) A press briefing

(D) An interview

GO ON TO THE NEXT PAGE

83. Why is the woman calling?

(A) To change an appointment

(B) To express appreciation

(C) To make a reservation

(D) To recommend a restaurant

84. What does the woman say she needs to decide about her party?

(A) What to serve

(B) When to hold it

(C) Where to hold it

(D) Who to invite

85. What does the speaker imply when she says, "They are filling up quickly"?

(A) The customers have eaten enough.

(B) The customers want to go home early.

(C) The hall has few nights left to reserve.

(D) The staff will finish their work soon.

86. When can listeners ask questions?

(A) As they are leaving

(B) At anytime

(C) During lunch

(D) In the afternoon session

87. What does the speaker mean when he says, "We'll be covering all the basics of running a small business"?

(A) They will apply for small business insurance.

(B) They will instruct listeners on many aspects of starting a business.

(C) They will interview listeners for a job at a small business.

(D) They will review all the skills learned at a previous seminar.

88. What will the listeners do next?

(A) Fill out a form

(B) Get into small groups

(C) Have lunch

(D) Listen to talks

89. What department does Robert most likely work in?

(A) Accounting

(B) IT

(C) Office administration

(D) Sales

90. What will Jocelyn do in less than a week?

(A) Hire a moving company

(B) Clean the new office

(C) Organize supplies

(D) Pack boxes

91. Why does the speaker say, "on second thought"?

(A) She wants the listeners to think about something again.

(B) She wants to do something different than what she first said.

(C) She thinks that time is running out for the move.

(D) She thinks that the move should happen sooner.

92. Who most likely are the listeners?

(A) Bookstore workers

(B) Club members

(C) Professors

(D) Students

93. What will listeners hear next?

(A) A book excerpt

(B) A movie summary

(C) A university lecture

(D) Questions and answers

94. What does the speaker ask the listeners to do?

(A) Come up on stage

(B) Get into small groups

(C) Make a line at the microphone

(D) Stand up if they have a question

Mr. Black's Schedule

	10:00	1:00	3:00
Monday 14	Recording		
Tuesday 15	Sales call		Interview
Wednesday 16	Board meeting	Teleconference	Client outing
Thursday 17	Business trip --------	----------------	---------->
Friday 18	Seminar	Presentation	

95. What type of business is the speaker in?

(A) Audio recording

(B) Electronics sales

(C) Restaurant business

(D) Musical instruments sales

96. Look at the graphic. When can Mr. Black visit the speaker's business?

(A) At 10:00 on Monday

(B) At 1:00 on Tuesday

(C) At 1:00 on Thursday

(D) At 3:00 on Friday

97. What does the speaker offer Mr. Black?

(A) A discount

(B) A free gift

(C) Free parking

(D) Free upgrades

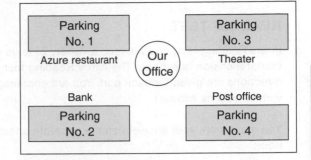

Parking No. 1		Parking No. 3
Azure restaurant	Our Office	Theater
Bank		Post office
Parking No. 2		Parking No. 4

98. What is mentioned about the current parking lot?

(A) It is being torn down.

(B) It is closing for repairs.

(C) It is giving employees security concerns.

(D) It is raising its prices.

99. Look at the graphic. Where does the speaker prefer the new parking to be located?

(A) Near Azure restaurant

(B) Near the bank

(C) Near the post office

(D) Near the theater

100. What is most important to the speaker when choosing a parking lot?

(A) Hours

(B) Location

(C) Price

(D) Safety

This is the end of the Listening test. Turn to Part 5 in your test book.

READING TEST

In the Reading test, you will read a variety of texts and answer several different types of reading comprehension questions. The entire Reading test will last 75 minutes. There are three parts, and directions are given for each part. You are encouraged to answer as many questions as possible within the time allowed.

You must mark your answers on the separate answer sheet. Do not write your answers in your test book.

PART 5

Directions: A word or phrase is missing in each of the sentences below. Four answer choices are given below each sentence. Select the best answer to complete the sentence. Then mark the letter (A), (B), (C), or (D) on your answer sheet.

---

101. After reading the incident report, the factory director realized his workers had different ------- on safety issues.

(A) looks
(B) sights
(C) views
(D) watches

102. In the financial industry, Mark Hudson has been known as an ------- business leader for many years.

(A) accomplish
(B) accomplishable
(C) accomplished
(D) accomplishment

103. The security software giant VESCO ------- their latest product around the world sometime next spring.

(A) has been launching
(B) has launched
(C) is launching
(D) will be launched

104. When an ------- version of Catfox browser is available, it will be automatically downloaded.

(A) invited
(B) edited
(C) interested
(D) updated

105. The employee had spent only a year in the IT department before getting a ------- to supervisor.

(A) promote
(B) promotion
(C) promotional
(D) promoted

106. ------- the hotel's billing error, the Smiths were excessively overcharged for their two-night stay.

(A) Due to
(B) Except for
(C) In case
(D) So that

107. The data transfer rates, usually from 100 to 150 kilobytes per second, ------- depending on the type of device you have.

(A) emerge
(B) convert
(C) record
(D) vary

108. Although Kyle Boyd was inexperienced in sales, his ------- cheerful character was a great benefit in selling products.

(A) naturally
(B) naturalness
(C) nature
(D) natural

109. The fashion magazine chose Amy Kitano as Designer of the Year for ------- a new line for young women.
    (A) create
    (B) created
    (C) creates
    (D) creating

110. It was obvious that Jim Barrow was not ------- prepared for his presentation since he could barely answer the questions.
    (A) fully
    (B) generously
    (C) securely
    (D) widely

111. Despite its convenient location, the new restaurant was not busy at all even ------- weekends.
    (A) around
    (B) for
    (C) in
    (D) on

112. The mayor announced the new city hall would have a special ceiling that two architectural firms ------- on.
    (A) collaborated
    (B) collaboration
    (C) collaborative
    (D) collaboratively

113. As the last meeting did not go well, the leader hopes to reach a ------- on the upcoming project this time.
    (A) consensus
    (B) definition
    (C) match
    (D) satisfaction

114. Mr. Patterson is a well-known business consultant whose career goal is to help his clients achieve -------.
    (A) theirs
    (B) them
    (C) themselves
    (D) those

115. Because of the last-minute venue change, the organizers had to contact all the attendees ------- had registered for the event.
    (A) that
    (B) what
    (C) which
    (D) whom

116. The purpose of the following survey on behavior analysis is to research ------- reactions to shocking news.
    (A) capable
    (B) formal
    (C) typical
    (D) terminal

117. Lisa Foster realized that working ------- from home was more difficult than she thought as there were so many distractions.
    (A) efficiencies
    (B) efficiency
    (C) efficient
    (D) efficiently

118. The marketing chief was satisfied with the survey results as ------- respondents found the new product "useful" or "very useful."
    (A) almost
    (B) most
    (C) mostly
    (D) the most

119. The development team had a small party to celebrate the completion of a home-use robot that can be ------- controlled by mobile phone.
    (A) hardly
    (B) jointly
    (C) manually
    (D) remotely

120. Gene Electronics' new 100-inch flat-screen TV will be available ------- five different colors next spring.
    (A) from
    (B) in
    (C) of
    (D) with

GO ON TO THE NEXT PAGE

121. The mining firm believed the vast region to be an immense storehouse of natural resources and thought it was a wise -------.
(A) invest
(B) invested
(C) investment
(D) investor

122. Hoping to improve the company's performance, the automaker's president decided to ------- its management structure.
(A) overestimate
(B) overhaul
(C) overlook
(D) overtake

123. The increased ------- for a thorough investigation showed how upset people are with the company's alleged secret funds.
(A) call
(B) called
(C) calling
(D) calls

124. The new recruit's project plan was so ------- that everyone in the department, including the manager, was quite impressed.
(A) elaborate
(B) elaborating
(C) elaborately
(D) elaboration

125. The study suggests that the elementary and middle school years are the best times for the ------- of a second language.
(A) acquisition
(B) buyout
(C) possession
(D) takeover

126. The newly-opened hotel is close to downtown and has luxurious amenities; -------, it is reasonably priced.
(A) in addition
(B) instead
(C) on the other hand
(D) otherwise

127. The data that the supervisor uploaded to the intranet was missing, which according to the technician, happens only -------.
(A) occasion
(B) occasional
(C) occasionally
(D) occasions

128. As visitors can have a full view of the office from the reception area, the manager told everyone to keep their desks -------.
(A) closely
(B) fairly
(C) orderly
(D) properly

129. In the interview, the company head said he has been successful because he always values integrity ------- profits.
(A) across
(B) over
(C) than
(D) upon

130. ------- the outcome is, it was a great honor for Sarah Daly to be considered for manager of the new branch.
(A) Indeed
(B) Nevertheless
(C) Whatever
(D) While

PART 6

Directions: Read the texts that follow. A word, phrase, or sentence is missing in parts of each text. Four answer choices for each question are given below the text. Select the best answer to complete the text. Then mark the letter (A), (B), (C), or (D) on your answer sheet.

Questions 131-134 refer to the following notice.

Attention all Marshburg City residents:

The Marshburg City Office will be under ------- **131.** from October 10 through October 21. All offices will be operating from the City Library for those two weeks, but will be closed from October 24 through October 28 ------- **132.** we move back into the City Office. Telephone and fax numbers will remain the same for the duration of the construction. ------- **133.**.

Our new office hours are as follows:
M–F 10:00 AM–4:00 PM
Closed Saturday and Sunday

------- **134.**, if any local residents wish to help with the move between October 24 and October 28, please sign up at the library. Lunch and drinks will be provided to anyone who volunteers.

131. (A) renovate
(B) renovated
(C) renovation
(D) renovator

132. (A) as
(B) if
(C) though
(D) whether

133. (A) Our mailing address can be found below.
(B) Our new phone numbers are listed on our Website.
(C) Our office hours, however, will be changing.
(D) Our office hours will remain the same.

134. (A) Additionally
(B) Second
(C) Therefore
(D) Yet

GO ON TO THE NEXT PAGE

Questions 135-138 refer to the following e-mail.

To: Samantha Patel
From: Perry Fonda
Subject: Help on November 8
Date: November 2

Hi Samantha,

I've got a ------- to ask. I'm meeting with the people from the Tolliver Fund next Tuesday, November 8
135.

at 4:00 and I could really use some backup. This is my first big chance to land an important client and

I don't want to -------. Since I'm fairly new, I'm not sure they will take me seriously ------- a senior
136.   **137.**

partner like you in the room. Do you have time, even to just stop in and introduce yourself? It would

really help. -------. Just a few tips from when you started out here.
138.

Thank you in advance.

Perry

135. (A) favor
(B) job
(C) request
(D) wish

136. (A) fail
(B) mistake
(C) stop
(D) upset

137. (A) among
(B) before
(C) except
(D) without

138. (A) After you look over the file, let me know what you think.
(B) If you are busy at that time, maybe you could give me some pointers.
(C) If you can't make it, I understand and I'll do my best.
(D) Let me know your schedule, and I'll try to match it.

Questions 139-142 refer to the following article.

> Junko Cosmetics announced Wednesday that it will ------- a new line of moisturizers just in time for
> **139.**
>
> the dry winter weather. -------. Junko CEO said of Skin Drink, "They're aimed at any person of any
> **140.**
>
> age who wants their skin to feel ------- and comfortable. We will offer a fragrance-free moisturizer and
> **141.**
>
> a type with sunscreen." The lotions ------- between £ 5.00 and £ 6.50 at any drugstore or cosmetics
> **142.**
>
> counter that sells the Junko brand.

Actual Test 2 side tabActual Test 2

139. (A) consider
(B) launch
(C) open
(D) test

140. (A) Like other Skin Drink products, the moisturizers include all natural ingredients.
(B) The company is keeping the product name under wraps until just before its release.
(C) The line, called Skin Drink, will feature four lotions for different types of skin.
(D) With its sales forecast looking gloomy, the future of the company is uncertain.

141. (A) smooth
(B) smoothen
(C) smoothly
(D) smoothness

142. (A) could price
(B) have been priced
(C) priced
(D) will be priced

GO ON / 77GO ON TO THE NEXT PAGE

77

JOB FAIR

1:00-5:00 PM
Sunday, November 13
Canary Family Fun Park

A unique and exciting job fair is going to be held in Canary Family Fun Park this month. It is focused

entirely on ------- jobs all in Canary Family Fun Park! If you've always wanted to work at the region's
        143.

number-one entertainment venue for people of all ages, come see us on Sunday, November 13. -------.
                                                                                              144.

Some of the jobs will be extended beyond the end of the year too! With ------- one application, you
                                                                          145.

will be considered for positions at all of the restaurants, hotels, and attractions at Canary Family Fun

Park.

Don't ------- this chance to get the job of your dreams!
        146.

---

143. (A) advertising
 (B) engineering
 (C) hospitality
 (D) research

144. (A) Be sure to include three letters of reference
  in your application and send it by November
  13.
 (B) Please encourage your friends and family to
  attend our grand opening event this
  weekend.
 (C) We are looking for experienced managers in
  all areas of marketing and advertising.
 (D) You will have the opportunity to apply for any
  of 150 temporary jobs.

145. (A) another
 (B) each
 (C) either
 (D) just

146. (A) win
 (B) grab
 (C) break
 (D) miss

PART 7

Directions: In this part you will read a selection of texts, such as magazine and newspaper articles, e-mails, and instant messages. Each text or set of texts is followed by several questions. Select the best answer for each question and mark the letter (A), (B), (C), or (D) on your answer sheet.

Questions 147-148 refer to the following coupon.

Now 30% OFF

at TOMAS BROWN

when you spend over $100 online.

OFFER ENDS November 1st

ENJOY SHOPPING

We will donate every $1 spent over $100 to Blue Triangle.

Terms

*Only valid online clothing purchases.
*Only valid in the U.S.
*Limit once per customer.
*Cannot be used in conjunction with any other offer.

147. What can this coupon be used for?

(A) A bag

(B) A shirt

(C) A watch

(D) Shoes

148. What limit is placed on the coupon?

(A) It can be used only by itself.

(B) It is only valid on certain brands.

(C) It is only valid on November 30.

(D) It is valid after spending $1.

GO ON TO THE NEXT PAGE

Questions 149-150 refer to the following notice.

ATTENTION: MEMBERS

Please be aware that there will be an annual maintenance check of the gymnasium and its facilities on November 9. This check ensures the safety of all equipment, studios, pool areas, changing rooms, and all other member locations.

The maintenance will last the entirety of November 9, starting from 6:00 AM. The gym will re-open to members at 6:00 AM on November 10. Due to this closure, the opening time on November 8 will be extended to 11:00 PM. Please note: this only includes the gymnasium. It does not include the studios or pool areas. Please contact the manager if you have any concerns.

We apologize for any inconvenience caused and thank you for your continued patronage.

149. When will the maintenance be completed?
(A) By noon on November 9
(B) By the beginning of November 10
(C) By lunchtime on November 10
(D) By the beginning of November 11

150. Which facilities can a member use later than usual on November 8?
(A) The dance studio
(B) The gymnasium
(C) The pool
(D) The sports shop

Questions 151-152 refer to the following text message chain.

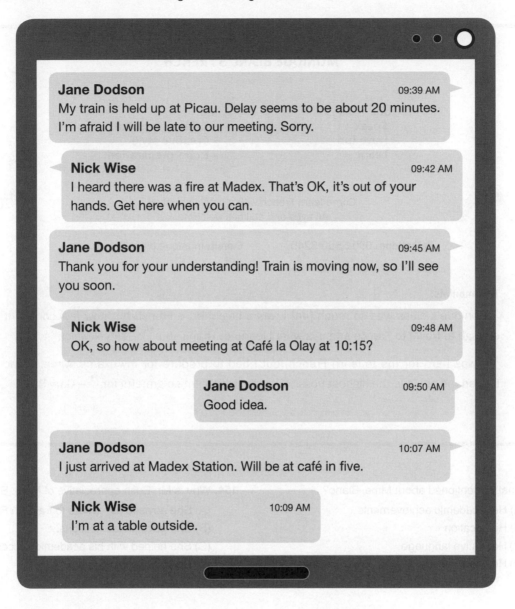

Jane Dodson 09:39 AM
My train is held up at Picau. Delay seems to be about 20 minutes. I'm afraid I will be late to our meeting. Sorry.

Nick Wise 09:42 AM
I heard there was a fire at Madex. That's OK, it's out of your hands. Get here when you can.

Jane Dodson 09:45 AM
Thank you for your understanding! Train is moving now, so I'll see you soon.

Nick Wise 09:48 AM
OK, so how about meeting at Café la Olay at 10:15?

Jane Dodson 09:50 AM
Good idea.

Jane Dodson 10:07 AM
I just arrived at Madex Station. Will be at café in five.

Nick Wise 10:09 AM
I'm at a table outside.

151. At 09:42 AM, what does Mr. Wise most likely mean when he writes, "it's out of your hands"?

(A) Another colleague will take over Ms. Dodson's project.
(B) Ms. Dodson isn't a specialist in that field.
(C) The delay started at Madex.
(D) The delay was not in Ms. Dodson's control.

152. Where was Ms. Dodson at 10:00?

(A) At Café la Olay
(B) At her office
(C) At Madex Station
(D) On a train

MONIQUE BLANC'S FRENCH

You:
- Speak
- Have fun
- Learn

Me:
- Relaxed lessons
- Creative style
- Exam preparation

Come learn French with a native speaker!
All ages and abilities welcome.

Telephone: 080-5555-3245   **E-mail:** monique.blanc@bisco.com

Testimonials:

"Monique's class was so much fun! I was a beginner in French but now feel confident enough to travel to France and use what I learned. Thank you!" — Mary Newman

"It was hard for me to learn French, but I had to prepare for my exams. Mme. Blanc helped me achieve the highest possible grade, which I'm so grateful for." — Gary Bush

153. What is mentioned about Mme. Blanc?

(A) Her academic achievements
(B) Her location
(C) Her native language
(D) Her work history

154. Why is Mr. Bush appreciative of Mme. Blanc?

(A) She advised him where to travel in France.
(B) She gave private lessons.
(C) She helped with his academic success.
(D) She gave a good grade.

Questions 155-157 refer to the following survey.

SILVER FERN HOTEL GROUP
Customer Satisfaction Survey

Please complete the following survey based on the experience of your stay with us.
Mark a number from 0 to 4 in the corresponding box, in accordance to the scale below.

Extremely dissatisfied	Dissatisfied	No opinion	Satisfied	Extremely satisfied
0	1	2	3	4

- Customer Service (reception, waiting/bar staff, housekeepers) 4
- Room Service (timeliness, ease, choice) 4
- The Restaurant (ambience, food, tableware) 4
- The Bar (ambience, choice of drinks) 1
- Cleanliness (all areas) 4
- Noise levels (external and internal) 3
- Location (distance from points of interest) 3
- Cost (general) 3
- Amenities (choice, functionality, age) 2

Other comments

Overall, I was very pleased with my stay at Silver Fern. The staff were exceptional, particularly Mr. Smyth, who went the extra mile to make my stay comfortable. However, even though the bar had a large variety of drinks available, I could not find my favorite cocktail and the bar staff did not know of it. I hope it will be on the menu when I return next year! I didn't have time to make use of the amenities, although the free shuttle service into town was an added bonus. Thank you again. I look forward to next time!

155. How does the customer rate the hotel?

(A) Average
(B) Excellent
(C) Mostly satisfying
(D) Poor

156. Who is Mr. Smyth?

(A) A hotel employee
(B) A hotel guest
(C) A hotel manager
(D) A taxi driver

157. What was the customer NOT satisfied with?

(A) The choice of amenities
(B) The distance from the town
(C) The diversity of drinks
(D) The friendliness of the staff

GO ON TO THE NEXT PAGE

Mobile phones are now said to provide us with twice as much information as libraries or schools do. This raises the question: should we continue to teach children in the traditional way? Education ministers and teachers are firmly on the yes side of this issue, but tech companies and most young people are calling for a new approach to learning.

Companies such as Poko and Djiib are pioneering the technology to make home-schooling or "anywhere-schooling" more possible and likely for the future. "The depth and breadth of knowledge a child can receive from this type of technology is much vaster than what a teacher can offer in the classroom," said Jim Frank, the CEO of Poko. "We are holding our children back by not changing the methods of education, as society and our lives develop."

Talks have been held by government officials in an attempt to fully comprehend this new idea and establish how viable it could be. The officials would like to hold a public meeting on October 3 so they can hear from parents and other concerned citizens. "For everyone's sake, I urge the public to attend this town hall meeting. We need the input from everybody on this important issue." Education minister Paul Simonson commented.

158. What is the article mainly about?

(A) A different way of schooling

(B) A new private school

(C) A special commemoration on October 3

(D) The future of mobile phones

159. What field does Jim Frank work in?

(A) Finance

(B) Government

(C) Publishing

(D) Technology

160. What does a government official encourage people to do?

(A) Start home-schooling their children

(B) Invest in tech companies

(C) Voice their opinions at a meeting

(D) Talk to some local teachers

Questions 161-163 refer to the following e-mail.

```
┌─────────────────────────────────────────────────────────────────────┐
│ ▣ ═══════════════════════  e-mail  ═══════════════════════            │
├─────────────────────────────────────────────────────────────────────┤
│ To:      rich.jack@hmail.com                                          │
│ From:    hotelworld@promotions.com                                    │
│ Subject: Hotel of the Week                                            │
│ Date:    Monday, October 3                                            │
└─────────────────────────────────────────────────────────────────────┘
```

HOTELWORLD
The World is Your Oyster.

HOTEL OF THE WEEK
Golden Arms Inn: Bleat, The United Kingdom

Situated on a brilliant, lush green piece of land in the English countryside, this inn is the perfect weekend getaway for Londoners or those looking to explore Northern England. There is a vast area of lawn surrounding the house, where guests can enjoy evening strolls, bowls, or even a spot of croquet. The inn itself displays a remarkable piece of architecture: reminiscent of the 19th century gothic style. Sit on the porch, under the archway and enjoy your free breakfast.

All rooms offer guests an insight into the inn's history, through careful restoration preserving the former charm. Each also has suite facilities (including a separate bath), queen-size beds, and 24-hour room service. Other amenities include a large dining hall, a ballroom, a library, an 18-hole golf course, and horse stables all within the grounds of the inn.

We are offering the second night's stay at a 50-percent discount, if you book before the end of the month. Do it now to avoid disappointment!

161. What is true of the inn?

(A) It displays modern architecture.
(B) It is located in a rural area.
(C) It is mainly for businesspeople.
(D) It offers a free lunch.

162. How are the guest rooms described?

(A) As cozy
(B) As historical
(C) As luxurious
(D) As spacious

163. How long is the discount?

(A) A week
(B) Two weeks
(C) Nearly a month
(D) A month and a half

Questions 164-167 refer to the following notice.

Distracted Driving Policy at Breztel, Inc.

Please read the new Distracted Driving Policy, sign and return to your supervisor.

In order to increase employee safety and eliminate unnecessary risks behind the wheel, Breztel, Inc. has enacted a Distracted Driving Policy, effective September 1. — [1] —. We are committed to ending the epidemic of distracted driving, and have created the following rules, which apply to any employee operating a company vehicle or using a company-issued cellphone while operating a personal vehicle:

* Employees may not use a handheld cellphone while operating a vehicle—whether the vehicle is in motion or stopped at a traffic light. This includes, but is not limited to: answering or making phone calls; engaging in phone conversations; and/or reading or responding to e-mails, instant messages, and/or text messages. — [2] —.
* If employees need to use their phones, they must pull over safely to the side of the road or another safe location.
* Additionally, employees should:
  (A) Turn cellphones off or put them on silent or vibrate mode before starting the car.
  (B) Consider changing their voice mail greetings to indicate that they are unavailable to answer calls or return messages while driving.
  (C) Inform clients, associates, and business partners of this policy as an explanation of why calls may not be returned immediately.

— [3] —. Any employee of Breztel, Inc. who is found to be out of compliance with the above regulations will first be given a written warning. — [4] —. A second infraction will result in a mandatory unpaid leave of absence of one week. The third infraction will result in the employee being terminated from Breztel, Inc.

---

164. What is the purpose of the new policy?
(A) To follow regional laws
(B) To prevent accidents
(C) To teach good driving techniques
(D) To remind drivers to stay awake

165. What is suggested regarding voice mail?
(A) It should be checked regularly.
(B) It should be turned off.
(C) It should state when the call will be returned.
(D) It should state why calls are not being answered.

166. What would an employee receive who violated the company policy twice?
(A) A position change
(B) A warning letter
(C) Termination from the company
(D) Suspension without pay

167. In which of the positions marked [1], [2], [3] and [4] does the following sentence best belong?

"This warning will be added to the employee's permanent personnel file."
(A) [1]
(B) [2]
(C) [3]
(D) [4]

Questions 168-171 refer to the following letter.

March 18

Dear Mr. Vaughn,

Thank you for taking the time to write of your unsatisfactory experience with our company and may I express my sincerest apologies about this matter. —[1]—. It is of utmost importance to meet our customers' expectations and in the instance that we fail, provide resolutions.

Therefore, we will accept your request and offer a replacement sofa of the same product number and color free of charge, which will be dispatched to you tomorrow morning. In light of the poor delivery service you received, we have conducted new training sessions for all drivers and I hope you recognize a difference tomorrow. —[2]—.

In addition, I would like to take this opportunity to offer you our personal services to show you we can do a much better job with our customer service. —[3]—. Please find enclosed a $50 voucher and my signed business card. If you decide to visit the store, please show the card to a staff member, who will personally assist you during your time there.

Thank you once again for bringing to our attention that there appears to be discrepancies within the company. —[4]—. We hope you will trust us again and continue to be a satisfied customer in the coming years.

Yours Sincerely,

Arun Devdas

Manager, Customer Services

---

168. Why did Mr. Devdas send the letter to Mr. Vaughn?

(A) To convey his regret
(B) To express his satisfaction
(C) To inform him about a company product
(D) To request new contact information

169. What did Mr. Devdas promise to Mr. Vaughn?

(A) To conduct training sessions soon
(B) To offer free delivery on his next order
(C) To provide a new sofa at no extra charge
(D) To respect Mr. Vaughn's decision

170. What will Mr. Vaughn receive by using the enclosed card?

(A) A free gift
(B) An extra discount
(C) An updated catalog
(D) Special assistance

171. In which of the positions marked [1], [2], [3], and [4] does the following sentence best belong?

"It is highly appreciated in ensuring growth and the future success of our business."

(A) [1]
(B) [2]
(C) [3]
(D) [4]

GO ON TO THE NEXT PAGE

□ ⊠

	Ken Brown 13:02	Hello to both of you! Have you finished the orders yet?
	Jack Taylor 13:12	Afternoon Ken. Not yet. It's taken longer than anticipated due to the unexpected fire drill.
	Ken Brown 13:14	Yes, that was unusual. Where are you up to?
	Jack Taylor 13:15	We were halfway through today's orders when the system shut down. Levi is back down in the stockroom, preparing boxes for the last half of orders.
	Ken Brown 13:15	OK. Have you remembered the orders in the black book?
	Jack Taylor 13:16	Oh, I totally blanked on those! I'll call down to Levi and get him to pick it up on his way back to the office.
	Ken Brown 13:17	It's OK, I'm on my way back to the office from the shop floor. I'll grab it.
	Levi O'Conner 13:25	Hi Ken, just checking in. The stockroom is a real mess. It'll take me a while to straighten things out.
	Ken Brown 13:27	No worries Levi. Just do as best you can and get back to the office as soon as possible. We need to get the order finished by 15:00 today.
	Levi O'Conner 13:28	Thanks Ken! If you have anyone to spare, I could use some help down here.
	Jack Taylor 13:30	I've just asked Bruce to leave the shop floor. He's on his way to give you a hand.
	Levi O'Conner 13:31	Good news. Thanks.

172. What are they mostly discussing?

(A) A fire drill

(B) A merchandise recall

(C) A new customer

(D) Order processing

173. At 13:16, what does Mr. Taylor mean when he writes, "I totally blanked on those!"?

(A) He cannot see well.

(B) He forgot all about something.

(C) He has a lot of free time.

(D) He is not ready to start working again.

174. Who will pick up the black book?

(A) Mr. Brown

(B) Mr. O'Conner

(C) Mr. Taylor

(D) Mr. Taylor's assistant

175. Where will Bruce go?

(A) To the entrance

(B) To the office

(C) To the shop

(D) To the stockroom

GO ON TO THE NEXT PAGE

E-Street Model X

There had been so many leaks about the new electric car from Matcha Motors, I was expecting to see no surprises at the unveiling this weekend. Was I ever wrong! Once I peeked inside the new model, I realized that this vehicle is a game-changer. Like the Model B, it has no instrument panels in front of either the driver or passenger. Instead, you control the car from a computer monitor mounted in the center. This makes sense for Matcha since it saves costly changes when shipping to either left-driving or right-driving countries. The technology is also a sight to see. From battery charge gauges to entertainment to climate control, the monitor in the Model X is simple and intuitive to use.

What's truly unbelievable about this model, though, is the price. Starting at just under $40,000, this is an e-car for the masses. Of course, to get the dual motor, you have to pay about $10,000 more, but it's worth it for those who like speed and longer distance driving on one charge.

Speaking of charge, Matcha Motors CEO promises 300 more charging stations across the country before the Model X ships. Yes, you'll have to wait two and a half more years for your Model X, but pre-orders are being taken on their Website, www.matchamotors.com. Just to reserve a car, you'll need to commit at least $4,000 depending on the extras you want. As for this reviewer, I'm hooked. I'm counting down the days until delivery . . .

—Shaun Hansen

To	Shaun Hansen <shaunh@wheels.com>
From	Olga Malayov <omalayov@matchamotors.com>
Subject	Review of the Model X

Dear Mr. Hansen,

Thank you for your glowing review of our latest model. We are sure you won't be disappointed once you are sitting behind the wheel of your new E-Street car. I had a few more pieces of information about the car I thought you might like to pass along to your readers.

Firstly, I'm sorry to say that there was a mistake in the press packet we handed out at the event you attended. The pricing for the second motor is about $2,000 less than you mentioned in your review. This makes the Model X even more attractive to consumers.

Secondly, we have upped our production targets and now expect drivers to take delivery of the Model X six months earlier than previously stated. By the end of next year, Matcha Motors will be manufacturing more vehicles than the country's top three automakers combined.

Lastly, we have had to start a waiting list for the Model X since the pre-orders exceeded even our high expectations. However, we do hope that because of our heightened production goals, we will be able to serve all consumers who want a Model X within the next three years.

Sincerely,
Olga Malayov

176. According to the review, on what feature does Matcha Motors save money?

(A) The batteries

(B) The control panels

(C) The motors

(D) The seats

177. Who most likely is Mr. Hansen?

(A) A Matcha Motors spokesperson

(B) A journalist

(C) A technology expert

(D) An advertising specialist

178. What does the extra motor on the Model X cost?

(A) $2,000

(B) $8,000

(C) $10,000

(D) $40,000

179. What does Ms. Malayov mention about production?

(A) It has been delayed.

(B) It has been sped up.

(C) It is being done overseas.

(D) It is being restructured.

180. In the review, the word "masses" in paragraph 2, line 2, is closest in meaning to

(A) public

(B) quantity

(C) variety

(D) wealth

Questions 181-185 refer to the following e-mail and information.

```
┌──────────────────────────────────────────────────────────┐
│ ▨ ▤▤▤▤▤▤▤▤▤▤▤▤▤▤▤    e-mail    ▤▤▤▤▤▤▤▤▤▤▤▤▤▤▤▤ │
├──────────────────────────────────────────────────────────┤
│ To:       info@yoganation.com                              │
│ From:     Evel Hun <e-hun@foro.com>                        │
│ Subject:  Package deals                                    │
│ Date:     Sunday, June 30                                  │
└──────────────────────────────────────────────────────────┘
```

Dear Sir/Madam,

I came across a copy of a pamphlet describing your package deals at the local gym and wonder if you could answer some questions.

I would like to get back into yoga and am interested in joining your group as often as possible. I noticed the BAI package allows me to practice whenever there is a class available. Could you tell me if you offer mature students a discount?

I picked up this flyer today but seeing as it's a weekend, you will not see my e-mail until Monday — by which time it'll be July 1. Would I still be entitled to a reduction in sign-up costs?

My friend and I are not sure which day is better to attempt the trial lesson. Could you make any suggestions?

I look forward to hearing from you.

Kind regards,
Evel Hun

 **YogaNation**

Please check out our monthly deals below if you're interested in becoming a permanent member of YogaNation.

PACKAGES	DETAILS	FEES (extra classes)
BAI	Attend however much you like	$400/month
PUR	Attend up to twelve classes a month	$360/month ($30/class)
GAR	Attend up to six classes a month	$210/month ($35/class)
CHA	A 'pay-as-you-go' system	$40/class

A membership fee of $200 for the year is charged as a one-time fee when initially purchasing packages.

Receive a 20-percent discount on membership with this pamphlet.

Valid until June 30.

181. What is the main purpose of the e-mail?

(A) To check if a price cut would be offered

(B) To inform the instructor of her attendance to regular classes

(C) To make the instructor aware of her interest

(D) To suggest starting a mature students' class

182. What should YogaNation do for Ms. Hun?

(A) Explain the deals in a more detailed way

(B) Recommend a good gym

(C) Respond with information about dates

(D) Sign her and her friend up for a trial lesson

183. Which package offers cheaper extra classes?

(A) BAI

(B) PUR

(C) GAR

(D) CHA

184. Who would pay $40 for a class?

(A) BAI members

(B) PUR members

(C) GAR members

(D) CHA members

185. How much at most would Ms. Hun pay to become a member?

(A) $200

(B) $400

(C) $560

(D) $600

GO ON TO THE NEXT PAGE

Redlands Community Center announces NEW adult classes for the winter

* Come join your friends and neighbors in interesting classes
* Learn a new skill or revive an old interest
* All classes are taught by local experts in their fields
* Choose from among the following classes:

- Outdoor Photography for Any Season
- Growing Your Own Herbs
- Introduction to Pilates
- Computer Basics

- French Cooking
- Sketching and Drawing
- Creative Writing
- Investing for Beginners

These and many others are listed on our Website: www.redlandscommctr.com. You can also fill out our online registration form and pay via credit card on the site. For questions, contact Jolene at joleneb@redlandscommctr.com. We look forward to seeing you in class!

---

www.redlandscommctr.com/registration

REGISTRATION FORM

Redlands Community Center Adult Learning

Name: Whitney Burke **Age:** 43 **Address:** 46 Wilderest Lane, Redlands

◊ Have you ever taken a Redlands Community Center class before? _NO_
◊ How did you hear about the classes? _My friend told me about them after taking a class._

Class ID	Class name	Teacher
RAD 105	Growing Your Own Herbs	Ralph Munez
RAD 148	Investing for Beginners	Jennifer Cho
RAD 197	Computer Basics	Neil Jackson
RAD 239	Advanced Photography	Suzanne Olsen

To	wburke@firemail.com
From	frankdodds@redlandscommctr.com
Date	October 28
Subject	Your registration for the Redlands classes

Dear Ms. Burke,

Thank you for registering for the Redlands Community Center classes. We were able to fit you into all classes except one. Unfortunately, Suzanne Olsen is unable to teach her class this winter. She has to relocate suddenly due to her husband's job. We are sorry for the inconvenience. We hope to offer this same class with a new instructor in the spring.

Also, since you mentioned in your application that you have a friend who has taken classes with us, I wanted to let you know about our referral discount. If you refer anybody to our classes, you both get 5 percent off the cost of all the classes for that term. Let us know your friend's name so we can offer him or her the discount.

Thanks again for registering. See you soon.

Frank Dodds

186. How can neighbors sign up for the classes?

(A) By visiting the center
(B) By completing a form
(C) By paying in advance
(D) By contacting staff

187. How did Ms. Burke find out about the courses?

(A) From a referral
(B) From a TV ad
(C) From the Internet
(D) From the notice

188. What can be said about Mr. Munez?

(A) He has taught the same course for many years.
(B) He is a local herb specialist.
(C) He is taking the same courses as Ms. Burke.
(D) He is moving out of the area.

189. Which class has an issue in the winter?

(A) RAD 105
(B) RAD 148
(C) RAD 197
(D) RAD 239

190. Why is one course unavailable?

(A) It is only offered in the spring.
(B) It was mistakenly added to the course list.
(C) The instructor is ill.
(D) The instructor is moving.

To	Customer Service <cs@steelworks.com>
From	Brian W <brianw@pershing.com>
Subject	My trusty iron
Date	November 29

To whom it may concern,

I have used my Press-on 400 iron for about six years and been quite satisfied with this reliable item. Recently, I had a problem that the temperature didn't rise. I checked the cord and there didn't seem to be any problem. I also cleaned off the surface, but it didn't change. I don't want to give up on this great iron, so I am wondering if it would be possible to have it repaired. Please let me know if there is a repair shop nearby in the Glendale Valley area. If not, I am willing to mail it outside of my immediate area if you'd let me know where to send it.

Thank you in advance for your help.

Brian Wilcox

---

e-mail

To:	Brian W <brianw@pershing.com>
From:	Customer Service <cs@steelworks.com>
Subject:	Re: My trusty iron
Date:	November 30

Dear Mr. Wilcox,

We are sorry to inform you that the Press-on 400 was discontinued about two years ago. We are unable to offer repair service on that model, but we value your loyalty and would like to retain you as a customer. To that end, I have enclosed a coupon for $30 off our newest model, the PressMagic 500, which has all the features of your iron, plus more. Our improved steaming features will reduce even difficult wrinkles. Additionally, the PressMagic can handle heavier fabrics than our previous models. We hope you will take advantage of our offer at any of the retail locations listed on the certificate.

We appreciate your business.

Jane Carver
Customer Relations
Steel Works

STEEL WORKS

Present this certificate at any of the following retail outlets for $30 off any Steel Works product.

B's Home Store	Appliances and More	Home Super Store	Johnson Goods
25081 Highway 53 Rosedale, UT	85 South Mall Drive Carsonville, NY	5903 E. Styx Way Glendale Valley, UT	898 Beverly St. Tatterville, NV

*This coupon is not valid in combination with any other promotion.
*This coupon may not be redeemed for cash.
*This coupon must be used on or before December 31.

191. What is wrong with Mr. Wilcox's product?

(A) The control button is broken.

(B) The cord is split.

(C) The heating element is broken.

(D) The steam function does not work.

192. Why can't Ms. Carver grant Mr. Wilcox's request?

(A) He does not have an extended warranty.

(B) He lives outside the store's range.

(C) His product has been recalled.

(D) His product is not being made anymore.

193. What is mentioned about the PressMagic 500?

(A) It has a better design.

(B) It has a higher heat range.

(C) It is more reliable.

(D) It works on thick clothes.

194. Where most likely would Mr. Wilcox use the coupon?

(A) At Appliances and More

(B) At B's Home Store

(C) At Home Super Store

(D) At Johnson Goods

195. How long can Mr. Wilcox use the coupon?

(A) For about one week

(B) For about two weeks

(C) For about one month

(D) For about one year

Three Brothers Catering

No job too small or too large — we aim to please!

Three Brothers Catering has been in business for over a decade and has pleased hundreds of hungry customers over the years. We can provide lunch or dinner for your corporate events, community organization or private party. No matter how many you're expecting, we have something sure to please everyone. Until the end of the month, first-time customers get free delivery on office lunches! Take a look at our menu (full color pictures!) online at www.3broscatering.com. If you like what you see, give us a call at 555-8139.

Three Brothers Catering

Three Brothers Catering

8391 Castle View Drive
Los Animas, NM

Customer Name: __Leslie Jones__   Date: __November 7__   Venue: __Jones and Co.__

Order	Qty.	Unit Price	Total
Variety of sandwiches	12	3.95	47.40
Green side salad	5	3.50	17.50
Variety of bottled drinks	12	1.00	12.00
Appetizer tray	1	12.00	12.00

e-mail

To:	rep@3broscatering.com
From:	ljones@jonesnco.com
Subject:	Changes to my order
Date:	November 5

Hi Joseph,

I hope it's not too late to make a few changes to my order for the day after tomorrow. I just got word that three people from our branch in Youngston will be joining us at our meeting. They won't be having lunch with us, but I will need beverages for them. So, that brings up the number to 15.

I also had a change in the salads. One person said he doesn't want a salad. Otherwise, everything else is fine. I understand that it's short notice for you, but it couldn't be helped. As this is our first order with your company, I hope we're still eligible for the special deal.

Thanks so much,
Leslie Jones

196. What is mentioned about Three Brothers Catering?

(A) It also offers cooking classes.
(B) It has won some awards.
(C) It is a new service.
(D) It opened more than ten years ago.

197. What event is Ms. Jones holding?

(A) A business lunch
(B) A grand opening
(C) A retirement party
(D) An open house

198. Why does Ms. Jones need to change her beverage order?

(A) More people are coming.
(B) More people would like coffee.
(C) Some people requested diet sodas.
(D) Some people will not be coming.

199. How many salads does Ms. Jones need?

(A) 3
(B) 4
(C) 5
(D) 12

200. What does Ms. Jones expect to receive?

(A) A 15-percent discount
(B) A free gift
(C) A loyalty program
(D) No delivery charge

Stop! This is the end of the test. If you finish before time is called, you may go back to Parts 5, 6, and 7 and check your work.

Actual Test

3

LISTENING TEST

In the Listening test, you will be asked to demonstrate how well you understand spoken English. The entire Listening test will last approximately 45 minutes. There are four parts, and directions are given for each part. You must mark your answers on the separate answer sheet. Do not write your answers in your test book.

PART 1 🎧09

Directions: For each question in this part, you will hear four statements about a picture in your test book. When you hear the statements, you must select the one statement that best describes what you see in the picture. Then find the number of the question on your answer sheet and mark your answer. The statements will not be printed in your test book and will be spoken only one time.

Statement (C), "They're sitting at the table," is the best description of the picture, so you should select answer (C) and mark it on your answer sheet.

1.

2.

GO ON TO THE NEXT PAGE

3.

4.

5.

6.

GO ON TO THE NEXT PAGE

PART 2 🎧 10

Directions: You will hear a question or statement and three responses spoken in English. They will not be printed in your test book and will be spoken only one time. Select the best response to the question or statement and mark the letter (A), (B), or (C) on your answer sheet.

7. Mark your answer on your answer sheet.

8. Mark your answer on your answer sheet.

9. Mark your answer on your answer sheet.

10. Mark your answer on your answer sheet.

11. Mark your answer on your answer sheet.

12. Mark your answer on your answer sheet.

13. Mark your answer on your answer sheet.

14. Mark your answer on your answer sheet.

15. Mark your answer on your answer sheet.

16. Mark your answer on your answer sheet.

17. Mark your answer on your answer sheet.

18. Mark your answer on your answer sheet.

19. Mark your answer on your answer sheet.

20. Mark your answer on your answer sheet.

21. Mark your answer on your answer sheet.

22. Mark your answer on your answer sheet.

23. Mark your answer on your answer sheet.

24. Mark your answer on your answer sheet.

25. Mark your answer on your answer sheet.

26. Mark your answer on your answer sheet.

27. Mark your answer on your answer sheet.

28. Mark your answer on your answer sheet.

29. Mark your answer on your answer sheet.

30. Mark your answer on your answer sheet.

31. Mark your answer on your answer sheet.

PART 3 🎧

Directions: You will hear some conversations between two or more people. You will be asked to answer three questions about what the speakers say in each conversation. Select the best response to each question and mark the letter (A), (B), (C), or (D) on your answer sheet. The conversations will not be printed in your test book and will be spoken only one time.

32. Who most likely is the woman?

(A) A clothing designer
(B) A department store clerk
(C) A researcher
(D) The man's colleague

33. Why is the man in a hurry?

(A) He is late to work.
(B) He is not feeling well.
(C) He is on his way to see someone.
(D) He just got an urgent call.

34. What does the man say about his purchase?

(A) It is a new brand.
(B) It is not for himself.
(C) It was easy to find.
(D) It was on sale.

35. Why is the woman worried?

(A) She has to speak in public.
(B) She will forget the changes.
(C) She cannot be on time.
(D) She will make a mistake.

36. What does the woman want to do now?

(A) Go home
(B) Practice more
(C) Visit the doctor
(D) Write some notes

37. Where will the speakers go next?

(A) To a cafeteria
(B) To a meeting room
(C) To the break room
(D) To the president's office

38. Where is this conversation most likely taking place?

(A) At a bank
(B) At a kitchenware store
(C) At a restaurant
(D) At a supermarket

39. What does the man complain about?

(A) Fewer choices
(B) Noisy atmosphere
(C) Poor quality
(D) Rude people

40. Why does the man say, "I'm afraid you've just lost some loyal customers"?

(A) He is not happy with the price increase.
(B) He will not visit the place anymore.
(C) Some people left because of bad service.
(D) Some people think the manager is incompetent.

41. Who most likely is the man?

(A) A customer service representative
(B) A librarian
(C) A post office worker
(D) A delivery person

42. What caused the woman's problem?

(A) A computer error
(B) A mistake in delivery
(C) A stock shortage
(D) A user oversight

43. What will the woman receive within two weeks?

(A) A coupon
(B) A refund
(C) Additional items
(D) Promotions

GO ON TO THE NEXT PAGE ▶

44. What are the speakers mainly discussing?
    (A) A manager's proposal
    (B) A new job candidate
    (C) A public service Website
    (D) A transportation delay

45. What will the woman do next?
    (A) Call a city information line
    (B) Check something on the Internet
    (C) Go to her manager's office
    (D) Visit a new client

46. Where does the man ask the woman to go?
    (A) To a client meeting
    (B) To a coffee shop
    (C) To a manager's office
    (D) To a train station

47. What did the woman do last week?
    (A) Attended a seminar
    (B) Had a job interview
    (C) Took a business trip
    (D) Went on vacation

48. What does the man say about the sales department?
    (A) It is moving to a new floor.
    (B) Its seminar was unsuccessful.
    (C) New employees started there recently.
    (D) The new head is unpopular.

49. What does the woman think the president should do?
    (A) Change the company policy
    (B) Communicate with all staff soon
    (C) Hire a new sales department manager
    (D) Instruct the manager to go easy

50. Why is the man calling the gym?
    (A) He forgot something there.
    (B) He wants to get some information.
    (C) He forgot to pick up an application form.
    (D) He wants to make sure they are open.

51. How does the man get to work?
    (A) By bicycle
    (B) By bus
    (C) By car
    (D) By train

52. Why might the man NOT join the gym?
    (A) It costs too much.
    (B) It is far from his house.
    (C) It does not have the equipment he likes.
    (D) It is not open at the times he needs.

53. What are the speakers mainly discussing?
    (A) A coworker's promotion
    (B) The man's work experience
    (C) The woman's assignment
    (D) Their boss's retirement

54. What does the man mean when he says, "I'm the wrong person to ask"?
    (A) He cannot make an objective judgment.
    (B) He has no preference in the matter.
    (C) He is not familiar with marketing.
    (D) He needs time to think of an answer.

55. What does the woman say about Steve?
    (A) He has an idea for a new product line.
    (B) He has been at the company the longest.
    (C) He has more experience than Iris.
    (D) He has to make an announcement soon.

56. What is the man asked to do?

(A) Fill out a survey
(B) Negotiate a contract
(C) Pay money
(D) Sign his name

57. Where are the women most likely working?

(A) At a bank
(B) At a construction company
(C) At a law office
(D) At a real estate office

58. What does Carol promise to do?

(A) Contact the man later
(B) Prepare more paperwork
(C) Talk to a bank officer
(D) Visit the man's company

---

59. What is the woman shopping for?

(A) A birthday gift
(B) A good-bye gift
(C) A retirement gift
(D) A wedding gift

60. What does the woman ask the man to do?

(A) Check the stockroom
(B) Give her a discount
(C) Recommend a different item
(D) Send her the item

61. What will the woman be doing tomorrow at noon?

(A) Attending a gathering
(B) Paying for the delivery
(C) Making food for a party
(D) Taking a colleague to the airport

```
┌─────────────────────────────────────┐
│            T-REX CINEMAS             │
│                                      │
│             Screen 1                 │
│  All Star Players    ▷ 5:30 – 7:40   │
│                      ▷ 8:00 – 10:10  │
│                                      │
│             Screen 2                 │
│  Brave And Braver    ▷ 5:40 – 7:30   │
│                      ▷ 7:50 – 9:40   │
└─────────────────────────────────────┘
```

62. What does the man say he is doing later?

(A) Sharing his thoughts
(B) Cooking dinner
(C) Going back to his office
(D) Meeting a friend

63. Look at the graphic. What time will the man probably watch a movie?

(A) 5:30
(B) 5:40
(C) 7:50
(D) 8:00

64. What type of movie is *Brave And Braver* most likely?

(A) A comedy
(B) A documentary
(C) A drama
(D) A science fiction

GO ON TO THE NEXT PAGE

Customer Satisfaction Survey	
Business	Comment
Anderson & Associates	Poor quality cleaning
Blackmoor, Inc.	Schedule problems
Parker & Sons	Too expensive
Vesper Group	Always satisfactory

Serenity Spa Options
- Massage ·············· $50
- Facial ················ $35
- Manicure ············· $25
- Pedicure ············· $20

❋ Or choose our Full Package for $100 when you show this online coupon.

65. Where do the speakers most likely work?

(A) At a cleaning business
(B) At a law firm
(C) At a rental agency
(D) At a training school

66. What explanation does the woman give for the poor quality comment?

(A) Lazy workers
(B) Low-quality supplies
(C) New management
(D) Untrained staff

67. Look at the graphic. Who will the woman most likely call soon?

(A) Anderson & Associates
(B) Blackmoor, Inc.
(C) Parker & Sons
(D) Vesper Group

68. Look at the graphic. How much will the woman pay?

(A) $25
(B) $35
(C) $50
(D) $100

69. When will the woman get a treatment?

(A) Today at 4:30
(B) Today at 5:00
(C) Tomorrow at 4:30
(D) Tomorrow at 5:00

70. Who will the woman bring with her?

(A) Her husband
(B) Her colleague
(C) Her daughter
(D) Her mother

PART 4 🎧 12

Directions: You will hear some talks given by a single speaker. You will be asked to answer three questions about what the speaker says in each talk. Select the best response to each question and mark the letter (A), (B), (C), or (D) on your answer sheet. The talks will not be printed in your test book and will be spoken only one time.

71. Where is the speaker?
    (A) At a community center
    (B) At a city office
    (C) At a computer repair shop
    (D) At a library

72. What does the speaker ask the listeners to do?
    (A) Learn about software
    (B) Deliver lunches
    (C) Recruit more volunteers
    (D) Use some devices

73. What is offered by local businesses?
    (A) Computer lessons
    (B) Discount coupons
    (C) Free software
    (D) Meals

74. What type of business is the message for?
    (A) An amusement park
    (B) A community center
    (C) A kids' theater
    (D) A school

75. How many days is the business closed in the summer?
    (A) One day
    (B) Two days
    (C) Three days
    (D) Never

76. What should a listener do for ticket pricing information?
    (A) Press "1"
    (B) Press "2"
    (C) Press "3"
    (D) Visit the Website

77. What is being advertised?
    (A) Air travel
    (B) A bus company
    (C) Train travel
    (D) A travel agency

78. What does the company offer customers?
    (A) Changeable tickets
    (B) Fast service
    (C) Low prices
    (D) Many destinations

79. According to the advertisement, what can be found on the Website?
    (A) Customer reviews
    (B) Scheduling information
    (C) Ticket prices
    (D) Tourist information

80. What is being reported?
    (A) A product design
    (B) A product display
    (C) A product recall
    (D) A product sales

81. What problem does the speaker mention?
    (A) The color
    (B) The functions
    (C) The price
    (D) The weight

82. What can customers get at the end of next month?
    (A) A discount
    (B) A feedback form
    (C) A free gift
    (D) A special invitation

GO ON TO THE NEXT PAGE

83. What is the audience asked to do?

(A) Be patient with the speaker
(B) Clap for the speaker at the end
(C) Refrain from taking pictures
(D) Wait until later to ask questions

84. Why does the speaker say, "I'm just going to bite the bullet and do this"?

(A) She is going to eat her lunch soon.
(B) She is going to speak even though she is afraid.
(C) She wants to hear what the audience thinks.
(D) She wants to stop violence in the town.

85. What will the speaker talk about next?

(A) How to involve people in voting
(B) How to solve the town's problems
(C) Ways to improve local schools
(D) Ways to recycle unwanted items

86. What has the listener asked the speaker to do?

(A) Design a piece of equipment
(B) Design a piece of luggage
(C) Make some handles
(D) Make some locks

87. What is mentioned about the speaker's business?

(A) It has won design awards.
(B) It is expanding overseas.
(C) It is having financial trouble.
(D) It is not a large firm.

88. What does the speaker imply when he says, "After all, that's only six weeks away"?

(A) The deadline is too soon.
(B) The order can be finished soon.
(C) The schedule is perfect.
(D) The summer is going quickly.

89. What does the speaker mean when she says, "What I'm about to say shouldn't be a surprise to anyone"?

(A) It is not the first time the company has tried to save money.
(B) It is unexpected that the speaker has to mention the topic again.
(C) The listeners have not understood the policy well before now.
(D) The listeners may have forgotten what the speaker said.

90. What unnecessary cost does the speaker want to reduce?

(A) Color toner
(B) Electricity
(C) Paper
(D) Computer server

91. What does the speaker ask the listeners to do to their computers?

(A) Change their settings
(B) Reset their passwords
(C) Save their files to the backup server
(D) Use a new printer

92. What is the seminar about?

(A) Building a new Website
(B) Helping local businesses
(C) Increasing visitors to Websites
(D) Updating Websites

93. What does the speaker mention about his experience?

(A) He designed his first Website 15 years ago.
(B) He has been helping businesses for a long time.
(C) He has received awards for his Web designs.
(D) He learned about new technology from attending seminars.

94. What are listeners encouraged to do during the presentations?

(A) Ask questions
(B) Make suggestions
(C) Take notes
(D) Use a recorder

SHOE SIZE CHART	
U.S.	Europe
6	36
7	38
8	40
9	42

FREE PUBLIC SEMINARS

sponsored by City Hospital

May 22	Exercise for Everyone, Young and Old
June 19	Healthy Diets for a Long Life
July 24	Healthy Eating Even on Vacation
August 21	Keeping Your Heart Happy

95. Why is the speaker calling?

(A) To ask for a refund

(B) To get return information

(C) To request a size chart

(D) To reschedule a trip

96. Look at the graphic. What size shoe does the speaker need?

(A) 36

(B) 38

(C) 40

(D) 42

97. Where is the speaker going soon?

(A) On a camping trip

(B) On a cruise

(C) On a walking tour

(D) On a work trip

98. Who most likely is the speaker?

(A) An administrator

(B) A doctor

(C) A city official

(D) A travel agent

99. What will the speaker do for the listener next week?

(A) Conduct a tour

(B) Host a party

(C) Perform an operation

(D) Speak at a seminar

100. Look at the graphic. When would Ms. Morris most likely attend a seminar?

(A) May 22

(B) June 19

(C) July 24

(D) August 21

This is the end of the Listening test. Turn to Part 5 in your test book.

GO ON TO THE NEXT PAGE

READING TEST

In the Reading test, you will read a variety of texts and answer several different types of reading comprehension questions. The entire Reading test will last 75 minutes. There are three parts, and directions are given for each part. You are encouraged to answer as many questions as possible within the time allowed.

You must mark your answers on the separate answer sheet. Do not write your answers in your test book.

PART 5

Directions: A word or phrase is missing in each of the sentences below. Four answer choices are given below each sentence. Select the best answer to complete the sentence. Then mark the letter (A), (B), (C), or (D) on your answer sheet.

101. Online reviewers of Hotel Lila complained that the rates were too expensive, but the Smiths thought they were -------.

(A) excessive
(B) fancy
(C) reasonable
(D) valuable

102. TGS Publishing is looking for an experienced ------- who can draw for our new series of children's books.

(A) illustrate
(B) illustrated
(C) illustration
(D) illustrator

103. Sophie Anderson started ------- own business, Real Wear Co., right after she graduated from high school.

(A) her
(B) hers
(C) herself
(D) she

104. If you wish to apply for the ------- of nighttime shift worker, please complete our online application form.

(A) employment
(B) obligation
(C) position
(D) responsibility

105. The survey results show that over 95 percent of participants have received information or promotions that are not ------- to them.

(A) relevance
(B) relevancy
(C) relevant
(D) relevantly

106. ------- the building expansion is close to completion, we will have to plan the opening ceremony.

(A) As long as
(B) Even though
(C) If only
(D) Now that

107. Suri Tech's products are not only high quality, but also ------- more economical than most brand-name items.

(A) ever
(B) highly
(C) much
(D) very

108. The shuttle runs between the shopping mall and Central Station ------- from 9:00 AM to 8:00 PM.

(A) continuation
(B) continuing
(C) continuous
(D) continuously

109. The administrative affairs division was having trouble deciding ------- they should cancel or postpone the company picnic.

(A) before
(B) even
(C) what
(D) whether

110. The sales representative was glad but nervous when she was told to ------- the CEO to a luncheon with a major client.

(A) accompany
(B) accomplish
(C) include
(D) involve

111. After he was transferred to the payroll department, Matt Bender needed some time to get ------- with the calculation software.

(A) acquaint
(B) acquainted
(C) acquainting
(D) acquaints

112. John Harris was promoted to manager three years after joining the company due to his ------- to the organization.

(A) contribute
(B) contributed
(C) contributing
(D) contribution

113. Incentive bonuses will be given twice a year, in June and December, depending on individual -------.

(A) background
(B) finance
(C) inspection
(D) performance

114. The exact date ------- the winners of the design competition will be announced has not been decided yet.

(A) when
(B) where
(C) which
(D) whose

115. When searching ------- the thousands of resources available online, it often takes some skills to get the results you want.

(A) beneath
(B) over
(C) through
(D) under

116. While the candidate has more than ------- experience for the job, the personnel chief thought he lacked a positive attitude.

(A) enormous
(B) enough
(C) expert
(D) extra

117. ------- speaking, the country's biofuel industry has improved greatly over the past few decades.

(A) Technological
(B) Technologically
(C) Technologies
(D) Technology

118. The marketing chief tried to fix his computer problem himself ------- than waiting for a technician to show up.

(A) better
(B) later
(C) rather
(D) other

119. The executive director thoroughly enjoyed his trip to a local branch as he was ------- treated by the employees there.

(A) effectively
(B) especially
(C) generally
(D) generously

120. If Elton Corp. could purchase the land at a fair price, they ------- to the new location by the end of the year.

(A) have been moved
(B) moved
(C) are moved
(D) will move

Actual Test 3

GO ON TO THE NEXT PAGE

115

121. As the wage hike negotiations didn't reach a consensus, the union was left with no choice but to ------- a strike.

(A) initiate
(B) initiation
(C) initiative
(D) initiatively

122. After several years of struggle, there are some ------- of recovery in the logistics industry.

(A) implications
(B) impressions
(C) indications
(D) interventions

123. At Acro Hill Hotel, visitors are sure to experience a comfortable stay ------- magnificent views from the rooftop terrace.

(A) enjoy
(B) enjoyed
(C) enjoying
(D) enjoys

124. Two teams were sitting at ------- sides of the table at the meeting, trying to push each of their plans through.

(A) opposing
(B) oppose
(C) opposite
(D) opposition

125. The national supermarket chain sought to ------- its debt by selling 50 of its 90 stores to a competitor.

(A) charge
(B) input
(C) offset
(D) release

126. In order to keep up ------- the latest technology in the industry, the automaker's president regularly reads several specialized magazines.

(A) along
(B) for
(C) to
(D) with

127. According to the pharmaceutical maker's report, it is estimated that ------- one in three people have some kind of food allergy.

(A) rough
(B) rougher
(C) roughly
(D) roughness

128. The experienced salesperson ------- mentored the new recruit for six months, leading him to remarkable achievements.

(A) enthusiastically
(B) periodically
(C) relatively
(D) potentially

129. Mildred Hospital is ranked ------- the best in the country for patient outcomes and state-of-the-art facilities.

(A) among
(B) highly
(C) providing
(D) that

130. A skilled pilot -------, Jeff Long is also an instructor at a flight school and a columnist for an aviation magazine.

(A) he
(B) him
(C) himself
(D) his

PART 6

Directions: Read the texts that follow. A word, phrase, or sentence is missing in parts of each text. Four answer choices for each question are given below the text. Select the best answer to complete the text. Then mark the letter (A), (B), (C), or (D) on your answer sheet.

Questions 131-134 refer to the following notice.

Eat Healthy, Be Active Community Workshop Series

The Eat Healthy, Be Active community workshops were developed by nutritionists and fitness ------- **131.** based on *The Dietary Guidelines for Health and Fitness* from the government. ------- of the six **132.** workshops in the series includes a lesson plan, learning objectives, hands-on activities, videos, and handouts. The workshops were designed for community educators, health promoters, nutritionists, and others to teach adults in a wide variety of community settings. These workshops will be offered free of charge at the River City Community Center every weekend in June. -------. Please enroll ------- the **133.** **134.** center or online at www.rivercitycommcenter.org.

131. (A) special
   (B) specialists
   (C) specialize
   (D) specializing

132. (A) Few
   (B) Each
   (C) Every
   (D) Total

133. (A) All participants will receive a continuing education certificate upon completion of the series.
   (B) Comments or suggestions to make the community center classes better are always welcome.
   (C) Since the renovations will take longer than expected, we've had to cancel some of the classes.
   (D) We're pleased to announce that the center now accepts all major credit cards, as well as cash.

134. (A) for
   (B) by
   (C) in
   (D) to

To: Gina Caruso
From: Yuki Madison
Date: July 5
Subject: Performance request

Dear Ms. Caruso,

I was in the audience at the Bluebird Café last Friday night and I was ------- impressed with your
135.
acoustic guitar and piano pieces. I'm in charge of booking musicians for the annual music festival in

Starling City and one of our performers has just -------. I know this is last-minute, but ------- there's
136.   137.
any way you could step in for her, I would be eternally grateful. -------. Could you look it over and get
138.
back to me at your earliest convenience?

Sincerely,

Yuki Madison
Organizer
Starling City Music Festival

135. (A) hardly
(B) nearly
(C) evenly
(D) deeply

136. (A) cancelled
(B) continued
(C) played
(D) attended

137. (A) even as
(B) if
(C) because
(D) moreover

138. (A) I won't be in the office until Friday, but I will
check my messages.
(B) I've attached a document with the fee offer
and other details.
(C) The festival is to be held July 30 and 31 at
Starling City Park.
(D) There are three other singers I'm considering
for the concert.

Questions 139-142 refer to the following notice.

Weekend Delays in the Valley Ridge Tunnel

Due to ongoing restoration and repair work in the Valley Ridge Tunnel by Valley Ridge City Engineers,

------- significant delays to weekend service on the 32, 89, 171 and 482 express buses in both
139.

directions through the end of the summer. Tunnel ------- will temporarily cause the closure of one
140.

tube, while two-way traffic is accommodated in the other tube. ------- The traffic on Friday nights
141.

going out of the city is expected to be especially heavy, so please allow ------- travel time whether in
142.

private vehicles or public transportation.

---

139. (A) expect
(B) expected
(C) expecting
(D) expects

140. (A) repairs
(B) services
(C) shutdown
(D) traffic

141. (A) As a result, there will only be one lane of traffic open in each direction.
(B) City buses can now accommodate baby strollers in a designated space.
(C) In fact, all roads in Valley Ridge have been inspected recently by city engineers.
(D) The engineers have said that the repair work could continue into next year.

142. (A) add
(B) addition
(C) additional
(D) additionally

GO ON TO THE NEXT PAGE

Dear Staff,

I have recently gotten a number of ------- regarding the state of the conference room on the fourth
143.

floor. Apparently, some of you have eaten your lunch in there and not ------- your trash with you when
144.

you leave. It makes it very unpleasant for people who have afternoon meetings in there. Please don't

put smelly food trash in the wastebaskets in that room. -------. If the problems persist, I may be forced
145.

to lock the room ------- lunch.
146.

Thank you very much.

Timothy Reynolds
Office Manager

---

143. (A) complaints
     (B) compliments
     (C) conflicts
     (D) controversies

144. (A) take
     (B) taken
     (C) taking
     (D) to take

145. (A) All of us can do better in submitting our time
         sheets on time.
     (B) For this type of trash, use the garbage can
         in the break room.
     (C) The president will address the importance of
         the recycling policy.
     (D) We will be catering the meeting, so get your
         order in soon.

146. (A) during
     (B) in
     (C) when
     (D) while

PART 7

Directions: In this part you will read a selection of texts, such as magazine and newspaper articles, e-mails, and instant messages. Each text or set of texts is followed by several questions. Select the best answer for each question and mark the letter (A), (B), (C), or (D) on your answer sheet.

Questions 147-148 refer to the following notice.

Attention: Residents of the Robinson Park District

This is notification of the temporary closing of Olonda Park for remodeling of the children's area and construction of the amphitheater for free concerts. It is expected to take 4–6 months for all of the work to be completed and we look forward to the big reopening festival next spring. It will be finished in time to celebrate the 100th anniversary of the founding of Meyer Springs, and we will hold a party in the park for the occasion. For the duration of Olonda Park's closure, we would like to encourage visitors to check out other nearby parks, such as Lindley Park and Jinat Park, which are conveniently located near schools in the area. If you have any questions, please send them to the office of the mayor (mayorsoffice@meyersprings.gov) or come to the next city council meeting on July 5.

147. Why is the park closing?
(A) To prepare for a big event next weekend
(B) To renovate and add a building
(C) To repair the park's roads and sidewalks
(D) To tear down old facilities

148. What are residents encouraged to do on July 5?
(A) Ask about construction in the park
(B) Express opposition to the city's plan
(C) Get a brochure regarding the new city parks
(D) Listen to the details of urban development

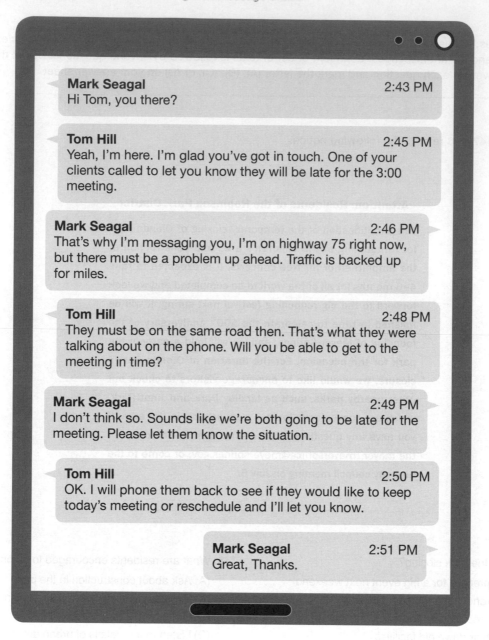

Mark Seagal   2:43 PM
Hi Tom, you there?

Tom Hill   2:45 PM
Yeah, I'm here. I'm glad you've got in touch. One of your clients called to let you know they will be late for the 3:00 meeting.

Mark Seagal   2:46 PM
That's why I'm messaging you, I'm on highway 75 right now, but there must be a problem up ahead. Traffic is backed up for miles.

Tom Hill   2:48 PM
They must be on the same road then. That's what they were talking about on the phone. Will you be able to get to the meeting in time?

Mark Seagal   2:49 PM
I don't think so. Sounds like we're both going to be late for the meeting. Please let them know the situation.

Tom Hill   2:50 PM
OK. I will phone them back to see if they would like to keep today's meeting or reschedule and I'll let you know.

Mark Seagal   2:51 PM
Great, Thanks.

149. What caused the meeting to be deferred?

(A) Because of a car breakdown
(B) Because of a traffic jam
(C) Because of a train delay
(D) Because of road construction

150. At 2:49 PM, what does Mr. Seagal mean when he says, "I don't think so"?

(A) He believes the data was incorrect.
(B) He cannot make it to the meeting on time.
(C) He disagrees with Mr. Hill's idea.
(D) He doubts the train will arrive on time.

Questions 151-152 refer to the following advertisement.

Waypoint is proud to announce the new Armada series of media players, being released this fall. These state-of-the-art devices are packed with space and choice. We know being able to watch and share the hottest videos on the go is important to keep current at work or school, so HD video comes standard in every Armada. Taking the music you love with you has become a staple today, and Waypoint has found a way to increase storage without losing the fidelity of the music. At the highest quality settings, the Armada 1 can hold 3,000 songs. Each step up generates another 3,000 more songs for your collection! If you decide that you want as much music as you can get, the Armada 5 can hold 15,000 songs at the highest quality. We are taking pre-orders now, so don't let this amazing device slip through your fingers.

151. What is true about the Armada series?

(A) They are available in many colors.
(B) They can hold movies.
(C) They can record music.
(D) They weigh less than other devices.

152. How many songs can an Armada 2 hold?

(A) 3,000
(B) 6,000
(C) 9,000
(D) 15,000

To	Melissa Scroggins
From	Harold Lloyd
Date	August 4
Subject	Conducting a class

Dear Melissa,

Thank you for asking me to conduct a lecture at your university. Although it means a great deal to me to be considered, I am unfortunately unable to accept your request at this time. I am currently required to be on site for the project my team is working on. With any luck, we will wrap it up around the first of the year, but there are, of course, no guarantees. I would be happy to discuss possible dates for next year, if your offer still stands. It always gives me great pleasure to see, speak to, and develop young minds passionate about physics. Towards the end of this year, if you could send me some details about which points or topics you would like me to speak about, I will get something prepared for your students. I also look forward to finally putting a face to your name after many months of e-mails.

Sincerely,

Dr. Harold Lloyd
Astrophysics Head, Andromeda Industries

153. When is Dr. Lloyd's project supposed to be complete?

(A) By January
(B) By March
(C) By August
(D) By December

154. What does Dr. Lloyd ask Ms. Scroggins to do?

(A) Meet him in person to discuss details
(B) Prepare a lecture at the university
(C) Send him an e-mail about the project proposal
(D) Send him some details about a lecture

Welcome to Schmidt's, Copper City's newest center for all of your home electronics and DIY needs. Please take this opening celebration coupon booklet to the store and choose the coupon that best suits you. For example, if you are looking to purchase new appliances for your home, present the first coupon to not only save 15 percent off the price of the product, but also get free home delivery. Or, if there is a TV you have in mind, the next coupon will give you free installation plus three months of satellite TV service! Finally, if you consider yourself handy around the house, the third coupon in here will entitle you to a complimentary set of tools. Let us know what you need and we will be happy to assist. We look forward to seeing you at Schmidt's Grand Opening Celebration, starting July 1.

155. Why is Schmidt's offering the coupons to customers?

(A) To begin their holiday sales week

(B) To celebrate the store's anniversary

(C) To celebrate the store's first day of operation

(D) To show customers that they appreciate them

156. How many services are offered with the coupons?

(A) 1

(B) 2

(C) 3

(D) 4

157. What kinds of items would customers most likely NOT find at Schmidt's?

(A) Automobile goods

(B) Home entertainment

(C) Kitchen appliances

(D) Paint brushes

Questions 158-160 refer to the following e-mail.

---

e-mail

To:	Rohm Ellington <rellington@vastmail.com>
From:	Pathway Tours <csr@pathwaytours.com>
Subject:	Canada tour
Date:	June 1

Dear Mr. Ellington,

Thank you for choosing Pathway Tours. This e-mail is a confirmation of your trip to Canada. We are happy to answer any questions that you might have about your tour, so please let us know if we can assist in any way. It looks like there will be a total of 38 people on this tour, so everyone will be sharing a room with one other guest. If you are traveling with more than one person, we can set up a family room for you. As we will be traveling to many restaurants and markets, please let us know if you or anyone you are traveling with has any allergies or restrictions with food.

The tour's flight is scheduled to leave at 9:32 AM, so we are requesting that everyone meet at the airport at 7:30 AM on the 17th. If you experience any trouble, contact one of the tour guides as soon as possible. The flight won't be able to wait, but if needed, one of them will meet you in Canada after your flight arrives. After arrival, the tour will be led by two guides, Ms. Gina Lyons and Mr. John Hogan. Both are Canadian born, and have lived in the area for most of their lives. They will show you not just the most popular spots, but also those hidden treasures that only locals know about.

Pamela Strathmore
CSR, Pathway Tours

---

158. What is the main purpose of the e-mail?

(A) To ask for assistance with guiding the tour
(B) To confirm a trip with a customer
(C) To offer a trip to a customer
(D) To tell a customer not to be late for the flight

159. Who will wait at the airport if a customer should miss a flight?

(A) A local travel agent
(B) A taxi driver
(C) A tour guide
(D) Ms. Strathmore

160. Why does Ms. Strathmore believe that the two guides are the best choice for this tour?

(A) They are both experts in the history of the area.
(B) They are very patient and will wait for others.
(C) They can speak the local dialect and translate.
(D) They were both born and raised in the area.

Questions 161-163 refer to the following questionnaire.

We at *Fair Trade Magazine* are asking our readers for feedback on the magazine. We want to know what you like and dislike about what you read every month. At the end of this period, we will be offering a prize to three randomly chosen participants. Everyone who sends us a filled out form will be entered into the contest.

Q. What sections in the magazine are your favorites?

A. Since my company has branches in multiple countries, I have to attend meetings all around the world, so the business etiquette section is a must-read. My other favorite is the largest section, the monthly report. It gives me invaluable insight into the business mind from the perspective of industry leaders.

Q. Do you have the least favorite section?

A. I think the least useful section is the cover story. It is usually a fluff piece about some hot shots or company presidents that don't tell the readers much about how they achieved success. It usually just details what he or she does when vacationing or away from the office. It doesn't encourage anyone who isn't a CEO or in upper management to read that. What about replacing this with articles of the regular people who work hard every day? Represent those of us who make Fair Trade possible.

Q. Are there other ways that we can improve the magazine?

A. Since the Website runs in conjunction with the magazine, how about bonus features for those who have a subscription to the magazine? It could have access to a members' section of the Website, or special features that have weekly updates or news about sales strategies, etc.

161. What does the reader enjoy about the etiquette pages?

(A) How employees in other countries work
(B) How other companies work
(C) How to act in unfamiliar situations
(D) How to greet new customers

162. Why does the reader believe the main article is not useful?

(A) It does not offer enough information.
(B) It does not profile famous people.
(C) It is too specialized for the general reader.
(D) It only covers easy subjects.

163. What does the reader propose for the magazine?

(A) Allowing readers to ask questions to famous leaders
(B) Arranging meetings between readers and newsmakers
(C) Creating a special section of the Website for some readers
(D) Giving an extra discount to magazine subscribers

GO ON TO THE NEXT PAGE

Questions 164-167 refer to the following article.

At Odds with Business, the new book by Ellison Waters, is a wonderful account of how anyone can easily overcome the toughest work decisions, if you have a little help along the way. —[1]—.

Mr. Waters said that this book is "the culmination of twenty-two years of hard work and experience, documenting all I picked up during my younger days." Waters' book, which is a partial biography and partial how-to book, begins with his childhood and takes us through his university days. —[2]—. For example, future competitors like Sam Nash opened the door to the business world for Mr. Waters.

He also includes choices he made early in his business life to show that failures can teach lessons and show us how not to do something. These failures can also be valuable to others so they won't make the same mistakes. —[3]—.

Understanding the techniques that Mr. Waters lists in his book won't make you the next industry giant, but it does give a bit of insight into how his mind works and how he uses his company to create new ideas. —[4]—. This book is recommended for anyone that is breaking into business or wants to learn new ways to create a product demand for your company.

164. What does the reviewer think of the book?

(A) It does not give enough business tips.

(B) It is a great way to learn business.

(C) It is hard to understand the writer's background.

(D) It spends too much time on failures.

165. What is stated in the first part of the book?

(A) Business books to read

(B) Business techniques

(C) Mr. Waters' business life

(D) Mr. Waters' school days

166. Who is Sam Nash?

(A) Mr. Waters' advisor

(B) Mr. Waters' partner

(C) Mr. Waters' relative

(D) Mr. Waters' rival

167. In which of the positions marked [1], [2], [3], or [4] does the following sentence best belong?

"After that, it moves on to introducing those who influenced him to become the business legend that he is today."

(A) [1]

(B) [2]

(C) [3]

(D) [4]

Questions 168-171 refer to the following article.

— [1] —. Many businessmen and women from around the globe will be coming to Los Angeles next week for the biggest trade show of the year. Leaders from electronics, computers, and gaming will be bringing out their best to show both consumers and competitors what is coming down the line.

As the week-long expo starts, we should expect to see many items, such as televisions, cameras, even new gaming consoles or mobile devices on display. — [2] —. More than 25,000 people are expected to be at the show for at least one of the five days, with many consumers attending all of the three public days of the show.

Non-industry individuals are considered vital to the show, as they will spend the most time with products, as well as give comments after use and receive free giveaways to show off back home. — [3] —. When asked, more than 40 percent of consumers polled said that seeing new products make them feel like kids in a candy store. Amazingly, 74 percent of confirmed attendees for this year said that they are coming to see the technical design of the products. — [4] —.

168. What is purpose of the event?

(A) To buy and sell new electronics

(B) To conduct marketing research

(C) To showcase future products

(D) To share technology advances

169. How many days is the event open to the general public?

(A) 1

(B) 3

(C) 5

(D) 7

170. According to the article, why do most people attend the event?

(A) To look at the product design

(B) To purchase the newest gadgets

(C) To talk with experts in the field

(D) To try new electronics before they're released

171. In which of the positions marked [1], [2], [3] or [4] does the following sentence best belong?

"Most of the surprises come during the first three days of the show, so we should know much more soon."

(A) [1]

(B) [2]

(C) [3]

(D) [4]

GO ON TO THE NEXT PAGE

◻ ⊠
▲

Drew Manson 12:34 PM	Hello, everyone. Thanks for joining me. With only three weeks left before we are due to present our group project, I was thinking we should see where we are, and if need be, ask for some help.
Michael Ino 12:35 PM	My team and I could definitely use some backup. We've hit the wall creatively.
Elaine Gregg 12:35 PM	I'd be glad to help out. What can I do?
Michael Ino 12:37 PM	Well, any thoughts about how we can show management how the product works in the real world? It doesn't translate well in presentation form.
Drew Manson 12:38 PM	Maybe we could show them a short demonstration of how it works. What do you think?
Michael Ino 12:40 PM	That's a good idea, but how can we get a demo unit built in less than three weeks? I'm worried that if it's rushed, it may not work at all. That would be a disaster.
Elaine Gregg 12:42 PM	I could have my team focus on the unit this week, and then pass it off to your team after that. When the time comes for the demo, it would be a great help if both teams knew how to use it properly, right?
Michael Ino 12:43 PM	That's a great idea. I'll let my team know that they will be working in tandem with you all.
Drew Manson 12:44 PM	Excellent. I look forward to hearing a progress report about it next week.

≡
▼

172. Why does Mr. Ino need help with his part of the project?

(A) He got a tough request from management.

(B) He has had trouble correcting some data.

(C) He must find cheaper materials.

(D) He wants to present the product well.

173. Who will work on the unit first?

(A) Mr. Ino's team

(B) Mr. Manson's team

(C) Ms. Gregg's team

(D) All IT staff

174. What will happen in a week?

(A) They will have a meeting with their managers.

(B) They will show their client a trial.

(C) They will start the new project.

(D) They will update Mr. Manson on the project.

175. At 12:37 PM, what does Mr. Ino mean when he says, "It doesn't translate well"?

(A) It is difficult to talk about the product effectively.

(B) It will be difficult to demonstrate in other countries.

(C) The pictures do not make sense to anyone else.

(D) The words are hard for many people to understand.

GO ON TO THE NEXT PAGE

Jericho, Inc. is looking for NEW TEAM MEMBERS to join us this summer. If you have experience with customer service and sales, we want to speak to you about a position. Our talented sales staff is trained to use both traditional and modern techniques, such as in newspaper and magazines, search engines, and commercials, to speak to individuals and companies about marketing and advertising of their products domestically and internationally.

Two men with a vision started the company in 1983, wanting to take the industry by storm. After their first eight years of operations, Jericho, Inc. is considered to be one of the top five companies in advertising today. We are looking for people who can be determined when it comes to advertising, sales, marketing, and negotiation. Over 200 million people have seen our campaigns, and we want to expand our vision by double this year. Big ideas are always welcome and we want to hear how you could transform our business into a world leader. Recent college graduates are encouraged to apply as well.

If interested, please contact Lance Everson at the Irvine office at 864-555-7093 or e-mail us at: jobsjericho@walls.com.

---

e-mail

To:	Lance Everson <jobsjericho@walls.com>
From:	Robert Gibson <robertgib11@smokeymt.edu>
Date:	May 20
Subject:	Job position

Dear Mr. Everson,

I am very interested in a position with Jericho, Inc. and would like to speak with you about a possible job opportunity at your earliest convenience. I am a senior at Smokey Mountain University and will be earning a degree in business economics at the end of this year. I am at the top of my class and am working part-time at Hunter & Michaels, a local advertising office in town. I share the passion of advertising and would like to use my experience in local advertising and marketing in a larger role. I am always thinking about new ways to introduce products into markets around the country, and would bring skills in Internet marketing and analytics to help ensure that our brands are seen by a larger percent of consumers. For these reasons, I feel that I would be a good fit for your company.

Thank you in advance for your consideration.

Robert Gibson

176. What kind of company is Jericho, Inc.?

(A) An advertising company

(B) An IT company

(C) A publisher

(D) A retailer

177. What is NOT mentioned in the advertisement?

(A) Staff training

(B) Sales figures

(C) Job qualifications

(D) Company history

178. What is the main purpose of the e-mail?

(A) To accept a job offer

(B) To apply for a job

(C) To ask about job details

(D) To follow up on an interview

179. What might prevent Mr. Gibson from getting the position?

(A) His current academic status

(B) His grades at school

(C) His major at the university

(D) Lack of recommendations

180. In the e-mail, the word "share" in line 5, is closest in meaning to

(A) divide

(B) give

(C) have

(D) match

GO ON TO THE NEXT PAGE

Meeting Agenda July 17	Time
Amory Brothers Representatives arrive	9:00 AM
Introductions and first proposal	9:30 AM
Multimedia showcase *Make sure to use the audio files with this.	10:00 AM
Discussions about how our company can achieve growth *May also be some Q & A during this time.	11:00 AM
Lunch with Amory Brothers President	12:00 PM
Group discussions with management from both companies	1:00 PM
Final negotiations *We are hoping to reach this part earlier, but will stress it at this time.	2:00 PM
Preliminary contracts drawn up	2:30 PM
End of the day's meeting	4:00 PM

MEMO

To: Mark Reynolds, Amy Abbott
From: Jennifer Tyson
Date: July 15
Subject: Meeting Agenda July 17

Hello, Mark and Amy,

Here is some information regarding the meeting with Amory Brothers on July 17th. I wanted to make sure to inform you of everything that should happen that day, since it is a big meeting for us.

This contract could help our company regain its foothold in the audio industry, and I know that I can count on you to help us do just that. When the reps from Amory arrive, please take them to meeting room D, where we will have everything ready to go for you.

Amory Brothers is a blue-chip company in the audio industry and works with everyone from the top singers to the best movie companies in the world. Their specialty is creating small equipment to offer assistance to space programs and governments that need to use the smallest audio listening devices available. They expect fast-thinking project leaders to respond to their concerns, and I know the two of you will show how we can be a leading part of the future in audio. I have every confidence they will see that we are the best choice for their future projects!

Jennifer Tyson
President, Hitbox Sound

181. What is the purpose of the meeting?

    (A) To explain a new audio device

    (B) To show new programs to representatives

    (C) To try to encourage a merger

    (D) To win a contract for the company

182. What does Ms. Tyson remind Mark and Amy to do during the showcase?

    (A) To answer the client's questions

    (B) To finish as quickly as possible

    (C) To explain as many details as they can

    (D) To use the prepared files

183. What does the client have leading technology in?

    (A) Audio equipment

    (B) Computers

    (C) Vehicles

    (D) Video equipment

184. What does Ms. Tyson NOT think about Amory Brothers?

    (A) They are a small company.

    (B) They are one of the best companies.

    (C) They need responsive companies to work with.

    (D) They will consider the contract beneficial.

185. When will Mark and Amy meet the visitors?

    (A) At 9:00 AM

    (B) At 9:30 AM

    (C) At 10:00 AM

    (D) At 12:00 PM

GO ON TO THE NEXT PAGE

Peter Solvang — A Brief Summary of the Artist's Work

• Early Period: Solvang worked in multiple colors (acrylic), using the broad brush strokes he would become famous for later in life.

• Mid-career: Solvang branched out with a few modern portraits during this time, bringing to mind the influence of Carson and Eustace.

• Final Works: In the decade before his death, Solvang expressed emotions only in black. The bold, dark strokes reflected their own light, he said.

Public Access Channel July Programming Schedule

Monday, July 17   Getting Started on Your Retirement Fund   17:00-17:15
Investment guru, Ravita Singh, tells viewers it's never too early to start investing for your retirement. Tune in for tips and warnings about the best and safest investments.

Tuesday, July 18   Taco Tuesday and Other Treats   15:30-16:00
Mexican chef Juanita Valdez shares another terrific recipe with us. Using ingredients easily found in any supermarket, you'll be able to please your hungry crowd tonight.

Wednesday, July 19   Peter Solvang Retrospective   20:00-21:30
Solvang has been called France's greatest modern painter. The second in a series, tonight's program examines the works in the middle of his seven-decade career.

Thursday, July 20   This Beautiful Old House   20:30-21:30
Owners of older houses have a lot of work to do. We make it easier with our weekly show that teaches you the basics of home repair and maintenance. Save money and DIY!

```
┌─────────────────────────────────────────────────────────────────────────┐
│ ▧  ▥▥▥▥▥▥▥▥▥▥▥▥▥▥          e-mail          ▥▥▥▥▥▥▥▥▥▥▥▥▥▥        │
├─────────────────────────────────────────────────────────────────────────┤
│  To:        Public Access Channel Information <pacinfo@pacabroadcasting.gov> │
│  From:      Riley Springer <rspringer@vastmail.com>                         │
│  Date:      July 20                                                         │
│  Subject:   Question about a program                                        │
├─────────────────────────────────────────────────────────────────────────┤
│                                                                            │
│   Hello,                                                                    │
│                                                                            │
│   I would like to know if you are re-broadcasting the program from last     │
│   night, about the painter. I only caught the last ten minutes of it, so I  │
│   don't know the name of it. I teach art history at the local college and   │
│   I'd like to use some of it in my class. Could you tell me how to view it  │
│   again or how to purchase a recording of it, if possible?                  │
│                                                                            │
│   Riley Springer                                                           │
│                                                                            │
└─────────────────────────────────────────────────────────────────────────┘
```

186. When did Peter Solvang use black paint only?

(A) In his early days

(B) Before he met Eustace

(C) During the middle of his career

(D) In the latter part of his life

187. What does the art TV program focus on?

(A) A tutorial on brush strokes

(B) An artist's portrait period

(C) Bright colors in nature

(D) Using acrylic in paintings

188. When does a show about money air?

(A) Monday

(B) Tuesday

(C) Wednesday

(D) Thursday

189. What program does Ms. Springer ask about?

(A) Getting Started on Your Retirement Fund

(B) Peter Solvang Retrospective

(C) Taco Tuesday and Other Treats

(D) This Beautiful Old House

190. What is mentioned about Ms. Springer?

(A) She is an artist.

(B) She is an investment banker.

(C) She owns an older home.

(D) She works in education.

GO ON TO THE NEXT PAGE

Auburn Motors Special Lease Offer

If you're not quite ready to make the commitment to buy a car for whatever reason, our lease option is perfect — and sometimes less costly in the long run than buying brand-new!

Lease any of our brand-new models* for just $200 per month for 36 months and pay only $2,500 at signing. That's a lower down payment than any of our competitors.

No security deposit. Walk-away anytime during lease agreement. For 36 months, take up the option to purchase a vehicle for value for money (cheaper than buying one). This offer will be made to qualified candidates. Thorough credit background check will be made by Verify, Inc.

*Wellspring 5000 sedan, Fox Trot XR sports car, Jasmine 33 hybrid, Emerald Bay mini van

Final Invoice for Car Lease

Name: Timothy Loins

Make/Model: Hybrid

Total time on lease: 12 months

Mileage Upon return: 12,389

Maintenance: New brake pads

Mileage charge	389 x 0.15	58.35
Local tax		49.50
Maintenance		245.25
Final month charge		200.00
Total		553.10

*Vehicle leases include 12,000 free miles per year. Above that, customers are charged $.15 per mile.

From	Timothy Lions <timothylions@bizplus.net>
To	Auburn Motors <info@auburnmotors.com>
Date	July 3
Subject	Car lease charges

I just received the final invoice from my car lease with Auburn Motors and I'm afraid there's been an error, probably just a clerical one. At the time I turned the car back in, I recorded the miles as 10,389.
I even took a picture of the odometer, which I've attached to this message. Please refund me the extra mileage charge.

Thank you,
Timothy Lions

191. How much did Mr. Lions likely pay as a down payment?

(A) $200
(B) $553.10
(C) $1,200
(D) $2,500

192. What type of car did Mr. Lions lease?

(A) Emerald Bay
(B) Fox Trot XR
(C) Jasmine 33
(D) Wellspring 5000

193. When did Mr. Lions return the vehicle?

(A) A week after signing the lease
(B) A few months after signing the lease
(C) One year after signing the lease
(D) Three years after signing the lease

194. How much is Mr. Lions asking to be refunded?

(A) $49.50
(B) $58.35
(C) $200.00
(D) $245.25

195. What has Mr. Lions sent with his e-mail?

(A) A picture of the car's control panel
(B) A picture of the car's exterior
(C) His original contract
(D) The lease advertisement

GO ON TO THE NEXT PAGE

San Marcos 25th Annual Home Decor Exhibition
July 21–24   9:30 AM–5:30 PM   Javier Center   San Marcos, CA

Program for July 21

• Opening Presentation   10:00 AM – 10:30 AM   Main Stage

       Exhibition organizer Felicia Knowles of Westbrook Designs will give a welcome speech.

• Trends in Home Fashion   11:30 AM – 12:30 PM   East Room

       Staff from local business Bridget Homes will explain what is trending now.

• Forecast for Next Year   1:30 PM – 2:00 PM   West Pavilion

       Design icon Robert Waxman will share his insights on hot designs in the coming year.

• New Exhibitors' Gallery   All Day   Center Section

       Don't miss the newest businesses showing off their products.

---

e-mail

From:	Marc Ephraim <mephraim@ephraimdes.com>
To:	Janessa Blackwell <jblackwell@ephraimdes.com>
Date:	July 17
Subject:	Home Decor Exhibition

Hi Janessa,

I was hoping you could help me with the upcoming event at Javier Center. My team and I can cover the booth itself, but we need to rotate some people to the gallery throughout the first day. I was wondering what your availability would be from 1:00 to 5:00? I could actually use two more people, so if you have any recommendations, let me know. One more thing. Could you look over the attached product list and confirm the price on CSH-45? I know that particular one costs more because of the specialty fabric, but I don't know what price we finally settled on.

Thanks a lot,
Marc Ephraim
Ephraim Designs

Ephraim Designs Exhibition Product List

	Item Number	Dimensions	Price
Upholstery Fabrics			
Woven	UF-WV21	Varies (remnants)	Individually labeled
Modern	UF-MO11	"	"
Traditional	UF-TR95	"	"
Small Cupboards			
Mottled Green	CPB-MG3	H85/W76/D40	$125
French Grey	CPB-FG5	"	$125
Provence Blue	CPB-PB7	"	$135
Mediterranean Blue	CPB-MB9	"	$130
Cushion Covers			
Floral	CSH-55	40x40	$45
Animals	CSH-32	40x40	$45
Designer	CSH-45	55x55	$50
Traditional	CSH-64	55x55	$50

196. Where can participants hear about future trends?

(A) Center Section
(B) East Room
(C) Main Stage
(D) West Pavilion

197. When does Mr. Ephraim want Ms. Blackwell's help?

(A) On July 21
(B) On July 22
(C) On July 23
(D) On July 24

198. In the e-mail, the word "cover" in line 2, is the closest in meaning to

(A) decorate
(B) hide
(C) wrap
(D) include

199. What item does Mr. Ephraim ask Ms. Blackwell about?

(A) The designer cushion cover
(B) The floral cushion
(C) The modern upholstery fabric
(D) The woven table cloth

200. What is common to the cupboards in the list?

(A) The color
(B) The material
(C) The price
(D) The size

Stop! This is the end of the test. If you finish before time is called, you may go back to Parts 5, 6, and 7 and check your work.

Actual Test

4

LISTENING TEST

In the Listening test, you will be asked to demonstrate how well you understand spoken English. The entire Listening test will last approximately 45 minutes. There are four parts, and directions are given for each part. You must mark your answers on the separate answer sheet. Do not write your answers in your test book.

PART 1 🎧 13

Directions: For each question in this part, you will hear four statements about a picture in your test book. When you hear the statements, you must select the one statement that best describes what you see in the picture. Then find the number of the question on your answer sheet and mark your answer. The statements will not be printed in your test book and will be spoken only one time.

Statement (C), "They're sitting at the table," is the best description of the picture, so you should select answer (C) and mark it on your answer sheet.

1.

2.

GO ON TO THE NEXT PAGE

3.

4.

5.

6.

GO ON TO THE NEXT PAGE

Directions: You will hear a question or statement and three responses spoken in English. They will not be printed in your test book and will be spoken only one time. Select the best response to the question or statement and mark the letter (A), (B), or (C) on your answer sheet.

7. Mark your answer on your answer sheet.

8. Mark your answer on your answer sheet.

9. Mark your answer on your answer sheet.

10. Mark your answer on your answer sheet.

11. Mark your answer on your answer sheet.

12. Mark your answer on your answer sheet.

13. Mark your answer on your answer sheet.

14. Mark your answer on your answer sheet.

15. Mark your answer on your answer sheet.

16. Mark your answer on your answer sheet.

17. Mark your answer on your answer sheet.

18. Mark your answer on your answer sheet.

19. Mark your answer on your answer sheet.

20. Mark your answer on your answer sheet.

21. Mark your answer on your answer sheet.

22. Mark your answer on your answer sheet.

23. Mark your answer on your answer sheet.

24. Mark your answer on your answer sheet.

25. Mark your answer on your answer sheet.

26. Mark your answer on your answer sheet.

27. Mark your answer on your answer sheet.

28. Mark your answer on your answer sheet.

29. Mark your answer on your answer sheet.

30. Mark your answer on your answer sheet.

31. Mark your answer on your answer sheet.

PART 3 🎧 15

Directions: You will hear some conversations between two or more people. You will be asked to answer three questions about what the speakers say in each conversation. Select the best response to each question and mark the letter (A), (B), (C), or (D) on your answer sheet. The conversations will not be printed in your test book and will be spoken only one time.

32. Where are the speakers going next week?
   (A) On a business trip
   (B) On a camping trip
   (C) To a client's office
   (D) To a holiday resort

33. How are the speakers going to get to their destination?
   (A) By airplane
   (B) By bus
   (C) By car
   (D) By train

34. What is mentioned about this Friday?
   (A) No company vehicles are available.
   (B) The man will spend time with his family.
   (C) The woman will move to a new place.
   (D) There is a company picnic.

35. What does the woman say she likes?
   (A) Greek food
   (B) Modern art
   (C) New cafés
   (D) Pop music

36. Where are the speakers planning to meet?
   (A) At a gallery
   (B) At a restaurant
   (C) At an art supply store
   (D) At the woman's apartment

37. What will the speakers do tomorrow at 7:30?
   (A) Cook dinner
   (B) Listen to an artist talk
   (C) Participate in an art class
   (D) Try a new restaurant

38. What does the man ask the woman about?
   (A) A college application
   (B) A promotional campaign
   (C) His checking account
   (D) His son's scholarship

39. Why does the woman say, "We've had a lot of calls about that today"?
   (A) Many people have complained that the line is busy.
   (B) She has talked with the same customer repeatedly.
   (C) She is tired of all the calls.
   (D) The new offer is popular.

40. What does the woman recommend to the man?
   (A) To ask a friend for advice
   (B) To come see her again
   (C) To call back later
   (D) To hurry up

41. Where are the speakers?
   (A) At an airport
   (B) At a luggage store
   (C) At a train station
   (D) At a travel agency

42. What is the problem?
   (A) The man forgot to make a reservation.
   (B) The man overcharged the woman.
   (C) The woman's item did not arrive with her.
   (D) The woman's name was spelled wrong.

43. Where will the woman probably go next?
   (A) To a clinic
   (B) To a hotel
   (C) To Atlanta
   (D) To her home

44. What are the speakers mainly discussing?
    (A) A customer order
    (B) A feedback form
    (C) A new Website
    (D) A trial product

45. What change does the woman suggest?
    (A) Decreasing the font size
    (B) Emphasizing the logo
    (C) Making the type darker
    (D) Modifying the whole design

46. What does the man mean when he says, "I think I can handle it"?
    (A) The man can set up the system by himself.
    (B) The man needs no feedback from the woman.
    (C) The woman does not have to see the designers.
    (D) The woman does not need to give the man a ride.

47. Who most likely is the man?
    (A) A credit card company representative
    (B) A customer service representative
    (C) A new customer
    (D) A store clerk

48. What is the woman's problem?
    (A) Her computer is not working.
    (B) Her order has not arrived yet.
    (C) Her order is incorrect.
    (D) Her payment method is not accepted.

49. What might the man do next?
    (A) Call the credit card company
    (B) Check the woman's purchase record
    (C) Explain a procedure
    (D) Transfer the woman's call

50. What are the speakers mainly discussing?
    (A) A food delivery service
    (B) A neighborhood event
    (C) The man's schedule
    (D) The woman's new job

51. What change would the woman like to see?
    (A) A variety of services
    (B) A different schedule
    (C) Friendlier staff
    (D) Lower prices

52. What does the woman say she will do?
    (A) Move to a different area
    (B) Change her jobs
    (C) Sign up for a service
    (D) Talk to her neighbors

53. What problem are the speakers discussing?
    (A) A customer complaint
    (B) A financial problem
    (C) A product recall
    (D) A supply problem

54. What does the woman imply when she says, "The summer will nearly be over by then"?
    (A) She is happy that it will be less hot then.
    (B) The company will close after summer.
    (C) The product will not be needed then.
    (D) The workers will be busier then.

55. What will happen at the end of the day?
    (A) A manufacturer will call back.
    (B) A clearance sale will begin.
    (C) The speakers will do an inventory.
    (D) The products will be put on the market.

56. What is mentioned about the speakers' company?

(A) It is doing well.

(B) It is hiring new employees.

(C) It is moving to an overseas location.

(D) It is spending more than it takes in.

57. What does the woman say she will do?

(A) Contact her friend

(B) Look at some contracts

(C) Make a reservation

(D) Visit a new branch office

58. What is the reason for the higher rent prices in the area?

(A) Better transportation

(B) Economic growth

(C) Improved safety

(D) New office building construction

59. What does Ellen dislike about her new place?

(A) The access to work

(B) The crowded station

(C) The color of the house

(D) The size of her room

60. What can be said about Seven Oaks Station?

(A) It is a new station.

(B) It is in the western part of the city.

(C) The women did not know about it.

(D) Two lines go through it.

61. What will Nina do next?

(A) Look for a new place

(B) Check the departure time

(C) Show Ellen an app

(D) Take a train

62. Who most likely is the man?

(A) A caterer

(B) A city official

(C) A grocery store manager

(D) A reporter

63. What is mentioned about the woman's business?

(A) It almost won the award last year.

(B) It relocated last year.

(C) It remodeled its office this year.

(D) It started this year.

64. What will happen next Monday?

(A) The contest results will be announced.

(B) The magazine issue will be released.

(C) The speakers will meet at the woman's office.

(D) The woman will have a job interview.

GO ON TO THE NEXT PAGE

```
HOTEL SINCLAIR

1. Room charge      .......... $80
2. Mini bar         .......... $17
3. Room service     .......... $12
4. Service charge   .......... $8

     Total          $117
```

ABC Furniture

Discount Coupon

Sofas, Couches	10% OFF!
Dining tables	20% OFF!
Beds	20% OFF!

9791196597504

(Expires July 31)

65. Look at the graphic. How much will be taken off of the bill?

(A) $8
(B) $12
(C) $17
(D) $80

66. What does the man say caused the problem?

(A) A cleaning staff mistake
(B) A computer error
(C) A name mix-up
(D) A reservation change

67. What will the man most likely do next?

(A) Call his supervisor
(B) Check something on the computer
(C) Give the woman a key
(D) Process a payment

68. What does the man mention about the item?

(A) It is his favorite color.
(B) It is suitable for his home.
(C) It is big for his place.
(D) It is within his budget.

69. Look at the graphic. What discount will the man get on his purchase?

(A) 10%
(B) 15%
(C) 20%
(D) 25%

70. What will the man most likely do next?

(A) Arrange delivery
(B) Check the price online
(C) Look for a different item
(D) Measure the item

PART 4 🔊 16

Directions: You will hear some talks given by a single speaker. You will be asked to answer three questions about what the speaker says in each talk. Select the best response to each question and mark the letter (A), (B), (C), or (D) on your answer sheet. The talks will not be printed in your test book and will be spoken only one time.

71. What type of business is the message for?
    (A) A hotel
    (B) An airline
    (C) An electronics store
    (D) An online clothing store

72. What are callers asked to have ready?
    (A) Their membership number
    (B) Their mobile phone number
    (C) Their order number
    (D) Their passport number

73. When is a caller directed to call back for a shorter wait time?
    (A) At 10:00 AM
    (B) At 5:30 PM
    (C) At 7:00 PM
    (D) At 8:30 PM

74. Why is the speaker meeting with the listeners?
    (A) To explain how some software works
    (B) To find out what they need in a new system
    (C) To inform new employees of company policies
    (D) To introduce a piece of equipment

75. According to the speaker, what is a benefit of his product over the competitor's?
    (A) It is cheaper.
    (B) It is faster.
    (C) It is higher quality.
    (D) It is lighter.

76. What will the listeners do next?
    (A) Listen to a presentation
    (B) Log into a new system
    (C) Use some office equipment
    (D) Watch a video

77. What is mentioned about the Air Space K shoes?
    (A) They are made for new runners only.
    (B) They are only available online.
    (C) They are the cheapest on the market.
    (D) They use a new type of fabric.

78. What does the store's technology do?
    (A) Make custom shoes
    (B) Measure foot size
    (C) Teach customers how to run
    (D) Show customers where to run

79. What does a customer have to do to get a free gift?
    (A) Bring in a coupon
    (B) Buy two pairs of shoes
    (C) Fill out a questionnaire
    (D) Say they heard the advertisement

80. Where are the listeners?
    (A) At a concert venue
    (B) At a grocery store
    (C) At a movie theater
    (D) At a sports venue

81. What will happen in five minutes?
    (A) A game will begin.
    (B) A performer will appear.
    (C) Another announcement will be made.
    (D) Snacks will be available.

82. What will listeners who show a subway card receive?
    (A) A copy of a magazine
    (B) A food discount
    (C) A free gift
    (D) A special seat

GO ON TO THE NEXT PAGE

83. What does the speaker mean when she says, "we will stop taking breakfast orders in about ten minutes"?

(A) The listeners should be in a hurry to leave.
(B) The listeners should decide what they want soon.
(C) The speaker is nearly finished with her shift.
(D) The speaker is running out of breakfast items.

84. What does the speaker suggest the listeners do?

(A) Order drinks separately
(B) Pay for their meals individually
(C) Share a common beverage
(D) Try an appetizer

85. What will the speaker bring the listeners soon?

(A) Coffee
(B) Menus
(C) Silverware
(D) Water

86. Who most likely is giving the report?

(A) A fire official
(B) A product designer
(C) A Web designer
(D) An IT staff member

87. What was the problem?

(A) A fire in the office damaged some equipment.
(B) A product was found to be defective.
(C) A Website had been hacked.
(D) An employee used an unsafe Website.

88. When will the problem be fully resolved?

(A) By tomorrow
(B) By the middle of next week
(C) At the end of next week
(D) Next month

89. What type of item is the speaker reporting on?

(A) A gadget
(B) A laptop computer
(C) A music player
(D) A video camera

90. What does the speaker imply when she says, "the store opened at 9:00 and it's almost 2:00 now"?

(A) The line at the cashier's is getting shorter.
(B) The popular item may be gone by now.
(C) The store clerks are tired already.
(D) The store will be closing soon.

91. When can a customer receive their online order?

(A) In three weeks
(B) In six weeks
(C) In about two months
(D) In six months

Expense Report					
Trip purpose: _Trade Show_			Department: _Sales_		
Name: _Catherine Snow_		Manager: _Isabelle Perkins_			
Date	Description	Air/Transp.	Hotel	Meals	Others
8/20, 23	RT flight to LA	$350			
8/20-22	3 nights stay		$800		
8/20-22	Meals			$300	
8/20-22	Rental car	$200			

92. Which department does the caller work in?

(A) Accounting
(B) Administration
(C) Personnel
(D) Sales

93. Look at the graphic. For what amount does Catherine have to produce receipts?

(A) $50
(B) $200
(C) $250
(D) $350

94. What is Catherine asked to do soon?

(A) Book the air tickets
(B) Bring a paper to the caller
(C) Change a reservation
(D) Fill out a form

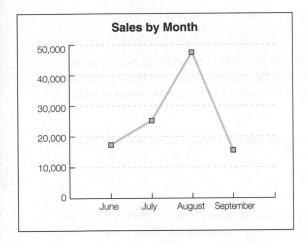

Sales by Month

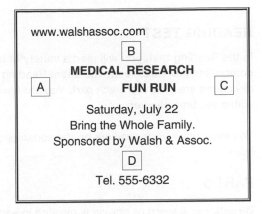

www.walshassoc.com

B

MEDICAL RESEARCH

A **FUN RUN** C

Saturday, July 22
Bring the Whole Family.
Sponsored by Walsh & Assoc.

D

Tel. 555-6332

95. Where most likely does the speaker work?

(A) At a cable services firm
(B) At a home furnishings company
(C) At a telecommunications company
(D) At a travel agency

96. Look at the graphic. When was the sale held?

(A) June
(B) July
(C) August
(D) September

97. What will Rachel talk about?

(A) A branch grand opening
(B) A new sales staff member
(C) Some new sales strategies
(D) The disappointing sales numbers

98. Where most likely does the speaker work?

(A) At a print shop
(B) At a sports gym
(C) In a business office
(D) In a shopping mall

99. Look at the graphic. Where does the speaker want to put the Web address?

(A) A
(B) B
(C) C
(D) D

100. What will the listeners do next?

(A) Attend an event
(B) Get a flyer printed
(C) Give their opinions
(D) Help the speaker hand out flyers

This is the end of the Listening test. Turn to Part 5 in your test book.

GO ON TO THE NEXT PAGE

READING TEST

In the Reading test, you will read a variety of texts and answer several different types of reading comprehension questions. The entire Reading test will last 75 minutes. There are three parts, and directions are given for each part. You are encouraged to answer as many questions as possible within the time allowed.

You must mark your answers on the separate answer sheet. Do not write your answers in your test book.

PART 5

Directions: A word or phrase is missing in each of the sentences below. Four answer choices are given below each sentence. Select the best answer to complete the sentence. Then mark the letter (A), (B), (C), or (D) on your answer sheet.

---

101. The express train that the division head took to work was delayed an hour because of mechanical -------.

(A) harm
(B) mistake
(C) revision
(D) trouble

102. Long-term testing was required to refine the business risk management process to make it more ------- and consistent.

(A) predict
(B) predictability
(C) predictable
(D) prediction

103. Two poster samples were presented to the team leader, but ------- struck him and the team had to think of something else.

(A) both
(B) each
(C) either
(D) neither

104. The nonprofit organization was fortunate to receive ------- assistance in the amount of $30,000 from the local bank.

(A) educational
(B) informative
(C) monetary
(D) personnel

105. Sunshine Security offers free on-site estimates with no ------- to buy for your home or business.

(A) obligate
(B) obligation
(C) oblige
(D) obliged

106. ------- the scheduled staff meeting, the assistant had to print out all the handouts for everyone.

(A) As far as
(B) Except for
(C) Just about
(D) Prior to

107. Although he was offered the position of overseas branch manager last week, Ian Lee is ------- considering if he should take the opportunity.

(A) almost
(B) only
(C) still
(D) yet

108. Owing ------- to the cooler-than-usual summer, the sales of air conditioners have dropped nationwide.

(A) large
(B) largely
(C) largeness
(D) larger

109. A voucher ------- to this e-mail in pdf format; please show it to the hotel clerk when you check in.
(A) attached
(B) attaching
(C) is attached
(D) is attaching

110. The magazine article succeeded in ------- public attention to the rural agricultural issues.
(A) directing
(B) forcing
(C) promoting
(D) reaching

111. Naomi Boomer rushed to the Fairmont Hotel, ------- she was scheduled to see her client.
(A) when
(B) where
(C) which
(D) who

112. The administrative manager thought that Central Park would be perfectly ------- for the company's outdoor event.
(A) suit
(B) suitability
(C) suitable
(D) suitably

113. The most noticeable ------- of the new smartphone series, Xtreme, is a fingerprint sensor to authenticate the user.
(A) fascination
(B) feature
(C) trademark
(D) treasure

114. The tour bus will stop at a spot to enjoy a panoramic view of the city ------- at least 20 minutes.
(A) by
(B) for
(C) until
(D) with

115. The CEO was delighted to hear the news that his firm recorded the ------- sales last quarter.
(A) higher
(B) highest
(C) lower
(D) lowest

116. The marketing chief was truly impressed with the new recruit's ------- analysis of the survey results.
(A) considerate
(B) desperate
(C) respectful
(D) thorough

117. Thanks to the success of its new products, Catty, Inc. was able to reduce its accumulated ------- by 8.5 million dollars last year.
(A) lose
(B) losing
(C) losses
(D) lost

118. This Website allows anyone who is interested in our city cleaning project ------- its progress.
(A) follow
(B) followed
(C) following
(D) to follow

119. As he ------- talked about his colorful career, the lecturer did not realize he had already gone over his time.
(A) confidentially
(B) cooperatively
(C) enormously
(D) passionately

120. With technology advancing so fast every day, ------- is critical for professionals and job seekers to stay up-to-date in their fields.
(A) it
(B) one
(C) that
(D) there

GO ON TO THE NEXT PAGE

121. In order to fully ------- the vision of our clients, we make every effort to establish a close relationship with them.
(A) realizable
(B) realization
(C) realize
(D) realized

122. Working for more than 20 years at a charity organization, Tim Davidson gained ------- in fund-raising activities.
(A) commitment
(B) comprehension
(C) expertise
(D) access

123. Everyone seemed exhausted after the long discussion; ------- the supervisor wrapped up the meeting quickly.
(A) accordingly
(B) likewise
(C) meanwhile
(D) nonetheless

124. The local bakery is famous for its ------- display of assorted bread and pastries in the window.
(A) appetite
(B) appetizer
(C) appetizing
(D) appetizingly

125. Please forward us the amount -------, which is indicated on the invoice, by the end of the month.
(A) counted
(B) balanced
(C) owed
(D) refunded

126. The botanist says that River City Garden benefits ------- from the mild climate of the area.
(A) rich
(B) richer
(C) richly
(D) richness

127. The waterfront development project ------- done a week ago, but it is nowhere near completion yet.
(A) had been
(B) should have been
(C) was
(D) would be

128. The division head was really looking forward to reading Molly Shannon's report, but she had not ------- finished yet.
(A) barely
(B) far
(C) quite
(D) very

129. The Emerson Group is dedicated to ------- people with limited finances or other special needs.
(A) help
(B) helped
(C) helping
(D) helps

130. To enforce the security, Madison Corp. decided to ------- a security guard at each of its three entrances.
(A) layout
(B) moving
(C) premises
(D) station

PART 6

Directions: Read the texts that follow. A word, phrase, or sentence is missing in parts of each text. Four answer choices for each question are given below the text. Select the best answer to complete the text. Then mark the letter (A), (B), (C), or (D) on your answer sheet.

Questions 131-134 refer to the following notice.

Harvey Collins: A Special Cinema Screening

Saturday 15 July

From *West End Lovers* to *All the Beautiful Tomorrows*, Harvey Collins' acting career ------- over five
131.

decades. Now, for the first time, the Creststone Picture House Archives has ------- together highlights
132.

from Mr. Collins award-winning career. Some clips from the collection are never-before-seen outtakes

and behind-the-scenes footage while filming in locations all over the world. Films will be introduced by

Creststone Archives Officer Kathryn Villa. -------.
133.

Seats are limited at this free event, so book yours soon. Please follow the link below for -------.
134.

https://www.eventbook/harveycollins/creststonearchives.com

131. (A) had spanned
    (B) is spanned
    (C) spanned
    (D) spans

132. (A) gone
    (B) got
    (C) moved
    (D) put

133. (A) She is in charge of all public inquiries about the works.
    (B) She will also be taking audience questions after each film.
    (C) The Creststone Cinema is undergoing renovation at this time.
    (D) There is a $5 charge for each adult, while children are free.

134. (A) discounts
    (B) lists
    (C) purchases
    (D) reservations

Questions 135-138 refer to the following e-mail.

To: cs@bbluggage.com
From: matildaikeda@greenmail.com
Subject: PakTek40
Date: August 10

To whom it may concern:

I bought your PakTek40 backpack about three weeks ago. I really like all the different pockets and

pouches. Since I bike to work, I need a lot of ------- to carry my stuff. -------. I tried applying a bit of
                               135.   **136.**

oil on it, but it won't move at all. I'm not sure ------- I should send it back to you or take it back to the
                                          137.

store where I bought it. Please let me know ------- to do to resolve this. Thank you.
                                              138.

135. (A) compartments
    (B) efforts
    (C) parts
    (D) alternatives

136. (A) I discovered yesterday that the small pouch
        in front has a tear on the bottom.
    (B) Just after getting home from the store,
        I spilled paint on it.
    (C) The straps are too short for me to use it on
        my bicycle.
    (D) Unfortunately, the main zipper got stuck and
        I haven't been able to fix it.

137. (A) as
    (B) if
    (C) though
    (D) where

138. (A) how
    (B) what
    (C) when
    (D) whom

Citywide Ferry Service to Launch Soon

The Rockridge _____ will be the first citywide ferry service to hit the water, with a launch coming in
                    139.

October. The two other planned routes will begin early next year. _____. The route includes a stop at
                                                                    140.

the City Center Terminal on the way from Rockridge to the _____ stop, Pier 7 in Brantley. Rides will
                                                           141.

cost $3.00, but fares won't be integrated with the rest of the city's transportation, meaning that riders

won't get a _____ transfer from boat to subway.
            142.

---

139. (A) bridge
(B) direction
(C) map
(D) route

140. (A) City officials are hoping to attract tourists to
the new park by offering free bus rides from
the station.
(B) Rockridge is getting the first service since
the area has among the longest commute
times in the city.
(C) The city council is expected to vote on the
new service's cost and stops at its next
monthly meeting.
(D) The ferry was traveling at the usual speed
when the accident occurred, according to
safety inspectors.

141. (A) final
(B) finalized
(C) finalize
(D) finally

142. (A) fast
(B) free
(C) complete
(D) secure

GO ON TO THE NEXT PAGE

Questions 143-146 refer to the following notice.

The annual company picnic will be held at Doe Reservoir Beach on Saturday, July 3, starting at 11:00 AM. All employees and their families ------- 143. . This year we again plan to ------- 144. volleyball, softball, swimming, and water-skiing (with at least three boats in the water!). ------- 145. . The company will provide basic barbecue fare (including vegetarian entrées) and sporting equipment, but all are ------- 146. to bring along their own fun. And don't forget your dessert! Please let Luke Harris know by June 21 how many people you'll be bringing. Looking forward to a wonderful time!

---

143. (A) are invited
     (B) invited
     (C) inviting
     (D) will be inviting

144. (A) promote
     (B) feature
     (C) operate
     (D) sustain

145. (A) All of us were happy to welcome our newest member, Josh, to the company last week.
     (B) If you have any ideas about the ceremony, please let Marie know before next Saturday.
     (C) Of course, the dessert contest will likely be the most popular part of the whole day.
     (D) Those who have used goods to donate to the charity, you can bring them up till July.

146. (A) encouraged
     (B) encouragement
     (C) encourager
     (D) encourages

PART 7

Directions: In this part you will read a selection of texts, such as magazine and newspaper articles, e-mails, and instant messages. Each text or set of texts is followed by several questions. Select the best answer for each question and mark the letter (A), (B), (C), or (D) on your answer sheet.

Questions 147-148 refer to the following memo.

After 40 years of service with Parker & Sons, Mr. Howard Trumbo will retire at the end of this month. Mr. Trumbo is known in the industry for his humor and hard work, and has said that he wants to use his golden years to travel and see parts of the globe he has never experienced before. We wish him all the best.

Ms. Janet Newsome, who has been selected to fill the seat, is expected to lead the company to a successful future after being our group leader for the last five years. The transition will take a few weeks, as new team members get acquainted with new responsibilities and tasks.

147. What is the purpose of the notice?

(A) To congratulate someone on winning a prize
(B) To give information about merger transition
(C) To inform staff about someone leaving the company
(D) To welcome a new team member to the company

148. What is true about Ms. Newsome?

(A) She retired a few weeks ago.
(B) She will go on a business trip abroad.
(C) She will transfer to a different office.
(D) She has led a team over years.

GO ON TO THE NEXT PAGE

Questions 149-150 refer to the following text message chain.

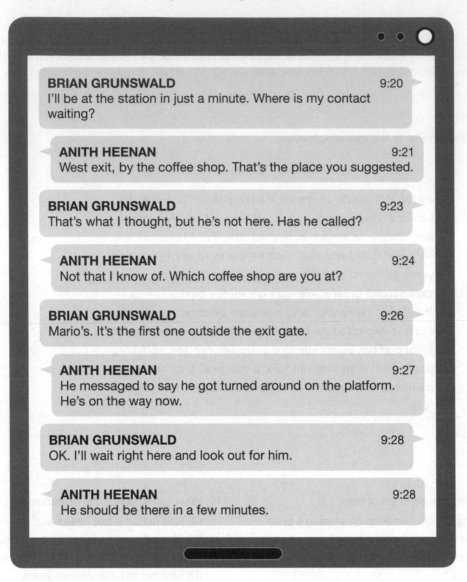

BRIAN GRUNSWALD   9:20
I'll be at the station in just a minute. Where is my contact waiting?

ANITH HEENAN   9:21
West exit, by the coffee shop. That's the place you suggested.

BRIAN GRUNSWALD   9:23
That's what I thought, but he's not here. Has he called?

ANITH HEENAN   9:24
Not that I know of. Which coffee shop are you at?

BRIAN GRUNSWALD   9:26
Mario's. It's the first one outside the exit gate.

ANITH HEENAN   9:27
He messaged to say he got turned around on the platform. He's on the way now.

BRIAN GRUNSWALD   9:28
OK. I'll wait right here and look out for him.

ANITH HEENAN   9:28
He should be there in a few minutes.

149. Where will Mr. Grunswald meet his contact?

(A) Beside the exit gate
(B) By a café
(C) Near the station
(D) On the platform

150. At 9:27, what does Ms. Heenan mean when she says, "he got turned around on the platform"?

(A) He got confused about the direction he needed to go.
(B) He started walking around the platform to look at things.
(C) He wanted to meet at a different place.
(D) He was walking in a large crowd.

The Conway Accounting Firm is proud to announce a getaway program for all employees! We want to show our appreciation for all the hard work you do during the year, and an office party isn't always the best answer, so starting the first week in September, we will be offering complimentary rotating day trips to various parts of the tri-state area.

These day trips will offer everyone a chance to relax, unwind him- or herself after the tough month of hard overtime. We want everyone to be able to enjoy these, so each trip will be within three hours of the office, and some of the choices include a day spa, first-class service at a lodge, or the virtual world at VirtuaPlex. There will be over 20 to choose from!

Everyone is eligible to use this program, but the dates are first come, first served; so don't wait too long. Sign up through the company intranet and look for the link marked "Employee Days" to select your day to getaway.

Actual Test 4

151. Why is the company offering day trips to the workers?

(A) As a reward for finishing a project
(B) As a thank-you for their effort
(C) As a thank-you for winning a prize
(D) As a year-end bonus for workers

152. What is NOT true about the programs?

(A) They are mainly outdoor activities.
(B) They are offered for free.
(C) They will not take long to travel to.
(D) They will start in early September.

In potentially bad news for their rivals, it is being reported that TES Systems and Holiday Technologies are entering a new business partnership to work together to increase market share in the very competitive technology market. Combined, the two companies will create one of the largest computer software companies in the world.

If approved, TES Systems will begin making parts for Holiday in an effort to increase margin by using cost-effective technology. It is reported that TES Systems uses refurbished materials, greatly reducing costs for the manufacturer. Although both companies are reluctant to use the word "merger," it looks to be the case in this situation. TES spokesman Greg Harrison said, "This partnership will help both companies increase profits, while benefiting each company with lower production costs."

153. What is the article mainly about?

(A) Company's fiscal condition

(B) A potential merger

(C) Developing new technology

(D) Raising recycling awareness

154. How does TES Systems keep costs down?

(A) They have an efficient manufacturing process.

(B) They outsource their manufacturing overseas.

(C) They will cut the costs by half.

(D) They use cheaper materials for their parts.

Attention: All Dream Net Employees

After a few months of negotiation, we have made the decision to bring in some new equipment to our office, and we want everyone to get a chance to be introduced to it, as well as learn how to use it. Starting on Monday, you will notice a section of the second floor will be blocked off in preparation of its installation. What is this new equipment? We think you will be very excited to learn that we will now be able to do the highest level Medical 3D printing, right here in the building.

As many of our clients have stated, this new technique is something they are interested in bringing to their network of rehabilitation clinics, and we believe that we can be the number one provider of these services. A number of our clients have stated their preference to use this technology with those they are trying to assist, and with the Wish Foundation, we can help those dreams become a reality. Whether it be a 3D printed hand or leg, we can now do our very best to be a part of the team that supports everyone in need.

Once installed, there will be a few basic training days, and then some more intensive programs for teams working directly with the machines. Questions or any other comments should be sent to Jackie Stevens at extension 49 or e-mail her at: jstevens@dreamnet.com.

155. Where will the new equipment be introduced?

(A) At a medical clinic
(B) At a new client's office
(C) At Dream Net's office
(D) At the Wish Foundation's office

156. What kind of work does the company most likely do?

(A) Aid people with disabilities
(B) Create images with high-tech scanners
(C) Sell office equipment
(D) Use technology to create servers

157. What will take place next week?

(A) The company will announce a partnership with the Wish Foundation.
(B) The company will discuss new product designs.
(C) The company will join a medical network.
(D) The company will offer training programs.

GO ON TO THE NEXT PAGE

Questions 158-160 refer to the following estimate.

Ken Brockton's Auto Repair

1928 Ball Road
Culver City, CA 90232
August 7

Damage	- Front left fender partially crushed - Front left headlight and casing - Bumper has cracks and paint scrapes
Repairs	- Repair and smooth front left fender - Replace headlight - Fix bumper cracks - Polish and wax bumper
Estimated Repair Time	4 days*
Estimated Cost	$850.00*
Insurance Details	- Automobile Insurance (pay for 60 percent) - Policy # 0323-268-9890
Auto Body Technician	Clark Flynn
Mechanic	Aaron Bernard
Customer	Nicholas Tunney 65 Arrow Lane Los Angeles, CA 90096 424-555-7404

Please note: Time and costs are subject to change. It is our policy to notify the customer of these changes before action is taken.

158. How many automobile parts will be fixed by the service?

(A) 1
(B) 2
(C) 3
(D) 4

159. When is the soonest the repairs could be finished?

(A) August 9
(B) August 11
(C) August 13
(D) August 15

160. What is indicated about the cost?

(A) An insurance company will partly cover it.
(B) It is due on August 30.
(C) It is the final amount.
(D) Mr. Tunney should pay $850.

---

e-mail

To:	Marcus Thorn <thorninyourside@nsm.com>
From:	Anthony Weldon Mtonyweldon@cwm.com>
Date:	September 23
Subject:	Cinema Write Magazine subscription

Hello Marcus,

I wanted to get in touch with you and say thank you for subscribing to our magazine for over ten years. It's because of supporters like you that we are able to continue delivering the #1 magazine for screenwriters in the world. —[1]—.

I noticed that your subscription is ending towards the end of next month, and thought I should see if you are ready to renew it today. Since you are in our top-rank subscribers, I am authorized to offer this "for your eyes only" special. —[2]—. With this special, you will receive a 60-percent discount on a two-year subscription, as well as receive commemorative copies of two original scripts used for the best picture winners from the last 50 years.

—[3]—. A chance to meet and interact with some of the hottest screenwriters in the business today! We will be having a Platinum Tier online course for everyone that wishes to attend. Here you can listen to experts, ask questions, and even get advice on how to best sell your script in today's market.

So what do you say, Marcus? Are you ready to continue with us and have the best to be delivered to your door every month? —[4]—.

Regards,
Anthony Weldon

---

161. When will Mr. Thorn's subscription expire?

(A) At the end of September
(B) At the beginning of October
(C) At the end of October
(D) At the beginning of November

162. Why is Mr. Thorn offered a special program?

(A) He has a top-level membership.
(B) He has donated a large amount of money.
(C) He has worked for the magazine for over ten years.
(D) He introduced the magazine to his friend.

163. In which of the positions marked [1], [2], [3], or [4] does the following sentence best belong?

"Act today and you will find something else coming to you as well."

(A) [1]
(B) [2]
(C) [3]
(D) [4]

Questions 164-167 refer to the following article.

Mayor West and the City Council today announced a plan to resurrect the riverbank area of our fine city. —[1]—. The plan, called the "Banks of Riverdale," will remove many of the older warehouses and buildings and replace them with more family friendly attractions to help visitor experience of downtown Riverdale. There will also be at least two new parks built next to the river with playgrounds, swings, and more for everyone to enjoy. —[2]—.

More than half of citizens polled said that the downtown area needed to be beautified to enhance what many consider to be one of the best cities in the region already. —[3]—. Project leaders said that this complete renovation of the area was considered years ago, but could only be funded now, thanks to the successful projects involving the city's sports teams and the revenue they are generating.

According to Mayor West, initial parts of the project will begin this spring, with the areas closest to the sports stadiums being renovated or removed first. From there, leaders are hoping new restaurants and shopping areas will catch on with those new and familiar to the area. —[4]—.

164. How will the city improve the waterfront area?

(A) By building restaurants and tourist sites
(B) By creating an amusement park for kids
(C) By making the river water safer and cleaner
(D) By moving warehouses to another part of the city

165. What is mentioned about Riverdale?

(A) It is close to a lake.
(B) It is looking for professional sports teams.
(C) It is opening a new stadium soon.
(D) It is seen as one of the top cities in the area.

166. Why did the city government decide to proceed with the renovation plan?

(A) The voters in the area agreed it upon after many debates.
(B) Money was finally available for it.
(C) They wanted to upgrade the city before a big sporting event.
(D) They wanted to update the city's look after criticism from the media.

167. In which of the positions marked [1], [2], [3], or [4] does the following sentence best belong?

"We are excited to hear more about this project as the plans become finalized over the next few weeks."

(A) [1]
(B) [2]
(C) [3]
(D) [4]

Questions 168-171 refer to the following notice.

We at Streamline would like to inform all our customers and clients that we are moving to larger offices next month. We have had such an unbelievable growth in the last few years thanks to all of you, and we wanted to say thank you for the kind reviews and helping spread the word about us. We at Streamline believe that the customer is the reason that we are here, and we want to make sure that we are doing the best we can to serve you.

Starting on September 1, we will begin our move across town to our new offices located in the Geraldine district. Our offices will be on the corner of 97th and Taft Street, in the Houseman Building, on floors one through five. Parking for the Houseman offices is in the rear of the building offering almost one hundred spaces. The first floor will be where most of the day-to-day operations will take place, our second floor will be for meetings and interviews, but on floors three through five, we are going to have production studios, where we will have some stages and sets to help create the perfect ideas for your business.

As we begin our transition into our new headquarters, we will make sure to have representatives at both the old and new locations, just in case you have questions. You can contact us via our Website at www.streamline.com or by calling 555-2389.

168. What is the reason Streamline has decided to change offices?

(A) The business has had much success recently.
(B) The customers asked them to move closer to downtown.
(C) They needed to make room for their new products.
(D) They streamlined their business operations.

169. Where should people park when visiting the new office?

(A) Behind the building
(B) In front of the building
(C) Next to the building
(D) Underneath the building

170. Which floor will a client visit if they give a presentation?

(A) On the first floor
(B) On the second floor
(C) On the third floor
(D) On the fourth floor

171. Why will some employees stay at the old office?

(A) To answer customers' questions
(B) To clean up old equipment
(C) To complete ongoing projects
(D) To meet some important customers

GO ON TO THE NEXT PAGE

GREG HUNT	Hello everyone. Any news about the exhibition next month?	11:30
TONY PLAYER	I received an e-mail about it yesterday. Didn't you get it?	11:31
JIM JONSON	I got it. Said we were all going to be sharing a room. Is that right?	11:33
GREG HUNT	What? How can we fit four of us in one room? We'll be stuffed in like sardines!	11:34
TONY PLAYER	How do they expect that to work? The rooms only have two beds.	11:36
JIM JONSON	That is a problem. I don't want to sleep on the floor for a week either.	11:37
RON BURKE	I'm here now. I asked management about the room. They said they would look into it.	11:39
GREG HUNT	Great. OK, let's think about how we will present the products this year.	11:39
TONY PLAYER	I was thinking that we should have some kind of interactive display.	11:40
JIM JONSON	I like that. Then people can try it out as we talk about it.	11:42
RON BURKE	Good plan. How about Tony and Jim handle the first presentation?	11:42
TONY PLAYER	OK. I'll work on it this afternoon.	11:44
JIM JONSON	What is the game plan for length of the demo? We don't want to go long.	11:47
GREG HUNT	No more than 10 to 15 minutes. We want as many people to see it as possible.	11:48
TONY PLAYER	We should prevent anyone from taking photos at the event as well.	11:49
RON BURKE	Of course. We wouldn't want competitors to "borrow" any ideas from us.	11:50
GREG HUNT	OK, let's get to work and meet again Friday with how we want to proceed.	11:51

172. What is the team preparing for?

    (A) A presentation for a client

    (B) An industry event

    (C) A competition

    (D) A sales meeting

173. Why did Mr. Burke contact management?

    (A) To ask about the project

    (B) To lower the cost

    (C) To request new equipment

    (D) To talk about the room size

174. Who will give the first speech?

    (A) Mr. Burke and Mr. Player

    (B) Mr. Hunt and Mr. Burke

    (C) Mr. Jonson and Mr. Hunt

    (D) Mr. Jonson and Mr. Player

175. At 11:47, what does Mr. Jonson mean when he says, "We don't want to go long"?

    (A) He does not like photo sessions.

    (B) He expects the event will end early.

    (C) He is reluctant to travel far.

    (D) He prefers the demo to be short.

To	Brian Sinclair
From	John Sheridan
Subject	New company policy
Date	July 17

Hi Brian,

Here's the draft for the new company summer shape-up program. I would appreciate some feedback from you on it.

Now that the summer is here, we would like to introduce an exciting new way for employees at Lang & Huston to begin the day. Starting at 8:00 AM, we will begin a 30-minute warm-up exercise class for everyone to attend. We are pushing everyone to be as healthy and active as possible this year! We will have a special guest to kick off our first week of morning sessions, but I don't want to spoil the surprise.

This will be a great way to stretch both our bodies and minds. After that, we will hold an office meeting to discuss what we can do to improve our daily missions. We want everyone to attend, so please make sure to be in Meeting Room A by 8:00 AM, starting Monday the 3rd.

John Sheridan
VP of Personnel
Lang & Huston, Inc.

To	John Sheridan
From	Brian Sinclair
Subject	RE: New company policy
Date	July 17

Hi John,

I am encouraged to read your e-mail about the morning shape-up program; however, I think we may have to make some changes to it. When I read it, I felt as though it was mandatory, and we cannot force anyone to join a workout class at work. How about we offer free classes to anyone that wants to have them? They would have to be offered at a few different times, since we can't exclude anyone from the opportunity. Also, we probably should also remove the special guest mystery. If you have someone special booked to make everyone excited to join, we should use that to encourage attendance. And why don't we schedule the sessions on the first and last day of the week, so we can begin and end the week with some team building?

Brian Sinclair
Sales Manager
Lang & Huston, Inc.

176. What does Mr. Sheridan want employees to do?

(A) Be industry leaders in health services
(B) Be more competitive with each other
(C) Have a better sales record than last year
(D) Have a workout with colleagues

177. In the first e-mail, the word "spoil" in paragraph 2, line 4, is closest in meaning to

(A) assist
(B) create
(C) repair
(D) ruin

178. When does Mr. Sinclair propose revealing a special guest?

(A) As late as possible
(B) At the first session
(C) Next Monday
(D) Sometime before August 3

179. What does Mr. Sinclair offer to do?

(A) Offer classes for recruits
(B) Open various times
(C) Register in advance
(D) Check personal preferences

180. Which days does Mr. Sinclair believe would be best for the classes?

(A) On Monday and Tuesday
(B) On Monday and Friday
(C) On Thursday and Friday
(D) On Saturday and Sunday

Office Supply Wholesale Order Form

Name:	Wolffe Marketing	**Shipping Address:**	2002 Republic Boulevard
Address:	66 Order Ave		Nashville, TN
	Springfield, IL		37201
	62702		
Date:	June 24		
Invoice #:	C2032		

Item	Qty.	Unit Price	Total Price
Printer paper (case)	10	$40.00	$400.00
Office desk 30x48x23	10	$100.00	$1,000.00
Office chairs (black)	10	$60.00	$600.00
Total			$2,000.00
Member Discount*: 10%			$1,800.00 (#OSW23789)
Tax**: 10%			$180.00
Total Cost			$1,980.00

*Member discount requires membership #
**No sales tax for orders shipped to KY, TN, MS, or AL

---

e-mail

To:	Customer Service <csr@osw.com>
From:	Leila Saldana <leilasaldana@packmail.com>
Subject:	Order #OSW23789
Date:	July 1

Attn: Customer Service Department

Our office ordered some new furniture for our new staff (order #2032) from your online store. The order was placed last month.

Everything arrived fine at our receiving address today, but there are two errors that do need attention. The office chairs that we ordered were black, but all ten that we received were red. While these are very nice chairs, we would prefer something a little more suited for our office design. Another problem is about the sales tax on the items I have bought. Can I get a price adjustment for that?

We would like to exchange the chairs as soon as possible, as our new employees start at the office on the 12th. I would like an authorization label to switch the chairs, as well as reimbursement for the shipping cost for returning them to your warehouse.

Thank you very much for your attention to this issue.

Sincerely,
Leila Saldana
Floor Manager
Wolffe Marketing

181. What can be inferred in the invoice?
    (A) The billing and shipping addresses are the same.
    (B) A shipping charge has been added.
    (C) Each item has the same quantity.
    (D) Only office furniture has been ordered.

182. How long did Wolffe Marketing wait for the supplies?
    (A) For a few days
    (B) For about a week
    (C) For a few weeks
    (D) For about a month

183. How much will Ms. Saldana get back?
    (A) $150
    (B) $180
    (C) $200
    (D) $380

184. What is Ms. Saldana requesting from the supply company?
    (A) A discount on their next purchase
    (B) Approval to return the order
    (C) An exchange permission form
    (D) Reimbursement for the entire order

185. What was the problem with the order?
    (A) The color of an item was wrong.
    (B) The items were shipped to the wrong address.
    (C) The number of items was wrong.
    (D) The price of the chairs was incorrect.

GO ON TO THE NEXT PAGE

Just moved and need your cable TV and Internet service set up? Having trouble with your cable services? Call Jim the Cable Guy today.

- Low prices
- Convenient service times
- Locally owned and operated

The following packages are available to most customers within the region.

TV+Internet $50/month	Internet only $25/month
- Includes 200 channels and HD for free - Standard speed Internet	- Standard speed Internet - Free installation (online orders only)
TV only $40/month	**Deluxe $75/month**
- Includes 200 channels - Extra charge for HD	- Includes 250 channels and HD - High-speed Internet and free installation

Jim the Cable Guy
Service Application

Name: Candace Bauman
Best time of day*: 12:00-1:00 Monday, Wednesday, or
                          Thursday, before noon on weekends
Address: 3801 San Carlos Drive Esposito, California
Phone: 555-2839
Type of residence: Apartment

*We can't guarantee we'll make it at these times, but we strive to match your schedule.

★ ★ ☆ ☆ ☆ I signed up for Jim's cable service in my new place and the man (not Jim) came to install it today. I was frustrated that he was 30 minutes late. Since I was on my lunch break, I ended up getting back to work late. He also made a lot of noise and broke one of my pictures hanging above the TV. Since I paid top dollar for your service, I expected a much more professional installer. — Candace

186. What is mentioned about the owner of Jim the Cable Guy?

(A) He has an engineering degree.
(B) He has owned the business for decades.
(C) He lives in the area.
(D) He recently moved to a new place.

187. In the application, the word "strive" in line 8 is closest in meaning to

(A) affect
(B) compete
(C) oppose
(D) try

188. When did an employee of Jim the Cable Guy most likely visit Ms. Bauman's home?

(A) On Monday morning
(B) On Wednesday noon
(C) On Friday noon
(D) On Saturday morning

189. Which package did Ms. Bauman get?

(A) Deluxe
(B) Internet only
(C) TV and Internet
(D) TV only

190. What did Ms. Bauman complain about?

(A) The behavior of the installer
(B) The cable service price
(C) The quality of her TV picture
(D) The speed of her Internet

To	Theodore Slate <tslate@jumbo.com>
From	Cassandra Holly <cholly@jumbo.com>
Date	Monday, September 26
Subject	Pop-up store

Hi Theo,

I was wondering if you could do some research for me? I want to put some of our top-selling products in a pop-up store somewhere in town for the week-long vacation starting on October 6. We've done well selling our products online, which is good. I'm just not sure how many residents around here know about our products. Could you look around and see if there are any empty storefronts or even outdoor venues where we could set up shop? Thanks.

Cassie

e-mail

To:	Cassandra Holly <cholly@jumbo.com>
From:	Customer Service <cs@steelworks.com>Theodore Slate <tslate@jumbo.com>
Date:	Monday, October 3
Subject:	Re: Pop-up store

Hi Cassandra,

I'm really excited about your idea to feature our homemade bags in a visible way in Oaktown.
I found several places that might be of interest for the pop-up store. I've attached a list to this message. I'm thinking maybe the first or second would be the best, since they are the biggest and are available now. Although from a traffic standpoint, the last one could be perfect since it's on a busy corner downtown.

Let me know what you think. I can set up appointments with the owners of these places if you'd like to see any of them.

Theo

Type Property	Location	Size	Details
Storefront	391 Main Street	45 m²	Available now
Mall space	Oaktown – east wing	42 m²	Expensive
Kiosk near station	Greenbay Station exit	31 m²	Security concerns
Storefront	208 Redmond Blvd.	40 m²	Available mid Oct.

191. Why does Ms. Holly want to have a pop-up store?

(A) She has extra merchandise to sell.

(B) She has just started her business.

(C) She hopes to gain more local customers.

(D) She wants to introduce a new product line.

192. What type of product does Mr. Slate's company make?

(A) Clothing

(B) Cosmetics

(C) Jewelry

(D) Purses

193. Why would the location on the Redmond Boulevard likely not be chosen?

(A) It is not available at the right time.

(B) It is too expensive.

(C) It is too far away.

(D) It is too small.

194. What does Mr. Slate offer to do?

(A) Do more research

(B) Make a list of properties

(C) Make some appointments

(D) Show Ms. Holly some new products

195. What is mentioned about the kiosk?

(A) It is close to a mall.

(B) It is downtown.

(C) It is the largest location.

(D) It might not be safe.

THE BROWN HOTEL
... in the heart of Center Grove

The Brown Hotel is one of Center Grove's most well-known landmarks, just off of King Square near the convention center. We feature an in-house coffee shop and a full-service dining room. Here are the specials for the month of September.

- Stay two weeknights for the price of one.*
- Groups booking 3 or more double rooms can receive a 20% off discount.**

   *Offer does not apply to Mondays if it is a national holiday.

   **Not to be combined with any other offer.

Itinerary for Exhibition in Center Grove
September 23 – 25

Saturday, September 23	
10:00 AM	Arrive in Center Grove
11:00 AM	Set up booth for exhibition
1:00 – 5:00 PM	Exhibition at Welch Convention Center
Sunday, September 24	
10:00 AM	Doors open at exhibition
10:00 AM – 4:00 PM	Exhibition
7:00 PM	Dinner with your team
Monday, September 25 (national holiday)	
9:00 AM	Breakfast meeting with Center Grove director
11:00 AM	Campaign planning with Center Grove team (working lunch)
3:30 PM	Flight back to Winchester

To	Kate Johnson <kjohnson@mytex.com>
From	Bradley Dexter <bdexter@mytex.com>
Date	Monday, September 11
Subject	Your upcoming trip

Hi Kate,

I understand you're going to the exhibition at Center Grove. I went last year and it was really fun. Our people at the branch office are very nice and they will show you a good time. Be sure to ask the director to take you to this great breakfast place right on the water called Stanley's. The omelets are fantastic.

Anyway, I found this advertisement about the Brown Hotel. That's where we stayed last year. It's really convenient to the exhibition venue and the views of the bay are great, so ask for a bayside room.

Hope you can get one of the two discounts they're offering this month.
Have a nice trip.

Bradley Dexter

196. What is mentioned about the Brown Hotel?

(A) It has just been renovated.

(B) It is a renowned place.

(C) It offers 24-hour room service.

(D) It serves mostly businesspeople.

197. What will Ms. Johnson and her team be doing around noon on Monday?

(A) Discussing a business strategy

(B) Eating out

(C) Taking down the booth

(D) Working at the exhibition

198. Why will the team not be eligible for the hotel's half price discount?

(A) They are not staying long enough.

(B) They are staying at the hotel on the weekend.

(C) They do not have a membership card for the hotel.

(D) They will not book enough rooms.

199. When could Ms. Johnson go to Stanley's with her colleagues?

(A) On Saturday lunchtime

(B) On Sunday morning

(C) On Sunday evening

(D) On Monday morning

200. What does Mr. Dexter recommend doing at the hotel?

(A) Asking for extra pillows

(B) Getting a room on a certain side

(C) Going to the music hall

(D) Visiting a gift shop

Stop! This is the end of the test. If you finish before time is called, you may go back to Parts 5, 6, and 7 and check your work.

Actual Test

5

LISTENING TEST

In the Listening test, you will be asked to demonstrate how well you understand spoken English. The entire Listening test will last approximately 45 minutes. There are four parts, and directions are given for each part. You must mark your answers on the separate answer sheet. Do not write your answers in your test book.

PART 1

Directions: For each question in this part, you will hear four statements about a picture in your test book. When you hear the statements, you must select the one statement that best describes what you see in the picture. Then find the number of the question on your answer sheet and mark your answer. The statements will not be printed in your test book and will be spoken only one time.

Statement (C), "They're sitting at the table," is the best description of the picture, so you should select answer (C) and mark it on your answer sheet.

1.

2.

GO ON TO THE NEXT PAGE

Actual Test **5**

3.

4.

5.

6.

GO ON TO THE NEXT PAGE

PART 2 🎧 ❪18❫

Directions: You will hear a question or statement and three responses spoken in English. They will not be printed in your test book and will be spoken only one time. Select the best response to the question or statement and mark the letter (A), (B), or (C) on your answer sheet.

7. Mark your answer on your answer sheet.

8. Mark your answer on your answer sheet.

9. Mark your answer on your answer sheet.

10. Mark your answer on your answer sheet.

11. Mark your answer on your answer sheet.

12. Mark your answer on your answer sheet.

13. Mark your answer on your answer sheet.

14. Mark your answer on your answer sheet.

15. Mark your answer on your answer sheet.

16. Mark your answer on your answer sheet.

17. Mark your answer on your answer sheet.

18. Mark your answer on your answer sheet.

19. Mark your answer on your answer sheet.

20. Mark your answer on your answer sheet.

21. Mark your answer on your answer sheet.

22. Mark your answer on your answer sheet.

23. Mark your answer on your answer sheet.

24. Mark your answer on your answer sheet.

25. Mark your answer on your answer sheet.

26. Mark your answer on your answer sheet.

27. Mark your answer on your answer sheet.

28. Mark your answer on your answer sheet.

29. Mark your answer on your answer sheet.

30. Mark your answer on your answer sheet.

31. Mark your answer on your answer sheet.

PART 3 🎧 19

Directions: You will hear some conversations between two or more people. You will be asked to answer three questions about what the speakers say in each conversation. Select the best response to each question and mark the letter (A), (B), (C), or (D) on your answer sheet. The conversations will not be printed in your test book and will be spoken only one time.

32. What are the speakers discussing?

(A) A company celebration

(B) An annual salary

(C) A leadership change

(D) A new product's sales

33. What did the man do last year?

(A) He got promoted.

(B) He moved departments.

(C) He overspent on a project.

(D) He planned an event.

34. What did the company president tell the woman to do?

(A) Book a larger venue

(B) Make a payment

(C) Increase sales soon

(D) Use less money

---

35. What is the purpose of the call?

(A) To cancel an appointment

(B) To change an appointment

(C) To confirm an appointment

(D) To make an appointment

36. When will the man go to the woman's office?

(A) This morning

(B) This afternoon

(C) Tomorrow at 3:00

(D) Tomorrow at 6:00

37. What does the woman remind the man about?

(A) His annual checkup

(B) His appointment next week

(C) His insurance information

(D) His payment from last month

---

38. Why is the man selling his couch?

(A) He bought a new one.

(B) He is moving overseas.

(C) It is rather old.

(D) It is too big for his new apartment.

39. What can be said about the woman?

(A) She has been in the man's apartment before.

(B) She is an apartment owner.

(C) She is having a party soon.

(D) She just moved to a new town.

40. What does the man imply when he says, "I'm showing it to somebody this afternoon"?

(A) He does not want the woman to buy his apartment.

(B) He may have found a buyer for the couch.

(C) He thinks someone is interested in his apartment.

(D) He wants to sell the couch quickly.

---

41. What is the woman's difficulty in making a decision?

(A) She has no suitable candidates.

(B) She has pressure from her boss.

(C) She has time pressure.

(D) She has two good choices.

42. Where do the speakers work?

(A) At a factory

(B) At a clothing store

(C) At a fast food restaurant

(D) At a supermarket

43. What does the man suggest?

(A) Advertising the position online

(B) Going to different stores to get data

(C) Having a joint interview

(D) Reading an essay from the candidates

---

44. What is the problem about the event?

    (A) It is largely over budget.

    (B) The speakers cannot find the venue.

    (C) The weather may be bad.

    (D) There are not enough participants.

45. What does the man say he will do?

    (A) Call a staff meeting

    (B) Inform the media about the event

    (C) Post a notice on the staff bulletin board

    (D) Put information on an internal network

46. When will the event probably be held?

    (A) Today

    (B) Thursday

    (C) Friday

    (D) Next Monday

47. Where does the man most likely work?

    (A) At a conference center

    (B) At a hotel

    (C) At a travel agency

    (D) At an airline

48. What is the purpose of the woman's trip?

    (A) Wedding

    (B) Business

    (C) Vacation

    (D) Family gathering

49. What will the woman give the man next?

    (A) Her contact information

    (B) Her credit card number

    (C) Her flight information

    (D) Her reservation number

50. What is mentioned about the man?

    (A) He is new at the office.

    (B) He wants to be president.

    (C) He was assigned a new project.

    (D) He would like to help the woman.

51. What does the woman mean when she says, "you have my vote"?

    (A) She hopes the man will run in an election.

    (B) She supports the man's idea.

    (C) She wants to elect the man to a managerial position.

    (D) She will give the man a good review.

52. Where will the man most likely go next?

    (A) To the City Hall

    (B) To the president's office

    (C) To the voting place

    (D) To the woman's office

53. What was changed over the weekend?

    (A) The computer network

    (B) The department spaces

    (C) The employees' desks

    (D) The office location

54. What does the woman say she needs to do?

    (A) Finish her report

    (B) Find her presentation notes

    (C) Get onto her computer

    (D) Give the man his assignment

55. What does the man offer to do for the woman?

    (A) Call the IT department

    (B) Change her password

    (C) Listen to her speech

    (D) Show her around the office

56. Why is the woman surprised?

(A) Her boss is leaving the company.
(B) Robert was late to the meeting.
(C) The applicants were not qualified.
(D) There are many job candidates.

57. What does Robert suggest?

(A) Advertising on more Websites
(B) Asking for some help
(C) Calling some universities
(D) Scheduling interviews soon

58. What will Tony probably do next?

(A) Fill out an application
(B) Enter data into a computer
(C) Interview a candidate
(D) Look through some applicants

59. Who most likely is the man?

(A) A board member
(B) A caterer
(C) A clerical assistant
(D) An organizer

60. What event is the woman calling about?

(A) A birthday party
(B) A retirement party
(C) An awards banquet
(D) An executive gathering

61. What will the man send the woman?

(A) A brochure
(B) A menu
(C) A price estimate
(D) A wine list

Rockford Natural History Museum Ticket Prices
• Regular Exhibits $18
—with audio tour $22
• Dinosaur Exhibit $10
—plus movie $14

62. Look at the graphic. How much did the man pay for his ticket?

(A) $10
(B) $14
(C) $18
(D) $22

63. What does the woman say about the movie?

(A) It explains the special exhibits.
(B) It has some special effects.
(C) It is very long.
(D) It runs every hour.

64. What does the man say he will do?

(A) Come back to the museum later
(B) Consider the woman's suggestion
(C) Join a museum club
(D) Watch the movie another day

Mystery	Biography
Science Fiction	Horror
History	Fantasy

Item No.	Fabric	Amount in Stock
C92	Cotton	18 meters
Ch19	Chiffon	1 meter
G05	Gauze	10 meters
W83	Wool	7 meters

65. What does the woman say about the book?

(A) It has gotten mixed reviews.

(B) It is difficult to read.

(C) It is popular.

(D) It is set in Europe.

66. Why does the man want to read the book?

(A) He needs to read it for an assignment.

(B) He wants to see if it is worth recommending.

(C) He read a rare review of the book.

(D) The woman highly recommended it.

67. Look at the graphic. What type of book is the man looking for?

(A) Fantasy

(B) History

(C) Horror

(D) Mystery

68. Where is this conversation most likely taking place?

(A) At a restaurant

(B) At a clothing store

(C) At a fabric store

(D) At an art store

69. What does the woman say she is doing this weekend?

(A) Going to a gallery

(B) Completing a piece of art

(C) Checking inventory

(D) Working at her company

70. Look at the graphic. Which fabric will the woman buy?

(A) C92

(B) Ch19

(C) G05

(D) W83

PART 4 🎧20

Directions: You will hear some talks given by a single speaker. You will be asked to answer three questions about what the speaker says in each talk. Select the best response to each question and mark the letter (A), (B), (C), or (D) on your answer sheet. The talks will not be printed in your test book and will be spoken only one time.

71. What event is the speaker attending next week?
(A) A building dedication
(B) A local festival
(C) A restaurant opening
(D) A winery tour

72. Why does the speaker ask the listener to contact her?
(A) To answer a question about the event
(B) To confirm an additional guest
(C) To cancel her attendance
(D) To give directions to the event

73. Who does the speaker mention is coming to visit?
(A) A business contact
(B) A business owner
(C) A friend
(D) A relative

74. Who most likely are the listeners?
(A) Book club members
(B) Bookstore employees
(C) Community leaders
(D) Cooking club members

75. According to the speaker, what will Mr. Pascal be doing soon?
(A) Demonstrating a skill
(B) Reading from his book
(C) Signing his book
(D) Taking questions from listeners

76. When did Mr. Pascal's interest in his chosen field start?
(A) After he wrote his first book
(B) In his childhood
(C) When he left France for the first time
(D) While he was in cooking school

77. Where is the announcement being made?
(A) On a boat
(B) On a tour bus
(C) On a train
(D) On an airplane

78. What is located near the snack bar?
(A) A tourist information counter
(B) Stairs to the exit
(C) The bathrooms
(D) The only available exit

79. Who speaks multiple languages?
(A) Restaurant servers
(B) Staff at a service center
(C) The snack bar employees
(D) The crew of the boat

80. What product is being advertised?
(A) A learning app
(B) A book series
(C) A language camp program
(D) A language private lesson

81. According to the advertisement, how does *Say Hello!* keep users motivated?
(A) By offering discounts regularly
(B) By offering level-up incentives
(C) By using interesting images
(D) By using popular music

82. What is mentioned about EduLang?
(A) It has received honors.
(B) It is a start-up in the software industry.
(C) It is the most popular company in the industry.
(D) It was started by technology experts.

GO ON TO THE NEXT PAGE

83. What department does the speaker work in?
   (A) Marketing
   (B) Payroll
   (C) Personnel
   (D) Sales

84. What does the speaker mean when she says, "I was hoping to finalize everything later today"?
   (A) She wants Dominic to call her soon.
   (B) She wants Dominic to hurry up.
   (C) She wants help on her final report.
   (D) She wants to leave early.

85. Who needs to visit the speaker's office today?
   (A) Dominic
   (B) George
   (C) The marketing boss
   (D) The payroll director

86. What type of radio program does the speaker host?
   (A) Classical music
   (B) Local news
   (C) Rock and roll
   (D) Talk show

87. According to the speaker, who is Marshall Young?
   (A) A bank employee
   (B) A local business leader
   (C) An orchestra conductor
   (D) A radio station worker

88. What does the speaker imply when he says, "Seating is limited"?
   (A) Listeners are eligible to reserve special tickets.
   (B) Listeners can get only front seats.
   (C) Listeners can reserve tickets for Wednesday only.
   (D) Listeners have to get tickets soon.

89. What is the main purpose of the call?
   (A) To congratulate a colleague
   (B) To inform a colleague of an award
   (C) To invite a colleague out for dinner
   (D) To request help from a colleague

90. What does the speaker mean when she says, "No one deserves this more than you"?
   (A) Everyone hoped the listener would win.
   (B) No other worker should get the award.
   (C) There is no one else on the speaker's team.
   (D) We all deserved a better result.

91. What is mentioned about the speaker's company this year?
   (A) It expanded to other places.
   (B) It hired many people.
   (C) It moved to a new location.
   (D) It won an award.

92. What kind of business is Stronghold, Inc.?
   (A) Information security
   (B) Investment
   (C) Law firm
   (D) Real estate

93. Why has this year been good for the company?
   (A) They expanded overseas.
   (B) They hired experienced employees.
   (C) Their reputation increased.
   (D) Their sales hit a record high.

94. What is the speaker offering the listeners?
   (A) Management positions
   (B) Extra security
   (C) Larger offices
   (D) Year-end bonuses

Store Sales by Week
(November)

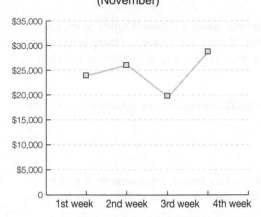

DIAMOND DEPARTMENT STORE
FLOOR DIRECTORY

4th Floor	Women's Wear
3rd Floor	Shoes
2nd Floor	Men's Wear
1st Floor	Cosmetics

95. What type of business is the speaker in?

(A) Hospitality
(B) Manufacturing
(C) Retail sales
(D) Construction

96. Look at the graphic. When will the store likely relocate?

(A) The 1st week in November
(B) The 2nd week in November
(C) The 3rd week in November
(D) The 4th week in November

97. What does the speaker say about sales?

(A) They are about the same year to year.
(B) They go up during seasonal campaigns.
(C) They have been lower than usual this year.
(D) They vary greatly within a month.

98. How often does the store have a sale?

(A) Every quarter
(B) Every six months
(C) Once a month
(D) Once a year

99. Look at the graphic. Where can a customer receive an extra discount today?

(A) On the 1st floor
(B) On the 2nd floor
(C) On the 3rd floor
(D) On the 4th floor

100. What would a customer do for a chance to win a prize?

(A) Fill out a survey
(B) Purchase a minimum amount of goods
(C) Show a coupon
(D) Use their loyalty card

This is the end of the Listening test. Turn to Part 5 in your test book.

READING TEST

In the Reading test, you will read a variety of texts and answer several different types of reading comprehension questions. The entire Reading test will last 75 minutes. There are three parts, and directions are given for each part. You are encouraged to answer as many questions as possible within the time allowed.

You must mark your answers on the separate answer sheet. Do not write your answers in your test book.

PART 5

Directions: A word or phrase is missing in each of the sentences below. Four answer choices are given below each sentence. Select the best answer to complete the sentence. Then mark the letter (A), (B), (C), or (D) on your answer sheet.

---

101. Cosmos House is a leading firm in the industry with a staff of over 200 ------- architects and designers.

(A) advanced
(B) calculated
(C) interested
(D) talented

102. Immigration ------- do not permit foreigners to work in the country without the appropriate status.

(A) regulate
(B) regulation
(C) regulations
(D) regulatory

103. ------- on Mr. Gibson's team contributed to the success of the new shoe line.

(A) Everyone
(B) Whoever
(C) One another
(D) Each other

104. We welcome your ------- to help us continually provide you with first-class service.

(A) motivation
(B) feedback
(C) invitation
(D) operation

105. This week only, easybuy.com is offering special discounts on ------- items.

(A) selected
(B) selecting
(C) selection
(D) selections

106. ------- the software company is relatively unknown, its new product could help it become popular.

(A) Although
(B) Despite
(C) In addition
(D) Until

107. While the delivery fee was supposed to be $300, the supplier charged the retailer $100 ------- on the bill.

(A) above
(B) high
(C) more
(D) up

108. Our customer care line is available seven days a week, ------- that no question goes unanswered.

(A) convincing
(B) deciding
(C) ensuring
(D) featuring

109. ------- for the marketing team, the sales campaign went exceptionally well and received wide media coverage.

(A) Fortunate
(B) Fortunately
(C) Fortune
(D) Fortunes

110. Wayfair Company is committed to ------- the latest software at affordable prices.

(A) provide
(B) provided
(C) provision
(D) providing

111. According to the specialist, wind turbines generally work ------- better in open, rural areas than mounted on rooftops in cities.

(A) far
(B) further
(C) less
(D) more

112. If you are a ------- to the digital version of *Movie Times*, you have access to our online archives.

(A) subscribe
(B) subscriber
(C) subscribers
(D) subscription

113. The division head was having a hard time choosing white ------- light gray for the wallpaper of his new office.

(A) and
(B) but
(C) nor
(D) or

114. The CEO always says that conducting ------- research and analysis can minimize the risk of failure.

(A) complicated
(B) redundant
(C) tentative
(D) thorough

115. Mark Tyler worked at Zane Industries in the early years of the company, ------- there were only a few employees.

(A) when
(B) where
(C) which
(D) whose

116. Despite her colleagues' enthusiasm about the merger, the news was ------- little interest to Lisa Olsen.

(A) at
(B) in
(C) of
(D) with

117. Although the job offer was almost too ------- to pass up, Lee Boule was reluctant to commute to a different state.

(A) attracting
(B) attraction
(C) attractive
(D) attractively

118. Please note that the accounting department will only provide ------- for expenses when a receipt is included with the form.

(A) reassessment
(B) reference
(C) reimbursement
(D) replica

119. As Amy Lynn ------- the speech every day since last week, her colleagues believe she is ready to deliver it.

(A) could have practiced
(B) had practiced
(C) has practiced
(D) practices

120. ------- your inquiry about joining our association, we will be more than happy to discuss membership details.

(A) Because
(B) Likewise
(C) Regarding
(D) With

GO ON TO THE NEXT PAGE

121. Milan Properties acquired Colton Tech's former sites, which ------- nearly one million square feet.
   (A) gross
   (B) net
   (C) sum
   (D) total

122. If the administrative manager had ------- his client Ms. Ford on the street, he would have said hello to her.
   (A) recognition
   (B) recognize
   (C) recognized
   (D) recognizing

123. If you return the product without a receipt, you will be given a store credit, which can be applied ------- your next purchase.
   (A) above
   (B) over
   (C) through
   (D) toward

124. Sue Ellis became a section chief three years ago and was ------- promoted to sales manager the next year.
   (A) chronologically
   (B) continually
   (C) sincerely
   (D) subsequently

125. The last chapter of ZDE Steel's corporate history features the company's ------- in the 1980s.
   (A) expand
   (B) expandable
   (C) expander
   (D) expansion

126. Under the company regulations, factory inspections have to be carried out ------- every two months.
   (A) during
   (B) once
   (C) then
   (D) within

127. With the most ------- carry-on luggage, travelers will avoid the inconveniences during the trip.
   (A) rigorous
   (B) comparable
   (C) vigorous
   (D) durable

128. The automobile company has announced a recall of over one million cars because their airbags were ------- manufactured.
   (A) defect
   (B) defective
   (C) defectively
   (D) defects

129. Some psychological treatments may have more ------- effects than other treatments.
   (A) last
   (B) lasting
   (C) lasted
   (D) lastly

130. To make an official purchase agreement, a director must hand in ------- from at least two potential vendors.
   (A) applications
   (B) estimates
   (C) requirements
   (D) comprises

PART 6

Directions: Read the texts that follow. A word, phrase, or sentence is missing in parts of each text. Four answer choices for each question are given below the text. Select the best answer to complete the text. Then mark the letter (A), (B), (C), or (D) on your answer sheet.

Questions 131-134 refer to the following notice.

Oak Grove Library Presents Business Lunch Hour

On Tuesday, November 7 from 11:30 AM to 12:30 PM, the Oak Grove Library will ------- a free
131.

Business Lunch Hour. Entrepreneurs and small business owners are invited to bring ------- own lunch
132.

and meet at the Oak Grove Library to learn digital skills to help their businesses grow. James Olson,

owner of Digital Age, will share ten ways you can boost your visibility online for free. This event is

presented in ------- with the Monroe Country Chamber of Commerce. -------.
133. **134.**

---

131. (A) cater
(B) establish
(C) host
(D) plan

132. (A) theirs
(B) them
(C) their
(D) themselves

133. (A) collaborate
(B) collaboration
(C) collaborative
(D) collaboratively

134. (A) For more information, call James at 555-2591.
(B) Participants will be charged a small fee at the door.
(C) The event will be called off in case of rain.
(D) The library will be closed on Monday, November 6.

San Marcos opening new store in Harriston

HARRISTON—Harriston is getting its first San Marcos. The coffee shop chain announced its ------- **135.**

for a store in Harriston on Tuesday. It says the store, due to open in February next year, is part of its

initiative, which ------- three years ago to invest in more rural communities across the nation. -------.
136. **137.**

San Marcos also plans to work with locally-owned businesses to supply products for the store.

Harriston officials have said they're excited about the store, believing it will help ------- more foot
138.

traffic to the downtown area.

---

135. (A) developments
(B) operations
(C) plans
(D) promises

136. (A) began
(B) had begun
(C) have begun
(D) will have begun

137. (A) Company officials say their goal is to create job opportunities for local youth.
(B) San Marcos grows its own beans in several Latin America and African countries.
(C) The investment is expected to be safe for retired couples and young people alike.
(D) Rural communities are usually the last to benefit from economic upturns.

138. (A) bring
(B) keep
(C) offer
(D) occur

Questions 139-142 refer to the following e-mail.

From: Henri Saveaux <hsaveaus@visitparis.fr>
To: Amalia Francis <amaliaf@bloggers.net>
Date: December 12
Subject: Permission to reprint

Dear Ms. Francis,

I work for a small publishing company in Paris. We put out an English tourist magazine about France

every quarter. We noticed your blog post on toursaroundtheworld.com. It was very ------- written
                                                                                      139.

and has some good pictures and maps. -------. Of course, we would pay you the ------- rate for
                                            140.   **141.**

contributions to our magazine. Your writing is so captivating—we're wondering if you'd like to be a

regular contributor. Please let us know if you agree to ------- or both offers.
                                                              142.

Thank you,

Henri Saveaux

---

139. (A) entertain
(B) entertaining
(C) entertainingly
(D) entertainment

140. (A) Each of our issues is focused on a different
city around the world, and next time it's
Berlin.
(B) Your illustrations were beautiful and we'd
like to hang them in our gallery in Paris.
(C) We think our readers would like it and are
wondering if we can print it in our February
issue.
(D) When you return to Paris, please visit our
new office near the River Seine.

141. (A) beneficial
(B) less
(C) reduced
(D) usual

142. (A) all
(B) either
(C) many
(D) neither

Museums Saver Ticket

Buy a museums saver ticket to the Fashion Museum, the Roman Museum, and Torrance Art Gallery and save big on entry prices! ------- **143.** . You can ------- **144.** a saver ticket online, at the front desks, or from the Tourist Information Center.

- Adults: £21.50
- Seniors (65 and over) / Students: £18.50
- Children (age 6–16): £11.75
- Groups of more than 20 people: £13.00 each

Season Ticket

------- **145.** value for entry for one full year to the Fashion Museum, the Roman Museum, and Torrance Art Gallery, the season ticket is also available in the same ways as described above. The season ticket is ------- **146.** if you live in the region or even if you just visit Torrance regularly.

- Adults: £30.00
- Seniors (65 and over) / Students: £25.00
- Children (age 6–16): £14.00

143. (A) All of the buildings are unfortunately closed for renovation at this time.
(B) You can buy three tickets to these three locations, all within ten minutes' walk of each other.
(C) There are more museums set to open in the Torrance area next year.
(D) When you visit Torrance by train, please get off at Torrance West Station.

144. (A) apply
(B) confirm
(C) purchase
(D) reserve

145. (A) Accessible
(B) Available
(C) Best
(D) Obvious

146. (A) perfect
(B) perfection
(C) perfectly
(D) perfectness

PART 7

Directions: In this part you will read a selection of texts, such as magazine and newspaper articles, e-mails, and instant messages. Each text or set of texts is followed by several questions. Select the best answer for each question and mark the letter (A), (B), (C), or (D) on your answer sheet.

Questions 147-148 refer to the following information.

In an effort to extend the life of your new Haven sweater, we would like to offer some advice and tips on how to take care of your new favorite top. First, since the material is very delicate, we do not recommend cleaning it in a conventional washer and dryer. The tossing and tumbling can cause the cloth to stretch, and after a few washes, it could possibly tear. Please take the sweater to a cleaning professional, such as a dry cleaner, to have it cleaned properly.

We also recommend keeping it in a dry, dark box when not wearing it, as it will help keep the colors bright and the materials fresh. Once taken out to wear, a soft felt brush should be used to clean lint or hair from the sweater. If you choose to use something else, it may work fine, but anything with coarse, plastic or metal bristles could cause damage to your top.

147. What could happen if the product is not taken to an experienced cleaner?

(A) It might get wrinkled.

(B) It might rip.

(C) It might shrink.

(D) The color might change.

148. According to the information, where should a user keep the product?

(A) In a bright room

(B) In a closet

(C) In a dry, covered container

(D) In a well-ventilated place

GO ON TO THE NEXT PAGE

Actual Test 5

This is a notice to all employees of Yongwater, Inc. in regard to the new vacation policy that will be implemented on October 1. All employees will be required to inform management at least two weeks prior to their target vacation date. If a time-off request comes up unexpectedly, we will review the need at that time. The updated policy is made to make sure that the company can continue operations without interruption, even if some employees are not available at their regular time. This will also enable the company to fill temporary positions if necessary. Please include the dates and reason for taking time-off and it will be reviewed by the management. Thank you for your cooperation.

149. What will happen in October?

(A) A new computer system will be introduced.
(B) New rules regarding holiday time will begin.
(C) The company will have temporary workers.
(D) The management will change.

150. When should an employee submit a document?

(A) At the beginning of every month
(B) About half a month before a day off
(C) In two weeks
(D) The next day

At Martinez Goods, we are working hard to create the things that we believe you will not want to live without. Therefore, we are proud to announce the Jericho 5000 line of microwaves. Our designers put in many hours of testing, including safety tests, to make sure that these appliances have all the features you need.

As someone who has purchased Jericho models in the past, we would like to invite you to participate in helping us decide what is important for the newest model of our line. We want to make the best product we can for our loyal customers, and with your help, we think we can. The survey below should only take about 5 – 7 minutes to complete, and as a thank-you, we will send a 10-percent-off coupon for your next purchase on our Website.

151. Who does Martinez Goods ask to join the survey?

(A) Any visitors to their Website
(B) Parents of young children
(C) Previous customers
(D) Their designers

152. What is a responder offered after filling out the survey?

(A) A voucher
(B) A free gift
(C) A link to a special sale
(D) A thank-you e-mail

Actual Test 5

Brad Young   1:32 PM
What did you think of the new human resources proposal Ray sent this morning? It seems like it will fit onto the company vision for the coming year nicely.

Jessica Imono   1:36 PM
I haven't had much time to look it over yet, but from what I've seen, it looks good.

Brad Young   1:37 PM
I wanted to get your input on something. Did you read the extra section marked "bonus" in the e-mail?

Jessica Imono   1:40 PM
No, where was it? I didn't see any attachments on the e-mail. Let me check again.

Brad Young   1:42 PM
It should either be attached or maybe a link on the bottom on the e-mail. I could forward it to you now.

Jessica Imono   1:43 PM
That would be great. It's definitely not here.

Brad Young   1:44 PM
OK. Check again in a few minutes and then we can talk about it.

153. What is the conversation topic?

(A) A company employee

(B) A company problem

(C) A personnel plan

(D) A missing item

154. At 1:43PM, what does Ms. Imono most likely mean when she writes, "It's definitely not here"?

(A) She cannot access a Web page.

(B) She cannot find the information.

(C) The e-mail must be missing.

(D) The information must be posted somewhere else.

Questions 155-157 refer to the following e-mail.

	e-mail
To:	Emerson Palmer <emersonp@nextmail.com>
From:	Reginald Teller <representative@dasexpress.com>
Date:	September 28
Subject:	Order #820-00812

Hello Mr. Palmer,

I am writing to you about your order with us for the digital antenna and speaker. Unfortunately, we had very strong storms near our warehouses this week, which caused some serious damage to our buildings. Therefore, we are unable to immediately ship the items you purchased. It will take 1-2 weeks for the buildings to be repaired and then another few days for order preparation before we anticipate orders resuming.

We have few options that you may choose for your order. First, approval of a delay will keep your order active, and we will ship it as soon as possible. Next, we can substitute a similar product and have it sent from another warehouse in the country to your location. Lastly, if you would prefer, we can cancel the order for you. Please let us know which is best for you in the next 48 hours. If we do not receive a response, we will keep the order active. We apologize for any inconvenience this may cause.

Thank you and have a nice day.

Reginald Teller
Service Representative

155. Why is the shipping delayed?

(A) Due to a delivery problem
(B) Due to inclement weather
(C) Due to mislabeling
(D) Due to a stock shortage

156. Which option is NOT given to the customer?

(A) An alternate item
(B) The order cancellation
(C) The later shipping of an item
(D) The refund for shipping costs

157. What will happen if Mr. Palmer does not respond in two days?

(A) The order will be canceled.
(B) The order will be charged.
(C) The order will be processed.
(D) The order will be delivered.

GO ON TO THE NEXT PAGE

Fall is almost upon us and now is the best time to get in shape for next year! At Gregg's Gym, we offer the most up-to-date techniques in aerobics, cardio, yoga, martial arts, muscle building, and weight loss programs. If you want to shed some pounds before the holidays, or just get some exercise, we have a plan for you.

Our off-season Body Saver series offer a little something for everyone. You can choose to take only one type of class for the full season, choose a pair of classes for the price of one, or use the mix-and-match system, joining any classes you want during your visit. Drop in and take a test drive with any of our qualified instructors and see how you can improve your well-being, and have fun while doing it.

Gregg's is open 7 days a week, from 6:00 AM to 12:00 AM every day, so we can fit into your schedule at any time you need. We are conveniently located at the corner of 17th and Winslow Avenue, right in the heart of the city, and only a two-block walk from the subway.

158. What is NOT mentioned in the ad?

(A) A type of exercise

(B) Business hours

(C) A location

(D) Requirements

159. According to the advertisement, what features does Gregg's have?

(A) A lot of staff members

(B) Right next to a station

(C) Open 24 hours a day

(D) Special offers

160. How can a person try out a service?

(A) By accompanying a friend

(B) By applying online

(C) By becoming a member at the site

(D) By going directly to the site

Questions 161-163 refer to the following e-mail.

To	Amelia Hunters <ahunters@sloanefoundation.com>
From	Rachel Benson <rbenson@nextmail.com>
Date	October 10
Subject	Sloane history exhibition

Hi Amelia,

I wanted to get in touch and see if you wanted to come with us to the Sloane history exhibition this weekend. —[1]—. It's supposed to be one of the best displays of the fall. —[2]—.

The arts director received permission to show everything in the museum's collection about our area's history and many things from our foundation will be included. There are so many items that I have wanted to see, but were always in the vault and unavailable to the public. —[3]— I know that you are a big fan of history and wouldn't want to miss a chance to see this.

If you can get back to me before 8:00 tomorrow night, I will be picking up tickets for everyone who wants to go at that time. —[4]—. There will be a group of us, maybe six or so, and we will be meeting at the office before heading over.

Rachel

161. What is the purpose of the e-mail?

(A) To ask Ms. Hunters to an event

(B) To get permission to leave work early

(C) To invite Ms. Hunters to lunch

(D) To respond to an e-mail

162. Where does Ms. Benson want to meet Ms. Hunters this weekend?

(A) At the box office

(B) At the city hall

(C) At the foundation office

(D) At the museum

163. In which of the positions marked [1], [2], [3], or [4] does the following sentence best belong?

"I heard that even the original designs for the city will be shown."

(A) [1]

(B) [2]

(C) [3]

(D) [4]

GO ON TO THE NEXT PAGE

```
┌─────────────────────────────────────────────────────────────────────┐
│ ▦▦▦▦▦▦▦▦▦▦▦▦▦▦▦▦▦          e-mail          ▦▦▦▦▦▦▦▦▦▦▦▦▦▦▦▦▦ │
├─────────────────────────────────────────────────────────────────────┤
│ To:      │ Amy Loughton <amyloughton01@parspace.com>                  │
│ From:    │ Kevin Redd <kevinredd@beldingnperk.com>                    │
│ Date:    │ August 25                                                  │
│ Subject: │ Sales Lead Position at Belding&Perk                        │
└─────────────────────────────────────────────────────────────────────┘
```

Hi Amy,

I wanted to thank you for coming to our office last week and speaking with me regarding the Sales Lead position. — [1] —. It was very nice meeting you and hearing your thoughts on what you could bring to our team, and some of the techniques you mentioned that could encourage sales in the coming years. — [2] —. I would like to offer you the position and wanted you to start with us on the 1st of the month.

We will need you to start off strong and, of course, have introductory meetings, as well as formal meetings with your teams. As our Sales Lead, we will need you to create goals and set deadlines for all of our teams, have biweekly update meetings with management, and assist in any large sales meetings. — [3] —. I don't want you to get buried during your initial weeks with us, so I will be working closely with you in the first month.

If you have any questions before or after your start date, please let me know. — [4] —.

Kevin Redd
Sales Manager, Belding & Perk

---

164. What does Mr. Redd like about the interview with Ms. Loughton?

(A) Her cheerful personality

(B) Her experience in sales

(C) Her management skills

(D) Her sales ideas

165. How will Ms. Loughton get ready for her first week at the company?

(A) She will attend training with other employees.

(B) She will complete assigned tasks.

(C) She will write a speech for her subordinates.

(D) She will have several meetings.

166. Who will help Ms. Loughton in September?

(A) Mr. Redd's assistant

(B) Sales team members

(C) The previous Sales Lead

(D) The Sales Manager

167. In which of the positions marked [1]. [2], [3], or [4] does the following sentence best belong?

"I know it sounds like quite a bit of work at first, but we believe that you can keep up."

(A) [1]

(B) [2]

(C) [3]

(D) [4]

Questions 168-171 refer to the following e-mail.

To	Jackson Waters <jwaters@noratech.com>
From	Emily Brewer <eb001@goerslove.com>
Date	Wednesday, November 1
Subject	Meeting about our products

Hi Mr. Waters,

I hope you are doing well. I wanted to see if it would be okay to reschedule tomorrow's meeting for the next week. We want to be able to share with you all of the most up-to-date product information we can, but won't receive the report until this evening. We would like to read and thoroughly go over the report before presenting it to you. Overall, it should take two or three days to read and confirm the product information.

Should we receive the product report earlier, I will, of course, let you know. We will have a little extra time to process and work with this information over the weekend, so we will have a demonstration prepared for you during the meeting. The beginning of next week should be fine for us. Would that be okay for you as well?

I look forward to hearing back from you and thank you for working with us on such an important project for both of our companies.

Thank you,
Emily Brewer

168. What is the purpose of the e-mail?

(A) To ask for an item description
(B) To ask to delay a meeting time
(C) To extend the meeting time
(D) To give an update on the meeting

169. How much time will the team spend going through the information?

(A) A few hours
(B) A day
(C) A few days
(D) A week

170. What does Ms. Brewer offer Mr. Waters?

(A) A completed unit
(B) A demo
(C) Printed reports
(D) Support documents

171. What day would Ms. Brewer most likely to meet with Mr. Waters?

(A) On Monday
(B) On Thursday
(C) On Friday
(D) On Saturday

GO ON TO THE NEXT PAGE

Questions 172-175 refer to the following online discussion.

Randal Bunch 11:34 AM		Has anyone seen Francis today? I was supposed to speak with him.
Ingrid Colane 11:35 AM		He got a phone call this morning and said he needed to leave. I think he was heading to a client's office.
Randal Bunch 11:35 AM		I see. Does anyone have an update on Kilnesmith?
Brian Lagerwood 11:40 AM		I think I can assist with that. I was working with Francis on that account.

— Ingrid Colane has exited the chat. —

Randal Bunch 11:41 AM		Great, thanks, Brian. I know that Francis has been working with them for quite some time. Do you think they will accept our offer?
Brian Lagerwood 11:41 AM		Francis and I have met with them multiple times over the last few months. It will come down to us or another company. They should decide by October 13.
Randal Bunch 11:44 AM		Hmm, OK. I was hoping to know by September. I need to know if there is anything we can do to encourage them to accept our offer. If they don't, it would set our finances back quite a bit for next fiscal year.
Brian Lagerwood 11:45 AM		Well, I heard that Bromley offered Klinesmith more money, but it was a short-time deal. Ours would be twice as long. Should we sweeten the pot?
Randal Bunch 11:46 AM		Maybe, but let's make sure that we can work with them on this. We can't afford to find another supplier in such a short amount of time.
Brian Lagerwood 11:47 AM		I will let you know as soon as I get an update.

172. What does Ms. Colane mention that Francis is doing?

(A) Going on a business trip

(B) Seeing with a client

(C) Trying to get a better deal

(D) Visiting a family member

173. How does Mr. Bunch describe a deal with Kilnesmith?

(A) Complex

(B) Demanding

(C) Essential

(D) Long-lasting

174. What has Mr. Lagerwood been involved with recently?

(A) Looking for a new location for a warehouse

(B) Meeting with a potential supplier

(C) Preparing for a business trip

(D) Working on financial details for next year

175. At 11:45 AM, what does Mr. Lagerwood most likely mean when he writes, "should we sweeten the pot?"

(A) He wants to know if he should explain why their contract is better.

(B) He wants to know if he should extend the time for them to decide.

(C) He wants to know if he should invite them for a meeting.

(D) He wonders if he should make a better offer.

GO ON TO THE NEXT PAGE

Shade: The Mark on Banker Hill

Written by Steven Bird
Directed by Lindy Allen

Richard Shade is a tough-talking, hard-boiled detective who knows the city like the back of his hand. He's had the respect of his peers since he was a fresh face on his first case. The city is dark and chilling and he feels that today is either his lucky day or maybe the worst day of his life. One of film's iconic crime detectives, Shade works outside the police and has many disputes with Maxwell Young, the one cop he trusts. Steven Bird has taken the original film and transformed it for today's audiences, using current technology to create the modern atmosphere that surrounds the story.

We also meet a mysterious woman, Gloria Grey, who believes someone is trying to steal her husband's inheritance, showing up at Shade's office and asking for his help. She lets herself in as Shade naps in his office, and proves to be a woman willing to do anything to get her hands on the money. The streets around Banker Hill are dangerous, but for someone like Richard Shade, it could be murder.

Running Time: 117 minutes

---

https://www.freshtomatoes.com/review

Shade: The Mark on Banker Hill is a remake of a classic movie, which tells us the story of a down-on-his-luck detective who is looking for a break. Originally, this was one of a series of films about Shade released in the 1950s and is now considered to be one of the classics of the genre.

This version of the Shade character has been given a softer side, and the private eye is now more of a fast-thinking joker. Stepping into the shoes of Richard Shade is Johnny Baxter, who has been cast historically as a more comedic and musical actor. But Baxter comes through with a performance that I believe the classic cast would be proud of. It's definitely a different take on the original, but Baxter handles the scenes like he was born for the role. Marianne Lewis is fantastic in the lead female role and will be seen as an up-and-coming star for sure. Since much of the story revolves around these two, it should be noted how well they work off of each other in the film, but there are memorable scenes with the rest of the small cast, too.

Shade is designed to be the first in a new film series for Grand Studios, and although this film isn't going to change the way we view crime movies, it is a good way to establish the characters in today's world.

176. Who is the person that Richard Shade has faith in?

(A) Gloria Grey
(B) Johnny Baxter
(C) Lindy Allen
(D) Maxwell Young

177. In the program, the word "fresh" in paragraph 1, line 2 is closest in meaning to

(A) additional
(B) energetic
(C) new
(D) raw

178. What is NOT true about the film?

(A) It's been reproduced.
(B) The director didn't change the original film.
(C) There are two main characters in the film.
(D) It has reflected the today's trend.

179. What change to the new version does the review focus on?

(A) The lead character
(B) The music
(C) The overall atmosphere
(D) The scenario

180. What kind of job is Mr. Baxter usually offered?

(A) Action
(B) Comedy
(C) Drama
(D) Horror

GO ON TO THE NEXT PAGE

Actual Test 5

To	Elijah Graham <elijah2019@inoutbox.com>
From	Tower Hotel <frontdesk@towerhotelten.com>
Date	September 5
Subject	Confirmation of reservation

Dear Mr. Graham,

We have received your request to book a room for October 3−12 and can confirm that we have Room 711 ready for you then. We can also confirm the wake-up call from October 4−6, at 5:30 AM for the three days.

The hotel and the surrounding areas will be very busy during your stay, as the Richmond Harvest Festival will be taking place. The city is expecting around 100,000 people to visit on at least one of the days during the week-long celebration. We appreciate your business and if there is anything we can do to make your stay even better, please do not hesitate to ask.

Service included	Wake-up call
	Complimentary breakfast
	Room cleaning
Room 711 at $92/night (Oct. 3−12, 9 nights)	Total: $828

Thank you for choosing Tower Hotel.

Jason Richards
Hospitality Manager
Tower Hotel, Richmond, Tennessee

To	Tower Hotel <frontdesk@towerhotelten.com>
From	Elijah Graham <elijah2019@inoutbox.com>
Date	September 6
Subject	Reservation and correction

Dear Mr. Richards,

Thank you for confirming the booking so quickly, but I noticed that there was an error with it. I will be leaving on the 11th, so I will not need the room on the 12th. Can you re-book and confirm the new dates?

Also, I was unaware of the Richmond Harvest Festival, so that may present a problem. I will be in town working with a client and I've requested a wake-up call not to be late. I am now worried that traffic may be difficult during the week. Do you offer shuttle service or hotel buses for your guests? I don't want to be late for my meetings because I have to wait for a public taxi.

Thank you,
Elijah Graham

181. When will the festival take place?

(A) At the end of September

(B) At the beginning of October

(C) In mid-October

(D) At the end of October

182. What service will the hotel provide for Mr. Graham?

(A) Refreshments

(B) Laundry

(C) Room service

(D) A free meal

183. When is Mr. Graham expected to have a meeting?

(A) On October 3–5

(B) On October 4–6

(C) On October 3–11

(C) On October 11–12

184. How many nights is Mr. Graham planning to stay at the hotel?

(A) 6

(B) 7

(C) 8

(D) 9

185. What does Mr. Graham ask the hotel about?

(A) A parking space

(B) The festival dates

(C) The room size

(D) Transportation

GO ON TO THE NEXT PAGE

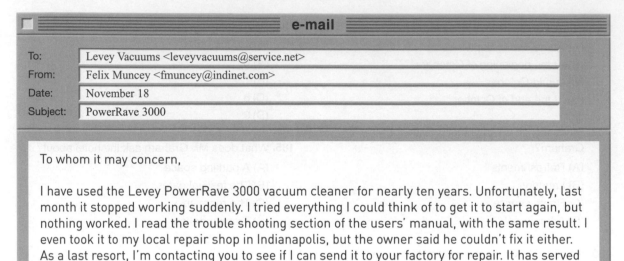

e-mail	
To:	Levey Vacuums <leveyvacuums@service.net>
From:	Felix Muncey <fmuncey@indinet.com>
Date:	November 18
Subject:	PowerRave 3000

To whom it may concern,

I have used the Levey PowerRave 3000 vacuum cleaner for nearly ten years. Unfortunately, last month it stopped working suddenly. I tried everything I could think of to get it to start again, but nothing worked. I read the trouble shooting section of the users' manual, with the same result. I even took it to my local repair shop in Indianapolis, but the owner said he couldn't fix it either. As a last resort, I'm contacting you to see if I can send it to your factory for repair. It has served me well all these years and I'd hate to have to replace it.

Thank you in advance for consideration.

Felix Muncey

e-mail	
To:	Felix Muncey <fmuncey@indinet.com>
From:	Levey Vacuums <leveyvacuums@service.net>
Date:	November 19
Subject:	RE: PowerRave 3000

Dear Mr. Muncey,

Thank you for your inquiry. We are sorry to hear that your PowerRave 3000 is no longer functioning. We regret to inform you that this model has been discontinued. However, since you liked the PowerRave so much, we're confident that you'll also like our new model, the Clean Machine XT (retail price: $250).

The Clean Machine XT is our newest model cleaner and has many attractive features. Its "one-of-a-kind material" means it is much lighter than any other comparable machine on the market, without sacrificing power. Also, the Clean Machine's revolutionary design allows for access into small corners and under furniture.

To honor your loyalty to the Levey vacuum brand, I'd like to offer you a discount on the purchase of the Clean Machine XT. I've attached the coupon to this message, so you can print it out and show it to one of our authorized outlets near you. We hope that we can retain you as a customer for many years to come.

Sincerely,
Marcia Lopez
Customer Care

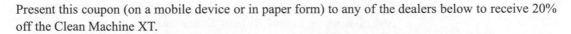

Date of issue: November 19

Present this coupon (on a mobile device or in paper form) to any of the dealers below to receive 20% off the Clean Machine XT.

Al's Vacuums	**Morristown Appliance**	**Flat Irons Appliance**	**S & B Vacuums**
Gary, IN	Morristown, IN	Evansville, IN	Indianapolis, IN

*Offer not good on any other make or model.
*Not to be combined with any other discounts or deals.
*Coupon expires six months after date of issue.

186. What is the purpose of the first e-mail?

(A) To ask about repair shops nearby
(B) To complain about a product
(C) To inquire about factory repair
(D) To request a refund

187. What makes the Clean Machine XT unique?

(A) Its power
(B) Its price
(C) Its size
(D) Its weight

188. How much is the vacuum with the coupon?

(A) $100
(B) $150
(C) $200
(D) $250

189. Which retailer is located in the same town as Mr. Muncey?

(A) Al's Vacuums
(B) Morristown Appliance
(C) Flat Irons Appliance
(D) S & B Vacuums

190. When will the coupon expire?

(A) On November 30
(B) On December 31
(C) On January 19
(D) On May 19

GO ON TO THE NEXT PAGE

Award-winning author Roland Evans has made us wait four long years, but finally, the follow-up to his best-selling smash *Surprise, Surprise!* is here. November 25 is the day to mark on your calendars: the release of *No Surprise Is a Good Surprise* in hardback. Mr. Evans was holed up in his mountain cabin for nearly six months last year finishing the book, according to his publicist. And it's worth the wait, say all reviewers lucky enough to get an advance copy.

Apparently, *No Surprise Is a Good Surprise* blends all the terrific characters and exciting actions readers loved in *Surprise, Surprise!* The question we're all asking now: is there a movie in the works, bringing these great books to the big screen? On that, Mr. Evans is being suspiciously quiet. We'll just have to see what surprise may await us.

Franklin Books Schedule of Events for December

Date	December 4 8:00 PM	December 7 3:00 PM	December 11 7:00 PM	December 14 1:00 PM	December 20 8:00 PM
Author	Lucia Tanak	Elise Pauley	Roland Evans	Emil Vargus	Erin Gutierrez
Type of book	Fantasy	Children's	Young Adult	History	Science Fiction

To	Johan Klein <jkdemon@fastline.com>
From	Franklin Books <customer@franklinbooks.com>
Date	December 21
Subject	Event calendar

Dear Mr. Klein,

Thank you for your message. We are sorry your experience at Mr. Evans's event was unsatisfactory. We do mention on our Website that seating is first come, first served as space is limited. If you arrived a bit late, as you indicated, it's not surprising you weren't able to get a seat. As for the long line for signatures, again, we cannot really help the popularity of our guest authors.

I will pass along your idea to have more than one event for each author. My supervisor takes customer feedback seriously. I hope you will join us again when another of your favorite authors comes to town.

Thank you.

Frannie Poleman
Franklin Books

191. What is mentioned about Mr. Evans?

(A) He has a shelter in the mountains.
(B) He is making a movie.
(C) He is taking a long vacation.
(D) He wants to quit writing.

192. What type of book is *No Surprise Is a Good Surprise*?

(A) Children's
(B) Fantasy
(C) Science Fiction
(D) Young adult

193. What can be said of Franklin Books?

(A) It closes at 8:00 PM.
(B) It did not hold morning events in December.
(C) It has a large event space.
(D) It holds an event once a week.

194. When did Mr. Klein likely attend an event at Franklin Books?

(A) On December 4
(B) On December 11
(C) On December 14
(D) On December 20

195. What does Ms. Poleman promise to do for Mr. Klein?

(A) Call him the next time an author comes
(B) Give his suggestion to her boss
(C) Save him a seat at an event
(D) Send him a discount coupon

GO ON TO THE NEXT PAGE

Questions 196-200 refer to the following e-mails and product information.

From	Jarvis Sloan <jsloan@allproav.net>
To	Stephanie Ross <sross@ultrawave.com>
Date	November 7
Subject	Presentation equipment

Dear Ms. Ross,

Thank you for your e-mail about our line of presentation equipment. I have attached a spec sheet to this e-mail. On the attachment, you will find a brief of features, plus the price ranges. For more details, including color pictures and a helpful video on each of these products, please see our Website at www. allproav.net. You can also set up an account and purchase any item directly from us via our Website.

Please don't hesitate to contact me if I can be of further assistance to you in meeting your company's audio-visual needs.

Sincerely,
Jarvis Sloan
All-Pro Audio-Visual, Inc.
555-2839

All-Pro Audio-Visual, Inc.

Projectors – portable and in-house
- Choose from 2.5 or 4 GB internal memory
- Wi-Fi connectivity
- USB capability
- Portable models are lightweight for easy travel
- LED lamp never needs replacing
- Price range $299-$495, depending on memory size

Screens
- Portable – easy set up and break down (includes travel case)
- Mounted (permanent) – electric or manual pull-down
- 92-120 inches
- Prices range from $99 to $159, depending on size

Smartboards
- Like a giant tablet in your conference room
- Interactive screen makes input from multiple people possible
- Multi-touch screen
- Dry-erase surface for drawing and writing
- Prices range from $559 to $999

The latest in presentation technology, these SMART boards are truly cutting-edge! Though a bit pricey, the collaboration they inspire makes it worth the cost.

```
┌─────────────────────────────────────────────────────────────────────┐
│ ═══════════════════════  e-mail  ═══════════════════════             │
├─────────────────────────────────────────────────────────────────────┤
│ To:       Jarvis Sloan <jsloan@allproav.net>                          │
│ From:     Stephanie Ross <sross@ultrawave.com>                        │
│ Date:     November 9                                                  │
│ Subject:  RE: Presentation equipment                                  │
└─────────────────────────────────────────────────────────────────────┘
```

Dear Mr. Sloan,

Thank you for your quick reply. While I'm interested in having a smartboard, the budget for our new start-up does not allow for this type of purchase right now. Please keep me informed of any reduction in price as you introduce new lines in the future.

For the moment, I'm interested in the cheapest projector, plus the 92-inch screen. Please let me know how I can purchase these, as I didn't see that information on the spec sheet.

Thank you for your help.

Stephanie Ross
Ultra Wave

196. Why does Mr. Sloan send the e-mail to Ms. Ross?

(A) To respond to her complaint
(B) To respond to her inquiry
(C) To schedule a meeting time with her
(D) To thank her for her business

197. According to the information, what is an advantage of a smartboard?

(A) Groups can work together more easily on it.
(B) It can be used as a video screen.
(C) It can be easily carried in a case.
(D) It is cheaper than a projector.

198. How much will Ms. Ross most likely pay for a screen?

(A) $99
(B) $159
(C) $299
(D) $495

199. What does Ms. Ross mention about the smartboard?

(A) Her boss does not understand its functions.
(B) Her company cannot afford to buy it.
(C) Her company does not need it.
(D) Her coworkers have never used one before.

200. What is implied about Ms. Ross?

(A) She did not look at the Website.
(B) She is the head of an established company.
(C) She is new at Mr. Sloan's company.
(D) She will give a presentation to Mr. Sloan.

Stop! This is the end of the test. If you finish before time is called, you may go back to Parts 5, 6, and 7 and check your work.

新制多益計分換算參考對照表

答對題數	聽力分數	答對題數	閱讀分數
96-100	480-495	96-100	460-495
91-95	435-490	91-95	410-475
86-90	395-450	86-90	380-430
81-85	355-415	81-85	355-400
76-80	325-375	76-80	325-375
71-75	295-340	71-75	295-345
66-70	265-315	66-70	265-315
61-65	240-285	61-65	235-285
56-60	215-260	56-60	205-255
51-55	190-235	51-55	175-225
46-50	160-210	46-50	150-195
41-45	135-180	41-45	120-170
36-40	110-155	36-40	100-140
31-35	85-130	31-35	75-120
26-30	70-105	26-30	55-100
21-25	50-90	21-25	40-80
16-20	35-75	16-20	30-65
11-15	20-55	11-15	20-50
6-10	15-40	6-10	15-35
1-5	5-20	1-5	5-20
0	5	0	5

註：上述表格僅供參考，實際計分以官方分數為準。

超完勝 新制多益高分5回 黃金試題1000題

Answer Sheet TEST NO. 1

測驗日	年	月	日
姓名	中文		
	英文		

答對題數	
成果	聽力
	閱讀

Listening Comprehension (Part I~IV)

NO.	ANSWER	NO.	ANSWER	NO.	ANSWER	NO.	ANSWER	NO.	ANSWER
1	a b c d	21	a b c	41	a b c d	61	a b c d	81	a b c d
2	a b c d	22	a b c	42	a b c d	62	a b c d	82	a b c d
3	a b c d	23	a b c	43	a b c d	63	a b c d	83	a b c d
4	a b c d	24	a b c	44	a b c d	64	a b c d	84	a b c d
5	a b c d	25	a b c	45	a b c d	65	a b c d	85	a b c d
6	a b c d	26	a b c	46	a b c d	66	a b c d	86	a b c d
7	a b c d	27	a b c	47	a b c d	67	a b c d	87	a b c d
8	a b c d	28	a b c	48	a b c d	68	a b c d	88	a b c d
9	a b c d	29	a b c	49	a b c d	69	a b c d	89	a b c d
10	a b c d	30	a b c	50	a b c d	70	a b c d	90	a b c d
11	a b c d	31	a b c	51	a b c d	71	a b c d	91	a b c d
12	a b c d	32	a b c	52	a b c d	72	a b c d	92	a b c d
13	a b c d	33	a b c	53	a b c d	73	a b c d	93	a b c d
14	a b c d	34	a b c	54	a b c d	74	a b c d	94	a b c d
15	a b c d	35	a b c	55	a b c d	75	a b c d	95	a b c d
16	a b c d	36	a b c	56	a b c d	76	a b c d	96	a b c d
17	a b c d	37	a b c	57	a b c d	77	a b c d	97	a b c d
18	a b c d	38	a b c	58	a b c d	78	a b c d	98	a b c d
19	a b c d	39	a b c	59	a b c d	79	a b c d	99	a b c d
20	a b c d	40	a b c	60	a b c d	80	a b c d	100	a b c d

Reading Comprehension (Part V~VII)

NO.	ANSWER	NO.	ANSWER	NO.	ANSWER	NO.	ANSWER	NO.	ANSWER
101	a b c d	121	a b c d	141	a b c d	161	a b c d	181	a b c d
102	a b c d	122	a b c d	142	a b c d	162	a b c d	182	a b c d
103	a b c d	123	a b c d	143	a b c d	163	a b c d	183	a b c d
104	a b c d	124	a b c d	144	a b c d	164	a b c d	184	a b c d
105	a b c d	125	a b c d	145	a b c d	165	a b c d	185	a b c d
106	a b c d	126	a b c d	146	a b c d	166	a b c d	186	a b c d
107	a b c d	127	a b c d	147	a b c d	167	a b c d	187	a b c d
108	a b c d	128	a b c d	148	a b c d	168	a b c d	188	a b c d
109	a b c d	129	a b c d	149	a b c d	169	a b c d	189	a b c d
110	a b c d	130	a b c d	150	a b c d	170	a b c d	190	a b c d
111	a b c d	131	a b c d	151	a b c d	171	a b c d	191	a b c d
112	a b c d	132	a b c d	152	a b c d	172	a b c d	192	a b c d
113	a b c d	133	a b c d	153	a b c d	173	a b c d	193	a b c d
114	a b c d	134	a b c d	154	a b c d	174	a b c d	194	a b c d
115	a b c d	135	a b c d	155	a b c d	175	a b c d	195	a b c d
116	a b c d	136	a b c d	156	a b c d	176	a b c d	196	a b c d
117	a b c d	137	a b c d	157	a b c d	177	a b c d	197	a b c d
118	a b c d	138	a b c d	158	a b c d	178	a b c d	198	a b c d
119	a b c d	139	a b c d	159	a b c d	179	a b c d	199	a b c d
120	a b c d	140	a b c d	160	a b c d	180	a b c d	200	a b c d

* 每題答案僅有一個，請參考下方＜範例＞的劃記方式。如未依規定劃記，或非用鉛筆書寫，致電腦無法讀取，由考生自行負責。

＜範例＞正確劃記方式：● 　錯誤劃記方式：○◐◑◒◓

應試文具：限用鉛筆（不得使用簽字筆、原子筆）

Answer Sheet

TEST NO. 2

超完勝 新制多益高分 5 回 黃金試題1000題

測驗日	年	月	日
姓名	中文		
	英文		

成果	答對題數
聽力	
閱讀	

Listening Comprehension (Part I~IV)

（NO. 1~100，每題 ANSWER 欄位為 a b c d 劃記選項）

Reading Comprehension (Part V~VII)

（NO. 101~200，每題 ANSWER 欄位為 a b c d 劃記選項）

* 每題答案僅有一個，請參考下方＜範例＞的劃記方式。如未依規定劃記，或非用鉛筆書寫，致電腦無法讀取，由考生自行負責。

＜範例＞正確劃記方式：● 　　錯誤劃記方式：◌ ○ ◍ ◑ ◐ ◉

應試文具：限用鉛筆（不得使用簽字筆、原子筆）

超完勝 新制多益高分5回 實金試題1000題

Answer Sheet

TEST NO. 3

測驗日	年	月	日
姓名	中文		
	英文		

	答對題數
成果	聽力
	閱讀

Listening Comprehension (Part I~IV)

Reading Comprehension (Part V~VII)

* 每題答案僅有一個，請參考下方＜範例＞的劃記方式。如未依規定劃記，或非用鉛筆書寫，致電腦無法讀取，由考生自行負責。

＜範例＞正確劃記方式：●　錯誤劃記方式：○⊙⊘◍①○

應試文具：限用鉛筆（不得使用簽字筆、原子筆）

超完勝 新制多益高分 5 回 黃金試題1000題

Answer Sheet TEST NO. 4

測驗日	年	月	日
姓名	中文		
	英文		

答對題數		
	聽力	
	閱讀	
成果		

Listening Comprehension (Part I～IV)

NO.	ANSWER	NO.	ANSWER	NO.	ANSWER	NO.	ANSWER
1	a b c d	21	a b c d	41	a b c d	61	a b c d
2	a b c d	22	a b c d	42	a b c d	62	a b c d
3	a b c d	23	a b c d	43	a b c d	63	a b c d
4	a b c	24	a b c d	44	a b c d	64	a b c d
5	a b c	25	a b c d	45	a b c d	65	a b c d
6	a b c	26	a b c d	46	a b c d	66	a b c d
7	a b c	27	a b c d	47	a b c d	67	a b c d
8	a b c	28	a b c d	48	a b c d	68	a b c d
9	a b c	29	a b c d	49	a b c d	69	a b c d
10	a b c	30	a b c d	50	a b c d	70	a b c d
11	a b c	31	a b c d	51	a b c d	71	a b c d
12	a b c	32	a b c d	52	a b c d	72	a b c d
13	a b c	33	a b c d	53	a b c d	73	a b c d
14	a b c	34	a b c d	54	a b c d	74	a b c d
15	a b c	35	a b c d	55	a b c d	75	a b c d
16	a b c	36	a b c d	56	a b c d	76	a b c d
17	a b c	37	a b c d	57	a b c d	77	a b c d
18	a b c	38	a b c d	58	a b c d	78	a b c d
19	a b c	39	a b c d	59	a b c d	79	a b c d
20	a b c	40	a b c d	60	a b c d	80	a b c d

NO.	ANSWER
81	a b c d
82	a b c d
83	a b c d
84	a b c d
85	a b c d
86	a b c d
87	a b c d
88	a b c d
89	a b c d
90	a b c d
91	a b c d
92	a b c d
93	a b c d
94	a b c d
95	a b c d
96	a b c d
97	a b c d
98	a b c d
99	a b c d
100	a b c d

應試文具：限用鉛筆（不得使用簽字筆、原子筆）

Reading Comprehension (Part V～VII)

NO.	ANSWER	NO.	ANSWER	NO.	ANSWER	NO.	ANSWER	NO.	ANSWER
101	a b c d	121	a b c d	141	a b c d	161	a b c d	181	a b c d
102	a b c d	122	a b c d	142	a b c d	162	a b c d	182	a b c d
103	a b c d	123	a b c d	143	a b c d	163	a b c d	183	a b c d
104	a b c d	124	a b c d	144	a b c d	164	a b c d	184	a b c d
105	a b c d	125	a b c d	145	a b c d	165	a b c d	185	a b c d
106	a b c d	126	a b c d	146	a b c d	166	a b c d	186	a b c d
107	a b c d	127	a b c d	147	a b c d	167	a b c d	187	a b c d
108	a b c d	128	a b c d	148	a b c d	168	a b c d	188	a b c d
109	a b c d	129	a b c d	149	a b c d	169	a b c d	189	a b c d
110	a b c d	130	a b c d	150	a b c d	170	a b c d	190	a b c d
111	a b c d	131	a b c d	151	a b c d	171	a b c d	191	a b c d
112	a b c d	132	a b c d	152	a b c d	172	a b c d	192	a b c d
113	a b c d	133	a b c d	153	a b c d	173	a b c d	193	a b c d
114	a b c d	134	a b c d	154	a b c d	174	a b c d	194	a b c d
115	a b c d	135	a b c d	155	a b c d	175	a b c d	195	a b c d
116	a b c d	136	a b c d	156	a b c d	176	a b c d	196	a b c d
117	a b c d	137	a b c d	157	a b c d	177	a b c d	197	a b c d
118	a b c d	138	a b c d	158	a b c d	178	a b c d	198	a b c d
119	a b c d	139	a b c d	159	a b c d	179	a b c d	199	a b c d
120	a b c d	140	a b c d	160	a b c d	180	a b c d	200	a b c d

* 每題答案僅有一個，請參考下方＜範例＞的畫記方式。如未依規定畫記，或非用鉛筆書寫，致電腦無法讀取，由考生自行負責。

＜範例＞正確劃記方式：● 　錯誤劃記方式：⊘ ○ ◐ ● ●

Answer Sheet TEST NO. **5**

超完勝 新制多益高分 5 回 **黃金試題1000題**

測驗日		年	月	日
姓名	中文			
	英文			

答對題數	
成果	聽力
	閱讀

Listening Comprehension (Part I～IV)

(答案卡 NO. 1～100，各題 ANSWER 選項 a b c d)

Reading Comprehension (Part V～VII)

(答案卡 NO. 101～200，各題 ANSWER 選項 a b c d)

應試文具：限用鉛筆（不得使用簽字筆、原子筆）

* 每題答案僅有一個，請參考下方＜範例＞的劃記方式。如未依規定劃記，或非用鉛筆書寫，致電腦無法讀取，由考生自行負責。

＜範例＞正確劃記方式：●　　錯誤劃記方式：⊙ ⊖ ◒ ◓ ◑ ●

百分百命中多益考題趨勢，
New TOEIC完整五回經典黃金試題，
超強詳解剖析解題關鍵！多益高分超簡單！

新制多益聽力測驗增加了「三人對話題」、「來回次數超過五次對話題」、「說話者意圖題」、「圖表整合題」；閱讀測驗增加了「句子插入題」、「說話者意圖題」及「多篇閱讀題」。新制題型考驗考生對英文資訊的整合能力。本書針對多益改制創新升級，依最新命題趨勢來編撰試題。試題本包含五回聽力閱讀模擬實戰考題，解析本包含聽力內容、詳盡中譯、解題句標示以及各題詳解，讓考生在短時間內快速提升應考能力，多益高分不再遙不可及！

❶ 考題命中新制多益出題方針！

針對新制多益命題趨勢，編寫高度擬真的聽力閱讀 **1000題**，題題切中考點，高效培養應試手感，如臨真實考場！

❷ 完整涵蓋多益出題題型與情境

題目涵蓋所有**多益題型**及多種**常考情境**，如電話留言、商家促銷、職場對話等，題型與主題完整，練習更全面，幫助熟悉出題模式，增加對新制多益題型及情境的熟悉度，上考場時看到題目沒在怕！

❸ 完整聽力對白稿及中譯！

聽力測驗附上完整的**中英對照文稿**，閱讀題目也附上篇章及題目**中譯**，作答後可藉由中英對照複習檢討，幫助快速理解失誤考題！

❹ 清楚標示解題關鍵句！

篇章題型皆貼心標示出**解題關鍵句**，幫助一眼找出破題關鍵，是做完考題後自我檢討的最佳幫手！

❺ 命中解題關鍵的超強詳解！

題題皆提供詳盡解題說明，除了點出**解題的關鍵資訊**以及羅列該題的**重點單字**外，另針對多益愛考的同義詞替換以及陷阱題目提供「**換句話說**」以及**陷阱選項分析**，幫助越過重重障礙奪高分！

❻ 貼心標示新制題型！

中譯本貼心標示出**新制題型**，在做自我檢討複習時，可重點留意新制題型出現位置、考題型態等，幫助在考前對新制題型瞭若指掌！

❼ 專業外師錄製的MP3！

聽力MP3由具有道地口音的專業外師所錄製，涵蓋多益聽力中重點測驗的**英美加澳**四國口音，讓考生快速熟悉各國口音特色，從容上陣應考！

寂天 文化事業股份有限公司
www.icosmos.com.tw   C1378-1624

超完勝
新制多益
高分5回

黃金試題
1000題

MP3

寂天雲 APP

或登入官網下載音檔
www.icosmos.com.tw

解析版

解析本

超完勝
新制多益
高分5回

黃金試題
1000題

解析版

解析本

Contents

PART 1 🎧 01

001 加

(A) A person is holding a camera in his hand.
(B) **A person is looking at a notebook.**
(C) A person is putting something in a box.
(D) A person is taking a picture.

中譯 (A) 有個人手裡拿著相機。
(B) 有個人正在看筆記本。
(C) 有個人正把某個東西放進盒子裡。
(D) 有個人正在拍照。

解析 照片中的男子坐著查看一本筆記本或記事本，因此 **(B)**「A person is looking at a notebook.」為最適當的描述；照片中的男子手上拿著東西，因此 **(A)** 當中刻意使用了「hold . . . in one's hand」的用法。

字彙 take a picture 拍照

---

002 英

(A) The bus is pulling into a parking lot.
(B) A car is picking up a passenger.
(C) Cars are lined up next to the bus.
(D) **People are boarding the bus.**

中譯 (A) 公車正開進停車場。
(B) 有輛車正在接乘客上車。
(C) 汽車在公車旁邊排成一列。
(D) 人們正在上公車。

解析 照片中背著書包的孩童們正在搭公車，因此 **(D)**「People are boarding the bus.」為最適當的描述；車子為靜止狀態，因此 **(A)** 的描述並不適當。

字彙 pull into 駛進
line up （使……）排成行／列
board 上（車、船、飛機等）

---

003 澳

(A) **They are crossing a street.**
(B) They are entering a driveway.
(C) They are turning a corner.
(D) They have their feet on the pedals.

中譯 (A) 他們正穿越街道。
(B) 他們正開進車道。
(C) 他們正轉過街角。
(D) 他們的腳踩在踏板上。

解析 照片中的人們正走在斑馬線上穿越馬路，因此 **(A)**「They are crossing a street.」為適當的描述；照片中並未出現車道（driveway）或街角（corner）。

字彙 cross 越過，橫渡
driveway （住宅通往馬路的）私人車道

004 (美)

(A) They are leaving a building.
(B) They are putting their luggage on the counter.
(C) They are shopping for coats.
(D) They are waiting in line.

中譯 (A) 他們正離開大樓。
(B) 他們正把行李放在櫃檯上。
(C) 他們正在逛街買外套。
(D) 他們排隊等候。

解析 照片中的人們在商店前方排隊等待入場,因此 (D)「They are waiting in line.」為最適當的描述;人們是往進入店家的方向排隊,因此「leaving a building」並不適當。

字彙 luggage 行李
wait in line 排隊等候

005 (澳)

(A) Chairs are being folded up.
(B) Screens are hanging from the ceiling.
(C) Seats are filled with people.
(D) A speaker is standing on the stage.

中譯 (A) 椅子正在被摺疊起來。
(B) 螢幕從天花板垂掛下來。
(C) 座位上坐滿了人。
(D) 有個演講者站在舞台上。

解析 照片中會議廳內的天花板上懸掛著螢幕,同時圍繞著講台,因此 (B)「Screens are hanging from the ceiling.」為最適當的描述;(A) 雖然螢幕下方有擺設椅子,但無法確認是否為摺疊起來的狀態。

字彙 fold up 把……摺疊起來
hang from the ceiling 從天花板上垂掛下來
be filled with 充滿
stage 舞臺

006 (美)

(A) A ship is being painted.
(B) A ship is docking at a pier.
(C) People are getting on a ship.
(D) People are standing on the beach.

中譯 (A) 一艘船正在被油漆。
(B) 有艘船正在停靠碼頭。
(C) 人們正在上船。
(D) 人們站在海灘上。

解析 照片中的人們站在海邊,因此 (D)「People are standing on the beach.」為最適當的描述;而船隻位在海的中央,因此 (B) 當中的「docking at a pier」並不適當。

字彙 dock 靠碼頭
pier 碼頭
get on 上(交通工具)

007 英美

Does your university still offer night classes?
(A) Yes, on Tuesdays and Thursdays.
(B) It has a library on campus.
(C) Many students go to the school.

中譯 你的大學仍有夜間課程嗎?
(A) 有,星期二和星期四上課。
(B) 校園裡有一間圖書館。
(C) 很多學生去上學。

解析 一般問句 本題詢問大學是否仍有夜間課程。(A) 採正面回答的方式,告知對方上課時間,故為正確答案。其餘選項皆為陷阱選項,僅是與學校有關的內容。

字彙 **offer** 提供

---

008 澳加

Whose mobile phone keeps ringing?
(A) It seems to be Jerry's.
(B) I think it's a good song.
(C) The caller is his sister.

中譯 誰的行動電話一直響?
(A) 好像是傑瑞的。
(B) 我覺得這是首好歌。
(C) 是他姊姊打來的。

解析 Whose 開頭的問句 本題詢問是誰的電話一直在響。(A) 表示可能是傑瑞的手機在響,故為正確答案。(C) 當中的「caller」指的是「打電話的人、來訪者」,為誘答陷阱。

字彙 **ring** (鐘、鈴等)鳴,響
seem 似乎

---

009 美澳

When did you go to the store?
(A) Across from the bank.
(B) I went this morning.
(C) The total was $24.92.

中譯 你什麼時候去商店的?
(A) 在銀行對面。
(B) 我今天早上去的。
(C) 總金額是 24.92 元。

解析 When 開頭的問句 本題詢問對方前往商店的時間。(B) 回答上午去過了,故為正確答案;(A) 和 (C) 的回答分別為位置和金額。

字彙 **total** 總額

010 加 英

The traffic is bad today.
(A) It's always like this on Fridays.
(B) The train was delayed due to the accident.
(C) I think that piece is fantastic.

中譯　今天的交通狀況不佳。
(A) 星期五都是這樣。
(B) 火車因為事故而誤點了。
(C) 我認為那個作品非常棒。

解析　**直述句**　本題提到今天交通的狀況不佳。(A) 表示週五總會碰上這種狀況，故為最適當的答覆。題目句中的 **traffic** 指的是路上的行人與車輛，因此 **(B)** 回答因事故導致火車誤點並不適當。

字彙　**due to** 因為，由於　**accident** 事故
piece（藝術、音樂等）作品

(02)

011 英 加

They haven't sold all of the new books by Mr. Martin, have they?
(A) Yes, if you want to see a movie.
(B) There are still a few left on the table over there.
(C) His latest book won an award.

中譯　他們還沒有把馬丁先生的新書全賣完，不是嗎？
(A) 是的，如果你想看電影的話。
(B) 那邊的桌上還有一些。
(C) 他最新的書得了獎。

解析　**附加問句**　本題詢問馬丁先生的新書是否都賣光了。**(B)** 表示還剩幾本，為最適當的答覆。

字彙　**see a movie** 看電影
win an award 得獎

012 澳 美

What was the last thing you read?
(A) It's a good way to spend a night.
(B) The event will last about 30 minutes.
(C) A great ghost story set in England.

中譯　你最近一次閱讀的東西是什麼？
(A) 那是打發夜晚時光的好方法。
(B) 那場活動將持續 30 分鐘左右。
(C) 一個背景在英國的精采鬼故事。

解析　**What 開頭的問句**　本題詢問對方最近看了哪些書。**(C)** 針對書進行介紹，故為最適當的答覆；**(B)** 當中「last」是動詞，意思為「（時間）持續」。

字彙　**last** 持續
set（故事、電影）以……為背景

013 英 澳

Is Mr. Stark still the president of Wolf's Creek?
(A) The company is growing.
(B) He retired last year.
(C) I think they sell auto parts.

中譯　沃夫克里克的總裁還是史塔克先生嗎？
(A) 公司正在成長。
(B) 他去年退休了。
(C) 我想他們販售汽車零件。

解析　**一般問句**　本題詢問史塔克先生是否還是公司的總裁。**(B)** 表示他退休了，故為最適當的答覆；**(A)** 和 **(C)** 的回答僅與公司有所關聯。

字彙　**retire** 退休　**auto part** 汽車零件

014 [加][美]

Why are the lights off in this room?
(A) There are four of them.
(B) No one was using it.
(C) The lunchroom is on the first floor.

中譯 這個房間的燈為什麼關了？
(A) 他們有四個人。
(B) 房間沒人。
(C) 餐廳在一樓。

解析 **Why 開頭的問句** 本題詢問把房間燈關掉的理由。**(B)** 表示現在沒人使用，也就是房間裡沒有人，故為適當的答覆。

字彙 lunchroom （學校、工廠等的）餐廳

---

015 [美][澳]

Where should we meet next time?
(A) Probably in the morning.
(B) Let's go to a restaurant.
(C) Once a week is best.

中譯 我們下次應該在哪裡見面？
(A) 也許在早上。
(B) 讓我們去家餐廳。
(C) 最好一星期一次。

解析 **Where 開頭的問句** 本題詢問下次見面的地點。**(B)** 針對地點提出建議，故為正確答案。**(A)** 和 **(C)** 的回答分別為時間和頻率。

---

016 [加][英]

How often do you visit your hometown?
(A) Every two years or so.
(B) It's a few hours from here.
(C) My parents still live there.

中譯 你多久回一次家鄉？
(A) 大約每二年一次。
(B) 從這裡去需要好幾個小時。
(C) 我父母還住在那裡。

解析 **How often 開頭的問句** 本題詢問頻率。**(A)** 回答出次數，故為適當的答覆；**(B)** 回答的是所需時間。

字彙 **or so** 大約

---

017 [美][澳]

Is she planning on flying to the conference?
(A) From Wednesday through Friday.
(B) She was, but all the flights were booked.
(C) These plans look great!

中譯 她打算搭飛機去參加大會嗎？
(A) 從星期三到星期五。
(B) 她原來計劃這樣，但所有的航班都訂滿了。
(C) 這些計劃看來很棒！

解析 **一般問句** 本題詢問是否打算搭飛機去參加會議。**(B)** 說明狀況來表達否定（她本來要搭飛機，但最後因買不到票而沒有搭），故為正確答案；**(A)** 回答的是時間；**(C)** 僅重複使用題目中的 **plan**，屬於陷阱選項。

字彙 **plan on** 計劃，打算

018 加美

Where did the marketing team go?
(A) They're at a seminar.
(B) It's all in this folder.
(C) We need two additional members.

中譯 行銷團隊去哪了？
(A) 他們去參加研討會。
(B) 都在這個檔案夾裡。
(C) 我們還需要二位成員。

解析 **Where 開頭的問句** 本題詢問行銷部前往的地點。(A) 表示他們去參加研討會，故為最適當的答覆；(B) 為陷阱選項，「in this folder」與 where 問句有關。

字彙 **seminar** 研討會，專題討論會
additional 額外的，另外的

🎧 02

019 英加

He's taken on a lot of extra responsibility, hasn't he?
(A) No, he arrived five minutes ago.
(B) We'll take extra precautions, of course.
(C) Yes, and it's rather surprising.

中譯 他承擔了很多額外的職責，不是嗎？
(A) 不，他五分鐘前到的。
(B) 當然，我們會格外謹慎。
(C) 是的，這相當令人吃驚。

解析 **附加問句** (C) 先是以 Yes 表示同意對方的看法，並告知自己的想法，故為最適當的答覆；(A) 和 (B) 與題目無關，不適合作為答案。

字彙 **take on** 承擔（責任），接受（挑戰）
precaution 預防措施　**rather** 相當

020 美澳

How did everything go at the convention?
(A) I'll try to be on time.
(B) In Los Angeles, I believe.
(C) Very well. I wish you had been there.

中譯 大會進行得順利嗎？
(A) 我會設法準時到。
(B) 我相信是在洛杉磯。
(C) 非常順利，我希望你當時在場。

解析 **How 開頭的問句** 本題詢問會議的狀況。(C) 表示非常順利，同時表達希望對方能夠在場，故為最適當的答覆。

字彙 **convention** 會議，大會　**on time** 準時

021 英加

I'm thinking about changing apartments.
(A) I pay nearly $2,000 a month.
(B) Oh, really? Why?
(C) We have only one more candidate.

中譯 我在考慮換間公寓。
(A) 我每個月付將近二千元。
(B) 噢，真的嗎？為什麼？
(C) 我們只剩一個應徵者了。

解析 **直述句** (B) 對於對方的想法表示驚訝，同時以 why 詢問對方理由，故為最適當的答覆。

字彙 **pay** 支付，付款給
candidate 候選人，應試者

022 澳美

Have all the attendees received a packet?
(A) Yes. I handed them out as they arrived.
(B) This package is addressed to someone else.
(C) No. We need to collect more data.

中譯 所有出席者都收到資料袋了嗎？
(A) 是的，我在他們到達時發給他們了。
(B) 這個包裹是寄給別人的。
(C) 不，我們需要收集更多資料。

解析 **一般問句** 本題詢問參加者是否都有收到資料袋。(A) 表示都有收到，並補充說明在大家抵達現場時便發送，故為適當的答覆；(B) 當中的「package」僅與「packet」發音相似，屬於答題陷阱。

字彙 **packet** 小包，小袋
hand out 分發，免費給予 **package** 包裹
address 在……（信封或包裹上）寫上姓名或地址
collect 收集

023 澳英

When is a good time to reach Mr. Thompson?
(A) He's in the office by 8:00 every morning.
(B) I'm sorry, we've run out of time.
(C) It opened last week.

中譯 何時方便聯絡湯普森先生？
(A) 他每天早上 8 點前就在辦公室了。
(B) 抱歉，我們沒時間了。
(C) 上星期開幕的。

解析 **When 開頭的問句** 本題詢問適合聯絡的時間。(A) 採間接回答的方式，表示他每天上午八點上班，最為適當；(C) 當中使用「it」，無法得知它指的是什麼，且該回答使用過去式，因此並不適當。

字彙 **run out of time** 沒有時間

024 加澳

Could you help me with next quarter's budget?
(A) Which floor are you going to?
(B) We went over by quite a bit.
(C) Yes, but I'm busy until noon.

中譯 你可以協助我做下一季的預算嗎？
(A) 你要去哪一樓？
(B) 我們預算超支許多。
(C) 可以，但我要忙到中午。

解析 **Could you 開頭的問句** 本題請求對方的協助。(C) 答應對方，並補充說明自己會忙到中午，故為最適當的答覆。

字彙 **quarter** 季度
go over 超過
quite a bit 很多

025 加美

His sales numbers are slipping, unfortunately.
(A) All of our accessories are on sale today.
(B) I don't have time right now.
(C) What should we do about it?

中譯 很遺憾，他的業績正在下滑。
(A) 我們所有的配件今天都特價。
(B) 我現在沒時間。
(C) 我們應該怎麼辦？

解析 直述句 本題指出銷售業績不佳的問題。slip 的意思為「下降、惡化、變差」。(C) 反問對方要怎麼解決這個問題，故為最適當的答覆。

字彙 sales number 銷量，業績　slip 下降
on sale 降價出售

026 美英

Should we buy these supplies online or at the store?
(A) Whichever is cheaper.
(B) I'd rather take the train.
(C) We accept all types of credit cards.

中譯 我們應該在網上訂購這些日用品還是去店裡買？
(A) 看哪邊比較便宜。
(B) 我寧願搭火車。
(C) 我們接受所有種類的信用卡。

解析 選擇疑問句 本題詢問購買的地方。(A) 表示只要是便宜的地方都好，故為最適當的答覆；(B)「I'd rather」具有選擇的概念，有時候會被用在正確答案中。

字彙 supply 生活用品　accept 接受

027 澳加

The new clients have been entered in the system, right?
(A) I'm just finishing the last one.
(B) No. They're staying overnight.
(C) Yes. They just left.

中譯 新客戶都已鍵入系統，對嗎？
(A) 我剛完成最後一位。
(B) 不，他們要過夜。
(C) 是的，他們剛離開。

解析 直述句 本題與附加問句相同，屬於向對方確認的句子。(A) 表示已經將客戶資料建檔完畢，故為最適當的答覆。

字彙 stay overnight 過夜

028 美澳

Who is that waiting in the conference room?
(A) The client suddenly postponed the meeting.
(B) It must be my 10:00 appointment.
(C) The equipment is all ready.

中譯 在會議室等候的那個人是誰？
(A) 客戶突然把會議延後。
(B) 一定是我十點約的人。
(C) 設備都準備好了。

解析 Who 開頭的問句 本題詢問會議室內的人是誰。(B) 並未回答人名，而是利用擬人化的方式回答「my 10:00 appointment」，故為最適當的答覆；若未充分理解問題的意思，可能會誤選 (A)，請特別注意。

字彙 postpone 使……延期，延緩

Have you decided on a section leader yet?
(A) All seats in this section are reserved.
(B) It's between Logan and Maria.
(C) Not everyone is happy about it.

中譯　你們決定好科長人選了嗎？
(A) 這一區的座位都有人預訂了。
(B) 從羅根和瑪麗亞二人中選一個。
(C) 不是每個人都滿意。

解析　一般問句　當該問題有很多種回答方式時，可以使用刪去法，選出最適當的答覆。本題詢問對方是否已做好人事上的決定。(B) 表示要從兩個人選中取一，故為最適當的答覆；(A) 僅重複使用題目中的 section，為陷阱選項。

字彙　decide on　決定，選定
section leader　部門、處、科、組等領導人
reserve　預訂，保留

You picked up the new brochures, didn't you?
(A) No, I'm just leaving to do that now.
(B) Whenever you decide to go is fine.
(C) Yes, they'll be ready tomorrow.

中譯　你去拿了新的廣告手冊，不是嗎？
(A) 沒有，我現在正要出發去拿。
(B) 不管你決定何時去都行。
(C) 是的，明天會準備好。

解析　附加問句　針對確認型的問句，無論是正面或反面的答覆，後方都必須連接相對應的內容。本題詢問是否有把新手冊帶過來，(A) 回答沒有，現在就去拿過來，故為正確答案；(C) 回答 Yes，但後方卻說明天會準備好，前後邏輯並不一致，因此不能作為答案。

Will the company change its name after the merger?
(A) Everyone agrees on the amount.
(B) Yes, to Vancouver.
(C) We have no intention of doing so.

中譯　合併後，公司會改名嗎？
(A) 大家都同意這個數量。
(B) 是的，去溫哥華。
(C) 我們不打算這麼做。

解析　一般問句　本題詢問公司合併後是否會更改名稱。(C) 給予否定答覆，最為適當；(A) 提到 amount，為數額的概念，答非所問。

字彙　merger　（公司、企業等的）合併
agree on　對⋯⋯一致同意
intention　意圖，打算

PART 3 03

Questions 32-34 refer to the following conversation. 英 澳

M	Excuse me. ㉜ I'm going to City Stadium to watch the baseball game with my son. Is this the bus we should take?
W	Yes, this bus goes to the stadium but I heard ㉝ there's long delay on Satellite Avenue because of road construction. If I were you, I'd take the subway.
M	Oh, I didn't know I could get there on the subway.
W	Yes, it's a new station. ㉞ Just get on the Blue Line and get off at 14th Street.
M	Thank you very much.

男：不好意思，㉜我和我兒子要去市立體育場看棒球賽。我們應該要搭這路公車嗎？
女：是的，這路公車去體育場，但我聽說，㉝衛星大道因為道路施工而嚴重塞車。如果我是你，我會搭地鐵。
男：噢，我不知道可以搭地鐵去那裡。
女：可以，是新設的站。㉞只要搭藍線，然後在14街下車就可以。
男：非常謝謝妳。

03

字彙 **delay** 延遲，耽擱　**road construction** 道路施工　**get off** 下車

032

Where is the man going?
(A) To a bus stop
(B) To a concert hall
(C) **To a sports venue**
(D) To a theater

中譯 男子要去哪裡？
(A) 去公車站　　　(B) 去音樂廳
(C) 去體育場館　　(D) 去劇院

解析 第一段話中，男子提到要和兒子去 City Stadium 看棒球比賽，因此男子前往的地方為體育場之類的運動場所。

換句話說 City Stadium → sports venue

字彙 **venue**（公共事件的）發生場所，會場　**theater** 劇場

033

What is mentioned about Satellite Avenue?
(A) It is a new street.
(B) **It is being repaired.**
(C) It is closed.
(D) It is near downtown.

中譯 關於衛星大道，文中說了什麼？
(A) 那是條新的街道。　(B) 那裡正在修馬路。
(C) 那裡關閉了。　　　(D) 那裡靠近鬧區。

解析 女子告訴男子前往體育場的方法時，提到衛星大道正在施工，可能會塞車，因此答案要選 (B)。

換句話說 road construction → being repaired

字彙 **repair** 修理，整修　**downtown** 城市商業區，鬧區

034

What does the woman suggest the man do?
(A) Catch a taxi
(B) Go home
(C) **Ride the Blue Line**
(D) Wait for the next bus

中譯 女子建議男子做什麼？
(A) 搭計程車　　　(B) 回家
(C) 搭藍線　　　　(D) 等下一班公車

解析 本題可由女子最後所說的話確認。女子建議男子搭乘藍線至第14街下車。

換句話說 get on the Blue Line → ride the Blue Line

字彙 **ride** 乘（車等），騎（馬等）

13

Questions 35-37 refer to the following conversation. 加 美

W	Well, Mr. French, from all I've heard today, ㉟ **you are our strongest choice for the position.** I just have a few more questions.	女：嗯，法藍奇先生，就我今天聽到的所有訊息，㉟你是我們這個職務的最強人選。只是，我還有幾個問題。
M	Of course. And please call me Chris. Mr. French sounds like my father.	男：當然。還有，請叫我克里斯。法藍奇先生聽起來好像我爸爸。
W	Okay, Chris. ㉟ ㊱ **Your résumé shows you started the job you now have just six months ago.** Why are you looking for a different job so soon?	女：好的，克里斯。㉟ ㊱你的履歷顯示，你現在的工作才做了僅僅六個月。你為什麼這麼快就要找不同的工作？
M	Actually, ㊲ **my wife got promoted to branch manager here in Oak City**, and we decided to relocate.	男：其實㊲是我太太升遷為橡樹市這裡的分公司經理，所以我們決定搬過來。

字彙 **strongest choice** 最佳選擇　**position** 職位，工作　**résumé** 履歷表　**branch** 分支機構　**relocate** 遷移，重新安置

035

Who most likely is the man?
(A) A branch manager
(B) A job candidate
(C) A job recruiter
(D) A reporter

中譯 男子最可能是誰？
(A) 一名分公司經理　(B) 一名應徵者
(C) 一名招聘人員　(D) 一名記者

解析 請由女子所說的話，確認男子的狀況。第一段話中，女子提到男子為適任該職位的有力人選；第二段話中，則提到男子的履歷表。由這兩句話可以看出男子為求職者。

換句話說 **our strongest choice for the position → job candidate**

字彙 **recruiter** 招聘人員

036

How long has the man been working in his current job?
(A) 2 months
(B) 3 months
(C) Half a year
(D) A year

中譯 男子目前的工作做多久了？
(A) 二個月　(B) 三個月
(C) 半年　(D) 一年

解析 由女子所說的話，可以得知本題的資訊。第二段話中，女子提到男子僅在目前的職場工作六個月。

換句話說 **six months → half a year**

037

What is mentioned about the man's family?
(A) His wife is not happy with his job.
(B) His wife got a new position.
(C) They are from Oak City.
(D) They do not want to relocate.

中譯 關於男子的家庭，文中說了什麼？
(A) 他太太不滿意他的工作。
(B) 他太太有新職位。
(C) 他們來自橡樹市。
(D) 他們不想搬家。

解析 對話最後，男子提到自己的妻子升為分公司經理一事，表示她換到新的職位，因此答案為 **(B)**。

換句話說 **got promoted to branch manager → got a new position**

Questions 38-40 refer to the following conversation. 加 英

W	Marcus, this is Sylvia from Three Rivers Inc. I'm sorry to do this to you at the last minute, ❸❽ **but I have to change our appointment tomorrow.** Something urgent came up and I have to leave the office early.
M	That's no problem, Sylvia. Do you have time earlier in the day, like around noon?
W	Actually, no. That's why I'm apologizing. I really have no time at all tomorrow. But the next day, ❸❾ **Thursday, I'm free in the morning.**
M	❸❾ **Works for me.** Why don't we say 10:00?
W	Sounds good, Marcus. Thanks so much for your understanding. ❹⓿ **I look forward to hearing your proposal for our joint project.**

女：馬可斯，我是三河公司的施薇亞。很抱歉在最後一刻這麼做，❸❽但我必須更改我們明天的約。發生了急事，我得提早下班。

男：沒關係，施薇亞。明天早一點，妳有空嗎，像是中午左右？

女：其實沒有。所以，我才要致歉。我明天真的完全沒有時間。但隔天，❸❾也就是星期四，我早上有空。

男：❸❾我可以。我們要不要約 10 點？

女：聽起來不錯，馬可斯。非常感謝你的諒解。❹⓿我期待聽到你關於我們合作計畫的提案。

字彙 at the last minute 最後一刻　appointment（尤指正式的）約會　urgent 緊急的　apologize 道歉
Why don't we say . . . 我們何不說定……　joint project 合作計畫

038

Why does the woman apologize?
(A) Because she has to cancel the appointment.
(B) Because she is late for the meeting.
(C) Because she needs to reschedule the meeting.
(D) Because she refused the man's offer.

中譯 女子為什麼道歉？
(A) 因為她必須取消約會。
(B) 因為她開會遲到。
(C) 因為她需要重新安排會議的時間。
(D) 因為她拒絕男子的提議。

解析 第一段話中，女子向男子道歉，表示欲更改隔日碰面的時間。因此答案要選 (C)，為調整會議時間而道歉。

換句話說 change our appointment → reschedule the meeting

字彙 cancel 取消　reschedule 重新安排……的時間
refuse 拒絕　offer 提議

---

039 新增題型

What does the man mean when he says, "Works for me"?
(A) He is agreeing with the place to meet.
(B) He is fine with a video chat.
(C) The suggested schedule is convenient for him.
(D) The woman works in his department.

中譯 當男子說：「我可以」時，他的意思是什麼？
(A) 他同意碰面的地點。　(B) 他可以接受視訊對談。
(C) 建議的時間對他方便。　(D) 女子在他的部門工作。

解析 男子說出「Works for me.」前，女子提到她週四上午有空。由此可以得知男子的回應為這個時間點他也有空的意思。

換句話說 free → convenient

字彙 convenient 方便的　department 部門

040

What will the speakers discuss at their meeting?
(A) A collaboration plan
(B) A merger
(C) The man's budget ideas
(D) The woman's qualifications

中譯 說話者在他們的會議中會討論什麼？
(A) 一項合作計畫　　　(B) 一項合併案
(C) 男子的預算構想　　(D) 女子的資格

解析 對話最後，女子提到期待男子對共同企畫的某項提案。由此可以推測兩人將進行一項合作計畫，且欲對此開會討論。

換句話說 joint project → collaboration plan

字彙 collaboration 合作　budget 預算
qualification 資格，能力

Questions 41-43 refer to the following conversation. 美 澳

M	Hi, Elizabeth. How are you? Did you do anything over the three-day weekend?	男：嗨，伊莉莎白，妳好嗎？這三天的週末假期，妳做了什麼嗎？
W	Oh, hi, Ben. Nothing special. ㊶ **Just worked in the garden.** You know, it was great weather to be outside. How about you?	女：噢，嗨，班。沒什麼特別，㊶只是在花園工作。你知道的，天氣很好，很適合待在戶外。你呢？
M	I took my family to the new amusement park on the west side of the city. It was absolutely packed with people. ㊷ **We couldn't find a parking spot for about 30 minutes.**	男：我帶家人去城市西部新開幕的遊樂園。那裡完全擠滿了人。㊷我們光找車位就找了大概 30 分鐘。
W	Sounds stressful. But I'm sure your kids loved it.	女：聽起來好焦慮。不過，我相信你小孩很愛那裡。
M	Yes, once we finally got into the park, they had a great time. The roller coaster was their favorite. ㊸ **I'll show you some pictures I took.**	男：是啊，等我們終於進到遊樂園裡，他們玩得很高興。他們最愛雲霄飛車。㊸我給妳看我拍的照片。

字彙 amusement park 遊樂園　be packed with 擠滿　parking spot 停車位

041

What did the woman do on the weekend?
(A) She did home repair works.
(B) She did some gardening.
(C) She visited an amusement park.
(D) She visited her parents.

中譯 女子週末時做了什麼？
(A) 她整修家裡。　　　(B) 她做了一些園藝工作。
(C) 她去了遊樂園。　　(D) 她去看她爸媽。

解析 本大題針對連假期間所做的事情進行對話。男子詢問女子週末做了些什麼事，女子表示自己在花園工作。

換句話說 worked in the garden → did some gardening

042

What did the man have trouble doing?
(A) Deciding where to go
(B) Finding his destination
(C) Getting a parking space
(D) Making a reservation

中譯 男子遇到什麼麻煩？
(A) 決定要去哪裡　　　(B) 找到他的目的地
(C) 找停車位　　　　　(D) 預訂

解析 第二段對話中，男子表示自己和家人去了一趟遊樂園，光找停車位就花了三十分鐘，因此男子所遭遇的困難為找尋停車位。

換句話說 couldn't find a parking spot → getting a parking space

字彙 destination 目的地　make a reservation 預訂

043

What will the woman probably do next?
(A) Call her children
(B) Look at some photos
(C) Take a break
(D) Talk about her holiday

中譯 女子接下來最可能做什麼？
(A) 打電話給她的小孩　(B) 看一些照片
(C) 休息一下　(D) 談她的假期

解析 最後一段對話，男子提到要給對方看照片，由此可以推測女子接下來將會看到照片。

換句話說 show you some pictures → look at some photos

字彙 take a break 休息

Questions 44-46 refer to the following conversation. 美 加

🎧03

M Hello, ㊹ I'd like to make a reservation for six for next Monday night. I also have a question about your menu.

W Okay. We have a lovely table with a view that would seat six. What would you like to know about the menu?

M One woman in our party has a dietary restriction. ㊺ She's allergic to soy, so she can't have any soy based products or oil on any of her food.

W That won't be a problem. ㊻ Our chef is familiar with this type of restriction. He can prepare everything without soy for her.

M ㊻ That's a relief. It hasn't been easy finding a suitable restaurant for her.

男：哈囉，㊹ 我要預訂下個星期一晚上，六個人的位子。我還有個關於菜單的問題。

女：好的。我們有張可以看到風景的桌子，可以坐六個人。你想知道關於菜單的什麼事？

男：我們裡面有個女子有飲食限制。㊺ 她對大豆過敏，所以，她不能吃任何的大豆製品，或者食物裡有大豆油。

女：沒有問題。㊻ 我們的大廚見慣了這種限制。他可以為她準備沒有大豆的菜。

男：㊻ 那太好了。要幫她找一間合適的餐廳很不容易。

字彙 with a view 可以看到風景　party （共同工作或活動的）一批人　dietary 飲食的　restriction 限制
be allergic to 對……過敏　prepare 準備　relief（痛苦、負擔等的）緩和，解除　suitable 適宜的，合適的

044

How many people will accompany the man to the restaurant?
(A) 3
(B) 4
(C) 5
(D) 6

中譯 有多少人會和男子一起去餐廳？
(A) 三個　(B) 四個
(C) 五個　(D) 六個

解析 本大題為欲訂位餐廳的顧客與店員間的對話。男顧客表示想要訂位，人數為六人，因此與該男子同行的人數為五人。

字彙 accompany 和……一起，陪同

045

What is mentioned about one of the man's party?
(A) She has a serious allergy.
(B) She is a vegetarian.
(C) She likes the table with a view.
(D) She will show up late.

中譯 關於男子一行人的其中一位，文中說了什麼？
(A) 她有嚴重過敏。　(B) 她是素食者。
(C) 她喜歡可看到風景的座位。　(D) 她會晚到。

解析 對話中提到對於菜單有特殊要求。第二段對話中，男子提到同行者中有人對大豆過敏，不能吃含有大豆的料理。這表示同行者中有人有嚴重的過敏問題。

換句話說 She's allergic to soy. → She has a serious allergy.

字彙 serious 嚴重的　vegetarian 素食者　show up 出席，露面

046 新增題型

Why does the man say, "That's a relief"?
(A) He is concerned his guests will not like the restaurant.
(B) He is glad the chef can do what he asks.
(C) He is happy to get a reservation at a busy time.
(D) He is worried that there will not be enough menu choices.

中譯 男子為什麼說:「那太好了」?
(A) 他擔心他的客人不喜歡這家餐廳。
(B) 他很高興主廚可以做到他要求的事。
(C) 他很高興在人多的時段可以訂到位子。
(D) 他擔心菜單的選擇不夠多。

解析 男子說出「That's a relief.」前,女子提到餐廳主廚善於處理各種餐飲要求,到時候會為顧客準備不含大豆的料理。由此可以得知男子之所以會鬆一口氣,是因為對於對方接受自己的要求感到開心。

字彙 concerned 擔心的

Questions 47-49 refer to the following conversation. 澳 英

W　Louis, ⑱ I've been getting complaints about the heater in Room C. I guess it's making a loud noise every time it turns on and off.

M　Hmm, I just fixed that last week. I guess ⑰ this community center is just getting old. I'll look at it after lunch.

W　It would be great if you could look at it now because there's a group coming at 1:00 to use the room. They're going to be listening to a lecture about the town's history.

M　Okay. ⑲ Let me get my tools and I'll go over there.

女:路易,⑱ 我一直接到關於 C 室暖氣的客訴。我猜想,每次開關時,它都會發出巨大的噪音。

男:嗯,我上星期才剛修好那台暖氣。我想,⑰ 這個社區活動中心就是老舊了。吃完午餐後,我會去檢查。

女:你可能現在去查看會比較好,因為一點會有一個團體要用那個房間。他們要聽一場關於本鎮歷史的演講。

男:好。⑲ 讓我去拿工具,然後我就過去。

字彙 complaint 客訴,抱怨　fix 修理　tool 工具

047

Where is the conversation taking place?
(A) In a community center
(B) In a hotel
(C) In a library
(D) In a retirement home

中譯 這段對話發生在哪裡?
(A) 在一個社區活動中心
(B) 在一家飯店
(C) 在一間圖書館
(D) 在一家養老院

解析 從對話內容或是說話者直接提及的話語中,可以得知對話所在地點。第一段對話中,男子提到社區活動中心老舊的問題,由此可以得知此段對話發生在社區活動中心裡。

048

What problem does the woman mention?
(A) The building is old.
(B) The construction outside is noisy.
(C) The heater is not working properly.
(D) The rooms are too cold.

中譯 女子提到什麼問題?
(A) 建築物老舊。　(B) 外面施工很吵。
(C) 暖氣無法順暢運作。　(D) 房間太冷。

解析 第一段對話中,女子提到有人不滿暖氣開關機時發出巨大的噪音,由此可以得知暖氣機無法正常運轉。

換句話說 making a loud noise → not working properly

18

049

What will the man do next?
(A) Call the maintenance department
(B) Have his lunch
(C) Listen to a lecture
(D) Retrieve his tools

中譯 男子接下來會做什麼？
(A) 打電話給維修部門　(B) 吃午餐
(C) 聽演講　　　　　　(D) 拿他的工具

解析 最後一段對話中，女子要求馬上修理，而男子隨後表示他
會帶工具前往現場。

換句
話說 get my tools → retrieve his tools

Questions 50-52 refer to the following conversation. 英 加

M	Wendy, ⑤⓪ congratulations on your Employee of the Year award. You deserve it after all your hard work on the new product line.
W	Oh, thanks, Russell. It's a bit embarrassing since ⑤① I was just part of a large group that worked really hard on the new line. It really was a team effort.
M	But you were the leader of the team. Their cheerleader, so to speak. I know you put in extra-long hours over several months.
W	Yes, it was a lot of work. But it paid off. ⑤② We have the number one tablet computer in the market now.

男：溫蒂，⑤⓪恭喜妳得到年度最佳員工獎。妳對新系列產品付出那麼多努力，這是妳應得的。

女：噢，謝謝，羅素。有點不好意思，因為⑤①我只是一個大團隊裡的一員，大家為了新產品真的很辛苦。這真的是團隊的努力。

男：但妳是團隊領導人，可以說是他們的啦啦隊。我知道，妳有好幾個月都投入特別長的工作時間。

女：是啊，有好多工作。但結果很成功。⑤②我們現在是市面上第一名的平板電腦。

字彙 deserve 值得，應得　hard work 努力工作　embarrassing 使人尷尬的，令人為難的
so to speak 可以說是，可謂是

050

Why is the man congratulating the woman?
(A) She got married.
(B) She got promoted.
(C) She received an honor.
(D) She won a contract.

中譯 男子為什麼向女子道賀？
(A) 她結婚了。　　　(B) 她升職了。
(C) 她得到殊榮。　　(D) 她爭取到一份合約。

解析 第一段對話中，男子恭喜女子獲頒年度最佳員工獎。

字彙 get married 結婚　get promoted 升職
receive an honor 獲得表揚，獲得殊榮
win a contract 爭取到合約

051

What does the woman say about her group?
(A) They have not worked with her before.
(B) They put in a lot of effort.
(C) They were not cooperative with her.
(D) They will get reassigned soon.

中譯 關於她的團隊，女子說了什麼？
(A) 他們以前沒有和她一起工作過。
(B) 他們花費很多精力。
(C) 他們不配合她。
(D) 他們很快會重新調派職務。

解析 對於男子的稱讚，女子謙虛表示整個團隊都很認真投入新系列產品的工作，自己僅是當中的一員罷了。自己所屬的團隊工作認真投入，也就是說團隊花費很多精力。

換句
話說 worked really hard → put in a lot of effort

字彙 put in effort 努力　cooperative 合作的，樂於合作的
reassign 重新分配，重新指定

052

What kind of products does the woman's company sell?
(A) Clothes
(B) Digital devices
(C) Automobile
(D) Medicine

中譯 女子的公司販賣何種產品？
(A) 衣服　　　　　(B) 數位裝置
(C) 汽車　　　　　(D) 藥品

解析 最後一段話中，女子提到在當前平板電腦市場中，自家產品的排名為第一。由此可以得知女子公司販售的商品為數位裝置。

換句話說 tablet computer → digital devices

字彙 device 設備，裝置

Questions 53-55 refer to the following conversation. 美 澳 新增題型

M Sarah, I'm having a lot of trouble with this catalog update. I was wondering if you could help me.

W Of course, Stephen. When I did the update a few years ago, I was surprised how much work it was. What seems to be the problem?

M ❺❸ It's the photographer. He doesn't understand that the pictures of the new products should look similar to the older ones.

W That doesn't sound good. Are you using Cathryn Jacobs, the photographer I used?

M No, she wasn't available. I went with someone she recommended, but now I wish I had waited until Ms. Jacobs was free. And it's too late now since ❺❹ the deadline is in two weeks.

W ❺❺ Maybe if I went with you to the studio, I could try to explain what we want.

M That would be great. I'm sorry to take up your time like this.

W It's no problem. I'm happy to help.

男：莎拉，我在更新型錄上遇到很多麻煩。不知道妳可不可以幫我。

女：當然可以，史蒂芬。當我幾年前更新時，我很驚訝有這麼多事要做。你覺得問題出在哪？

男：❺❸ 是攝影師。他不了解新產品的照片應該要看起來和舊的很像。

女：聽起來不妙。你是找我以前用的那位攝影師凱薩琳‧傑可布思嗎？

男：不是，她沒空。我用了她推薦的人，但我現在希望我當初能等到傑可布思女士有空時。而現在已經來不及了，因為 ❺❹ 二個星期後就要截稿了。

女：❺❺ 如果我和你一起去攝影棚，也許我可以試著解釋我們想要的效果。

男：那就太好了。很抱歉這樣佔用妳的時間。

女：沒問題的。我很樂意幫忙。

字彙 similar 相像的，類似的　available 有空的；可利用的　recommend 推薦，建議　deadline 截止期限　take up 佔據（地方或時間）

053

What is the man's problem?
(A) He cannot find a photographer for a project.
(B) He does not have enough pictures for a catalog.
(C) He does not have the right kind of pictures.
(D) His deadline is already past.

中譯 男子的問題是什麼？
(A) 他無法為一個專案找到攝影師。
(B) 他沒有足夠的照片做型錄。
(C) 他沒有合適的照片。
(D) 他已經過了截止期限。

解析 本大題的對話來回次數超過五次，屬於長篇對話。男子針對型錄更新一事請求女子的協助。第二段對話中，男子提出具體的問題，表示共事的攝影師無法理解新產品照片為何要與原有產品的照片相似。由此內容，可以推測出問題為沒有合適的照片。

字彙 past 過去了的

054

What will happen in two weeks?
(A) A photographer will be available.
(B) An update will be finished.
(C) The man will get a job.
(D) The woman will take over the project.

中譯 兩個星期後會發生什麼事？
(A) 有位攝影師會有空。　(B) 更新工作會完成。
(C) 男子會得到一份工作。　(D) 女子會接手專案。

解析 本題要掌握整篇對話的脈絡，才能順利解題。男子提到目前正忙於更新型錄，而距離截止日僅剩下兩週，所以無法更換攝影師。由此可以推測兩週後就得完成更新。

字彙 **take over** 接手，接管

055

03

What does the woman offer to do for the man?
(A) Accompany him to a photo shoot
(B) Call a different photographer
(C) Find a new studio
(D) Review a previous catalog

中譯 女子提議幫男子做什麼？
(A) 陪他去拍攝　　　　(B) 打電話給另一個攝影師
(C) 找一間新的攝影棚　(D) 回顧之前的型錄

解析 女子表示要與男子一同前往攝影棚，解釋他們想要的照片效果為何。由此可以得知女子的建議為陪同男子前往拍攝現場。

字彙 **review** 回顧，再檢查　**previous** 以前的

Questions 56-58 refer to the following conversation with three speakers. 加 澳 美 新增題型

W1 It looks like 56 **we're all ready for the facility inspection in Singapore. I've gotten our tickets** and Jane, you booked the hotel, right?

W2 Yes, I found a place very close to the facility. It will be just a ten-minute taxi ride away.

W1 So we don't need to rent a car?

M I've been to Singapore before. 57 **The public transit system is fantastic.** Nobody needs to use a car in the city center, especially visitors.

W1 That's good news since 58 **our boss wants us to keep expenses as low as possible.** Well, be sure to bring your inspection checklists and passports. See you tomorrow.

女1：看起來 56 我們都做好去查驗新加坡工廠的準備了。我已經拿到機票，而珍，妳已訂好飯店了，對嗎？

女2：是的，我找到一個很靠近工廠的地方，搭計程車只要十分鐘。

女1：所以，我們不需要租車？

男：我以前去過新加坡，57 大眾運輸系統非常好，沒有人需要在市中心開車，尤其是旅客。

女1：那真是好消息，因為 58 我們的老闆要我們儘量降低開支。嗯，務必要帶你們的檢核表和護照。明天見。

字彙 **facility**（包含多個建築物，有特定用途的）場所，設施　**inspection** 檢查　**be close to** 靠近，在……附近
public transit 大眾運輸　**expense** 開支，費用

056

What are the speakers mainly discussing?
(A) A business trip
(B) A new company policy
(C) Their new branch
(D) Their recent vacations

中譯 說話者討論的主題是什麼？
(A) 一次出差　　　　(B) 一項新的公司政策
(C) 他們的新分公司　(D) 他們最近的假期

解析 本篇文章為兩女一男的三人對話。當中提到視察工廠的行前準備事項為預訂飯店和機票，由此可以看出他們在討論出差一事。

換句話說 facility inspection, tickets, booked the hotel → business trip

字彙 **business trip** 出差　**policy** 政策　**recent** 最近的

21

057

What does the man mention about Singapore?
(A) It has a lot of good food.
(B) It has many sightseeing spots.
(C) It is a beautiful city.
(D) It is easy to get around.

中譯 關於新加坡，男子提到什麼事？
(A) 有很多好吃的食物。
(B) 有很多觀光景點。
(C) 是個美麗的城市。
(D) 要到各處去很方便。

解析 女1疑惑為何不需要租車，而男子則回應新加坡的大眾運輸系統十分發達，這句話表示在移動上相當便利，要去什麼地方都很方便。

換句話說 The public transit system is fantastic. → It is easy to get around.

字彙 sightseeing spot 觀光景點
get around 各處旅行，四處走動

058

What does the speakers' boss want them to do?
(A) Go over the inspection checklist
(B) Save on costs
(C) Stay in a specific hotel
(D) Treat a facility manager to dinner

中譯 說話者的老闆要他們做什麼？
(A) 察看檢核表
(B) 節省費用
(C) 住在特定的旅館
(D) 請工廠經理吃晚餐

解析 對話最後，女1提到老闆要求儘可能降低開支。由此可以得知老闆希望他們節省花費。

換句話說 keep expenses as low as possible → save on costs

字彙 go over 察看　cost 費用　specific 特定的
treat 請客，款待

Questions 59-61 refer to the following conversation. 加 美

W	Oh, no. I just realized ⑤⑨ I forgot something at my office. Can you turn around and go back to where you picked me up?
M	Uh, ⑥⓪ I can't do a U-turn right here. So, I'll have to go around the block.
W	That's fine. ⑤⑨ I can't believe I left such an important file for my meeting there. I'm just glad I remembered it before we got too far.
M	Okay, here we are. I'll wait here, but of course ⑥⓪ the meter will be running.
W	I understand. ⑥① I won't be long.

女：噢，不，我剛剛才想起，⑤⑨ 我把某個東西留在辦公室了。你可不可以調頭，回到你載我的地方？

男：呃，⑥⓪ 這裡不能迴轉。所以，我得繞著這個街區走。

女：沒關係。⑤⑨ 我不敢相信，我把開會要用的那麼重要的檔案留在那裡。我只是很高興，在我們沒有走太遠以前就想起來。

男：好，我們到了。我會在這裡等，但當然，⑥⓪ 表會繼續跳。

女：我了解。⑥① 我不會太久。

字彙 realize 明白，意識到　do a U-turn 迴轉　meter （計程車的）計費表

059

What is the woman's problem?
(A) She cannot find her ID.
(B) She forgot her purse.
(C) She is lost.
(D) She is missing some papers.

中譯 女子的問題是什麼？
(A) 她找不到她的身分證。　(B) 她忘了她的錢包。
(C) 她迷路了。　(D) 她把一些文件弄丟了。

解析 第一段對話中，女子提到她有東西忘在辦公室。第二段對話中，她又提到她不敢相信自己竟然忘了帶會議要用的重要資料。由這兩段內容，可以得知女子的問題為遺漏某些資料文件。

換句話說 forgot something, left such an important file → missing some papers

字彙 lost 迷路的

🎧 03

060

Who most likely is the man?
(A) A building security officer
(B) A taxi driver
(C) A traffic reporter
(D) Her colleague

中譯 男子最可能是誰？
(A) 大樓保全　(B) 計程車司機
(C) 交通路況播報員　(D) 她的同事

解析 女子請對方開回自己搭車的地方，而男子表示無法迴轉。對話最後，男子又提到會繼續跳表。綜合這些內容，女子應為乘客，男子則為計程車司機。

字彙 security officer 保全人員

061 新增題型

What does the woman imply when she says, "I won't be long"?
(A) She does not want to go to the meeting.
(B) She does not want to turn right.
(C) She prefers a short conversation.
(D) She will come back soon.

中譯 當女子說：「我不會太久」，她意指什麼？
(A) 她不想去參加會議。
(B) 她不想右轉。
(C) 她偏好簡短的對話。
(D) 她很快就回來。

解析 根據對話的脈絡，女子先回辦公室，接著再回來搭計程車。因此女子說自己不會花太久的時間，意思是她很快就會回來搭車。

換句話說 won't be long → come back soon

Questions 62-64 refer to the following conversation with three speakers. 美 英 澳 新增題型

M1 Thank you for coming, Ellen. We have something we want to ask you.	**男1：** 謝謝妳來，艾倫。我們有事想問妳。
M2 62 **How would you like to work at our overseas branch**, you know, the one in Shanghai?	**男2：** 62 妳想不想去我們的海外分公司工作，妳知道的，上海那邊的？
W Oh, I hadn't thought about it. I mean, 63 **I thought this meeting was going to be an employee evaluation or something. I thought that's why you're here, Mr. Evans.**	**女：** 噢，我從來沒想過。我的意思是，63 我本來以為這次會議是員工考核之類的事。我以為這也是你會出席的原因，伊文斯先生。
M2 Well, 63 **as head of personnel** I wanted to explain some of the details if you were to take us up on the offer.	**男2：** 嗯，63 身為人事部主管，如果妳打算接受我們提出的工作，我想解釋一些細節。

M1 We've heard good things about you from your supervisor and we thought the time was right to give you some more responsibility.

W I'm really flattered, uh, honored. Since it's quite sudden, can I have some time to think it over?

M2 Of course. But there are a lot of things my department needs to sort out, like visas. So ⑥④ we'll need an answer by the end of the month.

男 1：我們從妳主管那裡聽聞你表現優良，我們認為，該是給妳更多責任的時候了。

女　：我真是受寵若驚，呃，真是榮幸。由於事出突然，我可不可以有點時間仔細考慮一下？

男 2：當然。但是，我的部門有很多事情必須處理，像是簽證。所以，⑥④我們在月底之前必須得到回覆。

字彙 overseas branch 海外分公司　employee evaluation 員工考核　personnel 人事部門
detail 細節，詳情　supervisor 監督人，指導者　flattered 受寵若驚的　sudden 突然的
sort out 解決（問題），處理

062

What is the purpose of the meeting?
(A) To conduct an employee evaluation
(B) To discuss a new branch
(C) To interview a job candidate
(D) To offer a position

中譯 這次會議的目的是什麼？
(A) 進行員工考核
(B) 討論新的分公司
(C) 面試應徵者
(D) 給予工作機會

解析 本篇文章為兩男一女的三人對話。兩名男子向女子提議外派海外分公司工作一事，因此會議的目的為向女子提議新的工作職位。

063

Who most likely is Mr. Evans?
(A) The company president
(B) The overseas branch head
(C) The Personnel Department director
(D) The woman's direct supervisor

中譯 伊文斯先生最可能是誰？
(A) 公司的總裁
(B) 海外分公司負責人
(C) 人事部總監
(D) 女子的直屬上司

解析 女子以為開會的目的是要進行員工考核，所以伊文斯先生（男 2）才會在場。而後男 2 表示他身為人事部主管，要向女子說明外派細節才會過來。

換句話說 as a head of personnel → the Personnel Department director

064

What does the woman need to do by the end of the month?
(A) Find a new job
(B) Get a visa
(C) Make a decision
(D) Move to Shanghai

中譯 女子在月底前必須做什麼？
(A) 找新工作
(B) 申請簽證
(C) 做出決定
(D) 搬到上海

解析 女子表示需要時間考慮外派的提案，而後男 2 請她在月底前答覆，因此女子要在這個月底之前做好決定。

換句話說 need an answer → make a decision

Questions 65-67 refer to the following conversation and list. 澳 英

Name	Monthly Fee	Songs available /month	Devices
Music Depot	$8.50	unlimited	phone
PlayNow	$5.00	2,000	phone
Smartsound	$3.99	1,000	phone, PC
❻ X Hits	$9.50	unlimited	phone, PC

名稱	月費	歌曲數／月	裝置
音樂倉庫	$8.50	無限	手機
現在就播	$5.00	2,000	手機
聰明聲音	$3.99	1,000	手機、電腦
❻ 勁爆金曲	$9.50	無限	手機、電腦

🎧 03

W Hey, Mark, ❻ I found the list of music streaming services on the Internet. These services are pretty reasonable.

M Oh, thanks for this, Janice. ❻ I want to be able to listen to music anywhere, especially when I'm on the train. I guess I can go for the cheap one since I just like hip hop.

W ❻ I really like the idea of no limits since my musical taste is pretty varied. And I'd like to be able to listen to it on both my phone and PC.

女：嘿，馬克，❻ 我在網路上找到這個音樂串流服務業者的名單。這些服務費用都蠻公道的。

男：噢，謝謝妳，珍妮絲。❻ 我希望在哪裡都能聽音樂，尤其是搭火車時。我想我可以選便宜的那家，因為我只喜歡嘻哈。

女：❻ 我真的很喜歡無限的方案，因為我喜歡的音樂相當多元。而且我想要在手機和電腦上都能聽。

字彙 reasonable（價錢）公道的，不貴的　taste（個人的）品味　varied 各種各樣的

065

What does the woman say about the service?
(A) It is convenient.
(B) It is high-tech.
(C) It is priced fairly.
(D) It is very popular.

中譯 關於服務，女子說了什麼？
(A) 很方便。　(B) 是高科技。
(C) 價格很合理。　(D) 很受歡迎。

解析 第一段對話中，女子提到她發現一張音樂串流服務的方案，價格都實惠公道。

換句話說 pretty reasonable → priced fairly

字彙 price 給……定價　fairly 公平地，公正地

066

Where does the man like to listen to music in particular?
(A) At home
(B) At the gym
(C) At work
(D) On the train

中譯 男子特別喜歡在哪裡聽音樂？
(A) 在家裡　(B) 在健身房
(C) 工作時　(D) 在火車上

解析 男子提到他想在火車上聽音樂。選項直接列出對話中出現的「on the train」。

067 新增題型

Look at the graphic. Which service will the woman most likely choose?
(A) Music Depot
(B) PlayNow
(C) Smartsound
(D) X Hits

中譯 見圖表。女子最可能選擇哪一家的服務？
(A) 音樂倉庫　(B) 現在就播
(C) 聰明聲音　(D) 勁爆金曲

解析 本題為圖表整合題。最後一段對話中，女子提到她希望音樂可以無限暢聽，且同時使用手機和電腦收聽。由這兩點要求，可以推測出女子會選擇 X Hits 的方案。

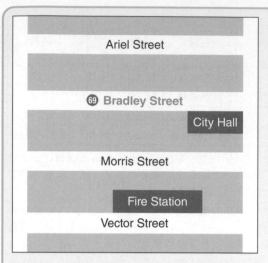

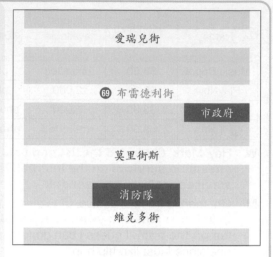

W　Mark, ❻❽ **the parade went really well last year.** We got so many positive comments. And now we have to decide where we want the parade to start this year. Of course, it should be somewhere downtown.

M　Well, we can't start it on Morris Street because it's too narrow. And Vector Street is out because of the fire station. That leaves two possible streets.

W　❻❾ **Why don't we start it at City Hall?** There is a big plaza to gather in front.

M　Sounds good. Now, all we need to do is get the permit.

W　I've already filled out the permit application form. I just need to add the starting place information and the time. ❼❶ **Then I'll drop it at the city office on my way home this evening.**

女：馬克，❻❽去年的遊行真的很成功。我們好評如潮。現在，我們必須決定今年的遊行要從哪裡開始。當然，應該是在市中心的某個地方。

男：嗯，我們不能從莫里斯街出發，因為那裡太窄了。還有，維克多街也去掉，因為有消防隊。那就還有二條街可選。

女：❻❾我們何不以市政府為起點？市政府前面有個大廣場可以集合。

男：聽起來不錯。現在我們只需要獲得核准。

女：我已經填好許可申請表。我只需要加上起點的資料和時間。❼❶然後，我今天下午回家的路上，會把它送去市政府。

字彙　**go well** 進展順利　**positive** 肯定的　**narrow** 狹窄的　**gather** 聚集，集合　**permit** 許可
fill out 填寫（表格、申請書等）　**application form** 申請表

068

What can be said about the parade?
(A) It was successful last year.
(B) It will be canceled this year.
(C) It will be held for the first time.
(D) Its budget was increased.

中譯　關於遊行，可以由文中得知什麼？
(A) 去年的遊行很成功。
(B) 今年的遊行將會取消。
(C) 將是第一次舉行。
(D) 遊行的預算增加了。

解析　第一段對話中，女子提到去年的遊行辦得十分順利，表示辦得很成功。

換句話說　went really well → successful

069 新增題型

Look at the graphic. Where will the parade start?
(A) On Ariel Street
(B) On Bradley Street
(C) On Morris Street
(D) On Vector Street

中譯 見圖表。遊行會從哪裡開始？
(A) 愛瑞兒街　　　(B) 布雷德利街
(C) 莫里斯街　　　(D) 維克多街

解析 本題為圖表整合題。女子建議遊行從市政府開始，而男子表示這是一個好點子，因此答案為布雷德利街。

070

What does the woman say she will do?
(A) Call City Hall
(B) Fill out a job application
(C) Help the man with the paperwork
(D) Visit a government office

中譯 女子說她會做什麼事？
(A) 打電話給市政府　　(B) 填寫工作應徵表
(C) 幫助男子處理文書工作　(D) 去到政府單位

解析 最後一段對話中，女子表示下班回家路上會順道去市府辦公室繳交許可申請書。市政府屬於政府機關，因此答案為 (D)。

換句話說 drop it at the city office → visit a government office

 04

PART 4 　04

Questions 71-73 refer to the following news report. 澳

Well, after more than ten years away, 71 hometown hero and basketball star Harrison Jones is finally returning home. Mr. Jones has just announced his retirement and relocation back here to Orangeton. 72 After nearly eight years in the professional league, Mr. Jones suffered an injury in a game last season. Though doctors did everything they could, he eventually had to give up playing. Since then 73 he's been to 20 different cities talking about his book and now he's coming back here to open up a sports gym chain.

嗯，離開家鄉十多年後，71本地英雄人物，籃球明星哈里森・瓊斯，終於要回來了。瓊斯先生不久前宣布退休，並搬回奧倫其頓這裡。72在職業聯盟打了將近八年後，瓊斯先生在上一季一場比賽中受傷，並從那之後一直深受傷勢之苦。雖然，醫師們盡了他們一切所能，他最終仍然不得不放棄打球。自那之後，73他已去過20個城市宣傳他的書，現在，他要回到這裡，開連鎖運動健身房。

字彙 return 返回　announce 宣布，宣告　retirement 退休　relocation 搬遷，重新安置　suffer 受苦，受折磨　injury 傷害，損傷　give up 放棄　chain 連鎖店

071

What is implied about Orangeton?
(A) It is experiencing a lot of growth.
(B) It is getting a professional sports team.
(C) It is Mr. Jones' place of birth.
(D) It is the speaker's favorite place.

中譯 關於奧倫其頓，可由文中得知什麼？
(A) 它正在飛速發展。
(B) 它正成立一支職業運動隊伍。
(C) 它是瓊斯先生的出生地。
(D) 它是說話者最喜歡的地方。

解析 本篇獨白為奧倫其頓地區的新聞報導。前半段提到家鄉英雄人物瓊斯先生回到家鄉（returning home），暗示瓊斯先生在奧倫其頓出生。

換句話說 hometown → place of birth

字彙 imply 暗指，意味著　experience 經歷，體驗　growth 發展，成長

072

How long was Mr. Jones a professional athlete?
(A) For 5 years
(B) For 8 years
(C) For 10 years
(D) For 20 years

中譯 瓊斯先生當職業運動員有多久？
(A) 五年
(B) 八年
(C) 十年
(D) 二十年

解析 報導中提到瓊斯先生於職業聯盟活躍將近八年的時間（nearly eight years）。

073

What did Mr. Jones recently do?
(A) Opened a store
(B) Left a hospital
(C) Played in a tournament
(D) Traveled around

中譯 瓊斯先生最近做了什麼？
(A) 開一家店
(B) 離開醫院
(C) 打錦標賽
(D) 四處旅行

解析 後半段報導中提及他的近況。瓊斯先生巡迴二十個城市宣傳自己的書，表示他為到各地進行演講而四處旅行。

Questions 74-76 refer to the following telephone message. 美

Hello, this is Vince Conklin. 74 I own the East End Diner on Main Street. A friend recommended 75 I call you to get an estimate on putting window coverings on our south facing windows. The customers are complaining about the late afternoon sun in the front part of our restaurant. 76 Could you give me a call at 555-2839 when you get this message? I'd like to get started on this as soon as possible since the weather is warming up.

哈囉，74我是文斯‧康克林，我是緬因街東城小吃的老闆。有個朋友建議 75 我打電話給你們，估一下在我們朝南的窗戶上裝窗簾的價格。顧客一直抱怨我們餐廳的正面在下午稍晚會曬到太陽。76你聽到這個留言後，可以打 555-2839 這個電話給我嗎？我想儘快開始處理這個問題，因為天氣開始熱起來了。

字彙 get an estimate 估價　customer 顧客

074

Who is the caller?
(A) A business owner
(B) The listener's friend
(C) An engineer
(D) A weather forecaster

中譯 打電話的人是誰？
(A) 商家老闆　　　　(B) 聽話者的朋友
(C) 工程師　　　　　(D) 氣象預報員

解析 前半段電話留言中，說話者表明了自己的身份，他提到自己是東城小吃的老闆（**own the East End Diner**），因此答案要選 (A)「a business owner」。

字彙 **forecaster** 預測者，推測者

04

075

What can the listener provide?
(A) A catering service
(B) Locally-grown food
(C) A new window
(D) A quotation

中譯 聽話者可以提供什麼？
(A) 外燴服務　　　　(B) 本地種植的食物
(C) 新的窗戶　　　　(D) 一份報價單

解析 本題詢問聆聽電話留言的人可以提供什麼東西。聆聽電話留言中提及的來電目的，便能得知答案。留言中提到他想在店內裝設窗簾，並請對方報價。由此可以得知，聽者將提供報價單給來電者。

換句話說 an estimate → a quotation

字彙 **locally-grown** 本地種植的　**quotation** 報價單

076

What does Mr. Conklin ask the listener to do?
(A) Call back quickly
(B) Contact his assistant
(C) Reply by e-mail
(D) Stop by his office

中譯 康克林先生要求聽話者做什麼？
(A) 快點回電話　　　(B) 聯絡他的助理
(C) 以電子郵件回覆　(D) 順路去他的辦公室

解析 留言最後提到請對方確認留言後回電，並表明希望儘快（**as soon as possible**）動工。

字彙 **contact** 聯絡，接觸　**assistant** 助理，助手
reply 回覆，回應　**stop by** 順路拜訪

Questions 77-79 refer to the following advertisement. 加

Does your house or apartment need a thorough cleaning but you just don't have the time? If you're an older couple who just can't keep up with the tasks or a busy working mom who's just plain tired, let Merry Workers help you out. ⑦ Our cheerful staff of cleaners can come in and do what might take you several days in a few hours. ⑱ It will give you a big lift to walk into your fresh-smelling and orderly house after a long day. ⑲ Call us today for a new customer discount of up to 25 percent, depending on the size of your place. 555-3829.

你的房子或公寓是否需要全面大掃除，但你就是沒有時間？如果，你們是較年長的夫婦，就是無法勝任這樣的粗活，或者你是忙碌的上班族媽媽，就是完全累攤了，讓「快活工人」幫助你擺脫困境。⑦我們朝氣蓬勃的清潔人員可以來你家，在幾個小時之內完成你可能要花好幾天才能做完的工作。在經過漫長的一天之後，走進你空氣清新、井井有條的家，⑱會讓你精神大振。⑲今天就撥打 555-3829 給我們，以獲得新客戶折扣優惠，依你家大小而定，可能高達 75 折。

字彙 **thorough cleaning** 大打掃，徹底清潔　**keep up with** 跟上……　**cheerful** 興高采烈的，情緒好的
give sb. a lift 使……情緒振奮　**orderly** 整齊的　**discount** 打折，減價　**depending on** 取決於，根據

077

What kind of business is being advertised?
(A) Childcare service
(B) **Cleaning service**
(C) Delivery service
(D) Elderly care service

中譯　文中是哪一種行業的廣告？
(A) 托兒服務　　　　(B) 清潔服務
(C) 送貨服務　　　　(D) 銀髮照護服務

解析　前半段廣告中，提到專人清掃的好處，中間還提及「我們朝氣蓬勃的清潔人員（Our cheerful staff of cleaners）」，由此可以得知本篇獨白為清潔服務的廣告。

字彙　childcare 兒童照護　delivery 投遞，交貨

078 新增題型

What does the speaker mean when she says, "It will give you a big lift"?
(A) The service will make listeners save money.
(B) The service will be used to make listeners feel lighter.
(C) **The service will make listeners happy.**
(D) The service will take listeners where they need to go.

中譯　當說話者說：「會讓你精神大振」，她的意思是什麼？
(A) 這項服務能讓聽話者省錢。
(B) 使用這項服務會讓聽話者感覺較輕鬆。
(C) 這項服務會讓聽話者快樂。
(D) 這項服務會帶聽話者去他們需要去的地方。

解析　「It will give you a big lift」的意思為「讓你精神大振、讓你更開心」。

換句話說　give you a big lift → make listeners happy

字彙　light 輕鬆的

079

Who can get a discount?
(A) Those who give a discount code
(B) Those who have a certain size house
(C) **Those who have not used the service before**
(D) Those who live in a certain area

中譯　誰可以得到折扣優惠？
(A) 那些有折扣代碼的人
(B) 那些房子是特定大小的人
(C) 那些以前沒有使用過這項服務的人
(D) 那些住在某些地區的人

解析　與折扣有關的內容通常會出現在廣告的後半段，當中提到將提供新顧客最高 75 折的優惠。

換句話說　new customer → those who have not used the service before

Questions 80-82 refer to the following broadcast. 英

Good evening. I'm Rex Madison with your news update. Our top story tonight is ⑳ **the approval of a new bridge over the Marble River**. While the river is our city's most visible landmark, it makes it rather inconvenient to get from one side of town to the other. Now we'll have two bridges to choose from. Taxpayers approved the bridge last November, but ㉑ **it has taken six months for city officials to choose a construction company.** They finally went with the lowest bidder, ㉒ **Nine Point Construction, a local business that expects to hire more than 50 people for the five-year project.**

晚安，我是雷克斯・麥迪森，為你播報最新消息。我們今晚的頭條新聞是，⑳ 在馬波河上新建一座橋樑的案子已通過。雖然，這條河是我們這個城最顯而易見的地標，但它讓人從城的一邊要去另一邊變得很不方便。現在，我們有二條橋可以選。納稅人去年十一月同意建橋，但 ㉑ 市政府官員花了六個月才選出建設公司。他們終於選了標價最低的廠商，㉒ 本地的九點營造公司，這個五年的工程預期將僱用超過 50 人。

字彙　approval 批准，同意　visible 顯而易見的，引人注目的　inconvenient 不方便的　taxpayer 納稅人
construction company 建設公司　bidder 投標人

080

What will the new bridge go over?
(A) A lake
(B) A river
(C) A valley
(D) Some train tracks

中譯 新橋將橫越什麼之上？
(A) 一座湖　　　　(B) 一條河
(C) 一座山谷　　　(D) 一些火車軌道

解析 本篇獨白為地方新聞的廣播，內容有關馬波河上新蓋的一座橋（a new bridge over the Marble River）。

081

Why was the project delayed?
(A) The citizens did not want to approve it.
(B) The city could not decide on a builder.
(C) The city did not have the money.
(D) The construction company had problems.

中譯 工程為什麼耽擱了？
(A) 市民不想批准。
(B) 市政府無法決定建商。
(C) 市政府沒有錢。
(D) 建設公司有問題。

解析 廣播中提到市府官員花了六個月的時間在選擇建設公司上，由此可以得知施工延後的原因為無法決定出建設業者。

換句話說 choose a construction company → decide on a builder

字彙 builder 建商

082

What is the construction company expected to do?
(A) Employ many people
(B) Give a press conference
(C) Start the bidding process
(D) Underbid its rivals

中譯 建設公司預計會做什麼？
(A) 僱用許多人　　　(B) 開記者會
(C) 啟動投標程序　　(D) 出價低於競爭對手

解析 新聞最後提到當地企業九點營造公司預計釋出五十個以上的工作職缺。

字彙 employ 僱用　press conference 記者會
bidding 投標，出價　process 過程，程序
underbid 出價低於

Questions 83-85 refer to the following talk. 澳

Just a quick word before we open this morning. As you know, we're having our big annual sale this weekend. ❸ Many customers wait to buy all their clothes at this sale, so it gets pretty busy. Based on last year's sales, ❸ business really picked up between 5:00 and 7:00 PM, so I need more of you for that time. I've adjusted the schedule and posted it on the bulletin board in the break room. Please check it before you leave today. Of course, ❸ anybody working a longer shift will be paid overtime, which is double your hourly wage.

在我們今天早上開門營業前，我很快講一下。你們都知道，這個週末就是我們的年度大特賣。❸ 很多顧客都等著在這次特賣中，買下他們所有的衣服，所以會非常忙。根據去年的業績來看，❸ 在下午五到七點間的生意真的比較好，所以，那段時間，我會需要更多人手。我已經調整班表並張貼在休息室的布告欄上。請在今天下班前去查看。當然，❸ 上班時間較長的人會有加班費，時薪會是二倍。

字彙 annual 年度的，每年的　based on 以……為根據，基於　pick up 增加，提高　adjust 調整
bulletin board 布告欄　shift 輪班　hourly wage 時薪

083

Where is the announcement taking place?
(A) At a bookstore
(B) At a clothing store
(C) At a grocery store
(D) At a shoe store

中譯 這項通知發生在哪裡？
(A) 在書店　　　　(B) 在服飾店
(C) 在雜貨店　　　(D) 在鞋店

解析 本篇獨白為商店內針對延長工作時間的通知。前半段提到顧客將於特賣期間前來購買衣服（clothes），由此可以推測本篇獨白會出現在販售服飾的地方。

084 新增題型

What does the speaker imply when she says, "business really picked up between 5:00 and 7:00 PM"?
(A) A lot of customers came during the evening.
(B) The customers used a shuttle bus to come to the store.
(C) A special discount was offered in the evening.
(D) Those who work in the evening were paid double.

中譯 當說話者說：「在下午五到七點間的生意真的比較好」，她意指什麼？
(A) 傍晚有很多客人來。　(B) 顧客搭接駁車來店裡。
(C) 傍晚有特別折扣。　　(D) 那些上晚班的人薪資加倍。

解析 獨白中提到大家在下午5點至7點間生意會很忙碌（business really picked up），暗示傍晚這段時間會有很多顧客上門。

085

What will listeners receive if they work longer this weekend?
(A) A bonus
(B) Free merchandise
(C) Higher salary
(D) A paid day off

中譯 如果聽話者這個週末工作時間較長，他們會得到什麼？
(A) 紅利獎金　　　(B) 免費商品
(C) 較高的薪水　　(D) 一天的有薪假

解析 獨白最後提到工作時間延長的人將領到原有薪資兩倍（double）的加班費，由此可以得知超時工作者將領到更高的薪水。

換句話說 wage → salary

字彙 merchandise 商品，貨物　salary 薪水　day off 休息日

Questions 86-88 refer to the following advertisement. 美

Are you unreasonably tired at the end of the day? Do you have trouble staying awake after lunch? ❻ **Then you need our all-natural energy supplement, Pep Pills. ❼ These supplements are nonaddictive and perfectly safe for people over 15.** Made with ginseng and vitamin B12, Pep Pills give you a big boost of energy quickly. Available in capsule or convenient gel form. Don't look for Pep Pills at the drug store. ❽ **They're only sold online at www. peppills.com.** Visit our Website for a free sample sent right to your door. No obligation, no charge.

你在一天結束時，是否感到異常疲累？你是否吃完午餐後，要保持清醒有困難？❻ 是的話，你就需要我們的全天然能量補給品沛普錠。❼ 這種補給品不會上癮，而且對15歲以上的人非常安全。沛普錠以人蔘和維他命B12為原料，能快速提振你的精神。有膠囊或是方便服用的凝膠狀可選。別去藥局找沛普錠，❽ 這只有在網上販售：www.peppills.com。請上我們的網站，免費試用品可直送到你家。不會強迫購買，不會收費。

字彙 unreasonably 不合理地，過分地　supplement 補給品　nonaddictive 不會上癮的
obligation （道義上或法律上的）義務　charge 費用，索價

086

What is being advertised?
(A) A drink
(B) A health food
(C) A medication
(D) A supplement

中譯　文中在廣告什麼？
(A) 飲料
(B) 健康食物
(C) 藥品
(D) 補給品

解析　本篇獨白為全天然能量補給品（**all-natural energy supplement**）的廣告。

087

Who can use the advertised product?
(A) Anyone
(B) Hospital patients only
(C) Students only
(D) Those over 15

中譯　誰可以使用廣告的產品？
(A) 任何人
(B) 只有住院的病人
(C) 只有學生
(D) 15 歲以上的人

解析　廣告中提到此款補給品不會使人上癮，且 15 歲以上的人都可以安心食用（**safe for people over 15**）。

088

Where can the product be purchased?
(A) At a health exhibition
(B) At all health food stores
(C) At any drugstore
(D) On the Web

中譯　這項產品可以在哪裡買到？
(A) 在健康醫療展
(B) 在所有的健康食品店
(C) 在任何一家藥局
(D) 在網路上

解析　廣告中提到此款產品僅於公司網站上販售。

換句話說　online → on the Web

字彙　exhibition 展覽　drugstore 藥局，藥妝店

Questions 89-91 refer to the following talk. 加

Just wanted to let everybody know before they leave for the weekend that the parking lot to the north side will be closed next week, Monday through Friday, for resurfacing. ❽❾ **That means we will be restricted to the east end parking lot, which is smaller.** ❾⓪ **I encourage you to carpool or take public transportation** because parking in that lot will be first come, first served. With only 25 spots, ❾❶ **some of you may have to find street parking, which is expensive and far from the office.**

在大家下班過週末前，我只是要告訴大家，北邊的停車場在下星期，也就是星期一到星期五，會關閉重鋪路面。❽❾ 那表示，我們只能受限於用東邊比較小的停車場。❾⓪ 我鼓勵你們共乘或搭乘大眾運輸工具，因為，那邊的停車場是先來先停。由於只有 25 個車位，❾❶ 你們有些人可能必須找路邊停車位，那會很貴而且離辦公室很遠。

字彙　resurface 為……鋪設新表面（路面）　restrict 限制　encourage 鼓勵
first come, first served 先來先得　spot 地點，場所

089

What is the talk mainly about?
(A) An expansion of the office
(B) A new employee's first day
(C) **Parking location changes**
(D) Public transportation fees

中譯 這段談話的主題是什麼？
(A) 辦公室擴建
(B) 一名新員工的第一天
(C) 停車地點改變
(D) 大眾運輸的費用

解析 本篇獨白的內容是通知員工因路面重鋪工程而將關閉（**closed**）北邊的停車場，請大家改使用東邊面積較小的停車場。因此本篇獨白為告知聽者停車地點的更動。

字彙 **expansion** 擴展，擴張　**location** 位置，場所　**fee** 費用

090

What are listeners encouraged to do?
(A) Keep their desks clean
(B) Participate in a survey
(C) **Ride to work together**
(D) Welcome a new employee

中譯 文中鼓勵聽話者做什麼？
(A) 保持桌面乾淨
(B) 參加民意調查
(C) 一起開車上班
(D) 歡迎一位新員工

解析 為節省停車空間，建議大家採取共乘的方式，或是搭乘大眾運輸工具。

換句話說 carpool → ride to work together

字彙 **participate in** 參加　**survey** 意見調查

091

According to the speaker, what might some listeners experience next week?
(A) **A long walk**
(B) Loud construction noise
(C) Low temperatures in the office
(D) A new desk assignment

中譯 根據說話者，有些聽話者下星期可能會經歷什麼事？
(A) 走很遠的路　　　(B) 巨大的工程噪音
(C) 辦公室的低溫　　(D) 新的座位分配

解析 獨白中聽到因停車空間有限，一部分的人需要支付較高的停車費把車停到距離辦公室較遠的（**far from the office**）停車地點。由此可以得知部分員工需要步行較長的距離至公司。

字彙 **temperature** 溫度　**assignment** 分配，指派

Questions 92-94 refer to the following announcement and receipt. 英

Fern Grove Department Store	
♪♪ Thank you for shopping with us today. ♪♪	
Women's blouse	$55.00
Tax (10%)	$5.50
❾❹ Total	$60.50
We appreciate our customer's feedback: www.ferngrovedepart.com	

芬葛羅芙百貨公司	
♪♪ 感謝您今天的惠顧 ♪♪	
女用襯衫	$55.00
稅（10%）	$5.50
❾❹ 總計	$60.50
我們歡迎顧客的回饋意見。 www.ferngrovedepart.com	

Attention customers. Thank you for shopping with us at Fern Grove Department Store today. As a reminder, our annual sale is ongoing on all floors. ❷ **Discounts between 40 and 60 percent can be found on all items in some sections, such as kids' clothing and women's shoes.** ❸ **The sale ends tomorrow at closing, so don't delay.** Remember to bring your receipt and parking ticket for validation to any of our customer service desks throughout the store. ❹ **Free parking is offered for those with purchases over 50 dollars.** ❸ **We will be closing in 30 minutes, at 8:00, as usual.**

各位顧客請注意。感謝您今天光臨芬葛羅芙百貨購物。提醒您，我們各樓層正在進行年度大特賣。❷ 在某些區，如童裝和女鞋區，所有的品項都打 4 到 6 折。❸ 特賣會到明天打烊為止，所以腳步要快。記得您的收據和停車票券到我們店內的任一顧客服務檯驗證。❹ 凡消費滿 50 元者，都可以免費停車。❸ 我們將在 30 分鐘後，如常在 8 點結束營業。

字彙 reminder 提醒（的話） ongoing 進行的 delay 拖延，耽擱 validation 確認，批准

092

What discount can a customer get on a child's jacket at most?
(A) 30 percent
(B) 40 percent
(C) 50 percent
(D) 60 percent

中譯 顧客買兒童外套，最多可以打幾折？
(A) 7 折　(B) 6 折
(C) 5 折　(D) 4 折

解析 本大題為百貨公司內的廣播。當中提到兒童服飾（kids' clothing）和女鞋（women's shoes）等區，提供 40%–60% 的折扣，即原價去掉 40%–60%，也就是中文的「打六到四折」。兒童夾克屬於兒童服飾，因此最高有 60% 折扣，也就是可打四折。

093

When does the sale end?
(A) This afternoon at 5:00
(B) Tonight at 8:00
(C) Tomorrow at 12:00
(D) Tomorrow night at 8:00

中譯 特賣何時結束？
(A) 今天下午 5 點　(B) 今天晚上 8 點
(C) 明天 12 點　(D) 明天晚上 8 點

解析 廣播中段提到優惠只到隔日百貨公司打烊為止（tomorrow at closing），最後又提到平時的打烊時間為晚上八點，因此可以得知優惠結束時間為明天晚上八點。

094 新增題型

Look at the graphic. What can the customer receive?
(A) An extra discount
(B) A free gift
(C) Free parking
(D) A refund

中譯 見圖表。顧客可以得到什麼？
(A) 額外折扣　(B) 免費禮物
(C) 免費停車　(D) 退款

解析 本題為圖表整合題。廣播中提到折扣內容以及針對消費滿 50 元以上的顧客，提供免費停車的服務。根據收據上的內容，消費總額為 60.50 元，因此適用免費停車。

字彙 refund 退款

Questions 95-97 refer to the following excerpt of meeting and layout. 澳

office area	storage room
studio	⑨⑥ meeting room

辦公區	儲藏室
攝影棚	⑨⑥ 會議室

⑨⑤ Thanks everyone for your hard work on the next issue. Our subscribers are really going to like the beautiful photographs we're adding to the magazine. Now I'd like to mention a change to the office renovation plans. I've talked with the architect and she said that to get the most light in our studio, we should add one more set of windows. ⑨⑥ That will mean the room next to the studio will be smaller. ⑨⑦ I'd like to hear from anyone who has any objections or concerns about this now. What do you think?

⑨⑤ 謝謝你們每一位對下一期雜誌所投入的努力。我們的訂戶真的會喜歡我們放進雜誌裡的美麗照片。現在,我想要提一下,辦公室的整修工程計畫有個地方要修改。我和建築師談過,她說,如要讓光線儘可能地照進我們的攝影棚,我們應該再加一組窗戶。⑨⑥ 那表示,攝影棚旁邊的房間會比較小。⑨⑦ 現在,我想聽聽任何反對或擔憂的人的意見。你們認為呢?

字彙 **subscriber** 訂閱者 **renovation** 整修,重建 **architect** 建築師 **objection** 反對 **concern** 擔心,關心 **storage** 儲藏,儲存

095

What industry does the speaker work in?
(A) Architecture
(B) Construction
(C) Medical
(D) Publishing

中譯 說話者在哪一行工作?
(A) 建築　　　　(B) 營造
(C) 醫療　　　　(D) 出版

解析 獨白中提到 next issue、subscribers、magazine 等關鍵字,可以得知說話者任職於出版業。

096 新增題型

Look at the graphic. Which room will be smaller after the renovation?
(A) The meeting room
(B) The office area
(C) The storage room
(D) The studio

中譯 見圖表。整修後,哪個房間會比較小?
(A) 會議室　　　(B) 辦公區
(C) 儲藏室　　　(D) 攝影棚

解析 本題為圖表整合題。依照獨白中提及的辦公室整修計畫,預計會縮小(**smaller**)攝影棚隔壁位置的空間。根據設計圖,攝影棚隔壁為會議室,由此可以得知會議室會變小間。

097

What most likely will the listeners do next?
(A) Discuss the office layout
(B) Have lunch together
(C) Plan a new product
(D) Speak with an architect

中譯 聽話者接下來最可能做什麼?
(A) 討論辦公室的格局　(B) 一起吃午餐
(C) 設計一項新產品　　(D) 和建築師談話

解析 之後要做的事,通常會出現在獨白最後。說話者針對空間變小一事,詢問大家的意見,由此可以得知之後他將與員工們討論辦公室空間配置的問題。

字彙 **layout** 格局,布局

Questions 98-100 refer to the following announcement and timetable. 美

Platform	Time	Destination
1	15:30	Arendale
2	15:35	Hastings Cross
99 3	15:45	Gilmore Station
4	15:48	Green River

月台	時間	終點
1	15:30	艾倫戴爾
2	15:35	赫斯汀斯十字
99 3	15:45	吉爾摩車站
4	15:48	綠河

Attention passengers. 98 Please be aware that we've had a change of time for one of our trains leaving soon. 99 The express to Gilmore Station will leave ten minutes later than scheduled. We apologize for this delay. If you are taking the express to Gilmore Station, please go to Platform 3. The local to Green River is leaving from Platform 4. As a reminder, 100 cars 5 to 9 are for passengers with reserved tickets only. If you have an unreserved ticket, please enter at the front of the train, in cars 1 to 4.

各位旅客請注意。98 請留意，我們即將發車的一班火車時間有更改。99 往吉爾摩車站的快車將比預訂時間晚十分鐘發車。我們為誤點致歉。如果您要搭乘往吉爾摩車站的快車，請前往第三月台。往綠河的慢車將從第四月台發車。提醒您，100 第五到第九節車廂只供持預售票乘客使用。如果您買的不是預售票，請從火車前面，第一到第四車廂上車。

04

字彙 passenger 乘客，旅客　aware 知道的　express 快車　platform 月台　reserved 預訂的
unreserved 未預訂的　enter 進入

098

Who most likely is the speaker?
(A) A passenger
(B) A train conductor
(C) A train driver
(D) A train station staff

中譯 說話者最可能是誰？
(A) 一名乘客　　　　(B) 一名火車列車長
(C) 一名火車司機　　(D) 一名火車站員工

解析 廣播中提及列車延誤、月台通知等內容，因此說話者應為火車站員工。

字彙 train conductor 火車車長

099 新增題型

Look at the graphic. What time is the train to Gilmore Station going to leave?
(A) 15:35
(B) 15:45
(C) 15:48
(D) 15:55

中譯 見圖表。往吉爾摩車站的火車幾點會發車？
(A) 15:35　　　　(B) 15:45
(C) 15:48　　　　(D) 15:55

解析 本題為圖表整合題。廣播中提到前往吉爾摩車站的快速列車預計延後 10 分鐘發車（ten minutes later than scheduled）。而時刻表中的原定發車時間為 15 點 45 分，因此答案要選 15 點 55 分。

100

Where should passengers with reserved tickets go?
(A) Car 1
(B) Car 2
(C) Car 4
(D) Car 8

中譯 買預售票的乘客應該去哪裡？
(A) 第一節車廂　　(B) 第二節車廂
(C) 第四節車廂　　(D) 第八節車廂

解析 廣播中提及第五至九節車廂僅限事先預訂車票的乘客搭乘（passengers with reserved tickets only），因此選擇選項中的第八節車廂較為適當。

PART 5

101

If you would like to book one of our meeting rooms, please let us know if you need any ------- such as a projector or a video camera.

(A) equipment
(B) amenities
(C) instruments
(D) materials

中譯 如果你想預訂我們的會議室,請告知你是否需要任何設備,如投影機或攝影機。

(A) 設備   (B) 娛樂消遣設施
(C) 樂器   (D) 材料

解析 本題要選出符合題意的名詞。**such as** 後方連接「投影機或攝影機」,空格應填入通稱這兩樣東西的單字,因此選擇 **equipment** 較為適當。

字彙 **equipment** 設備
amenity 娛樂消遣設施
instrument 樂器   **material** 材料

102

AtoZ Industry offers plenty of ------- office furniture and supplies suitable for your needs.

(A) rent
(B) rental
(C) renter
(D) rents

中譯 艾圖利工業有許多符合你需求的辦公家具和用品可供出租。

(A) 租用   (B) 供出租的
(C) 承租人   (D) 租用

解析 空格位在介系詞 **of** 和名詞片語 **office furniture** 之間,因此空格適合填入形容詞 **rental**,用來形容後方名詞。**rent** 可以當作動詞或名詞使用,**renter** 為名詞,兩者填入空格後,會變成複合名詞,但是皆不符合題意。而 **rents** 則是現在式第三人稱單數動詞。

字彙 **plenty of** 很多,大量
rental 供出租的

103

If you have a problem installing our software on your computer, you can call ------- send an e-mail to our customer service staff.

(A) and
(B) nor
(C) or
(D) to

中譯 如果你在你的電腦上安裝我們的軟體有困難,你可以打電話或發電子郵件給我們的客服人員。

(A) 並且   (B) 也不
(C) 或者   (D) 給

解析 空格位在動詞 **call** 和 **send** 之間,根據題意適合填入連接詞 **or**,表示兩者擇一的概念。

字彙 **install** 安裝

104

The city council ------- receives architectural proposals created by a group of graduate students.

(A) recently
(B) similarly
(C) highly
(D) regularly

中譯 市議會經常收到由一群研究生所創作的建築提案。

(A) 最近   (B) 相似地
(C) 非常   (D) 經常

解析 選項中,能搭配現在式動詞 **receives** 使用,又符合題意的副詞為 **regularly**。

字彙 **similarly** 相似地

105

As the keynote speech was cancelled at the last minute, the event organizer had to find a -------.
(A) replace
(B) replaceable
(C) replacing
(D) replacement

中譯 由於主題演講在最後一刻取消，主辦單位必須找替代代方案。
(A) 代替　　　　　(B) 可替換的
(C) 代替　　　　　(D) 代替

解析 空格位在句尾，且前方連接不定冠詞 a，因此適合填入名詞 replacement。

字彙 keynote speech 主題演講
organizer（競賽、活動的）籌辦者
replacement 代替者，代替物

106

The leader talked at length about how practical his project plan was ------- all of his team members agreed to proceed.
(A) in case
(B) given that
(C) until
(D) whether

中譯 領導者花了很長的時間談他的專案計畫有多可行，直到他的團隊成員都同意進行該計畫。
(A) 以防萬一　　　(B) 鑒於
(C) 直到　　　　　(D) 是否

解析 本題要選出適合連接空格前後方句子的連接詞。空格前方表達「領導者進行說明」，空格後方表達「團隊成員全都同意進行他的計畫」，選項中適合填入的單字為 until，表示持續的動作到此結束。

字彙 at length 長時間地　practical 可實施的
proceed 繼續進行　in case 以防萬一
given that 鑒於，考慮到

107

Sarah Luther had to hurry back to her office to attend a ------- seminar for the new intranet system.
(A) numerous
(B) mandatory
(C) versatile
(D) voluntary

中譯 莎拉‧路德不得不匆忙趕回辦公室，以參加一個必須出席的新內網系統研討會。
(A) 許多的　　　　(B) 強制的
(C) 多才多藝的　　(D) 自願的

解析 本題為形容詞詞彙題。句中提及莎拉「不得不」快點回辦公室出席某個研討會，因此空格最適合填入 mandatory，表示「強制的、必須履行的」。

字彙 numerous 許多的　mandatory 強制的，義務的
versatile 多才多藝的，多功能的　voluntary 自願的

108

Because of a heating problem, the sales team had to hold their meeting in an ------- cold room.
(A) exceed
(B) exceeded
(C) exceeding
(D) exceedingly

中譯 由於暖氣出了問題，業務團隊不得不在一個極為寒冷的房間開會。
(A) 超過　　　　　(B) 超過
(C) 極度的　　　　(D) 極度地

解析 本題要選出填入冠詞 an 和名詞片語 cold room 之間的單字。選項中最適合用來修飾形容詞 cold 的是副詞 exceedingly。

字彙 exceedingly 極度地

109

All employees are required to acknowledge that ------- have been informed of the new company policy and agree to it in all respects.
(A) theirs
(B) them
(C) themselves
(D) they

中譯 所有員工都要覆函告知他們已知悉公司的新政策並且完全同意。
(A) 他們的 (B) 他們
(C) 他們自己 (D) 他們

解析 關係代名詞 that 和 have 之間缺少主詞，因此空格適合填入 they，用來代替主詞 All employees。按照文法規則，所有格代名詞 theirs 可以置於主詞的位置，但是根據本題題意，填入 theirs 並不適當。

字彙 be required to 按照要求去做
acknowledge 確認收到（信或電子郵件）
inform 通知，告知 in all respects 各方面，全部

110

Melba Logistics is a licensed carrier ------- rapid and safe transportation services all over the world.
(A) forwarding
(B) equipping
(C) providing
(D) receiving

中譯 梅爾巴物流公司是有執照的運輸業者，在全球各地提供快速又安全的運輸服務。
(A) 轉寄 (B) 裝備
(C) 提供 (D) 接收

解析 本題為動詞詞彙題，空格要填入動詞加 ing 形成的現在分詞，從空格到 world 都是形容詞，修飾前方的 a licensed carrier。根據題意，表達物流業者「提供」運輸服務較為適當。

字彙 licensed 領有執照的 carrier 從事運輸的人或公司
rapid 快速的 forward 轉寄 equip 裝備，配備
provide 提供

111

More than 300 people ------- 50 different countries took part in the 15th International Conference on Environmental Science.
(A) among
(B) from
(C) over
(D) through

中譯 來自 50 個不同國家的 300 多位人士，參加了第十五屆國際環境科學大會。
(A) 在……之中 (B) 來自
(C) 越過 (D) 穿過

解析 本題為介系詞詞彙題。from 表達出身或來源。空格填入 from 後，表示「來自五十個國家的三百多人」。

字彙 take part in 參加，出席

112

With the board members -------, Mr. Henderson will assume the post of chairperson next month.
(A) endorsable
(B) endorse
(C) endorsement
(D) endorser

中譯 在董事會的支持下，韓德森先生下個月將接任主席一職。
(A) 可被認可的 (B) 認可
(C) 認可 (D) 背書人

解析 空格前方為所有格，因此要填入名詞。雖然 endorsement 和 endorser 皆為名詞，但是表達得到董事會的「支持、贊同」，便能擔任主席最符合題意，因此答案要選 endorsement。

字彙 board 董事會 assume 就任 post 職位
endorsement 支持，認可

113

If you have any problems with or questions about the network access -------, please ask our IT department.
(A) selection
(B) advance
(C) protocol
(D) sequence

中譯 如果你有任何關於網路存取協定的麻煩或問題,請向我們的資訊部門詢問。
(A) 選擇 　　　　(B) 前進
(C) 協定 　　　　(D) 次序

解析 本題為名詞詞彙題,要選出適合搭配 network access 使用的單字。根據題意,表達「網路存取協定」較為適當,因此答案為 protocol。

字彙 selection 選擇　advance 前進,發展
protocol 協定　sequence 次序

114

According to the financial advisor, conducting ------- research beforehand is crucial for buying stocks.
(A) detail
(B) detailed
(C) detailing
(D) details

中譯 根據理財顧問的意見,事前進行詳細的研究對購買股票至關重要。
(A) 詳述 　　　　(B) 詳細的
(C) 詳述 　　　　(D) 細節

解析 空格位在動名詞 conducting 和名詞 research 之間,應填入形容詞。過去分詞 detailed 可以扮演形容詞的角色,填入空格後表示「詳細研究」,最符合題意。

字彙 financial advisor 理財顧問　conduct research 進行研究
beforehand 預先,事先　crucial 至關重要的　stock 股票
detailed 詳細的

115

The personnel chief considers that asking an unexpected question can be useful to judge candidates ------- interviewing them.
(A) as well as
(B) unless
(C) still
(D) when

中譯 人事主管認為在面試時,問一個意想不到的問題有助評斷應徵者。
(A) 還有 　　　　(B) 除非
(C) 仍然 　　　　(D) 當……時

解析 本題要選出適當的連接詞,置於 interviewing 前方。根據題意,表達「在人事部主管面試求職者的時候」最為適當,因此答案為 when。

字彙 personnel chief 人事主管　consider 認為
unexpected 出乎意料的　judge 判斷,評判

116

Rather than partially modifying it, the team manager thought they should reconsider the ------- design of the new product.
(A) center
(B) extra
(C) main
(D) whole

中譯 團隊經理認為,他們應該重新考慮新產品的整體設計,而不是部分修改就好。
(A) 中心的 　　　　(B) 額外的
(C) 主要的 　　　　(D) 全部的

解析 partially 前方連接 rather than,表示比較的概念。空格要填入 whole,與 partially 形成對比,才符合題意。

字彙 rather than 而不是……　partially 部分地　modify 修改

117

As the contract is coming to an end, the company will have to remove all possessions and ------- the rented property by the end of the week.

(A) vacancies
(B) vacancy
(C) vacant
(D) vacate

中譯 隨著合約即將到期，這家公司必須在本週結束前，搬走所有物品並清空承租的房子。
(A) 空位　　　　　　(B) 空位
(C) 空的　　　　　　(D) 空出

解析 空格前方有對等連接詞 and，空格後方連接定冠詞開頭的名詞片語 the rented property，表示空格為動詞的位置。and 前方出現 remove all possessions，表示 and 後方應為 vacate the rented property，前後文才有連貫性。

字彙 remove 移動，搬開　possession 所有物　property 房產　vacancy 空位　vacate 空出

118

The consumer trends report found that people have recently spent ------- money on vacations and have saved it instead.

(A) fewer
(B) less
(C) many
(D) more

中譯 消費趨勢報告指出，人們近來較少花錢度假，而是把錢存起來。
(A) 較少的　　　　　(B) 較少的
(C) 許多的　　　　　(D) 更多的

解析 選項中，可以用來修飾不可數名詞 money 的單字為 less 和 more。根據題意，後方提到取而代之的是存錢，因此空格填入 less，表示「少花一點錢」較為適當。

字彙 consumer 消費者　instead 反而，卻

119

The new laptop, TGX 800, received many good reviews as it has been ------- improved from its old model and is a lot easier to use.

(A) mostly
(B) drastically
(C) scarcely
(D) temporarily

中譯 新款筆電 TGX 800 得到許多好評，因為它與舊款相比大幅改進，也比舊款容易使用得多了。
(A) 主要地　　　　　(B) 大幅地
(C) 幾乎沒有　　　　(D) 暫時地

解析 空格前方提到產品廣受好評，空格應填入副詞，用來修飾後方動詞 improved。根據題意，填入副詞 drastically 最為適當。

字彙 improve 改進　mostly 主要地，大部分地
drastically 大幅地　scarcely 幾乎沒有，幾乎不
temporarily 暫時地

120

The CEO is extremely concerned that the company's stock price ------- steadily over the past few weeks.

(A) has dropped
(B) has been dropping
(D) is dropping
(D) will drop

中譯 公司的股價過去幾星期來一直下跌，這讓執行長極為擔心。
(A) 已下跌　　　　　(B) 一直下跌
(C) 正在下跌　　　　(D) 將下跌

解析 主要子句的時態為現在式，而句尾出現 over the past few weeks，表示過去一段時間，因此空格應填入現在完成進行式 has been dropping 較為適當。

字彙 extremely 極其　stock price 股價
steadily 逐漸地，不斷地　drop （價格、溫度等）下降

121

-------, the product launch went quite smoothly even though several urgent changes were made.
(A) Surprise
(B) Surprised
(C) Surprising
(D) Surprisingly

中譯 儘管緊急修改了幾個地方，產品發表會出乎意料地相當順利。
(A) 驚訝　　　　　(B) 感到驚訝的
(C) 令人驚訝的　　(D) 出乎意料地

解析 即使拿掉空格，該句仍為一個結構完整的句子，因此空格適合填入副詞 Surprisingly，用來修飾完整句。

字彙 launch 發表會　smoothly 順利地

122

Mason Engineering has ------- some major changes over the year to become more customer-focused.
(A) underestimated
(B) undergone
(C) undermined
(D) understood

中譯 曼森工程過去一年來歷經了一些重大改革，變得更加以客戶為中心。
(A) 低估　　　　　(B) 經歷
(C) 暗中破壞　　　(D) 了解

解析 根據題意，公司為了達到目標，「經歷」很大的變化，因此空格適合填入 undergo 的過去分詞 undergone。

字彙 customer-focused 以客戶為中心　underestimate 低估
undergo 經歷　undermine 暗中破壞

123

An e-mail was sent to notify all the participants that the event would take place at Hamilton Hall ------- Celia Hall.
(A) prior to
(B) instead of
(C) though
(D) thus

中譯 已寄出一封電子郵件通知所有參加者，活動改到漢彌爾頓廳舉行，而不是在西利亞廳。
(A) 在……之前　　(B) 而不是
(C) 雖然　　　　　(D) 因此

解析 空格位在名詞和名詞之間，因此不能填入 (C) 或 (D)。根據題意，instead of 才能表達「告知參加者活動場所從西利亞廳改成漢彌爾頓廳」。

字彙 notify 通知，告知　participant 參加者
prior to 在……之前

124

There were nearly 1,000 people ------- at the protest against the discontinuation of free bus passes for seniors.
(A) present
(B) presentation
(C) presented
(D) presenter

中譯 有將近一千人參加這場抗議不再提供銀髮族免費公車乘車證的活動。
(A) 出席的　　　　(B) 出示
(C) 展出　　　　　(D) 節目主持人

解析 選項中，形容詞 present 適合用來修飾前方的 1,000 people。過去分詞 presented 帶有被動的含意，不適合填入空格。

字彙 nearly 幾乎，差不多　protest 抗議，反對
discontinuation 終止，廢止　senior 年長者
present 出席的

125

The collected personal information will not be disclosed to third parties without prior -------, except under court order.
(A) analysis
(B) **consent**
(C) discussion
(D) engagement

中譯 除了法院命令之外，未經事先同意，所收集的個人資料不會透露給第三方。
(A) 分析
(B) 同意
(C) 討論
(D) 約定

解析 根據題意，consent 最適合搭配空格前方的 prior 一起使用，表示「事先同意」之意。

字彙 personal information 個人資料　disclose 公開
third party 第三方　prior 在前的　except 除……之外
analysis 分析　consent 同意，贊成
discussion 討論，商議　engagement 約定；訂婚

126

Compromise does not always resolve the issues ------- contain underlying interpersonal conflicts.
(A) what
(B) **that**
(C) where
(D) whose

中譯 妥協不一定都能解決那些含有更深層人際衝突的問題。
(A) 所……的事物
(B) 那些……
(C) ……的地方
(D) 那個／些人的

解析 本題為關係代名詞考題。空格前方為 the issues，而這項問題便是指空格後方連接的 contain underlying interpersonal conflicts（包含深層的人際關係衝突）。另外，空格後方連接動詞 contain，因此填入關係代名詞主格 that 較為適當。

字彙 compromise 妥協　resolve 解決　underlying 深層的，潛在的
interpersonal 人際的　conflict 矛盾，衝突

127

Jade Private Hospital has established an excellent reputation in the community for its high ------- to patient satisfaction.
(A) commit
(B) **commitment**
(C) committal
(D) committed

中譯 傑德私立醫院因為它全心致力於讓病人滿意，而在社會上樹立了優良的聲譽。
(A) 使……致力於
(B) 投入
(C) 收監
(D) 投入的

解析 空格位在 its high 和介系詞 to 之間，表示空格適合填入名詞。雖然 commitment 和 committal 皆為名詞，但是填入 commitment，表達「為了讓病患滿意而做的努力」較為適當。

字彙 establish 建立，確立　reputation 名譽，聲望
satisfaction 滿意，滿足　commit 使……致力於
commitment 投入，奉獻　committal 收監

128

As the restaurant has been -------, the owner is considering expanding his business in the region.
(A) productive
(B) **prosperous**
(C) strategic
(D) struggling

中譯 由於餐廳生意一直很好，老闆考慮在這一區擴大營業。
(A) 多產的
(B) 興旺的
(C) 戰略的
(D) 艱難為生的

解析 老闆考慮擴展事業，因此空格適合填入 prosperous，表達「生意興隆」。struggling 表示相反意思，為「經營不善」之意。

字彙 expand 擴大　region 地區　productive 多產的
prosperous 興旺的，繁榮的　strategic 戰略的
struggling 艱難為生的，苦苦掙扎的

129

At the lecture, the renowned chef told the audience ------- such an easy recipe could result in such a delicious dish.
(A) as if
(B) despite
(C) how
(D) then

中譯 在講座上，這位知名的主廚告訴觀眾，這麼簡單的一份食譜如何能做出那麼美味的一道菜。
(A) 彷彿
(B) 儘管
(C) 如何
(D) 那麼

解析 空格後方連接子句，表示空格適合填入連接詞，因此請先刪去介系詞 (B) 和副詞 (D)。空格填入 how 的話，表示「如何用簡單的食譜做出美味的菜餚」，最符合題意。

字彙 lecture 講座　renowned 有名的　audience 觀眾
recipe 食譜，烹飪法　result in 導致，結果是

130

Even after spending long hours trying to fix it, the IT worker could not iron ------- the problem with the network.
(A) down
(B) off
(C) out
(D) over

中譯 即使花了很多時間試圖修理，資訊人員還是無法解決網路的問題。
(A) 向下
(B) 停止
(C) 去掉
(D) 在……之上

解析 iron out 的意思為「解決」，根據題意，最適合搭配後方受詞 the problem 一起使用。

字彙 iron out 解決，消除

PART 6

Questions 131-134 refer to the following email. 電子郵件

To:	Amanda Green
From:	Exciting Travel Co.
Subject:	Visit Costa Rica
Date:	March 19

Exciting Travel's Top Three Reasons You Should Visit Costa Rica

1. ------- **131.** you crave adventure, Costa Rica is definitely the place for you. You can go white-water rafting, kayaking, scuba diving, cliff diving, sky diving… the list is endless.

2. ------- **132.** . Both public and private beaches are sure to please lovers of sun and sand like ------- **133.** .

3. Costa Rica has been called the happiest country on Earth, and for good reason. The

收件者：亞曼達・葛林
寄件者：刺激旅遊公司
主旨：造訪哥斯大黎加
日期：3 月 19 日

刺激旅遊推薦你去哥斯大黎加旅遊的三大理由：

1. 131 如果你渴望冒險，哥斯大黎加肯定是你該去的地方。你可以玩激流泛舟、划獨木舟、水肺潛水、懸崖跳水、跳傘……，可玩的無限多。

2. 132 由於海岸線將近一千英里長，世界最美的海灘有些就位於哥斯大黎加。不管是公共的還是私人的海灘，一定都會讓像 133 你一樣的陽光與沙灘愛好者開心。

3. 哥斯大黎加被譽為地球上最快樂的國家，這其來有自。那裡的人愛好和平又友善，而且

people are peaceful, friendly and go out of their way to make every visitor feel at home.

For details about our travel ------ to Costa Rica, please visit our Website: www.excitingtravel.net.

134.

費盡心思要讓每一位遊客感到賓至如歸。

更多關於我們哥斯大黎加 **134** 套裝行程的細節，請上我們的網站：www.excitingtravel.net。

字彙 **crave** 渴望獲得，懇求　**definitely** 肯定地，毫無疑問　**white-water** 激起白色浪花的水面，激流
please 使……高興，使……滿意　**good reason** 充分的理由　**go out of one's way to** 費盡心思，特地

131

(A) If
(B) Probably
(C) Where
(D) Whether

中譯 (A) 如果　　　　　(B) 很可能
(C) 在……的地方　(D) 是否

解析 空格應填入連接詞，連接逗點前後的子句。if 表示條件，根據題意，填入 **if** 後，表達「如果你渴望冒險，哥斯大黎加肯定是你該去的地方」最為適當。

132 新增題型

(A) Costa Rica has a world-famous rainforest and many environmental organizations give tours of it.
(B) If you have kids, you'll definitely want to take advantage of our resort's six swimming pools.
(C) We have several great travel deals to Costa Rica, but they expire soon so don't put it off — call today.
(D) With almost 1,000 miles of coastline, Costa Rica is home to some of the world's loveliest beaches.

中譯 (A) 哥斯大黎加有世界知名的雨林，許多環保組織會舉行雨林之旅。
(B) 如果你有小孩，你一定會想利用我們度假中心的六座游泳池。
(C) 我們有好幾種很棒的哥斯大黎加行程，但優惠很快就會到期，所以別再拖了，今天就打電話。
(D) 由於海岸線將近一千英里長，世界最美的海灘有些位於哥斯大黎加。

解析 三個值得探訪的理由中，第二個理由與海邊有關，因此空格適合填入介紹哥斯大黎加海灘的句子。

字彙 **rainforest** 雨林　**environmental** 環境的
organization 組織，機構　**expire** 到期，結束
put off 延遲，拖延　**coastline** 海岸線

133

(A) ourselves
(B) them
(C) themselves
(D) yourself

中譯 (A) 我們自己　　(B) 他們
(C) 他們自己　　(D) 你自己

解析 根據前後文意，對廣告郵件收件者，應使用代名詞 **yourself** 稱呼。

134

(A) agency
(B) insurance
(C) package
(D) tips

中譯 (A) 代理機構　　(B) 保險
(C) 套裝行程　　(D) 祕訣

解析 本篇電子郵件主要是旅行社在宣傳哥斯大黎加旅遊的套裝行程，因此應表示欲知有關哥斯大黎加旅遊「套裝行程（**travel package**）」的細節，請上官網查詢。而空格後方又連接 to Costa Rica，因此不適合填入 (A)。

字彙 **agency** 代理機構，代辦處　**insurance** 保險

Questions 135-138 refer to the following article. 文章

Media Company to Relocate to Stamford

STAMFORD—Blasted, a live-streaming media company ------- in Westville, plans to move within the
135.
next few months to an office park in Stamford's south end. The firm is set to make the move during the second quarter of this year after ------- a long-term
136.
lease for 9,500 square feet at Brookbend Center.

"Brookbend Center has been home to many high technology companies ------- its founding, and we're
137.
pleased Blasted is making Brookbend its future home," property manager Jonathan Turner said in a statement. Situated next to the Norton River, Brookbend Center covers 40 acres. It features a conference room that can hold up to 200 people, an auditorium, and six meeting rooms. -------.
138.

媒體公司將搬到史坦福

　　史坦福快訊——布萊思提德是一家 ⑬⑤ 位於威士特維爾的直播媒體公司，它計畫在接下來幾個月內搬到史坦福南區的一處商業園區。該公司將在 ⑬⑥ 簽下布魯克班中心 9,500 平方英呎空間的長期租約後，在今年第二季開始搬遷。

　　「布魯克班中心 ⑬⑦ 從成立後，就一直是許多高科技公司的大本營，我們很高興布萊思提德選了布魯克班作它未來的根據地，」物業經理強納森·特納在聲明中說。位於諾頓河邊的布魯克班中心佔地 40 英畝。它的特色是有一間可容納近 200 人的大型會議室、一間大禮堂和六間小型會議室。⑬⑧ 辦公中心還包含一間自助餐廳、1,457 個停車位和好幾條步道。

字彙 office park 辦公園區，商業園區　be set to 設定，調定　make the move 搬家　second quarter 第二季 lease 租約　square feet 平方英呎　founding 建立，創立　statement 聲明　situated 坐落在 feature 以……為特色　hold 容納　up to 將近　auditorium 大禮堂

135

(A) base
(B) based
(C) is basing
(D) was based

中譯 (A) 將……的基地設於
　　(B) 以……為基地
　　(C) 將……的基地設於
　　(D) 以……為基地

解析 空格所在句子的主詞為 **Blasted**，動詞為 **plans**，名詞片語 **a live-streaming media company** 為主詞 **Blasted** 的同位語，因此空格適合填入分詞形態 **based**，表示「以……為基地」，即「位於、將總部設於」。

字彙 base 將……的基地設於

136

(A) creating
(B) losing
(C) proposing
(D) signing

中譯 (A) 創造
　　(B) 喪失
　　(C) 提議
　　(D) 簽署

解析 主詞 **The firm** 指的就是即將搬遷的公司 **Blasted**。空格後方連接受詞 **a long-term lease**，根據前後文意，只有動詞 **sign** 適合與該受詞搭配使用，意思為「簽署」。

字彙 propose 提議，建議　sign 簽署，簽字

(A) by
(B) since
(C) until
(D) yet

中譯 (A) 透過　　　　　(B) 自從
　　 (C) 直到　　　　　(D) 尚未

解析 本題要選出適當的介系詞，連接後方的 **its founding**。**has been** 表示時態為現在完成式，適合搭配使用的介系詞為 **since**，填入後表示「自從」公司創立以來。

138 新增題型

(A) Mr. Turner is taking applications from other prospective tenants for an available office unit.
(B) The company will expand its domestic manufacturing capacity after the move, sources say.
(C) The office center also includes a cafeteria, 1,457 parking spaces, and several walking trails.
(D) Time will tell if the move by Blasted will result in higher earnings for their struggling products.

中譯 (A) 特納先生正接受其他想承租空辦公室的潛在承租戶的申請。
　　 (B) 消息來源說，該公司在搬家後，將擴大它的國內產能。
　　 (C) 辦公中心還包含一間自助餐廳、1,457 個停車位和好幾條步道。
　　 (D) 時間會說明，布萊思提德的搬遷是否能為他們苦苦求生的產品帶來較高收益。

解析 文章第二段談論的是與布魯克班中心有關的內容，空格前方介紹了中心內的設施，空格適合填入補充說明其他特色的敘述，因此答案為 (C)。

字彙 **prospective** 可能的，潛在的　**tenant** 承租人，房客　**domestic** 國內的；家庭的　**capacity** 生產力　**walking trail** 步道　**earnings** 收入，利潤

Questions 139-142 refer to the following memo. 備忘錄

MEMORANDUM

To: All Employees
From: Oscar Mendelson
Date: May 25
Subject: Welcoming our new employee

I'm happy to announce that Ms. Joanne Remnick is joining Medifast, Inc. to fill the open position in customer service. Joanne ------- for more than five years in
139.
customer service at BioServe. She earned several employee-of-the-month awards while there and she comes ------- recommended by her superiors.
140.

Joanne's direct supervisor will be Robert Vesper, so if you have questions, you can ------- with Robert before
141.
she starts.

We are delighted to have Joanne join the Medifast team. Joanne's first day will be Tuesday, June 13. -------
142.

備忘錄

收件者：所有員工
寄件者：奧斯卡·孟德爾森
日期：5 月 25 日
主旨：歡迎新員工

　　我很高興宣布，喬安妮·雷米尼克小姐將加入麥迪費斯特公司，補客服的空缺。喬安妮曾在生物服務公司的客服部 **139** 任職五年多。她在那裡多次獲得當月最佳員工獎，她的主管都 **140** 大力推薦她。

　　喬安妮的直屬長官會是羅伯·維士帕，所以如果你們有任何問題，你們可以在她開始上班之前找羅伯 **141** 談。

　　我們很高興有喬安妮加入麥迪費斯特的團隊。喬安妮會在 6 月 13 日星期二開始上班。**142** 如果你們在辦公大樓看到喬安妮，記得歡迎她加入公司。

字彙 **memorandum (memo)** 備忘錄　**open position** 空缺　**(direct) supervisor** （直屬）長官

139

(A) is working
(B) will have worked
(C) worked
(D) works

中譯 (A) 正在工作　(B) 將已工作
(C) 工作過　(D) 工作

解析 本篇文章為介紹新進員工的公司內部備忘錄。空格所在句子陳述了新進員工喬安妮的經歷，根據文意，表達她「過去五年任職於生物服務公司」較為適當，因此答案為過去式動詞 **worked**。

140

(A) highly
(B) mainly
(C) mostly
(D) fairly

中譯 (A) 非常　(B) 主要地
(C) 大部分地　(D) 相當地

解析 選項中，**highly** 最適合搭配空格後方的動詞 recommended 一起使用，表示「強力、積極地」推薦。**fairly** 放在形容詞或副詞前方使用時，意思為「相當地、頗為」，此外還有「公正地」之意，皆不符合文意。

字彙 **highly** 非常，高度地　**mainly** 主要地
mostly 大部分地，大多數地　**fairly** 相當地；公正地

141

(A) share
(B) solve
(C) talk
(D) think

中譯 (A) 分享　(B) 解決
(C) 談話　(D) 思索

解析 選項中，適合與空格後方 with 搭配使用的動詞只有 **talk** 和 **think**。**talk with** 的意思為「與……談話」，符合前後文意；**think with** 的意思為「與……意見一致」。

字彙 **share** 分享，分配　**solve** 解決，解答

142 新增題型

(A) As we will have safety inspectors here next week, please don't be late to work.
(B) If you see Joanne around the building, be sure to welcome her to the company.
(C) Joanne was one of our best employees in customer service and we will miss her.
(D) Please make sure to submit your suggestion for employee of the month by then.

中譯 (A) 由於我們這裡下星期有安全檢查，上班請不要遲到。
(B) 如果你們在辦公大樓看到喬安妮，記得歡迎她加入公司。
(C) 喬安妮是我們客服部的最佳員工之一，我們會懷念她。
(D) 請確認你們在那時之前交出本月最佳員工的建議名單。

解析 文章前半段為新進員工的介紹，後半段則談到新進員工開始工作一事，因此最後適合連接歡迎新進員工加入的說詞。**(A)** 和 **(D)** 皆與此無關；**(C)** 則是針對退休員工所說的話。

字彙 **safety inspector** 安全檢查員
submit 交出

Questions 143-146 refer to the following e-mail. 電子郵件

To:	Atlas Property Management Agency
From:	Rita Hanson, Buildmore Co.
Date:	May 13
Subject:	Necessary repairs

As a follow-up to our conversation on May 12, this is a ------- for repairs at our office located in the Bradford
143.
Building, Number 301. The office was in need of these
repairs ------- we moved in, not through any fault,
144.
abuse, or negligence on our part. These are the items in
need of repair: one inner office door (latch broken) and
the heating unit on south side of office (doesn't turn on
and off properly).

------- It regrettably interferes with our ability -------
145.   146.
business in this location. Please let me know when you
will be making the repairs.

Sincerely,

Rita

收件者：艾提勒斯物業管理公司
寄件者：麗塔・韓森，比爾德莫爾公司
日期：5 月 13 日
主旨：必要的整修

　　這封電子郵件是我們 5 月 12 日談話的後續，我們 ⑱ 要求修理位於布萊德福德大樓 301 室的辦公室。這間辦公室 ⑭ 在我們搬進去時就需要修理這些東西，並非因我方的過失、不當使用或疏失所致。這些是需要修理的物品：辦公室的一扇內門（門閂損壞）以及辦公室南邊的暖氣（無法順利開關）。

　　⑭ 當然，我們希望這件事能儘快處理。很遺憾，它妨礙了我們在這個地方 ⑭ 辦公的效率。請讓我知道，你們何時要修理。

誠摯地，

麗塔

字彙 repair 修理，修補　**follow-up** 後續（行動），跟進（行動）　**abuse** 濫用，虐待　**negligence** 疏忽，粗心
latch 門閂　**regrettably** 令人遺憾地，可惜地　**interfere** 妨礙，干涉

143

(A) bill
(B) quote
(C) reply
(D) request

中譯 (A) 帳單　　　　　(B) 報價
(C) 回覆　　　　　(D) 要求

解析 本篇電子郵件為「要求」房產管理公司進行修繕的內容，因此空格適合填入 request。bill 和 quote 皆與金額有關，不適合填入；reply 適合搭配介系詞 to 一起使用。

字彙 bill 帳單　quote 報價　reply 回覆，回應
request 要求，請求

144

(A) although
(B) because
(C) when
(D) whether

中譯 (A) 雖然　　　　　(B) 因為
(C) 當……時　　　(D) 是否

解析 前方提及辦公室需要修理，後方則表示並非自己所造成的。因此 we moved in 前方適合填入 when，表示時間點「我們搬進來時」，最符合前後文意。

50

145　新增題型

(A) Our firm has recently earned several awards for design and efficiency.
(B) This office has many great attributes like spaciousness and natural light.
(C) We look forward to hearing back from you about our collaboration proposal.
(D) We would like this matter to be taken care of as soon as possible, of course.

中譯
(A) 我們公司最近得到好幾個關於設計與效率的獎項。
(B) 這間辦公室有許多很棒的特點，如寬敞的空間和自然光。
(C) 我們期待收到您對我們合作案的回音。
(D) 當然，我們希望這件事能儘快處理。

解析　選項中，表達要求儘快來修理的敘述為 (D)。(A) 和 (C) 與公司業務有關；(B) 則是提及辦公室的優點，皆不符合前後文意。(D) 當中的 this matter 指的是需要修理的問題。

字彙　efficiency 效率　attribute 特性，特質
spaciousness 寬敞　natural light 自然光
proposal 計畫，提案

146

(A) conducting
(B) conducted
(C) conducts
(D) to conduct

中譯
(A) 正在經營　(B) 經營過
(C) 經營　(D) 經營

解析　本題要選出適當的動詞形態。空格所在句已經有主詞和動詞，而 ability 後面常接不定詞 to V，用來修飾 ability，因此答案為 (D)。

字彙　conduct 經營，管理

PART 7

Questions 147-148 refer to the following product instructions. 產品說明書

TopSpeed

Thank you for purchasing the Trine Blender TopSpeed. We pride ourselves on easy-to use high-quality kitchen appliances and utensils.

To start using your new blender, first you will need to remove the pieces from the container and begin setup. 147 The blender base is heavy, so please be aware it might fall out if the package is opened from the bottom.

The contents of the box will include: one base, two blade attachments, one pitcher attachment, and four serving cups. Before using, make sure to thoroughly clean all parts of the machine. Choose the blades needed 148 (one large and one small blade; other sizes sold separately) and screw the blade attachment to the base. Once secured, it will be ready to use. Next, plug it in, add your ingredients, and make sure the pitcher is on tight. You will be then ready to use the Trine Blender TopSpeed.

全速

感謝你購買三倍攪拌機「全速」。我們以生產容易使用的高品質廚房小家電和用具而自豪。

如要開始使用你的新攪拌機，首先你需要把零件從包裝箱中取出，然後開始組裝。147 攪拌機的底座很重，因此，如果從箱子底部打開，要小心它可能會掉出來。

箱子裡的內容物包括：一個底座，二個附送的攪拌刀片，一個隨附的壺和四個杯子。在使用之前，務必要徹底清潔機器的所有部分。選擇所需的攪拌刀片 148（一個大的和一個小的攪拌刀片，其他尺寸另行販售），把它鎖到底座上。一旦鎖好，就可以使用了。接下來，插上電源，放入你的食材，確認壺身卡緊。那麼，你就已準備好使用三倍攪拌機「高速」了。

字彙 trine 三倍的　pride oneself on 以……自豪　appliance 設備,器具　utensil 器皿,用具　container 容器　setup 安裝,設置　blade 刀片　attachment 附件,附屬物　pitcher 壺,罐　thoroughly 徹底地,完全地　separately 個別地,分開地　screw (用螺絲釘等)固定　secured 牢固的　plug in 插上……的插頭　ingredient (烹調的)材料

147

What should customers pay attention to when removing the product?
(A) The installation instructions
(B) The sharpness of the blades
(C) The type of knife to open the box with
(D) The way the box is opened

中譯 消費者把產品拿出來時,要注意什麼?
(A) 安裝說明
(B) 攪拌片的鋒利
(C) 用以打開箱子的刀子種類
(D) 箱子打開的方式

解析 本篇文章為攪拌機使用說明。第二段中提到:「The blender base is heavy, so please be aware it might fall out if the package is opened from the bottom.」,可以得知要注意開箱的方向,表示顧客在取出產品時,得留意箱子打開的方式。

字彙 installation instruction 安裝說明
sharpness 鋒利,銳利

148

How many types of blades are included in the box?
(A) 1
(B) 2
(C) 3
(D) 4

中譯 箱子裡包含幾種攪拌刀片?
(A) 一種　(B) 二種
(C) 三種　(D) 四種

解析 第三段的第一句話提到內附兩種攪拌刀片,而後又提到:「one large and one small blade; other sizes sold separately」,表示刀片分成大與小兩種尺寸。

Questions 149-150 refer to the following text message chain. 簡訊對話 新增題型

Steve Bedrosian 9:34 AM	史蒂夫·培卓西安 上午 9:34
Hey Mark, sorry to bother you. I know it's almost time for your appointment with the new client, but I have a favor to ask.	嘿,馬克,抱歉打擾你。我知道已經快到你和新客戶約的時間了,但我要請你幫個忙。
Mark Fitz 9:37 AM	馬克·費茲 上午 9:37
Sure, What's up?	當然,怎麼了?
Steve Bedrosian 9:39 AM	史蒂夫·培卓西安 上午 9:39
149 I'm stuck in meetings at the office all day, so I was wondering if you could swing by our westside office and grab the design documents for the Bunker Hill project on your way back here for the meeting this evening.	149 我整天都要待在公司開會,所以,不知道你回來這裡的路上,可不可以順路去我們的西區辦公室,拿今天晚上會議要用的邦克丘建案的設計文件。
Mark Fitz 9:41 AM	馬克·費茲 上午 9:41
No problem. I'm heading into my customers office now. It's not too far, so I can stop and get them after we finish here. Is the project back on the schedule?	沒問題。我現在要進去我客戶的辦公室了。那裡並沒有太遠,所以我們這邊結束後,我可以中途停一下去拿那些文件。建案要回歸原先的時程表了嗎?

Steve Bedrosian   **9:43 AM**

Thanks. I appreciate it. We are having discussions about using the designs either to restructure the original BH project or possibly using them to start the new Wilder project next spring.

Mark Fitz   **9:48 AM**

Wow, that's good to hear! I was hoping it would be picked up again for something. ⑮⓪ I really liked the way it was shaping up when it was pitched. I'll message you once I have them and am heading your way.

史蒂夫・培卓西安   上午 9:43

謝啦，很感激。我們正在討論是要用這些設計來調整原先的邦克丘建案，還是可能用它們來開啟明年春天新的懷俪德建案。

馬克・費茲   上午 9:48

哇，很高興聽到這消息！我原先就希望這案子能被選中並重啟。⑮⓪我真的喜歡在推案時，它發展的方式。等我拿到文件，往你那裡去時，我會發簡訊給你。

字彙 bother 打擾　client 客戶　be stuck in 被困在，陷入　swing by 順路拜訪　grab 快速拿
appreciate 非常感謝　have discussions 進行討論　restructure 重建，調整

149

What is preventing Mr. Bedrosian from getting the meeting documents?
(A) He has to go to Bunker Hill.
(B) He has to stay at the company.
(C) His colleague took a day off.
(D) The documents are not ready yet.

中譯 什麼事讓培卓西安先生無法拿到會議要用的文件？
(A) 他必須去邦克丘。
(B) 他必須待在公司。
(C) 他的同事休假。
(D) 文件還沒準備好。

解析 9 點 39 分的訊息中提到：「I'm stuck in meetings at the office all day」，表示史蒂夫・培卓西安先生因為開會，整天都待在辦公室裡，沒辦法去拿資料。

字彙 prevent 阻止，妨礙　colleague 同事

150 新增題型

At 9:48 AM, what does Mr. Fitz mean when he writes, "I really liked the way it was shaping up"?
(A) He thought that the design of the project was good.
(B) He thought that the meeting was well organized.
(C) He thought that the project was losing unnecessary things.
(D) He thought that the schedule would work.

中譯 上午 9:48，當費茲先生寫道：「我真的喜歡它發展的方式」，他的意思是什麼？
(A) 他認為，建案設計得很好。
(B) 他認為，會議安排得井井有條。
(C) 他認為，這個建案丟棄了多餘的東西。
(D) 他認為，這個時程表可行。

解析 shape up 的意思為「（往好的方向）進展」，因此透過該則訊息的內容可以得知，他認為這項建案的設計很棒。

字彙 organized 有系統的，有組織的
unnecessary 不需要的，多餘的

Questions 151-152 refer to the following notice. 通知

Rosa's Italian Homestead is proud to announce that we will be reopening our 52nd Street location on Saturday, April 16, and we would like to invite everyone to come see our new look and menu. For over 30 years, we have served the area the finest dishes possible, but wanted to modernize and update our design and the meals for you.

　　蘿莎義大利農莊很自豪地宣布，我們位於五十二街的店將在 4 月 16 日星期六重新開幕，我們想要邀請大家來看看我們煥然一新的餐廳和菜單。三十多年來，我們一直盡可能為本地供應最好的菜餚，但也想要現代化，並為我們的客戶更新餐廳的設計和餐點。

To show our gratitude for your time in the Mariemont area, we will be offering a few special items that will only be available this month! ⓲ Come and enjoy traditional Sicilian Pasta alla Norma, Manicotti, and a fresh seafood plate of Pesce spada alla ghiotta.
ⓘ During the first week, we will be offering a special three-course meal for the price of a large pizza.
Come in and experience the fresh new tastes at Rosa's!

為了感謝您在馬利葉蒙特地區的時光，我們將推出幾道只有本月供應的特殊餐點！⓲ 請來享受傳統的西西里諾瑪義大利麵、管狀通心粉和一道新鮮海鮮料理——美味旗魚排。ⓘ 第一個星期，我們會供應一套含三道菜的特餐，只要一個大披薩的價格。來蘿莎體驗全新的風味吧！

字彙 location 場所　finest dish 最好的菜　modernize 現代化　gratitude 感謝　plate 盤子

151

When will the special discount end?
(A) In a few days
(B) At the end of the week
(C) At the end of the month
(D) At the end of next month

中譯 優惠何時結束？
(A) 幾天後
(B) 週末
(C) 本月底
(D) 下個月底

解析 題目中出現 special discount（優惠活動），指的是可以用大披薩的價格享用三道特別料理，而優惠活動的時間是 During the first week（第一週期間），因此活動將至週末結束（at the end of the week）。

152

Which kind of plate is Rosa's NOT offering in the special reopening menu?
(A) A large pizza
(B) Manicotti plate
(C) Seafood plate
(D) Sicilian pasta

中譯 蘿莎重新開幕的特別菜單中，不供應哪一道菜？
(A) 大披薩
(B) 管狀通心粉
(C) 海鮮盤
(D) 西西里義大利麵

解析 文中提到：「Sicilian Pasta alla Norma, Manicotti, and a fresh seafood plate of Pesce spada alla ghiotta」，當中未出現的餐點為 (A)。後方優惠活動內容中才提到 a large pizza。

Questions 153-154 refer to the following e-mail. 電子郵件

To:	James McCullen
From:	Sebastian Bludd
Subject:	The Winterholm Project
Date:	April 20

Dear Mr. McCullen,

The Winterholm Project has been given clearance to start, but I think I am going to need your help on a few things. ⓘ This will be my first time as lead of a new construction site, but I know you've had a lot of experience in situations like this, so I would appreciate your input.

收件者：詹姆斯・麥考倫
寄件者：賽巴斯提安・布拉德
主旨：溫特洪建案
日期：4 月 20 日

親愛的參考倫先生：

　　溫特洪建案已獲批准可以動工，但我想我有幾件事需要你幫忙。ⓘ 這是我第一次當新工地的負責人，但我知道，對像這樣的狀況，你有很豐富的經驗，因此我很感激你的參與。

First, we only have 14 months to complete it, ⑮ **but we will have to start construction in November, so the winter air will make it more difficult for our construction team.** Do you think we should start with the smaller construction crew and add more later? It will be a large structure, and we will need quite a bit of time for creating the best workspaces for all of our recruits. I understand that speed is as important as quality in this matter, but I want to do it right. Let me know what ideas you can come up with.

Sebastian Bludd

首先，我們的工期只有 14 個月，⑮ 但我們必須在 11 月開工，因此冬季的天氣會讓我們的建築團隊工作更加困難。你認為，我們應該先用小一點的營造團隊，之後再加人嗎？這會是一個大型的建物，我們會需要相當多時間來為我們新來的人手創造一個最好的工作環境。我了解，在這件事上速度和品質一樣重要，但我想把事情做好。讓我知道，你有什麼想法。

賽巴斯提安·布拉德

字彙 clearance 批准，許可　construction site 建築工地　experience 經驗　input 投入，輸入
complete 完成　structure 建築物　workspace 工作區，工作空間　recruit 新成員
come up with the idea 提出想法

153

Why does Mr. Bludd ask Mr. McCullen for his advice?
(A) He does not want to be responsible for the project.
(B) He has no experience in construction.
(C) He thinks he needs approval to start it.
(D) He trusts his opinion about the project.

中譯 布拉德先生為什麼尋求麥考倫先生的建議？
(A) 他不想負責這個建案。
(B) 他對營建沒有經驗。
(C) 他認為，他需要得到同意才能開工。
(D) 他信任他對這個建案的意見。

解析 第一段最後提到麥考倫先生有豐富的經驗，所以「I would appreciate your input」，布拉德先生想要徵求麥考倫先生的想法，這段話表示布拉德先生信任對方的意見。另外，第一段還提到：「This will be my first time as lead of a new construction site」，這句話僅表示布拉德先生沒有領導的經驗，無法得知他是否沒有營建方面的經驗。

字彙 opinion 意見

154

What problem does Mr. Bludd mention?
(A) The placement of the offices
(B) The price of the building
(C) The size of the land
(D) The weather during construction

中譯 布拉德先生提到什麼問題？
(A) 辦公室的位置
(B) 大樓的價格
(C) 土地的大小
(D) 建造期間的天氣

解析 第二段布拉德先生提及自己的煩惱，表示他們將於 11 月動工，但冬天寒冷的空氣（the winter air）可能會讓營建團隊工作更加辛苦；文中並未提到其餘選項的內容。

字彙 placement 布局，放置

ATTENTION: ALL EMPLOYEES

⑮ **The Annual Summer Warehouse Sale will begin on June 5!** All employees can participate in the sale, which will offer merchandise for 60-80 percent off and includes anything currently housed in our warehouse located near the main office. ⑮ **That means televisions, ovens, radios, and more.**

⑮ **We have updated the Employee Sale section of the company intranet** so that you can start searching the catalog now! Please note, once the sale begins, the Web page data may be incorrect, as it will take some time to update sales that week. All items will be sold on a first come first served basis, so don't wait if you see something you are interested in.

Make sure to bring your company badge with you for entry into the warehouse. ⑮ **The sale will only last two weeks**, so take advantage of this once-a-year savings opportunity!

全體員工請注意

⑮ 一年一度的夏季清倉大拍賣將從 6 月 5 日開始！所有員工都能參加特賣會，商品將打四到二折，包括任何目前存放在總公司附近倉庫裡的所有商品。⑮ 那表示有電視、烤箱、收音機等多樣商品。

⑮ 我們已更新公司內網上的員工特賣區，這樣你們現在就可以開始搜尋型錄！請注意，一旦特賣會開始，網頁的資訊可能不正確，因為更新那個星期的銷售狀況要花點時間。所有的商品都是先來先買，所以如果你看到有興趣的東西，別等了。

要進入倉庫，務必要帶著你的員工識別證。⑮ 特賣會只有兩個星期，所以把握這個一年一次的省錢機會吧！

字彙 warehouse 倉庫　include 包含　currently 現在，目前　house 儲藏　incorrect 不正確的　badge 證章　entry 進入（權）　last 持續　savings 節省，節約　opportunity 機會

155

What kind of products will be available at the sale?
(A) Electronics
(B) Kitchen utensils
(C) Office equipment
(D) Summer clothing

中譯 特賣會有什麼樣的產品可買？
(A) 電器用品　(B) 廚房用具
(C) 辦公設備　(D) 夏季服飾

解析 第一段提到特賣的產品有 televisions、ovens、radios 等，可以統稱為電器用品。

156

When does the sale end?
(A) June 5
(B) June 19
(C) June 30
(D) July 1

中譯 特賣會何時結束？
(A) 6 月 5 日　(B) 6 月 19 日
(C) 6 月 30 日　(D) 7 月 1 日

解析 第一句話提到從 6 月 5 日開始進行特賣活動，最後一句話又提到特價期間為期兩週（will only last two weeks），因此特價結束時間為 6 月 5 日加上兩週的時間，答案為 6 月 19 日。

157

How can people find out about sale items before the sale begins?
(A) By accessing a Website
(B) By asking for a list
(C) By contacting someone in the main office
(D) By visiting the warehouse

中譯 人們如何在特賣會開始前得到特賣商品的資訊？
(A) 上網　(B) 要一份清單
(C) 聯絡在總公司的某個人　(D) 去倉庫

解析 第二段提到只要上公司網站的員工特賣區（the Employee Sale section of the company intranet），便能確認特惠品項，因此答案為上網確認。

字彙 access 進入　ask for 要求

Questions 158-160 refer to the following advertisement. 廣告

JD Turk Cleaners will come to your office, store, or warehouse and create a safe clean working environment for your team. We have been in business for six years and have been the recipient of numerous awards for our thoroughness and work attitude. You can put your faith in us to take care of your office, wherever it may be. We have members of our staff ready at any time required by you. 🄸59 **Our team leader Glen Matthews has over 20 years of experience in the field, and will be able to get the job done for you.**

We don't want to interrupt your important work time, so 🄸58 **we are available 24 hours a day and seven days a week, whenever you need us.** 🄸60 **To contact JD Turk, you can call our office number: 916-555-2342 or send us a message to jdturk@mailme.com or you can send forms to our address:**

4023 Sacred Heart Boulevard,
San Difrangeles,
CA 94207

JD 特克清潔公司會到你的辦公室、商店或倉庫，為你的團隊創造一個安全乾淨的工作環境。我們已開業六年，因為我們的仔細徹底和工作態度，已經獲得許多獎項。你可以信任我們會照顧好你的辦公室，不管地點在哪裡。不論你要求的時間為何，我們的員工都隨時準備好可以上工。🄸59 我們的團隊經理葛蘭‧馬修斯在這一行的經驗超過 20 年，能夠做好你交付的工作。

我們不想干擾你們重要的工作時間，因此，🄸58 我們一週七天，每天 24 小時待命，不管你什麼時間需要我們都行。🄸60 要聯絡 JD 特克，你可以打我們公司的電話：916-555-2342，或寄信到 jdturk@mailme.com，或者，你可以寄表單到我們的地址：

加州 94204 聖地法藍磯市聖心大道 4023 號

字彙 **recipient** 接受者，受領者 **thoroughness** 徹底，完全 **attitude** 態度 **faith** 信任，信賴 **interrupt** 打斷，打擾

158

What is true about JD Turk Cleaners?
(A) They can finish the job quickly.
(B) They can work at any time.
(C) They only hire the top workers in the industry.
(D) They started their business 20 years ago.

中譯 關於 JD 特克清潔公司，下列何者為真？
(A) 他們可以很快完成工作。
(B) 他們可以在任何時間工作。
(C) 他們只僱用業界的頂尖工人。
(D) 他們 20 年前創立。

解析 第二段提到：「we are available 24 hours a day and seven days a week, whenever you need us」，表示隨時都能提供服務。

字彙 **hire** 僱用 **industry** 行業

159

What does Mr. Matthews do?
(A) He answers the phone at the office.
(B) He hires new employees for the company.
(C) He is the field manager for JD Turk.
(D) He responds to all e-mails directly.

中譯 馬修斯先生的工作為何？
(A) 他在辦公室接聽電話。
(B) 他為公司僱用新員工。
(C) 他是 JD 特克的現場經理。
(D) 他直接回覆所有電子郵件。

解析 本題要從文中找出與葛蘭‧馬修斯有關的資訊。當中介紹此人為 team leader，還說他「has over 20 years of experience in the field」，表示他應該是 field manager。

字彙 **field** 實地，現場 **respond** 回答 **directly** 直接地

160

How can a customer NOT contact JD
Turk Cleaners?
(A) By mail
(B) By phone
(C) Via e-mail
(D) Via the Website

中譯 顧客無法以何種方式聯絡 JD 特克清潔公司？
(A) 透過郵件
(B) 透過電話
(C) 透過電子郵件
(D) 透過網站

解析 廣告文最後列出聯絡 JD 特克的方式，提供電話、電子郵件以及公司地址，當中並未提到 (D)，故為正確答案。

字彙 via 經由，透過

Questions 161-163 refer to the following article. 文章

⑯ Garibaldi Security Services was celebrating today after receiving word that they had received the prized Londo Award for Internet protection and safeguarding of clients. GSS is responsible for over 235 customers, and had zero server failures of service during the time frame of the award. In recent years, GSS has overcome past mistakes and become a leader in security technology, as well as new security measures to prevent loss of corporate and consumer information.

This is the first time that GSS has won the award, and a spokesperson said, "This award recognizes all of the efforts our company has made in the last year to ensure that our clients can trust us with their privacy." ⑯ The spokesperson continued to say that the reorganization of the company five years ago helped create a stronger commitment to staying on top of new hacking techniques and espionage from outside sources. ⑯ GSS is also looking to expand their services in the next year, in an effort to maximize profits and name recognition.

⑯ 加里波底資安服務公司今天在慶功，因他們接到消息，他們因網路防護與保護客戶資料安全而獲得重量級的隆鐸獎。加里波底負責的客戶超過 235 位，在獎項評選期間內，伺服器完全沒有故障。近年來，加里波底克服了過去的錯誤，成為資安科技的領頭羊，還有新的安全措施以防止企業和消費者資料流失。

這是加里波底第一次得到這個獎，發言人說：「這個獎認可了我們公司在過去一年，為確保客戶可放心交付隱私給我們而做的全部努力。」⑯ 發言人繼續說道，公司五年前的改組，有助於在新的駭客技術和外部間諜活動的掌握上投入更多努力。⑯ 加里波底也計畫明年要擴大他們的服務範圍，以期讓利潤最大化並建立品牌認同。

字彙 prized 非常有價值的　protection 保護，防護　time frame 時間範圍　measure 措施，方法
spokesperson 發言人　recognize 認可，表彰　reorganization 改組，重整
stay on top of 在……居領先地位　espionage 間諜活動　maximize 達到最大值　profit 利潤

161

What is the article mainly about?
(A) A company recognized for outstanding service
(B) A failure of a newly established company
(C) A major change in personnel at an IT company
(D) A recent trend in the information technology industry

中譯 這篇文章的主題是什麼？
(A) 一家公司因傑出的服務而受表揚
(B) 一家新創公司的失敗
(C) 一家資訊公司的重大人事變動
(D) 資訊科技業近年的趨勢

解析 第一句寫道：「they had received the prized Londo Award for Internet protection and safeguarding of clients」，表示該公司獲頒獎項，本篇文章便是針對此項消息進行報導。

字彙 outstanding 傑出的　establish 建立，創辦

162

Why did the company restructure five years ago?
(A) To expand their business overseas
(B) To get better ideas to support clients
(C) To purchase updated technology
(D) To replace older workers

中譯 公司五年前為什麼要改組？
(A) 為了將業務擴展到海外
(B) 為了找到更好的構想以支援客戶
(C) 為了購買最近的技術
(D) 為了汰換舊員工

解析 本題要找出與公司五年前重整有關的內容。文中寫道：「the reorganization of the company five years ago helped create a stronger commitment to staying on top of new hacking techniques and espionage from outside sources」，表示公司掌握了新型態的駭客攻擊手法，以及外部間諜活動，因此可以得知公司重整為的是提供客戶更好的支援。

字彙 replace 取代，替換

163

What is the company NOT looking to do in the near future?
(A) Improve brand awareness
(B) Make their profits
(C) Expand their business
(D) Pursue government contracts

中譯 公司在不久的將來並未計畫做什麼？
(A) 提高品牌知名度　　(B) 獲利
(C) 擴展業務　　(D) 尋求政府的合約

解析 最後一句話寫道：「expand their services in the next year」、「maximize profits and name recognition」，由此便能確認 (A)、(B)、(C) 的敘述。而文中並未提到與政府合約有關的內容。

字彙 pursue 追求　contract 合約，契約

Questions 164-167 refer to the following advertisement. 廣告

(164) Do you want to spend your summer working as a mentor to children? If so, come join us for an exciting six-week program at Camp Crystal.
—[1]—. (165) We will spend two weeks working and training together at camp, doing all the fun things you remember from your own childhood.

We have three areas at Camp Crystal where children can learn and have fun. —[2]—. Sharing the duties and helping with chores set the example of teamwork. Campers will help create the decorations and meals in the cabins.

—[3]—. Next, in the forest that surrounds the camp, everyone will see wildlife up-close and personally, as many kinds of interesting animals live around Camp Crystal. In past treks, we've seen everything from insects to foxes and bears! Trained outdoor leaders supervise all nature walks, so there won't be any danger of getting hurt or lost.

(164) 你想利用暑假來當兒童的輔導老師嗎？如果是，來水晶營加入我們的行列，共度令人興奮的六週課程。(165) 我們會以二週的時間在營地一起工作和訓練，做那些你童年記憶裡的所有樂事。

水晶營地有三區可供兒童學習與玩樂。(167) 首先，在住宿區，我們一起生活、烹煮、打掃和玩樂。分擔工作責任以及協助日常工作建立團隊合作的榜樣。營隊學員要協助裝飾木屋與準備三餐。

接下來，在營地四周的森林裡，每個人都能近距離親眼看到野生生物，因為有很多有趣的動物住在水晶營地四周。我們以前在健行時曾看過各種動物，從昆蟲到狐狸和熊都有！受過訓練的戶外領隊會監督所有在大自然的健行活動，所以不會有任何受傷或迷路的危險。

Finally, in our most popular area, we have a large lake, where counselors and campers alike will enjoy swimming, boat rides and if they are lucky, they might see Old Jason, a large tortoise that has lived near the lake for 100 years!

166 We also offer music, cooking, and painting lessons at an additional cost. If you have a class that you can teach, please let us know. Come to Camp Crystal and see what everyone is screaming about! —[4]—.

最後，在我們最受歡迎的區域有一大片湖，指導老師和營隊學員都可以在這裡享受游泳、划船的樂趣，如果他們幸運的話，還可能看到老傑生，一隻住在湖邊快一百年的大陸龜！

166 我們也提供額外付費的音樂、烹飪和繪畫課。如果，你有能教授的課，請告訴我們。來水晶營，看看讓大家尖叫的都是什麼事！

字彙 **mentor** 導師　**duty** 責任，義務　**chore** 例行工作　**surround** 圍繞，包圍　**wildlife** 野生生物　**trek** 徒步旅行，健行　**supervise** 監督，管理　**counselor** （營隊的）指導老師，輔導員

164

What is the main purpose of the advertisement?
(A) To draw tourists to Camp Crystal
(B) To hire new camp counselors for the summer
(C) To inform people of changes in Camp Crystal
(D) To introduce outdoor summer activities

中譯 這則廣告的主要目的是什麼？
(A) 為了吸引旅客來水晶營
(B) 為了僱用夏季營隊的新指導老師
(C) 為了通知人們水晶營的變動
(D) 為了介紹夏季的戶外活動

解析 第一句話寫道：「spend your summer working as a mentor to children」，接著又寫道：「come join us for an exciting six-week program at Camp Crystal」，表示本篇文章為廣告文，目的是招募夏季營隊指導孩童的老師。

字彙 **draw** 吸引，招來　**outdoor** 戶外的，露天的

165

How long will employees train before the camp begins?
(A) A few days
(B) A week
(C) Half a month
(D) A month

中譯 在營隊開始前，員工會受訓多久？
(A) 幾天　　　　　(B) 一個星期
(C) 半個月　　　　(D) 一個月

解析 文中提到：「spend two weeks working and training together at camp」，可以得知訓練期為兩週。(C) 將 two weeks 改寫成 half a month，故為正確答案。

166

Which additional lessons does Camp Crystal NOT offer?
(A) Cooking
(B) Horseback riding
(C) Music
(D) Painting

中譯 水晶營沒有提供哪種額外課程？
(A) 烹飪　　　　　(B) 騎馬
(C) 音樂　　　　　(D) 繪畫

解析 本題要找出提及附加課程的內容。最後一段寫道：「We also offer music, cooking, and painting lessons at an additional cost.」，當中並未提及 (B)，故為正確答案。

In which of the positions marked [1], [2], [3], and [4] does the following sentence best belong?

"First, in the lodging area, we live, cook, clean, and have fun as a group."

(A) [1]
(B) [2]
(C) [3]
(D) [4]

中譯 在標記 [1]、[2]、[3] 和 [4] 的地方,下列這句話最適合放在何處?「首先,在住宿區,我們一起生活、烹煮、打掃和玩樂。」

(A) [1]　　　　(B) [2]
(C) [3]　　　　(D) [4]

解析 文中介紹水晶營分成三個區域,題目提供的句子中,關鍵線索為句首的「First」。該句話適合放在 [2] 的位置,而後在下一段才介紹可以近距離看到野生動物的地方。

字彙 lodging 寄宿的地方

Questions 168-171 refer to the following e-mail. 電子郵件

To:	Sarah McGinly
From:	Frank Tyson
Subject:	Our products
Date:	April 14

Dear Ms. McGinly,

We recently received an e-mail from you about our lineup of educational products that you recently used and we appreciate your wonderful words about your experience with them. —[1]—. We always love hearing from those who are satisfied with our products and ⓻ would be excited to offer you a chance to help decide what kinds of future apps, games, and software we will release.

In our customer beta program, you would be sent versions of apps or computer software that we are currently working on. You would be able to download and use them for free ⓼ and all we need for you to do is answer short questionnaires and give feedback via our preferred customer Website.

—[2]—. ⓽ If interested, please fill out the form attached, which includes sections such as preferences of what kind of apps and software you would most enjoy beta testing and how often you would want to be included in the test. —[3]—. ⓽ Once we receive these forms and after we find products you are most interested in, we will contact you to start your first test period. —[4]—.

Thanks and have a wonderful day.

Frank Tyson, Product Manager
Brain Games Entertainment

收件者:莎拉・麥金利
寄件者:法蘭克・泰森
主旨:我們的產品
日期:4 月 14 日

親愛的麥金利女士:

我們最近收到一封關於妳近期使用我們教育系列產品的電子郵件,我們很感謝妳使用後的美言。我們一直很喜愛聽到那些滿意我們產品的人的意見,⓻ 而且很興奮地要提供妳一個機會,幫助我們決定未來將推出何種應用程式、遊戲和軟體。

在我們的消費者試用版程式中,妳會收到我們正在設計的應用程式或電腦軟體。妳可以免費下載並使用,⓼ 而我們需要妳做的只是回答簡短的問卷,並透過我們的貴賓客戶網站提供回饋意見。

⓽ 如果有興趣,請填寫隨函附上的表格,裡面包括了像是妳最想測試的應用程式和軟體種類,以及妳想要參加測試的頻率等等。⓽ 我們也需要妳簽一份保密協議,這樣妳才可加入貴賓客戶計畫。⓽ 一旦我們收到這些表格,並找到妳最有興趣的產品後,我們就會和妳聯絡,開始妳的第一個測試期。

感謝妳,祝妳有個美好的一天。

法蘭克・泰森　產品經理
大腦遊戲娛樂公司

字彙 **lineup** 系列(產品、商品)　**educational** 教育的,有教育意義的　**release** 發行,發表　**questionnaire** 問卷　**preference** 偏好(的人事物)　**period** 期間

168

What type of product would Brain Games NOT send to Ms. McGinly?
(A) Apps
(B) **Books**
(C) Games
(D) Software

中譯　大腦遊戲公司不會寄哪種產品給麥金利女士？
(A) 應用程式
(B) 書籍
(C) 遊戲
(D) 軟體

解析　第一段最後寫道：「offer you a chance to help decide what kinds of future apps, games, and software we will release」，當中並未提到書本。

169

What would Ms. McGinly have to do as part of the program?
(A) Come to the office to work
(B) Fill out reports for the manager
(C) **Respond to questions about the products**
(D) Speak to reporters about the new products

中譯　作為計畫一部分，麥金利女士必須做什麼？
(A) 進辦公室工作
(B) 寫報告給經理
(C) 回答關於產品的問題
(D) 和記者談新產品

解析　第二段寫道：「all we need for you to do is answer short questionnaires and give feedback」，表示麥金利女士須回答與產品有關的問題。

170

What should Ms. McGinly do to participate in the program?
(A) Call Mr. Tyson directly
(B) Download an application form
(C) **Send back the attachment**
(D) Visit Brain Games Entertainment

中譯　麥金利女士應該做什麼才能參與計畫？
(A) 直接打電話給泰森先生
(B) 下載申請書
(C) 把附件寄回去
(D) 造訪大腦遊戲娛樂公司

解析　第三段寫道：「If interested, please fill out the form attached」，後半段又提到「Once we receive these forms」，表示麥金利女士如果想參加這項計畫，就要填寫附件（attachment），並寄回公司。

字彙　send back 送回，發回　attachment 附件，附加裝置

171 新增題型

In which of the positions marked [1], [2], [3], and [4] does the following sentence best belong?
"We would also need you to sign a secrecy agreement to be included in the preferred customer program."
(A) [1]
(B) [2]
(C) **[3]**
(D) [4]

中譯　在標記 [1]、[2]、[3] 和 [4] 的地方，下列這句話最適合放在何處？「我們也需要妳簽一份保密協議，這樣妳才可加入貴賓客戶計畫。」
(A) [1]
(B) [2]
(C) [3]
(D) [4]

解析　題目列出的句子為該公司向麥金利女士要求的事項。當中出現 also，表示適合放在第三段當中，置於要求事項之一的 fill out the form attached 後方，也就是 [3] 的位置。

字彙　secrecy agreement 保密協議

Questions 172-175 refer to the following online discussion. 線上討論 新增題型

Steve Banner 2:23 PM	**史蒂夫・班納** 下午 2:23

Steve Banner　　　　　　　　　　2:23 PM
Hi, Brand and Kate. Thanks for giving me a few minutes. I need to ask about the traffic on our Website. I have checked the data and it shows that customer traffic has been declining sharply for the last few days. Any ideas what's happening?

Brand Thompson　　　　　　　　　2:24 PM
There was a special report on the news a few days ago saying that ⑰ **one of our products caused an injury, which might have something to do with it**.

Kate Marna　　　　　　　　　　　2:26 PM
What? I hadn't heard anything about this. What happened?

Steve Banner　　　　　　　　　　2:27 PM
This is news to me as well. Can you fill us in, Brand?

Brand Thompson　　　　　　　　　2:30 PM
A local news channel interviewed a parent about learning to ride a bicycle with training wheels, the Cubby 200. ⑰ **The parent said that the wheels just popped off, which made the child fall and scrape up his legs and face a bit.**

Steve Banner　　　　　　　　　　2:32 PM
Why was this not brought to my attention? ⑰ **We need to contact this parent and extend our apologies, as well as we offer a replacement.** Let's try to turn this around to show that we do care about our products and customers.

Kate Marna　　　　　　　　　　　2:34 PM
Brand, ⑰ **message me which news station it was, and I will get in touch with them** so I can help straighten out the situation. ⑰ **Let's put out this fire before it's too late!**

Brand Thompson　　　　　　　　　2:35 PM
OK. I'll have to find the information, but I will send it over today.

Steve Banner　　　　　　　　　　2:37 PM
OK. Thanks for the update. Looks like concerned parents are hearing about this by word of mouth, causing the traffic drop, so you two need to work together to help get these customers back.

史蒂夫・班納　　　　　　　　　　下午 2:23
嗨，布倫德和凱特。謝謝你們撥時間給我。我需要問一下我們網站的流量。我查看了數據，顯示這幾天顧客的流量急遽下滑。知道發生什麼事了嗎？

布倫德・湯普生　　　　　　　　　下午 2:24
幾天前，新聞裡有篇特別報導指出，⑰我們的一個產品導致有人受傷，可能和這件事有關。

凱特・瑪娜　　　　　　　　　　　下午 2:26
什麼？我完全沒聽到這個消息。發生什麼事？

史蒂夫・班納　　　　　　　　　　下午 2:27
我也是第一次聽到。你可以告訴我們詳情嗎，布倫德？

布倫德・湯普生　　　　　　　　　下午 2:30
一個地方新聞頻道訪問一名家長，問他與學習騎有輔助輪的腳踏車——巧比 200——相關的事。⑰那名家長說，輔助輪突然就脫落，害小孩摔倒，腿和臉有點刮傷。

史蒂夫・班納　　　　　　　　　　下午 2:32
這件事怎麼沒有讓我知道？⑰我們必須和這位家長聯絡，表達我們的歉意，同時，我們還要表明要換一台車。讓我們設法扭轉情勢，顯示我們的確關心我們的產品和顧客。

凱特・瑪娜　　　　　　　　　　　下午 2:34
布倫德，發簡訊⑰告訴我是哪家新聞台，我會和他們聯絡，這樣我才能協助把情況處理好。⑰讓我們在失控前，撲滅火勢！

布倫德・湯普生　　　　　　　　　下午 2:35
好，我得去找一下資料，不過，我今天會發過去。

史蒂夫・班納　　　　　　　　　　下午 2:37
好，謝謝更新狀況。看起來擔心的家長口耳相傳得知這件事，造成流量下滑，所以，你們兩個必須合作，幫忙把將些顧客拉攏回來。

字彙 traffic 流量　　decline 下降，衰退　　fill sb. in 向⋯⋯提供（額外或漏聽的資訊）　　pop off 突然脫落
scrape 擦傷，刮破　　bring sth. to sb.'s attention 讓某人得知某事　　extend apologies 致歉
get in touch with 與⋯⋯聯絡　　straighten out 解決（問題），成功應付（困境）　　by word of mouth 口頭地

172

What caused a drop in Website traffic?

(A) A defective product
(B) A hike in prices
(C) A new company policy
(D) A piece of incorrect information

中譯 什麼造成網站流量下滑？
(A) 有瑕疵的產品　　(B) 價格上漲
(C) 新的公司政策　　(D) 一則錯誤的訊息

解析 湯普生先生在 2 點 24 分和 2 點 30 分的訊息，說明顧客流量下降的可能原因。由「one of our products caused an injury, which might have something to do with it」和「the wheels just popped off」得知產品瑕疵導致意外發生，這件事被媒體播報後，使得網站的顧客流量減少；文中並未提到其餘選項的內容。

字彙 defective 有缺陷的　hike （物價等的）上漲

173

How will they try to solve the problem?

(A) By giving a new Cubby 200
(B) By sending an apology letter
(C) By using the media to promote their products
(D) By warning customers not to use a product

中譯 他們將如何設法解決問題？
(A) 送一輛新的巧比 200
(B) 寄一封道歉信
(C) 利用媒體來宣傳他們的產品
(D) 提醒消費者不要使用某個產品

解析 下午 2 點 32 分的訊息中，班納先生提到：「We need to contact this parent and extend our apologies, as well as we offer a replacement.」，表示要向對方道歉，同時更換成新產品，而需要替換的產品便是 the Cubby 200；雖然當中有提到要聯絡對方道歉，但並未提到要用寫信的方式，因此 (B) 並不正確。

字彙 promote 宣傳，推銷（商品等）

174

Who will contact certain news media?

(A) Mr. Banner
(B) Mr. Thompson
(C) Ms. Marna
(D) Their boss

中譯 誰會聯絡特定的新聞媒體？
(A) 班納先生　　　(B) 湯普生先生
(C) 瑪娜女士　　　(D) 他們的老闆

解析 下午 2 點 34 分的訊息中，瑪娜小姐提到：「I will get in touch with them」，此處的 them 指的是前面提及的新聞台。

175 新增題型

At 2:34 PM, what does Ms. Marna mean when she writes, "Let's put out this fire before it's too late!"?

(A) They need to encourage other employees of the company to do better.
(B) They need to address the issue quickly before they lose more customers.
(C) They need to start offering more discounts to customers who are loyal to the company.
(D) They need to keep the customers updated.

中譯 在下午 2:34 處，當瑪娜女士寫道：「讓我們在失控前，撲滅火勢！」，她的意思是什麼？
(A) 他們必須鼓勵公司的其他員工做得更好。
(B) 他們必須在失去更多顧客前處理這個問題。
(C) 他們必須開始提供公司的忠實顧客更多折扣優惠。
(D) 他們必須讓顧客知道最新狀況。

解析 「put out this fire」字面上的意思為「滅火」，表示「迅速解決問題」之意，可與「fix the problem」交替使用。該句話指的是儘快解決問題以免流失顧客，因此選擇 (B) 最為適當。

字彙 loyal 忠誠的，忠實的

Questions 176-180 refer to the following information and application form. 資訊 申請表

176 Expanse Engineering has started an online board for employees who wish to rent, buy, sell, or trade housing, furniture, appliances, and more. There is a small fee for positing, but replying or trading in the employee lounge is always free. To post an ad, please fill out all of the required information on the application, pay the fee.

177 Price

Item listing (under 50 words)	$2.00
Item listing (50-99 words)	$3.00
180 Item listing (100 words or more)	$4.00
Pictures	$0.1 per picture

176 廣闊工程公司已啟用線上布告欄,供想要租賃、購買、販賣或交換住宅、家具、家電和其他物品的員工使用。貼文需支付一筆小額費用,但回文或在員工休息室交易則一律免費。要張貼廣告,請填寫所有申請表上的必填資料,並繳交費用。

177 收費

商品刊登資訊(50 字內)	$2.00
商品刊登資訊(50–99 字)	$3.00
180 商品刊登資訊(100 字或以上)	$4.00
照片	每張 $0.1

Employee name: Mary Logan
Section: Sales/Furniture
Date: March 23

Item Description:

178 I am preparing to move after this fiscal year and want to sell some of my furniture. I have three things for sale. First is a large wooden dresser with four drawers. I've had it for four years and it is in excellent condition. I also have a small, white computer desk that is big enough for working, but won't get in the way inside a room. Finally is a small refrigerator that can hold several containers and up to around six drink cans. I would like to sell them together, but will sell piece by piece if needed. **179** Check out the pictures for each piece included and contact me to make an offer!

180 Words: 114

Photos attached: 3

How many days posted: 30 days

員工姓名:瑪麗·羅根
類別:販賣/家具
日期:3 月 23 日

商品說明:

178 我準備在這個會計年度後搬家,想要賣掉一些家具。我有三樣東西要賣。第一個是有四個抽屜的木製大梳妝台。我用了四年,狀況很好。我還有一張小的白色電腦桌,大到夠工作之用,但放在房間裡也不會擋路。最後是一台小冰箱,可以放好幾個保鮮盒和最多約六瓶罐裝飲料。我想要三個一起賣,但如果有需要,也可以一個一個賣。**179** 請查看各別物品所附的照片,並聯絡我出價!

180 字數:114

所附照片:3

張貼天數:30 天

字彙 **housing** 住宅,住房供給 **fiscal year** 會計年度 **dresser** 梳妝台 **get in the way** 擋路,妨礙 **container** 容器 **make an offer** 出價

176

What kind of services does the company board offer?
(A) Exchanging goods
(B) Collecting unwanted items
(C) Delivering appliances
(D) Translating documents

中譯 公司布告欄提供何種服務?
(A) 以物易物　　　　　(B) 收集多餘的物品
(C) 運送家電用品　　　(D) 翻譯文件

解析 第一篇文章中提到:「online board for employees who wish to rent, buy, sell, or trade housing, furniture, appliances, and more」,表示提供的服務為讓人在網路布告欄上從事各種物品的交易;文中並未提及 (B)、(C)、(D) 的內容。

字彙 **exchange** 交換 **goods** 商品,貨物 **translate** 翻譯

177

How is the price of the service determined?
(A) By the category
(B) By the number of items
(C) By the number of words
(D) By the posting period

中譯 服務的價格如何決定?
(A) 根據種類而定
(B) 根據物品的數量
(C) 根據字數
(D) 根據貼文的時長

解析 第一篇文章中有價目表,由此表格便能得知服務費用取決於刊登資訊的字數和附件照片的數量。

178

Why is Ms. Logan selling the items?
(A) She is going to buy new ones.
(B) She is leaving the company.
(C) She needs the money.
(D) She will relocate.

中譯 羅根女士為什麼要賣東西?
(A) 她要買新的。
(B) 她要離職。
(C) 她需要錢。
(D) 她要搬家。

解析 第二篇文章中提到:「I am preparing to move after this fiscal year and want to sell some of my furniture.」,羅根女士自行告知欲出售的原因。

179

How can a person know about the condition of the items?
(A) By contacting a Web administrator
(B) By looking at photos online
(C) By sending Ms. Logan an e-mail
(D) By visiting Ms. Logan's place

中譯 要如何得知物品的狀況?
(A) 和網站管理人聯絡
(B) 看線上的照片
(C) 寄電子郵件給羅根女士
(D) 造訪羅根女士住的地方

解析 第二篇文章最後提到:「Check out the pictures for each piece included」,並附上三張照片,表示能從網路上查看照片,以確認物件的狀態。

字彙 administrator 管理人

180

How much did Ms. Logan probably spend for the advertisement?
(A) $2.10
(B) $3.30
(C) $4.30
(D) $9.30

中譯 羅根女士很可能花多少錢登這則廣告?
(A) 2.10 元
(B) 3.30 元
(C) 4.30 元
(D) 9.30 元

解析 第二篇文章最後顯示物件介紹字數為 114 字,附件照片為 3 張。根據第一篇文章的價目表,字數在 100 字以上時,價格為 4 元,照片單張為 0.1 元,因此總額為 4.3 元。

Questions 181-185 refer to the following schedule and e-mail. 行程 電子郵件

New Hires – Orientation Schedule
April 3rd-7th

Schedule	Times
Welcome Breakfast	8:00 AM – 10:00 AM
Introduction to Policies and Procedures	10:15 AM – 11:05 AM
System Training (Customer Service Reps Only) – Lana Carney	11:15 AM – 12:00 PM
System Training (Engineers) – Vince Turner	11:15 AM – 12:00 PM
Lunch	12:15 PM – 1:15 PM
185 System Training (Inside and Outside Sales) – Richard Bird	1:15 PM – 2:00 PM
185 System Training (Management Trainees) – Lori Stevens	1:15 PM – 2:00 PM
Breakout Session with Division Managers (Division Leads Only)	1:30 PM – 2:00 PM
Breakout Session into Department groups – Manager Introductions	2:15 PM – 3:00 PM
181 Team Breakout Session – All Groups	3:15 PM – 4:45 PM
End of Orientation Day	5:00 PM

新進人員——員工訓練時間表
4/3-4/7

時程	時間
早餐歡迎會	上午 8:00–10:00
介紹規定與程序	上午 10:15–11:05
系統訓練（只有客服代表）——拉娜·卡妮	上午 11:15–下午 12:00
系統訓練（工程師）——文斯·特納	上午 11:15–下午 12:00
午餐	下午 12:15–1:15
185 系統訓練（內勤與外勤業務）——理察·伯德	下午 1:15–2:00
185 系統訓練（培訓管理人員）——蘿莉·史蒂文斯	下午 1:15–2:00
與部門經理分組會議（只有科室主管）	下午 1:30–2:00
部門分組會議——經理介紹	下午 2:15–3:00
181 團隊分組會議——所有部門	下午 3:15–4:45
員工訓練結束	下午 5:00

To: 185 Richard Bird; Lori Stevens
From: Vince Turner
Subject: Orientation Schedule
Date: March 31, 2:43 PM

Hello Rich and Lori,

I know that orientation for new employees is coming up next week, but a Towson manager asked me if I had time to work with them directly next week to assist with 183 building their new database. They would need me to be at their offices in the morning to start the process. 182 185 If possible, I would need to switch training times with one of you.

184 Normally I wouldn't ask, but this is a Top 10 client, so I didn't want to say no. Since I was the captain of

收件者：185 理察·伯德；蘿莉·史蒂文斯
寄件者：文斯·特納
主旨：員工訓練時間表
日期：3月31日 下午 2:43

哈囉，理察和蘿莉

　　我知道新進員工訓練就在下星期，但道森公司有個經理問我，下星期是否有時間直接和他們一起工作，協助他們 183 建立新的資料庫。他們需要我早上待在他們的辦公室，以便開始作業。182 185 如果可能，我需要和你們其中一位換訓練時間。

　　184 通常，我不會開口要求，但這是前十大的客戶，所以我不想拒絕。因為我是我們資料庫的領導人，他們說需要我過去，

the ship for our databases, they said they needed me to come in and guide them through it. I feel it is important for me to show loyalty to our customers for the installation.

It would only be from Monday to Wednesday, but I think it would be easier for all involved if we could reschedule the entire week. Can either of you switch times with me so I can work with Towson in the mornings?

Thank you,
Vince Turner

帶領他們完成作業。我覺得在建置資料庫上，展現我對客戶的忠誠，對我來說很重要。

這只會從星期一到星期三，但我想如果能重新安排整個星期的時程，對所有的相關人士會比較容易些。你們兩位誰可以和我換時間，好讓我能在早上去和道森的人工作？

謝謝你們，
文斯・特納

字彙 orientation （對新生的）環境、工作等介紹　come up 即將發生　build 建造，建立
installation 安裝，設置　involved 有關的　entire 整個的，全部的

181

How long will the session take for the team?
(A) For half an hour
(B) For 45 minutes
(C) For an hour
(D) For one and a half hours

中譯 團隊分組會議的時間有多久？
(A) 半小時　　　　　(B) 45 分鐘
(C) 一小時　　　　　(D) 一個半小時

解析 請從日程表中找出與團隊會議有關的項目。「Team Breakout Session – All Groups」的時間為下午 3 點 15 分至 4 點 45 分，總共歷時 90 分鐘，也就是 (D) 一個半小時。

182

What is the purpose of the e-mail?
(A) To ask what will be discussed at the orientation
(B) To determine which managers are attending
(C) To find out who is running the training programs
(D) To request a change in schedule

中譯 這封電子郵件的目的是什麼？
(A) 詢問員工訓練時要討論什麼
(B) 決定哪幾位經理要參加
(C) 找出誰要主持訓練課程
(D) 要求更改時間表

解析 電子郵件中，特納先生先簡單敘述自己的工作狀況後，提到「If possible, I would need to switch training times with one of you.」，表示要求更動時間表。

字彙 determine 決定　run 開辦，管理

183

In the e-mail, the word "building" in paragraph 1, line 2, is closest in meaning to
(A) adding
(B) creating
(C) enlarging
(D) revising

中譯 在電子郵件中，第一段第二行的「building」一字，意思最接近下列何字？
(A) 加　　　　　　　(B) 創造
(C) 增大　　　　　　(D) 訂正

解析 第一段第二行「building their new database」當中的動詞 build 指的是「建立」資料庫。選項中，意思最為接近的單字是 (B) creating。

字彙 enlarge（使……）增大　revise 訂正

184

Why doesn't Mr. Turner want to turn down the customer's request?
(A) He promised to help them anytime.
(B) **They are an important company.**
(C) They cannot use the database without him.
(D) They paid for a tour.

中譯 特納先生為什麼不想拒絕客戶的要求？
(A) 他答應隨時幫助他們。
(B) 他們是重要的公司。
(C) 沒有他，他們就無法使用資料庫。
(D) 他們支付旅費。

解析 電子郵件中提及客戶的要求，並提到：「Normally I wouldn't ask, but this is a Top 10 client, so I didn't want to say no.」，表明無法拒絕客戶的原因。Top 10 client 指的是公司的重要客戶（important company）。

185

When would Mr. Turner like to talk to new engineers?
(A) 11:15 AM
(B) **1:15 PM**
(C) 1:30 PM
(D) 5:00 PM

中譯 特納先生想要在何時對新工程師演講？
(A) 上午 11:15 　　(B) 下午 1:15
(C) 下午 1:30 　　(D) 下午 5:00

解析 電子郵件的收件者為理察・伯德和蘿莉・史蒂文斯，寄件者特納先生提到想與其中一人換時段。而第一篇日程表中，理察和蘿莉負責的時段為下午 1 點 15 分到 2 點，因此答案為 (B)。

Questions 186-190 refer to following information, e-mail and invoice. 資訊 電子郵件 發票 新增題型

Damaged Baggage

186 If your checked baggage arrives damaged, you'll need to report the damage within seven days of receiving your bag. You can contact one of our ground staff at the airport or send a message to our Customer Service section. cs@forwardair.com

Forward Airlines responsibility for damaged baggage is limited. Please see full details of our Baggage Policy here. Forward Airlines Baggage Policy

189 As a general rule, we do not assume responsibility for normal wear and tear to baggage. This includes:

* Cuts, scratches, scuffs, dents and marks that may occur despite careful handling

* 189 Damage to, or loss of, protruding parts of the baggage including: straps, pockets, pull handles, hanger hooks, wheels, external locks, security straps, or zippers

* Unsuitably-packed luggage (e.g. over-packed)

行李破損

186 如果你的托運行李在送達時有破損，你必須在拿到行李後七天內報告損壞情形。你可以在機場聯絡我們的任一位地勤人員，或發訊息給我們的客戶服務部門：cs@forwardair.com。

前進航空對破損行李的責任範圍有限。我們的完整行李規定內容請見：前進航空行李須知。

189 一般而言，我們對於行李的正常磨損並不負責。這包括：
* 雖然小心搬運，仍可能產生的割痕、刮傷、拖行磨損、凹陷和污漬。
* 189 行李突出部分的損壞及遺失，包括：帶子、口袋、拉桿把手、衣架掛鉤、輪子、外加行李鎖、行李帶或拉鍊。
* 未適當打包的行李（例如：超重）。

To:	Forward Airlines Customer Services <cs@forwardair.com>
From:	Beverly Rodriguez <brodriguez@pronto.net>

收件者：前進航空客戶服務 <cs@forwardair.com>
寄件者：貝芙莉・羅德里格茲 <brodriguez@pronto.net>

Subject:	Damaged luggage
Date:	May 22

To whom it may concern,

I recently returned to Los Angeles from Hong Kong on Forward Airlines. I was dismayed to see that my checked suitcase had been damaged. ⑱ **I took it to a luggage repair shop the same day and got it fixed.** I have attached the bill to this message. I expect to be reimbursed for the full amount of the repair. ⑱ **This is my first bad experience with Forward Airlines** and I hope to have this problem resolved quickly.

Beverly Rodriguez

主旨：行李破損
日期：5 月 22 日

敬啟者：

　　我最近搭乘前進航空由香港返回洛杉磯。看到我的托運行李箱受損，讓我很沮喪。⑱當天，我就把行李送去一家行李店修理，把它修好了。我把帳單附在這封信裡。我期待能得到修理費的全額賠償。⑱這是我搭乘前進航空以來的第一次不好的經驗，我希望這個問題能很快解決。

貝芙莉・羅德里格茲

THREE STAR LUGGAGE REPAIR

⑱ Date received	May 17
Customer name	Beverly Rodriguez
Bag type	Large rolling bag, black
⑲ **Bag maker**	Stenson, Inc.
Invoice number	5V803
Staff member	Yannick
Date finished	May 21

⑱ **Description of repair:**
Replacement of retracting handle mechanism

⑲ **Note: All repairs completed according to manufacturer's standard using parts from original manufacturer.**

Subtotal	$35.50
Tax	$5.00
Total	$40.50

三星行李修理

⑱ 收件日	5 月 17 日
顧客姓名	貝芙莉・羅德里格茲
行李種類	大型拖式，黑色
⑲ **製造廠商**	史戴森公司
請款單號碼	5V803
員工姓名	亞尼克
完工日期	5 月 21 日

⑱ 修理說明：
更換伸縮把手裝置

⑲ 備註：所有的修理工作都依照製造商的標準完成，使用原廠零件。

小計	35.50 元
稅	5.00 元
合計	40.50 元

字彙 baggage 行李　ground staff（機場）地勤人員　scuff 磨損痕跡　dent 凹陷　protrude 突出
dismayed 沮喪的　reimburse 賠償，歸還　retract 縮回，收回

186

What is true about the information?
(A) Customers should report the damage within a week.
(B) Damaged luggage is covered by insurance.
(C) Customers should bring their luggage to the office.
(D) Worn baggage is dealt separately.

中譯 關於公告資訊，下列何者為真？
(A) 顧客需在一星期內報告受損。
(B) 行李箱破損有保險可理賠。
(C) 顧客須帶行李到辦公室。
(D) 破舊的行李箱會分開處理。

解析 第一篇文章中提到：「need to report the damage within seven days of receiving your bag」，選項 (A) 將 within seven days 改寫為 within a week。

字彙 worn 破舊的

187

When did Ms. Rodriguez arrive in Los Angeles?
(A) May 15
(B) May 17
(C) May 21
(D) May 22

中譯 羅德里格茲女士何時抵達洛杉磯？
(A) 5 月 15 日
(B) 5 月 17 日
(C) 5 月 21 日
(D) 5 月 22 日

解析 電子郵件中提到：「I took it to a luggage repair shop the same day」，由此可以得知發票上的收件日（Date received：May 17）便是抵達日。

188

What does Ms. Rodriguez imply in her e-mail?
(A) She has flown on Forward Airlines before.
(B) She has recently moved overseas.
(C) She repaired the luggage by herself.
(D) She flew to Hong Kong.

中譯 羅德里格茲女士在她的電子郵件中暗示什麼？
(A) 她以前搭過前進航空。
(B) 她最近搬到國外。
(C) 她自己修好行李箱。
(D) 她飛到香港。

解析 電子郵件中提到：「This is my first bad experience with Forward Airlines」，表示她之前有搭乘過前進航空；羅德里格茲女士從香港飛往洛杉磯，因此 (D) 並不正確。

189

Why might Forward Airlines deny Ms. Rodriguez's claim?
(A) She did not report it to the proper staff.
(B) She had a damaged handle.
(C) She had over-packed her bag.
(D) She didn't make the claim.

中譯 前進航空為什麼可能拒絕羅德里格茲女士的要求？
(A) 她未向負責人員通報此事。
(B) 她損壞的是把手。
(C) 她的行李超重。
(D) 她未提出索賠。

解析 根據發票上的修理說明（Description of repair），可以得知更換了把手。回到第一篇文章，後半段提到前進航空不負賠償責任的項目有：「Damage to, or loss of, protruding parts of the baggage including: straps, pockets, pull handles, . . .」，因此羅德里格茲女士無法獲得修理把手的賠償金。

字彙 report 通報　make the claim 提出索賠

190

What is mentioned about the repair?
(A) It cost less than expected.
(B) It was finished earlier than requested.
(C) The item was sent to the manufacturer.
(D) The replacement parts were from Stenson, Inc.

中譯 關於修理，文中提到什麼？
(A) 它的費用比預期少。
(B) 它比要求的時間提早修好。
(C) 行李箱被送回原廠。
(D) 更換的零件來自史戴森公司。

解析 根據發票上的內容，行李箱的製造商為「史戴森公司」。下方備註部分（Note）寫道：「All repairs completed according to manufacturer's standard using parts from original manufacturer.」，表示更換後的把手同為史戴森公司的產品。

Castle Clothing Order Summary

Customer: Eric Pratchett
5400 Hanover Rd. Smith Village, Ca 94423
Order Date: May 14
Ship Date: May 17

Item #	Item name	Color	Qty.	Unit Price	Total
SW99	Sweater	Blue	1	$50.00	$50.00
CR67	Men's pants	Gray/Black	2	$80.00	$160.00
⑲² BL02	Light blazer	Brown	1	$150.00	⑲⁴ $150.00
SH14	Shirt	White	2	$40.00	$80.00
				Subtotal	$440.00
				Total Order	$440.00

* For residents of CA, tax is included in unit price.
⑲¹ **No shipping charges for orders over $300

城堡服飾 訂單摘要

顧客：艾瑞克·普萊契特
加州 94423 史密斯村 漢諾瓦路 5400 號
訂單日期：5 月 14 日
出貨日期：5 月 17 日

商品 #	品名	顏色	數量	單價	總數
⑲² BL02	毛衣	藍	1	50.00 元	50.00 元
CR67	男褲	灰／黑	2	80.00 元	160.00 元
⑲² BL02	薄西裝外套	棕	1	150.00 元	⑲⁴ 150.00 元
SH14	襯衫	白	2	40.00 元	80.00 元
				小計	440.00 元
				訂單總計	440.00 元

* 加州州民的稅金已含於單價內
** ⑲¹ 訂單金額達 300 元以上免運

To:	Eric Pratchett <ericpratchett@strongly.net>
From:	Castle Clothing Customer Care <cccc@castleclothing.com>
Subject:	Your order
Date:	May 29

Dear Mr. Pratchett,

⑲² Unfortunately, the following item that you ordered is now out of stock: #BL02. Although we try our best to maintain 100-percent accuracy with inventory, there are rare occasions where we experience an inventory error.

⑲⁵ Attached is a description of an item that is similar to the one you purchased that we currently have in stock. ⑲⁴ This item is cheaper than the one you purchased, so the difference would be refunded. ⑲³ Please let us know if you would like this one as a replacement or if you would like to wait until your original item becomes available.

Sincerely,
Raleigh McIntosh
Castle Clothing Customer Care

收件者：艾瑞克·普萊契特 <ericpratchett@strongly.net>
寄件者：城堡服飾客戶服務 <cccc@castleclothing.com>
主旨：你的訂單
日期：5 月 29 日

親愛的普萊契特先生：

⑲² 很不巧，下列您所訂購的商品目前無庫存：#BL02。雖然我們已盡力讓庫存量維持百分之百正確，但少數時候會有庫存量錯誤的情形發生。

⑲⁵ 附件是我們庫存中與您購買商品類似的產品說明。⑲⁴ 這件商品比您所購買的商品便宜，因此會退還差價。⑲³ 請告知我們，您是否要更換成這件商品，或者您要等到您原先訂購的商品有貨。

誠摯地，
萊禮·麥金塔
城堡服飾客戶服務

Graveline Sports Jacket

This jacket for men is light enough to wear on a warm spring day or with a sweater underneath on a chilly day. 🕙 **Made of 100-percent breathable cotton**, the jacket has five front buttons, two roomy side pockets, and one inner breast pocket. The wind-blocking stand-up collar is stylish and practical. 🕙 **Available in a variety of colors for $140 (incl. Tax).**

葛佛林運動外套

這件男士外套輕薄到可以在溫暖的春季穿，也可以在裡面加件毛衣在寒冷的天氣穿。🕙 以百分之百透氣的純棉製成，外套有五顆前扣，二個寬大的側口袋，一個內面的胸袋。可擋風的立領時尚又實用。🕙 有多種顏色可選，售價140 元（含稅）。

字彙 quantity (qty.) 數量　unit price 單價　shipping charge 運費　out of stock 無庫存，無現貨 maintain 維持，保持　accuracy 正確性，準確性　inventory 存貨，存貨清單　rare 罕有的 difference 差額，差別　refund 退款，退還　underneath 在……下面，在……底下 chilly 寒冷的，冷颼颼的　breathable 透氣的　roomy 寬大的　practical 實用的，實際的

191

What can be inferred in the order form?
(A) It was shipped on the day of the purchase.
(B) Additional tax has been charged.
(C) The items were shipped at no charge.
(D) The items can be returned.

中譯 從訂單中可看出什麼？
(A) 它在購買日當天出貨。
(B) 額外收取稅金。
(C) 這些商品沒有收運費。
(D) 這些商品可退貨。

解析 訂購單最後寫道：「No shipping charges for orders over $300」。訂購總額為 440 元，因此適用免運配送。

192

Which item Mr. Pratchett ordered is NOT immediately available?
(A) Black pants
(B) Gray pants
(C) The blue sweater
(D) The brown blazer

中譯 普萊契特先生訂購的商品，哪一個當下沒有貨？
(A) 黑色長褲
(B) 灰色長褲
(C) 藍色毛衣
(D) 棕色西裝外套

解析 第二篇文章為販售商寄給顧客艾瑞克・普萊契特的電子郵件。當中提到：「the following item that you ordered is now out of stock: #BL02」，表示 BL02 號商品目前缺貨。回到第一篇的訂購單中，BL02 號商品為棕色薄西裝外套。

193

What information does Mr. McIntosh want?
(A) A credit card number
(B) A customer's decision
(C) The delivery address
(D) The item number

中譯 麥金塔先生想要什麼資料？
(A) 信用卡卡號
(B) 顧客的決定
(C) 送貨地址
(D) 商品編號

解析 電子郵件後半段提到：「Please let us know if you would like this one as a replacement or if you would like to wait until your original item becomes available.」，請顧客告知是決定要換成其他商品，還是繼續等缺貨商品補貨。

194

How much can Mr. Pratchett get a refund on a new jacket?
(A) $10
(B) $40
(C) $50
(D) $80

中譯 普萊契特先生的新外套可退回多少錢？
(A) 10 元
(B) 40 元
(C) 50 元
(D) 80 元

解析 訂購單中的 **BL02** 號商品為 150 元，用來替代的運動外套為 **140** 元。電子郵件第二段中提到會退還差額（**the difference would be refunded**），表示若普萊契特先生購買外套，便能收到 10 元的差額。

195

What material is BL02 most likely made of?
(A) Silk
(B) Nylon
(C) Cotton
(D) Wool

中譯 BL02 最可能以什麼材質製成？
(A) 絲
(B) 尼龍
(C) 棉
(D) 羊毛

解析 電子郵件中提到附件為與 **BL02** 號類似的商品。而在該商品說明中提到：「**Made of 100-percent breathable cotton**」，這表示 **BL02** 號商品最有可能是棉製的。

Questions 196-200 refer to following schedule, list and e-mail.

行程　清單　電子郵件　新增題型

ITINERARY FOR SINGAPORE TRIP		新加坡之旅行程表	
May 10 – 13		5 月 10 － 13 日	
㊫ Wednesday, May 10		**㊫ 5 月 10 日 星期三**	
•4:00 PM	Arrive in Singapore	• 下午 4 時	抵達新加坡
•7:00 PM	Dinner with team (at your discretion)	• 下午 7 時	團體晚餐（自行決定）
Thursday, May 11		**5 月 11 日 星期四**	
•10:00 AM–4:00 PM	Tour of manufacturing facility, led by Mr. Chang	• 上午 10 時—下午 4 時	參觀製造廠，由張先生帶隊
•7:00 PM	Dinner cruise with Mr. Chang	• 下午 7 時	和張先生的晚餐巡航之旅
㊗ Friday, May 12		**㊗ 5 月 12 日 星期五**	
•10:00 AM	**Sightseeing around Singapore**	• 上午 10 時	遊覽新加坡
•2:00 PM	Presentation by product development team	• 下午 2 時	產品開發團隊簡報
•6:30 PM	Dinner reservations at Waverly Point	• 下午 6 時 30 分	有訂位威佛利岬餐廳晚餐
Saturday, May 13		**5 月 13 日 星期六**	
•10:00 AM	Check out of hotel	• 上午 10 時	退房
•12:00 noon	Flight departs for San Francisco	• 中午 12 時	班機起飛往舊金山

Where to Eat in Singapore

Pavilion

Located in the Western Hotel, Pavilion offers travelers a taste of home when away from home. We will ⑲⑧ **pair** your meal with a great glass of wine.

Open 7 days/week

Fortini

⑲⑦ **Don't ask for the menu. We don't have one. Allow our award-winning chef to choose for you.** We promise you won't regret it.

Open 7 days/week

Aubergine

French chef Paul Desautel left his comfortable Parisian life to start Aubergine five years ago. One of Singapore's most delightful restaurants.

⑲⑦ **Closed Wednesdays**

Chantilly

Located in the heart of Marina Bay, Chantilly takes fusion very seriously. Combines the best culinary tastes from around the world.

Closed Mondays

To:	Jocelyn Woods
From:	Brandon Ainsley
Subject:	Recommendation
Date:	April 28

Hi Jocelyn,

I heard you're going to Singapore. That's fantastic! ⑲⑨ **You absolutely cannot miss this great restaurant called Fortini.** It sounds Italian and they do have delicious Italian dishes, but they serve so much more. I've been there three times and each time I come away thinking that was the best meal I've ever had. ⑳⓪ **And you don't need to worry about Megan either, since the chef always has something terrific for vegetarians. I** guarantee you all will love it!

Safe travels,
Brandon Ainsley

新加坡美食指南

涼亭

涼亭位於西方飯店內，遠離家鄉的旅客家鄉味。我們會為你的餐點 ⑲⑧ 搭配一杯極佳葡萄酒。

每週營業七天

佛提尼

⑲⑨ 別要菜單，我們沒有。請容我們的得獎主廚為你選擇。我們保證你不會失望。

每週營業七天

茄子

法國主廚保羅・迪薩泰五年前拋下舒適的巴黎人生活，開了茄子餐廳。新加坡最令人愉快的餐廳之一。

⑲⑦ 星期三公休

香提莉

位於濱海灣中心的香提莉，非常認真看待無國界料理。融合來自全球的最佳烹飪風味。

星期一公休

收件者：喬瑟琳・伍茲
寄件者：布蘭登・安斯理
主旨：推薦
日期：4月28日

嗨，喬瑟琳：

我聽說妳要去新加坡，那真是太棒了！⑲⑨妳絕對不能錯過這家叫作佛提尼的餐廳。它聽起來像義大利名字，而他們也的確有美味的義大利菜，但他們供應的料理還有好多。我去過那裡三次，每一次我離開的時候，都在想那是我吃過最棒的一餐。⑳⓪還有，妳也不需要擔心梅根，因為主廚永遠有準備給素食者吃的超美味料理。我保證，你們都會愛死它！

旅途平安，
布蘭登・安斯理

字彙 **itinerary** 旅行計畫　**discretion** 決定權　**manufacturing facility** 製造工廠　**sightseeing** 觀光，遊覽　**depart** 出發，離開　**traveler** 旅客，遊客　**regret** 懊悔，惋惜　**culinary** 烹飪的　**terrific** 極度的，非常好的　**guarantee** 保證

196

According to the schedule, when will the team visit some tourist places?
(A) Wednesday
(B) Thursday
(C) Friday
(D) Saturday

中譯 根據行程表，旅行團何時造訪一些觀光景點？
(A) 星期三
(B) 星期四
(C) 星期五
(D) 星期六

解析 行程表中在新加坡觀光（**Sightseeing around Singapore**）的時間從 **5** 月 **12** 日星期五上午 **10** 點開始。

197

Which restaurant will the team be unable to visit on the first day?
(A) Pavilion
(B) Fortini
(C) Aubergine
(D) Chantilly

中譯 旅行團第一天無法去哪一家餐廳？
(A) 涼亭
(B) 佛提尼
(C) 茄子
(D) 香提莉

解析 行程表第一天為 **5** 月 **10** 日星期三。而餐廳清單中，茄子餐廳為週三公休（**Closed Wednesdays**），表示第一天無法前往茄子餐廳。

198

In the list, the word "pair" in line 3, is the closest in meaning to
(A) combine
(B) double
(C) keep
(D) treat

中譯 在清單中，第三行的「pair」一字，意思最接近下列何者？
(A) 結合
(B) 加倍
(C) 維持
(D) 招待

解析 美食指南清單中第三行：「**pair your meal with a great glass of wine**」當中的 **pair . . . with . . .** 表示把料理與美酒「配對、結合」。選項中，意思最為接近的單字為 **combine**，因此答案為 **(A)**。

字彙 **combine** 結合，聯合　**double** 使……加倍

199

What is mentioned about the restaurant Mr. Ainsley recommends?
(A) It has no menu.
(B) It has outdoor seating.
(C) It serves fusion food.
(D) It serves only vegetarian food.

中譯 關於安斯理先生推薦的餐廳，文中提到什麼？
(A) 它沒有菜單。
(B) 它有戶外座位。
(C) 它供應無國界料理。
(D) 它只供應素食。

解析 電子郵件中推薦的餐廳為佛提尼。美食指南清單中。佛提尼的介紹為「**Don't ask for the menu. We don't have one.**」，表示該餐廳為無菜單料理。雖然郵件中提到餐廳能提供素食主義者很棒的料理，但是並未強調該餐廳僅提供素食料理，因此 **(D)** 並不正確。

What is implied about a member of the group?
(A) She went to the diner before.
(B) She doesn't like Italian food.
(C) She has a dietary restriction.
(D) She is not going on the trip.

中譯 關於旅行團的一位成員，可由文中得知什麼？
(A) 她以前去過那家餐廳。
(B) 她不喜歡義大利菜。
(C) 她有飲食的限制。
(D) 她不參加這次旅行。

解析 電子郵件中提到：「you don't need to worry about Megan either, since the chef always has something terrific for vegetarians」，表示梅根為素食主義者，挑選餐廳時要特別留意這一點，由此可以得知當中有人在飲食方面有所限制。

字彙 dietary restriction 飲食限制

Actual Test 2

001 㕲

(A) One person is taking a drink from a bottle.
(B) One person is writing on a computer.
(C) They're listening to a speaker on a stage.
(D) They're sitting around a rectangular table.

中譯 (A) 有個人正從瓶子裡倒酒喝。
(B) 有個人正在電腦上寫東西。
(C) 他們正在聽舞台上的講者演講。
(D) 他們圍著一張長方形桌而坐。

解析 照片中有幾個人圍坐方形桌子且旁談笑風生，因此答案要選 (D)「They're sitting around a rectangular table.」。

字彙 take a drink 喝一杯
rectangular 長方形的

002 㴸

(A) They're drying off with towels.
(B) They're playing with a ball.
(C) They're running toward the sea.
(D) They're standing near a net.

中譯 (A) 他們正用毛巾擦乾。
(B) 他們在玩球。
(C) 他們跑向大海。
(D) 他們站在網子附近。

解析 照片中有幾個人站在沙灘排球場的球網附近，因此 (D)「They're standing near a net.」為最適當的描述；而照片中並未出現球，因此 (B) 當中的「playing with a ball」並不適當。

字彙 dry off 擦乾

003 㤥

(A) Coffee is being poured into cups.
(B) Plates with food sit near a glass.
(C) A spoon has been left in the cup.
(D) A table is covered with vegetables.

中譯 (A) 咖啡正在被倒進杯子裡。
(B) 好幾盤食物放在玻璃杯附近。
(C) 杯子裡有一根湯匙。
(D) 桌上擺滿蔬菜。

解析 照片中玻璃杯旁擺著裝有食物的盤子，因此答案要選 (B)「Plates with food sit near a glass.」；(A) 使用進行式，但是照片中並未出現任何人物動作，因此該描述並不適當。

字彙 pour into 倒進……中
be covered with 被……所覆蓋

004 美

(A) They're adding ingredients to a dish.
(B) They're cleaning some cooking utensils.
(C) They're cooking something in large pans.
(D) They're serving food in a tent.

(A) 他們正把食材加進料理中。
(B) 他們正在清潔一些烹飪用具。
(C) 他們正在大平底鍋裡煮東西。
(D) 他們在帳蓬裡供應餐點。

解析 雖然四個選項皆與食物有關，但只有 (D)「They're serving food in a tent.」描寫人們在戶外的篷子下提供餐點，故為最適當的答案。

字彙 serve 提供（食物或飲料）

005 澳

(A) All flowers are being placed in baskets.
(B) Flowers are being planted in front of a door.
(C) Some plants are growing over a window.
(D) Some plants are hanging near a wall.

中譯 (A) 所有的花都正被放在籃子裡。
(B) 花正被種在門前。
(C) 有些植物長得高過窗戶。
(D) 有些植物懸掛在牆邊。

解析 照片中栽種著植物的花盆被懸掛在牆邊，因此 (D)「Some plants are hanging near a wall.」為最適當的描述；(C) 當中的 over 指的是「超過……」。(A) 使用進行式，但是照片中並未出現任何人物動作，因此該描述並不適當。

字彙 basket 籃子　plant 種植，栽種
hang 懸掛，吊

006 美

(A) He's bending down to pick something up.
(B) He's leaning on the side of the car.
(C) He's opening the car window.
(D) He's pointing at something in front of the car.

中譯 (A) 他正彎下身撿東西。
(B) 他正靠在汽車側邊上。
(C) 他正打開汽車的窗戶。
(D) 他正指著車子前面的某個東西。

解析 照片中的男子看起來像是交通警察，他站在車子前方將手指向左方，因此 (D)「He's pointing at something in front of the car.」為最適當的描述。

字彙 bend down 彎腰，俯身
pick up 撿起，拾起　lean 倚，靠

007 美 加

How often does the interoffice mail get delivered?
(A) Twice a day.
(B) Which ones are for me?
(C) Take a 15-minute break.

中譯 各部門間的郵件多久送一次？
(A) 一天二次。
(B) 哪些是給我的？
(C) 休息 15 分鐘。

解析 How often 開頭的問句 本題詢問次數。(A) 回答一天兩次，故為適當答覆。

字彙 interoffice （同一組織的）各部門間的，各辦公室間的
break 暫停，休息

---

008 澳 英

Are they planning to work on Saturday?
(A) Yes, it works both ways.
(B) I don't know where they are.
(C) Yes, and Sunday.

中譯 他們打算星期六工作嗎？
(A) 是的，二種都適用。
(B) 我不知道他們在哪裡。
(C) 是的，還有星期日。

解析 一般問句 本題詢問週六是否要工作。(C) 回答 Yes，並告知週日也要工作，故為最適當的答覆。(A) 故意出現 work 與題目重複，但是題目中的 work 指的是工作，而 (A) 的 work 是「行得通」的意思。

字彙 work 工作；行得通

---

009 美 加

Where is the extra copy paper?
(A) We're out of paper cups.
(B) By the plant over there.
(C) Just $9.99 per pack.

中譯 多的影印紙放在哪裡？
(A) 我們的紙杯沒了。
(B) 在那邊的植物旁邊。
(C) 一包只要 9.99 元。

解析 Where 開頭的問句 本題詢問其他的影印紙在哪裡。(B) 告知位置在盆栽旁邊，故為適當的答覆；(A) 僅重複使用題目句中的 paper，為陷阱選項。

字彙 extra 額外的　copy paper 影印紙

---

010 英 澳

You saw the new museum exhibit, didn't you?
(A) Yes, and it was fantastic.
(B) Only if you let me pay.
(C) No one was at the meeting place.

中譯 你去看過博物館的新展覽了，不是嗎？
(A) 是的，展覽很棒。
(B) 只要你讓我付錢。
(C) 會面地點沒有人。

解析 附加問句 本題向對方確認是否看過博物館新的展覽。(A) 回答自己的感想，表示很不錯，故為適當的答覆。

字彙 exhibit 展覽（品）

011 英美

Didn't Sarah submit her application?
(A) Not yet. By tomorrow at noon, she said.
(B) She told me to meet her at the station.
(C) Her report was 15 pages long.

中譯 莎拉沒有提出申請嗎？
(A) 還沒有，她說明天中午以前。
(B) 她叫我去車站和她碰面。
(C) 她的報告有 15 頁之長。

解析 **一般問句** 雖然本題為 Didn't 開頭的問句，但並不影響句意。這句話詢問莎拉是否已繳交申請表。(A) 表示尚未繳交，並補充說對方預計何時繳交，故為最適當的答覆。

字彙 **application** （通常指書面的）申請

012 加澳

I think we should get this agreement in writing.
(A) There is writing on both sides of the paper.
(B) Nobody can agree on the remodeling.
(C) Good thinking. Please request it.

中譯 我認為，我們應該把這份協議寫下來。
(A) 這張紙二面都寫了東西。
(B) 對於改組一事，大家無法取得一致意見。
(C) 很好的想法。請提出要求。

解析 **直述句** (C) 對於對方的想法表示同意，故為最適當的答覆；(A) 的「writing」和 (B) 的「agree」皆為答題陷阱。

字彙 **agreement** 協議
in writing 以書面形式（尤指文件或合約）
request 要求，請求給予

013 澳美

Why did the sales team leave early today?
(A) Because it cost too much.
(B) They went to a seminar.
(C) To get a repair estimate.

中譯 業務團隊今天為什麼提早離開？
(A) 因為太貴了。
(B) 他們去參加研討會。
(C) 去拿修理的估價單。

解析 **Why 開頭的問句** 本題詢問業務部提早下班的原因。(B) 表示他們去參加研討會，故為最適當的答覆；(A) 和 (C) 分別使用了 because 和表示「為了」的不定詞（to get）來回答，乍看之下皆適合作為 why 問句的答案，但是後方連接的內容與問題無關。

字彙 **cost** 花費　**estimate** 估價，估計

014 英澳

Do you know when Ms. Travers is going to Sydney?
(A) I haven't heard the price.
(B) With all of her subordinates.
(C) Sometime in August.

中譯 你知道崔維斯女士何時要去雪梨嗎？
(A) 我還沒聽到價錢。
(B) 帶著她所有的下屬。
(C) 八月的某個時候。

解析 **一般問句** 本題乍看之下像是一般問句，實際上是詢問前往雪梨的時間。(C) 回答八月的某個時間點，故為最適當的答覆。當題目為 Do you know 開頭的間接問句時，後方的內容為答題關鍵。

字彙 **subordinate** 下屬

015 (加)(美)

What is the accounting head doing in Melissa's office?
(A) Don't ask me.
(B) The accounts were reviewed twice.
(C) Let me call you right back.

中譯 會計部主管在梅莉莎辦公室做什麼？
(A) 別問我。
(B) 這些帳戶被審閱過二次。
(C) 我馬上回電話給你。

解析 What 開頭的問句 本題詢問特定人士在別人的辦公室裡做什麼。(A) 採迴避式回答法，表示自己並不知情，故為最適當的答覆。(B) 的選項有 accounts，是「帳戶」的意思，為陷阱選項。

字彙 accounting 會計

---

016 (英)(加)

When do you suppose he'll make his decision?
(A) I'm supposed to be in Detroit today.
(B) It could take a while.
(C) A one-in-ten chance, I'd say.

中譯 你認為他何時會做出決定？
(A) 我今天應該在底特律。
(B) 可能要一段時間。
(C) 我認為，十分之一的機會。

解析 When 開頭的問句 本題詢問做決定的時間。(B) 表示應該需要花上一些時間，為三個選項中最適當的答覆。題幹的 suppose 是「認為」的意思，在這裡的用法與 think 接近。

字彙 one-in-ten 十分之一　chance 機會，可能性

---

017 (澳)(英)

How are you getting to the conference tomorrow?
(A) Just ten minutes from here.
(B) By train, I'd expect.
(C) Tuesday, November the 15th.

中譯 你明天要如何去參加會議？
(A) 離這裡只有 10 分鐘。
(B) 我預計要搭火車。
(C) 11 月 15 日星期二。

解析 How 開頭的問句 本題詢問交通方式。(B) 表示搭火車前往，故為適當的答覆。

字彙 conference （正式的）會議，大會

---

018 (美)(澳)

Has she spoken to Mr. Sears about her time-off request?
(A) Yes, and he approved it.
(B) No. I haven't been trained yet.
(C) Wherever she goes, she'll be successful.

中譯 她和席爾斯先生說她要請假了嗎？
(A) 是的，而且他批准了。
(B) 沒有，我還沒受過訓。
(C) 不論她做哪一行，她都會成功。

解析 一般問句 雖然本題使用現在完成式提問，但不需要因此感到困難。本題詢問是否有向席爾斯先生提出請假申請，題目中的 request 是「要求」的意思。(A) 採取正面的回應，並表示對方已經准假，故為最適當的答覆。

字彙 time-off 請假，休假

82

019 美 加

When can we expect an answer about this?
(A) Every third Saturday at noon.
(B) I've stopped going to the gym.
(C) In about three days.

中譯 我們預計何時能得到這件事的答案?
(A) 每月第三個星期六中午。
(B) 我不再去健身房了。
(C) 大約三天。

解析 **When** 開頭的問句　本題詢問何時能收到答覆。**(C)** 提出未來的時間點,故為最適當的答覆;**(A)** 提出的內容屬於定期發生的狀況,並不適合作為答覆。

字彙 **gym** 健身房

---

020 澳 英

🎧 06

The new temp is working out, isn't he?
(A) Yes. We've had record heat.
(B) Yes, as far as I know.
(C) Just a moment. I'll get him.

中譯 新來的臨時雇員工作挺順利的,不是嗎?
(A) 是的,高溫創紀錄。
(B) 是的,就我所知。
(C) 稍等一下。我去找他。

解析 **附加問句**　本題以問句確認新臨時工的工作表現是否良好。問句中的 **work out** 是「進行順利」的意思,而這個片語也常指「鍛鍊、健身」。**(B)** 表示據自己所知是如此,故為最適當的答覆。考題中經常以「**as far as I know**」作為確認型問句的答覆。

字彙 **temp** 臨時雇員　**record heat** 破紀錄的高溫
as far as 就……

---

021 美 澳

Could you order takeout for us for lunch?
(A) Sure. What do you want?
(B) The tickets are all sold out.
(C) What time did you arrive?

中譯 午餐你可以幫我們點外賣嗎?
(A) 當然,你們要什麼?
(B) 票都賣完了。
(C) 你何時到的?

解析 **Could you** 開頭的問句　本題詢問午餐能否幫忙叫外送。**(A)** 同意此要求,並反問對方要點什麼,故為最適當的答覆。

字彙 **be sold out** (門票等)全部售完　**arrive** 到達

---

022 英 加

Who called for Ms. Carson this morning?
(A) He didn't leave his name.
(B) About 8:00 AM.
(C) I heard her train was delayed.

中譯 今天早上是誰打電話找卡森女士?
(A) 他沒有留下姓名。
(B) 大約上午 8 時。
(C) 我聽說她的火車誤點了。

解析 **Who** 開頭的問句　本題詢問打電話過來的人是誰。**(A)** 回答對方並未告知姓名,等同於表示不知道對方是誰,故為最適當的答覆。

字彙 **leave** 留下

023 [美][澳]

Do you think Paul will accept the offer?
(A) There are many factories in that area.
(B) We should congratulate him.
(C) He's leaning toward yes.

中譯 你認為保羅會接受提議嗎？
(A) 那個地區有很多工廠。
(B) 我們應該恭喜他。
(C) 他傾向於同意。

解析 一般問句 本題針對保羅是否會接受提案，詢問對方想法。(C) 表示他應該會接受，故為適當的答覆。「lean toward」的意思為「傾向於⋯⋯」。

字彙 factory 工廠 lean toward 傾向

---

024 [英][美]

I just realized my phone ran out of battery.
(A) These phones are too heavy.
(B) We're all out of that size.
(C) Here's my charger.

中譯 我剛剛才發現我的手機沒電了。
(A) 這些手機太重了。
(B) 我們完全沒有那個尺寸。
(C) 這是我的充電器。

解析 直述句 本題表示剛才發現手機沒電了。對此 (C) 拿出自己的充電器，故為最適當的答覆。

字彙 run out of 用完，耗盡 charger 充電器

---

025 [加][澳]

Are they planning to stay overnight?
(A) I'm not sure, but I'll ask.
(B) We were there just for the weekend.
(C) Actually, I disagree.

中譯 他們打算留下來過夜嗎？
(A) 我不確定，但我會問問。
(B) 我們只有週末待在那裡。
(C) 其實，我不同意。

解析 一般問句 本題詢問是否有要住一晚。(A) 表示自己不太清楚，得問問看，為選項中最適當的答覆。

字彙 stay overnight 留下來過夜
disagree 不同意，不一致

---

026 [加][英]

Where did these flowers come from?
(A) They went to London last year.
(B) A thank-you gift from Mr. Allen.
(C) They haven't been authorized.

中譯 這些花是從哪來的？
(A) 他們去年去倫敦。
(B) 艾倫先生的謝禮。
(C) 他們沒有得到授權。

解析 Where 開頭的問句 本題詢問花的來源。(B) 表示是謝禮，故為適當的答覆。雖然名詞片語並未顯示時態，但是仍能作為答案，請特別留意。

字彙 authorize 授權

027 (澳)(美)

He isn't sure he wants to go with us.
(A) Well, it's his choice.
(B) Never give up on your dreams.
(C) Those aren't my only options.

中譯　他不確定他是否想和我們一起去。
(A) 嗯，那是他的決定。
(B) 永遠別放棄你的夢想。
(C) 那些不是我唯一的選擇。

解析　直述句　本題需要確實掌握題意，才能順利解題。這句話表示他不確定是否會跟我們一起去。(A) 回答那是他本人的選擇，為三個選項中最適當的答覆。

字彙　option 選擇（權）

028 (英)(加)

Should we make the copies now or wait until tomorrow?
(A) The coffee has gotten cold.
(B) We might have last-minute changes.
(C) Not around here.

中譯　我們應該現在製作副本，還是等到明天再做？
(A) 咖啡冷了。
(B) 我們也許最後一刻還會改。
(C) 不在這裡。

解析　選擇疑問句　本題詢問影印的時間點。(B) 採間接回答的方式，回答可能會突然出現需要修改的內容，等同於表示現在不適合，故為適當的答覆。

字彙　last-minute 最後一刻的

029 (美)(英)

It's going to be a long day.
(A) That's right. By 7:00.
(B) True. But we'll get through it somehow.
(C) All of the employees are gone.

中譯　這會是漫長的一天。
(A) 沒錯，7 點以前。
(B) 真的，但我們總會有辦法度過的。
(C) 所有的員工都離開了。

解析　直述句　「It's going to be a long day.」帶有擔心未來可能會很辛苦的意涵在內。(B) 表示同意，並回答我們一定能夠做好，故為最適當的答覆。

字彙　get through 通過，完成　somehow 以某種方法

030 (加)(澳)

The reports have been finalized, haven't they?
(A) Yes, they were looking for you.
(B) Not yet. The oven is still heating up.
(C) I'm just checking them for the last time.

中譯　那些報告定稿了，不是嗎？
(A) 是的，他們在找你。
(B) 還沒，爐子還在加熱。
(C) 我只是最後再檢查一次。

解析　附加問句　本題確認是否已經完成報告。(C) 表示在最後的確認階段，故為最適當的答覆。

字彙　finalize 定稿，最後確定
heat up 變熱

Do you mind if I switch seats with you?
(A) Not at all.
(B) Yes, I'm almost there.
(C) There's no need to switch cars.

中譯 你介意我和你換座位嗎？
(A) 完全不介意。
(B) 是的，我快到那裡了。
(C) 不需要換車。

解析 一般問句 針對 Do you mind if 開頭的問句，回答沒關係是表示不介意，回答不可以則是表示介意，因此適當的答覆為 (A)。

字彙 switch 交換，調換

PART 3 07

Questions 32-34 refer to the following conversation. 澳 英

W Hi. ㉜ I'll be away from home on holiday for the month of October. I was wondering if I could suspend my home Internet service while I'm gone.
M Yes, you can, but ㉝ you'll have to pay a suspension fee, $5.00 a month.
W I guess that's all right. Can you set that up for me now?
M Of course. To start the process, ㉞ I'll need your name and home address.

女：嗨，㉜我十月要離家度假，我在想是否可以在出門期間暫停我的家用網路服務。
男：是的，可以，㉝但妳必須支付停用的費用，一個月五元。
女：我想沒問題。你可以現在幫我設定嗎？
男：當然可以。㉞我需要妳的姓名和住家地址以啟動程序。

字彙 away from 離開 suspend 暫時取消（擱置） suspension fee 暫停服務的費用

032

What will the woman do in October?
(A) Attend a seminar
(B) Go on vacation
(C) Study abroad
(D) Take a business trip

中譯 女子十月要做什麼？
(A) 參加研討會　　　　(B) 去度假
(C) 出國留學　　　　　(D) 去出差

解析 女子在第一句話便表示她十月份會休假一個月，人不在家裡。

換句話說 be away from home on holiday → go on vacation

字彙 business trip 出差

033

What does the man say about the suspension of service?
(A) It cannot be done.
(B) It has to be longer than a month.
(C) The procedure needs to be done online.
(D) There will be a charge.

中譯 關於暫停服務，男子說了什麼？
(A) 無法完成　　　　　(B) 必須多於一個月
(C) 手續必須在線上完成　(D) 會有費用

解析 男子提到一個月得繳交服務暫停費用 5 元，表示仍需要收費。

換句話說 suspension fee → charge

字彙 procedure 手續，程序　charge 收費，費用

034

What information will the woman give next?
(A) Her account number
(B) Her e-mail address
(C) Her home address
(D) Her phone number

中譯 女子接下來要給什麼資料？
(A) 她的帳號 　　　　(B) 她的電子郵件地址
(C) 她的住家地址 　　(D) 她的電話號碼

解析 男子在最後詢問女子的姓名和住址。選項直接使用男子所述的「home address」。

字彙 account 帳戶

Questions 35-37 refer to the following conversation. 加 美

W　Hello. My name is Megan Roberts and ㉟ I have an appointment for a personal yoga session with Ms. Jackson tomorrow morning, but ㊱ I'm not going to be able to make it. Does she have time tomorrow afternoon?

M　She is booked all day tomorrow and for the rest of the week, I'm afraid. Looks like she's totally booked the whole next week, too. ㊲ If you're fine with someone else, Ms. Dalton is available tomorrow afternoon.

W　I've heard she's good, too. ㊲ Okay, I'll try her.

女：哈囉，我是梅根・羅勃茲，㉟我明天早上預約了一堂和傑克森女士的私人瑜珈課，㊱但我沒辦法去。她明天下午有空嗎？

男：抱歉，她明天整天和這星期的其餘時間都約滿了。看起來，她下星期也都約滿了。㊲如果妳可以上其他人的課，達頓女士明天下午有空。

女：我聽說她也很好。㊲好的，我試試看。

字彙 session （從事某項活動的）一段時間，一節

035

Who most likely is Ms. Jackson?
(A) A receptionist
(B) A school owner
(C) A student
(D) An instructor

中譯 傑克森女士最可能是誰？
(A) 接待人員 　　　　(B) 學校所有人
(C) 學生 　　　　　　(D) 教練

解析 女子在第一句話中便提到自己跟傑克森女士預約了瑜珈課程，由此可以得知傑克森女士為瑜珈老師。

字彙 receptionist 接待人員　instructor 教練

036

Why is the woman calling?
(A) To book an appointment
(B) To cancel an appointment
(C) To confirm an appointment
(D) To reschedule an appointment

中譯 女子為什麼打電話？
(A) 預訂約會 　　　　(B) 取消約會
(C) 確認約會 　　　　(D) 重新安排約會時間

解析 女子表示上午沒辦法上課，詢問是否可以改到下午。由此可以得知女子打電話的目的為更動預約時間。

字彙 confirm 確認，證實

037

What did the woman decide to do?
(A) Call the man back later
(B) Choose a different person
(C) Make an appointment next week
(D) Talk to Ms. Jackson

中譯 女子決定做什麼？
(A) 稍候回電話給男子 　(B) 選另外一個人
(C) 預訂下星期的約會 　(D) 和傑克森女士談談

解析 男子向她推薦另一位達頓老師，而後女子表示願意試試看。由此可以得知女子最後選擇上另一位老師的課。

07

Questions 38-40 refer to the following conversation. 加 英

W Oh, David, I was looking for you. ❸❽ **Do you have a minute to look at the new logos?** The design firm sent them to me this morning and well, see for yourself.	女：噢，大衛，我正在找你。❸❽ 你有沒有時間看看新的商標？設計公司今天早上寄來給我，然後，嗯，你自己看吧。
M Oh, wow, these are really different from what I expected.	男：噢，哇，這些真的和我預期的不一樣。
W Yes, but I can't quite put my finger on what is wrong. The color? The size?	女：是的，但我不太能確切指出哪裡有問題。顏色？大小？
M I think ❸❾ **the company name is hard to read on these two. And this one is too busy.** You know, too many lines and . . .	男：我想 ❸❾ 這二個商標很難看出公司名。還有，這個太雜亂。妳知道的，太多線條和……。
W ❸❾ **That's it. We need something simple and clean.** ❹⓿ **I'll let the designers know.** Hopefully, they'll come up with better ones.	女：❸❾ 就是這樣。我們需要簡單清楚的設計。❹⓿ 我會告知設計師。希望他們能想出比較好的設計。

字彙 put one's finger on 確切地指出　busy 雜亂的，使人眼花撩亂的　come up with （針對問題等）想出，提供

038

What are the speakers discussing?
(A) **A company symbol**
(B) A new building design
(C) A painting
(D) A photograph

中譯 說話者在討論什麼？
(A) 公司的標誌　　　(B) 新大樓的設計
(C) 一幅畫　　　　　(D) 一張照片

解析 第一段對話中，女子表示想要討論一下新的標誌，而後便針對新標誌提出想法。因此該篇對話的主旨為公司的標誌。

換句話說 logo → symbol

039 新增題型

What does the woman mean when she says, "That's it"?
(A) She has said what she wants to say.
(B) She is amused by his opinion.
(C) **She thinks the man made a good point.**
(D) She wants to end the conversation.

中譯 當女子說：「就是這樣」時，她的意思是什麼？
(A) 她已經說了她想說的話。
(B) 她被他的意見逗得很開心。
(C) 她認為男子說到重點了。
(D) 她想結束這段對話。

解析 男子表示設計過於複雜，文字不方便閱讀。而後女子說出「That's it.」，同時表示需要更簡單明瞭的標誌。由此可以得知女子認為男子說出了重點。

字彙 amused 被逗樂的，愉快的　point 要點，論點

040

What does the woman say she will do?
(A) Ask another coworker for help
(B) **Contact an artistic firm**
(C) Hire a different firm
(D) Think of new slogans

中譯 女子說她要做什麼？
(A) 請另一位同事幫忙
(B) 聯絡美術公司
(C) 僱用另一家公司
(D) 想新的廣告標語

解析 最後一段對話中，女子表示要向設計師說出他們剛才討論的想法，也就是要聯絡設計師，並表達他們的意見。

字彙 coworker 同事

Questions 41-43 refer to the following conversation. 澳 美

W I see the Charleston Line isn't running this morning. What happened?	女：我發現，查爾斯頓線今天早上沒開。發生什麼事了？
M ㊶ **There was a signal malfunction near Dearing Station.** They think the storm last night shut down the signals.	男：㊶ 迪爾林車站附近號誌故障。他們認為，昨天晚上的暴風雨造成號誌停止運作。
W How long do you think before the line is running again?	女：你認為要多久這條路線才會恢復通車？
M Hard to say. They've been working on it for an hour or so and I haven't heard an update. ㊷ **The latest information is on our Website.** ㊸ **Here's a card with the Website address.**	男：很難說。他們已經修了大約一個小時，而我還沒有聽到最新消息。㊷ 最新消息會公布在我們的網站上。㊸ 這張卡上有網址。

字彙 **signal** 信號，交通指示燈　**malfunction** 故障　**line** 交通線　**run** （車、船）行駛

041

What is the cause of the delay?
(A) A mechanical problem
(B) A staffing problem
(C) A traffic jam
(D) A car accident

中譯 延誤的原因是什麼？
(A) 機械問題　　　　(B) 人手問題
(C) 交通壅塞　　　　(D) 車禍

解析 第一段對話中，男子提到迪爾林車站附近的指示燈故障。由此可以得知是機械出問題才導致誤點。

換句話說 signal malfunction → mechanical problem

字彙 **staffing** 員工總數，人員配備　**traffic jam** 交通壅塞

042

Who most likely is the man?
(A) A mechanic
(B) A passenger
(C) A station worker
(D) A Website designer

中譯 男子最可能是誰？
(A) 技工　　　　　　(B) 乘客
(C) 車站員工　　　　(D) 網站設計師

解析 女子不斷提出火車相關的問題，男子逐一答覆。且在最後一段對話中，男子表示可以在公司網站上查詢最新消息，由此可知男子應為站務人員。

字彙 **mechanic** 技工

043

What does the man give the woman?
(A) A line map
(B) A refund
(C) A URL of his company
(D) An update on the delay

中譯 男子給女子什麼？
(A) 路線圖
(B) 退款
(C) 他公司的網址
(D) 關於延誤狀況的最新消息

解析 最後一段對話中，男子交給女子一張上頭寫著公司網址的卡片。(D) 相較於 (C) 不夠直接，公司網址公布的最新消息，不一定只會包括延誤狀況。

換句話說 Website address → URL

07

Questions 44-46 refer to the following conversation. 澳 英 新增題型

W	Hi, there. ㊹ **I'd like to sign up for the boat tour tomorrow.** Uh, do you have any space left in the morning?
M	How many people are there?
W	Two adults and two children.
M	In that case, you'll have to take the afternoon tour. ㊺ **The boats are not that big, actually.** They only hold eight people.
W	I see. And ㊹ **they go by the floating markets where we can buy souvenirs, right**?
M	That's right. The vendors sell all kinds of accessories and food. It's one of our most popular tours.
W	Excellent. ㊻ **My friend recommended we do this tour.** ㊹ **It's one of the main reasons we came here.**

女：嗨，你好，㊹ 我想報名明天的乘船旅遊。呃，早上還有空位嗎？

男：有多少人？

女：二名成人和二名兒童。

男：那樣的話，妳得參加下午的行程。㊺ 其實船沒有那麼大，只能載八個人。

女：了解。另外想問，㊹ 船隻經過水上市場，我們可以在那裡買到紀念品，對嗎？

男：沒錯。小攤商販賣各種配件和食物。那是我們最受歡迎的行程之一。

女：太棒了。㊻ 我朋友推薦我們參加這個行程。㊹ 這是我們來這裡的主要原因之一。

字彙 **sign up for** 報名參加（活動或課程）　**in that case** 既然那樣，如果是那樣的話　**floating market** 水上市場
souvenir 紀念品　**vendor** 小販

044

What will the woman's family most likely do tomorrow?
(A) Go fishing
(B) Purchase mementos
(C) Return home
(D) See a friend

中譯 女子一家明天最可能做什麼？
(A) 去釣魚
(B) 購買紀念品
(C) 回家
(D) 見一個朋友

解析 請從前半段對話中，掌握女子的意圖。第一段對話中，女子提到她想報名乘船遊覽行程，對話中間詢問是否有機會可前往水上市場購買紀念品，最後又提到她們一家人前來這裡的主因。由這些內容可以得知，女子一家人明天最可能做的事為買紀念品。

換句話說 buy souvenirs → purchase mementos

字彙 **memento** 紀念品，引起回憶的東西

045

What does the man mention about the boat?
(A) It is fast.
(B) It is small.
(C) It needs some repairs.
(D) It runs only once a day.

中譯 關於船隻，男子說了什麼？
(A) 船很快。
(B) 船很小。
(C) 船需要修理。
(D) 一天只開一班。

解析 本題可以從男子所說的話中得知答案。他提到船並不大。

換句話說 not that big → small

046

How did the woman hear about the tour?
(A) From a brochure
(B) From a friend
(C) From a TV show
(D) From an online advertisement

中譯 女子如何得知這個行程？
(A) 從廣告小冊　　(B) 從朋友處
(C) 從電視節目　　(D) 從線上廣告

解析 最後一段對話中，女子提到她是因為朋友推薦才來參加這個行程。

字彙 brochure 小冊子

Questions 47-49 refer to the following conversation. 美 加

M　Amy, now that we're all moved in, we have to let our neighbors know about us. How should we advertise?

W　Hmm. ㊼ **After paying the rent and deposit on this place, we have hardly any money left for advertising.**

M　True, but I think if we can get some local people in here for their morning coffee, they'll tell their friends, who will tell their friends . . .

W　Yeah, ㊽ **word of mouth doesn't cost us a thing.** But to start it off, why don't we use social media?

M　Okay. ㊾ **I'll post a picture of some of our drinks and pastries on my social networking sites.**

男：艾美，既然我們全都搬好了，我們得讓鄰居認識我們。我們該如何宣傳？

女：嗯，㊼在付完這個地方的租金和押金後，我們幾乎沒剩什麼錢可以打廣告了。

男：的確是，但我想，如果我們可以讓一些本地人早上來這裡喝咖啡，他們會告訴朋友，他們又會告訴他們的朋友……。

女：是啊，㊽口頭宣傳不花我們一分錢。但要開始宣傳的話，我們為什麼不利用社群媒體？

男：好。㊾我會貼一張可以呈現部分飲料和糕點的照片在我的社群網站上。

字彙 rent 租金　deposit 押金，保證金　word of mouth 口耳相傳

047

What does the woman imply about the finances?
(A) The speakers are in debt to the bank.
(B) The speakers are making a lot of money.
(C) The speakers have enough money for advertising.
(D) The speakers do not have extra money.

中譯 關於財務，女子暗示什麼？
(A) 說話者欠銀行錢。
(B) 說話者賺很多錢。
(C) 說話者有足夠的錢打廣告。
(D) 說話者沒有多餘的錢。

解析 第一段對話中，女子提到付完租金和押金後，已經沒有錢可以用在廣告上。因此這段話表示說話者們沒有多餘的錢。

換句話說 have hardly any money → do not have extra money

字彙 in debt 負債　make money 賺錢，致富

048 新增題型

Why does the woman say, "word of mouth doesn't cost us a thing"?
(A) She believes there is a cheaper way.
(B) She does not like what the man said.
(C) She is not sure how much advertising costs.
(D) She knows referrals are free.

中譯 為什麼女子說：「口頭宣傳不花我們一分錢」？
(A) 她相信會有較便宜的方法。
(B) 她不喜歡男子說的話。
(C) 她不確定廣告要花多少錢。
(D) 她知道推薦是不花錢的。

解析 對話中，女子提到：「word of mouth doesn't cost us a thing」，此句話可以改寫成「referrals are free」，因此答案為 (D)。

字彙 referral 推薦，介紹

049

What does the man say he will do?
(A) Give free drinks out
(B) Take a class in finance
(C) Talk to some friends
(D) Upload a photo online

中譯 男子說他會做什麼？
(A) 發送免費飲料　　　　(B) 上一門財經課程
(C) 找一些朋友聊聊　　　(D) 上傳照片到網路上

解析 最後一段話中，男子提到要將飲料和糕點的照片上傳到社群網站。由此可以得知男子將會把照片上傳到網路上。

換句話說 post a picture → upload a photo

字彙 take a class 修一門課

Questions 50-52 refer to the following conversation. 英 加

M Hi. I'm in a bit of a hurry. ⑤⓪ I need to see my client in 30 minutes. Which lunch specials do you think are quickest to make?

W Well, ⑤① all our meals are made to order, but the hamburger plate is fairly fast. It comes with a choice of salad or soup.

M Hmm, what's your soup today?

W Potato cream with bacon.

M I think I'll have a salad and the hamburger plate. ⑤② And an iced tea.

W Got it. ⑤② I'll be right out with your drink.

男：嗨，我有點趕時間，⑤⓪必須在 30 分鐘內去見客戶。妳覺得哪種午間特餐能最快做好？

女：嗯，⑤①我們所有餐點都是針對顧客需求特別製作的，但漢堡餐相當快。它的附餐還可以選沙拉或湯。

男：嗯，今天是什麼湯？

女：培根馬鈴薯濃湯。

男：那我要點沙拉和漢堡餐。⑤②還有一杯冰茶。

女：好的。⑤②我馬上送你的飲料過來。

字彙 made to order 訂做的

050

Why is the man in a hurry?
(A) He has a job interview.
(B) He has an appointment.
(C) He needs to catch a train.
(D) He wants to get home quickly.

中譯 男子為什麼趕時間？
(A) 他要去面試工作。　　(B) 他有約。
(C) 他必須去趕火車。　　(D) 他想快點回到家。

解析 男子提到三十分鐘後要和客戶見面，表示他待會有約所以趕時間。appointment 是約會的意思。

換句話說 see my client → has an appointment

字彙 in a hurry 趕時間

051

What is mentioned about the food at the restaurant?
(A) It is all from local suppliers.
(B) It is all organic.
(C) It is prepared ahead of time.
(D) It is prepared when ordered.

中譯 關於餐廳的食物，文中提到什麼？
(A) 全都來自本地供應商。
(B) 全都是有機的。
(C) 是事先準備好的。
(D) 是點餐之後才做的。

解析 女子為餐廳員工，提到餐點皆為現點現做，也就是客人點完餐後，才會開始料理。

換句話說 made to order → prepared when ordered

字彙 supplier 供應商　organic 有機的　ahead of time 提前

052

What will the woman bring the man first?
(A) A hamburger
(B) A salad
(C) An iced tea
(D) Potato soup

中譯 女子會先送什麼給男子？
(A) 漢堡
(B) 沙拉
(C) 冰茶
(D) 馬鈴薯湯

解析 最後一段話中，女子提到會先為男子送上飲料，而男子點的飲料為冰茶。

Questions 53-55 refer to the following conversation. 澳 美

W ⑤3 **Thank you for joining us on our program today**, Mr. Sullivan. You've been busy in these past few months, giving talks and interviews.

M Uh, yes, it's all been a bit overwhelming. When ⑤4 **my research on oceans was published**, I had no idea people would be so interested.

W ⑤3 **Could you tell our viewers** what's next for ⑤4 **your proposal to clean the world's oceans**?

M Well, that's a good question. No one has taken on the project I suggested. I'm still hopeful though, that some private company or a group of governments will contribute the necessary funds for it. It's very urgent, as you know.

W Yes, I know. ⑤5 **Now, let's show a video you and your team made to explain the project in more detail.**

女：⑤3 謝謝你今天上我們的節目，蘇利文先生。過去這幾個月來，你都忙著演講和接受訪問。

男：呃，是的，這有點令人措手不及。⑤4 當我發表關於海洋的研究時，我不知道人們會這麼感興趣。

女：⑤3 你是否可以告訴我們的觀眾，⑤4 關於清理全球海洋的提案，你下一步計畫是什麼？

男：啊，那是個好問題。還沒有人接下我提的計畫。但我仍然希望有私人公司或一些政府能提供計畫所需的資金。你知道的，情況很緊急。

女：是的，我知道。⑤5 你和你的團隊有拍攝一支影片詳細解釋這個計畫，現在讓我們播來看看吧。

07

字彙 overwhelming 難以抵擋的，無法抗拒的　private 私人的，私立的　contribute 捐助，提供

053

Where most likely are the speakers?
(A) At a university
(B) At an awards ceremony
(C) In a radio station
(D) In a TV studio

中譯 說話者最可能在哪裡？
(A) 一所大學　　　　(B) 一個頒獎典禮
(C) 一個廣播電台　　(D) 一個電視台的攝影棚

解析 第一段對話中，女子感謝對方來參加節目；第二段對話中，提到觀眾（**our viewers**），由此可以推測說話者們正在電視攝影棚內錄製電視節目。

字彙 ceremony 儀式，典禮

054

What is the man's research about?
(A) Environmental concerns
(B) Political issues
(C) Private sector growth
(D) World economy

中譯 男子的研究是關於什麼？
(A) 環境問題　　　　(B) 政治議題
(C) 私部門的成長　　(D) 世界經濟

解析 第一段對話中，男子提到自己有出書，內容為對海洋的研究；第二段對話中，女子向男子詢問有關海洋淨化的下一步計畫。由這兩處可以得知男子研究的是與環境有關的議題。

字彙 concern 擔心，憂慮的事情　political 政治的

055

What will the speakers do next?
(A) Continue with an interview
(B) Listen to audience questions
(C) Look at some data
(D) Watch a video

中譯 說話者接下來會做什麼？
(A) 繼續訪問　　　(B) 接聽觀眾的問題
(C) 看一些資料　　(D) 觀看一段影片

解析 最後一段對話中，女子提到播放影片一事。

換句
話說 show a video → watch a video

Questions 56-58 refer to the following conversation with three speakers. 澳 美 加 新增題型

W1	Mr. Stuart, 56 I hope your toothache is better now. When would you like to schedule your next appointment?	女1：史都華先生，56 希望你的牙痛現在比較好了。你的下一次看診想要排在什麼時候？
M	Uh . . . how about the same day and time next week, Thursday, August 4th at 10:00 AM?	男：呃……，下個星期的同一天同一個時間，8月4日星期四上午10點如何？
W1	Dr. McCloud may be away that day. Let me check with her. Oh, there she is. Dr. McCloud, will you be here next Thursday?	女1：麥克勞德醫師那天可能不在。讓我問她一下。噢，她來了。麥克勞德醫師，你下個星期四會在嗎？
W2	No, 57 I have to attend an annual dental conference.	女2：不會，57 我得去參加牙科年會。
M	I see. Well, 58 I can come here next Friday, the 5th.	男：了解。嗯，58 我可以下個星期五來，5號。
W2	58 I'll be back by then, so I can see you in the afternoon.	女2：58 那時我已經回來了，所以，我下午可以給你看診。

字彙 toothache 牙痛　attend 參加，出席　annual 一年一度的，每年的

056

Who most likely is the man?
(A) A dentist
(B) A medical assistant
(C) A patient
(D) A receptionist

中譯 男子最可能是誰？
(A) 牙醫　　　　　(B) 醫療助理
(C) 病人　　　　　(D) 接待人員

解析 本篇文章為兩女一男的三人對話。第一段對話中，女1向男子史都華先生表示希望他的牙痛有好轉，接著問他下一次約診時間，由此可以得知男子為前來看牙醫的病患。

057

What is mentioned about Dr. McCloud?
(A) She is completely booked this week.
(B) She is leaving the office soon.
(C) She will go to a conference.
(D) She will take a break now.

中譯 關於麥克勞德醫師，文中提到什麼？
(A) 她這個星期的約診全都排滿了。
(B) 她很快就要離開辦公室。
(C) 她將要去參加會議。
(D) 她現在要休息一下。

解析 女2回答女1的問題，表示女2為麥克勞德醫生。麥克勞德醫生回答她得參加牙科年會。(A) 中的 book 是「預定」的意思。

換句
話說 attend an annual dental conference →
go to a conference

字彙 completely 完全地　take a break 休息，小憩

058

When will Mr. Stuart's next appointment be?
(A) Next Thursday morning
(B) Next Thursday afternoon
(C) Next Friday morning
(D) Next Friday afternoon

中譯 史都華先生的下次約診是何時？
(A) 下個星期四早上
(B) 下個星期四下午
(C) 下個星期五早上
(D) 下個星期五下午

解析 男子表示 5 號下星期五他有空，接著女 2 表示她那天會在，那就下午見，因此史都華先生下次看診的時間為下週五下午。

Questions 59-61 refer to the following conversation with three speakers. 英 澳 美 新增題型

M1 ⑤⑨ Tomorrow, we have to take inventory in the stockroom, so I'll need you both to stay a bit later. Say, two hours.

W Fine with me. I could use the overtime.

M2 Uh, ⑥⓪ I have a class that starts at 7:30. I can't miss it since I was absent twice already. The third absence and you have to drop the class.

M1 Okay, John, you can leave in time for your class. If we aren't done yet, Sarah and I will finish up. Is that all right with you, Sarah?

W Sure. ⑥① I don't have any plans tomorrow.

男 1：⑤⑨ 我們明天必須盤點倉庫的庫存，所以，我需要你們二個留晚一點，大約二小時。

女：我沒問題。我可以加班。

男 2：呃，⑥⓪ 我 7 點半有課。我不能再去，因為我已經缺席二次了。第三次缺課，就得退出這門課了。

男 1：好，約翰，你可以及早離開去上課。如果我們還沒點完，莎拉和我會做完。妳可以嗎，莎拉？

女：當然。⑥① 我明天沒有什麼事要做。

字彙 take inventory 盤點存貨　could use 想要；需要　overtime 加班　absent 缺席的　in time 及早，及時

059

What will the speakers do at the store tomorrow?
(A) Get ready for a sale
(B) Make a list of stock
(C) Pack items in boxes
(D) Put out new merchandise

中譯 說話者明天在店裡要做什麼？
(A) 準備特賣會　(B) 列出存貨清單
(C) 把商品裝箱　(D) 製造新商品

解析 本篇文章為兩男一女的三人對話。第一段對話中，男 1 提到明天要盤點倉庫的庫存，因此「列出庫存清單」為最適當的答案。

換句話說 take inventory → make a list of stock

字彙 get ready 準備好　make a list 列一張表
stock 存貨　pack 包裝　put out 生產，製造

060

Why is John unable to stay late tomorrow?
(A) He has a doctor's appointment.
(B) He has another job.
(C) He is going out of town.
(D) He is in school.

中譯 約翰明天為什麼無法留到很晚？
(A) 他要去看醫生。
(B) 他有另一個工作。
(C) 他要出城。
(D) 他還在求學。

解析 第二段對話中，名為約翰的男生提到自己 7 點 30 分有課，表示他要去上課，所以不能待太晚。

換句話說 I have a class → He is in school.

95

061

What can be said about the woman? (A) She does not like to work overtime. (B) **She has some free time tomorrow.** (C) She is not sure of her schedule. (D) She wants to get promoted.	中譯 關於女子，可由文中得知什麼？ (A) 她不喜歡加班。 (B) 她明天有空。 (C) 她不確定她的時間。 (D) 她想要升職。

解析 對話中，女子表示自己可以加班，最後又提到自己明天沒有計畫，代表她明天有空。

換句話說 I don't have any plans tomorrow. → She has some free time tomorrow.

字彙 be sure of 肯定，確信

Questions 62-64 refer to the following conversation and advertisement. 英 澳

Lacy's October Sale
7th – 13th

The earlier you shop, the more you SAVE!

25% OFF! Friday thru Sunday
❻❹ **20% OFF!** **Monday** and Tuesday
15% OFF! Wednesday
10% OFF! Thursday

蕾西百貨十月特賣會
7–13 日

越早買，省越多！

75 折！ 星期五到星期日
❻❹ 8 折！ 星期一和星期二
85 折！ 星期三
9 折！ 星期四

M Jennifer, ❻❷ **I need to get a new jacket** and you said you wanted a new shirt, right? What do you say we go to the sale at Lacy's? Looking at this advertisement, we can save money if we go there this weekend.

W Not only do I need a new shirt, but I also need a pair of shoes. The problem is ❻❸ **I'm going to be out of town to go to my cousin's wedding ceremony this weekend.** I'll be back Sunday night.

M Don't worry. ❻❹ **We can go after work on Monday.**

男：珍妮佛，❻❷ 我需要買件新夾克，而妳之前說想要件新襯衫，對吧？我們要不要去蕾西百貨的特賣會？看看這個廣告，如果我們這個週末去的話，可以省錢。

女：我不只需要新襯衫，我也需要一雙新鞋。問題是，❻❸ 我這個週末要出城去參加我表姊的婚禮。星期日晚上才回來。

男：別擔心，❻❹ 我們可以星期一下班後再去。

062

What does the man want to buy? (A) A bag (B) **A jacket** (C) A pair of shoes (D) A shirt	中譯 男子想要買什麼？ (A) 一個袋子 (B) 一件夾克 (C) 一雙鞋 (D) 一件襯衫

解析 第一段對話中，男子表示自己需要一件新夾克。

063

What will the woman do this weekend?
(A) **Attend an event**
(B) Buy some clothes
(C) Relax at home
(D) Take a business trip

中譯 女子這個週末要做什麼？
(A) 參加一個活動
(B) 買一些衣服
(C) 在家放鬆休息
(D) 去出差

解析 第一段對話中，女子表示這個週末她要去參加親戚的結婚典禮，等同於她要參加活動的概念。event 是「活動」的意思。

換句話說 go to my cousin's wedding ceremony → attend an event

字彙 relax 放鬆

064 新增題型

Look at the graphic. What discount will the speakers most likely get?
(A) 10 percent
(B) 15 percent
(C) **20 percent**
(D) 25 percent

中譯 見圖表。說話者最可能得到多少折扣？
(A) 9 折
(B) 85 折
(C) 8 折
(D) 75 折

解析 本題為圖表整合題。男子提議週一下班後去逛街，而廣告中，週一提供的優惠為八折。

Questions 65-67 refer to the following conversation and schedule. 加 英 新增題型

Board Meeting Schedule November 1	
66 10:00	Ms. Erin Sinclair
10:30	Mr. Leo Anderson
11:30	Sales team
12:00	President Matt Moore

董事會時程表 11/1	
66 10:00	艾琳・辛克萊兒女士
10:30	里歐・安德森先生
11:30	業務團隊
12:00	麥特・摩爾總裁

W Thanks for making the agenda for the board meeting, William. I'm afraid there's going to have to be a change though.

M Oh, really? What's that?

W 65 My boss, Ms. Sinclair has an urgent matter to handle with a client tomorrow morning. She won't get back here until 11:00.

M I see. I'm sure we can switch some things around.

W Actually, 66 it's all taken care of. I've already asked the sales team to present their report earlier.

M Oh, great. Then 67 I'll remake the agenda and send it out to everyone before I leave tonight.

W Sorry for the extra work.

M Don't mention it.

女：謝謝你製作董事會的議程表，威廉。但恐怕會有變動。

男：噢，真的嗎？是什麼？

女：65 我的上司，辛克萊兒女士明天早上有個緊急事項要和客戶處理。她要到11點才會回來。

男：了解。我確定，我們可以把事情掉換一下。

女：其實，66 全都處理好了。我已經要求業務團隊提早簡報。

男：噢，太好了。67 那我就重排議程，在我今晚下班前寄給大家。

女：抱歉增加你的工作。

男：不會，別客氣。

字彙 agenda 議程　present 提出，展現

065

What will the woman's boss do
before 11:00 tomorrow?
(A) Attend the board meeting
(B) Interview candidates
(C) Prepare for the presentation
(D) See a client

中譯 女子的上司明天 11 時前要做什麼？
(A) 參加董事會
(B) 面試應徵者
(C) 準備簡報
(D) 見客戶

解析 第二段對話中，女子表示明天上午她的老闆跟客戶有急事
要處理，表示老闆要去見客戶。

換句話說 handle with a client → see a client

066 新增題型

Look at the graphic. What time will
the sales team present their report?
(A) 10:00
(B) 10:30
(C) 11:30
(D) 12:00

中譯 見圖表。業務團隊何時做報告？
(A) 10
(B) 10:30
(C) 11:30
(D) 12

解析 本題為圖表整合題。對話中段，女子表示已經要求業務部提
前報告，而辛克萊兒小姐原本要報告的時間為上午 10 點。

067

What does the man say he will do?
(A) Edit a schedule
(B) Finish a report
(C) Send an invitation
(D) Talk to the sales team

中譯 男子說他會做什麼？
(A) 編輯時程表
(B) 完成報告
(C) 寄出邀請函
(D) 找業務團隊談

解析 男子為製作會議時間表的人，在後半段對話中，他提到會
重新修正時間表。

換句話說 remake the agenda → edit a schedule

字彙 edit 編輯，剪輯

Questions 68-70 refer to the following conversation and list.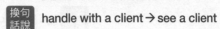

Products	Band Material	Band Color
Chater 400	Metal	Silver
Elling 2Z	Metal	Gold
Millseed CR	Leather	Brown
⑥⑨ Vextron 7T	Leather	Black

產品	錶帶材質	錶帶顏色
嘉特 400	金屬	銀
艾林 2Z	金屬	金
米爾西德 CR	皮革	棕
⑥⑨ 維克斯壯 7T	皮革	黑

M Hello, I heard about your sale on watches. Can I
see them?

W Yes, but only certain brands are discounted.
These over here. This Charter 400 is a best seller.

M Okay, I'll try it. Ah, no. ⑥⑧ **I don't like the feel of
the band. It's too itchy.** Can I try a different one?

W Of course. Maybe you would like a leather band
better. Here's a stylish one in brown.

男：哈囉，我聽說你們的手錶在促銷，我
可以看看嗎？

女：好的，但只有某些品牌有折扣。這邊
這些。這只嘉特 400 是暢銷款。

男：好，我試戴看看。啊，不行，⑥⑧我
不喜歡錶帶的觸感。好癢。我可以試
別只嗎？

女：當然可以。你也許會比較喜歡皮錶
帶。這只棕色的很時尚。

M ⑥⑨ Ah, that feels better, but do you have a black one?

W Not in the store currently. But ⑦⓪ I can order it for you and have it sent to your house, free of charge.

M Sounds good. Thank you.

字彙 itchy 發癢的　leather 皮革

男：⑥⑨ 啊，那感覺好多了，但你們有黑色的嗎？

女：目前店裡沒有。⑦⓪ 但我可以幫你訂，然後送到你家去，免費。

男：聽起來很棒。謝謝妳。

068

What was wrong with the first watch the man tried?
(A) It was not the right color.
(B) It was too expensive.
(C) It was too heavy.
(D) It was uncomfortable.

中譯 男子試戴的第一只手錶有什麼問題？
(A) 顏色不對。
(B) 太貴了。
(C) 太重了。
(D) 戴起來不舒服。

解析 第二段對話中，男子表示戴了錶帶之後會發癢，等同於戴起來不太舒服的意思。

換句話說 too itchy → uncomfortable

字彙 uncomfortable 令人不舒服的，不自在的

---

069 新增題型

Look at the graphic. Which watch will the man probably order?
(A) Charter 400
(B) Elling 2Z
(C) Millseed CR
(D) Vextron 7T

中譯 見圖表。男子很可能會訂購哪一只手錶？
(A) 嘉特 400
(B) 艾林 2Z
(C) 米爾西德 CR
(D) 維克斯壯 7T

解析 本題為圖表整合題。後半段對話中，男子試戴皮製錶帶後，詢問是否有黑色錶帶，而後女子表示會幫他訂購。目錄中黑色皮製錶帶的手錶為維克斯壯 7T。

070

What does the woman offer the man for free?
(A) An extra band
(B) Delivery service
(C) Gift wrapping
(D) Parking

中譯 女子提議免費給男子什麼？
(A) 另外送一條錶帶
(B) 送貨服務
(C) 禮物包裝
(D) 停車

解析 最後一段對話中，女子表示可將手錶免費送至男子家，換言之即提供免費配送服務。

字彙 wrapping 包裝

Questions 71-73 refer to the following telephone message. 澳

Hello, my name is Samantha and ❼ **I own a print shop in your neighborhood.** I noticed your company has just moved here and I wanted to let you know what we do. In addition to the usual printing and copying, we offer Website and logo design services. For new customers such as yourself, we are priced very competitively, say . . . on business cards, if you need some with your new address. ❼ **We offer the quickest turnaround of all shops in this area,** even same-day service on certain jobs. ❼ **I'll be dropping a flyer by your office later this week.** Hopefully, we can speak then about your printing needs. Thank you.

哈囉，我是莎曼珊，❼ 我在你們附近開了一家印刷行。我注意到你們公司剛搬來這裡，我想讓你們了解我們的業務。除了一般的列印和影印之外，我們也提供網站和商標設計服務。對於像你們這樣的新客戶，我們的定價相當有競爭力，就以名片來說，如果你們有印一些新地址名片的需求，❼ 我們的處理時間是這一區所有商店中最快的，某些服務甚至是當天取貨。❼ 這星期稍晚，我會放一張傳單在你們辦公室。希望到時候，我們可以談談你們的印刷需求。謝謝你。

字彙 **neighborhood** 鄰近地區，街坊　**notice** 注意到　**competitively** 有競爭力地　**turnaround** 處理時間　**flyer** 小（廣告）傳單

071

Who most likely is the speaker?
(A) An IT employee
(B) A police officer
(C) A postal worker
(D) A store owner

中譯 說話者最可能是誰？
(A) 資訊工程員工
(B) 警官
(C) 郵政人員
(D) 商店店主

解析 前半段電話留言中，說話者表明自己的身份，並表示自己經營一家印刷店。

換句話說 own a print shop → store owner

字彙 **postal** 郵政的

072

According to the speaker, what is unique about her business?
(A) It is the cheapest.
(B) It is the fastest.
(C) It is the largest.
(D) It is the oldest.

中譯 根據說話者，她的商店有什麼獨特處？
(A) 最便宜。
(B) 最快。
(C) 最大。
(D) 最老。

解析 本篇電話留言的目的為宣傳印刷店，因此當中會提及具有競爭力的特點。後半段留言中，提到他們店的特點為該區域作業速度最快的，甚至可在當天完成印刷。

換句話說 quickest → fastest

073

What does the speaker say she will do soon?
(A) Move to a different location
(B) Open a new branch
(C) Post an advertisement
(D) Visit the listener's office

中譯 說話者說，她很快會做什麼事？
(A) 搬到不同的地點　　(B) 開一家新分店
(C) 張貼廣告　　(D) 造訪聽話者的辦公室

解析 留言中提到預計於這週前往辦公室發送傳單（dropping a flyer by your office），表示會去到聽話者的辦公室。

字彙 post 張貼

Questions 74-76 refer to the following broadcast. 美

Good news for local hockey fans. **❼❹ It looks like we'll be getting our first professional hockey team here in Stanleyville.** The owner of the Pirates, a team that has played for over a decade in Greenborough, released a written statement earlier today saying he's moving his team here. **❼❺ Among the many attractions to this area were the energetic fans and world-class ice arena,** the statement said. We sent a reporter to City Hall and, **❼❻ as you'll see after the commercial break, Stanleyville Mayor Evans had a very enthusiastic reaction to the historic announcement.** Don't go away.

本地曲棍球迷的好消息。❼❹ 看來，我們史丹利維爾即將迎來第一支職業曲棍球隊了。在葛林保若打了超過十年的海盜隊，他們的老闆今天稍早發了一份書面聲明，表示要把球隊移來這裡。聲明指出，❼❺ 本區有許多吸引人的特點，其中包括了熱情的球迷和世界級的溜冰場。我們派了一位記者去市政府採訪，❼❻ 你在廣告後會看到，史丹利維爾市的市長伊凡斯非常熱情地回應這個歷史性的宣布。別走開。

字彙 release 發表，公布　written 書面的　attraction 吸引人的事物　commercial break 廣告時間　enthusiastic 熱情的

074

What is the broadcast mainly about?
(A) A new sports facility
(B) A new sports team
(C) A retiring player
(D) A sports tournament

中譯 這段廣播的主題是什麼？
(A) 一個新的運動場所
(B) 一支新的運動隊伍
(C) 一位退休的球員
(D) 一項運動錦標賽

解析 本篇獨白為史丹利維爾地區的新聞廣播，播報的是首支專業曲棍球隊將移至此區的消息。

075

What is mentioned about Stanleyville?
(A) It has a new mayor.
(B) It has an excellent ice rink.
(C) It has hosted sporting events before.
(D) It has more than one professional team.

中譯 關於史丹利維爾，文中提到什麼？
(A) 有一位新市長。
(B) 有一流的溜冰場。
(C) 以前主辦過體育活動。
(D) 有不止一支職業隊伍。

解析 球隊選擇移籍到此區，原因是該區域擁有許多粉絲和世界級的冰上競技場。由此段話可以得知此地擁有優秀的溜冰場地。文中的 arena 的意思是「周圍有觀眾席的的比賽場地」。

換句話說 world-class ice arena → excellent ice rink

字彙 host 主辦，主持

076

What will listeners hear next?
(A) A city leader's speech
(B) A reporter's story
(C) A weather report
(D) Advertisements

中譯 聽眾接下來會聽到什麼？
(A) 一位城市領導人的演說
(B) 一位記者的報導
(C) 一則氣象預報
(D) 廣告

解析 雖然廣播最後有提到將公開伊凡斯市長的反應，但表示是在廣告過後（after the commercial break），因此聽者會先聽到廣告。

換句話說 commercial break → advertisements

字彙 speech 演說，致詞

Question 77-79 refer to the following announcement. 加

⑰ Attention Tally Ho Wine shoppers. ⑱ It is now 7:45 and our store will close in 15 minutes. Please bring your selections to the front for checkout. We are open from 10:00 AM to 9:00 PM Monday through Friday and ⑱ 10:00 AM to 8:00 PM on Saturday and Sunday. For your convenience, ⑲ we also have a Website where you can purchase all of the items you see in our store, plus some bottles of wine that are available online only. To access the shopping feature, just use your loyalty card number and create a password. The address is www. tallyhowines.com.

⑰ 各位塔利何酒窖的顧客請注意，⑱ 現在是 7 時 45 分，本店即將在 15 分鐘後打烊。請將你所選的商品拿到前面的收銀台結帳。我們的營業時間是星期一到星期五，上午 10 點到下午 9 點，⑱ 星期六和星期日是上午 10 點到下午 8 點。
為了讓你方便，⑲ 我們也有網站，所有你在店內看到的商品都可以那裡買到，另外還有一些只在網上販售的酒品。要使用購物功能，只要用你的會員卡卡號，然後設定一組密碼即可。網址是 www.tallyhowines.com。

字彙 selection 被選中的人或物　checkout（超市等的）收銀台　shopping feature 購物功能

077

What type of store is the announcement for?
(A) A deli
(B) A department store
(C) A grocery store
(D) A wine shop

中譯 這則廣播是關於什麼樣的商店？
(A) 熟食店
(B) 百貨公司
(C) 雜貨超市
(D) 酒品專賣店

解析 廣播通知開頭便提到商店名稱為「Tally Ho Wine」，由此可以得知該商店為酒品專賣店。

078

When is the announcement most likely being made?
(A) On Monday
(B) On Wednesday
(C) On Friday
(D) On Sunday

中譯 這則廣播最可能在何時播送？
(A) 星期一
(B) 星期三
(C) 星期五
(D) 星期日

解析 廣播中提到現在時間為 7 點 45 分，距離關門還有 15 分鐘，而後又提到週六和週日的營業時間至晚上 8 點結束，因此該廣播的播送時間選擇週日最為適當。

079

What is mentioned about the online option?
(A) It offers more selection than the store.
(B) It has recently been redone.
(C) It is cheaper than the store.
(D) It is secure.

中譯 關於網上的選擇，文中提到什麼？
(A) 提供比店內更多的選擇。
(B) 最近才重新調整過。
(C) 比店內便宜。
(D) 很安全。

解析 廣播中間提到網站，並表示部分酒品僅限網路販售（available online only）。這段話表示相較於店內販售的品項，網站上所販售的產品有更多選擇（more selection）。

字彙 secure 安全的

Question 80-82 refer to following news report. 英

And now we turn to regional news. ⑧⓪ **The government has released the economic numbers for last quarter** and for the first time in three years, there has been an upturn in production and job growth. The report cites two industries in particular that are responsible for the good news, biotechnology and manufacturing. We've been covering the biotech boom a lot recently, so we thought we'd get a different perspective today. ⑧① ⑧② **Our reporter Kevin Chang sat down with the president of KRL Manufacturing to ask about his company's recent growth.**

現在來看地方新聞。⑧⓪ 政府公布了上一季的經濟數字，三年來第一次在生產與就業成長上有所好轉。報告特別舉出二種帶來這個好消息的產業，生物科技與製造業。我們最近報導了很多生技業蓬勃發展的狀況，因此，我們今天想換個角度。⑧① ⑧② 記者凱文‧張和 KRL 工業的總裁日前坐下來談論了他公司最近的成長。

字彙 regional news 地方新聞　quarter 季度，四分之一　upturn 好轉，向上　cite 舉出，引……為證
in particular 尤其是，特別是　biotechnology 生物科技　manufacturing 工業，製造業　cover 採訪，報導
perspective （思考問題的）角度，觀點

080

What is the speaker mainly discussing?
(A) A new government policy
(B) A new local facility
(C) Personnel changes at his work
(D) Recent economic news

中譯 說話者主要在討論什麼？
(A) 一個新的政策
(B) 一家新的本地機構
(C) 他工作上的人事變動
(D) 最近的經濟新聞

解析 本篇獨白為地方新聞報導。開頭提到政府公布了上一季的經濟數據，稍後會介紹特定公司的成長趨勢，因此說話者探討的是最近的經濟消息。

字彙 personnel 人事（部門）
economic 經濟的

081

Who most likely is Kevin Chang?
(A) A biotechnology expert
(B) A company owner
(C) A government spokesperson
(D) A news person

中譯 凱文・張最可能是誰？
(A) 一位生物科技專家
(B) 一家公司的老闆
(C) 一位政府發言人
(D) 一位新聞從業人員

解析 請務必要聽清楚提及凱文・張的片段。當中介紹稍後要談論的內容，以及記者凱文・張和他要採訪的對象。

換句話說 reporter → news person

字彙 expert 專家

082

What will listeners hear next?
(A) An advertisement
(B) A biotechnology report
(C) A press briefing
(D) An interview

中譯 聽眾接下來會聽到什麼？
(A) 一段廣告
(B) 一則生物科技的報導
(C) 一場記者會
(D) 一段訪問

解析 記者要向 KRL 製造業者的董事長提問，由此可以推測聽者稍後將聽到的是訪談內容。

Questions 83-85 refer to the following telephone message. 澳

Hi, Carlos. **❽ I just wanted to tell you how wonderful our awards ceremony was, thanks to your great recommendation of the Four Leaf banquet hall.** The staff there was so helpful and the food was wonderful. I understand why you go back there every year for your firm's party. I actually asked them about having our end-of-year party there also. They were booked on the night we had chosen, but my coworkers and I loved it so much, **❽ we're thinking about changing nights. ❽ They are filling up quickly, so you should probably confirm your party date with them soon.** Anyway, take care, Carlos!

嗨，卡洛斯，❽ 我只想告訴你，多虧你大力推薦四葉宴會館，我們的頒獎典禮辦得很成功。那裡的工作人員幫了很大的忙，食物也美味極了。我理解你為什麼每年都回去找他們辦你公司的派對。我其實也問了他們，在那裡辦我們公司尾牙的事。我們選的那一天晚上，已經有人預訂了，但我同事和我都愛死那裡了，❽ 我們正在考慮要改成其他天晚上。❽ 他們很快就會訂滿，所以你可能要趕快和他們確定你們派對的日期。好了，保重囉，卡洛斯！

字彙 coworker 同事　fill up （使……）充滿，（使……）填滿　confirm 確定

083

Why is the woman calling?
(A) To change an appointment
(B) To express appreciation
(C) To make a reservation
(D) To recommend a restaurant

中譯 女子為什麼打電話？
(A) 為了更改約會
(B) 為了表達謝意
(C) 為了預訂
(D) 為了推薦一家餐廳

解析 電話留言通常會在前半段提及來電目的。開頭提到感謝對方推薦的場地（**thanks to your great recommendation**），活動辦得很成功。由此可以看出來電目的為表達感謝之意。

字彙 appreciation 感謝；欣賞

084

What does the woman say she
needs to decide
about her party?
(A) What to serve
(B) When to hold it
(C) Where to hold it
(D) Who to invite

女子說，她需要決定關於派對的什麼？
(A) 要供應什麼餐點
(B) 何時要舉辦
(C) 在哪裡舉辦
(D) 要邀請誰

解析 後半段留言中提到尾牙的計畫。當中表示為了能順利預訂場地，考慮更改尾牙舉行的時間（**changing nights**），表示他們得決定何時舉辦。

085 新增題型

What does the speaker imply when
she says, "They are filling up
quickly"?
(A) The customers have eaten
enough.
(B) The customers want to go home
early.
(C) The hall has few nights left to
reserve.
(D) The staff will finish their work
soon.

中譯 當說話者說：「他們很快就會訂滿」，她的意思是什麼？
(A) 顧客已經吃飽。
(B) 顧客想早點回家。
(C) 會館可以預定的時間只剩下幾個晚上。
(D) 工作人員很快就會結束工作。

解析 最後提到場地很快就會被訂滿，建議聽者儘快敲定派對日期。這表示能接受預訂的日子所剩不多。

Questions 86-88 refer to the following talk. 加

Welcome to today's seminar on starting your own
business. 87 We'll be covering all the basics of
running a small business, from advertising to
financing to location. 88 You'll be hearing from real
business owners on each of the topics this
morning. Then, after lunch, we'll have the speakers
lead small group discussions so you can ask specific
questions on your situation. 86 We ask that you hold
your questions until the afternoon sessions. Also,
we'd like you to fill out a survey at the end of the
seminar. You'll find it in the information packets on
each chair. Just drop them in the box at the door as
you leave. Well, let's get started.

歡迎參加今天有關自行創業的研討會。87 我們會討論所有經營一家小企業的基本要素，從廣告到財務到地點。88 在今天早上的每個主題裡，你會聽到真正企業主的說法。然後，在午餐之後，我們會讓講者帶領小組討論，這樣你就可以問與自身狀況有關的具體問題。86 請你們把問題留在下午的課程再問。此外，我們想請你們在研討會結束時填寫一份問卷。你們可以在每張椅子上的資料袋裡找到問卷。請在你離開時，把問卷投進門邊的箱子裡。我們開始吧。

字彙 financing 財政，金融　information packet 資料袋

086

When can listeners ask questions?
(A) As they are leaving
(B) At anytime
(C) During lunch
(D) In the afternoon session

中譯 聽眾何時可以提問？
(A) 在他們離開時
(B) 隨時都可以
(C) 午餐時
(D) 下午的課程時

解析 本篇文章為課程流程的介紹。關於提問部分，當中建議將問題留到（**hold your questions**）下午再提問，表示提問時間安排在下午。

What does the speaker mean when he says, "We'll be covering all the basics of running a small business"?
(A) They will apply for small business insurance.
(B) They will instruct listeners on many aspects of starting a business.
(C) They will interview listeners for a job at a small business.
(D) They will review all the skills learned at a previous seminar.

中譯 當說話者說:「我們會討論所有經營一家小企業的基本要素」,他的意思是什麼?
(A) 他們會申請小企業保險。
(B) 他們會在創業的許多面向上指導聽眾。
(C) 他們會就一份在一家小企業的工作面試聽眾。
(D) 他們會複習上一次研討會學到的所有技巧。

解析 演講中會談到經營小型企業所需的所有基本知識 (**all the basics**),包含廣告、財務、地點等方面。由此可以得知會提供聽者多方面 (**many aspects**) 的指導。

字彙 instruct 指導,訓練 aspect 方面 review 複習

088

What will the listeners do next?
(A) Fill out a form
(B) Get into small groups
(C) Have lunch
(D) Listen to talks

中譯 聽眾接下來會做什麼?
(A) 填寫一份表格 (B) 分成小組
(C) 吃午餐 (D) 聽演講

解析 本篇文章為課程開始前的說明,上午將由企業家針對各類主題進行演說,表示聽者稍後便要聆聽演講。課程結束後依序為 (C) 午餐時間、(B) 小組討論、(A) 填寫問卷。

Questions 89-91 refer to the following excerpt from a meeting. 加

Since we have less than a week before the move, I wanted to go over our assignments again. ⑧⑨ **Robert, your team will of course be in charge of the computer equipment.** I mean, the movers we've hired will box it all up, but I'd like you to supervise and make sure everything is set up correctly at the new office. ⑨⓪ **Jocelyn, you're in charge of supplies. Again, you just have to make sure to label the boxes the movers pack and then put everything away in an organized way.** Finally, Luis, can you update the Website to show our new location? Well, ⑨① **on second thought, Luis, wait until the actual move-in day, December 12.** Thanks everyone.

由於再不到一個星期就要搬家,我想要再仔細把我們各自的分工檢查一遍。⑧⑨ 羅伯,你的小組負責電腦設備,這毫無疑問。我是說,我們請的搬家師傅會把設備裝箱,但我想要你監督指揮,並且確定每樣東西在新辦公室都正確設定好。⑨⓪ 喬瑟琳,妳負責辦公用品。同樣地,妳只需要確定搬家師傅打包好的箱子都貼上了標籤,然後把所有東西都井井有條地歸位。最後,路易斯,你可以更新網站,以顯示我們的新地址嗎?嗯,⑨① 我再想一想,路易斯,還是等到真正搬進去那天,也就是 12 月 12 日再做好了。謝謝大家。

字彙 assignment (分派的) 任務,工作 in charge of 負責 supplies 日用品 organized way 井然有序地 on second thought 進一步考慮後,轉念一想 move-in day 搬進新居之日

089

What department does Robert most likely work in?
(A) Accounting
(B) IT
(C) Office administration
(D) Sales

中譯 羅伯最可能在什麼部門工作?
(A) 會計部 (B) 資訊部
(C) 管理部 (D) 業務部

解析 本篇獨白內容為搬遷之前確認工作分配。當中提到由羅伯的部門負責電腦設備,由此可以推測他所任職的部門與電腦相關。

字彙 administration 行政管理

090

What will Jocelyn do in less than a week?
(A) Hire a moving company
(B) Clean the new office
(C) Organize supplies
(D) Pack boxes

中譯 喬瑟琳在不到一星期內會做什麼？
(A) 僱用一家搬家公司
(B) 打掃新辦公室
(C) 整理辦公用品
(D) 裝箱

解析 獨白中段提及喬瑟琳要負責的工作。當中請她負責辦公用品，並在箱子貼上標籤，把東西井然有序地分類好（organized）。由此段話可以得知她將負責整理辦公用品。

字彙 organize 整理，安排

091 新增題型

Why does the speaker say, "on second thought"?
(A) She wants the listeners to think about something again.
(B) She wants to do something different than what she first said.
(C) She thinks that time is running out for the move.
(D) She thinks that the move should happen sooner.

中譯 說話者為什麼說：「再想一想」？
(A) 她想要聽話者再考慮一下某件事。
(B) 她想要做一件和她一開始說的不一樣的事。
(C) 她認為搬家的時間愈來愈緊迫。
(D) 她認為要快點搬家。

解析 說話者說出「on second thought」推翻前方所述的話。「再次考慮」表示她要做的事情跟一開始說的不一樣。

字彙 run out 用完，耗盡

Questions 92-94 refer to the following introduction. 英

❷ We are indeed lucky to have an award-winning history professor addressing our book club tonight. Actually, Dr. Fleming recently retired from teaching and is touring around the country promoting his new book on Egyptian treasure. There's even talk of a movie version of his fascinating tale. ❸ First he's going to read an excerpt of his book *Jewels in the Sand*. Then he'll take questions from the audience. We have a wireless microphone so everyone can hear you. ❹ If you'd like to ask a question, just stand and someone will bring the microphone to you. Okay, without further ado, please welcome Dr. Fleming.

❷ 我們真的很幸運，能請到獲獎的歷史教授今晚來我們讀書俱樂部演講。事實上，佛萊明博士最近從教職退休，正巡迴全國宣傳他關於埃及寶藏的新書。甚至傳出要將他極吸引人的故事改編為電影。❸ 首先，他會讀一段他的著作《沙中寶石》的內容，然後，他會接受觀眾的提問。我們有無線麥克風，這樣大家都能聽到你說話。❹ 如果你想提問，只要站起來，就會有人拿麥克風給你。好了，我就閒話少說，請歡迎佛萊明博士。

字彙 award-winning 獲獎的　address 向……發表演說　fascinating 迷人的，吸引人的
excerpt（演講、書、電影等的）摘錄　wireless 無線的　without further ado 不再浪費時間，乾脆，立即

092

Who most likely are the listeners?
(A) Bookstore workers
(B) Club members
(C) Professors
(D) Students

中譯 聽眾最可能是誰？
(A) 書店工作人員
(B) 俱樂部會員
(C) 教授
(D) 學生

解析 本篇獨白為讀書俱樂部的活動講者介紹，由此可以得知聽者應為讀書俱樂部的會員。

093

What will listeners hear next?
(A) A book excerpt
(B) A movie summary
(C) A university lecture
(D) Questions and answers

中譯 聽眾接下來會聽到什麼？
(A) 一段書摘　　　(B) 電影摘要
(C) 大學講座　　　(D) 問與答

解析 介紹完講者後，接著說明活動流程。中段提及講者將擷取書中內容閱讀給大家聽（read an excerpt of his book），表示聽眾將聽到書本的摘錄。(B) 選項的 summary 也是「摘要」的意思，不過整個選項的意思是「電影摘要」，所以與問題不符合。

字彙 summary 摘要

094

What does the speaker ask the listeners to do?
(A) Come up on stage
(B) Get into small groups
(C) Make a line at the microphone
(D) Stand up if they have a question

中譯 說話者要求聽眾做什麼？
(A) 到舞台上去
(B) 分成小組
(C) 排隊用麥克風
(D) 如果要問問題就站起來

解析 後半段中提到如果有問題想發問，可以直接站起來（just stand），旁邊會有人遞上麥克風。

字彙 make a line 排成一列

Questions 95-97 refer to the following telephone message and schedule. 澳

Mr. Black's Schedule

	10:00	1:00	3:00
Monday 14	Recording		
Tuesday 15	Sales call		Interview
Wednesday 16	Board meeting	Teleconference	Client outing
Thursday 17	Business trip --------	--------------	------>
96 Friday 18	Seminar	Presentation	

布雷克先生的行程表

	10:00	1:00	3:00
星期一 14	錄音		
星期二 15	拜訪客戶		訪問
星期三 16	董事會	視訊會議	帶客戶出遊
星期四 17	出差 --------	--------------	------>
96 星期五 18	研討會	簡報	

Hello, Mr. Black? 95 **This is Regina Worthy from Capel Studios returning your call about reserving a recording studio on November 14th.** I'm afraid we won't be open November 14th, 15th, or 16th. We're renovating our studios on those days. 96 **We'll re-open on Thursday the 17th**, so if you can call me back, I'll book a session for you. I'm sorry for the inconvenience this may cause you, Mr. Black. The good news is that 97 **we'll be offering a grand re-opening special—you'll get 10 percent off your total price within five days of our re-opening.** We look forward to hearing from you soon. Thank you.

哈囉，布雷克先生？95 我是卡沛兒錄音室的蕾吉娜‧沃爾西，就你要預訂 11 月 14 日錄音室的事情回電話給你。很抱歉，我們 11 月 14 日、15 日和 16 日不營業。這幾天，我們正在整修錄音室。96 我們會在 17 日星期四重新開幕，所以如果你可以回我電話，我會幫你預訂一個時段。很抱歉這可能會造成你的不便，布雷克先生。好消息是，97 我們會提供重新開幕的特別活動——在重新開幕的五天內，你的總費用都會打九折。期待很快能接到你的電話。謝謝你。

字彙 recording studio 錄音室　renovate 整修，翻新

095

What type of business is the speaker in?
(A) Audio recording
(B) Electronics sales
(C) Restaurant business
(D) Musical instruments sales

中譯 說話者從事哪一行？
(A) 錄音
(B) 電器銷售
(C) 餐廳經營
(D) 樂器銷售

解析 說話者在前半段電話留言中提到「卡沛兒錄音室」，並表示自己是為預約錄音室一事打電話給對方。

換句話說 recording studio → audio recording

096 新增題型

Look at the graphic. When can Mr. Black visit the speaker's business?
(A) At 10:00 on Monday
(B) At 1:00 on Tuesday
(C) At 1:00 on Thursday
(D) At 3:00 on Friday

中譯 見圖表。布雷克先生何時能去造訪說話者的公司？
(A) 星期一 10 點
(B) 星期二 1 點
(C) 星期四 1 點
(D) 星期五 3 點

解析 本題為圖表整合題。留言中提到 14 至 16 日並未開放錄音室，要到 17 日才會重新開放。但是根據布雷克先生的行程表，他 17 日要出差，得到 18 日週五下午三點才有空前往。

097

What does the speaker offer Mr. Black?
(A) A discount
(B) A free gift
(C) Free parking
(D) Free upgrades

中譯 說話者提議給布雷克先生什麼？
(A) 折扣
(B) 免費禮物
(C) 免費停車
(D) 免費升級

解析 後半段留言中，提到重新開放後的五天內，都能享有總額九折的優惠。

換句話說 percent off → discount

Questions 98-100 refer to the following excerpt from a meeting and map. 美

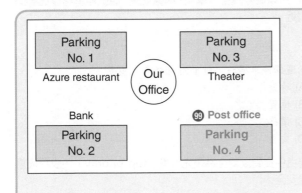

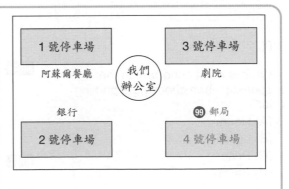

I'll try to keep this last agenda item brief. We've been informed by the building manager that ⑨⑧ **the cost for our parking spaces in this building will be doubled next year** uh, starting in January. We really can't afford that, so we need to find a new parking lot. Here's a map of the surrounding area. It looks like we have four choices but numbers 1 and 2 are pretty far away, so they're out. ⑨⑨ **Number 4 is not the cheapest, but it's more secure than number 3** since they have a guard on duty 24 hours. ⑨⑨ ⑩⑩ **I think security should be our top priority.** What do you all think?

我會盡量讓這最後一項議程簡短。大樓經理通知我們，⑨⑧ 我們在這棟大樓裡的停車位費用，明年將要漲為二倍，呃，從一月開始。我們真的無法負擔那樣的費用，所以我們需要找新的停車場。這是附近地區的地圖。看起來我們有四個選擇，但1號和2號相當遠，所以出局。⑨⑨ 4號不是最便宜的，但比3號安全，因為24小時都有警衛值勤。⑨⑨ ⑩⑩ 我認為安全應該是我們的優先考量。你們大家覺得呢？

字彙 **surrounding** 周圍的，附近的　**brief** 簡短的　**afford** 支付得起　**priority** 優先事項，優先權

098

What is mentioned about the current parking lot?
(A) It is being torn down.
(B) It is closing for repairs.
(C) It is giving employees security concerns.
(D) It is raising its prices.

中譯 關於目前的停車場，文中提到什麼？
(A) 正在拆除。
(B) 現在關閉進行整修。
(C) 讓員工有安全疑慮。
(D) 要調漲價格。

解析 本篇獨白討論的是選定新的停車場。當中表示目前大樓的停車費用將調漲至兩倍（**doubled**），因此答案要選價格調漲。

字彙 **tear down** 拆除　**raise** 增加，提高

099 新增題型

Look at the graphic. Where does the speaker prefer the new parking to be located?
(A) Near Azure restaurant
(B) Near the bank
(C) Near the post office
(D) Near the theater

中譯 見圖表。說話者比較喜歡新停車場在哪個位置？
(A) 靠近阿蘇爾餐廳
(B) 靠近銀行
(C) 靠近郵局
(D) 靠近劇院

解析 本題為圖表整合題。獨白中提及雖然四號停車場的費用並非最便宜的，但是比三號停車場安全，因為以安全為優先考量，所以偏好四號停車場。根據地圖，四號停車場位在郵局附近。

100

What is most important to the speaker when choosing a parking lot?
(A) Hours
(B) Location
(C) Price
(D) Safety

中譯 在選擇停車場時，什麼對說話者最重要？
(A) 時數
(B) 位置
(C) 價格
(D) 安全

解析 獨白中提到以安全為優先考量（**top priority**），表示最重視安全。

換句話說 security → safety

PART 5

101

After reading the incident report, the factory director realized his workers had different ------- on safety issues.
(A) looks
(B) sights
(C) views
(D) watches

中譯 看過事故報告後，工廠廠長發現，他的工人對安全問題有不同的看法。
(A) 外表　　　　(B) 景象
(C) 看法　　　　(D) 看守

解析 本題要選出適當的名詞。根據題意，表達對安全議題有不同的「看法」較為適當。

字彙 incident（不愉快或不尋常的）事件　sight 景象；視覺

102

In the financial industry, Mark Hudson has been known as an ------- business leader for many years.
(A) accomplish
(B) accomplishable
(C) accomplished
(D) accomplishment

中譯 多年來，在財經界大家都知道馬克‧哈德森是位很有成就的企業領導人。
(A) 完成　　　　(B) 可完成的
(C) 有成就的　　(D) 成就

解析 空格位在冠詞 an 和名詞 business 之間，應填入形容詞。(A) 是動詞，(D) 是名詞，這兩個先刪去；(B) 和 (C) 皆為形容詞，當中表達「成功的企業領袖」較符合題意，因此答案為 (C)。

字彙 financial 財政的，金融的　accomplished 有成就的

103

The security software giant VESCO ------- their latest product around the world sometime next spring.
(A) has been launching
(B) has launched
(C) is launching
(D) will be launched

中譯 安全防護軟體巨頭 VESCO 將在明年春天於全球推出最新產品。
(A) 一直推出　　(B) 已推出
(C) 正要推出　　(D) 將被推出

解析 本題考的是時態，next spring 表示未來，適合搭配現在進行式 -ing 一起使用。(D) 不合適是因為 will be launched 是被動式，不符合題意。

字彙 giant（成功且有影響力的）大公司　launch 啟動，推出

104

When an ------- version of Catfox browser is available, it will be automatically downloaded.
(A) invited
(B) edited
(C) interested
(D) updated

中譯 當貓狐瀏覽器有升級版可用時，它會自動下載。
(A) 被邀請的　　(B) 編輯過的
(C) 感興趣的　　(D) 更新的

解析 本題為形容詞詞彙題。根據題意，表達「有『最新』版本的軟體可用時，便會自動下載」較為適當。

字彙 automatically 自動地　edit 編輯，剪輯

105

The employee had spent only a year in the IT department before getting a ------- to supervisor.
(A) promote
(B) promotion
(C) promotional
(D) promoted

中譯 這名員工只在資訊部待了一年就升職成主管。
(A) 使……晉升　　　(B) 晉升
(C) 晉升的　　　　　(D) 被晉升

解析 空格位在冠詞 a 的後方、介系詞 to 的前方，因此只能填入名詞。

字彙 get a promotion 得到晉升

106

------- the hotel's billing error, the Smiths were excessively overcharged for their two-night stay.
(A) Due to
(B) Except for
(C) In case
(D) So that

中譯 由於飯店的帳務系統出錯，史密斯一家住宿二晚的費用被超收很多。
(A) 由於　　　　　　(B) 除了……之外
(C) 以防萬一　　　　(D) 如此一來

解析 空格後方連接片語，而 error 後方連接子句，因此空格可以填入 (A) 或 (B)。帳單有誤為原因，因此空格適合填入 Due to。

字彙 excessively 過度地，極度地　overcharge 索價過高

107

The data transfer rates, usually from 100 to 150 kilobytes per second, ------- depending on the type of device you have.
(A) emerge
(B) convert
(C) record
(D) vary

中譯 數據傳輸速率通常在每秒 100 到 150 千位元，會依你的裝置種類而有差異。
(A) 浮現　　　　　　(B) 轉變
(C) 記錄　　　　　　(D) 呈現差異

解析 本題要選出意思適當的動詞。主詞為「數據傳輸速度」，表達「速度會因使用者的裝置而『有所不同』」較為適當。

字彙 device 設備，裝置　emerge 浮現，顯露　convert 轉變
vary 呈現差異

108

Although Kyle Boyd was inexperienced in sales, his ------- cheerful character was a great benefit in selling products.
(A) naturally
(B) naturalness
(C) nature
(D) natural

中譯 雖然凱爾・波伊德沒有銷售經驗，但他與生俱來的樂天性格在銷售產品上是很大的優勢。
(A) 天生地　　　　　(B) 自然狀態
(C) 自然　　　　　　(D) 自然的

解析 空格位在所有格形容詞和形容詞 cheerful 之間，因此適合填入副詞 naturally。

字彙 inexperienced 缺乏經驗的，經驗不足的　benefit 優勢，利益
naturally 天生地，自然地

109

The fashion magazine chose Amy Kitano as Designer of the Year for ------- a new line for young women.

(A) create
(B) created
(C) creates
(D) creating

中譯　時尚雜誌選出北野艾美為年度設計師，因為她為年輕女性設計一系列新產品。

(A) 創造　　　　　(B) 創造過
(C) 創造　　　　　(D) 創造

解析　空格位在介系詞 for 後方，且連接名詞片語 a new line，因此只能填入具備主動式意味的動名詞 (D)。

110

It was obvious that Jim Barrow was not ------- prepared for his presentation since he could barely answer the questions.

(A) fully
(B) generously
(C) securely
(D) widely

中譯　顯然，吉姆‧貝羅並未充分準備好他的報告，因為他幾乎回答不出問題。

(A) 充分地　　　　(B) 慷慨地
(C) 安全地　　　　(D) 廣泛地

解析　本題要選出意思適當的副詞。根據題意，若幾乎沒辦法回答問題，表示他並未「充分」準備好，因此空格適合填入 fully。

字彙　obvious 明顯的，顯著的　barely 幾乎沒有，僅僅
fully 充分地，完全地　generously 慷慨地，豐富地
securely 安全地　widely 廣泛地，大大地

111

Despite its convenient location, the new restaurant was not busy at all even ------- weekends.

(A) around
(B) for
(C) in
(D) on

中譯　儘管這家新餐廳的位置很方便，但它即使在週末也一點都不忙。

(A) 圍繞　　　　　(B) 持續（一段時間）
(C) 在……期間　　(D) 在……時候

解析　weekends 表示時間，前方適合加上 on，表示「在週末」。in 適合搭配週、月份或年份使用。

112

The mayor announced the new city hall would have a special ceiling that two architectural firms ------- on.

(A) collaborated
(B) collaboration
(C) collaborative
(D) collaboratively

中譯　市長宣布新的市政廳將會有一片特別的天花板，這是由兩家建築事務所合作設計的。

(A) 合作過　　　　(B) 合作
(C) 合作的　　　　(D) 合作地

解析　空格位在 that 引導的子句中，主詞為 two architectural firms，空格適合填入動詞。collaborate on 的意思為「在……上合作」。

字彙　collaborate 合作

113

As the last meeting did not go well, the leader hopes to reach a ------- on the upcoming project this time.

(A) consensus
(B) definition
(C) match
(D) satisfaction

中譯 由於上次會議並不順利，主管希望這一次在即將進行的專案上能達成共識。
(A) 共識　　(B) 定義
(C) 比賽　　(D) 滿意

解析 本題要選出意思適當的名詞。reach a consensus on 的意思為「在……上達成共識」。

字彙 reach a consensus on 在……上達成共識
definition 定義，解釋

114

Mr. Patterson is a well-known business consultant whose career goal is to help his clients achieve -------.

(A) theirs
(B) them
(C) themselves
(D) those

中譯 派特森先生是位知名的商業顧問，他的生涯目標就是幫助客戶達到他們的目標。
(A) 他們的　　(B) 他們
(C) 他們自己　　(D) 那些

解析 空格要填入適合代替 clients 的複數代名詞，同時可以搭配 achieve 使用的選項。因此空格適合填入 theirs，表示「clients' goals」。

115

Because of the last-minute venue change, the organizers had to contact all the attendees ------- had registered for the event.

(A) that
(B) what
(C) which
(D) whom

中譯 因為活動場地在最後一刻更改，主辦單位必須聯絡所有已經報名參加活動的人。
(A) 那些……（的人事物）
(B) 凡是……（的事物）
(C) 那些……（的事物）
(D) 那些……（的人）

解析 本題要選出適合連接空格前後的詞彙。空格後方連接動詞，因此適合填入關係代名詞主格，且由於先行詞為人物，因此選擇 that 較為適當。

字彙 venue 會場，舉行地點　register 登記，註冊

116

The purpose of the following survey on behavior analysis is to research ------- reactions to shocking news.

(A) capable
(B) formal
(C) typical
(D) terminal

中譯 以下這項關於行為分析的調查，其目的在研究人們對於震撼新聞的典型反應。
(A) 有能力的　　(B) 正式的
(C) 典型的　　(D) 末期的

解析 本題要選出適合修飾 reactions 的形容詞。根據題意，表達「研究對令人震驚的新聞的『典型』反應」較為適當。

字彙 reaction to 對……的反應　capable 有能力的
formal 正式的　typical 典型的，有代表性的
terminal 末期的

117

Lisa Foster realized that working ------- from home was more difficult than she thought as there were so many distractions.
(A) efficiencies
(B) efficiency
(C) efficient
(D) efficiently

Actual Test 2　PART 5

中譯　麗莎・佛斯特了解到，要以高效率在家工作，比她以為的要困難得多，因為有太多讓人分心的事物。
(A) 效率　　　　　　　(B) 效率
(C) 效率高的　　　　　(D) 效率高地

解析　本題要選出適當的詞性，填入動名詞 **working** 和介系詞片語 **from home** 之間。**(D)** 為副詞，最適合與動詞 **work** 搭配使用，表示「有效率地」。雖然 **(A)** 和 **(B)** 也能夠與 **working** 連接，但是並不符合題意。

字彙　**distraction** 分散注意力的事物　**efficiently** 效率高地

118

The marketing chief was satisfied with the survey results as ------- respondents found the new product "useful" or "very useful."
(A) almost
(B) most
(C) mostly
(D) the most

中譯　行銷部主管對調查結果很滿意，因為大部分受訪者認為新產品「有用」或「很有用」。
(A) 幾乎　　　　　　　(B) 大部分的
(C) 大部分地　　　　　(D) 最多的

解析　空格用來修飾後方名詞 **respondents**。**(B)** 和 **(D)** 當中，填入 **(B)** 最符合題意，意思為「大部分的、大多數的」。**(D) the most** 則是「最多」的意思。

119

The development team had a small party to celebrate the completion of a home-use robot that can be ------- controlled by mobile phone.
(A) hardly
(B) jointly
(C) manually
(D) remotely

中譯　研發團隊開了個小派對，以慶祝完成了可以用行動電話遠端遙控的家用機器人。
(A) 幾乎不　　　　　　(B) 共同地
(C) 用手地　　　　　　(D) 遙遠地

解析　空格後方連接「透過手機操控」，選項中最符合題意的單字為「遠端」操控。

字彙　**completion** 完成，實現　**jointly** 共同地，聯合地
manually 用手地，手工地　**remotely** 遙遠地，遠距離地

120

Gene Electronics' new 100-inch flat-screen TV will be available ------- five different colors next spring.
(A) from
(B) in
(C) of
(D) with

中譯　金恩電子的新型 100 吋平面電視，將在明年春天上市，有 5 種不同顏色。
(A) 出自　　　　　　　(B) 以
(C) 屬於　　　　　　　(D) 有

解析　根據題意，表示「產品以五種不同的顏色上市」。介系詞 **in** 後方要連接方法或材料，表示「以、用……」。

121

The mining firm believed the vast region to be an immense storehouse of natural resources and thought it was a wise -------.
(A) invest
(B) invested
(C) investment
(D) investor

中譯 這家礦業公司相信這片廣大地區蘊藏著無限的自然資源，並認為這是一個明智的投資。
(A) 投資
(B) 投資過
(C) 投資
(D) 投資者

解析 空格前方連接冠詞加上形容詞，因此空格適合填入名詞 (C) 或 (D)。主詞 it 指的是「投資行為」，因此答案要選 (C)。

字彙 vast 廣闊的　immense 巨大的，無邊無際的
storehouse 倉庫，(資訊或知識等的) 寶庫
investment 投資

122

Hoping to improve the company's performance, the automaker's president decided to ------- its management structure.
(A) overestimate
(B) overhaul
(C) overlook
(D) overtake

中譯 汽車公司總裁決定全面檢視公司的管理結構，期望能改善公司業績。
(A) 高估
(B) 全面檢視
(C) 俯瞰
(D) 超過

解析 本題要從 over 開頭的動詞中，選出最符合題意的動詞。根據題意，表達「為改善公司的業績，總裁決定『全面檢視』管理結構」最為適當。

字彙 performance 業績，工作表現　overestimate 高估
overhaul 全面檢查，大修　overlook 俯瞰；忽略
overtake 超過，趕上

123

The increased ------- for a thorough investigation showed how upset people are with the company's alleged secret funds.
(A) call
(B) called
(C) calling
(D) calls

中譯 徹底調查的呼聲增加，顯示人們對這家公司被指控有祕密資金一事有多不滿。
(A) 要求
(B) 要求過
(C) 要求
(D) 要求

解析 空格位在「冠詞＋修飾語」以及介系詞 for 之間，因此適合填入名詞。call for 的意思為「對……的要求」。

字彙 thorough 徹底的，完全的　investigation 調查，偵查
alleged 被指控的

124

The new recruit's project plan was so ------- that everyone in the department, including the manager, was quite impressed.
(A) elaborate
(B) elaborating
(C) elaborately
(D) elaboration

中譯 那位新進人員的專案計畫非常詳盡，因此部門裡的每個人，包括經理在內，都印象相當深刻。
(A) 詳盡的
(B) 詳述
(C) 詳盡地
(D) 詳細闡述

解析 空格位在 so 和 that 之間，適合填入形容詞或副詞。(A) 為形容詞，(C) 為副詞，而 was 後方適合連接形容詞，當作補語。

字彙 elaborate 詳盡的，精心製作的

125

The study suggests that the elementary and middle school years are the best times for the ------- of a second language.

(A) acquisition
(B) buyout
(C) possession
(D) takeover

中譯 研究顯示，小學與中學時期是習得外語的最佳年齡段。

(A) 習得　　　　　(B) 買斷
(C) 擁有　　　　　(D) 接管

解析 second language 的意思為「第二外語」，最適合與此搭配的選項為 acquisition，意思為「取得、習得」。(C) possession 也有「取得」的意思，但是多半針對「財產」的取得。

字彙 acquisition 習得，獲得　buyout 買斷，全部買下　takeover 接管，繼任

126

The newly-opened hotel is close to downtown and has luxurious amenities; -------, it is reasonably priced.

(A) in addition
(B) instead
(C) on the other hand
(D) otherwise

中譯 新開幕的飯店離鬧區很近，擁有豪華的便利設施；此外，價格還很合理。

(A) 此外　　　　　(B) 反而
(C) 另一方面　　　(D) 否則

解析 空格前後各連接一個子句，且前後都是提出優點，並非相反的內容，因此答案要選 (A)，表示進一步說明。

字彙 reasonably 合理地

127

The data that the supervisor uploaded to the intranet was missing, which according to the technician, happens only -------.

(A) occasion
(B) occasional
(C) occasionally
(D) occasions

中譯 主管上傳到內網的數據不見了，根據技術人員的說法，這種情形偶爾才會發生。

(A) 場合　　　　　(B) 偶爾的
(C) 偶爾地　　　　(D) 場合

解析 空格的解題關鍵在於前方的 which happens（發生什麼事）。happen 為完全不及物動詞，因此空格適合填入副詞。

字彙 occasion 場合；重大活動　occasionally 偶爾地

128

As visitors can have a full view of the office from the reception area, the manager told everyone to keep their desks -------.

(A) closely
(B) fairly
(C) orderly
(D) properly

中譯 因為訪客從接待區就可以看到整個辦公室，經理告訴大家要保持桌面整齊。

(A) 緊密地　　　　(B) 公平地
(C) 整齊的　　　　(D) 恰當地

解析 空格前方為動詞 keep 連接受詞 their desks，因此空格要填入形容詞。選項中，(A)、(B)、(D) 皆為副詞，只有 (C) 為形容詞。

字彙 orderly 整齊的，有條理的

129

In the interview, the company head said he has been successful because he always values integrity ------- profits.
(A) across
(B) over
(C) than
(D) upon

中譯 公司老闆在訪問中表示，他一直很成功是因為他總是把正直看得比獲利還要重要。
(A) 橫越 　　　　　(B) 在……之上
(C) 比……更 　　　(D) 在……上面

解析 根據題意，表達的是「比起後方的 A，更重視前方的 B」，因此答案範圍可以縮小至 (B) 和 (C)。當中 than 的範圍有所限制，意思為「超過（某個數量、時間、距離等）」；over 所指的範圍較廣，表示「超過……」，且動詞 value 更適合搭配 (B) 一起使用。

字彙 value 重視，尊重　integrity 正直　profit 利益

130

------- the outcome is, it was a great honor for Sarah Daly to be considered for manager of the new branch.
(A) Indeed
(B) Nevertheless
(C) Whatever
(D) While

中譯 不管結果如何，對莎拉・達利來說，被列為新公司經理的候選名單就是個很大的榮耀。
(A) 的確 　　　　　(B) 儘管
(C) 不管什麼樣的 　(D) 當……的時候

解析 本題要選出引導子句 the outcome is 的連接詞。根據題意，表達「無論結果如何」較為適當，因此要填入 whatever 來引導副詞子句。(A) 為副詞，(B) 為連接副詞，(D) 為連接詞，填入後文法皆不正確。

字彙 outcome 結果，結局

PART 6

Questions 131-134 refer to the following notice. 通知

Attention all Marshburg City residents:

The Marshburg City Office will be under ------- from
131.
October 10 through October 21. All offices will be operating from the City Library for those two weeks, but will be closed from October 24 through October 28
------- we move back into the City Office. Telephone
132.
and fax numbers will remain the same for the duration of the construction. -------.
133.

Our new office hours are as follows:
M–F 10:00 AM–4:00 PM
Closed Saturday and Sunday

馬希伯格市的全體市民請注意：

馬希伯格市政府大樓從 10 月 10 日到 10 月 21 日將進行 ⑬ 整修。在這二星期裡，所有單位將在市立圖書館辦公，但 10 月 24 日到 10 月 28 日不上班，⑬ 因為我們要搬回市政府大樓。工程期間，電話和傳真號碼不變，⑬ 然而，我們的辦公時間有變動。

我們的新辦公時間如下：
星期一到星期五 上午 10 點到下午 4 點
星期六與星期日不上班

------- **134.**, if any local residents wish to help with the move between October 24 and October 28, please sign up at the library. Lunch and drinks will be provided to anyone who volunteers.

134 此外，如果任何本地居民想要協助 10 月 24 日到 10 月 28 日的搬遷，請到圖書館報名。凡志願幫忙者，我們都提供午餐和飲料。

字彙 **under renovation** 整修中　**operate** 工作，運作　**remain** 保持不變　**duration** 持續期間
local resident 本地居民　**volunteer** 自願

131

(A) renovate
(B) renovated
(C) **renovation**
(D) renovator

中譯 (A) 整修
(B) 整修過
(C) 整修
(D) 整修者

解析 空格前方為介系詞 **under**，後方連接表示時間的副詞片語，因此空格要填入名詞。**(C)** 和 **(D)** 皆為名詞，根據前後文意，表達「將重新翻修」較為適當。**under renovation** 屬於常見用語。

132

(A) **as**
(B) if
(C) though
(D) whether

中譯 (A) 因為
(B) 如果
(C) 雖然
(D) 是否

解析 空格前後連接的子句中皆有動詞，因此要填入連接詞。翻修工程導致必須暫時搬離的狀況，之後「因為」要重回辦公室，所以搬遷期間會暫時關閉。

133 新增題型

(A) Our mailing address can be found below.
(B) Our new phone numbers are listed on our Website.
(C) **Our office hours, however, will be changing.**
(D) Our office hours will remain the same.

中譯 (A) 我們的郵寄地址列在下面。
(B) 我們的新電話號碼列在我們的網站上。
(C) 然而，我們的辦公時間有變動。
(D) 我們的辦公時間不變。

解析 空格後方列出新的辦公時間，因此空格適合填入表示辦公時間有所更動的內容。

字彙 **below** 在下面，在……下面

134

(A) **Additionally**
(B) Second
(C) Therefore
(D) Yet

中譯 (A) 此外
(B) 其次
(C) 因此
(D) 然而

解析 空格為副詞的位置。後方提及非辦公時間的相關資訊，以及其他新資訊，因此空格填入 **(A)** 較為適當，表示補充說明的概念。

Questions 135-138 refer to the following e-mail. 電子郵件

To:	Samantha Patel
From:	Perry Fonda
Subject:	Help on November 8
Date:	November 2

收件者：莎曼珊‧佩托
寄件者：派瑞‧方達
主旨：在 11 月 8 日提供協助
日期：11 月 2 日

Hi Samantha,

I've got a ------- to ask. I'm meeting with the people
　　　　　　135.
from the Tolliver Fund next Tuesday, November 8 at
4:00 and I could really use some backup. This is my first
big chance to land an important client and I don't want
to -------. Since I'm fairly new, I'm not sure they will take
　136.
me seriously ------- a senior partner like you in the
　　　　　　137.
room. Do you have time, even to just stop in and
introduce yourself? It would really help. -------. Just a
　　　　　　　　　　　　　　　　138.
few tips from when you started out here.

Thank you in advance.

Perry

嗨，莎曼珊：

　　我要請妳 ⑬ 幫個忙。我和托利維基金的人約在下星期二 11 月 8 日 4 點碰面，而我真的需要一些支援。這是我第一次有望贏得重要客戶的大好機會，我不想 ⑬ 搞砸。因為我還很菜，我不確定 ⑬ 沒有像妳這樣的資深夥伴在場的話，他們是否會認真看待我。妳有空嗎，就算只是中間進來介紹一下妳自己都好？那真的會很有幫助。⑬ 如果妳那個時間要忙，也許妳可以給我一些指點。只要一些妳在這裡工作剛起步時的撇步。

先謝謝你。

派瑞

字彙 land 獲得，贏得　take ... seriously 認真對待　stop in 中途停留，順道拜訪　in advance 事先，預先

135

(A) favor
(B) job
(C) request
(D) wish

中譯 (A) 幫助　(B) 工作　(C) 要求　(D) 希望

解析 本篇文章為請求對方幫忙的電子郵件，因此要用 a favor to ask，表示「請你幫個忙」。

字彙 favor 幫助，恩惠

136

(A) fail
(B) mistake
(C) stop
(D) upset

中譯 (A) 失敗　(B) 犯錯　(C) 停止　(D) 攪亂

解析 文中表示這是他第一次能取得重要客戶的機會，因此表達不想「失敗」較符合文意。此外，want to 後面應該加上原形動詞，所以選 fail 才正確。

字彙 upset 攪亂；使……煩心

137

(A) among
(B) before
(C) except
(D) without

中譯 (A) 在……之中　(B) 在……之前　(C) 除……之外　(D) 沒有

解析 空格適合填入 without，表達如果「沒有」資深同事在場，他們可能不會重視我，因此向對方請求幫助。

(A) After you look over the file, let me know what you think.
(B) If you are busy at that time, maybe you could give me some pointers.
(C) If you can't make it, I understand and I'll do my best.
(D) Let me know your schedule, and I'll try to match it.

中譯
(A) 在妳看過檔案之後，請告訴我妳的想法。
(B) 如果妳那個時間要忙，也許妳可以給我一些指點。
(C) 如果妳無法趕到，我可以理解，我會盡力而為。
(D) 告訴我妳的行程，我會努力配合。

解析 空格前方提到希望對方能順道過來一趟，空格後方則請對方告訴自己一些剛開始工作時的技巧，因此當中的空格適合填入 (B)，表達「如果您沒空過來，請給我一些指點。」最符合前後文意。

字彙 look over 瀏覽，檢查　pointer 建議；跡象
match 使……相配

Questions 139-142 refer to the following article. 文章

Junko Cosmetics announced Wednesday that it will ------- a new line of moisturizers just in time for the dry
139.
winter weather. -------. Junko CEO said of Skin Drink,
140.
"They're aimed at any person of any age who wants their skin to feel ------- and comfortable. We will offer a
141.
fragrance-free moisturizer and a type with sunscreen."
The lotions ------- between £ 5.00 and £ 6.50 at any
142.
drugstore or cosmetics counter that sells the Junko brand.

君可化妝品星期三宣布將 ⑬ 推出新系列保濕產品，正好趕上乾燥的冬季氣候之用。⑭ 這個系列名為「肌膚飲品」，將主打四種適合不同膚質的乳液。君可執行長談到肌膚飲品：「它們的客群是任何想讓皮膚變得 ⑭ 光滑又舒服的人，且不分年齡皆可使用。我們會推出一款無香味的保濕霜和一種有防曬作用的產品。」乳液的 ⑭ 定價會落在 5 到 6.5 英鎊之間，任何販售君可品牌產品的藥局或是藥妝店都可買到這款乳液。

字彙 cosmetics 化妝品　moisturizer 保濕霜，潤膚霜　aim 瞄準，對準　fragrance-free 無香味的

139

(A) consider
(B) launch
(C) open
(D) test

中譯
(A) 考慮　　(B) 推出
(C) 打開　　(D) 測試

解析 本篇文章為介紹新產品的報導。後方提及產品的特色、價格區間、販售地點等資訊，因此空格適合填入「推出」保濕產品系列。

140 新增題型

(A) Like other Skin Drink products, the moisturizers include all natural ingredients.
(B) The company is keeping the product name under wraps until just before its release.
(C) The line, called Skin Drink, will feature four lotions for different types of skin.
(D) With its sales forecast looking gloomy, the future of the company is uncertain.

中譯
(A) 就像其他肌膚飲品系列產品一樣，保濕霜所含均為天然原料。
(B) 直到上市之前，公司對產品名稱一直保密。
(C) 這個系列名為「肌膚飲品」，將主打四種適合不同膚質的乳液。
(D) 由於銷售預測看來不樂觀，公司前景未明。

解析 該系列為新產品，因此 (A) 並不適當；而空格後方有提到產品名稱，因此也不適合填入 (B)；(D) 的敘述與新產品的介紹無關；而 (C) 說明新產品的名稱和分類，因此最適合填入空格中。

字彙 ingredient 原料　keep . . . under wraps 將……保密
release 發行，發表　forecast 預測　gloomy 悲觀的
uncertain 未知的，不確定的

141

(A) smooth
(B) smoothen
(C) smoothly
(D) smoothness

中譯 (A) 光滑的　　　　(B) 使……光滑
(C) 光滑地　　　　(D) 光滑

解析 空格前方為動詞 feel，後方連接對等連接詞 and，表示空格與 and 後方的詞性需一致，因此答案為形容詞 (A)，連接 and comfortable。此外，feel 是感官動詞，所以後面也可以直接加形容詞。

字彙 smooth 光滑的

142

(A) could price
(B) have been priced
(C) priced
(D) will be priced

中譯 (A) 可能使……定價為　(B) 一直定價為
(C) 定價　　　　　　　(D) 將定價為

解析 本篇文章報導新產品上市一事，因此選項中最適合用未來式表達產品的價格區間。

Questions 143-146 refer to the following information. 資訊

JOB FAIR

1:00-5:00 PM
Sunday, November 13
Canary Family Fun Park

A unique and exciting job fair is going to be held in Canary Family Fun Park this month. It is focused entirely on ------- jobs all in Canary Family Fun Park!
143.
If you've always wanted to work at the region's number-one entertainment venue for people of all ages, come see us on Sunday, November 13. -------.
144.
Some of the jobs will be extended beyond the end of the year too! With ------- one application, you will be
145.
considered for positions at all of the restaurants, hotels, and attractions at Canary Family Fun Park.

Don't ------- this chance to get the job of your dreams!
146.

就業博覽會

11 月 13 日星期日
下午 1:00–5:00
加那利家庭歡樂園區

　　一場獨特而令人興奮的就業博覽會本月將在加那利家庭歡樂園區舉行。主要招聘加那利家庭歡樂園區的所有 ⓭ 接待服務工作！如果你一直想要在本地首屆一指、老少咸宜的娛樂空間工作，11 月 13 日星期天來找我們。⓮ 你有機會應徵上 150 個短期的任一臨時工作，其中有些工作也會延長到今年底之後！⓯ 只要一份申請書，你就會被列入加那利家庭歡樂園區內所有餐廳、飯店和景點的工作考慮人選。

　　別 ⓰ 錯過這次得到你夢想工作的機會！

字彙 entirely 完全，徹底　attraction 景點；有吸引力的事物

143

(A) advertising
(B) engineering
(C) hospitality
(D) research

中譯 (A) 廣告　　　　(B) 工程
(C) 接待服務　　(D) 研究

解析 本篇文章為就業博覽會的資訊。當中提到加那利家庭歡樂園區內餐廳、飯店、觀光景點的職缺，這些皆屬於觀光服務業。

字彙 engineering 工程學，工程設計
hospitality 接待服務，餐旅業

(A) Be sure to include three letters of reference in your application and send it by November 13.
(B) Please encourage your friends and family to attend our grand opening event this weekend.
(C) We are looking for experienced managers in all areas of marketing and advertising.
(D) You will have the opportunity to apply for any of 150 temporary jobs.

中譯 (A) 你的應徵信須包含三封推薦信，並在 11 月 13 日前寄出。
(B) 請鼓勵你的朋友和家人參加我們本週末的盛大開幕。
(C) 我們正在尋找行銷與廣告各領域上有經驗的經理人。
(D) 你有機會應徵上 150 個的任一短期臨時工作。

解析 空格前方表示「歡迎想找工作的朋友前來」，空格後方則提到「某些工作還可以延長合約」，因此可以推測該空格適合填入與短期約聘有關的敘述；空格前方要求應徵者直接參加就業博覽會，而 (A) 要求附上推薦信，前後文意不一致，因此並不適合填入。

字彙 reference 推薦，推薦信　encourage 鼓勵
experienced 有經驗的　temporary 臨時的，短期的

145

(A) another
(B) each
(C) either
(D) just

中譯 A) 另一個　(B) 每一個
(C) 不是……就是……　(D) 只要

解析 空格後方提到可以申請園內所有餐廳、飯店、觀光景點的職缺，因此最適合填入的選項為 just。

146

(A) win
(B) grab
(C) break
(D) miss

中譯 (A) 贏得　(B) 抓取
(C) 打破　(D) 錯過

解析 空格最適合填入動詞 miss，表達千萬別「錯過」就業的機會。

字彙 grab 抓取，奪取

PART 7

Questions 147-148 refer to the following coupon. 折價券

Now 30% OFF
at TOMAS BROWN
when you spend over $100 online.

OFFER ENDS November 1st

ENJOY SHOPPING

We will donate every $1 spent over $100 to Blue Triangle.

Terms
147 *Only valid online clothing purchases.
*Only valid in the U.S.
*Limit once per customer.
148 *Cannot be used in conjunction with any other offer.

現正 7 折
只要在湯馬斯布朗的線上購物滿 100 元

優惠到 11/1 止

購物愉快

凡購買藍色三角產品，每滿百元，我們就捐出一元。

條件
147 * 只限線上購買衣服。
* 優惠只限美國。
* 每人只能享有一次優惠。
148 * 不得與其他任何優惠合併使用。

字彙 donate 捐獻，捐贈　term 條件，條款　valid 有效的，合法的　in conjunction with 與……一起

147

What can this coupon be used for?
(A) A bag
(B) A shirt
(C) A watch
(D) Shoes

中譯 這張優惠券可以用來買什麼？
(A) 袋子
(B) 襯衫
(C) 手錶
(D) 鞋子

解析 優惠券下方 Terms 處寫道：「Only valid online clothing purchases.」，表示僅限用於線上購買服飾類，而選項中只有 (B) 屬於服飾類。

148

What limit is placed on the coupon?
(A) It can be used only by itself.
(B) It is only valid on certain brands.
(C) It is only valid on November 30.
(D) It is valid after spending $1.

中譯 優惠券上列了什麼限制？
(A) 只能單獨使用。
(B) 只有某些品牌可用。
(C) 只在 11 月 30 日有效。
(D) 消費 1 元後，即可使用。

解析 Terms 處最後一行寫道：「Cannot be used in conjunction with any other offer.」，表示該優惠券無法與其他優惠同時合併使用。(A) 表示僅能單獨使用，為優惠券使用的限制。

字彙 place a limit 限制　by oneself 獨自，單獨地

Questions 149-150 refer to the following notice. 通知

ATTENTION: MEMBERS

Please be aware that there will be an annual maintenance check of the gymnasium and its facilities on November 9. This check ensures the safety of all equipment, studios, pool areas, changing rooms, and all other member locations.

The maintenance will last the entirety of November 9, starting from 6:00 AM. ⑭⑨ **The gym will re-open to members at 6:00 AM on November 10.** Due to this closure, the opening time on November 8 will be extended to 11:00 PM. ⑮⓪ **Please note: this only includes the gymnasium. It does not include the studios or pool areas.** Please contact the manager if you have any concerns.

We apologize for any inconvenience caused and thank you for your continued patronage.

注意：所有會員

　　請注意，健身房及其設施將在 11 月 9 日進行年度維修檢查。這項檢查確保所有設備、教室、泳池區、更衣室和其他會員使用場所的安全。

　　維修工作將會持續 11 月 9 日一整天，從上午 6 時開始。⑭⑨ 健身房將在 11 月 10 日上午 6 時重新開放給會員使用。由於這項關閉之故，11 月 8 日的營業時間將延長到晚上 11 時。⑮⓪ 請注意：這只包含健身房，並不包含教室或泳池區。如果你有任何疑慮，請聯絡經理。

　　我們為造成任何不便致歉，謝謝你持續惠顧。

字彙 maintenance 維修，保養　gymnasium 健身房　facility 設施，設備　ensure 保證　entirety 全部，完全
extend 延長，擴展　continued 持續的，連續的　patronage 惠顧，贊助

149

When will the maintenance be completed?
(A) By noon on November 9
(B) By the beginning of November 10
(C) By lunchtime on November 10
(D) By the beginning of November 11

中譯 維修工作何時完成？
(A) 11 月 9 日中午前
(B) 11 月 10 日前
(C) 11 月 10 日午餐時間前
(D) 11 月 11 日前

解析 本篇文章為健身房定期維護保養的公告。透過第二段內容，便能確認相關日程。當中提到「The gym will re-open to members at 6:00 AM on November 10.」，由此可以推測答案為 (B)，維護保養至 11 月 10 日前結束。

Which facilities can a member use later than usual on November 8?
(A) The dance studio
(B) **The gymnasium**
(C) The pool
(D) The sports shop

中譯 在 11 月 8 日，哪項設施會員可以使用得比平常晚？
(A) 舞蹈教室　　(B) 健身房
(C) 游泳池　　(D) 體育用品店

解析 後半段文章中提及與閉館有關的延長開放政策。當中表示「Due to this closure, the opening time on November 8 will be extended to 11:00 PM. Please note: this only includes the gymnasium.」，提醒 11 月 8 日延長開放的只有健身房而已。

Questions 151-152 refer to the following text message chain. 簡訊對話 新增題型

Jane Dodson	09:39 AM

My train is held up at Picau. Delay seems to be about 20 minutes. I'm afraid I will be late to our meeting. Sorry.

Nick Wise	09:42 AM

I heard there was a fire at Madex. That's OK, ⑮ **it's out of your hands**. Get here when you can.

Jane Dodson	09:45 AM

Thank you for your understanding! Train is moving now, so I'll see you soon.

Nick Wise	09:48 AM

OK, so how about meeting at Café la Olay at 10:15?

Jane Dodson	09:50 AM

Good idea.

⑯ Jane Dodson	10:07 AM

I just arrived at Madex Station. Will be at café in five.

Nick Wise	10:09 AM

I'm at a table outside.

珍‧達德森　　上午 9:39
我的火車卡在皮考。似乎會誤點約 20 分鐘。恐怕開會要遲到。對不起。

尼克‧懷斯　　上午 9:42
我聽說梅德克斯有火災。沒關係，⑮ 那不是妳能控制的事。等你可以再過來這裡。

珍‧達德森　　上午 9:45
謝謝你的體諒！火車現在動了，所以我很快就能和你見面。

尼克‧懷斯　　上午 9:48
好，那麼 10 點 15 分在拉歐蕾咖啡館見如何？

珍‧達德森　　上午 9:50
好主意。

⑯珍‧達德森　　上午 10:07
我剛到梅德克斯車站。5 分鐘內到咖啡館。

尼克‧懷斯　　上午 10:09
我在戶外區。

字彙 **hold up** 延誤　**out of one's hands** 不受某人控制

151 新增題型

At 09:42 AM, what does Mr. Wise most likely mean when he writes, "it's out of your hands"?
(A) Another colleague will take over Ms. Dodson's project.
(B) Ms. Dodson isn't a specialist in that field.
(C) The delay started at Madex.
(D) **The delay was not in Ms. Dodson's control.**

中譯 上午 9 點 42 分，當懷斯先生寫道：「那不是妳能控制的事」，他的意思最可能指什麼？
(A) 另一個同事會接手達德森女士的專案。
(B) 達德森女士不是那個領域的專家。
(C) 誤點從梅德克斯開始。
(D) 誤點不是達德森女士能控制的。

解析 達德森小姐透過文字簡訊表示因為火車誤點，所以沒辦法準時赴約。「out of one's hands」的意思為「超出掌控範圍、場面失控」，因此懷斯先生在 9 點 42 分的訊息中寫道：「it's out of your hands」，表示火車誤點並非達德森小姐能控制的事情。

字彙 **take over** 接管　**specialist** 專家　**field** 領域

152

Where was Ms. Dodson at 10:00?
(A) At Café la Olay
(B) At her office
(C) At Madex Station
(D) On a train

中譯 達德森女士 10 點時在哪裡？
(A) 拉歐蕾咖啡館　　(B) 她的辦公室
(C) 梅德克斯車站　　(D) 火車上

解析 達德森小姐在 10 點 7 分的訊息中表示自己剛到梅德克斯車站，因此答案為 (D)。要再過五分鐘才會抵達咖啡廳，因此不能選 (A)。

Questions 153-154 refer to the following advertisement. 廣告

MONIQUE BLANC'S FRENCH

You:
- Speak
- Have fun
- Learn

Me:
- Relaxed lessons
- Creative style
- Exam preparation

153 Come learn French with a native speaker!
All ages and abilities welcome.

Telephone: 080-5555-3245
E-mail: monique.blanc@bisco.com

Testimonials:

"Monique's class was so much fun! I was a beginner in French but now feel confident enough to travel to France and use what I learned. Thank you!" — Mary Newman

"It was hard for me to learn French, 154 but I had to prepare for my exams. Mme. Blanc helped me achieve the highest possible grade, which I'm so grateful for." — Gary Bush

莫妮克・布蘭卡的法文課

你：
—說
—學得愉快
—學習

我：
—輕鬆自在的課程
—有創意的風格
—準備考試

153 來和母語者學法文！
任何年紀、程度都歡迎

電話：080-5555-3245
電子郵件：monique.blanc@bisco.com

學員推薦：

「莫妮克的課好有趣！我是法文的初學者，但現在有足夠的信心去法國旅行，並且運用我的所學。謝謝你！」——瑪麗・紐曼

「之前學法文對我來說很困難，154 但我必須準備考試。布蘭卡女士幫助我拿到最高一級，我非常感激。」——蓋瑞・布希

字彙 preparation 準備　ability 能力　testimonial （人、物的性格、品質等的）推薦書　confident 自信的　achieve 達到，得到　grateful 感激的，感謝的

What is mentioned about Mme. Blanc?
(A) Her academic achievements
(B) Her location
(C) Her native language
(D) Her work history

中譯 關於布蘭卡女士，文中提到什麼？
(A) 她的學術成就　　(B) 她的所在地
(C) 她的母語　　　　(D) 她的工作經歷

解析 本篇文章為學法語的廣告。當中提到「Come learn French with a native speaker!」，由此可以得知布蘭卡女士的母語為法語；廣告中並未提及其餘選項。

字彙 academic 學院的，學術的　achievement 成就

Why is Mr. Bush appreciative of Mme. Blanc?
(A) She advised him where to travel in France.
(B) She gave private lessons.
(C) She helped with his academic success.
(D) She gave a good grade.

中譯 布希先生為什麼感謝布蘭卡女士？
(A) 她向他推薦法國的旅遊地點。
(B) 她教授私人課程。
(C) 她幫助他取得學業成功。
(D) 她分數打很高。

解析 布希先生的推薦文中提到：「Mme. Blanc helped me achieve the highest possible grade, which I'm so grateful for.」，表示感謝對方的幫助，讓自己得以考到最高的分數。(C) 將 achieve the highest possible grade 改寫成 academic success，故為正確答案。

Questions 155-157 refer to the following survey. 民意調查

SILVER FERN HOTEL GROUP
Customer Satisfaction Survey

Please complete the following survey based on the experience of your stay with us. Mark a number from 0 to 4 in the corresponding box, in accordance to the scale below.

Extremely dissatisfied	0
Dissatisfied	1
No opinion	2
Satisfied	3
Extremely satisfied	4

- Customer Service (reception, waiting/bar staff, housekeepers) — 4
- Room Service (timeliness, ease, choice) — 4
- The Restaurant (ambience, food, tableware) — 4
- 157 • **The Bar (ambience, choice of drinks)** — 1
- Cleanliness (all areas) — 4
- Noise levels (external and internal) — 3
- Location (distance from points of interest) — 3
- Cost (general) — 3
- Amenities (choice, functionality, age) — 2

Other comments

155 Overall, I was very pleased with my stay at Silver Fern. 156 The staff were exceptional, particularly Mr. Smyth, who went the extra mile to make my stay comfortable. 157 However, even though the bar had a large variety of drinks available, I could not find my favorite cocktail and the bar staff did not know of it. I hope it will be on the menu when I return next year! I didn't have time to make use of the amenities, although the free shuttle service into town was an added bonus. Thank you again. I look forward to next time!

銀蕨飯店集團
顧客滿意度調查

請以您在我們這裡的住宿經驗為準，完成下面的調查。依照下面的量表，在對應的空格內標出 0 到 4 的數字。

極不滿意	0
不滿意	1
沒意見	2
滿意	3
極為滿意	4

- 顧客服務
  (接待、服務生／酒吧工作人員、房務人員) 4
- 客房服務 (及時性、自在程度、選擇多寡) 4
- 餐廳 (氣氛、食物、餐具) 4
- 157 ·酒吧 (情調、飲品的選擇) 1
- 清潔 (所有區域) 4
- 噪音程度 (外面與裡面) 3
- 地點 (與景點的距離) 3
- 費用 (整體上) 3
- 便利設施 (選擇多寡、功能、年齡) 2

其他意見

155 整體而言，我很滿意我在銀蕨的住宿經驗。156 員工很優秀，尤其是史密斯先生，他付出額外心力讓我住的舒適自在。157 然而，即使酒吧有很多不同飲品可以選，我還是找不到我最愛的雞尾酒，而且吧檯的人沒聽過這種雞尾酒。我希望，明年我再來時酒單上會有！我沒有時間使用便利設施，但進城的免費接駁車有加分。再次謝謝你們。期待下次來！

Actual Test 2   PART 7

字彙 corresponding 對應的　in accordance to 依照　extremely 極其，非常　timeliness 及時，時效性
tableware （總稱）餐具　ambience 氣氛，情調　external 外面的，外部的　internal 內部的，內在的
distance 距離，路程　overall 總體上　exceptional 優秀的　go the extra mile 付出比別人期待更多的努力

155

How does the customer rate the hotel?
(A) Average
(B) Excellent
(C) Mostly satisfying
(D) Poor

中譯 這位顧客對飯店評價如何？
(A) 普通
(B) 很好
(C) 大部分滿意
(D) 很差

解析 本文為飯店的顧客滿意度調查表。各項目的分數介於 3 至 4 分，且下方的其他意見欄中寫道：「pleased with my stay」，因此答案為 (C)。

字彙 average 普通的，一般的

156

Who is Mr. Smyth?
(A) A hotel employee
(B) A hotel guest
(C) A hotel manager
(D) A taxi driver

中譯 史密斯先生是誰？
(A) 一名飯店員工
(B) 一名飯店客人
(C) 一名飯店經理
(D) 一名計程車司機

解析 與史密斯先生有關的內容出現在其他意見欄中。當中寫道：「The staff were exceptional, particularly Mr. Smyth, who went the extra mile to make my stay comfortable.」，由此段話可以得知史密斯先生為 staff，而 staff 指的就是 hotel employee。

157

What was the customer NOT satisfied with?
(A) The choice of amenities
(B) The distance from the town
(C) The diversity of drinks
(D) The friendliness of the staff

中譯 這位顧客對什麼不滿意？
(A) 便利設施的選擇
(B) 與市區的距離
(C) 飲品的多樣性
(D) 員工的友善程度

解析 調查表中「酒吧」的分數最低，在其他意見欄中，提到未提供自己最喜歡的雞尾酒，由此可以得知不滿意的點在於飲品種類不夠多樣。

字彙 diversity 多樣性　friendliness 友善，親切

Questions 158-160 refer to the following article. 文章

Mobile phones are now said to provide us with twice as much information as libraries or schools do. ⓖⒽ **This raises the question: should we continue to teach children in the traditional way?** Education ministers and teachers are firmly on the yes side of this issue, but tech companies and most young people are calling for a new approach to learning.

ⓖⒾ **Companies such as Poko and Djiib are pioneering the technology to make home-**

據說，現在行動電話提供給我們的資訊量是圖書館或學校的二倍。ⓖⒽ 這就帶出這個問題：我們應該繼續以傳統方式教孩子嗎？教育部門主管和教師在這個議題上都強烈贊成，但科技公司和大部分年輕人卻要求新的學習方法。

ⓖⒾ 像波可和迪吉布這樣的公司正在開創科技，使在家自學或「隨處學習」在未

schooling or "anywhere-schooling" more possible and likely for the future. "The depth and breadth of knowledge a child can receive from this type of technology is much vaster than what a teacher can offer in the classroom," said ⑯ **Jim Frank, the CEO of Poko**. "We are holding our children back by not changing the methods of education, as society and our lives develop."

Talks have been held by government officials in an attempt to fully comprehend this new idea and establish how viable it could be. The officials would like to hold a public meeting on October 3 so they can hear from parents and other concerned citizens. "For everyone's sake, ⑯ **I urge the public attend this town hall meeting. We need the input from everybody on this important issue.**" Education minister Paul Simonson commented.

來更有可能。「兒童能從這種科技接收到的知識深度與廣度，比教師在課堂所能提供的要大得多，」⑯波可公司執行長吉姆‧法蘭克表示。「隨著社會和我們生活的進步，我們不改變教育的方式就是在阻礙我們的孩子。」

政府官員已舉辦對談以全面了解這種新的概念，並確立它的可行性有多大。官員想在 10 月 3 日舉辦公開會議，如此一來，他們可以聽到家長與其他關心此議題市民的意見。「為了大家好，⑯我呼籲大家出席這次在市政廳的會議。在這個重要議題上，我們需要每個人的意見，」教育局局長保羅‧西蒙森評論道。

字彙 **raise a question** 提出問題，引出問題 **traditional** 傳統的 **firmly** 堅定地 **approach** 方法 **pioneer** 做⋯⋯的先鋒 **depth** 深度 **breadth** 寬度 **vast** 龐大的，巨大的 **fully** 完全地，充分地 **comprehend** 了解，理解 **establish** 確立，建立 **viable** 可實行的 **urge** 催促，呼籲

158

What is the article mainly about?
(A) A different way of schooling
(B) A new private school
(C) A special commemoration on October 3
(D) The future of mobile phones

中譯 這篇文章的主題是什麼？
(A) 一種不同的教育方式
(B) 一所新的私立學校
(C) 10 月 3 日的一場特殊紀念活動
(D) 行動電話的未來

解析 本篇報導探討在教育上導入新的學習方式。當中的關鍵句為：「**should we continue to teach children in the traditional way?**」，而後提出專家對於其他教育方式的意見。

字彙 **schooling** 學校教育 **commemoration** 紀念（活動）

159

What field does Jim Frank work in?
(A) Finance
(B) Government
(C) Publishing
(D) Technology

中譯 吉姆‧法蘭克在哪個領域工作？
(A) 財經界
(B) 政府
(C) 出版界
(D) 科技業

解析 第二段引用了吉姆‧法蘭克所說的話，並介紹此人為波可的執行長。此段寫道：「**Companies such as Poko and Djiib are pioneering the technology to make homeschooling or "anywhere-schooling" more possible and likely for the future.**」，由此段話可以得知波可為與教學技術領域有關的公司。

字彙 **finance** 財政，金融 **publishing** 出版（業）

160

What does a government official encourage people to do?
(A) Start home-schooling their children
(B) Invest in tech companies
(C) Voice their opinions at a meeting
(D) Talk to some local teachers

中譯 政府官員鼓勵人們做什麼？
(A) 開始讓他們的孩子在家自學
(B) 投資科技公司
(C) 在會議上說出他們的意見
(D) 和當地教師談話

解析 第三段提到政府官員將舉行會議討論新的教學方式，而後提到教育局局長的建議：「I urge the public to attend this town hall meeting. We need the input from everybody on this important issue.」，表示他希望大家不但來參加會議，也可在開會時表達自己的想法。此處 input 表示「意見」。

字彙 invest 投資　voice （用言語）表達

Questions 161-163 refer to the following e-mail. 電子郵件

To:	rich.jack@hmail.com	收件者：rich.jack@hmail.com
From:	hotelworld@promotions.com	寄件者：hotelworld@promotions.com
Subject:	Hotel of the Week	主旨：本週最佳飯店
Date:	Monday, October 3	日期：10 月 3 日 星期一

HOTELWORLD
The World is Your Oyster.

HOTEL OF THE WEEK
Golden Arms Inn: Bleat, The United Kingdom

⑯ **Situated on a brilliant, lush green piece of land in the English countryside**, this inn is the perfect weekend getaway for Londoners or those looking to explore Northern England. There is a vast area of lawn surrounding the house, where guests can enjoy evening strolls, bowls, or even a spot of croquet. The inn itself displays a remarkable piece of architecture: reminiscent of the 19th century gothic style. Sit on the porch, under the archway and enjoy your free breakfast.

⑯ **All rooms offer guests an insight into the inn's history, through careful restoration preserving the former charm.** Each also has suite facilities (including a separate bath), queen-size beds, and 24-hour room service. Other amenities include a large dining hall, a ballroom, a library, an 18-hole golf course, and horse stables all within the grounds of the inn.

⑯ **We are offering the second night's stay at a 50-percent discount, if you book before the end of the month.** Do it now to avoid disappointment!

旅館世界
世界任你遨遊。

本週最佳旅館
金手臂旅店：英國比利特

⑯ 位於英格蘭鄉間一片鮮麗蒼翠綠地上的這家旅店，是倫敦人或其他想要探索北英格蘭者的完美週末度假地。旅店四周圍繞著一大片草地，客人可以在這裡享受夜間漫步之樂，玩草地滾球遊戲，甚至是玩槌球。旅店本身是一件卓越的建築作品：懷舊的 19 世紀哥德式風格。你可以坐在門廊上和拱形建築下享用免費早餐。

⑯ 所有房間透過仔細修復而保留過往風華，讓旅客深入了解旅店的歷史。每間房也有套房的設備（包含分開的浴缸）、加大尺寸的床以及 24 小時的客房服務。其他便利設施包括一間大餐廳、一間晚宴廳、一座圖書館、一座 18 洞高爾夫球場以及馬廄，全都在旅店的範圍內。

⑯ 如果在月底前預訂，我們提供第二晚半價優惠。現在就訂，以免向隅！

字彙 The world is your oyster. 你可以隨心所欲。　situate 使……坐落於　lush 蒼翠繁茂的
getaway 旅遊的地方　stroll 散步　display 陳列，顯露　remarkable 非凡的，卓越的
reminiscent 使人憶起……的　porch 門廊　insight into 深刻的理解　restoration 修復
preserve 保留　stable 馬廄　ground 地面，土地

161

What is true of the inn?
(A) It displays modern architecture.
(B) **It is located in a rural area.**
(C) It is mainly for businesspeople.
(D) It offers a free lunch.

中譯 關於旅店，下列何者為真？
(A) 它展現出現代建築風格。
(B) 它位於鄉村地區。
(C) 它主要接商務客。
(D) 它供應免費午餐。

解析 文中提到：「Situated on a brilliant, lush green piece of land in the English countryside」，表示旅館位於鄉村地區，因此答案為 (B)。

字彙 rural 鄉村的，農村的

162

How are the guest rooms described?
(A) As cozy
(B) **As historical**
(C) As luxurious
(D) As spacious

中譯 如何形容客房？
(A) 舒適的
(B) 歷史的
(C) 豪華的
(D) 寬敞的

解析 第二段提到：「All rooms offer guests an insight into the inn's history, through careful restoration preserving the former charm.」，由此可以得知客房的特色為具有歷史意義。

字彙 cozy 舒適的，愜意的　luxurious 豪華的，奢侈的
spacious 寬敞的，無邊無際的

163

How long is the discount?
(A) A week
(B) Two weeks
(C) **Nearly a month**
(D) A month and a half

中譯 折扣期間有多久？
(A) 一個星期
(B) 二個星期
(C) 將近一個月
(D) 一個半月

解析 與優惠有關的內容出現在文章最後。當中提到：「We are offering the second night's stay at a 50-percent discount, if you book before the end of the month.」，此封電子郵件的寄件日為 10 月 3 日，只要在這個月底前預訂都能享有住宿第二晚半價優惠，表示優惠期間為期一個月左右。

Distracted Driving Policy at Breztel, Inc.

Please read the new Distracted Driving Policy, sign and return to your supervisor.

⓭ In order to increase employee safety and eliminate unnecessary risks behind the wheel, Breztel, Inc. has enacted a Distracted Driving Policy, effective September 1. —[1]—. We are committed to ending the epidemic of distracted driving, and have created the following rules, which apply to any employee operating a company vehicle or using a company-issued cellphone while operating a personal vehicle:

* Employees may not use a handheld cellphone while operating a vehicle—whether the vehicle is in motion or stopped at a traffic light. This includes, but is not limited to: answering or making phone calls; engaging in phone conversations; and/or reading or responding to e-mails, instant messages, and/or text messages. —[2]—.

* If employees need to use their phones, they must pull over safely to the side of the road or another safe location.

* Additionally, employees should:

(A) Turn cellphones off or put them on silent or vibrate mode before starting the car.

⓭ (B) Consider changing their voice mail greetings to indicate that they are unavailable to answer calls or return messages while driving.

(C) Inform clients, associates, and business partners of this policy as an explanation of why calls may not be returned immediately.

—[3]—. Any employee of Breztel, Inc. who is found to be out of compliance with the above regulations will first be given a written warning. —[4]—. ⓭ A second infraction will result in a mandatory unpaid leave of absence of one week. The third infraction will result in the employee being terminated from Breztel, Inc.

布里茲托公司分心駕駛政策

　　請詳讀新的分心駕駛政策，簽名後交回給你的主管。

　　⓭為了提升員工安全並消除駕駛時的非必要風險，布里茲托公司制定分心駕駛政策，9月1日生效。我們致力要消除氾濫的分心駕駛現象，並已制定下列規定，適用於任何一位駕駛公司車輛或在駕駛私人車輛時使用公司配發行動電話的員工：

* 員工在駕駛時不得使用手持行動電話——無論車輛是在行進中或是停在交通號誌前。這包含，但不限於：接聽或撥打電話；講電話；以及／或閱讀或回覆電子郵件、即時訊息，以及／或發送簡訊。

* 如果，員工需要使用行動電話，他們必須把車開到路邊或其他安全地點停妥。

* 此外，員工應該：

（A）在啟動汽車前將行動電話關閉或轉為靜音或震動模式。

⓭（B）考慮更改他們語音信箱的問候語，表明在開車時無法接聽電話或回覆簡訊。

（C）告知客戶、同事和商業夥伴這項政策，以解釋為什麼可能無法立即回電。

　　任何被發現未遵守上述規定的布里茲托員工，第一次會給予書面警告。⓭這次警告將紀錄到該員工的永久個人檔案中。⓭第二次違規將被強制休一星期的無薪假。第三次違規將導致該名員工被布里茲托公司免職。

字彙 distracted 分心的　eliminate 消除，排除　risk 風險，危險　enact 制定（法律）
be committed to 致力於　epidemic 流行，泛濫　operate 操作　handheld 手持的，手提式的
engage in 從事於，忙於　pull over 把……（車輛）開到路邊　vibrate mode 震動模式
compliance 服從，遵守　infraction 違法（行為）　terminate 解僱，終止

164

What is the purpose of the new policy?
(A) To follow regional laws
(B) **To prevent accidents**
(C) To teach good driving techniques
(D) To remind drivers to stay awake

中譯 新政策的目的是什麼？
(A) 為了遵守地方法律
(B) 為了避免事故
(C) 為了教導良好的駕駛技術
(D) 為了提醒駕駛人保持清醒

解析 本文為公司的駕駛政策公告。當中提到：「In order to increase employee safety and eliminate unnecessary risks behind the wheel」，由此可以得知此項政策的目的為預防駕駛時發生的事故。

字彙 purpose 目的　prevent 防止，預防

165

What is suggested regarding voice mail?
(A) It should be checked regularly.
(B) It should be turned off.
(C) It should state when the call will be returned.
(D) **It should state why calls are not being answered.**

中譯 關於語音信箱，文中建議什麼？
(A) 應該要經常檢查。
(B) 應該要關閉。
(C) 應該說明何時會回電話。
(D) 應該說明為什麼沒接電話。

解析 與語音留言有關的內容為：「Consider changing their voice mail greetings to indicate that they are unavailable to answer calls or return messages while driving.」，因此答案為 (D)，當中建議改用語音留言告知無法接電話的原因。

166

What would an employee receive who violated the company policy twice?
(A) A position change
(B) A warning letter
(C) Termination from the company
(D) **Suspension without pay**

中譯 違反公司政策二次的員工會得到什麼？
(A) 職位調動
(B) 警告信
(C) 被公司解僱
(D) 留職停薪

解析 與違反規定有關的內容出現在文章的最後，當中提到：「A second infraction will result in a mandatory unpaid leave of absence of one week.」，而選項將 a mandatory unpaid leave of absence 改寫成 suspension without pay。

字彙 violate 違反，違犯　termination 解僱，終止
suspension 停職，暫停

Actual Test 2

PART 7

In which of the positions marked [1], [2], [3] and [4] does the following sentence best belong?

"This warning will be added to the employee's permanent personnel file."

(A) [1]
(B) [2]
(C) [3]
(D) [4]

中譯 在標記 [1]、[2]、[3] 和 [4] 的地方，下列這句話最適合放在何處？「這次警告將紀錄到該員工的永久個人檔案中。」

(A) [1]　　　　　(B) [2]
(C) [3]　　　　　(D) [4]

解析 題目列出的句子中提到「This warning」，要找出其對應的內容。[4] 前方便提到 a written warning，表示違反規定的員工將會收到書面警告，後方接著表示警告將會添加至人事檔案中，較符合前後文意。

字彙 permanent 永久的

Questions 168-171 refer to the following letter. 信件

March 18

Dear Mr. Vaughn,

Thank you for taking the time to write of your unsatisfactory experience with our company and 168 **may I express my sincerest apologies about this matter**. —[1]—. It is of utmost importance to meet our customers' expectations and in the instance that we fail, provide resolutions.

Therefore, we will accept your request and 169 **offer a replacement sofa of the same product number and color free of charge**, which will be dispatched to you tomorrow morning. In light of the poor delivery service you received, we have conducted new training sessions for all drivers and I hope you recognize a difference tomorrow. —[2]—.

In addition, I would like to take this opportunity to offer you our personal services to show you we can do a much better job with our customer service. —[3]—. Please find enclosed a $50 voucher and my signed business card. If you decide to visit the store, 170 **please show the card to a staff member, who will personally assist you during your time there.**

Thank you once again for bringing to our attention that there appears to be discrepancies within the company. —[4]—. We hope you will trust us again and continue to be a satisfied customer in the coming years.

Yours Sincerely,
Arun Devdas
Manager, Customer Services

3 月 18 日

親愛的沃恩先生：

謝謝你花時間寫下對敝公司的不滿經驗，168 請容我對此事表達我衷心的歉意。滿足顧客的期望是我們最重要的事，而在我們無法做到時，則提供解決之道。

因此，我們接受你的要求，169 免費更換一組相同型號與顏色的沙發，貨品將在明天早上送去給你。有鑑於你之前遭受到的粗劣運送服務，我們已對所有司機進行新的訓練課程，我希望你明天能看出不同。

此外，我想藉此機會提供我們的私人服務給你，以向你表明我們的客服可以做得更好。請見隨信附上的 50 元優惠券和我簽名的名片。如果你決定到門市去，170 請將名片出示給店員看，他們會親自全程協助你。

再次謝謝你讓我們知道，公司內似乎有不一致之處。171 非常感謝能確保我們公司的成長以及未來的成功。我們希望你能再次信任我們，並在未來仍是滿意的客戶。

誠摯地，
阿倫・德夫達斯
客服部經理

字彙 sincere 衷心的，真誠的　utmost 最大的，極度的　meet 滿足，符合　expectation 期望，預期　instance 情況　resolution 解決　dispatch 發送，派遣　in light of 有鑑於，根據　enclosed 隨函附上的　voucher 現金券，優惠券　discrepancy 不一致，差異

Why did Mr. Devdas send the letter to Mr. Vaughn?
(A) **To convey his regret**
(B) To express his satisfaction
(C) To inform him about a company product
(D) To request new contact information

中譯 德夫達斯先生為什麼寄這封信給沃恩先生？
(A) 為了表達他的懊悔
(B) 為了表達他的滿意
(C) 為了告知他公司的一項產品
(D) 為了詢問新的聯絡資料

解析 本文為公司客服人員回應沙發配送客訴的道歉信。信件開頭提到：「express my sincerest apologies about this matter」，選項改寫成 convey his regret。

字彙 convey 表達，傳達　regret 懊悔，遺憾

169

What did Mr. Devdas promise to Mr. Vaughn?
(A) To conduct training sessions soon
(B) To offer free delivery on his next order
(C) **To provide a new sofa at no extra charge**
(D) To respect Mr. Vaughn's decision

中譯 德夫達斯先生給沃恩先生什麼承諾？
(A) 會很快進行訓練課程
(B) 他的下一筆訂單免運費
(C) 免費提供一組新沙發
(D) 尊重沃恩先生的決定

解析 第二段提到與配送有關的內容：「a replacement sofa of the same product number and color free of charge」，選項改寫成 provide a new sofa at no extra charge。

字彙 respect 尊重，尊敬

170

What will Mr. Vaughn receive by using the enclosed card?
(A) A free gift
(B) An extra discount
(C) An updated catalog
(D) **Special assistance**

中譯 沃恩先生使用隨信附上的名片會得到什麼？
(A) 一份免費禮物　　(B) 一次額外折扣
(C) 一份最新的型錄　(D) 特別協助

解析 店家出錯時，經常會提供顧客額外的服務。第三段提到將提供個人服務（offer you our personal services），同時送上五十元的優惠券和名片，而後又提到：「show the card to a staff member, who will personally assist you during your time there」，表示沃恩先生能獲得「特別服務（special assistance）」

字彙 assistance 援助，幫助

---

171 新增題型

In which of the positions marked [1], [2], [3], and [4] does the following sentence best belong?
"It is highly appreciated in ensuring growth and the future success of our business."
(A) [1]
(B) [2]
(C) [3]
(D) **[4]**

中譯 在標記 [1]、[2]、[3] 和 [4] 的地方，下列這句話最適合放在何處？「非常感謝能確保我們公司的成長以及未來的成功。」
(A) [1]　　　　　　(B) [2]
(C) [3]　　　　　　(D) [4]

解析 [1] 位在第一段向對方致歉的段落中；[2] 位在第二段表示要賠償對方的段落中；[3] 位在提供額外服務的段落中；[4] 位在最後一段感謝顧客批評與指教的段落中。而題目列出的句子表示「非常感謝能確保我們公司的成長以及未來的成功」，較符合最後一段的主題，故該句話置於 [4] 最為適當。

字彙 appreciate 感謝

Questions 172-175 refer to the following online discussion. 線上討論 新增題型

Ken Brown 13:02	**肯‧布朗** 13:02
Hello to both of you! Have you finished the orders yet?	哈囉，二位好！你們完成訂單了嗎？
Jack Taylor 13:12	**傑克‧泰勒** 13:12
Afternoon Ken. Not yet. It's taken longer than anticipated due to the unexpected fire drill.	午安，肯。還沒有。由於意料之外的消防演習，出貨時間比預期的要久。
Ken Brown 13:14	**肯‧布朗** 13:14
Yes, that was unusual. Where are you up to?	是啊，那很罕見。你們進行到哪裡了？
Jack Taylor 13:15	**傑克‧泰勒** 13:15
We were halfway through today's orders when the system shut down. ⑰ Levi is back down in the stockroom, preparing boxes for the last half of orders.	當系統關閉時，我們正處理完今天一半的訂單。⑰ 列維回去倉庫，準備箱子裝剩下一半的貨。
Ken Brown 13:15	**肯‧布朗** 13:15
OK. Have you remembered the orders in the black book?	好。你們記得黑色本子裡記的訂單吧？
Jack Taylor 13:16	**傑克‧泰勒** 13:16
Oh, ⑰ I totally blanked on those! I'll call down to Levi and get him to pick it up on his way back to the office.	噢，⑰ 我完全忘了那些！我會打電話下去給列維，叫他回辦公室時順路去拿。
Ken Brown 13:17	**肯‧布朗** 13:17
⑰ It's OK, I'm on my way back to the office from the shop floor. I'll grab it.	⑰ 沒關係，我正要從店裡回辦公室。我會去拿。
Levi O'Conner 13:25	**列維‧歐康納** 13:25
Hi Ken, just checking in. The stockroom is a real mess. It'll take me a while to straighten things out.	嗨，肯，只是打個招呼。倉庫真是一團亂，我得花一些時間才能把東西整理好。
Ken Brown 13:27	**肯‧布朗** 13:27
No worries Levi. Just do as best you can and get back to the office as soon as possible. We need to get the order finished by 15:00 today.	別擔心，列維。就盡你所能，然後盡快回辦公室。我們必須在今天 15:00 前把訂單處理完畢。
Levi O'Conner 13:28	**列維‧歐康納** 13:28
Thanks Ken! If you have anyone to spare, I could use some help down here.	謝啦，肯！如果，你還有人手，我這裡需要人幫忙。
Jack Taylor 13:30	**傑克‧泰勒** 13:30
⑰ I've just asked Bruce to leave the shop floor. He's on his way to give you a hand.	⑰ 我剛剛叫布魯斯離開店裡。他已經過去幫你了。
Levi O'Conner 13:31	**列維‧歐康納** 13:31
Good news. Thanks	好消息。謝啦。

字彙 anticipate 預期，預料　fire drill 消防演習　shut down 關閉　stockroom 倉庫，儲藏室
blank 一時忘記　shop floor 店鋪銷售區

172

What are they mostly discussing?
(A) A fire drill
(B) A merchandise recall
(C) A new customer
(D) **Order processing**

中譯 他們主要在討論什麼？
(A) 一次消防演習
(B) 一次產品召回
(C) 一位新顧客
(D) 訂單處理流程

解析 本文為工作上的對話，因預料之外的消防演習，導致訂單處理延誤。

字彙 processing 過程，步驟

173 新增題型

At 13:16, what does Mr. Taylor mean when he writes, "I totally blanked on those!"?
(A) He cannot see well.
(B) **He forgot all about something.**
(C) He has a lot of free time.
(D) He is not ready to start working again.

中譯 在 13:16 時，當泰勒先生寫道：「我完全忘了那些！」，他的意思是什麼？
(A) 他看不清楚。
(B) 他完全忘記某件事。
(C) 他很有空。
(D) 他還沒準備好再開始工作。

解析 blank 的意思為「沒有想法、一片空白」。13 點 16 分的訊息中提到：「I totally blanked on those!」，回答前方布朗先生的提問：「Have you remembered the orders in the black book?」，表示完全忘記這件事，而選項改寫成 forgot all about something，因此答案為 (B)。

174

Who will pick up the black book?
(A) **Mr. Brown**
(B) Mr. O'Conner
(C) Mr. Taylor
(D) Mr. Taylor's assistant

中譯 誰會去拿黑色本子？
(A) 布朗先生
(B) 歐康納先生
(C) 泰勒先生
(D) 泰勒先生的助理

解析 布朗先生在 13 點 17 分的訊息中提到：「I'm on my way back to the office from the shop floor. I'll grab it」，因此答案為 (A)，本來是由泰勒先生去拿，但他忘了這件事。

175

Where will Bruce go?
(A) To the entrance
(B) To the office
(C) To the shop
(D) **To the stockroom**

中譯 布魯斯會去哪裡？
(A) 去門口
(B) 去辦公室
(C) 去店裡
(D) 去倉庫

解析 泰勒先生在 13 點 30 分的訊息中提到：「I've just asked Bruce to leave the shop floor. He's on his way to give you a hand.」，當中提到布魯斯這個名字，而 you 根據 13 點 28 分的訊息，指的是列維·歐康納。根據泰勒先生在 13 點 15 分傳送的訊息，當中提到他人在倉庫，因此布魯斯要前往的地方為倉庫。

字彙 entrance 入口，門口，進入

E-Street Model X

There had been so many leaks about the new electric car from Matcha Motors, I was expecting to see no surprises at the unveiling this weekend. Was I ever wrong! Once I peeked inside the new model, I realized that this vehicle is a game-changer. Like the Model B, it has no instrument panels in front of either the driver or passenger. Instead, you control the car from a computer monitor mounted in the center. ⑯ This makes sense for Matcha since it saves costly changes when shipping to either left-driving or right-driving countries. The technology is also a sight to see. From battery charge gauges to entertainment to climate control, the monitor in the Model X is simple and intuitive to use.

What's truly unbelievable about this model, though, is the price. Starting at just under $40,000, this is an e-car for the ⑱ masses. Of course, ⑰ to get the dual motor, you have to pay about $10,000 more, but it's worth it for those who like speed and longer distance driving on one charge.

Speaking of charge, Matcha Motors CEO promises 300 more charging stations across the country before the Model X ships. Yes, you'll have to wait two and a half more years for your Model X, but pre-orders are being taken on their Website, www.matchamotors.com. Just to reserve a car, you'll need to commit at least $4,000 depending on the extras you want. ⑰ As for this reviewer, I'm hooked. I'm counting down the days until delivery . . .

—Shaun Hansen

To: Shaun Hansen <shaunh@wheels.com>
From: Olga Malayov <omalayov@matchamotors.com>
Subject: Review of the Model X

Dear Mr. Hansen,

Thank you for your glowing review of our latest model. We are sure you won't be disappointed once you are sitting behind the wheel of your new E-Street car. I had a few more pieces of information about the car I thought you might like to pass along to your readers.

Firstly, I'm sorry to say that there was a mistake in the press packet we handed out at the event you attended. ⑱ The pricing for the second motor is about $2,000 less than you mentioned in your review.

E-Street X 型車

　　關於馬查汽車的新款電動車已經有好多小道消息流出，我原本預期這個週末的發表會不會看到什麼驚喜，我可錯了！當我瞥見新車裡面，我就知道這輛車會顛覆傳統。就像 B 型車一樣，它無論是駕駛座還是副駕座前都沒有儀表板。取而代之的是，你從一個架在中間的電腦螢幕上控制汽車。⑯這對馬查來說很合理，因為不管是把車運送到左駕或右駕的國家，它都可以省下改裝的大筆費用。科技的部分也很值得一看。從電池充電表、娛樂功能到恆溫控制，X 型車的螢幕都很簡單且可憑直覺使用。

　　但是，這款車真正令人不可思議的地方是價錢。起跳價格不到 4 萬元，這是一輛給⑱大眾使用的電動車。當然，⑰想要雙馬達的話，你得多付大約一萬元，但對那些喜歡速度和充一次電就能跑較長距離的人來說很值得。

　　說到充電，馬查汽車執行長保證在 X 型車出貨前，全國會有超過 300 個充電站。是的，你必須再等 2 年半才能拿到你的 X 型車，但他們的網站上正進行預訂：www.matchamotors.com。只是要預訂一輛車，你就必須繳至少 4 千元，看你想要的附加配備而定。⑰作為撰寫此評論的人，我已經迷上它了。我正在倒數離出貨還有幾天……

——尚恩·韓森

收件者：尚恩·韓森 <shaunh@wheels.com>
寄件者：歐嘉·瑪拉約夫
　　　　<omalayov@matchamotors.com>
主旨：X 型車評

親愛的韓森先生：

　　謝謝你對我們最新款車讚譽有加的評論。我們相信，等你坐在你的新 E-Street 車的方向盤後時，你不會失望的。我這裡還有幾個關於這輛車的資訊，我想你可能想傳遞給你的讀者。

　　首先，我很抱歉地說，在你參加的那場活動上，我們分送的新聞資料袋裡有錯。⑱第二個馬達的價格大約比你在評論所說的少 2 千元。這讓 X 型車對消費者更有吸引力了。

This makes the Model X even more attractive to consumers.

⑰⑨ Secondly, we have upped our production targets and now expect drivers to take delivery of the Model X six months earlier than previously stated. By the end of next year, Matcha Motors will be manufacturing more vehicles than the country's top three automakers combined.

Lastly, we have had to start a waiting list for the Model X since the pre-orders exceeded even our high expectations. However, we do hope that because of our heightened production goals, we will be able to serve all consumers who want a Model X within the next three years.

Sincerely,
Olga Malayov

⑰⑨ 第二，我們提高了我們的生產目標，駕駛人現在預期收到 X 型的時間會比之前所說的早六個月。明年底之前，馬查汽車所製造的汽車將比全國前三名的汽車製造商加起來的還多。

最後，我們已經開啟候補名單，因為預訂的數量甚至超過我們預期的高標。然而，我們真的希望，由於我們拉高了生產目標，我們能在未來三年內供應所有想要 X 型的消費者。

誠摯地，
歐嘉・瑪拉約夫

PART 7

字彙 leak（祕密等的）洩漏　unveiling 揭幕　peek 窺視，偷看
game-changer 改變形勢（或商業領域）的產品（或事件）　instrument panel 儀表板　mount 固定
intuitive 直覺的　commit 投入（時間或金錢）　hooked 入迷的，上癮的　glowing 熱烈讚揚的
pass along to 傳遞給　press packet 新聞資料袋　exceed 超過，超出

176

According to the review, on what feature does Matcha Motors save money?
(A) The batteries
(B) The control panels
(C) The motors
(D) The seats

中譯 根據評論，馬查汽車在什麼功能上省了錢？
(A) 電池
(B) 控制面板
(C) 馬達
(D) 座位

解析 本文為針對新電動車的評論。與節省費用有關的內容出現在第一段：「**This makes sense for Matcha since it saves costly ...**」。其前方提到以電腦螢幕取代儀表板，無論是左駕或右駕國家都適用，能省下改裝費用。**(B)** 將文中的 instrument panels 改寫成 control panels，故為正確答案。

177

Who most likely is Mr. Hansen?
(A) A Matcha Motors spokesperson
(B) A journalist
(C) A technology expert
(D) An advertising specialist

中譯 韓森先生最可能是誰？
(A) 馬查汽車的發言人
(B) 記者
(C) 技術專家
(D) 廣告專家

解析 韓森先生為撰寫評論的人。選項中與 reviewer 最有關聯的職業為 **(B)**。

字彙 journalist 記者

178

What does the extra motor on the
Model X cost?
(A) $2,000
(B) $8,000
(C) $10,000
(D) $40,000

中譯 在 X 型車上多裝一個馬達要多少錢？
(A) 2,000 元   (B) 8,000 元
(C) 10,000 元   (D) 40,000 元

解析 與價格有關的內容出現在評論中段處，以及電子郵件的第二段。評論中提到：「**to get the dual motor, you have to pay about $10,000 more**」，但電子郵件中發出了更正的說明：「**The pricing for the second motor is about $2,000 less than you mentioned in your review.**」，因此答案為一萬元減去兩千元，等於八千元。

179

What does Ms. Malayov mention
about production?
(A) It has been delayed.
(B) It has been sped up.
(C) It is being done overseas.
(D) It is being restructured.

中譯 關於生產，瑪拉約夫女士提到什麼？
(A) 已經落後了。   (B) 已經加快了。
(C) 正在海外進行。   (D) 正在重建。

解析 請從電子郵件中確認瑪拉約夫小姐提及的內容。與生產有關的內容出現在第三段當中：「**Secondly, we have upped our production targets and now expect drivers to take delivery of the Model X six months earlier than previously stated.**」，表示生產速度有加快，因此答案為 **(B)**。

字彙 speed up（使……）加速   restructure 重建

180

In the review, the word "masses" in
paragraph 2, line 2, is closest in
meaning to
(A) public
(B) quantity
(C) variety
(D) wealth

中譯 在評論中，第二段第二行的「masses」一字，意義最接近下列何者？
(A) 大眾   (B) 數量
(C) 多樣化   (D) 財富

解析 **this is an e-car for the masses** 前方提到車子的價格便宜到令人難以置信，只要四萬元以下就可入手，因此適合解釋成此款電動車是為「大眾」所設計的車款。選項中，單字 **public** 的意思為「大眾」。

字彙 variety 多樣化，變化

Questions 181-185 refer to the following e-mail and information. [電子郵件] [資訊]

To:	info@yoganation.com
From:	Evel Hun <e-hun@foro.com>
Subject:	Package deals
Date:	Sunday, June 30

Dear Sir/Madam,

I came across a copy of a pamphlet describing your
package deals at the local gym and wonder if you
could answer some questions.

I would like to get back into yoga and ⑱ **am interested in
joining your group as often as possible.** I noticed the

收件者：info@yoganation.com
寄件者：伊佛・漢 <e-hun@foro.com>
主旨：套裝優惠
日期：6 月 30 日 星期日

敬啟者：

    我在本地一家健身房偶然拿到一份說明你們套裝優惠課程的小冊子，不知道你能否回答幾個問題。

    我想要重新上瑜珈課，⑱ 想要盡可能常去上你們的課。我注意到 BAI 套裝課程

BAI package allows me to practice whenever there is a class available. Could you tell me ⑱ **if you offer mature students a discount**?

I picked up this flyer today but seeing as it's a weekend, you will not see my e-mail until Monday — by which time it'll be July 1. ⑱ **Would I still be entitled to a reduction in sign-up costs?**

⑱ **My friend and I are not sure which day is better to attempt the trial lesson. Could you make any suggestions?**

I look forward to hearing from you.

Kind regards,
Evel Hun

可以只要有課就去上。你可以告訴我，⑱ 你們是否提供成年學員折扣優惠？

我今天才拿到這份廣告，但由於是週末，你們要到星期一才會看到我的電子郵件，到那時候就已經是 7 月 1 日了。⑱ 我還有權享有報名費的減價優惠嗎？

⑱ 我朋友和我不確定要選哪一天去試上課程比較好。你可以給我們建議嗎？

期待收到你的回覆。

祝安好，
伊佛・漢

YogaNation

Please check out our monthly deals below if you're interested in becoming a permanent member of YogaNation.

PACKAGES	DETAILS	FEES (extra classes)
⑱ BAI	Attend however much you like	$400/month
PUR	Attend up to twelve classes a month	$360/month (⑱ $30/class)
GAR	Attend up to six classes a month	$210/month ($35/class)
CHA	A 'pay-as-you-go' system	⑱ $40/class

⑱ **A membership fee of $200 for the year is charged as a one-time fee when initially purchasing packages.**

Receive a 20-percent discount on membership with this pamphlet.

Valid until June 30.

瑜珈國

如果，你有興趣成為瑜珈國的永久會員，請查看我們下列的每月優惠。

套裝課程	內容	費用（外加課程）
⑱ BAI	想上幾堂就上幾堂	$400 ／月
PUR	每月最多 12 堂	$360 ／月 （⑱ $30 ／堂）
GAR	每月最多 6 堂	$210 ／月 （$35 ／堂）
CHA	預付制	⑱ $40 ／堂

⑱ 會員年費 $200 在最初購買套裝課程時收取一次。
出示本傳單會費打 8 折。
優惠到 6 月 30 日止。

字彙 come across 偶然碰見（發現） describe 形容，敘述 mature student 成年學生
be entitled to 有權利，有資格 reduction 減少，降低 charge 索價，收費 initially 最初

181

What is the main purpose of the e-mail?
(A) To check if a price cut would be offered
(B) To inform the instructor of her attendance to regular classes
(C) To make the instructor aware of her interest
(D) To suggest starting a mature students' class

中譯 這封電子郵件的主要目的是什麼？
(A) 為了確認是否可以有減價優惠
(B) 為了通知教練她要上固定課程
(C) 為了讓教練注意到她的興趣
(D) 為了建議開一班給成年學生的課

解析 本文為針對瑜伽課程提問的電子郵件，主要在詢問是否有提供成人學生優惠。

字彙 price cut 減價，降價

182

What should YogaNation do for Ms. Hun?
(A) Explain the deals in a more detailed way
(B) Recommend a good gym
(C) Respond with information about dates
(D) Sign her and her friend up for a trial lesson

中譯 瑜珈國應該為漢女士做什麼？
(A) 把優惠內容解釋得更詳細
(B) 建議一家好的健身房
(C) 回覆關於日期的資訊
(D) 為她和她朋友報名體驗課程

解析 漢女士透過電子郵件詢問是否有優惠，以及請對方建議哪一天可以參加體驗課程。由此可以得知瑜伽國要回覆漢女士日期的資訊。

183

Which package offers cheaper extra classes?
(A) BAI
(B) PUR
(C) GAR
(D) CHA

中譯 哪個套裝課程所涵蓋的外加課程較便宜？
(A) BAI
(B) PUR
(C) GAR
(D) CHA

解析 根據課程資訊，括號內為額外課程的價格，當中最便宜的為價格三十元的 PUR 課程。

184

Who would pay $40 for a class?
(A) BAI members
(B) PUR members
(C) GAR members
(D) CHA members

中譯 誰會付 40 元一堂的課？
(A) BAI 學員   (B) PUR 學員
(C) GAR 學員   (D) CHA 學員

解析 根據課程資訊，單堂課四十元的課程為 CHA 課程。

185

How much at most would Ms. Hun pay to become a member?
(A) $200
(B) $400
(C) $560
(D) $600

中譯 漢女士最多有可能要花多少錢成為會員？
(A) 200 元   (B) 400 元
(C) 560 元   (D) 600 元

解析 漢女士在電子郵件中提到她想要盡可能多上一點課。課程資訊中，BAI 課程寫到能隨心所欲參加課程，而 BAI 課程的報名費為 400 元。另外，課程資訊最後提到一年的會費為 200 元，因此漢女士最多得支付 600 元。

Redlands Community Center announces NEW adult classes for the winter

* Come join your friends and neighbors in interesting classes
* Learn a new skill or revive an old interest
186 * All classes are taught by local experts in their fields
* Choose from among the following classes:

- Outdoor Photography for Any Season
- French Cooking
- Growing Your Own Herbs
- Sketching and Drawing
- Introduction to Pilates
- Creative Writing
- Computer Basics
- Investing for Beginners

These and many others are listed on our Website: www.redlandscommctr.com. 186 You can also fill out our online registration form and pay via credit card on the site. For questions, contact Jolene at joleneb@redlandscommctr.com. We look forward to seeing you in class!

紅土社區活動中心宣布冬季新成人課程

* 來和你的朋友及鄰居一起上有趣的課程
* 學一項新的技能或重溫舊有的興趣
188 * 所有課程都由各自領域的本地專家教授
* 有下列課程可選：

- 任一季戶外攝影
- 法式料理
- 自己種香草
- 素描與繪畫
- 皮拉提斯入門
- 創意寫作
- 電腦基礎
- 新手投資

這些課程以及許多其他課程列在我們的網站上：www.redlandscommctr.com。186 你也可以填寫線上註冊表，並在網站上刷卡繳費。如有疑問，請聯絡裘琳：joleneb@redlandscommctr.com。我們期待在課堂上見到你！

REGISTRATION FORM
Redlands Community Center Adult Learning

Name: Whitney Burke **Age:** 43
Address: 46 Wilderest Lane, Redlands

◊ Have you ever taken a Redlands Community Center class before? NO

◊ How did you hear about the classes? 187 My friend told me about them after taking a class.

Class ID	Class name	Teacher
RAD 105	188 Growing Your Own Herbs	Ralph Munez
RAD 148	Investing for Beginners	Jennifer Cho
RAD 197	Computer Basics	Neil Jackson
189 RAD 239	Advanced Photography	Suzanne Olsen

註冊表
紅土社區活動中心成人學習

姓名：惠特妮・柏克 年齡：43
地址：紅土懷爾德雷斯特路 46 號

- 你之前曾上過紅土社區活動中心的課嗎？ 沒有
- 你如何得知這些課程？187 我朋友來上過課後告訴我的。

課程編號	課程名稱	教師
RAD 105	188 自己種香草	拉斐爾・穆內
RAD 148	新手投資	珍妮佛・趙
RAD 197	電腦基礎	尼爾・傑克生
189 RAD 239	進階攝影	蘇珊・歐森

To:	wburke@firemail.com
From:	frankdodds@redlandscommctr.com
Subject:	October 28
Date:	Your registration for the Redlands classes

Dear Ms. Burke,

Thank you for registering for the Redlands Community Center classes. We were able to fit you into all classes except one. ⑱ **Unfortunately, Suzanne Olsen is unable to teach her class this winter. ⑲ She has to relocate suddenly due to her husband's job.** We are sorry for the inconvenience. We hope to offer this same class with a new instructor in the spring.

Also, since you mentioned in your application that you have a friend who has taken classes with us, I wanted to let you know about our referral discount. If you refer anybody to our classes, you both get 5 percent off the cost of all the classes for that term. Let us know your friend's name so we can offer him or her the discount.

Thanks again for registering. See you soon.

Frank Dodds

收件者：wburke@firemail.com
寄件者：frankdodds@redlandscommctr.com
日期：10 月 28 日
主旨：你所註冊的紅土課程

親愛的柏克女士：

　　謝謝妳註冊紅土社區活動中心的課程。我們可以安排妳上所有的課程，除了一門以外。⑱ 很不巧，蘇珊·歐森今年冬天無法教課。⑲ 由於她先生的工作之故，她忽然必須搬家。很抱歉造成不便。我們希望春天時，能有新老師開設相同的課程。

　　還有，因為妳在註冊時提到妳有朋友來上我們的課程，我想告訴妳，我們有推薦折扣優惠。如果妳推薦任何人來上我們的課，你們二人那一期的所有課程都打 95 折。請告知我們妳朋友的名字，好讓我們可以給他折扣。

　　再次謝謝妳註冊。稍後見。

法蘭克·達茲

字彙 revive （使……）復原，（使……）甦醒　relocate （使……）搬遷，重新安置　inconvenience 不便，麻煩
referral discount 推薦的折扣

186

How can neighbors sign up for the classes?
(A) By visiting the center
(B) By completing a form
(C) By paying in advance
(D) By contacting staff

中譯 街坊鄰居要如何報名課程？
(A) 造訪中心　　　(B) 完成表格
(C) 預先付費　　　(D) 聯絡員工

解析 三篇文章分別為社區中心的課程介紹、柏克小姐的報名表以及社區中心回覆給柏克小姐的電子郵件。課程介紹最後有提到課程的報名方式：「fill out our online registration form」，選項改寫成 completing a form，因此答案為 (B)。

187

How did Ms. Burke find out about the courses?
(A) From a referral
(B) From a TV ad
(C) From the Internet
(D) From the notice

中譯 柏克女士如何發現這些課程？
(A) 有人推薦
(B) 從電視廣告
(C) 從網際網路
(D) 從公告

解析 柏克小姐的報名表中，其中一項問題為：「How did you hear about the classes?」，後方寫道：「My friend told me about them after taking a class.」，由此可以得知柏克小姐是透過朋友介紹才知道這門課程。

188

What can be said about Mr. Munez?
(A) He has taught the same course for many years.
(B) He is a local herb specialist.
(C) He is taking the same courses as Ms. Burke.
(D) He is moving out of the area.

中譯 關於穆內先生，可由文中得知什麼？
(A) 他同樣一門課教了很多年。
(B) 他是本地的香草專家。
(C) 他和柏克女士選一樣的課程。
(D) 他要搬到別的地方。

解析 介紹文寫道：「All classes are taught by local experts in their fields」，在報名表中，穆內先生負責的課程為「Growing Your Own Herbs」，表示他是 a local herb specialist。

Which class has an issue in the winter?
(A) RAD 105
(B) RAD 148
(C) RAD 197
(D) RAD 239

中譯 哪一門課這個冬天有問題？
(A) RAD 105　　　(B) RAD 148
(C) RAD 197　　　(D) RAD 239

解析 電子郵件提到了某課程的問題，當中提到柏克小姐所報名的課程中，蘇珊・歐森老師的課程無法順利開課，蘇珊・歐森老師的課程編號為 RAD 239。

Why is one course unavailable?
(A) It is only offered in the spring.
(B) It was mistakenly added to the course list.
(C) The instructor is ill.
(D) The instructor is moving.

中譯 為什麼有一門課無法開班？
(A) 它只有春天才開班。
(B) 它被誤加到課程名單裡。
(C) 老師生病了。
(D) 老師要搬家。

解析 蘇珊・歐森老師的課程無法開課，其後方便提到無法開課的原因為：「She has to relocate suddenly due to her husband's job.」，選項將 relocate 改寫成 moving，因此答案為 (D)。

字彙 mistakenly 錯誤地　add 增加　ill 生病的，不舒服的

Questions 191-195 refer to the following e-mails and coupon. 電子郵件 折價券 新增題型

To:	Customer Service <cs@steelworks.com>
From:	Brian W <brianw@pershing.com>
Subject:	My trusty iron
Date:	November 29

To whom it may concern,

I have used my Press-on 400 iron for about six years and been quite satisfied with this reliable item. ⑲ Recently, I had a problem that the temperature didn't rise. I checked the cord and there didn't seem to be any problem. I also cleaned off the surface, but it didn't change. I don't want to give up on this great iron, so I am wondering if it would be possible to have it repaired. ⑭ Please let me know if there is a repair shop nearby in the

收件者：客戶服務 <cs@steelworks.com>
寄件者：布萊恩・W<brianw@pershing.com>
主旨：我可靠的熨斗
日期：11 月 29 日

敬啟者：

　　我的 Press-on 400 熨斗已經用了大約六年，我一直很滿意這個可靠的產品。⑲ 最近，我遇到溫度不會上升的問題。我檢查了電源線，看起來似乎沒有任何問題。我也清了表面，但情況沒變。我不想放棄這個很棒的熨斗，因此，我在想不知道它是否能修。⑭ 請告知在格蘭戴爾威利地區附近是否有維修站。如果沒有，要是你們能告訴我要寄到哪裡去，我

Glendale Valley area. If not, I am willing to mail it outside of my immediate area if you'd let me know where to send it.

Thank you in advance for your help.

Brian Wilcox

很樂意把它寄到我現住地區以外的地方。

先謝謝你的協助。

布萊恩・威爾考克斯

To:	Brian W <brianw@pershing.com>
From:	Customer Service <cs@steelworks.com>
Subject:	Re: My trusty iron
Date:	(191) November 30

Dear Mr. Wilcox,

(192) **We are sorry to inform you that the Press-on 400 was discontinued about two years ago. We** are unable to offer repair service on that model, but we value your loyalty and would like to retain you as a customer. To that end, I have enclosed a coupon for $30 off our newest model, the PressMagic 500, which has all the features of your iron, plus more. Our improved steaming features will reduce even difficult wrinkles. (193) **Additionally, the PressMagic can handle heavier fabrics than our previous models.** We hope you will take advantage of our offer at any of the retail locations listed on the certificate.

We appreciate your business.

Jane Carver
Customer Relations
Steel Works

收件者：布萊恩・W<brianw@pershing.com>
寄件者：客戶服務 <cs@steelworks.com>
主旨：關於：我可靠的熨斗
日期：(191) 11 月 30 日

親愛的威爾考克斯先生：

(192) 我們很遺憾通知你，Press-on 400 大約二年前已停產。我們無法提供該型號的維修，但我們很珍視你的產品忠誠度，想要留住你這個顧客。因此，我隨信附上我們最新款 PressMagic 500 的 30 元折價券，你的熨斗有的功能它都有，還有更多新功能。我們的改良蒸氣功能，就連最難消除的皺紋也能熨平。(193) 此外，PressMagic 可以處理比前幾代產品更厚重的布料。我們希望你會把我們的優惠用於列在折價券上的零售店裡。

我們感謝你的惠顧。

珍・卡佛
客戶關係
鋼鐵作業

STEEL WORKS

Present this certificate at any of the following retail outlets for $30 off any Steel Works product.

B's Home Store	Appliances and More	(194) Home Super Store	Johnson Goods
25081 Highway 53 Rosedale, UT	85 South Mall Drive Carsonville, NY	5903 E. Styx Way Glendale Valley, UT	898 Beverly St. Tatterville, NV

*This coupon is not valid in combination with any other promotion.

*This coupon may not be redeemed for cash.

(195) *This coupon must be used on or before December 31.

鋼鐵作業

在下列任何零售店出示這張優惠券，任何鋼鐵作業的產品折價 30 元。

B 氏家用品店	不止有家電	(194) 家居超級商店	強生用品店
猶他州羅斯戴爾 53 號公路 25081 號	紐約州卡森維爾南摩爾路 85 號	猶他州格蘭戴爾威利東史戴克斯路 5903 號	內華達州塔特維爾比佛利街 898 號

* 本優惠券不得與其他任何促銷合併使用。
* 本優惠券不得兌換現金。
(195) * 本優惠券需在 12 月 31 日（含）之前使用。

字彙 reliable 可靠的，可信賴的　surface 表面　be willing to 願意，樂意　immediate 目前的
discontinue 停止，中止　retain 留住，保持　to that end 為了那個目的　enclose 隨信（或包裹）附上
certificate 憑證　in combination with 與……結合　redeem 將優惠券等兌換成現金（或物品）

191

What is wrong with Mr. Wilcox's product?
(A) The control button is broken.
(B) The cord is split.
(C) The heating element is broken.
(D) The steam function does not work.

中譯 威爾考克斯先生的用品有什麼問題？
(A) 控制鈕故障。
(B) 電源線裂開。
(C) 加熱元件故障。
(D) 蒸氣功能故障。

解析 第一篇文章為因熨斗壞掉，而向公司詢問如何修理的電子郵件。當中提到熨斗的問題為：「I had a problem that the temperature didn't rise」，選項將此段話改寫成「The heating element is broken.」。

字彙 split 裂開，破裂　heating element 加熱元件

192

Why can't Ms. Carver grant Mr. Wilcox's request?
(A) He does not have an extended warranty.
(B) He lives outside the store's range.
(C) His product has been recalled.
(D) His product is not being made anymore.

中譯 卡佛女士為什麼無法答應威爾考克斯先生的要求？
(A) 他沒有延長保固。
(B) 他住在商店服務範圍之外。
(C) 他的產品已被召回。
(D) 他的產品已停產。

解析 第二篇文章為針對第一封電子郵件的回信。信中提到由於威爾考克斯先生入手的產品早已停產（discontinued），因此無法接受他的維修要求。(D) 表示該產品已經不再生產，故為正確答案。

字彙 grant 同意，准予　warranty （商品的）保固卡　recall 召回

193

What is mentioned about the PressMagic 500?
(A) It has a better design.
(B) It has a higher heat range.
(C) It is more reliable.
(D) It works on thick clothes.

中譯 關於 PressMagic 500，文中提到什麼？
(A) 它的設計較好。
(B) 它的熱度範圍較大。
(C) 它較可靠。
(D) 它可以用在厚重的衣服上。

解析 取代 Press-on 400 的最新機型為 PressMagic 500，第二封電子郵件中提到該機型的功能升級，能夠熨燙更厚的布料。選項將 handle heavier fabrics 改寫成 works on thick clothes，因此答案為 (D)。

字彙 thick 厚的

194

Where most likely would Mr. Wilcox use the coupon?
(A) At Appliances and More
(B) At B's Home Store
(C) At Home Super Store
(D) At Johnson Goods

中譯 威爾考克斯先生最可能在哪裡使用折價券？
(A) 不只有家電
(B) B 氏家用品店
(C) 家居超級商店
(D) 強生用品店

解析 第一封電子郵件中段提到：「Please let me know if there is a repair shop nearby in the Glendale Valley area.」，由此可以推測威爾考克斯先生應該住在格蘭戴爾威利附近。而根據優惠券中列出的店家名單，位在格蘭戴爾威利的店家為「家居超級商店」。

195

How long can Mr. Wilcox use the coupon?
(A) For about one week
(B) For about two weeks
(C) For about one month
(D) For about one year

中譯 威爾考克斯先生使用折價券的期限有多久？
(A) 大約一星期
(B) 大約二星期
(C) 大約一個月
(D) 大約一年

解析 優惠券中寫道：「This coupon must be used on or before December 31.」，而威爾考克斯先生收到電子郵件的日期為 11 月 30 日，表示優惠券的效期為一個月左右。

Questions 196-200 refer to the following advertisement, order form, and e-mail.

廣告 訂單表格 電子郵件 新增題型

Three Brothers Catering
No job too small or too large — we aim to please!

196 Three Brothers Catering has been in business for over a decade and has pleased hundreds of hungry customers over the years. We can provide lunch or dinner for your corporate events, community organization or private party. No matter how many you're expecting, we have something sure to please everyone. 200 Until the end of the month, first-time customers get free delivery on office lunches! Take a look at our menu (full color pictures!) online at www.3broscatering.com. If you like what you see, give us a call at 555-8139.

Three Brothers Catering

三兄弟外燴
沒有什麼工作會太輕鬆或太困難——我們的目標是讓人滿意！

196三兄弟外燴已營運超過 10 年，在這些年裡，讓許多飢餓的顧客得到滿足。我們可以為你的企業活動、社區組織或私人派對提供午餐或晚餐。不管你期待有多少量，我們一定能端出讓大家都滿意的東西。200在這個月底前，新客戶的公司午餐外送免運費！請看我們在 www.3broscatering.com 上的菜單（全彩照片！）如果，你喜歡你所看到的，請撥打電話 555-8139。

三兄弟外燴

Three Brothers Catering

8391 Castle View Drive
Los Animas, NM

Customer Name: <u>Leslie Jones</u>
Date: <u>November 7</u>   Venue: <u>Jones and Co.</u>

Order	Qty.	Unit Price	Total
Variety of sandwiches	12	3.95	47.40
⑲ Green side salad	5	3.50	17.50
Variety of bottled drinks	12	1.00	12.00
Appetizer tray	1	12.00	12.00

三兄弟外燴

新墨西哥州洛杉尼馬堡景道 8391 號

顧客姓名：<u>萊思莉·瓊斯</u>
日期：<u>11/7</u>   地點：<u>瓊斯公司</u>

貨品	數量	單價	小計
綜合三明治	12	3.95	47.40
⑲ 綠色配菜沙拉	5	3.50	17.50
綜合瓶裝飲料	12	1.00	12.00
開胃菜拼盤	1	12.00	12.00

To: rep@3broscatering.com
From: ljones@jonesnco.com
Subject: Changes to my order
Date: November 5

Hi Joseph,

I hope it's not too late to make a few changes to my order for the day after tomorrow. ⑲⑲ **I just got word that three people from our branch in Youngston will be joining us at our meeting.** They won't be having lunch with us, but I will need beverages for them. So, that brings up the number to 15.

I also had a change in the salads. ⑲ **One person said he doesn't want a salad.** Otherwise, everything else is fine. I understand that it's short notice for you, but it couldn't be helped. ⑳ **As this is our first order with your company, I hope we're still eligible for the special deal.**

Thanks so much,
Leslie Jones

收件者：rep@3broscatering.com
寄件者：ljones@jonesnco.com
主旨：更改訂單
日期：11 月 5 日

嗨，約瑟夫，

希望現在更改我後天的訂單還來得及。⑲⑲ 我剛剛得到消息，會有三個我們楊斯頓分公司的人來參加我們的會議。他們不會和我們一起吃午餐，但我需要幫他們點飲料，因此，那會讓數量加到 15。

沙拉的數量也要改。⑲ 有個人說他不要沙拉。除此之外，其他的都沒問題。我知道這是臨時通知，但我別無選擇。⑳ 由於這是我們跟你公司的第一份訂單，我希望我們仍有享有特別優惠。

非常感謝，
萊思莉·瓊斯

字彙 catering 承辦酒席，外燴　aim 打算，想要　decade 十年　corporate 公司的，團體的
the day after tomorrow 後天　beverage 飲料　short notice 臨時通知　eligible 有資格的，具備條件的

196

What is mentioned about Three Brothers Catering?
(A) It also offers cooking classes.
(B) It has won some awards.
(C) It is a new service.
(D) It opened more than ten years ago.

中譯 關於三兄弟外燴，文中提到什麼？
(A) 它也開烹飪班。   (B) 它得過一些獎。
(C) 它是新公司。   (D) 它開業超過十年。

解析 第一篇文章為三兄弟外燴的外燴餐飲服務廣告。當中提到：「has been in business for over a decade」，由此可以推測該家業者開業超過十年。

197

What event is Ms. Jones holding?
(A) A business lunch
(B) A grand opening
(C) A retirement party
(D) An open house

中譯　瓊斯女士主辦什麼活動？
(A) 商業午餐
(B) 盛大開幕
(C) 退休派對
(D) 開放參觀日

解析　訂購單上的訂購人為瓊斯小姐，同時為電子郵件的寄件人。她透過電子郵件告知訂單更動事項，同時提到：「three people from our branch in Youngston will be joining us at our meeting」，由此可以得知活動為公司的餐會。

字彙　grand opening 盛大開幕

198

Why does Ms. Jones need to change her beverage order?
(A) More people are coming.
(B) More people would like coffee.
(C) Some people requested diet sodas.
(D) Some people will not be coming.

中譯　為什麼瓊斯女士需要更改她的飲料訂單？
(A) 有更多人要來。
(B) 有更多人想要咖啡。
(C) 有些人要求無糖汽水。
(D) 有些人不來。

解析　電子郵件中提到人數臨時增加三個人，必須為他們準備飲料。也就是表示因為有更多的人要參加，所以才要更改飲料訂購數量。

199

How many salads does Ms. Jones need?
(A) 3
(B) 4
(C) 5
(D) 12

中譯　瓊斯女士需要幾份沙拉？
(A) 3
(B) 4
(C) 5
(D) 12

解析　電子郵件中提到與沙拉有關的內容為：「One person said he doesn't want a salad.」，表示訂單中的沙拉數量要扣掉一份，而原本訂單中的沙拉數量為五份，因此答案要選 **(B)**。

200

What does Ms. Jones expect to receive?
(A) A 15-percent discount
(B) A free gift
(C) A loyalty program
(D) No delivery charge

中譯　瓊斯女士期待得到什麼？
(A) 打 85 折
(B) 免費禮物
(C) 老顧客方案
(D) 免運費

解析　電子郵件最後，瓊斯小姐提到：「As this is our first order with your company, I hope we're still eligible for the special deal.」，表示希望能獲得特別優惠。回到第一篇廣告，當中提到：「Until the end of the month, first-time customers get free delivery on office lunches!」，選項將 free delivery 改寫成 no delivery charge，因此答案為 (D)。

Actual Test 3

001 加

(A) **The men are looking at a screen.**
(B) The men are sitting in chairs.
(C) The woman is cleaning a window.
(D) The woman is drinking something.

中譯 (A) 男子們在看螢幕。
(B) 男子們坐在椅子上。
(C) 女子正在清理窗戶。
(D) 女子正在喝東西。

解析 照片中兩名男子正盯著螢幕看,因此 (A)「The men are looking at a screen.」為最適當的描述;無法由照片確認戴眼鏡的男子是否坐著,因此 (B) 並不適當。

字彙 screen 螢幕

002 美

(A) **People are standing near tables.**
(B) People are eating at tables.
(C) Tables are piled with papers.
(D) People are moving files off the tables.

中譯 (A) 大家站在桌邊。
(B) 大家在桌邊吃東西。
(C) 桌子上堆滿文件。
(D) 大家正把桌上的檔案移開。

解析 照片中的人們站在桌子旁邊,因此 (A)「People are standing near tables.」為最適當的描述;桌上只有看到筆電,因此 (C) 和 (D) 皆不適當。

字彙 be piled with 堆滿⋯⋯

003 澳

(A) They are running along a bank of a lake.
(B) **A man is fishing in a lake.**
(C) They are getting in a boat.
(D) A man is putting his fishing pole together.

中譯 (A) 他們沿著湖岸邊跑步。
(B) 男子正在湖邊釣魚。
(C) 他們正在上船。
(D) 男子正在組裝釣魚桿。

解析 照片中的男子正在釣魚,因此 (B)「A man is fishing in a lake.」為最適當的描述;照片中並未出現與 running、getting in、putting together 等描述相符的人物動作。

字彙 run along 沿著⋯⋯跑步
put together 組裝
fishing pole 釣魚桿

004 英

(A) Cars are going into a tunnel.
(B) Cars are parking in a garage.
(C) **Cars are traveling along a road.**
(D) Cars are yielding to a motorcycle.

中譯 (A) 車子正進入隧道。
(B) 車子正停入車庫。
(C) 車子在路上行駛。
(D) 車子正停下，讓機車先過。

解析 照片中的車輛行駛在道路上，因此答案要選 (C)「Cars are traveling along a road.」；照片中並未出現 tunnel、garage 和 motorcycle。

字彙 garage 車庫　yield 停車讓道

---

005 澳

(A) They are dancing in a hall.
(B) **Some people are holding hands in a circle.**
(C) They are watching a live performance.
(D) Some people are walking out of a building.

中譯 (A) 他們在大廳跳舞。
(B) 有些人牽著手圍成一個圓圈。
(C) 他們在看現場演出。
(D) 有些人正走出大樓。

解析 照片中可明顯看到一群人在戶外牽著手圍成一個圈，因此 (B)「Some people are holding hands in a circle.」為適當的描述。

字彙 hold hands 牽手

---

006 美

(A) A man is paying for some items.
(B) A woman is giving an item to a man.
(C) A man is taking pictures at a fair.
(D) **A woman is carrying a bag in her hand.**

中譯 (A) 男子在付錢買東西。
(B) 女子在將某物品交給男子。
(C) 男子正在博覽會上拍照。
(D) 女子手上提著一個袋子。

解析 照片中有一名女子在結帳櫃檯，手舉起袋子，似乎要把袋子交給某個人，因此答案為 (D)「A woman is carrying a bag in her hand.」；照片中並未看到男人的身影。

字彙 fair 博覽會，市集

09

PART 2

007 澳 美

Where do you want to meet?
(A) In front of the station.
(B) She can't find the files.
(C) Tomorrow at 1:00.

中譯 你想在哪裡碰面？
(A) 車站前方。
(B) 她找不到檔案。
(C) 明天 1 點。

解析 Where 開頭的問句　本題詢問地點。(A) 告知對方地點，故為適當的答覆；(C) 適合用來回答 when 開頭的問句。

008 英 美

Could you let us know as soon as possible?
(A) Not as far as I know.
(B) That route is always delayed.
(C) Yes, of course. I'll call you.

中譯 你可以儘快告知我們嗎？
(A) 就我所知不需要。
(B) 那條路線的班車總是會誤點。
(C) 好的，沒問題。我再打給你們。

解析 Could you 開頭的問句　本題要求對方盡快告知。(C) 表示同意，並提到會回電給對方，故為適當的答覆；(A) 使用「as far as」，僅與題目中的「as soon as」類似，屬於答題陷阱。

字彙 route 路線

009 加 澳

When are you leaving for your vacation?
(A) It was less than $1,500.
(B) I've never seen such crowds.
(C) Not until Wednesday.

中譯 你什麼時候要去度假？
(A) 價格低於 1,500 元。
(B) 我從沒看過這麼多人潮。
(C) 要等到週三。

解析 When 開頭的問句　本題詢問時間點。(C) 使用「not until」來回答，為適當的答覆。

字彙 crowd 人潮，人群

010 英 加

Should we update the price on the Website?
(A) I haven't heard of that brand before.
(B) No. Let's wait till the end of the day.
(C) It has doubled in five years.

中譯 我們應該更新網站上的價格嗎？
(A) 我從沒聽過那個牌子。
(B) 不用。我們等到下班看看。
(C) 五年內增加了一倍。

解析 一般問句　本題詢問對方意見。(B) 表達否定的想法，為最適當答覆；(C) 利用題目中的 price 回答相關內容，屬於陷阱選項。

011 澳 加

How long has Ms. Mason been in that meeting?
(A) I wish the line would move more quickly.
(B) Since 11:00 this morning.
(C) The small conference room.

中譯 梅森小姐開會開多久了？
(A) 我希望排隊隊伍能移動得快些。
(B) 從今天早上 11 點開始。
(C) 小會議室。

解析 **How long 開頭的問句** 本題詢問時間長短。(B) 使用 since 來回答，為適當的答覆；(C) 利用題目中的 meeting 回答相關內容，屬於陷阱選項。

字彙 conference room 會議室

---

012 美 英

The user reviews have been mostly positive, haven't they?
(A) Yes, over 80 percent gave three stars or more.
(B) No, I haven't reviewed the plans yet.
(C) The movie was just so-so, in my opinion.

中譯 使用者評價大多是正面的，對嗎？
(A) 是的，超過 80% 的人給三顆星以上的評價。
(B) 不是，我還沒仔細看過計畫。
(C) 我認為此電影滿普通的。

解析 **附加問句** 本題是確認使用者是否都給予正面評價。(A) 表示肯定，並說明大部分的人都給了三顆星以上的分數，為最適當的答覆；其餘選項僅利用題目中的 review 回答相關內容，屬於陷阱選項。

字彙 review 評價；仔細看過

---

013 加 澳

Why hasn't the mail been delivered yet?
(A) I'll call to make a reservation.
(B) Maybe because of the bad weather.
(C) There's a post office around the corner.

中譯 為什麼郵件還沒有送到？
(A) 我會打電話訂位。
(B) 也許是因為氣候不佳。
(C) 轉角有間郵局。

解析 **Why 開頭的問句** 本題詢問原因，因此必須找出合理的回答。(B) 表示由於氣候因素，導致郵件尚未送達，為最適當的答覆；(C) 僅利用題目中的 mail 回答相關內容，屬於陷阱選項。

---

014 美 英

It's the end of the month already.
(A) I left my phone in the taxi.
(B) It seems we're all booked.
(C) We've been so busy. The time has flown by.

中譯 已經到月底了。
(A) 我的手機掉在計程車上。
(B) 看來我們都被訂滿了。
(C) 我們一直都好忙。時間過得真快。

解析 **直述句** 本題提到已經到月底了，帶有「時間過得真快」的意涵在內。(C) 對此表示有同感，故為最適當的答覆。

字彙 Time flies by. 光陰似箭。

015 美 澳

What do you want me to do with the old monitors?
(A) I'd like everyone's attention, please.
(B) Let's try to sell them online.
(C) No one is monitoring their progress.

中譯 你希望我怎麼處理老舊的螢幕？
(A) 我想請大家注意一下。
(B) 我們試著在網路賣賣看。
(C) 沒有人在監督他們的進度。

解析 **What 開頭的問句** 本題詢問該如何處理舊的電腦螢幕。對此 (B) 建議上網賣掉，為最適當的答覆；題目中的「monitor」指的是電腦的「螢幕」，但是 (C) 當中的「monitor」指的是「監督、監控」的意思。

字彙 monitor 螢幕；監督

---

016 英 加

Who knows when the president is going to make a decision on the project?
(A) I guess we should just work on other things.
(B) She knows everyone in the room.
(C) These reports are the most current.

中譯 有誰知道董事長什麼時候要對專案做出決定嗎？
(A) 我猜我們應該先設法處理其他事情。
(B) 她認識這會議室裡的每個人。
(C) 這些是最新的報告。

解析 **Who knows 開頭的問句** 本題詢問的是誰知道「董事長何時才會做出決定」。(A) 表示我們應該先處理其他工作，也就是指「沒人知道董事長何時才會做出決定，可能會花上一段時間」的意思，因此為最適當的答覆。

字彙 work on 設法處理

---

017 加 美

How do you spell your last name?
(A) F-U-L-L-E-R.
(B) Originally from Germany.
(C) Using black ink, always.

中譯 請問你的姓氏怎麼拼？
(A) F-U-L-L-E-R。
(B) 源自於德國。
(C) 請務必使用黑色墨水。

解析 **How 開頭的問句** 本題詢問姓氏的拼法。(A) 直接告知拼法，故為最適當的答覆。

字彙 spell 拼字

---

018 澳 美

Is it possible to change the staff meeting next week?
(A) Our best wishes to you in the future.
(B) Possible, but difficult. Why?
(C) We are open until 7:00.

中譯 有可能更改下週的員工會議嗎？
(A) 我們祝你將來一切順利。
(B) 有可能，但有點困難。怎麼了嗎？
(C) 我們營業到 7 點。

解析 **一般問句** 本題詢問是否能更改時間，回答可使用肯定或否定。(B) 表示可行但有難度，同時反問對方更動的原因，為選項中最適當的答覆。

019 英加

When does the customer want the service to begin?
(A) Through the end of the year.
(B) It's just $59 per month.
(C) On May 1.

中譯 顧客何時想開始使用此服務？
(A) 一直到年底。
(B) 每個月只要 59 元。
(C) 5 月 1 日。

解析 **When 開頭的問句** 本題詢問時間點。(C) 回答日期，故為最適當的答覆；(A) 適合用於回答「為期多久」的提問。

字彙 per month 每個月

---

020 澳美

Has she gone home for the day or is she coming back to the office?
(A) She lives in Springville.
(B) She doesn't need a call back.
(C) She said she'll return by 5:00.

中譯 她已經下班回家，還是會再回到公司？
(A) 她住在春維爾。
(B) 她不需要人家回電。
(C) 她說她 5 點前會回來。

解析 **一般問句** 本題詢問她已經下班回家或是還會再回到辦公室。(C) 表示她說下午 5 點前會回辦公室，故為最適當的答覆。

🎧10

---

021 英澳

Where are the completed applications?
(A) In this folder.
(B) It'll be hard to find a qualified applicant.
(C) Talking with Ms. Simpson.

中譯 填好的申請表在哪裡？
(A) 在資料夾裡。
(B) 我們會很難找到合格的應試者。
(C) 正在和辛普森小姐說話。

解析 **Where 開頭的問句** 本題詢問申請表的位置。(A) 表示在檔案夾裡，故為最適當的答覆；(B) 使用 applicant，僅與題目中的 applications 發音相似，屬於陷阱選項。

字彙 qualified 合格的，符合資格的

---

022 加英

Conference Room B is free now, isn't it?
(A) It holds 15 people.
(B) Check the schedule.
(C) It's free for groups of five or more.

中譯 會議室 B 現在沒人用，對嗎？
(A) 可容納 15 人。
(B) 請查看排程表。
(C) 可免費招待五人以上的團體。

解析 **附加問句** 本題確認現在會議室是否無人使用，題目中的「free」意思為「閒置的」。對此 (B) 請對方確認排程表，為最適當的答覆；(C) 當中的「free」意思為「免費的」。

字彙 free 閒置的；免費的　hold 容納

023 (美)(加)

Are there any spaces left for the seminar?
(A) Only two, I'm afraid.
(B) The seminar's about marketing.
(C) When should I pay for it?

中譯 座談會還有任何空位嗎？
(A) 恐怕只剩兩個。
(B) 座談會的主題跟行銷有關。
(C) 我什麼時候該付款？

解析 一般問句 本題詢問座談會是否還有空位。(A) 表示只剩下兩個位子，為最適當的答覆；(B) 僅重複使用題目中的 seminar。

字彙 pay for 付款買

---

024 (澳)(英)

Has Mr. Powell read the contract yet?
(A) His contact information has been updated.
(B) Instead of your assistant.
(C) I left it on his desk this morning.

中譯 包威爾先生已經看過合約內容了嗎？
(A) 他的聯絡資料已經更新了。
(B) 代替你的助理。
(C) 我今天早上把合約放在他桌上了。

解析 一般問句 本題詢問包威爾先生是否看過合約書。(C) 回答已經放在他的桌上，間接表示合約書已交給他，因此為最適當的答覆；(A) 是使用與題目中 contract 形音皆相近的單字 contact，屬於陷阱選項。

字彙 contract 合約　update 更新

---

025 (美)(澳)

The sales team went to the conference, didn't they?
(A) Yes, we have a double room.
(B) No, it was canceled at the last minute.
(C) I'm not sure where the reports are.

中譯 業務團隊去參加會議了，對嗎？
(A) 是的，我們有雙人房。
(B) 不是的，會議最後一刻取消了。
(C) 我不確定報告在哪裡。

解析 附加問句 本題是確認業務部是否去參加會議了。(B) 直接回答未參加的原因，故為最適當的答覆；(A) 表示肯定，但後方原因與題目毫無關聯。

字彙 at the last minute 最後一刻

---

026 (加)(英)

None of the new recruits are coming to the after-work party.
(A) I guess they're busy.
(B) There are ten of them in all.
(C) It was held at the restaurant on the corner.

中譯 沒有一個新進人員會來參加下班後的派對。
(A) 我猜他們在忙。
(B) 他們共有十人。
(C) 派對在轉角的餐廳舉辦。

解析 直述句 本題表達新進員工不會出席派對。對此 (A) 表示他們可能很忙，為最適當的答覆；(C) 為陷阱選項，若只聽到題目中的 party，可能會誤選。

027 美 澳

Who should we get to redecorate the lobby?
(A) They might deliver. Let me check.
(B) I'll ask around for a recommendation.
(C) Ms. Clark has a degree in finance.

中譯 我們該找誰重新裝潢大廳？
(A) 他們可能會送貨。我查查看。
(B) 我會四處問問看有沒有推薦的人選。
(C) 克拉克小姐具有財經學位。

解析 **Who 開頭的問句** 本題需要確實理解題意，才能順利解題。這句話其實是問要把某項工作交給誰。**(B)** 表示會請周圍的人推薦，故為最適當的答覆；**(C)** 回答人名，若只聽到 **who** 可能會誤選該選項。

字彙 **recommendation** 推薦　**degree** 學位

028 加 美

Do you want to announce the plans tomorrow?
(A) Yes, let's go out of town for the weekend.
(B) No. We should do it today.
(C) I just want some peace and quiet.

中譯 你想要明天宣布計畫嗎？
(A) 是的，我們週末出城吧。
(B) 不，我們應該今天宣布。
(C) 我只想要有點寧靜的時光。

解析 **一般問句** 本題詢問明天是否會宣布計畫。**(B)** 回答 No 表示否定，同時表明應於今日宣布，故為最適當的答覆；**(A)** 和 **(C)** 僅利用題目中的 **plan** 回答相關內容，屬於答題陷阱。

字彙 **peace and quiet** 寧靜

029 英 加

All of the surveys have been returned.
(A) Some of them went to lunch down the street.
(B) I didn't know she'd returned already.
(C) We should go through them as soon as possible.

中譯 所有問卷均已繳回。
(A) 他們之中有些人去外面吃午餐了。
(B) 我不曉得她已經回來了。
(C) 我們應儘快瀏覽問卷內容。

解析 **直述句** 本題表示已經收回所有的問卷。**(C)** 表示現在應該盡快檢視問卷內容，為最適當的答覆；**(A)** 和 **(B)** 分別利用題目中的「**all of**」和「**returned**」來回應，答非所問。

字彙 **return** 繳回，回來

030 加 美

Do you mind closing the window?
(A) Not at all.
(B) Yes, they're all sold out.
(C) There isn't room for everyone.

中譯 你介意關窗嗎？
(A) 完全不介意。
(B) 是的，全部售罄。
(C) 沒有容納大家的空間。

解析 **一般問句** 針對「**Do you mind**」開頭的問句，**(A)** 表示不介意，為最適當的答覆。若要表達介意，可回答「**Yes, I need some fresh air.**（是，我需要呼吸一下新鮮空氣）。」，等同於表示「請不要關窗」。

031 英 澳

I don't remember the last time I enjoyed a movie so much.
(A) It's only playing for another three days.
(B) You remember my brother, David.
(C) You're right. It was really good.

中譯 我都不記得上一次看電影看得這麼過癮是什麼時候了。
(A) 電影只會再播映三天。
(B) 你記得我哥哥大衛對吧?
(C) 你說得沒錯,這部電影真的很好看。

解析 直述句 本題表示不記得上一次享受看電影的樂趣是什麼時候的事了,等同於「剛才看的電影非常棒」的意思。對此 (C) 表示認同他的想法,故為最適當的答覆。

PART 3

Questions 32-34 refer to the following conversation. 澳 英

W   Hello, I'm with the Mystery Shopper Network. ㉜ **We conduct research about shoppers' experiences in various stores.** I see you have a bag from Nelson Marks department store. Would you mind if I asked you some questions?

M   Um, actually, ㉝ **I'm meeting someone in a few minutes.**

W   I understand. It won't take long. Were you shopping for yourself today or for someone else?

M   ㉞ **I bought a birthday present for my son, a shirt and tie.** I really have to go now. Sorry.

女:哈囉,我是「神秘購物者網絡」的員工。㉜我們研究購物者在各種店家消費的經驗。我看到您拿著尼爾森馬克思百貨公司的袋子。您介意回答我一些問題嗎?

男:嗯,㉝其實我過幾分鐘要與人碰面。

女:我了解。不會占用您太多時間的。您今天是為自己或別人買東西呢?

男:㉞我為我兒子買生日禮物,是一件襯衫和領帶。我現在真的要走了,抱歉。

字彙 conduct research 進行研究

032

Who most likely is the woman?
(A) A clothing designer
(B) A department store clerk
(C) A researcher
(D) The man's colleague

中譯 女子最有可能是什麼身分?
(A) 服裝設計師　　(B) 百貨公司店員
(C) 研究人員　　(D) 男子的同事

解析 第一段對話中,女子表示自己任職於「神秘購物者網絡」,調查顧客的購物體驗,由此可以得知女子的職業為研究員。

換句話說 conduct research → researcher

033

Why is the man in a hurry?
(A) He is late to work.
(B) He is not feeling well.
(C) He is on his way to see someone.
(D) He just got an urgent call.

中譯 男子為什麼趕時間?
(A) 他上班要遲到了。　(B) 他身體不舒服。
(C) 他正要去見某人。　(D) 他剛接到一通緊急電話。

解析 第一段對話中,男子提到自己幾分鐘後要去跟某人碰面,表示他正趕著去見某個人。

換句話說 meeting someone → on his way to see someone

What does the man say about his purchase?
(A) It is a new brand.
(B) It is not for himself.
(C) It was easy to find.
(D) It was on sale.

中譯 男子對他所購買的物品提出什麼說法？
(A) 該物品是某個新品牌。　(B) 該物品並非自用。
(C) 該物品很容易尋得。　(D) 該物品在打折。

解析 最後一段對話中，男子提到他買了兒子的生日禮物。由此可以得知他並非購買自己的東西，而是買禮物給兒子。

換句話說 birthday present for my son → not for himself

Questions 35-37 refer to the following conversation. 加 美

W I'm so nervous about my presentation, Jared. ㉟ **I'm worried I'll just forget what to say.**

M You'll be fine. You've practiced many times and you have your notes in order, right?

W Yes, I do. ㊱ **Maybe I can just go through it one more time, very quickly.**

M No. It's almost 3:00. ㊲ **We have to go to the conference room.** If you can't remember what to say, just look at your notes. You can do it!

女：我對發表簡報感到很緊張，傑瑞德。㉟ 我很擔心會忘記該說的內容。

男：妳會沒事的。妳已經練習多次，而且筆記已經照順序排好了，對嗎？

女：對的。㊱ 也許我可以再快速排練一次。

男：沒辦法，已經快 3 點。㊲ 我們該去會議室了。如果妳不記得該說什麼，就看一下筆記。妳辦得到的！

字彙 in order 照順序　go through 排練，練習

034

Why is the woman worried?
(A) She has to speak in public.
(B) She will forget the changes.
(C) She cannot be on time.
(D) She will make a mistake.

中譯 女子為何憂心忡忡？
(A) 她必須公開演講。　(B) 她會忘掉異動的情況。
(C) 她無法準時。　(D) 她會犯錯。

解析 第一段對話中，女子提到她很擔心自己會忘記要發表的內容，也就是擔心自己會出錯。

換句話說 forget what to say → make a mistake

036

What does the woman want to do now?
(A) Go home
(B) Practice more
(C) Visit the doctor
(D) Write some notes

中譯 女子現在想怎麼做？
(A) 回家　　　　(B) 多加練習
(C) 去看醫生　　(D) 寫點筆記

解析 第二段對話中，女子提到她想再次練習要發表的內容，由此可以得知她希望再多練習一下。

換句話說 go through it one more time → practice more

037

Where will the speakers go next?
(A) To a cafeteria
(B) To a meeting room
(C) To the break room
(D) To the president's office

中譯 說話者待會兒要去哪裡？
(A) 自助餐館
(B) 會議室
(C) 休息室
(D) 董事長的辦公室

解析 對話最後，男子提到沒有時間練習了，現在得趕快前往會議室。

換句話說 conference room → meeting room

Questions 38-40 refer to the following conversation. 英 加

M	Excuse me. I'm looking for the manager.
W	I'm the general manager. How can I help you?
M	㊳ ㊴ I just wanted to ask why the menu has changed. I come here a lot with my family and we have enjoyed the variety in the past, but now there are hardly any main dishes. They all seem like appetizers.
W	We decided to make the change to attract more people here after work. You know, to serve food that goes well with alcohol.
M	That's too bad. ㊵ I'm afraid you've just lost some loyal customers. I wish you could've kept at least some of our favorite dishes.

男：不好意思。我想找經理。

女：我是總經理。請問能幫您什麼忙？

男：㊳ ㊴ 我只是想問一下，菜單為什麼換了。我常和家人來這裡，過去很享受多樣化的菜色，但現在卻幾乎沒甚麼主菜可點。餐點都像是開胃菜。

女：因為我們決定改變菜單來吸引更多下班後的人。你知道的，就是提供比較下酒的菜色。

男：太可惜了。㊵ 你們恐怕已經失去一些老顧客。我希望你們至少可以保留幾道我們喜歡的菜色。

字彙 **appetizer** 開胃菜　**go well with** 和……好搭配

038

Where is this conversation most likely taking place?
(A) At a bank
(B) At a kitchenware store
(C) At a restaurant
(D) At a supermarket

中譯 此對話最有可能發生在哪一種場所？
(A) 銀行　　　　　　　(B) 廚具店
(C) 餐廳　　　　　　　(D) 超市

解析 對話中段處，男子詢問為何菜單有所更動，並抱怨沒有主餐可點，表示此篇對話發生的地點在餐廳。

字彙 **kitchenware** 廚具

039

What does the man complain about?
(A) Fewer choices
(B) Noisy atmosphere
(C) Poor quality
(D) Rude people

中譯 男子在抱怨什麼？
(A) 選擇變少　　　　　(B) 環境吵雜
(C) 品質不佳　　　　　(D) 人員無禮

解析 男子提到以前曾跟家人一起來過這家餐廳，吃過很多不同的料理，但現在只剩下開胃菜之類的料理，幾乎沒有什麼主餐可選。這段話表示他不滿意主餐的選擇變少了。

字彙 **atmosphere** 環境，氛圍　**rude** 無禮的

---

040 新增題型

Why does the man say, "I'm afraid you've just lost some loyal customers"?
(A) He is not happy with the price increase.
(B) He will not visit the place anymore.
(C) Some people left because of bad service.
(D) Some people think the manager is incompetent.

中譯 男子為何說「你們恐怕已經失去一些老顧客」？
(A) 他對於漲價的情況不是很高興。
(B) 他不會再來此處。
(C) 有些人因為服務差勁而離去。
(D) 有些人認為經理能力不足。

解析 男子提到餐廳將失去一些常客。由這句話可以推測他不滿意餐廳提供的菜單，未來不會再前來用餐。

字彙 **incompetent** 能力不足的

Questions 41-43 refer to the following conversation. 澳 美

W	Hello, I ordered some books on your Website a few days ago and I just received the package today. There are two copies of three of the books, but I only ordered one each. The order number is CW-AM-395.	女：哈囉，我幾天前在你們網站訂了幾本書，今天才收到包裹。我訂的書裡，有三種都重複寄兩本，但我每種書都只有訂一本。我的訂單編號是 CW-AM-395。
M	㊶ **I can help you with that.** Oh, I think I see what happened. ㊷ **You already had some of the titles in your shopping basket and then you added them into your basket again a few days ago. That's how you ended up with multiple copies.**	男：㊶ 我可以幫您處理。喔，我知道發生什麼事了。㊷ 您的購物車裡原本已經有放入幾本書目，幾天前您又放進同樣的書。這就是您最後會拿到重複書籍的關係。
W	Well, I don't want more than one copy of each book.	女：但我不想要每種書都多買。
M	I understand. Just send back the books you don't want. ㊸ **You should get your money back within two weeks.**	男：我了解。您只要寄回不想留的書籍即可。㊸ 您兩週內就能收到退款。

字彙 **copy** 一冊　**title** 書目　**end up with** 最後會

041

Who most likely is the man?
(A) A customer service representative
(B) A librarian
(C) A post office worker
(D) A delivery person

中譯 男子最有可能是什麼身分？
(A) 客服代表　(B) 圖書館員
(C) 郵局工作人員　(D) 送貨人員

解析 第一段對話中，男子表示要給予對方協助。女子為訂購書籍的顧客，男子為她解決問題，表示男子為客服中心的員工。

042

What caused the woman's problem?
(A) A computer error
(B) A mistake in delivery
(C) A stock shortage
(D) A user oversight

中譯 女子遭遇什麼問題？
(A) 電腦記錄錯誤　(B) 送貨缺失
(C) 庫存短缺　(D) 使用者的疏忽

解析 第一段對話中，女子告知自己所碰到的問題，而後男子指出造成問題發生的確切原因。他提到先前女子已經將書加入購物車內，幾天後又重複了同樣的動作，所以才會收到兩套相同的書籍。由此段話可以得知問題發生的原因為女子的失誤所致，而女子為網站的使用者，因此答案為 (D)。

字彙 **stock shortage** 庫存短缺　**oversight** 疏忽

043

What will the woman receive within two weeks?
(A) A coupon
(B) A refund
(C) Additional items
(D) Promotions

中譯 女子會在兩週內收到什麼？
(A) 折價券
(B) 退款
(C) 額外商品
(D) 促銷優惠

解析 最後一段對話中，男子請女子將書寄回，並告知她兩週內會收到退款。

換句話說 **get your money back → refund**

Questions 44-46 refer to the following conversation. 加 美

W	William, **㊹** I just heard the Red Line has a problem. It has completely stopped running.
M	Oh, no. Many of our employees use the Red Line to get home. We'd better make an announcement since it's almost the end of the day.
W	Can we wait just a minute? **㊺** I'd like to find out what alternate services the train company is offering. I'll look on their Website.
M	Good idea. **㊻** I have to meet with the personnel manager, Ms. Selleck, for a few minutes. Come to her office when you have the information.

女：威廉，**㊹** 我剛聽說紅線出了問題。該線完全停駛。

男：喔，不會吧，我們很多員工都搭紅線回家。都快下班了，我們最好趕快宣布這項消息。

女：我們可以再等一下嗎？**㊺** 我想了解看看鐵路局有沒有提出替代的服務方案。我查一下他們的網站。

男：好主意。**㊻** 我必須和人事經理賽爾拉克小姐見面幾分鐘。妳找好資料後，就來她的辦公室。

字彙 alternate 替代的

044

What are the speakers mainly discussing?
(A) A manager's proposal
(B) A new job candidate
(C) A public service Website
(D) A transportation delay

中譯 說話者主要在討論什麼？
(A) 經理的提案
(B) 新的求職者
(C) 公共服務網站
(D) 某交通運輸工具誤點

解析 第一段對話中，女子提到紅線列車發生問題，所以暫時停駛，而後兩人針對員工的交通備案進行討論，表示目前的問題為交通工具出問題而導致的誤點。

字彙 job candidate 求職者

045

What will the woman do next?
(A) Call a city information line
(B) Check something on the Internet
(C) Go to her manager's office
(D) Visit a new client

中譯 女子接下來會怎麼做？
(A) 撥打市政府的諮詢專線
(B) 上網找資料
(C) 前往經理的辦公室
(D) 造訪新客戶

解析 第二段對話中，女子提到她要上火車公司的網站，查看是否有針對問題提供替代方案。

換句話說 look on their Website → check something on the Internet

046

Where does the man ask the woman to go?
(A) To a client meeting
(B) To a coffee shop
(C) To a manager's office
(D) To a train station

中譯 男子要求女子前往何處？
(A) 參加客戶會議
(B) 前往咖啡廳
(C) 前往一位經理的辦公室
(D) 前往火車站

解析 對話最後，男子提到他要去見人事部經理賽爾拉克小姐，如果有什麼進展，請女子到經理的辦公室找他。

Questions 47-49 refer to the following conversation. 英 澳 新增題型

M	Oh, hi, Molly. I heard you got back yesterday. ❼ **How was your trip?**
W	It was great, Peter. ❼ **Very relaxing. Watching the sunset on the beach was fantastic.** So . . . what's been going on here?
M	Well, you missed a lot last week. There was a big shake-up in the sales department and two people left.
W	You're kidding! What happened?
M	❽ **The new sales manager has been making changes that people don't like.** I guess those two salespeople couldn't take it anymore.
W	❾ **It sounds like the president should have a long talk with the sales manager. Just to tell him to go slow with the changes.**

男：	喔，嗨，莫莉。我聽說妳昨天剛回來。❼妳這次旅行好玩嗎？
女：	我玩得很開心，彼得。❼我感到非常放鬆。可以在海邊欣賞夕陽，真是很棒的經驗。那……公司這邊還好嗎？
男：	妳上週錯過好多事。業務部門人事整頓，有兩個人離職。
女：	你開玩笑的吧！發生什麼事了？
男：	❽新上任的業務經理做了一些大家不喜歡的改變。我想那兩個業務員再也受不了。
女：	❾看來董事長應該跟業務經理促膝長談。建議他做出改變時應該放慢腳步。

字彙 sunset 夕陽　shake-up （機構的）重大調整，人事改組

047

What did the woman do last week?
(A) Attended a seminar
(B) Had a job interview
(C) Took a business trip
(D) Went on vacation

中譯 女子上週做了什麼事？
(A) 參加座談會
(B) 參加面試
(C) 出差
(D) 度假

解析 第一段對話中，男子詢問對方旅行的感想，而後女子提到海邊的日落，並表示自己過得很悠閒，由此可以得知女子剛旅遊回來。

換句話說 trip → vacation

048

What does the man say about the sales department?
(A) It is moving to a new floor.
(B) Its seminar was unsuccessful.
(C) New employees started there recently.
(D) The new head is unpopular.

中譯 關於業務部門，男子說了什麼？
(A) 該部門要遷移至新樓層。
(B) 該部門的座談會成效不佳。
(C) 最近有新進員工。
(D) 新主管不受歡迎。

解析 由對話中段的內容可以得知女子不在的期間公司所發生的變化。當中提到員工們不喜歡業務經理進行的改革，由此可以得知新的主管不太受員工歡迎。

字彙 unpopular 不受歡迎的

049

What does the woman think the president should do?
(A) Change the company policy
(B) Communicate with all staff soon
(C) Hire a new sales department manager
(D) Instruct the manager to go easy

中譯 女子認為董事長應該怎麼做？
(A) 更改公司政策
(B) 盡快與所有員工溝通
(C) 僱用新的業務部經理
(D) 勸導業務經理腳步放緩

解析 對話最後，女子提出自己的想法，表示董事長應該要跟業務經理談談，請他放緩改革的速度。

換句話說 tell him to go slow → instruct the manager to go easy

字彙 instruct 勸導　go easy 放輕鬆

Questions 50-52 refer to the following conversation.

M	Hi, ⑤⓪ I visited your gym for a free trial today and I'm afraid I left my bicycle helmet there. It's black with a red stripe.
W	Yes, I see it here in the lost and found box.
M	Oh, good. Can I come get it now?
W	Well, we're closing in about five minutes. We open at 6:00 tomorrow morning.
M	Okay, I do need it since ⑤① I ride my bike to work. But I live fairly close by, so I can pick it up on the way to work.
W	Great. Uh, what did you decide about joining our gym?
M	⑤② I'm still considering it. It's a bit more expensive than my old gym.

男：嗨，⑤⓪ 我今天到你們健身房免費體驗，我恐怕將自行車的安全帽留在那裡。那是黑底紅條紋的樣式。

女：有的，我有看到安全帽在失物招領箱。

男：太好了。我現在可以過去拿嗎？

女：我們再五分鐘就關門了。明天早上6點會營業。

男：好，因為 ⑤① 我騎腳踏車上班，所以我一定要有安全帽。但我家離健身房相當近，我可以上班前順便過去拿。

女：太好了。呃，那關於加入我們健身房一事，您決定得怎麼樣呢？

男：⑤② 我還在考慮。費用比我以前參加的健身房貴了點。

字彙 free trial 免費體驗　lost and found 失物招領處　fairly 相當地　close by 附近

050

Why is the man calling the gym?
(A) He forgot something there.
(B) He wants to get some information.
(C) He forgot to pick up an application form.
(D) He wants to make sure they are open.

中譯 男子為何聯絡健身房？
(A) 他有物品遺留在健身房。
(B) 他想了解某些資訊。
(C) 他忘了拿申請表。
(D) 他想確定健身房是否營業。

解析 男子提到自己把腳踏車安全帽忘在健身房，因此打電話向對方確認東西是否還在。

換句話說 left my bicycle helmet → forgot something

051

How does the man get to work?
(A) By bicycle
(B) By bus
(C) By car
(D) By train

中譯 男子如何上班?
(A) 騎自行車
(B) 搭公車
(C) 開車
(D) 搭火車

解析 本題針對對話中較不重要的資訊出題。對話中段處,男子提到自己騎腳踏車上班,想在隔天上班的時候去拿安全帽。

換句話說 ride my bike → by bicycle

052

Why might the man NOT join the gym?
(A) It costs too much.
(B) It is far from his house.
(C) It does not have the equipment he likes.
(D) It is not open at the times he needs.

中譯 男子為何可能不會加入健身房?
(A) 費用過高。
(B) 離家太遠。
(C) 沒有他喜歡的健身器材。
(D) 營業時間不符他的需求。

解析 最後一段對話中,男子提到他還在考慮要不要報名,因為價格比他以前去的地方還高。由此可以得知男子是因為費用較高,所以不去這間健身房。

換句話說 a bit more expensive → It costs too much.

Questions 53-55 refer to the following conversation. 澳 美

W I heard ⑬ the boss is finally going to announce a new marketing manager this week. Who do you think would do a better job, Steve or Iris?

M Oh, ⑭ I'm the wrong person to ask. You know Iris was the one who trained me. She's kind of been like a mentor to me since I started here.

W That's right, I remember. You have a good reason to prefer Iris. ⑮ As far as experience, though, Steve has more since he's been here for ten years.

M That's true. But, I'll still root for Iris.

女:我聽說 ⑬ 老闆終於要在本週宣布新的行銷經理。史提夫跟艾瑞絲,你覺得這兩人誰比較適任?

男:喔, ⑭ 這件事不應該問我。妳知道訓練我的人是艾瑞絲。從我進公司,她就像導師一樣督導我。

女:沒錯,我記得。你確實有偏好艾瑞絲的理由。⑮ 但是以經驗來說,史提夫勝出,因為他在公司已經十年。

男:沒錯。但我還是會支持艾瑞絲。

字彙 as far as 以……來說　root for 支持

053

What are the speakers mainly discussing?
(A) A coworker's promotion
(B) The man's work experience
(C) The woman's assignment
(D) Their boss's retirement

中譯 說話者主要在討論什麼事?
(A) 同事升遷
(B) 男子的工作經歷
(C) 女子分配到的工作
(D) 上司退休

解析 第一段對話中,女子提到這週老闆將公布新的行銷經理,詢問男子誰更適合擔任新的經理。前半段對話中,都在針對候選人進行討論,選項中最貼切的對話主旨為同事的升遷。

054 新增題型

What does the man mean when he says, "I'm the wrong person to ask"?
(A) **He cannot make an objective judgment.**
(B) He has no preference in the matter.
(C) He is not familiar with marketing.
(D) He needs time to think of an answer.

中譯 男子說「這件事不應該問我」是什麼意思？
(A) 他無法做出客觀的判斷。
(B) 他對此事件持中立態度。
(C) 他不熟悉行銷領域。
(D) 他需要時間思考答案。

解析 男子表示：「I'm the wrong person to ask.」，接著提到自己強力支持艾瑞絲的原因。由此段話可以得知，他無法對此問題做出客觀的判斷。

字彙 objective 客觀的　matter 事件

055

What does the woman say about Steve?
(A) He has an idea for a new product line.
(B) He has been at the company the longest.
(C) **He has more experience than Iris.**
(D) He has to make an announcement soon.

中譯 女子對史提夫有何看法？
(A) 他對新產品線有想法。
(B) 他是公司最資深的人員。
(C) 他的經驗比艾瑞絲豐富。
(D) 他必須儘快宣布消息。

解析 女子比較兩位候選人的經歷，表示史提夫工作已經十年，比艾瑞絲的經驗更多。

Questions 56-58 refer to the following conversation with three speakers. 加 美 澳 新增題型

W1 ⑤⑥ Here is the final contract, ready for your signature, Mr. Allen.

M ⑤⑦ I appreciate your hard work on selling my house. I didn't expect it to happen so quickly. I guess it's a good market for sellers right now.

W1 Yes, you're right. We are very busy in this office at the moment. Uh, now, on this page we'll need a witness to sign, so I've asked my assistant to join us. Carol, can you come over here and sign your name here under Mr. Allen's?

W2 Yes, Okay. There you go.

M Well, is that all? Any more paperwork to do?

W1 Not at this time. We'll take this to the buyers and start the payment process. You should receive the money within about six weeks.

W2 ⑤⑧ I'll send you an e-mail when everything has been finalized.

M Thank you both so much.

女1：艾倫先生，⑤⑥最終定案的合約已經準備好，只等您簽名了。

男：⑤⑦很感謝妳大力幫忙我賣房子。沒想到可以這麼快賣掉。我想目前的房市對賣房的人來說是好時機。

女1：您說得沒錯。我們現在很忙。嗯，那現在這一頁我們需要見證人的簽名，所以我已經請助理來幫忙。卡蘿，你可以過來一下，在艾倫先生的簽名下方，簽上你的名字嗎？

女2：好的。簽好了。

男：就這樣嗎？還有其他文書作業嗎？

女1：現階段已經沒有了。我們會將此合約交給買方，然後開始進行付款程序。您大約六週內會收到款項。

女2：⑤⑧所有程序均完成後，我會傳一封電子郵件給您。

男：非常感謝妳們兩位。

字彙 signature 簽名　witness 證人，見證人　payment 付款

056

What is the man asked to do?
(A) Fill out a survey
(B) Negotiate a contract
(C) Pay money
(D) Sign his name

中譯 男子被要求做什麼事？
(A) 填寫問卷　　　　(B) 協商合約
(C) 付款　　　　　　(D) 簽名

解析 本篇文章為兩女一男的三人對話。第一段對話中，女 1 請男子在最終版合約書上簽名。

換句話說 ready for your signature → sign his name

字彙 negotiate 協商

057

Where are the women most likely working?
(A) At a bank
(B) At a construction company
(C) At a law office
(D) At a real estate office

中譯 女子們最有可能在哪裡上班？
(A) 銀行　　　　　　(B) 建設公司
(C) 律師事務所　　　(D) 房地產公司

解析 第一段對話中，男子感謝女子努力工作幫自己賣掉房子，而後的對話內容為房屋買賣最後階段的討論，由此段話可以推測兩名女子在房地產公司工作。

字彙 real estate 房地產

058

What does Carol promise to do?
(A) Contact the man later
(B) Prepare more paperwork
(C) Talk to a bank officer
(D) Visit the man's company

中譯 卡蘿承諾什麼事？
(A) 晚一點會聯絡該男子　(B) 準備更多文書作業事宜
(C) 與銀行行員洽談　　　(D) 造訪該男子的公司

解析 女 2 為卡蘿，她在對話最後提到所有項目完成後，會傳送電子郵件給男子，也就是指卡蘿之後會再跟男子聯絡。

換句話說 send you an e-mail → contact the man later

Questions 59-61 refer to the following conversation. 加 英 新增題型

W Hi. Could you help me? ⑤⑨ I'm looking for a going-away present for my colleague who is moving to a different state next week. Do you have any suggestions?	女：嗨，你可以幫我嗎？我有同事下週要搬到其他州了，⑤⑨ 所以我想找個道別禮物送他。你可以推薦一下合適的禮物嗎？
M How about this nice travel umbrella? It has a convenient strap.	男：這一把不錯的旅用傘怎麼樣？它有便利掛繩。
W That looks great. I think he'll like this brown one. Could I get it gift-wrapped?	女：看起來很棒。我想他會喜歡棕色的。可以幫我包裝為禮物的樣子嗎？
M Of course. If you'll just wait a few minutes.	男：當然可以。請稍候幾分鐘即可。
W Actually, I need to do one more errand and then get back to my office for a meeting. ⑥⓪ Could I have it delivered later today?	女：其實我還必須要去辦個事情，然後回公司開會。⑥⓪ 你們能今天晚一點送來給我嗎？
M We can get it to you tomorrow morning. Will that be soon enough?	男：我們可以明天早上送達。這樣來得及嗎？
W Yes, I guess so. ⑥① We're having a party for my coworker at lunchtime, so I definitely need to have it before then.	女：我想可以。⑥① 我們午餐時間要幫那位同事開派對，所以我絕對要在派對前拿到禮物。
M I will make sure it's there in the morning.	男：我會確保明天早上送達。

字彙 going-away present 道別禮物　strap 掛繩　errand（短程）差事

059

What is the woman shopping for?
(A) A birthday gift
(B) A good-bye gift
(C) A retirement gift
(D) A wedding gift

中譯 女子要購買什麼物品？
(A) 生日禮物
(B) 離別禮物
(C) 退休禮物
(D) 結婚禮物

解析 第一段對話中，女子提到自己正在找要送給同事的餞別禮物。

換句話說 going-away present → good-bye gift

060

What does the woman ask the man to do?
(A) Check the stockroom
(B) Give her a discount
(C) Recommend a different item
(D) Send her the item

中譯 女子要求男子做什麼事？
(A) 查看存貨
(B) 給予折扣
(C) 推薦不同的品項
(D) 將商品寄給她

解析 對話中段處，女子詢問對方是否能把禮物送到辦公室；雖然在對話開頭，女子請男子推薦禮物，但女子對於男子推薦的禮物很滿意，因此不能選 (C)。

換句話說 have it delivered → send her the item

061

What will the woman be doing tomorrow at noon?
(A) Attending a gathering
(B) Paying for the delivery
(C) Making food for a party
(D) Taking a colleague to the airport

中譯 女子明天中午會做什麼事？
(A) 參加聚會
(B) 等物品到貨後付款
(C) 準備派對所需的食物
(D) 載送同事去機場

解析 男子表示會在隔天上午為她送貨，而後女子提到午餐時間時，要為那名同事舉辦歡送派對，希望禮物能在派對前送達。由此可以得知明天中午女子要參加活動。

換句話說 having a party → attending a gathering

Questions 62-64 refer to the following conversation and timetable. 英 澳

T-REX CINEMAS	
Screen 1	
All Star Players	▷ 5:30 – 7:40
	▷ 8:00 – 10:10
Screen 2	
63 **Brave And Braver**	▷ 5:40 – 7:30
	▷ 7:50 – 9:40

霸王龍電影院	
第一廳	
全星玩家	▷ 5:30 – 7:40
	▷ 8:00 – 10:10
第二廳	
63 勇者無懼	▷ 5:40 – 7:30
	▷ 7:50 – 9:40

M Hello. One ticket for *All Star Players* at 5:30, please.

男：哈囉。請給我一張 5:30 的《全星玩家》電影票。

W	Oh, I'm sorry. That time slot is sold out. Would you like to wait for the later showing?
M	Uh, I can't. ⑥² **I'm having dinner with a friend at 8:00.** I guess ⑥³ **I'll see** *Brave and Braver* then. I heard it was good.
W	Yes, ⑥⁴ **I saw it yesterday myself.** It was very funny.

女：喔，很抱歉。這個時段的票已經賣完了。您想等晚一點的場次嗎？

男：呃，我沒辦法。⑥² 我 8 點要和朋友吃晚餐。⑥³ 我想我看《勇者無懼》好了。聽說很好看。

女：是的，⑥⁴ 我昨天看了。非常好笑。

PART 3

062

What does the man say he is doing later?
(A) Sharing his thoughts
(B) Cooking dinner
(C) Going back to his office
(D) Meeting a friend

中譯 男子說晚一點要做什麼？
(A) 分享心得 　　(B) 煮晚餐
(C) 回到辦公室 　(D) 見朋友

解析 本篇對話發生在電影院售票處。男子看不成原本想看的時段的電影，且他提到八點要和朋友一起吃晚餐，無法改看下一個時段；對話中並未提到男子要親自下廚做晚餐（dinner），因此答案不能選 (B)。

換句話說 having dinner with a friend → meeting a friend

063 新增題型

Look at the graphic. What time will the man probably watch a movie?
(A) 5:30
(B) 5:40
(C) 7:50
(D) 8:00

中譯 見圖表。男子大概會在哪個時段看電影？
(A) 5:30 　　　(B) 5:40
(C) 7:50 　　　(D) 8:00

解析 本題為圖表整合題。男子決定改看他有空的時段播映的電影《勇者無懼》，而當中提及晚上八點要和朋友吃晚餐，因此可以推測他看的是 5 點 40 分開演的《勇者無懼》。

064

What type of movie is *Brave and Braver* most likely?
(A) A comedy
(B) A documentary
(C) A drama
(D) A science fiction

中譯 《勇者無懼》最有可能是什麼類型的電影？
(A) 喜劇
(B) 紀錄片
(C) 劇情片
(D) 科幻片

解析 最後一段對話中，女子提到她昨天看過那部電影，非常好笑，由此可以推測電影的類型為喜劇片。

Questions 65-67 refer to the following conversation and survey. 美 加 新增題型

Customer Satisfaction Survey	
Business	**Comment**
Anderson & Associates	Poor quality cleaning
⑥⁷ Blackmoor, Inc.	Schedule problems
Parker & Sons	Too expensive
Vesper Group	Always satisfactory

顧客滿意度問卷調查	
公司	評價
安德森暨相關事業	打掃品質不佳
⑥⁷ 黑沼公司	行程安排有問題
帕克森斯	價格高昂
維斯柏集團	滿意度向來極佳

M	Rachel, we've gotten the results of our customer satisfaction survey back and I'm not too pleased about some of the comments.	男：瑞秋，我們已經拿到顧客滿意度問卷調查的結果，我對於一些評語不是很開心。
W	Oh, really, Mr. Danvers? Which ones are concerning to you?	女：噢，真的嗎，丹佛斯先生？您擔心哪些評語？
M	Well, for example, ⑥⑤ "poor quality of cleaning" from Anderson & Associates.	男：像是 ⑥⑤ 安德森暨相關事業的「打掃品質不佳」評語。
W	Right. ⑥⑥ I spoke with Mr. Anderson and explained we had a new person in training at that time and it wouldn't happen again.	女：是的。⑥⑥ 我已經和安德森先生談過，並說明我們當時還在訓練新人，這個情況已經不會再發生。
M	⑥⑦ What about this one, "schedule problems"? We can surely do something about that.	男：⑥⑦ 那「行程安排有問題」這個評語怎麼說？這我們一定能有所改善。
W	Of course. ⑥⑦ I will call the customer right away and work out a better timetable for them.	女：當然。⑥⑦ 我會馬上聯絡顧客，並且協調出對顧客比較方便的時間。

字彙 satisfaction survey 滿意度問卷調查　comment 評語　work out 協調，想出

065

Where do the speakers most likely work?
(A) At a cleaning business
(B) At a law firm
(C) At a rental agency
(D) At a training school

中譯 說話者最有可能在哪裡上班？
(A) 清潔公司　　　　(B) 律師事務所
(C) 租賃管理公司　　(D) 技術訓練學校

解析 前半段對話針對公司的客戶滿意度調查結果進行討論。第二段對話中，男子提到調查結果寫道：「poor quality of cleaning」，由此可以推測說話者們從事與清潔相關的工作。

字彙 rental agency 租賃管理公司

066

What explanation does the woman give for the poor quality comment?
(A) Lazy workers
(B) Low-quality supplies
(C) New management
(D) Untrained staff

中譯 對於品質不佳的評價，女子提出什麼解釋？
(A) 人員偷懶　　　　(B) 用具的品質差勁
(C) 新的管理人員　　(D) 人員訓練不足

解析 第二段對話中，針對負評，女子提到她問過安德森先生，並說明當時有一名新進員工正在接受培訓。這表示是由於尚未訓練好員工，導致清潔品質不佳的結果。

換句話說 new person in training → untrained staff

067 新增題型

Look at the graphic. Who will the woman most likely call soon?
(A) Anderson & Associates
(B) Blackmoor, Inc.
(C) Parker & Sons
(D) Vesper Group

中譯 見圖表。女子最有可能儘快聯絡哪家公司？
(A) 安德森暨相關事業
(B) 黑沼公司
(C) 帕克森斯
(D) 維斯柏集團

解析 本題為圖表整合題。後半段對話中，男子提到時間安排問題，而後女子表示她現在馬上就打電話向客戶確認。查看調查表中的「行程安排有問題」，為黑沼公司提出的意見，表示女子要打電話給黑沼公司。

Questions 68-70 refer to the following conversation and coupon. 澳 美 新增題型

Serenity Spa Options
- Massage ················$50
- Facial ·····················$35
- Manicure ···············$25
- Pedicure ·················$20

68 *Or choose our Full Package for $100 when you show this online coupon.

寧靜 SPA 服務項目
- 按摩 ··················· 50 元
- 做臉 ··················· 35 元
- 手部美甲·············· 25 元
- 足部美甲·············· 20 元

68 * 亦可出示此網路折價券，即可用 100 元購買全套服務。

W Hello, **68 69** I'd like to reserve two spots for your full package spa treatment tomorrow.

M Tomorrow, let me see—we only have time in the afternoon. Would that be okay?

W Yes. Actually, the later the better since I have to work until 4:30.

M Fine, then **69** I'll put you down for 5:00. Do you have any coupons?

W Oh, yes, I almost forgot about that. **68** I have the coupon on my phone.

M Great. Just show it when you pay.

W Thanks. **70** My coworker and I are really looking forward to getting your full package.

女： 哈囉，**68 69** 我想預約明天兩人名額，參加你們的全套 SPA 療程服務。

男： 明天是嗎，我看一下——明天只剩下午可預約。時間可以嗎？

女： 可以的。其實越晚越好，因為我 4 點半才下班。

男： 好的，**69** 那我幫您預約 5 點。您有任何折價券嗎？

女： 噢，有的，我差點忘了。**68** 我手機裡有存折價券。

男： 好的。您結帳時出示折價券即可。

女： 謝謝你。**70** 我同事和我真的很期待體驗你們的全套服務。

字彙 treatment 療程

068

Look at the graphic. How much will the woman pay?
(A) $25
(B) $35
(C) $50
(D) $100

中譯 見圖表。女子將支付多少金額？
(A) 25 元 　　(B) 35 元
(C) 50 元 　　(D) 100 元

解析 本題為圖表整合題。第一段對話中，女子提到她想預約全套療程，後方又提到自己有折價券，而折價券上方寫道只要出示此券，便能以一百元的價格享用全套療程。

069

When will the woman get a treatment?
(A) Today at 4:30
(B) Today at 5:00
(C) Tomorrow at 4:30
(D) Tomorrow at 5:00

中譯 女子何時會去做 SPA 療程？
(A) 今天 4:30
(B) 今天 5:00
(C) 明天 4:30
(D) 明天 5:00

解析 由第一段對話，可以得知女子想預約隔天，而男子幫她預約 5 點，也就是說女子將於明天 5 點去做療程；4 點 30 分為女子下班的時間。

070

Who will the woman bring with her?
(A) Her husband
(B) **Her colleague**
(C) Her daughter
(D) Her mother

中譯 女子會帶誰一起去？
(A) 她的先生　　　　(B) 她的同事
(C) 她的女兒　　　　(D) 她的母親

解析 最後一段對話中，女子提到她跟同事都很期待全套療程，表示她將跟同事一同前往。

換句話說 coworker → colleague

PART 4 12

Questions 71-73 refer to the following talk. 澳

Thank you all for your help today. Digitizing all of the library's resources is a big job. Obviously, ⑫ **we need more volunteers to help, so if you know of anyone, let me know.** ⑪ **I'll be holding an information session for new volunteers next week here at City Library.** It should only take two hours or so to show people how to use the scanner and software. Of course, there's no pay, but we have plenty of free parking and ⑬ **some local restaurants have offered to deliver lunches to our volunteers.**

感謝大家今天的協助。將所有圖書館資源數位化是一項大工程。⑫我們明顯需要更多志工來幫忙，所以如果大家有認識的人選，請告訴我。⑪我下週會在市立圖書館這裡為新志工舉辦說明會。應該只需要兩小時左右，目的在於向大家展示掃描器和軟體的使用方法。當然，這是無酬工作，但我們有免費停車位，⑬某些當地餐廳亦表示，可提供免費餐點給我們的志工。

字彙 digitize 數位化　resource 資源　information session 說明會

071

Where is the speaker?
(A) At a community center
(B) At a city office
(C) At a computer repair shop
(D) **At a library**

中譯 說話者身在何處？
(A) 社區活動中心　　(B) 市府辦公室
(C) 電腦維修店　　　(D) 圖書館

解析 本篇獨白在徵求協助圖書館資料數位化的志工，當中提及說明會和市立圖書館。

072

What does the speaker ask the listeners to do?
(A) Learn about software
(B) Deliver lunches
(C) **Recruit more volunteers**
(D) Use some devices

中譯 說話者要求聽話者做什麼事？
(A) 了解軟體　　　　(B) 外送午餐
(C) 招募更多志工　　(D) 使用某些裝置

解析 獨白中提到需要更多的志工（more volunteers），並要求聽者告知能前來當志工的人選。

174

073

What is offered by local businesses?
(A) Computer lessons
(B) Discount coupons
(C) Free software
(D) Meals

中譯 當地企業提供了什麼？
(A) 電腦課　　　　　(B) 折價券
(C) 免費軟體　　　　(D) 餐點

解析 獨白最後提到當地有一些餐廳願意提供午餐（deliver lunches）給志工。

Questions 74-76 refer to the following recorded message. 美

❼❹ Thank you for calling the Chelsea Fun Park information line. The Chelsea Fun Park is open seven days a week from 10:00 AM to 7:00 PM. ❼❺ We are closed on some national holidays except in the summer months, June through August. We also close once a month for maintenance. A list of closing days is listed on our Website at www. chelseafunpark.com. If you wish to hear a listing of special events, please press "1". For information about accessibility and facilities for families, please press "2". ❼❻ For prices and group discounts, please press "3".

❼❹ 感謝您致電雀爾喜遊樂園區服務專線。雀爾喜遊樂園區每週開放七天，營業時間為早上 10 點至晚上 7 點。❼❺ 我們在一些國定假日不開放，但六月至八月的暑假期間皆營業。我們亦一個月休園一次，進行養護工作。在我們的網站列有休園時間表：www.chelseafunpark.com。若您想了解特殊活動，請按「1」。如需了解無障礙設施與親子設施，請按「2」。❼❻ 如需了解票價和團體折扣，請按「3」。

字彙 seven days a week 全年無休　national holiday 國定假日　maintenance 養護
accessibility 無障礙環境，交通可及性

074

What type of business is the message for?
(A) An amusement park
(B) A community center
(C) A kids' theater
(D) A school

中譯 這是哪種公司行號適用的訊息？
(A) 遊樂園　　　　　(B) 社區活動中心
(C) 兒童電影院　　　(D) 學校

解析 本篇獨白為企業自動回覆的語音訊息，開頭處便提到業者名稱。

換句話說 fun park → amusement park

075

How many days is the business closed in the summer?
(A) One day
(B) Two days
(C) Three days
(D) Never

中譯 該公司行號於夏季休息幾天？
(A) 一天　　　　　　(B) 兩天
(C) 三天　　　　　　(D) 從不休息

解析 獨白中提到遊樂園通常在國定假日時會閉園，夏季六至八月之間除外，但這三個月會每個月閉園一次進行定期維護，表示夏季這三個月的總休館日為三天。

076

What should a listener do for ticket pricing information?
(A) Press "1"
(B) Press "2"
(C) Press "3"
(D) Visit the Website

中譯 聽話者應如何取得票價資訊？
(A) 按「1」　　　　(B) 按「2」
(C) 按「3」　　　　(C) 前往網站

解析 獨白中提到按下「3」，便能查詢價格與團體優惠，因此如果要查詢門票價格，必須按「3」。

Thinking of taking a trip? Forget the hassle of the airport and the crowds at train stations. **77 Travel with us on Blue Star Bus Lines.** When you use Blue Star, just show up at any of our conveniently located terminals, many of which feature free park-and-ride services, and leave the driving to us. **78 Blue Star also offers flexible ticketing. If you want to return early or stop over at a different city, you can change your ticket with no penalty up to 24 hours in advance. 79 For more information, including testimonials from satisfied customers, please visit our Website, www.bluestarbuses.com.**

您是否想旅行呢?請將喧囂的機場和火車站的擁擠人潮拋諸腦後。**77** 歡迎搭乘我們的「藍星巴士」。若您要搭乘藍星,您只要前往任一個地點便利的藍星轉運站即可(許多轉運站提供免費停車轉乘的服務),讓我們載您前往目的地。**78** 藍星巴士亦提供彈性的票價。如果您想提早返回,或中途在不同城市停留,於 24 小時前換票而不需另繳罰金。**79** 如需了解更多資訊,包括顧客滿意度的見證,請至我們的網站 www.bluestarbuses.com。

字彙 hassle 喧囂　park-and-ride service 停車轉乘服務　penalty 罰金

077

What is being advertised?
(A) Air travel
(B) A bus company
(C) Train travel
(D) A travel agency

中譯 廣告主題為何?
(A) 航空旅遊業
(B) 巴士公司
(C) 火車旅遊業
(D) 旅行社

解析 廣告開頭便提到「Blue Star Bus Lines」,可以得知本篇獨白為巴士公司的廣告。之後還提到轉運站、轉乘服務、購票服務等。請特別注意,不要誤選成 (D) 旅行社。

078

What does the company offer customers?
(A) Changeable tickets
(B) Fast service
(C) Low prices
(D) Many destinations

中譯 該公司向顧客提供什麼?
(A) 可改期的票券
(B) 快速服務
(C) 低價
(D) 許多目的地

解析 獨白中提到公司提供免費停車轉乘服務 (free park-and-ride services) 和彈性票價服務 (flexible ticketing)。後者指的是只要在 24 小時前換票,就毋需支付罰金。

字彙 changeable 可更改的

079

According to the advertisement, what can be found on the Website?
(A) Customer reviews
(B) Scheduling information
(C) Ticket prices
(D) Tourist information

中譯 根據廣告內容,網站上會列出什麼資訊?
(A) 顧客評價
(B) 行程資訊
(C) 票價
(D) 觀光資訊

解析 廣告最後提到網站上有顧客的推薦文,建議上網查看。

換句話說 testimonials → reviews

Questions 80-82 refer to the following report. 英

⑧ I've been asked to report on the progress of the product redesign. ⑧ Since we received feedback from customers that our travel iron was too heavy to use, the product design team has worked hard to come up with a way to fix the problem. They found a different material to make the iron, so the finished product should be about half a kilogram lighter. We hope to have the new product ready to ship to stores by the end of next month. ⑧ **We are planning to send out coupons to all the customers on our mailing list at that time.**

⑧ 我應要求報告產品重新設計的進度。⑧ 自從得知顧客反應我們的旅用熨斗太重而不便使用後,產品設計團隊即竭力設法解決此問題。他們找到了別種製造熨斗的材質,所以成品的重量應該會少半公斤。我們希望新品下個月底就能到各門市鋪貨。⑧ 我們預計屆時向所有郵件清單上的顧客寄出折價券。

字彙 iron 熨斗　come up with 想出　finished product 成品　mailing list 郵件清單

080

What is being reported?
(A) A product design
(B) A product display
(C) A product recall
(D) A product sales

中譯 報導主題為何?
(A) 產品設計
(B) 產品展示
(C) 產品召回
(D) 產品銷量

解析 說話者提到他收到要求,因此告知產品重新設計(**product redesign**)的進展。

081

What problem does the speaker mention?
(A) The color
(B) The functions
(C) The price
(D) The weight

中譯 說話者提及哪方面的問題?
(A) 顏色
(B) 功能
(C) 價格
(D) 重量

解析 說話者提到收到顧客反應自家的旅行用熨斗的重量太重(**too heavy**),由此可以得知問題出在重量(**weight**)。

字彙 weight 重量

082

What can customers get at the end of next month?
(A) A discount
(B) A feedback form
(C) A free gift
(D) A special invitation

中譯 顧客可於下個月底獲得何物?
(A) 折扣
(B) 意見反饋表
(C) 免費贈禮
(D) 特殊邀請函

解析 獨白最後提到下個月底才會推出輕便的產品,到時候會提供顧客優惠券。

換句話說 coupons → discount

Questions 83-85 refer to the following speech. 澳

Thank you all for coming today. I will cover three main points in my lecture about making our town more eco-friendly. And then I'll be taking questions from all of you, concerned citizens. ⑧ **If you don't mind holding your questions to the end, that will help me.** To be honest, ⑧ **I'm a bit nervous**. It's the first time I've given this speech in front of such a large group. But I'm committed to making a difference in our community, so ⑧ **I'm just going to bite the bullet and do this**. ⑧ **My first point is about increasing our recycling efforts.**

感謝大家今天前來。我的演講將涵蓋三大重點，主旨是如何讓我們的城鎮更加環保。然後我會回答關心本鎮的各位市民的提問。⑧ 如果不介意的話，希望大家將問題保留到最後，那會對我有幫助。老實說，⑧ 我有點緊張。這是我第一次在這麼多人面前演講。但我致力於要為社區帶來改變，⑧ 我就咬緊牙關做這件事吧。⑧ 我的第一個重點是如何提升回收效用。

字彙 **cover** 涵蓋 **take questions** 回答問題 **be committed to** 決心做，致力於 **bite the bullet** 咬緊牙關應付
recycling 回收

083

What is the audience asked to do?
(A) Be patient with the speaker
(B) Clap for the speaker at the end
(C) Refrain from taking pictures
(D) Wait until later to ask questions

中譯 聽眾被要求進行何事？
(A) 耐心對待說話者　　(B) 最後為說話者鼓掌
(C) 忍住不要拍照　　　(D) 等到晚一點再提問

解析 本篇獨白為針對地方環境問題演講的開場白，說話者要求聽者的內容出現在獨白中段處。當中請聽眾將問題保留（**holding**）至演講結束後再發問。

字彙 **clap** 鼓掌 **refrain from** 克制，忍住

084 新增題型

Why does the speaker say, "I'm just going to bite the bullet and do this"?
(A) She is going to eat her lunch soon.
(B) She is going to speak even though she is afraid.
(C) She wants to hear what the audience thinks.
(D) She wants to stop violence in the town.

中譯 說話者為何說「我就咬緊牙關做這件事吧」？
(A) 她很快就要吃午餐。
(B) 她即使害怕也要演講。
(C) 她想了解聽眾有何想法。
(D) 她想制止城裡的暴力問題。

解析 **bite the bullet** 的意思為「咬緊牙關忍受」。說話者在該句話前方提到她第一次在眾人面前演講，十分緊張，但仍鼓起勇氣想要為社會帶來一些變化。

換句話說 **nervous → afraid**

字彙 **violence** 暴力

085

What will the speaker talk about next?
(A) How to involve people in voting
(B) How to solve the town's problems
(C) Ways to improve local schools
(D) Ways to recycle unwanted items

中譯 說話者接下來要談論什麼問題？
(A) 如何鼓勵大家踴躍投票
(B) 如何解決城裡的問題
(C) 改善當地學校的辦法
(D) 回收廢棄物品的方法

解析 說話者稍後要談的內容出現在獨白的最後。她提到第一項重點為針對回收再利用付出更多努力，由此可以推測她應該會講解回收再利用廢棄物品的方法，選項中與回收有關的主題為 (D)。

字彙 **unwanted** 不需要的

Questions 86-88 refer to the following telephone message. 美

Hi, this message is for Wendell Jasper. This is Frederick Booker from Booker Manufacturing. I'm pleased to hear you liked the design and quality of the luggage handles you ordered from us a few months ago. But, well, **86 this current order for lock components has me a bit concerned.** As you know, **87 we're a relatively small operation**—only 20 full-time staff and technicians working the equipment. Uh, so your order of 6,000 units by the end of the summer is going to be a challenge. **88 After all, that's only six weeks away.** Give me a call back at your earliest convenience to discuss this. Thanks.

嗨，這是給溫道爾・賈斯柏的留言。我是布克爾製造公司的費德烈克・布克爾。我很開心聽到您喜歡幾個月前向我們訂購的行李箱把手設計和品質。不過，**86** 我有點擔心您最新下訂鎖頭組件的這份訂單。因為您也知道，**87** 我們算小規模營運的公司——只有 20 名全職人員和技師在處理設備。因此，在今年夏天要完成您 6,000 份組件的訂單並非易事。**88** 畢竟，只剩下六週了。方便的話，希望您儘早回電給我討論一下此事。謝謝您。

字彙 component 組件　relatively 相對地　operation 營運　full-time staff 全職人員　after all 畢竟 at your earliest convenience 在您方便時儘早

086

What has the listener asked the speaker to do?
(A) Design a piece of equipment
(B) Design a piece of luggage
(C) Make some handles
(D) Make some locks

中譯 聽話者要求說話者做什麼事？
(A) 設計一台設備
(B) 設計一個行李箱
(C) 製造一些把手
(D) 製造一些鎖頭

解析 說話者在電話留言中提到他有點擔心行李箱鎖組件的訂單（order for lock components），由此可以得知聽者曾委託說話者製作鎖的組件；(C) 製作把手的訂單已經完成，時間點早於製作鎖的訂單。

087

What is mentioned about the speaker's business?
(A) It has won design awards.
(B) It is expanding overseas.
(C) It is having financial trouble.
(D) It is not a large firm.

中譯 關於說話者的公司，文中說了什麼？
(A) 贏過設計獎項。
(B) 正在拓展海外分部。
(C) 具有財務問題。
(D) 並非大型公司。

解析 說話者提到自家公司的規模相對較小（relatively small operation），等同於表示說話者的公司並非一間大公司。

088 新增題型

What does the speaker imply when he says, "After all, that's only six weeks away"?
(A) The deadline is too soon.
(B) The order can be finished soon.
(C) The schedule is perfect.
(D) The summer is going quickly.

中譯 當說話者說「畢竟，只剩下六週了」時，他意指什麼？
(A) 交貨期太早了。
(B) 能很快完成訂單。
(C) 行程安排得很完美。
(D) 夏季時光過得很快。

解析 說話者提到雖然接下了六千個鎖的訂單，但由於公司規模較小，讓他有點擔心這筆訂單。留言最後提到「只剩下六週了」，表示交期很趕。

Okay, let's move on to the next item. ⑧⑨ **What I'm about to say shouldn't be a surprise to anyone.** We've been trying to save on our office costs, as you know, by reducing our electricity and paper usage. I noticed recently that we spend a lot of unnecessary money on color copies. ⑨⓪ **I'd like to ask that for in-house documents, you only use black ink.** Of course, for presentations, if you absolutely need to have a graphic or picture in color, go ahead. But otherwise, ⑨① **please change your print function settings to "black and white only"** the next time you print.

好的,我們繼續討論下一個事項。⑧⑨ 我現在要說的話,大家應該不會太驚訝。我們一直試著節省辦公室的基本花費,你們也知道,也就是省電與節約用紙。我發現我們最近在彩色列印上花了不少冤枉錢。⑨⓪ 我希望要求大家,如果是公司內部要用的文件,請用黑白列印就好。當然,如果是絕對需要搭配彩色圖表或照片的簡報,還是可以使用彩色列印。但除此之外,之後列印文件時,⑨① 請大家將列印功能設定改為「僅黑白列印」。

字彙 electricity 電力　usage 用量　in-house 公司內部的

089 新增題型

What does the speaker mean when she says, "What I'm about to say shouldn't be a surprise to anyone"?
(A) It is not the first time the company has tried to save money.
(B) It is unexpected that the speaker has to mention the topic again.
(C) The listeners have not understood the policy well before now.
(D) The listeners may have forgotten what the speaker said.

中譯 當說話者說「我現在要說的話,大家應該不會太驚訝」時,他意指什麼?
(A) 這不是該公司第一次試圖省錢。
(B) 說話者在無預警情況下,再度提及此話題。
(C) 聽話者之前不太清楚政策。
(D) 聽話者可能忘了說話者說過什麼。

解析 說話者提到會議討論項目,並說接下來要討論的項目大家都不會太驚訝(**What I'm about to say shouldn't be a surprise to anyone.**),接著提到公司一直在節省辦公費用(**save on our office costs**),因此選擇 (A) 最為適當。

090

What unnecessary cost does the speaker want to reduce?
(A) Color toner
(B) Electricity
(C) Paper
(D) Computer server

中譯 說話者希望降低何種不必要的費用?
(A) 彩色碳粉匣　　　(B) 電費
(C) 紙張　　　　　(D) 電腦伺服器

解析 獨白談論節省辦公費用,其中談到花費太多錢在彩色列印上,因此建議使用黑白列印。由此可以得知她想要省下購買彩色碳粉匣的費用;(B) 和 (C) 皆為先前已經減少使用的項目。

091

What does the speaker ask the listeners to do to their computers?
(A) Change their settings
(B) Reset their passwords
(C) Save their files to the backup server
(D) Use a new printer

中譯 說話者要求聽話者在電腦上進行何事?
(A) 更改設定
(B) 重設密碼
(C) 將檔案儲存至備份伺服器
(D) 使用新的印表機

解析 獨白中要求將印表機的設定改成「黑白列印」(**change your print function settings to "black and white only"**),表示她要求更改電腦的設定。

Questions 92-94 refer to the following introduction. 英

Thank you all for coming to ❷ **this seminar today about increasing your company's Website traffic.** Even if you've had a Web presence for a while, I'll be teaching you some new tricks to get some more clicks. ❸ **Over the last 15 years, I've helped hundreds of businesses with their Websites**, so I'm sure you'll learn a lot today. In the first hour, I'll give a presentation about getting new people to your site. Then, in the next hour, I'll talk about keeping customers once they've visited your site. Of course, ❹ **if you have any questions, go ahead and interrupt me.** Well, let's get started.

感謝大家今天前來參加 ❷ 這場增加公司網站流量的座談會。即使你們已經成立網站一陣子，我還是會教導大家運用一些小訣竅，來提升點擊率。❸ 過去 15 年來，我已幫助上百家企業改善網站，所以我想各位今天也能獲益良多。在第一個小時，我用簡報說明吸引新顧客來到網站的方法。接下來一個小時，我會談談如何留住曾造訪過網站的顧客。當然，❹ 大家如有任何疑問，歡迎直接中斷我講話而提問。好，那我們開始吧。

字彙 traffic 流量　Web presence 網路身分　trick 小訣竅　give a presentation 報告　interrupt 中斷

092

What is the seminar about?
(A) Building a new Website
(B) Helping local businesses
(C) Increasing visitors to Websites
(D) Updating Websites

中譯 此座談會的目的為何？
(A) 架構新網站
(B) 協助當地企業
(C) 增加網站造訪人次
(D) 更新網站

解析 本文為座談會開場白，說話者介紹座談會的內容，並表明目的為增加公司網站的來訪人數。

換句話說 Website traffic → visitors to Websites

093

What does the speaker mention about his experience?
(A) He designed his first Website 15 years ago.
(B) He has been helping businesses for a long time.
(C) He has received awards for his Web designs.
(D) He learned about new technology from attending seminars.

中譯 說話者提了何種自身經驗？
(A) 他於 15 年前設計自己的第一個網站。
(B) 他長年協助各企業。
(C) 他獲得網頁設計獎項。
(D) 他藉由參加研習會來了解新科技。

解析 說話者自我介紹，並表示過去十五年來，曾協助過數百家企業，提供與網站有關的協助。(B) 表示曾幫助企業很長一段時間，故為最適當的答案。

094

What are listeners encouraged to do during the presentations?
(A) Ask questions
(B) Make suggestions
(C) Take notes
(D) Use a recorder

中譯 聽話者被鼓勵於報告過程中做何事？
(A) 提問問題
(B) 提出建議
(C) 做筆記
(D) 錄音

解析 獨白中提到歡迎隨時發問（go ahead and interrupt me），表示鼓勵聽者提出問題。

Questions 95-97 refer to the following telephone message and chart. (澳)

SHOE SIZE CHART	
U.S.	Europe
6	36
7	38
96 8	40
9	42

鞋碼表	
美國	歐洲
6	36
7	38
96 8	40
9	42

Hi, I have a question about a pair of shoes I ordered from your online store. I received them yesterday, but unfortunately, they don't fit. **96** I'm a size 7 here in the US and I ordered the correct size, according to the size conversion chart on your Website. But it seems I need one size up. **95** I'm wondering, how soon can I get a larger pair sent to me if I return these today? **97** I'm leaving on a business trip next week and I'd really like to have these comfortable shoes since I'll be doing a lot of walking. Please call me back at 555-2839.

嗨，我在你們網路商店訂了一雙鞋，但我有個疑問。我昨天收到了，但可惜的是不合腳。**96** 我在美國這裡通常穿穿 7 號的鞋，而根據你們網站上的尺寸對照表，我訂的也是正確的尺寸。但我好像需要穿大一號。**95** 不曉得如果我今天退貨，多久能收到再大一號的鞋？**97** 我下週就要出差，我真的很想穿這雙舒服的鞋款，因為我到時候需要走很多路。請撥打 555-2839 回電給我。

字彙 conversion 轉換

095

Why is the speaker calling?
(A) To ask for a refund
(B) To get return information
(C) To request a size chart
(D) To reschedule a trip

中譯 說話者為何打電話？
(A) 要求退款　　　(B) 取得退貨資訊
(C) 索取鞋碼表　　(D) 重新安排行程

解析 說話者在電話留言中提到他購買了一雙鞋，但尺寸不合，所以想要詢問換貨事宜。後半段留言中，還詢問今天換貨的話，何時能收到新鞋子。由這些內容，可以得知說話者為取得退換貨資訊才打電話。

096 新增題型

Look at the graphic. What size shoe does the speaker need?
(A) 36
(B) 38
(C) 40
(D) 42

中譯 見圖表。說話者需要的鞋碼為何？
(A) 36　　　　　　(B) 38
(C) 40　　　　　　(D) 42

解析 本題為圖表整合題。說話者提到，根據聽者公司網站上的尺寸表，自己穿的是美國尺寸 7 號的鞋子，但收到貨發現自己應該要穿大一號的鞋子。尺寸表中美國尺寸 7 號加上一號為 8 號，也就是歐洲尺寸 40 號。

097

Where is the speaker going soon?
(A) On a camping trip
(B) On a cruise
(C) On a walking tour
(D) On a work trip

中譯 說話者即將前往何處？
(A) 露營　　　　　(B) 搭遊輪
(C) 健行之旅　　　(D) 出差

解析 留言最後，說話者提到自己下週出差時，需要穿到這雙鞋，由此可以得知他下週要出差。

換句話說 business trip→work trip

Questions 98-100 refer to the following telephone message and information. 美

FREE PUBLIC SEMINARS	
	sponsored by City Hospital
May 22	Exercise for Everyone, Young and Old
⑩ June 19	**Healthy Diets for a Long Life**
July 24	Healthy Eating Even on Vacation
August 21	Keeping Your Heart Happy

免費的大眾座談會	
	由市立醫院贊助
5 月 22 日	老少咸宜的運動
⑩ 6 月 19 日	延年益壽的健康飲食習慣
7 月 24 日	度假也能吃得健康
8 月 21 日	維護心臟健康

Hello. This message is for Penelope Morris. ⑱ **My name is Stanley Evans, head administrator at City Hospital.** I received your e-mail about wanting a tour of the hospital for your group of city officials. ⑲ **I would be happy to lead that for you. Of the dates you gave, next Wednesday at 3:00 is the best for me.** Please confirm by phone or e-mail with the group number. To answer your other question, yes, we have free monthly seminars for the public. ⑩ **It sounds like you'd be interested in the one called Healthy Diets for a Long Life.** Look on our Website for more details. Looking forward to meeting you soon, Penelope.

哈囉，這是給潘妮洛普・莫里斯的留言。⑱我是市立醫院院長史丹利・艾文斯。我收到您的來信，詢問市府官員們想到我們醫院參觀的事。⑲我十分樂意擔任您們的嚮導。您所提的日期裡，我下週三 3 點最方便。請您以電話或電子郵件確認來訪的團體人數。關於您的其他疑問，是的，我們每個月都有為民眾舉辦免費入場的座談會。⑩感覺上您對「延年益壽的健康飲食習慣」座談會感興趣。請您到我們的網站了解更多細節。期待很快與您相見，潘妮洛普。

字彙 head administrator 行政長官　public 民眾　sponsor 贊助

098

Who most likely is the speaker?
(A) An administrator
(B) A doctor
(C) A city official
(D) A travel agent

中譯 說話者最有可能是什麼身分？
(A) 行政人員　　(B) 醫師
(C) 市府官員　　(D) 旅行社人員

解析 說話者在留言開頭表明自己的身份為行政主管（**head administrator**）。

099

What will the speaker do for the listener next week?
(A) Conduct a tour
(B) Host a party
(C) Perform an operation
(D) Speak at a seminar

中譯 說話者將於下週為聽話者進行何事？
(A) 導覽　　　　(B) 舉辦派對
(C) 開刀　　　　(D) 於座談會演講

解析 說話者表示自己很樂意為對方導覽，並提到下週三最為合適。由此段話可以得知說話者將為聽者進行導覽；(D) 說話者回答聽者其他的問題時有提到座談會，但並未提到要為聽者在座談會中做什麼事。

字彙 operation 手術

100 新增題型

Look at the graphic. When would Ms. Morris most likely attend a seminar?
(A) May 22
(B) June 19
(C) July 24
(D) August 21

中譯 見圖表。莫里斯小姐最有可能參加哪一場座談會？
(A) 5 月 22 日　　(B) 6 月 19 日
(C) 7 月 24 日　　(D) 8 月 21 日

解析 說話者提到聽者似乎對於長壽健康餐食感興趣，而相關座談會的時間為 6 月 19 日，因此莫里斯小姐最有可能會參加 6 月 19 日的座談會。

PART 5

101

Online reviewers of Hotel Lila complained that the rates were too expensive, but the Smiths thought they were -------.

(A) excessive
(B) fancy
(C) reasonable
(D) valuable

中譯 萊拉飯店的線上評價內容，均抱怨房價過高，但史密斯夫婦卻認為很合理。
(A) 多餘的　　　　　(B) 浮華的
(C) 合理的　　　　　(D) 寶貴的

解析 逗點前方的子句表達對費用的不滿，but 後方要連接與此相反內容的句子，因此根據題意，選擇「史密斯夫婦認為是『合理的』價格」較為適當。

字彙 rate 價格　excessive 過多的　reasonable 合理的　valuable 寶貴的

102

TGS Publishing is looking for an experienced ------- who can draw for our new series of children's books.

(A) illustrate
(B) illustrated
(C) illustration
(D) illustrator

中譯 TGS 出版社誠徵經驗豐富、可繪製新系列童書插畫的插畫家。
(A) 用圖說明　　　　(B) 圖解的
(C) 插畫　　　　　　(D) 插畫家

解析 空格後方連接 who 開頭的子句，表示空格受到子句的修飾，適合填入表示人物的名詞。根據題意，表示公司在找尋經驗豐富的「插畫家」較為適當。

字彙 illustrator 插畫家

103

Sophie Anderson started ------- own business, Real Wear Co., right after she graduated from high school.

(A) her
(B) hers
(C) herself
(D) she

中譯 蘇菲・安德森高中畢業後，馬上自行創業，成立她的「真實服飾公司」。
(A) 她的　　　　　　(B) 她的（人事物）
(C) 她自己　　　　　(D) 她

解析 本題要選出適當的人稱代名詞，選項中只有所有格形容詞能修飾空格後方的「形容詞＋名詞」，因此答案為 (A)。所有格形容詞後頭經常跟著 own，one's own 的意思為「自己的……」，為常見的用法。

104

If you wish to apply for the ------- of nighttime shift worker, please complete our online application form.

(A) employment
(B) obligation
(C) position
(D) responsibility

中譯 如果你想應徵夜班作業員一職，請填寫我們的線上應徵工作申請表。
(A) 就業　　　　　　(B) 義務
(C) 職位　　　　　　(D) 責任

解析 空格前方出現 apply for，後方連接與職稱有關的單字，因此最適合填入 position，表示工作職缺。

字彙 apply for 應徵　employment 就業　responsibility 責任

105

The survey results show that over 95 percent of participants have received information or promotions that are not ------- to them.
(A) relevance
(B) relevancy
(C) relevant
(D) relevantly

中譯 市調結果顯示，超過 95% 的受訪者均接收過與自己不相關的資訊或促銷訊息。
(A) 相關性 　　　　　(B) 相關性
(C) 相關的 　　　　　(D) 相關地

解析 空格位在形容詞子句中，且置於 be 動詞和「to + 名詞」之間，適合使用 be relevant to（與……有關）。

字彙 relevant 相關的

106

------- the building expansion is close to completion, we will have to plan the opening ceremony.
(A) As long as
(B) Even though
(C) If only
(D) Now that

中譯 既然該建築的拓展工程已近完工，我們該開始計畫開幕儀式。
(A) 只要 　　　　　(B) 儘管
(C) 要是 　　　　　(D) 既然

解析 本題要選出適當的詞彙，用來連接從屬子句「the building expansion . . .」和逗點後面的主要子句「we will . . .」。根據題意，表達「『既然』建築擴建已經接近尾聲」較為適當，因此空格適合填入 now that。

107

Suri Tech's products are not only high quality, but also ------- more economical than most brand-name items.
(A) ever
(B) highly
(C) much
(D) very

中譯 蘇利科技公司的產品不僅品質優良，還比多數名牌商品要經濟實惠得多了。
(A) 從來 　　　　　(B) 極其
(C) 更加 　　　　　(D) 非常

解析 空格後方連接形容詞比較級 more economical，表示空格適合填入副詞 much，用來修飾同為副詞的 more。

字彙 economical 經濟實惠的　brand-name 名牌的

108

The shuttle runs between the shopping mall and Central Station ------- from 9:00 AM to 8:00 PM.
(A) continuation
(B) continuing
(C) continuous
(D) continuously

中譯 此接駁車於早上九點至晚上八點持續往返購物商場與中央車站。
(A) 持續 　　　　　(B) 持續
(C) 持續的 　　　　　(D) 持續地

解析 空格位在兩個介系詞片語之間，若先將介系詞片語遮住的話，解題關鍵為 The shuttle runs，表示空格適合填入副詞 continuously，修飾動詞 runs。

字彙 continuously 持續地

109

The administrative affairs division was having trouble deciding ------- they should cancel or postpone the company picnic.
(A) before
(B) even
(C) what
(D) whether

中譯 行政事務部門在是否應取消或延期公司野餐一事猶豫不決。
(A) 在……之前
(B) 甚至
(C) ……的事物
(D) 是否

解析 空格前方出現動詞 decide，後方連接的子句句型為 A or B。因此空格最適合填入 whether，用來表達二擇一的概念。

字彙 administrative affairs 行政事務

110

The sales representative was glad but nervous when she was told to ------- the CEO to a luncheon with a major client.
(A) accompany
(B) accomplish
(C) include
(D) involve

中譯 當這名業務代表得知可陪同執行長參加與重要客戶的午餐會時，她既高興又緊張。
(A) 陪同
(B) 達成
(C) 包括
(D) 涉及

解析 本題要選出適當的動詞。空格後方連接人物受詞 CEO、介系詞 to 以及表示活動的名詞，因此空格最適合填入 accompany，形成「accompany sb. to N.」（陪同……參加……）。

字彙 luncheon 午餐會　accompany 陪同　involve 涉及

111

After he was transferred to the payroll department, Matt Bender needed some time to get ------- with the calculation software.
(A) acquaint
(B) acquainted
(C) acquainting
(D) acquaints

中譯 參特 · 班德爾調職到薪資管理部門後，需要一點時間來熟悉工時計算軟體。
(A) 使……熟悉
(B) 熟悉的
(C) 使……熟悉
(D) 使……熟悉

解析 選項列出動詞 acquaint 的各種詞類變化，意思為「使……熟悉」。空格前後分別連接 get 和 with，表示要從 (B) 和 (C) 中選出答案。be acquainted with 的意思為「熟悉、上手」。

字彙 payroll （公司員工的）在職人員工資表
get acquainted with 熟悉，上手

112

John Harris was promoted to manager three years after joining the company due to his ------- to the organization.
(A) contribute
(B) contributed
(C) contributing
(D) contribution

中譯 約翰 · 哈里斯因為對公司的貢獻良多，在加入公司的三年後被升為經理。
(A) 貢獻
(B) 貢獻過
(C) 貢獻
(D) 貢獻

解析 due to 的 to 是介系詞，適合搭配名詞一起使用，因此空格要填入名詞。

字彙 promote 升遷　contribution 貢獻

113

Incentive bonuses will be given twice a year, in June and December, depending on individual -------.
(A) background
(B) finance
(C) inspection
(D) performance

中譯 公司將視個人表現，一年發放兩次的績效獎金，發放時間是六月和十二月。
(A) 背景　　　　　　(B) 財務
(C) 視察　　　　　　(D) 表現

解析 根據題意，表達「公司會根據個人『表現』發放獎金」最為適當。

字彙 finance 財務　performance 表現

114

The exact date ------- the winners of the design competition will be announced has not been decided yet.
(A) when
(B) where
(C) which
(D) whose

中譯 目前尚未決定公布設計大賽贏家的確切日期。
(A) 何時　　　　　　(B) 何地
(C) 哪一個　　　　　(D) 何者的

解析 空格後方連接主詞和動詞，接著又連接動詞 has not been decided，因此空格適合填入關係副詞 when，用來引導形容詞子句，並修飾表示時間的先行詞 The exact date。

字彙 exact 確切的

115

When searching ------- the thousands of resources available online, it often takes some skills to get the results you want.
(A) beneath
(B) over
(C) through
(D) under

中譯 在網上遍尋上千筆可用資源時，經常需要運用一些技巧，才能找到想要的結果。
(A) 在……之下　　　(B) 在……之上
(C) 遍及　　　　　　(D) 在……之下

解析 本題要選出適合搭配動詞 search 一起使用的介系詞。search through 最符合題意，其意思為「搜遍、查遍」。

字彙 beneath 在……之下
search through 遍尋

116

While the candidate has more than ------- experience for the job, the personnel chief thought he lacked a positive attitude.
(A) enormous
(B) enough
(C) expert
(D) extra

中譯 雖然此求職者的工作經驗足以勝任此職位，但人資部長認為他缺乏積極的態度。
(A) 大量的　　　　　(B) 足夠的
(C) 專家　　　　　　(D) 額外的

解析 空格後方連接名詞，前方則是連接比較級 more than，因此該空格適合填入形容詞。enough 和 expert 這兩個形容詞都能搭配名詞 experience 使用，但是只有 enough 能與 more than 一起使用。

字彙 lack 缺乏　enormous 大量的

117

------- speaking, the country's biofuel industry has improved greatly over the past few decades.
(A) Technological
(B) **Technologically**
(C) Technologies
(D) Technology

中譯 以技術層面來說，此國家的生質燃料產業於過去數十年來進步良多。
(A) 技術層面的　　　(B) 技術層面地
(C) 技術　　　(D) 技術

解析 speaking 後方連接的是一個結構完整的句子，且當中只有一個動詞，因此逗點前方要使用副詞片語。

118

The marketing chief tried to fix his computer problem himself ------- than waiting for a technician to show up.
(A) better
(B) later
(C) **rather**
(D) other

中譯 行銷總長試著自行修理電腦問題，而不是等技術人員前來。
(A) 較佳的　　　(B) 較晚的
(C) 而不是　　　(D) 其他的

解析 根據題意，表達「而不是等到技術人員出現」較為適當，因此答案為 (C)，rather 搭配 than 使用，其意思為「而不是」；(A) 和 (B) 為形容詞；(D) 搭配 than 的意思為「除了」，與句意不合。

119

The executive director thoroughly enjoyed his trip to a local branch as he was ------- treated by the employees there.
(A) effectively
(B) especially
(C) generally
(D) **generously**

中譯 執行總監此次到分公司出差十分開心，因為當地的員工均大方款待他。
(A) 有效地　　　(B) 尤其是
(C) 一般　　　(D) 大方地

解析 空格位於 be 動詞和一般動詞 treated 之間，故要填入適當的副詞。根據題意，表達「當地員工大方地、慷慨地待人」最為適當。

字彙 treat 對待　effectively 有效地
generously 大方地，慷慨地

120

If Elton Corp. could purchase the land at a fair price, they ------- to the new location by the end of the year.
(A) have been moved
(B) moved
(C) are moved
(D) **would move**

中譯 如果艾爾頓企業能以合理價格買下該土地，他們就會在年底前遷移至新地點。
(A) 已被遷移　　　(B) 已遷移
(C) 被遷移　　　(D) 將遷移

解析 看到「If . . . could purchase」（條件子句裡有過去式），表示此句型是表示未來或現在不太可能會發生，或與事實相反的假設。根據文意，此句應為「與未來相反的假設」，其主要子句使用 would + V，故選 (D)。

121

As the wage-hike negotiations didn't reach a consensus, the union was left with no choice but to ------- a strike.

(A) initiate
(B) initiation
(C) initiative
(D) initiatively

中譯 由於在調薪協商上雙方無法達成共識，工會別無選擇，只能策動罷工。
(A) 開始　　　　　　(B) 開始
(C) 倡議　　　　　　(D) 主動地

解析 「(have) no choice but to V.」的意思為「除了……別無選擇」，不定詞 to 後方要連接原形動詞。

字彙 wage-hike 調薪　union 工會　strike 罷工　initiate 發起

122

After several years of struggle, there are some ------- of recovery in the logistics industry.

(A) implications
(B) impressions
(C) indications
(D) interventions

中譯 經過多年的苦撐，物流產業終於出現一些復甦的跡象。
(A) 暗示　　　　　　(B) 印象
(C) 跡象　　　　　　(D) 干預

解析 本題要找出適當的名詞，搭配 of 及其後方的名詞 recovery 一起使用。根據題意，表達「物流產業出現復甦的跡象」較為適當。

字彙 struggle 苦撐，掙扎　recovery 復甦　logistics 物流 implication 暗示　indication 跡象　intervention 干預

123

At Acro Hill Hotel, visitors are sure to experience a comfortable stay ------- magnificent views from the rooftop terrace.

(A) enjoy
(B) enjoyed
(C) enjoying
(D) enjoys

中譯 來到艾克羅山丘飯店的旅客，絕對能享受從頂樓露台觀賞美景的舒適住宿體驗。
(A) 享受　　　　　　(B) 享受過
(C) 享受　　　　　　(D) 享受

解析 空格前方為一個結構完整的句子，因此動詞 enjoy 要用來引導後方的片語，而空格後方連接受詞，因此填入 enjoying 較為適當。

字彙 magnificent 絕美的

124

Two teams were sitting at ------- sides of the table at the meeting, trying to push each of their plans through.

(A) opposing
(B) oppose
(C) opposite
(D) opposition

中譯 兩組人馬分坐會議桌兩側，試圖促成各自的每項計劃。
(A) 對立的　　　　　(B) 反對
(C) 相反的　　　　　(D) 反對

解析 空格位在介系詞 at 和名詞 sides 之間，適合填入形容詞，用來修飾後方名詞。

字彙 push sth. through 促成，使……通過 oppose 反對　opposite 相反的

125

The national supermarket chain sought to ------- its debt by selling 50 of its 90 stores to a competitor.
(A) charge
(B) input
(C) offset
(D) release

中譯 這家國營連鎖超市有 90 家門市，它欲將其中 50 家賣給競爭對手來抵銷債務。
(A) 收費　　　　　(B) 輸入
(C) 抵銷　　　　　(D) 釋放

解析 根據題意，業者希望嘗試做某件事來讓債務消失。選項中，offset 的意思為「補償、抵銷」，表達「藉由出售超市來抵銷債務」最符合題意。

字彙 seek 尋求　debt 債務　charge 收費　input 輸入　offset 抵銷

126

In order to keep up ------- the latest technology in the industry, the automaker's president regularly reads several specialized magazines.
(A) along
(B) for
(C) to
(D) with

中譯 為了跟上業界的最新科技，此汽車製造商的董事長會經常會閱讀一些專業雜誌。
(A) 沿著　　　　　(B) 為了
(C) 到　　　　　　(D) 和

解析 keep up with 的意思為「跟上、趕上」。根據題意，表達「跟上業界最新科技」較為適當。

字彙 keep up with 跟上

127

According to the pharmaceutical maker's report, it is estimated that ------- one in three people have some kind of food allergy.
(A) rough
(B) rougher
(C) roughly
(D) roughness

中譯 根據藥廠的報告，大約有三分之一的人都會對某種食物過敏。
(A) 粗略的　　　　(B) 較粗略的
(C) 大約　　　　　(D) 粗略

解析 空格後方連接的 one in three people 是 that 子句的主詞，故空格適合填入副詞。

字彙 estimate 預估　rough 粗略的　roughly 大約

128

The experienced salesperson ------- mentored the new recruit for six months, leading him to remarkable achievements.
(A) enthusiastically
(B) periodically
(C) relatively
(D) potentially

中譯 此資深業務員熱心教導了新人六個月，讓新人獲得亮眼成績。
(A) 熱心地　　　　(B) 定期地
(C) 相對地　　　　(D) 潛在地

解析 本題要選出適合搭配動詞 mentor 使用的副詞。根據題意，表達「熱心地指導新進員工」最為適當，因此答案為 (A)。

字彙 mentor 教導　enthusiastically 熱心地　periodically 定期地　potentially 潛在地

129

Mildred Hospital is ranked ------- the best in the country for patient outcomes and state-of-the-art facilities.

(A) among
(B) highly
(C) providing
(D) that

中譯 邁德瑞醫院在患者預後與先進設施方面，均為國內排名數一數二的醫院。
(A) 在……之中
(B) 極其
(C) 提供
(D) 上述提過的人事物

解析 空格前方使用被動語態 be ranked，後方連接名詞片語 the best，因此空格要填入介系詞，引導後方的名詞片語。(B) 為副詞，(C) 是動名詞，(D) 是代名詞。

字彙 state-of-the-art 先進的
rank . . . among 將……排名為

130

A skilled pilot -------, Jeff Long is also an instructor at a flight school and a columnist for an aviation magazine.

(A) he
(B) him
(C) himself
(D) his

中譯 傑夫・龍本身是一名技術高超的機長，亦擔任飛行學校的講師與航空雜誌的專欄作家。
(A) 他
(B) 他
(C) 他自己
(D) 他的

解析 該句話列出此人物兼任多項職業。空格後方加上逗點，表示前方形成一個名詞片語，因此空格適合填入表示強調的反身代名詞，無論是否有空格都不影響題意。

字彙 skilled 技術高超的　aviation 航空

PART 6

Questions 131-134 refer to the following notice. 通知

Eat Healthy, Be Active Community Workshop Series

The Eat Healthy, Be Active community workshops were developed by nutritionists and fitness ------- based on *The Dietary Guidelines for Health and Fitness* from the
131.
government. ------- of the six workshops in the series
132.
includes a lesson plan, learning objectives, hands-on activities, videos, and handouts. The workshops were designed for community educators, health promoters, nutritionists, and others to teach adults in a wide variety of community settings. These workshops will be offered free of charge at the River City Community Center every weekend in June. -------. Please enroll ------- the center or online at
133.　　　　　　　　**134.**
www.rivercitycommcenter.org.

「健康吃、動起來」社區研習系列

「健康吃、動起來」社區研習會，是由一群營養師與健身 ⑬ 專家根據政府的《健康與健身飲食指導方針》所制定。本系列的六堂研習會中，⑫ 每一堂課均包含課程計畫、學習目標、實踐活動、影片與講義。此研習會是為當地的教育工作者、健康促進專業人員、營養師以及其他人員設計的，目的是在各種社區環境中進行成人教育。六月的每個週末，均於河市社區中心免費授課。⑬ 所有學員完成此系列研習會後，均可獲得進修教育證書。請 ⑭ 在中心裡或至 www.rivercitycommcenter. org 網站報名。

字彙 develop 制定　learning objective 學習目標　hands-on 實踐的　nutritionist 營養師
a wide variety of 各種各樣　enroll 報名

131

(A) special
(B) **specialists**
(C) specialize
(D) specializing

(A) 特殊的　　　　　(B) 專業人士
(C) 專攻　　　　　　(D) 專攻

解析　空格後方連接 based on，因此形容詞 (A) 和原形動詞 (C) 皆不適合填入空格裡。被動語態 were developed 後方的 by 連接人物名詞 nutritionists，而後方又連接對等連接詞 and，表示空格適合填入人物名詞 specialists。

字彙　specialize 專攻

132

(A) Few
(B) **Each**
(C) Every
(D) Total

中譯　(A) 很少　　　　　(B) 每一個
(C) 每個　　　　　(D) 總數

解析　本題要找出句子的主詞。該句話的動詞為 includes，空格引導 of the six workshops，因此主詞要選第三人稱單數。Every 要改寫成 Every one of 才正確；Total 要改寫成 A total of 或 The total of 才正確。根據前後文意，表達「六堂研習會中『每一堂』都包含……」較為適當，因此最適合填入 (B)。

133 新增題型

(A) **All participants will receive a continuing education certificate upon completion of the series.**
(B) Comments or suggestions to make the community center classes better are always welcome.
(C) Since the renovations will take longer than expected, we've had to cancel some of the classes.
(D) We're pleased to announce that the center now accepts all major credit cards, as well as cash.

中譯　(A) 所有學員完成此系列研習會後，均可獲得進修教育證書。
(B) 我們總是歡迎您提出改善社區中心課程的建言。
(C) 由於翻新工程的時間超乎預期，我們必須取消部分課程。
(D) 我們很開心宣布，中心現可接受各大信用卡與現金。

解析　空格前方提到免費提供研習會，空格後方則說明報名的方法，因此空格填入 (A) 最符合前後文意，表達報名參加課程者，上完課後能取得證書。

字彙　continuing education 進修教育

134

(A) for
(B) by
(C) **in**
(D) to

中譯　(A) 為了
(B) 藉由
(C) 在……裡面
(D) 到

解析　空格後方連接表示地點的名詞 the center，因此空格要填入適當的介系詞，答案為 (C)；(B) 連接表示地點的名詞時，意思為「在……旁邊、身邊」。

Questions 135-138 refer to the following e-mail. 電子郵件

To:	Gina Caruso
From:	Yuki Madison
Date:	July 5
Subject:	Performance request

Dear Ms. Caruso,

I was in the audience at the Bluebird Café last Friday night and I was ------- impressed with your acoustic
135.
guitar and piano pieces. I'm in charge of booking musicians for the annual music festival in Starling City and one of our performers has just -------. I know this
136.
is last-minute, but ------- there's any way you could
137.
step in for her, I would be eternally grateful. -------.
138.
Could you look it over and get back to me at your earliest convenience?

Sincerely,

Yuki Madison
Organizer
Starling City Music Festival

收件者：吉娜・卡盧索
寄件者：由紀・麥迪森
日期：7月5日
主旨：表演請求

親愛的卡盧索小姐：

　　我上週五晚上在藍鳥咖啡廳欣賞表演，對於你的原聲吉他與鋼琴演奏印象 ⑬⑤ 深刻。我負責為史達林市的年度音樂節預約樂手的檔期，其中一位演奏者剛 ⑬⑥ 取消演出。我知道時間上很趕，但 ⑬⑦ 如果有任何辦法你能替補她的位子，我真的感激不盡。⑬⑧ 我已經附上演出報價與其他細節的文件。可否請你看一下，然後方便的話儘早回覆我嗎？

誠摯地，

由紀・麥迪森
主辦人
史達林市音樂節

Actual Test 3   PART 6

字彙 performance 表現　step in 介入，頂替　eternally 永遠地

135

(A) hardly
(B) nearly
(C) evenly
(D) deeply

中譯 (A) 幾乎不　　　(B) 幾乎
(C) 平均地　　　(D) 深刻地

解析 本題要選出適合修飾 impressed 的副詞。本文為邀請某位音樂家演出的電子郵件，根據前後文意，表達印象「深刻」最為適當。

字彙 evenly 平均地　deeply 深刻地

136

(A) cancelled
(B) continued
(C) played
(D) attended

中譯 (A) 取消　　　(B) 持續
(C) 演奏　　　(D) 參加

解析 空格位在說明為何邀請對方演出的文句，表達「有位表演者臨時『取消』演出」最符合前後文意。

137

(A) even as
(B) if
(C) because
(D) moreover

中譯 (A) 正當　　　(B) 如果
(C) 因為　　　(D) 再者

解析 空格後方連接 there's any way you could step in for her，因此要填入連接詞。若要假設能代替她參加，最適合填入 if。

193

(A) I won't be in the office until Friday, but I will check my messages.
(B) I've attached a document with the fee offer and other details.
(C) The festival is to be held July 30 and 31 at Starling City Park.
(D) There are three other singers I'm considering for the concert.

中譯 (A) 我到週五前都不會進辦公室，但我會查看訊息。
(B) 我已經附上演出報價與其他細節的文件。
(C) 音樂節的舉辦時間是 7 月 30 日和 31 日，地點在史達林市公園。
(D) 我也在考慮邀請其他三位歌手來這場音樂會。

解析 空格前方邀請對方演出，空格後方請對方研究「某樣東西」後回覆。因此可以推測空格要填入與演出有關的「某樣東西」。

字彙 fee 費用

Questions 139-142 refer to the following notice. 通知

Weekend Delays in the Valley Ridge Tunnel

Due to ongoing restoration and repair work in the Valley Ridge Tunnel by Valley Ridge City Engineers, ------- **139.** significant delays to weekend service on the 32, 89, 171 and 482 express buses in both directions through the end of the summer. Tunnel ------- **140.** will temporarily cause the closure of one tube, while two-way traffic is accommodated in the other tube. ------- **141.** The traffic on Friday nights going out of the city is expected to be especially heavy, so please allow ------- **142.** travel time whether in private vehicles or public transportation.

谷脊隧道週末誤點通知

由於谷脊市工程師仍持續修復和維修谷脊隧道，因此 ⓭⓭ 預計到夏天結束前，週末雙向通行此隧道的 32 號、89 號、171 號與 482 號的快捷公車將嚴重誤點。隧道 ⓭⓰ 維修工程將導致其中一條隧道暫時關閉，而另一條隧道則會容納雙向通車。⓭⓱ 因此，雙向車道均僅各開放一個線道。週五晚上出城的交通預計會格外壅塞，因此無論是自駕或搭乘大眾交通運輸工具，請做好車程時間 ⓭⓲ 增加的心理準備。

字彙 significant 顯著的　accommodate 容納

139

(A) expect
(B) expected
(C) expecting
(D) expects

中譯 (A) 預計
(B) 預計過
(C) 預計
(D) 預計

解析 從 Due to 至 the summer 為止，該句話缺少動詞，表示空格要填入動詞。選項列出的動詞 expect，其意思為「預計」，而空格後方連接受詞 significant delays，因此適合填入原形動詞，將該句話變成祈使句。

140

(A) repairs
(B) services
(C) shutdown
(D) traffic

中譯 (A) 維修　　　　(B) 服務
(C) 關閉　　　　(D) 交通

解析 本文為公告文，告知隧道的修復和維護工程影響交通一事。前方提到 restoration and repair work in the Valley Ridge Tunnel，因此表達因為「tunnel repairs」導致道路封閉，最符合前後文意。

字彙 shutdown 關閉

141 新增題型

(A) As a result, there will only be one lane of traffic open in each direction.
(B) City buses can now accommodate baby strollers in a designated space.
(C) In fact, all roads in Valley Ridge have been inspected recently by city engineers.
(D) The engineers have said that the repair work could continue into next year.

中譯 (A) 因此，雙向車道均僅各開放一個線道。
(B) 市公車現可於指定空間收納嬰兒推車。
(C) 事實上，市府工程師近期已巡察谷脊市的所有道路。
(D) 工程師表示，維修工程可能會延續到明年。

解析 空格前後分別提到道路封閉和週五晚上交通壅塞，因此空格適合填入 (A)，補充說明交通擁塞的原因；(B) 的敘述與本文無關；(C) 和 (D) 與交通壅塞無關。

142

(A) add
(B) addition
(C) additional
(D) additionally

中譯 (A) 新增 　　　　(B) 增加的人或物
(C) 增加的 　　　　(D) 此外

解析 空格位在動詞 allow 和名詞片語 travel time 之間，而後 whether 連接介系詞片語，因此空格最適合填入形容詞，用來修飾空格後方的 travel time。

Questions 143-146 refer to the following memo. 備忘錄

Dear Staff,

I have recently gotten a number of ------- regarding the
　　　　　　　　　　　　　　　　　　　143.
state of the conference room on the fourth floor.
Apparently, some of you have eaten your lunch in there
and not ------- your trash with you when you leave. It
　　　144.
makes it very unpleasant for people who have afternoon
meetings in there. Please don't put smelly food trash in the
wastebaskets in that room. -------. If the problems persist, I
　　　　　　　　　　　　　145.
may be forced to lock the room ------- lunch.
　　　　　　　　　　　　　146.

Thank you very much.

Timothy Reynolds
Office Manager

親愛的職員：

　　我近期接獲許多針對四樓會議室使用狀況的 ❶⓭ 投訴。顯然有些人在該會議室吃午餐，且未於離開前 ❶⓮ 帶走垃圾。導致下午需要到會議室開會的人非常不悅。請勿將味道重的廚餘丟到會議室的廢紙簍。❶⓯ 此類垃圾請丟到休息室的垃圾桶。如果此問題未改善，我將不得不於午餐 ❶⓰ 期間上鎖該會議室。

謝謝大家。

提摩西‧雷諾斯
辦公室經理

字彙 state 狀態　unpleasant 不悅的　wastebasket 廢紙簍

143

(A) complaints
(B) compliments
(C) conflicts
(D) controversies

中譯 (A) 投訴
(B) 表揚
(C) 衝突
(D) 爭議

解析 本文為公司備忘錄，提出會議室垃圾的問題。辦公室經理接到與會議室有關的事項，應為員工的抱怨或抗議。

字彙 compliment 表揚　controversy 爭議

144

(A) take
(B) taken
(C) taking
(D) to take

中譯 (A) 帶走　　　　(B) 帶走
　　　(C) 帶走　　　　(D) 帶走

解析 對等連接詞 and 前方使用現在完成式 have eaten，因此後方也使用相同時態 have taken 較為適當。當中 have 可以被省略，因此答案要選 (B)。

145 新增題型

(A) All of us can do better in submitting our time sheets on time.
(B) For this type of trash, use the garbage can in the break room.
(C) The president will address the importance of the recycling policy.
(D) We will be catering the meeting, so get your order in soon.

中譯 (A) 我們大家在準時交出時間表方面可以做得更好。
　　　(B) 此類垃圾請丟到休息室的垃圾桶。
　　　(C) 董事長將會說明回收政策的重要性。
　　　(D) 我們將為會議準備外燴服務，所以請儘早訂餐。

解析 空格前方的內容是叮嚀勿將食物廚餘丟進垃圾桶，空格後方表示否則午休時間會將會議室的門鎖上，所以空格適合填入與前方內容有關的叮嚀，因此最適合填入句子是 (B)。

字彙 address 說明

146

(A) during
(B) in
(C) when
(D) while

中譯 (A) 期間　　　　(B) 在……裡面
　　　(C) 何時　　　　(D) 在……的時候

解析 空格置於一個結構完整的句子中，且後方連接名詞 lunch，表示空格要填入介系詞。(C) 和 (D) 皆為連接詞，因此不適合；根據前後文意，選擇「在……期間」最為適當。

PART 7

Questions 147-148 refer to the following notice. 通知

Attention: Residents of the Robinson Park District

147 This is notification of the temporary closing of Olonda Park for remodeling of the children's area and construction of the amphitheater for free concerts. It is expected to take 4–6 months for all of the work to be completed and we look forward to the big reopening festival next spring. It will be finished in time to celebrate the 100th anniversary of the founding of Meyer Springs, and we will hold a party in the park for the occasion. For the duration of Olonda Park's closure, we would like to encourage visitors to check out other nearby parks, such as Lindley Park and Jinat Park, which are conveniently located near schools in the area. **148** If you have any questions, please send them

羅賓森公園區的居民請注意

147 特此通知，歐倫達公園因兒童區翻新與建造圓形劇場（供免費音樂會使用）等工程，需暫時關閉。我們預計於 4 到 6 個月內完工，並期待明年春季舉行再次開放的盛大活動。我們將及時完工，以便慶祝梅爾泉創建一百週年，我們屆時將於公園舉辦派對。在歐倫達公園關閉期間，我們鼓勵訪客前往鄰近的其他公園，例如交通便利且靠近該區學校的林利公園和吉那特公園。**148** 如有任何疑問，請

to the office of the mayor (mayorsoffice@meyersprings. gov) or come to the next city council meeting on July 5.

寄送電子郵件至市長辦公室（mayorsoffice@meyersprings. gov），或參加 7 月 5 日舉辦的下一場市政會議。

字彙 district 區　notification 通知　amphitheater 圓形劇場

147

Why is the park closing?
(A) To prepare for a big event next weekend
(B) To renovate and add a building
(C) To repair the park's roads and sidewalks
(D) To tear down old facilities

中譯 公園為何關閉？
(A) 為了準備下週末舉辦的盛大活動
(B) 為了翻新與新增建物
(C) 為了維修公園的道路和人行道
(D) 為了拆除老舊設施

解析 本文為公告文，告知關閉公園一事，第一句話便提出關閉的原因：「for remodeling of the children's area and construction of the amphitheater for free concerts」，由此可以得知是為了改造公園並增建建築物，才會暫時關閉公園。

字彙 tear down 拆除

148

What are residents encouraged to do on July 5?
(A) Ask about construction in the park
(B) Express opposition to the city's plan
(C) Get a brochure regarding the new city parks
(D) Listen to the details of urban development

中譯 文中鼓勵居民於 7 月 5 日進行何事？
(A) 針對公園工程提問
(B) 表達反對市府計畫
(C) 索取新市立公園的相關手冊
(D) 聆聽都會發展的詳細介紹

解析 本文最後提及與 7 月 5 日有關的內容。當中表示如有任何疑問，可以傳送電子郵件至市長辦公室，或是參加 7 月 5 日舉行的市政會議。這段話表示如有與工程相關的疑問，建議於 7 月 5 日的會議中提出。

字彙 opposition 反對　urban 都會的

Questions 149-150 refer to the following text message chain. [簡訊對話] [新增題型]

Mark Seagal	2:43 PM	馬克・席格	下午 2:43
Hi Tom, you there?		嗨，湯姆，你在嗎？	
Tom Hill	2:45 PM	湯姆・希爾	下午 2:45
Yeah, I'm here. I'm glad you've got in touch. One of your clients called to let you know they will be late for the 3:00 meeting.		我在。很高興你有聯絡我。你的其中一名客戶打來告知，他們 3 點的會議會遲到。	
Mark Seagal	2:46 PM	馬克・席格	下午 2:46
That's why I'm messaging you, I'm on highway 75 right now, but there must be a problem up ahead. ⑭⑨ **Traffic is backed up for miles.**		這就是我傳訊給你的原因，我人在 75 號高速公路上，但前方交通一定有狀況。⑭⑨ 已經塞車塞了好幾英里。	
Tom Hill	2:48 PM	湯姆・希爾	下午 2:48
⑭⑨ **They must be on the same road then.** That's what they		⑭⑨ 那他們一定也在同一條路上。因	

were talking about on the phone. Will you be able to get to the meeting in time?

Mark Seagal   2:49 PM
⓯ I don't think so. Sounds like we're both going to be late for the meeting. Please let them know the situation.

Tom Hill   2:50 PM
OK. I will phone them back to see if they would like to keep today's meeting or reschedule and I'll let you know.

Mark Seagal   2:51 PM
Great, Thanks.

為他們在電話上也這麼說。你有辦法趕回來開會嗎？

馬克・席格   下午 2:49
⓯ 我想應該沒辦法。看來我們會議都會遲到。請讓他們知道這個情況。

湯姆・希爾   下午 2:50
好的。我會回電給他們，看他們是想保留今天的會議或改時間，我再跟你說。

馬克・席格   下午 2:51
太好了，謝謝。

字彙 be backed up 堵塞

149

What caused the meeting to be deferred?
(A) Because of a car breakdown
(B) **Because of a traffic jam**
(C) Because of a train delay
(D) Because of road construction

中譯 會議延期的原因為何？
(A) 因為車子拋錨
(B) 因為交通堵塞
(C) 因為火車誤點
(D) 因為道路維修工程

解析 本文為文字簡訊，談論無法準時參加會議一事。馬克・席格在 2 點 46 分的訊息中寫道：「Traffic is backed up for miles.」，接著湯姆・希爾的回覆為：「They must be on the same road then.」，表示客戶也塞在同一條路上。由此段對話可以得知，無法準時開會的原因是交通壅塞。

字彙 defer 延期　breakdown 拋錨

150 新增題型

At 2:49 PM, what does Mr. Seagal mean when he says, "I don't think so"?
(A) He believes the data was incorrect.
(B) **He cannot make it to the meeting on time.**
(C) He disagrees with Mr. Hill's idea.
(D) He doubts the train will arrive on time.

中譯 在下午 2:49，席格先生說「我想應該沒辦法」的意思為何？
(A) 他認為資料不正確。
(B) 他無法準時回去開會。
(C) 他不認同希爾先生的想法。
(D) 他不確定火車是否會準時抵達。

解析 希爾先生在 2 點 48 分的訊息中詢問席格先生：「Will you be able to get to the meeting in time?」，席格先生回答：「I don't think so.」，意思是指他無法準時回去開會。

字彙 incorrect 不正確的　doubt 懷疑

Questions 151-152 refer to the following advertisement. 廣告

Waypoint is proud to announce the new Armada series of media players, being released this fall. These state-of-the-art devices are packed with space and choice. ⓯ We know being able to watch and share the hottest videos on the go is important to keep current at work or school, so HD video comes standard in every Armada. Taking the

　　航點公司在此自豪地宣布，今年秋季即將釋出全新的亞媒達媒體播放器系列。此先進裝置擁有不同容量和選擇。⓯ 我們知道為了跟上職場或學校的流行，隨時隨地觀賞和分享最火紅的影片是件重要的事。因此在每一

música you love with you has become a staple today, and Waypoint has found a way to increase storage without losing the fidelity of the music. 152 **At the highest quality settings, the Armada 1 can hold 3,000 songs. Each step up generates another 3,000 more songs for your collection!** If you decide that you want as much music as you can get, the Armada 5 can hold 15,000 songs at the highest quality. We are taking pre-orders now, so don't let this amazing device slip through your fingers.

部亞媒達上，播放 HD 畫質影片是標準配置。能讓自己最愛的音樂如影隨形，已是現代人的習慣。因此航點公司設法增加儲存容量，但不會犧牲音樂的音質。152 在最高音質的設定下，亞媒達 1 號可儲存 3,000 首歌曲。型號編號每往上加一級，表示能再多儲存 3,000 首歌曲！如果您希望儲存的歌曲量愈多愈好，亞媒達 5 號在最高音質設定下，可儲存 15,000 首歌曲。我們現在開放預購，因此千萬別錯過這項驚人的裝置。

字彙 staple 重要部分　fidelity 保真度，精確性　generate 產生　pre-order 預購
slip through one's fingers 某人事物被某人錯過

151

What is true about the Armada series?
(A) They are available in many colors.
(B) They can hold movies.
(C) They can record music.
(D) They weigh less than other devices.

中譯 以下針對亞媒達系列的敘述，何者為真？
(A) 具有多種顏色可選。
(B) 可播放電影。
(C) 可錄製音樂。
(D) 重量比其他裝置輕巧。

解析 本文為新推出的媒體播放器產品廣告。前半段提到產品的特色：「HD video comes standard in every Armada」，表示可以放電影。文中並未提及其他選項。

字彙 weigh 有……重量

152

How many songs can an Armada 2 hold?
(A) 3,000
(B) 6,000
(C) 9,000
(D) 15,000

中譯 亞媒達 2 號可儲存幾首歌曲？
(A) 3,000
(B) 6,000
(C) 9,000
(D) 15,000

解析 廣告中後段提到亞媒達 1 號可以儲存三千首歌曲，每上升一個等級，就能多儲存三千首歌。因此可以推算出亞媒達 2 號能儲存六千首歌曲。

Questions 153-154 refer to the following e-mail. 電子郵件

To : Melissa Scroggins
From : Harold Lloyd
Date : August 4
Subject : Conducting a class

收件者：梅莉莎・史格金斯
寄件者：哈洛・洛伊德
日期：8 月 4 日
主旨：教課事宜

Dear Melissa,

Thank you for asking me to conduct a lecture at your university. Although it means a great deal to me to be considered, I am unfortunately unable to accept your request at this time. I am currently required to be on site for the project my team is working on. 153 **With any luck, we**

親愛的梅莉莎：

感謝妳邀請我到貴校授課。雖然有此機會對我而言是一件大事，但可惜我這次無法接受妳的請求。我目前必須在場支援我團隊所負責的專案。153 運氣好的話，我們大概可在一月結

will wrap it up around the first of the year, but there are, of course, no guarantees. I would be happy to discuss possible dates for next year, if your offer still stands. It always gives me great pleasure to see, speak to, and develop young minds passionate about physics. Towards the end of this year, ⑭ **if you could send me some details about which points or topics you would like me to speak about**, I will get something prepared for your students. I also look forward to finally putting a face to your name after many months of e-mails.

Sincerely,

Dr. Harold Lloyd
Astrophysics Head, Andromeda Industries

案，但當然，我無法保證確切時間。如果妳的工作邀請仍有效的話，我很樂意與妳討論明年可授課的日期。我一直樂見熱衷物理的年輕人、與之交流，並培養他們的能力。到年底之前，⑭如果妳能將希望我傳授的重點或主題的細節寄給我，我會為妳的學生準備講解內容。我也很期待在這麼多個月的電子郵件往來後，終於能夠見到妳本人。

誠摯地，

哈洛・洛伊德博士
天體物理學部主任 安卓米達工業

字彙 site 現場　wrap sth. up 將……做總結　There are no guarantees. 無法保證。　stand 有效
passionate 熱衷的，熱忱的　put a face to a name 見到本人

153

When is Dr. Lloyd's project supposed to be complete?
(A) By January
(B) By March
(C) By August
(D) By December

中譯 洛伊德博士的專案預計何時完成？
(A) 一月前　　　　(B) 三月前
(C) 八月前　　　　(D) 十二月前

解析 本封電子郵件為針對受邀至大學授課的答覆。洛伊德博士表示無法接受邀請，同時提到：「With any luck, we will wrap it up around the first of the year」。the first of the year 指的便是一月。

154

What does Dr. Lloyd ask Ms. Scroggins to do?
(A) Meet him in person to discuss details
(B) Prepare a lecture at the university
(C) Send him an e-mail about the project proposal
(D) Send him some details about a lecture

中譯 洛伊德博士要求史格金斯小姐做什麼事？
(A) 當面和他討論細節
(B) 準備去大學授課的內容
(C) 寄電子郵件給他告知提案內容
(D) 傳送授課的細節內容

解析 洛伊德博士在電子郵件中表示，雖然現在婉拒對方，但如果往後仍有機會的話，希望與對方討論更詳細的內容。選項將 some details about which points or topics you would like me to speak about 改寫成 some details about a lecture，因此答案為 (D)；當中並未提到要見面討論，因此不能選 (A)。

Questions 155-157 refer to the following information. 資訊

⑮ Welcome to Schmidt's, Copper City's newest center for all of your home electronics and DIY needs. ⑮ Please take this opening celebration coupon booklet to the store and choose the coupon that best suits you. For example, if you are looking to purchase new appliances for

⑮歡迎來到庫柏市最新開幕的舒密茲中心。我們販售各種您所需的家電及 DIY 用品。⑮請攜帶此歡慶開幕的折價套券前往門市，選用最適合您的折價券。例如若您想為家裡購

your home, **⑯ present the first coupon to not only save 15 percent off the price of the product, but also get free home delivery.** Or, if there is a TV you have in mind, **⑯ the next coupon will give you free installation plus three months of satellite TV service!** Finally, if you consider yourself handy around the house, **⑯ the third coupon in here will entitle you to a complimentary set of tools.** Let us know what you need and we will be happy to assist. We look forward to seeing you at Schmidt's Grand Opening Celebration, starting July 1.

買新家電，⑯ 請出示第一張折價券，不但即可享有 85 折優惠，還可以享有免費運送到府的服務。或者若您考慮購買電視，⑯ 下一張折價券可讓您享有免費安裝，還附贈三個月的衛星電視服務！最後，若您是善於自己動手打理房子的人，⑯ 第三張折價券即可讓您享有一套免費的工具組。歡迎告知您的需求，我們將樂意協助您。十分期待能在 7 月 1 日的舒密茲盛大開幕儀式與您相見。

字彙 booklet 小冊子　suit 適合　satellite 衛星　handy 手巧的　entitle 賦予……權利　complimentary 免費的，贈送的

155

Why is Schmidt's offering the coupons to customers?
(A) To begin their holiday sales week
(B) To celebrate the store's anniversary
(C) To celebrate the store's first day of operation
(D) To show customers that they appreciate them

中譯 舒密茲為何主動向顧客提供折價券？
(A) 為了展開一週假期促銷的活動
(B) 為了歡慶開店週年
(C) 為了歡慶第一天營業
(D) 為了向顧客表示感謝之意

解析 本文第二句話寫道：「take this opening celebration coupon booklet to the store」，由此可以得知舒密茲為慶祝開幕提供折價券。(C) 表示為慶祝開幕首日，故為正確答案。

156

How many services are offered with the coupons?
(A) 1
(B) 2
(C) 3
(D) 4

中譯 折價券提供幾項服務？
(A) 1　　　　(B) 2
(C) 3　　　　(D) 4

解析 本題只要掌握文中的 first coupon、the next coupon 及 the third coupon，便能輕鬆解題。第一張為提供八五折優惠和免費送貨服務，第二張為提供免費安裝和三個月衛星電視服務，第三張為免費贈送一套工具組。

157

What kinds of items would customers most likely NOT find at Schmidt's?
(A) Automobile goods
(B) Home entertainment
(C) Kitchen appliances
(D) Paint brushes

中譯 顧客最不可能在舒密茲找到何種商品？
(A) 汽車用品
(B) 家庭娛樂設備
(C) 廚房電器
(D) 油漆刷

解析 本文第一句話介紹舒密茲：「Copper City's newest center for all of your home electronics and DIY needs」，家電產品包含 (B) 和 (C)，(D) 屬於 DIY 用具，並未包含 (A) 汽車用品。

To : Rohm Ellington <rellington@vastmail.com>
From : Pathway Tours <csr@pathwaytours.com>
Date : Canada tour
Subject : June 1

Dear Mr. Ellington,

Thank you for choosing Pathway Tours. 158 **This e-mail is a confirmation of your trip to Canada.** We are happy to answer any questions that you might have about your tour, so please let us know if we can assist in any way. It looks like there will be a total of 38 people on this tour, so everyone will be sharing a room with one other guest. If you are traveling with more than one person, we can set up a family room for you. As we will be traveling to many restaurants and markets, please let us know if you or anyone you are traveling with has any allergies or restrictions with food.

The tour's flight is scheduled to leave at 9:32 AM, so we are requesting that everyone meet at the airport at 7:30 AM on the 17th. 159 **If you experience any trouble, contact one of the tour guides as soon as possible. The flight won't be able to wait, but if needed, one of them will meet you in Canada after your flight arrives.** After arrival, the tour will be led by two guides, Ms. Gina Lyons and Mr. John Hogan. 160 **Both are Canadian born, and have lived in the area for most of their lives. They will show you not just the most popular spots, but also those hidden treasures that only locals know about.**

Pamela Strathmore
CSR, Pathway Tours

收件者：羅姆・艾靈頓
　　　　<rellington@vastmail.com>
寄件者：遊徑旅行社
　　　　<csr@pathwaytours.com>
主旨：加拿大旅行團
日期：6月1日

親愛的艾靈頓先生：

　　感謝您選擇遊徑旅行社為您服務。 158 此封電子郵件的目的，在於向您確認加拿大旅行的行程。若您對行程有任何問題，我們均樂意回答，歡迎告知我們您需要的協助。此次旅行團總計38人參加，因此房間的分配方式是兩人一間。若您與一人以上的親友同行，我們可為您安排家庭房。由於我們會前往許多餐廳和市集，若您本人或同行親友有任何食物過敏或飲食限制，請不吝告知我們。

　　此行程班機的表定起飛時間為早上9點32分，因此我們要求大家能在17號的早上7點半到機場集合。 159 若在前來途中遇到任何狀況，請儘快聯絡其中一名導遊。雖然班機不會等你，但如有必要，其中一名導遊會在您自行抵達加拿大後去接你。抵達加拿大後，將由吉娜・里昂斯小姐與約翰・霍根先生帶團。 160 他們兩位均為加拿大人，且在當地居住了大半輩子。他們不僅會帶大家參觀熱門景點，還會讓大家一睹只有當地人才知道的秘境。

潘蜜拉・史崔斯摩
遊徑旅行社客服代表

字彙 confirmation 確認　restriction 限制　spot 景點　hidden 隱藏的　treasure 寶藏　local 當地人
CSR (customer service representative) 客服代表

158

What is the main purpose of the e-mail?
(A) To ask for assistance with guiding the tour
(B) To confirm a trip with a customer
(C) To offer a trip to a customer
(D) To tell a customer not to be late for the flight

中譯 此封電子郵件的主要目的為何？
(A) 尋求帶團方面的協助
(B) 與顧客確認行程
(C) 主動向顧客推薦行程
(D) 告知顧客不可誤機

解析 本封電子郵件為寄給顧客的加拿大旅遊行程的確認信。(B) 將 a confirmation of your trip to Canada 改寫成 confirm a trip with a customer，故為正確答案；(D) 為寄件者欲提醒的項目之一。

159

Who will wait at the airport if a customer should miss a flight?
(A) A local travel agent
(B) A taxi driver
(C) **A tour guide**
(D) Ms. Strathmore

中譯 如果顧客趕不上飛機，何者會在機場等候？
(A) 當地的旅行社業者　　(B) 計程車司機
(C) 導遊　　　　　　　(D) 史崔斯摩小姐

解析 請找出文中與 miss a flight 有關的內容。第二段提到班機起飛時間，並寫道：「If you experience any trouble」，接著假設對方錯過班機的處理方式：「if needed, one of them will meet you in Canada after your flight arrives」，此處的 them 指的是前方提過的 one of the tour guides，因此答案要選 (C)；史崔斯摩小姐為本封電子郵件的寄件人，她亦是旅行社的客服人員。

160

Why does Ms. Strathmore believe that the two guides are the best choice for this tour?
(A) They are both experts in the history of the area.
(B) They are very patient and will wait for others.
(C) They can speak the local dialect and translate.
(D) **They were both born and raised in the area.**

中譯 史崔斯摩小姐為何認為此兩名導遊是本次行程的最佳人選？
(A) 他們均為熟悉當地歷史的專家。
(B) 他們非常有耐心，會等候他人。
(C) 他們會說當地方言且具備翻譯能力。
(D) 他們都是當地土生土長的居民。

解析 導遊的相關說明出現在電子郵件最後。針對 Gina Lyons 和 John Hogan 提到：「Both are Canadian born, and have lived in the area for most of their lives.」，表示兩人都在當地出生和成長，因此答案為 (D)。

字彙 local dialect 當地方言

Questions 161-163 refer to the following questionnaire. 問卷

We at *Fair Trade Magazine* are asking our readers for feedback on the magazine. We want to know what you like and dislike about what you read every month. At the end of this period, we will be offering a prize to three randomly chosen participants. Everyone who sends us a filled out form will be entered into the contest.

Q. What sections in the magazine are your favorites?
A. Since my company has branches in multiple countries, ⑯ I have to attend meetings all around the world, so the business etiquette section is a must-read. My other favorite is the largest section, the monthly report. It gives me invaluable insight into the business mind from the perspective of industry leaders.

Q. Do you have the least favorite section?
A. I think the least useful section is the cover story. It is usually a fluff piece about some hot shots or company presidents that don't tell the readers

《公平貿易雜誌》想請讀者針對雜誌內容提出意見反饋。我們想了解您對每個月雜誌內容的好惡想法。問卷期結束時，我們將贈送禮物給隨機抽出的三位受訪者。填妥問卷且回傳即可獲得抽獎資格。

問：您最喜歡本雜誌的哪些單元？
答：由於我的公司在多國都有分公司，⑯ 因此我必須到世界各地開會，所以商業禮儀單元是我必讀的部分。我另外一個喜歡的單元是篇幅最大的月報。此單元能讓我從產業領導人的角度，得知寶貴的商業見解。

問：您有最不喜歡的單元嗎？
答：⑯ 我覺得最不實用的單元是封面故事。此單元通常是一些娛樂性質的文章，而且介紹的紅人或公司

much about how they achieved success. It usually just details what he or she does when vacationing or away from the office. It doesn't encourage anyone who isn't a CEO or in upper management to read that. What about replacing this with articles of the regular people who work hard every day? Represent those of us who make Fair Trade possible.

Q. Are there other ways that we can improve the magazine?

A. Since the Website runs in conjunction with the magazine, **163** how about bonus features for those who have a subscription to the magazine? It could have access to a members' section of the Website, or special features that have weekly updates or news about sales strategies, etc.

董事長不會透露太多他們的成功之道。這單元通常只是詳細介紹這類人士度假或在非工作時間所做的事。這對於不是執行長或高階主管的讀者而言,並不具鼓舞效用。何不替換為每天努力奮鬥的市井小民的文章?請介紹在我們之中促成公平貿易的那些人。

問:我們還有其他方法改進本雜誌嗎?
答:既然網站和雜誌並行運作,**163** 何不讓雜誌訂閱者享有一些專題報導的福利呢?例如可登入網站的會員專區,或者是每週更新的特別專題報導,或涵蓋銷售策略新資訊等等。

字彙 randomly 隨機地　section 單元　must-read 必讀的東西　invaluable 寶貴的　perspective 見解 fluff 不具重要性的娛樂　hot shot 紅人　represent 介紹,呈現　in conjunction with 與……並行 subscription 訂閱　strategy 策略

161

What does the reader enjoy about the etiquette pages?
(A) How employees in other countries work
(B) How other companies work
(C) **How to act in unfamiliar situations**
(D) How to greet new customers

中譯 此讀者喜歡禮儀單元的什麼內容?
(A) 員工在其他國家的工作方式
(B) 其他公司運作的方式
(C) 如何在陌生情境下表現得體
(D) 如何接待新顧客

解析 本文為針對某雜誌讀者的 Q & A。etiquette pages 出現在第一題的回答當中。讀者提到必讀商業禮儀專欄的理由為「I have to attend meetings all around the world」,由此可以得知讀者偏好了解如何在不熟悉的狀況下行動。

162

Why does the reader believe the main article is not useful?
(A) **It does not offer enough information.**
(B) It does not profile famous people.
(C) It is too specialized for the general reader.
(D) It only covers easy subjects.

中譯 此讀者為何認為主文章不實用?
(A) 資訊不足。
(B) 沒有介紹名人。
(C) 對一般讀者而言過於艱深。
(D) 僅介紹淺顯易懂的主題。

解析 題目的 main article 指的是第二題回答中的 cover story,讀者回答這個專欄最沒有幫助,接著提到:「It is usually a fluff piece about some hot shots or company presidents that don't tell the readers much about how they achieved success.」,表示當中的故事多是娛樂性質的文章,沒有提到他們的成功之道,(A) 表示資訊不夠充分,意思最為貼近。

字彙 profile 介紹　specialized 專門的

163

What does the reader propose for the magazine?
(A) Allowing readers to ask questions to famous leaders
(B) Arranging meetings between readers and newsmakers
(C) Creating a special section of the Website for some readers
(D) Giving an extra discount to magazine subscribers

中譯 此讀者對此雜誌提出什麼建議？
(A) 讓讀者能向知名領導人發問
(B) 安排讀者和新聞人物會面
(C) 為某些讀者特別設立網站專區
(D) 為雜誌訂閱者提供額外折扣

解析 對雜誌的建議出現在第三題的回答中。當中提到：「bonus features for those who have a subscription to the magazine」，建議網站增設會員專區，提供一週新聞、銷售策略特別報導等。選項將其改寫成 a special section of the Website。

Questions 164-167 refer to the following article. 文章

At Odds with Business, the new book by Ellison Waters, is a wonderful account of how anyone can easily overcome the toughest work decisions, if you have a little help along the way. —[1]—.

Mr. Waters said that this book is "the culmination of twenty-two years of hard work and experience, documenting all I picked up during my younger days." 165 Waters' book, which is a partial biography and partial how-to book, begins with his childhood and takes us through his university days. —[2]—. 166 For example, future competitors like Sam Nash opened the door to the business world for Mr. Waters. He also includes choices he made early in his business life to show that failures can teach lessons and show us how not to do something. These failures can also be valuable to others so they won't make the same mistakes. —[3]—.

Understanding the techniques that Mr. Waters lists in his book won't make you the next industry giant, but it does give a bit of insight into how his mind works and how he uses his company to create new ideas. —[4]—. 164 This book is recommended for anyone that is breaking into business or wants to learn new ways to create a product demand for your company.

艾利森‧華特斯的新作《不一樣的商業觀點》的內容相當精采，它描述任何人如何透過過程中的一點幫助，來輕鬆克服最艱難的工作決策。

華特斯先生表示：「本書集結我二十二年來奮鬥的心路歷程，記錄我年輕時期所獲得的歷練。」165 華特斯的著作結合自傳與工具書的內容，由他的童年開始，一路帶領我們到他的大學時光。167 接下來的內容，則開始介紹對他影響深遠、造就他成為今日商界傳奇的各方人士。166 例如山姆‧納許等日後競爭者，為華特斯先生開啟了商界的大門。他亦以自己早期從商所做的選擇為借鏡，說明如何從失敗中汲取教訓，並引以為鑑。這些失敗經驗對他人而言彌足珍貴，讓大家不會犯下相同的錯誤。

了解華特斯先生於本書列出的技巧，雖然不會讓您成為業界的明日巨擘，卻能讓您一窺他的思維模式，以及他運用公司創造新點子的方式。164 本書適合商業新手，或想學新方法來為公司創造產品需求量的讀者。

字彙 account 記錄，描述　overcome 克服　culmination 集結　document 記錄　partial 部分的
biography 自傳　competitor 競爭者　break into 成功打入（某行業或領域）　demand 需求

164

What does the reviewer think of the book?
(A) It does not give enough business tips.
(B) **It is a great way to learn business.**
(C) It is hard to understand the writer's background.
(D) It spends too much time on failures.

中譯 此位書評家對此著作有何評價？
(A) 書中提供的商業訣竅不足。
(B) 此書是學習商業的絕佳方式。
(C) 難以了解作者的背景。
(D) 花太多篇幅講解失敗經驗。

解析 本文為新書評論報導。開頭介紹書籍內容，最後一段則提出對本書的想法：「**This book is recommended for anyone that is breaking into business or wants to learn new ways to create a product demand for your company.**」，表示評論撰寫者認為閱讀本書是學習商業知識的好方法。

165

What is stated in the first part of the book?
(A) Business books to read
(B) Business techniques
(C) Mr. Waters' business life
(D) **Mr. Waters' school days**

中譯 此書的第一部分介紹什麼內容？
(A) 適合閱讀的商業類書籍
(B) 商業技巧
(C) 華特斯先生的從商生涯
(D) 華特斯先生的學生時代

解析 書本的編排和內容出現在第二段。當中針對本書提到：「**a partial biography and partial how-to book, begins with his childhood and takes us through his university days**」，由此可以得知本書前半部談論的是作者學生時代的故事。

166

Who is Sam Nash?
(A) Mr. Waters' advisor
(B) Mr. Waters' partner
(C) Mr. Waters' relative
(D) **Mr. Waters' rival**

中譯 山姆・納許是誰？
(A) 華特斯先生的顧問
(B) 華特斯先生的合夥人
(C) 華特斯先生的親戚
(D) 華特斯先生的競爭對手

解析 文中寫道：「**future competitors like Sam Nash**」，由此可以推測山姆・納許是華特斯的競爭對手。

字彙 relative 親戚

167 新增題型

In which of the positions marked [1], [2], [3], or [4] does the following sentence best belong?
"After that, it moves on to introducing those who influenced him to become the business legend that he is today."
(A) [1]
(B) **[2]**
(C) [3]
(D) [4]

中譯 在標記 [1]、[2]、[3] 和 [4] 的地方，下列這句話最適合放在何處？「接下來的內容，則開始介紹對他影響深遠、造就他成為今日商界傳奇的各方人士。」
(A) [1]   (B) [2]
(C) [3]   (D) [4]

解析 題目列出的句子與書的編排和內容有關，因此最有可能置於第二段當中。句子提到接著會介紹影響作者的人，後面就舉例說明，因此本句最適合放在 [2] 的位置。

字彙 move on 繼續前進

Questions 168-171 refer to the following article. 文章

—[1]—. Many businessmen and women from around the globe will be coming to Los Angeles next week for the biggest trade show of the year. ⑯ Leaders from electronics, computers, and gaming will be bringing out their best to show both consumers and competitors what is coming down the line.

As the week-long expo starts, we should expect to see many items, such as televisions, cameras, even new gaming consoles or mobile devices on display. —[2]—. More than 25,000 people are expected to be at the show for at least one of the five days, ⑯ with many consumers attending all of the three public days of the show.

Non-industry individuals are considered vital to the show, as they will spend the most time with products, as well as give comments after use and receive free giveaways to show off back home. —[3]—. When asked, more than 40 percent of consumers polled said that seeing new products make them feel like kids in a candy store. ⑰ Amazingly, 74 percent of confirmed attendees for this year said that they are coming to see the technical design of the products. —[4]—.

世界各地的商界人士將於下週在洛杉磯齊聚一堂，參加今年最盛大的貿易展。⑯電子業、電腦業與電玩領域的大企業均將秀出最棒的產品，讓消費者與競爭對手了解未來的發展趨勢。

我們預計可在為期一週的展覽中，看見許多展品，像是電視、相機，甚至是新電動遊戲機或行動裝置。⑰多數驚人展品將於展覽的頭三天現身，所以我們很快就能得知更多消息。五天展期中，預計至少有一天會有超過2萬5千人的觀展人數，⑯許多消費者亦會參加開放大眾參觀的三天展期。

非業界人士是此展覽的重點族群，因為他們會投入多數時間了解產品，也會提出使用後的評價，並獲得免費贈品拿回家炫耀一番。在接受民意調查時，超過40%的消費者表示，目睹新品讓他們覺得像是小孩進入糖果店般興奮。⑰令人驚訝的是，確定前來今年展覽的觀展者中，74%表示他們想了解產品在技術層面的設計概念。

字彙 on display 展示   giveaway 贈品   poll 民意調查   individual 個人

168

What is purpose of the event?
(A) To buy and sell new electronics
(B) To conduct marketing research
(C) To showcase future products
(D) To share technology advances

中譯 此活動的目的為何？
(A) 買賣新的電子商品
(B) 進行行銷研究
(C) 展示未來產品
(D) 分享科技進展

解析 本文為貿易展的相關報導。文中提到：「Leaders from electronics, computers, and gaming will be bringing out their best to show both consumers and competitors what is coming down the line.」，表示能搶先看到即將上市的產品。因此本活動的目的為介紹往後要推出的產品。

字彙 advance 進展

169

How many days is the event open to the general public?
(A) 1
(B) 3
(C) 5
(D) 7

中譯 此活動開放幾天讓一般大眾觀展？
(A) 1
(B) 3
(C) 5
(D) 7

解析 與開放民眾參觀有關的內容出現在報導第二段最後：「all of the three public days of the show」，表示開放三天的時間，因此答案為 (B)。

170

According to the article, why do most people attend the event?
(A) To look at the product design
(B) To purchase the newest gadgets
(C) To talk with experts in the field
(D) To try new electronics before they're released

中譯 根據文章，為什麼多數人會參加此活動？
(A) 想目睹產品設計
(B) 為了購買最新的裝置
(C) 想與業界專家交談
(D) 想在新的電子商品上市前試用看看

解析 報導最後提到：「Amazingly, 74 percent of confirmed attendees for this year said that they are coming to see the technical design of the products.」，由此段話可以推測出參加貿易展的原因。(A) 將 see the technical design of the products 改寫成 look at the product design，故為正確答案。

字彙 gadget 裝置

171 新增題型

In which of the positions marked [1], [2], [3] or [4] does the following sentence best belong?
"Most of the surprises come during the first three days of the show, so we should know much more soon."
(A) [1]
(B) [2]
(C) [3]
(D) [4]

中譯 在標記 [1]、[2]、[3] 和 [4] 的地方，下列這句話最適合放在何處？「多數驚人展品將於展覽的頭三天現身，我們很快就能得知更多消息。」
(A) [1]
(B) [2]
(C) [3]
(D) [4]

解析 題目列出的句子與活動日程有關。during the first three days of the show 與開放民眾參觀有關，相關內容出現在第二段中間。[2] 前方提到將會展示即將上市的產品，後方則提到三天的公開活動將會有很多人前來參加，而本句表示很快就能知道更多細節，故最適合置於 [2]。

Questions 172-175 refer to the following online discussion. 線上討論 新增題型

Drew Manson	12:34 PM
Hello, everyone. Thanks for joining me. With only three weeks left before we are due to present our group project, I was thinking we should see where we are, and if need be, ask for some help.	

德魯．曼森	下午 12:34
哈囉，大家好。感謝大家參與討論。目前離團隊專案簡報的時間還剩三個禮拜，我想大家應該了解一下進度，看是否有需要尋求協助。	

Michael Ino	12:35 PM

My team and I could definitely use some backup. We've hit the wall creatively.

Elaine Gregg	12:35 PM

I'd be glad to help out. What can I do?

Michael Ino	12:37 PM

⑰ Well, any thoughts about how we can show management how the product works in the real world? ⑯ It doesn't translate well in presentation form.

Drew Manson	12:38 PM

Maybe we could show them a short demonstration of how it works. What do you think?

Michael Ino	12:40 PM

That's a good idea, but how can we get a demo unit built in less than three weeks? I'm worried that if it's rushed, it may not work at all. That would be a disaster.

Elaine Gregg	12:42 PM

⑱ I could have my team focus on the unit this week, and then pass it off to your team after that. When the time comes for the demo, it would be a great help if both teams knew how to use it properly, right?

Michael Ino	12:43 PM

That's a great idea. I'll let my team know that they will be working in tandem with you all.

Drew Manson	12:44 PM

Excellent. ⑭ I look forward to hearing a progress report about it next week.

麥可・伊諾	下午 12:35

我的團隊和我肯定需要一點後援。我們已經進入靈感撞牆期。

伊蓮・格瑞格	下午 12:35

我很樂意幫忙。需要我怎麼做呢？

麥可・伊諾	下午 12:37

⑰ 我們不知道如何向管理層展示產品在真實世界怎麼用，大家有什麼想法嗎？⑯ 因為這有點難用簡報呈現。

德魯・曼森	下午 12:38

也許我們可以用簡短的操作示範來說明產品的使用方式。你覺得怎麼樣？

麥可・伊諾	下午 12:40

好主意。但我們該怎麼樣在不到三週的時間內，做好一個示範機組。我擔心如果趕鴨子上架，也許會徒勞無功。到時候就慘了。

伊蓮・格瑞格	下午 12:42

⑱ 我可以讓我的團隊在本週專心製作機組，然後在下週轉交給你的團隊。如果兩個團隊都知道機組如何正確使用，到時要示範時會大有幫助，對不對？

麥可・伊諾	下午 12:43

這主意真棒。我會讓我的團隊知道將與你們合作的事。

德魯・曼森	下午 12:44

太好了。⑭ 我期待你們下週回報進度。

字彙 backup 後援　translate 轉化　demonstration (demo) 操作示範　disaster 災難　work in tandem with 與……協同工作

172

Why does Mr. Ino need help with his part of the project?
(A) He got a tough request from management.
(B) He has had trouble correcting some data.
(C) He must find cheaper materials.
(D) He wants to present the product well.

中譯 關於此專案，伊諾先生負責的部分為何需要協助？
(A) 管理層對他提出刁鑽的要求。
(B) 他在修正部分數據上遇到難題。
(C) 他必須找到較低價的材料。
(D) 他想好好地展示產品。

解析 本文為針對公司案子討論的線上聊天。12 點 37 分的訊息中寫道：「any thoughts about how we can show management how the product works in the real world?」，伊諾先生想好好向公司管理層展示產品，卻不知道該怎麼做。文中並未提及其他選項的內容。

字彙 correct 修正

173

Who will work on the unit first?
(A) Mr. Ino's team
(B) Mr. Manson's team
(C) Ms. Gregg's team
(D) All IT staff

中譯 誰會先處理機組？
(A) 伊諾先生的團隊
(B) 曼森先生的團隊
(C) 格瑞格小姐的團隊
(D) 所有的資訊科技部職員

解析 伊諾先生和格瑞格小姐分別在在 12 點 40 分和 12 點 42 分的訊息中提到「unit」。格瑞格小姐表示：「I could have my team focus on the unit this week, and then pass it off to your team after that.」，由此話可以得知格瑞格小姐的團隊會先著手處理。

174

What will happen in a week?
(A) They will have a meeting with their managers.
(B) They will show their client a trial.
(C) They will start the new project.
(D) They will update Mr. Manson on the project.

中譯 一週後會發生什麼事？
(A) 他們將與經理們開會。
(B) 他們會向客戶展示試用品。
(C) 他們將展開新專案。
(D) 他們會向曼森先生更新專案的進度。

解析 與下週有關的內容出現在曼森先生最後的訊息中：「I look forward to hearing a progress report about it next week.」，表示他們一週後要向曼森先生報告案子的最新進展。

字彙 trial 試用

175 新增題型

At 12:37 PM, what does Mr. Ino mean when he says, "It doesn't translate well"?
(A) It is difficult to talk about the product effectively.
(B) It will be difficult to demonstrate in other countries.
(C) The pictures do not make sense to anyone else.
(D) The words are hard for many people to understand.

中譯 下午 12:37 的時候，伊諾先生說「因為這有點難呈現」的意思為何？
(A) 產品解釋起來有困難。
(B) 難以在其他國家展示。
(C) 其他人都看不懂圖片的意思。
(D) 文字內容對許多人而言艱澀難懂。

解析 translate 的意思為「用另外的方式解釋、說明」。根據前後文意，這句話指的是「我無法採適當的方式說明」，由此可以推測他難以好好解說產品。

Questions 176-180 refer to the following job advertisement and e-mail. 徵才廣告 電子郵件

⑲ Jericho, Inc. is looking for new team members to join us this summer. If you have experience with customer service and sales, we want to speak to you about a position. ⑰ Our talented sales staff is trained to use both traditional and modern techniques, such as in newspaper and magazines, search engines, and commercials, to speak to individuals and companies about marketing and advertising of their products domestically and internationally.

⑲傑瑞寇公司欲找尋可於今年夏季加入我們的新血。若您有顧客服務與銷售業務方面的經驗，我們想向您介紹一項職務。⑰我們才華洋溢的業務人員受到良好訓練，能運用傳統與現代技巧，例如報章雜誌、搜尋引擎與廣告，來向個人與公司說明如何在國內外做產品的行銷與廣告。

⑰ Two men with a vision started the company in 1983, wanting to take the industry by storm. **⑯** After their first eight years of operations, Jericho, Inc. is considered to be one of the top five companies in advertising today. **⑰** We are looking for people who can be determined when it comes to advertising, sales, marketing, and negotiation. Over 200 million people have seen our campaigns, and we want to expand our vision by double this year. Big ideas are always welcome and we want to hear how you could transform our business into a world leader. **⑲** Recent college graduates are encouraged to apply as well.

If interested, please contact Lance Everson at the Irvine office at 864-555-7093 or e-mail us at: jobsjericho@walls.com.

To :	Lance Everson <jobsjericho@walls.com>
From :	Robert Gibson <robertgib11@smokeymt.edu>
Date :	May 20
Subject :	Job position

Dear Mr. Everson,

⑱ I am very interested in a position with Jericho, Inc. and would like to speak with you about a possible job opportunity at your earliest convenience. **⑲** I am a senior at Smokey Mountain University and will be earning a degree in business economics at the end of this year. I am at the top of my class and am working part-time at Hunter & Michaels, a local advertising office in town. I **⑳** share the passion of advertising and would like to use my experience in local advertising and marketing in a larger role. I am always thinking about new ways to introduce products into markets around the country, and would bring skills in Internet marketing and analytics to help ensure that our brands are seen by a larger percent of consumers. For these reasons, I feel that I would be a good fit for your company.

Thank you in advance for your consideration.

Robert Gibson

---

⑰ 本公司是由兩名具有遠見、欲掀起業界風暴的男士於 1983 年所創建。⑯ 他們經營傑瑞寇公司八年後，已使其名列為現今五大廣告公司之一。⑰ 我們在找尋在廣告、業務、行銷與協商方面具有決心的人才。已有超過兩億人看過我們的廣告，我們希望今年能夠將目標擴大一倍。我們願意隨時傾聽各種遠見，了解各位如何讓本公司領先全球的想法。⑲ 我們同樣鼓勵剛大學畢業的新鮮人前來應徵。

有意應徵的人，請撥打 864-555-7093 洽詢爾灣分處的藍斯・艾佛森，或寄送電子郵件至 jobsjericho@walls.com。

收件者：藍斯・艾佛森
　　　　<jobsjericho@walls.com>
寄件者：羅伯特・吉布森
　　　　<robertgib11@smokeymt.edu>
日期：5 月 20 日
主旨：職缺

親愛的艾佛森先生：

⑱ 我對傑瑞寇公司的職缺非常感興趣，希望能儘早與您洽談可能的工作機會。⑲ 我是史莫基山大學的大四生，今年年底將拿到商業經濟學的學位。我是班上的頂尖學生，並於鎮上當地的杭特麥克斯廣告公司打工。我對廣告業 ⑳ 具有熱忱，希望能將我當地的廣告行銷經驗運用於責任更重大的職位。我一直都在思考能讓產品打進國內各市場的新方法，甚至能為公司貢獻網路行銷與分析的技能，以確保我們的品牌能見度能拉高。基於上述原因，我認為自己十分符合貴公司的徵才需求。

感謝您的考慮，在此先表達謝意。

羅伯特・吉布森

字彙 **domestically** 國內地　**take ... by storm** 在……掀起風暴　**determined** 有決心的　**negotiation** 協商　**transform** 使……轉變　**senior** 大四生　**analytics**（電腦的）分析法

176

What kind of company is Jericho, Inc.?

(A) An advertising company
(B) An IT company
(C) A publisher
(D) A retailer

中譯 傑瑞寇公司是什麼類型的公司？
(A) 廣告公司　　　　　(B) 資訊科技公司
(C) 出版社　　　　　　(D) 零售商

解析 第一篇文章為傑瑞寇公司的徵人廣告。第一段針對職缺進行說明，第二段則針對公司進行介紹。當中提到：「the top five companies in advertising」，表示傑瑞寇公司是一家廣告公司。

字彙 publisher 出版社　retailer 零售商

177

What is NOT mentioned in the advertisement?

(A) Staff training
(B) Sales figures
(C) Job qualifications
(D) Company history

中譯 此廣告未提及什麼事？
(A) 人員教育訓練　　　(B) 銷售數據
(C) 適任條件　　　　　(D) 公司歷史

解析 (A) 人員教育訓練出現在第一段：「Our talented sales staff is trained」；(C) 適任條件出現在第二段：「We are looking for people who can be determined when it comes to advertising, sales, marketing, and negotiation.」；(D) 公司歷史出現在第二段第一句話中；文中並未提到公司銷售數據。

字彙 sales figures 銷售數據
qualification 任職資格，適任條件

178

What is the main purpose of the e-mail?

(A) To accept a job offer
(B) To apply for a job
(C) To ask about job details
(D) To follow up on an interview

中譯 此封電子郵件的主要目的為何？
(A) 接受工作邀約　　　(B) 應徵工作
(C) 詢問詳細的職務內容　(D) 追蹤訪談的後續事宜

解析 第一句話寫道：「I am very interested in a position with Jericho, Inc. and would like to speak with you about a possible job opportunity」，表示吉布森先生想要應徵工作。

字彙 follow up on 後續追蹤……

179

What might prevent Mr. Gibson from getting the position?

(A) His current academic status
(B) His grades at school
(C) His major at the university
(D) Lack of recommendations

中譯 吉布森先生的哪一項條件可能會讓他無法被錄用？
(A) 他目前仍在就學　　(B) 他的在校成績
(C) 他的大學主修科系　(D) 缺乏推薦人

解析 廣告中提到正在找尋今夏能加入公司的成員。後半段提到：「Recent college graduates are encouraged to apply as well.」，表示應屆畢業生也可應徵。但吉布森先生在電子郵件中提到：「I am a senior at Smokey Mountain University and will be earning a degree in business economics at the end of this year.」，由此可以推測他尚未畢業，無法於今年夏天到職。

字彙 status 狀態

180

In the e-mail, the word "share" in line 4, is closest in meaning to
(A) divide
(B) give
(C) have
(D) match

中譯 在電子郵件中，第四行的「share」與下列何者意思最相近？
(A) 劃分　　　(B) 賦予
(C) 具備　　　(D) 符合

解析 動詞 share 出現在「I share the passion of advertising」當中，表示「具備、擁有」對廣告的熱忱。選項中意思最為接近的單字為 have。

Questions 181-185 refer to the following schedule and memo. 行程表 備忘錄

Meeting Agenda July 17	Time	7 月 17 日會議議程	時間
⑱ Amory Brothers Representatives arrive	9:00 AM	⑱艾莫瑞兄弟公司的代表到場	上午 9:00
Introductions and first proposal	9:30 AM	簡介與第一次提案	上午 9:30
Multimedia showcase ⑱ *Make sure to use the audio files with this.	10:00 AM	多媒體演示 ⑱* 確保搭配使用音訊檔。	上午 10:00
Discussions about how our company can achieve growth *May also be some Q & A during this time.	11:00 AM	討論如何提升公司成長 * 可於此時段採用問答形式。	上午 11:00
Lunch with Amory Brothers President	12:00 PM	與艾莫瑞兄弟公司的董事長餐敍	下午 12:00
Group discussions with management from both companies	1:00 PM	兩家公司的管理層進行團體討論	下午 1:00
Final negotiations *We are hoping to reach this part earlier, but will stress it at this time.	2:00 PM	最終協商 * 雖然我們希望能提早進入此階段，但先將議程壓在這個時間點。	下午 2:00
⑱ Preliminary contracts drawn up	2:30 PM	⑱起草初步合約	下午 2:30
End of the day's meeting	4:00 PM	結束當日會議	下午 4:00

MEMO

To:	Mark Reynolds, Amy Abbott
From:	Jennifer Tyson
Date:	July 15
Subject:	Meeting Agenda July 17

Hello, Mark and Amy,

Here is some information regarding the meeting with Amory Brothers on July 17th. I wanted to make sure to inform you of everything that should happen that day, since it is a big meeting for us.

備忘錄

收件人：馬克・雷諾斯；艾咪・亞伯特
寄件人：珍妮佛・泰森
日期：7 月 15 日
主旨：7 月 17 日會議議程

哈囉，馬克與艾咪：

　　我附上 7/17 與艾莫瑞兄弟公司開會的相關資訊。我想確保你們知道當天的所有流程，因為這對我們來說是場重大會議。

181 This contract could help our company regain its foothold in the audio industry, and I know that I can count on you to help us do just that. **185** When the reps from Amory arrive, please take them to meeting room D, where we will have everything ready to go for you.

184 Amory Brothers is a blue-chip company in the audio industry and works with everyone from the top singers to the best movie companies in the world. **183** Their specialty is creating small equipment to offer assistance to space programs and governments that need to use the smallest audio listening devices available. They expect fast-thinking project leaders to respond to their concerns, and I know the two of you will show how we can be a leading part of the future in audio. I have every confidence they will see that we are the best choice for their future projects!

Jennifer Tyson
President, Hitbox Sound

181 這份合約可幫助我們公司在音響產業重新立足，我知道我能倚重你們來幫公司爭取到這份合約。**185** 艾莫瑞公司的代表到場時，請帶他們到 D 會議室，我們會在那裡為你們將一切準備好。

184 艾莫瑞兄弟公司是音響產業的績優公司，全球的大牌歌手到頂尖的電影公司都是他們的合作對象。**183** 他們專門打造小型設備，來為需要使用最小音訊裝置的太空計畫與政府機關提供協助。他們希望能有腦筋動得快的專案領導人來回應他們的關切的事，我知道你們兩位能展現出公司引領未來音響界的能力。我很有自信，他們一定會知道我們是未來專案合作的最佳人選！

珍妮佛・泰森
熱門音響公司董事長

字彙 management 管理層 preliminary 初步的 draw sth. up 起草某事 regain 重獲 foothold 立足點 count on 倚重 specialty 專長 concern 關切之事

181

What is the purpose of the meeting?
(A) To explain a new audio device
(B) To show new programs to representatives
(C) To try to encourage a merger
(D) To win a contract for the company

中譯 此會議的目的為何？
(A) 說明新的音響裝置
(B) 向代表人員演示新計畫
(C) 試圖促成合併案
(D) 為公司贏得合約

解析 兩篇文章分別為會議日程表和提醒員工的公司備忘錄。日程表下方寫道：「**Preliminary contracts drawn up**」，表示該會議的目的是透過協商簽訂合約；(B) 僅為會議中的某一項目，並非會議目的。

182

What does Ms. Tyson remind Mark and Amy to do during the showcase?
(A) To answer the client's questions
(B) To finish as quickly as possible
(C) To explain as many details as they can
(D) To use the prepared files

中譯 泰森小姐提醒馬克和艾咪需於演示時做什麼事？
(A) 回答客戶的問題
(B) 儘快完成
(C) 儘可能說明許多細節
(D) 使用預先準備好的檔案

解析 請找出與 showcase 有關的內容。日程表第三項寫道：「***Make sure to use the audio files with this.**」，表示泰森要求馬克和艾咪使用事先準備好的音檔。

183

What does the client have leading technology in?
(A) Audio equipment
(B) Computers
(C) Vehicles
(D) Video equipment

中譯 客戶在什麼領域擁有先進科技？
(A) 音響設備　　　　(B) 電腦
(C) 交通工具　　　　(D) 攝影器材

解析 公司備忘錄第三段中提到與客戶艾莫瑞兄弟公司有關的說明：「Their specialty is creating small equipment to offer assistance to space programs and governments that need to use the smallest audio listening devices available.」，(A) 將 audio listening devices 改寫成 audio equipment，故為正確答案。

184

What does Ms. Tyson NOT think about Amory Brothers?
(A) They are a small company.
(B) They are one of the best companies.
(C) They need responsive companies to work with.
(D) They will consider the contract beneficial.

中譯 泰森小姐對艾莫瑞兄弟公司的評價不包括哪一項？
(A) 他們是一家小公司。
(B) 他們是頂尖的公司之一。
(C) 他們需要與反應快的公司合作。
(D) 他們會認為這是份有利的合約。

解析 公司備忘錄第三段中提到：「Amory Brothers is a blue-chip company」，與 (A) 的小型公司敘述相異。

字彙 responsive 反應快的　beneficial 有利的

185

When will Mark and Amy meet the visitors?
(A) At 9:00 AM
(B) At 9:30 AM
(C) At 10:00 AM
(D) At 12:00 PM

中譯 馬克與艾咪何時會與訪客開會？
(A) 上午 9:00　　　(B) 上午 9:30
(C) 上午 10:00　　(D) 中午 12:00

解析 公司備忘錄中提到：「When the reps from Amory arrive, please take them to meeting room D」，艾莫瑞兄弟公司的代表抵達時間為 9 點，故為正確答案。

Questions 186-190 refer to the following summary, schedule, and e-mail.

摘要　時間表　電子郵件　新增題型

Peter Solvang— A Brief Summary of the Artist's Work

• Early Period: Solvang worked in multiple colors (acrylic), using the broad brush strokes he would become famous for later in life.

• ⑱ Mid-career: Solvang branched out with a few modern portraits during this time, bringing to mind the influence of Carson and Eustace.

• ⑱ Final Works: In the decade before his death, Solvang expressed emotions only in black. The bold, dark strokes reflected their own light, he said.

彼得・沙爾芬——藝術家作品之概要

• 早期生涯：沙爾芬運用各色壓克力顏料，搭配寬大筆觸，這種風格也使他爾後聲名大噪。

• ⑱ 中期成就：沙爾芬在此時期受到卡爾森和伊斯坦斯的影響，開始嘗試現代肖像畫。

• ⑱ 晚期作品：在他逝世前的十年裡，沙爾芬僅以黑色作畫來表達情緒。他表示：「大膽的暗色筆觸，能映照出畫作自身的光芒。」

Public Access Channel July Programming Schedule

⑱ Monday, July 17
Getting Started on Your Retirement Fund
17:00 – 17:15

Investment guru, Ravita Singh, tells viewers it's never too early to start investing for your retirement. Tune in for tips and warnings about the best and safest investments.

Tuesday, July 18
Taco Tuesday and Other Treats
15:30 – 16:00

Mexican chef Juanita Valdez shares another terrific recipe with us. Using ingredients easily found in any supermarket, you'll be able to please your hungry crowd tonight.

⑲ Wednesday, July 19
Peter Solvang Retrospective
20:00 – 21:30

Solvang has been called France's greatest modern painter. **⑰ The second in a series, tonight's program examines the works in the middle of his seven-decade career.**

Thursday, July 20
This Beautiful Old House
20:30 – 21:30

Owners of older houses have a lot of work to do. We make it easier with our weekly show that teaches you the basics of home repair and maintenance. Save money and DIY!

To :	Public Access Channel Information <pacinfo@pacabroadcasting.gov>
From :	Riley Springer <rspringer@vastmail.com>
Date :	July 20
Subject :	Question about a program

Hello,

⑲ I would like to know if you are re-broadcasting the program from last night, about the painter. I only caught the last ten minutes of it, so I don't know the name of it. **⑳ I teach art history at the local college** and I'd like to use some of it in my class. Could you tell me how to view it again or how to purchase a recording of it, if possible?

Riley Springer

公共開放頻道七月節目表

⑱ 7 月 17 日 週一
著手規劃退休基金
17:00-17:15

投資達人拉菲塔・辛將告訴觀眾為退休人生做好投資永不嫌晚。請準時收看，了解最棒且安全的投資秘訣以及須注意事項。

7 月 18 日 週二
週二墨西哥塔可餅與其他小吃
15:30 -16:00

墨西哥大廚胡安妮塔・費德茲將與我們分享另一道美味食譜。運用可於超市輕鬆取得的食材，您今晚就能讓飢腸轆轆的家人贊不絕口。

⑲ 7 月 19 日 週三
彼得・沙爾芬回憶錄
20:00 – 21:30

沙爾芬向來被譽為法國最偉大的現代畫家。**⑰ 此系列今晚將播出第二集，主要介紹他七十載畫家生涯的中期畫作。**

7 月 20 日 週四
絕美老屋大改造
20:30 – 21:30

老屋屋主其實需要操心很多事。每週一集的此節目將幫助你化繁為簡，教導房屋修繕與養護的基本法則。開始自己動手做，省下一筆錢！

收件者：	公共開放頻道資訊 <pacinfo@pacabroadcasting.gov>
寄件者：	萊莉・施普林格 <rspringer@vastmail.com>
日期：	7 月 20 日
主旨：	節目相關問題

你好：

　　⑲ 我想知道你們是否還會重播昨晚的畫家節目。我只有看到最後十分鐘，所以不曉得節目名稱是什麼。**⑳ 我在本地大學教導藝術史，**因此我希望能以此節目做為教課素材。是否可以告訴我該如何觀賞重播，或者如何購買該集影片，如果有的話？

萊莉・施普林格

字彙 brush stroke 筆觸　branch out 開展新工作　portrait 肖像畫　bring . . . to mind 想起　influence 影響　guru 達人　tune in 收看　retrospective 回顧展　DIY 自己動手做　re-broadcast 重播

186

When did Peter Solvang use black paint only?
(A) In his early days
(B) Before he met Eustace
(C) During the middle of his career
(D) In the latter part of his life

中譯 彼得・沙爾芬何時開始只用黑色顏料作畫？
(A) 早期生涯
(B) 遇見伊斯坦斯之前
(C) 繪畫生涯中期
(D) 人生晚期

解析 第一篇摘要中，與黑色有關的內容出現在「Final Works」段落。Final Works 指的是人生晚期的作品，因此答案為 (D)。

187

What does the art TV program focus on?
(A) A tutorial on brush strokes
(B) An artist's portrait period
(C) Bright colors in nature
(D) Using acrylic in paintings

中譯 該藝術節目著重哪個部分？
(A) 繪畫筆觸的教學
(B) 藝術家的肖像畫時期
(C) 大自然中的明亮色彩
(D) 運用壓克力顏料作畫

解析 電視節目表中與藝術有關的節目為「彼得・沙爾芬回憶錄」，當中的說明為：「the works in the middle of his seven-decade career」。回到第一篇摘要，中期作品（Mid-career）的特色為肖像畫，因此答案為 (B)。

字彙 tutorial 教學

188

When does a show about money air?
(A) Monday
(B) Tuesday
(C) Wednesday
(D) Thursday

中譯 與理財有關的節目會何時播出？
(A) 週一
(B) 週二
(C) 週三
(D) 週四

解析 電視節目表中與錢有關的節目為「著手規劃退休基金」，該節目的播出時間為星期一。

字彙 air 播出

189

What program does Ms. Springer ask about?
(A) Getting Started on Your Retirement Fund
(B) Peter Solvang Retrospective
(C) Taco Tuesday and Other Treats
(D) This Beautiful Old House

中譯 施普林格小姐詢問的是哪個節目？
(A) 著手規劃退休基金
(B) 彼得・沙爾芬回憶錄
(C) 週二墨西哥塔可餅與其他小吃
(D) 絕美老屋大改造

解析 寄件人施普林格小姐表示：「I would like to know if you are re-broadcasting the program from last night, about the painter.」，而該封電子郵件的寄件日期為 7 月 20 日。前一天 7 月 19 日播出與畫家有關的節目為「彼得・沙爾芬回憶錄」。

190

What is mentioned about Ms. Springer?
(A) She is an artist.
(B) She is an investment banker.
(C) She owns an older home.
(D) **She works in education.**

中譯 關於施普林格小姐，文中提到什麼資訊？
(A) 她是藝術家。
(B) 她是投資銀行家。
(C) 她擁有老屋。
(D) 她是教職人員。

解析 電子郵件中寫道：「I teach art history at the local college」，表示她從事教育工作；她教授藝術史，並不表示她就是一名藝術家。

Questions 191-195 refer to the following advertisement, invoice, and e-mail.

廣告 發票 電子郵件 新增題型

Auburn Motors Special Lease Offer

If you're not quite ready to make the commitment to buy a car for whatever reason, our lease option is perfect—and sometimes less costly in the long run than buying brand-new!

Lease any of our brand-new models* for just $200 per month for 36 months and ⑲ **pay only $2,500 at signing**. That's a lower down payment than any of our competitors.

No security deposit. Walk-away anytime during lease agreement. For 36 months, take up the option to purchase a vehicle for value for money (cheaper than buying one). This offer will be made to qualified candidates. Thorough credit background check will be made by Verify, Inc.

⑲ *Wellspring 5000 sedan, Fox Trot XR sports car, Jasmine 33 hybrid, Emerald Bay mini van

奧本汽車公司租車特價活動

如果您因為任何原因而尚未做好心理準備來購車，我們的租車服務恰恰適合您——長期來看，還有可能比購買新車更加划算！

連續租賃我們的全新車款* 36 個月，每月僅需 200 元，⑲ 簽合約時僅需事先支付 2500 元。這樣的首付款比我們的其他競爭對手低廉許多。

不需押金。還可於租約期間隨時解約。而連續租車 36 個月的方案，約滿後還可選擇購買物有所值的車（價格比一般購車更低）。此優惠適用於合格的租車方。我們將委託「核實公司」來檢驗信用背景。

⑲ * 泉源 5000 房車、福斯托特 XR 跑車、茉莉 33 油電混合車、翡翠灣多功能休旅車。

Final Invoice for Car Lease

Name: Timothy Loins

⑲ **Make/Model: Hybrid**
Mileage Upon return: 12,389

⑲ **Total time on lease: 12 months**
Maintenance: New brake pads

⑲ Mileage charge 389 x 0.15	58.35
Local tax	49.50
Maintenance	245.25
Final month charge	200.00
Total	553.10

⑲ *Vehicle leases include 12,000 free miles per year. Above that, customers are charged $0.15 per mile.

租車結算發票

租車人：提摩西・里昂斯

⑲ 車款：油電混合車
歸還時的里程數：12,389

⑲ 總租車時間：12 個月

保養項目：新煞車來令片

⑲ 里程數費用 389 x 0.15	58.35
地方稅	49.50
保養費	245.25
結算月收費	200.00
總金額	553.10

⑲ * 租車方案包含每年 1 萬 2 千英里的免費里程數。超過免費額度則每英里收取 0.15 元。

From :	Timothy Lions <timothylions@bizplus.net>
To :	Auburn Motors <info@auburnmotors.com>
Date :	July 3
Subject :	Car lease charges

I just received the final invoice from my car lease with Auburn Motors and I'm afraid there's been an error, probably just a clerical one. At the time I turned the car back in, ⑲ **I recorded the miles as 10,389.** ⑲ **I even took a picture of the odometer, which I've attached to this message.** Please refund me the extra mileage charge.

Thank you,
Timothy Lions

寄件者：提摩西・里昂斯
　　　　<timothylions@bizplus.net>
收件者：奧本汽車公司
　　　　<info@auburnmotors.com>
日期：7 月 3 日
主旨：租車費用

　　我剛收到奧本汽車公司寄來的租車結算發票，我想發票內容有誤，可能只是誤植。我歸還汽車時，⑲ 自己記錄的里程數是 10,389 英里。⑲ 我甚至有拍下里程表的照片，並隨此信附上照片。請退還超收我的里程費用。

謝謝您
提摩西・里昂斯

Actual Test 3　PART 7

字彙 costly 昂貴的　brand-new 全新的　security deposit 押金　clerical 辦公室工作的　odometer 里程表

191

How much did Mr. Lions likely pay as a down payment?
(A) $200
(B) $553.10
(C) $1,200
(D) $2,500

中譯 里昂斯先生付了多少首付款？
(A) 200 元
(B) 553.10 元
(C) 1,200 元
(D) 2,500 元

解析 根據租車廣告的內容，簽約時只需支付 2500 元即可。根據第二篇發票，里昂斯先生簽下了汽車租賃契約，簽約當下即付了簽約金 2500 元。

192

What type of car did Mr. Lions lease?
(A) Emerald Bay
(B) Fox Trot XR
(C) Jasmine 33
(D) Wellspring 5000

中譯 里昂斯先生租了哪一種車款？
(A) 翡翠灣
(B) 福斯托特 XR
(C) 茉莉 33
(D) 泉源 5000

解析 發票中顯示里昂斯先生租的車款為 hybrid。回到廣告的最後一行，hybrid 對應的車種為 Jasmine 33。

193

When did Mr. Lions return the vehicle?
(A) A week after signing the lease
(B) A few months after signing the lease
(C) One year after signing the lease
(D) Three years after signing the lease

中譯 里昂斯先生何時還車？
(A) 簽完租車合約後的一個禮拜
(B) 簽完租車合約後的幾個月
(C) 簽完租車合約後的一年
(D) 簽完租車合約後的三年

解析 發票上的「Total time on lease」為 12 個月，指的是簽約後一年要歸還車輛。

194

How much is Mr. Lions asking to be refunded?
(A) $49.50
(B) $58.35
(C) $200.00
(D) $245.25

中譯 里昂斯先生要求退款多少錢？
(A) 49.50 元
(B) 58.35 元
(C) 200.00 元
(D) 245.25 元

解析 發票上的「Mileage Upon return」為 12,389，但里昂斯先生在電子郵件中表明：「I recorded the miles as 10,389」。另外發票下方註明提供每年 12,000 英里的免費里程。這表示里昂斯先生被多收取的里程費用（Mileage charge）為 58.35 元，因此他要求退還此筆費用。

195

What has Mr. Lions sent with his e-mail?
(A) A picture of the car's control panel
(B) A picture of the car's exterior
(C) His original contract
(D) The lease advertisement

中譯 里昂斯先生隨電子郵件附上了什麼？
(A) 汽車儀表板的照片　　(B) 汽車外觀的照片
(C) 原合約　　(D) 租車廣告

解析 電子郵件的附件為要求退費的證明照片。當中寫道：「I even took a picture of the odometer, which I've attached to this message.」，(A) 將 odometer 改寫成 control panel，故為正確答案。

字彙 control panel 儀表板　exterior 外觀

Questions 196-200 refer to the following information, e-mail, and list.

資訊　電子郵件　清單　新增題型

San Marcos 25ᵗʰ Annual Home Decor Exhibition

⑲⑦ July 21 – 24　　9:30 AM – 5:30 PM
Javier Center　San Marcos, CA

Program for July 21

• Opening Presentation
10:00 AM – 10:30 AM
Main Stage

Exhibition organizer Felicia Knowles of Westbrook Designs will give a welcome speech.

• Trends in Home Fashion
11:30 AM – 12:30 PM
East Room

Staff from local business Bridget Homes will explain what is trending now.

• ⑲⑥ Forecast for Next Year
1:30 PM – 2:00 PM
West Pavilion

Design icon Robert Waxman will share his insights on hot designs in the coming year.

聖馬克斯 25 週年家飾展覽

⑲⑦ 7 月 21–24 日　　早上 9:30 – 下午 5:30
加州聖馬克斯哈維偏中心

7 月 21 日節目表

• 開幕致詞
上午 10:00-10:30
主要舞台

展覽主辦單位西布魯克設計公司的費莉西亞・諾爾斯將帶來迎賓致詞。

• 居家時尚的趨勢
上午 11:30- 下午 12:30
東側展廳

當地的布利基家飾公司人員將解說目前流行的趨勢。

• ⑲⑥ 明年趨勢預測
下午 1:30-2:00
西側展館

設計界的指標人物羅伯特・魏斯曼將分享他對於明年熱門設計風格的見解。

- New Exhibitors' Gallery
  All Day
  Center Section

Don't miss the newest businesses showing off their products.

- 新展覽藝廊
  全日開放
  中央展區

別錯過新創的家飾公司展示產品。

From :	Marc Ephraim <mephraim@ephraimdes.com>
To :	Janessa Blackwell <jblackwell@ephraimdes.com>
Date :	July 17
Subject :	Home Decor Exhibition

Hi Janessa,

I was hoping you could help me with the upcoming event at Javier Center. My team and I can ⑲⑧ **cover** the booth itself, ⑲⑦ **but we need to rotate some people to the gallery throughout the first day.** I was wondering what your availability would be from 1:00 to 5:00? I could actually use two more people, so if you have any recommendations, let me know. One more thing. ⑲⑨ **Could you look over the attached product list and confirm the price on CSH-45?** I know that particular one costs more because of the specialty fabric, but I don't know what price we finally settled on.

Thanks a lot,
Marc Ephraim
Ephraim Designs

寄件人：馬克・艾弗倫
　　　<mephraim@ephraimdes.com>
收件人：珍妮莎・伯萊克威
　　　<jblackwell@ephraimdes.com>
日期：7 月 17 日
主旨：家飾展覽

嗨，珍妮莎：

　　關於即將在哈維爾中心舉辦的活動，我希望妳能幫幫我。我和團隊可自行 ⑲⑧ 負責攤位，⑲⑦ 但參展第一天時，我們需要更多人手來輪流看顧藝廊區。我想了解一下，妳 1 點到 5 點之間何時有空檔？我其實還需要兩個人手，所以如果妳還有其他推薦人選，麻煩告訴我。還有一件事，⑲⑨ 可以麻煩妳看一下隨附的產品清單，確認 CSH-45 的價格嗎？我知道這件產品因為布料特殊而價格較高，但我不清楚我們最後說好的價格是多少。

十分感謝，
馬克・艾弗倫
艾弗倫設計公司

Ephraim Designs Exhibition Product List

	Item Number	Dimensions	Price
Upholstery Fabrics			
Woven	UF-WV21	Varies (remnants)	Individually labeled
Modern	UF-MO11	"	"
Traditional	UF-TR95	"	"
Small Cupboards			
Mottled Green	CPB-MG3	⑳⓪ H85/W76/D40	$125
French Grey	CPB-FG5	"	$125
Provence Blue	CPB-PB7	"	$135
Mediterranean Blue	CPB-MB9	"	$130

艾弗倫設計公司展覽產品清單

	品項編號	尺寸	價格
椅套布料			
平織布款	UF-WV21	各種尺寸（零碼布）	個別標示
現代款	UF-MO11	"	"
傳統款	UF-TR95	"	"
小櫥櫃			
波紋綠	CPB-MG3	⑳⓪ H85/W76/D40	$125
法式灰	CPB-FG5	"	$125
普羅旺斯藍	CPB-PB7	"	$135
地中海藍	CPB-MB9	"	$130

⑲ Cushion Covers				⑲ 靠枕套			
Floral	CSH-55	40x40	$45	花卉款	CSH-55	40x40	$45
Animals	CSH-32	40x40	$45	動物款	CSH-32	40x40	$45
⑲ Designer	CSH-45	55x55	$50	⑲ 設計師款	CSH-45	55x55	$50
Traditional	CSH-64	55x55	$50	傳統款	CSH-64	55x55	$50

字彙 exhibition 展覽　give a welcome speech 發表迎賓致詞　pavilion 展館　rotate 輪流　dimension 尺寸　upholstery 家飾　remnant 零碼布　mottled 波紋的

196

Where can participants hear about future trends?
(A) Center Section
(B) East Room
(C) Main Stage
(D) West Pavilion

中譯 觀展者可於何處聆聽未來趨勢的演講？
(A) 中央展區
(B) 東側展廳
(C) 主要舞台
(D) 西側展館

解析 與 future trends 有關的內容出現在日程表中的「明年趨勢預測」，其活動地點在西側展館。

197

When does Mr. Ephraim want Ms. Blackwell's help?
(A) On July 21
(B) On July 22
(C) On July 23
(D) On July 24

中譯 艾弗倫先生何時需要伯萊克威小姐的協助？
(A) 7 月 21 日
(B) 7 月 22 日
(C) 7 月 23 日
(D) 7 月 24 日

解析 第二篇文章為電子郵件，寄件人艾弗倫先生向收件人伯萊克威小姐請求協助。當中提到：「My team and I can cover the booth itself, but we need to rotate some people to the gallery throughout the first day.」，表示請伯萊克威小姐第一天前來支援。根據第一篇資訊，展覽於 7 月 21 日開始，因此答案為 (A)。

198

In the e-mail, the word "cover" in line 1, is the closest in meaning to
(A) decorate
(B) hide
(C) wrap
(D) include

中譯 在電子郵件中，第二行的「cover」意思與下列何者最相近？
(A) 裝飾
(B) 隱藏
(C) 包裝
(D) 包含

解析 動詞 cover 位在「My team and I can cover the booth itself」中，意思為「包含、負責」。選項中，意思最為相似的單字為 include，意思為「包含」。

字彙 hide 隱藏

199

What item does Mr. Ephraim ask Ms. Blackwell about?
(A) The designer cushion cover
(B) The floral cushion
(C) The modern upholstery fabric
(D) The woven table cloth

中譯 艾弗倫先生詢問伯萊克威小姐哪項產品的問題？
(A) 設計師款靠枕套
(B) 花卉款靠枕
(C) 現代款椅套布料
(D) 平織布款桌布

解析 請從電子郵件確認答案。當中詢問：「**Could you look over the attached product list and confirm the price on CSH-45?**」。至第三篇清單中確認，可以得知為 Cushion Covers 當中的 Designer。

What is common to the cupboards in the list?
(A) The color
(B) The material
(C) The price
(D) The size

中譯 櫥櫃清單裡一致的資訊為何？
(A) 顏色
(B) 材質
(C) 價格
(D) 尺寸

解析 請確認清單中的 cupboards 項目。當中各類櫥櫃的共同點為尺寸（dimensions），選項改寫成 size，因此答案為 (D)。

字彙 **material** 材質

Actual Test 3

PART 7

Actual Test 4

001 (加)

(A) She's touching a piece of equipment.
(B) She's talking with someone near a copier.
(C) She's looking at a video monitor.
(D) She's playing an instrument.

中譯 (A) 她正在觸摸設備。
(B) 她在跟影印機附近的某人說話。
(C) 她正看著錄影螢幕。
(D) 她正在彈奏樂器。

解析 照片中的女子正在操作機器,因此 **(A)**「She's touching a piece of equipment.」為最適當的描述。

字彙 copier 影印機　instrument 樂器

002 (美)

(A) He's cutting some grass.
(B) He's cleaning a window.
(C) He's operating a construction vehicle.
(D) He's painting something on a road.

中譯 (A) 他正在除草。
(B) 他在清理窗戶。
(C) 他在操作工程車。
(D) 他在路上畫記。

解析 照片中的男子正在操作工程車,因此答案為 **(C)**「He's operating a construction vehicle.」;照片中並未出現 cutting、cleaning、painting 等動作。

字彙 construction vehicle 工程車

003 (澳)

(A) A dog is being petted.
(B) A man is riding a bicycle.
(C) Some people are looking down at a dog.
(D) A dog is sitting on a bench.

中譯 (A) 狗狗正在被撫摸。
(B) 男子在騎自行車。
(C) 有些人正往下看著狗狗。
(D) 有隻狗坐在長凳上。

解析 照片中的孩子們正俯視跑在他們前方的小狗,因此 **(C)**「Some people are looking down at a dog.」為最適當的描述;孩子並未跟小狗有所接觸,因此 **(A)** 的描述並不適當。

字彙 pet 撫摸　look down 往下看

004 美

(A) Lights are hanging from the ceiling.
(B) Pictures are arranged by the door.
(C) Tables have been set for a meal.
(D) Windows are open near the door.

中譯 (A) 燈具懸掛於天花板。
(B) 照片排列在門邊。
(C) 餐桌已排好餐具準備用餐。
(D) 門附近的窗戶是打開的。

解析 照片中餐桌上已擺好用餐時所需的餐具,因此 (C)「Tables have been set for a meal.」為適當的描述。

字彙 arrange 排列
set a table for a meal 在餐桌上擺餐具準備用餐

---

005 澳

(A) They're driving through traffic.
(B) Some people are getting in a car.
(C) They're stopping at a signal.
(D) Some people are leaving a building.

中譯 (A) 他們正開車穿越車潮。
(B) 有些人正在上車。
(C) 他們停在紅綠燈前。
(D) 有些人正離開大樓。

解析 照片中人們站在道路上,準備上計程車的後座,因此 (B)「Some people are getting in a car.」為適當的描述。

字彙 traffic 車潮,交通 get in 進入(車輛)

---

006 英

🎧 13

(A) Motorcycles are being fixed.
(B) Motorcycles are parked end to end.
(C) Motorcycles are being washed.
(D) Motorcycles are parked next to each other.

中譯 (A) 有人正在修理機車。
(B) 機車前後接排停靠。
(C) 機車正在被清洗。
(D) 機車並排停靠。

解析 照片中的兩台摩托車並排停放,因此答案為 (D)「Motorcycles are parked next to each other.」;摩托車是並排的狀態,因此 (B) 並不正確。

字彙 end to end 前後相連
next to each other 並排

007 美 加

Would you be able to help me later?
(A) Sure. How about 3:00?
(B) I'm afraid I didn't catch his name.
(C) No. They're out at the moment.

中譯 你晚一點能幫我嗎?
(A) 當然可以。3 點怎麼樣?
(B) 我恐怕沒記住他的名字。
(C) 不行,他們現在在外面。

解析 Would you 開頭的問句 本題提出要求,詢問是否能幫自己的忙。(A) 表示同意,並提到在特定時間幫忙,故為適當的答覆。

字彙 catch one's name 記住某人的姓名

---

008 澳 英

Why do we need new security badges?
(A) No one can stay past 8:00 PM.
(B) Because she got a new one.
(C) The building has a new system.

中譯 我們為什麼需要配戴新的安全出入證?
(A) 沒有人能待到晚上 8 點以後。
(B) 因為她有新的出入證。
(C) 因為大樓設了新系統。

解析 Why 開頭的問句 如果不知道 security badges 是什麼,可能難以順利解題。本題詢問的是需要新的安全出入證的理由。(C) 表示因為大樓安裝了新的系統,故為最適當的答覆;(B) 故意使用 because 來回答 why 開頭的問句,為答題陷阱。

字彙 security 安全 past 超過

---

009 美 加

Who is supposed to sign my time sheet?
(A) She already filled it out online.
(B) Ask Mr. Peters.
(C) I have no more questions.

中譯 誰該幫我簽工時單?
(A) 她已經在線上填單。
(B) 問問彼得斯先生。
(C) 我沒有問題了。

解析 Who 開頭的問句 針對本題的提問,(B) 採取迴避式答覆,要求詢問他人,故為最適當的答覆。

字彙 be supposed to 應該

---

010 英 澳

The supplies are being delivered tomorrow, aren't they?
(A) You picked him yourself, didn't you?
(B) Yes, as far as I know.
(C) Just $4.99 for shipping.

中譯 補給用品明天會到貨,對嗎?
(A) 你親自選他的,對嗎?
(B) 是的,就我所知是明天。
(C) 運費只要 4.99 元。

解析 附加問句 本題以問句確認補給用品是否會在明天送達。(B) 表示據聽者所知是如此,為最適當的答覆;(C) 僅與題目中的 delivered 有所關聯,為陷阱選項。

字彙 supplies 補給用品 shipping 運輸

011 英 美

I was told this is the newest version of the software.
(A) There's a mistake on my bill.
(B) That's right. It's version 4.0.
(C) Can you make a copy of this contract?

中譯 有人跟我說這是此軟體的最新版本。
(A) 我的帳單有誤。
(B) 沒錯，是 4.0 版。
(C) 你可以影印一份此合約嗎？

解析 直述句 本題題目表示聽說這是最新版的軟體。(B) 表示同意，同時補充其他資訊，故為最適當的答覆。

字彙 version 版本

012 加 英

What do you want me to do with these reports?
(A) The report said Highway 50 is closed today.
(B) I want all staff informed immediately.
(C) Could you file them away for me?

中譯 你希望我怎麼處理這些報告？
(A) 報告指出 50 號高速公路今天封閉。
(B) 我希望立即通知所有員工。
(C) 你可以幫我歸檔嗎？

解析 What 開頭的問句 本題詢問該如何處理報告。(C) 請對方整理資料，為選項中最適當的答覆；(B) 僅是利用題目中的「you want me」，回答「I want」，為陷阱選項。

字彙 file . . . away 將……歸檔

013 加 美

Where are the new clients going?
(A) On a tour with the manager.
(B) I'm always thinking ahead.
(C) Wherever they will fit securely.

中譯 新客戶要去哪裡？
(A) 和經理四處遊覽。
(B) 我總是未雨綢繆。
(C) 只要能把它們固定好的地方就行。

解析 Where 開頭的問句 本題詢問位置。(A) 針對他們的動作進行說明，為選項中最適當的答覆。參觀或介紹公司或工廠的設施時，可以使用原意為「旅遊」的英文單字「tour」表示，如同 (A)「They are going on a tour with the manager」。

字彙 on a tour 遊覽　think ahead 未雨綢繆

014 英 澳

How much rice should we order?
(A) Until nearly 6:00.
(B) Same as last time—10 kilos.
(C) From the outlet over there.

中譯 我們應訂購多少米？
(A) 直到將近 6 點為止。
(B) 和上次一樣——10 公斤。
(C) 從專賣店那裡訂。

解析 How much 開頭的問句 本題詢問訂購量。(B) 回答與上次相同的量：十公斤，為適當的答覆；(A) 和 (C) 的回答分別對應詢問時間和位置的問句。

字彙 outlet 專賣店

Actual Test 4

PART 2

14

015 加美

When does the next bus leave for the airport?
(A) Tickets are $25 per person.
(B) Do you prefer a window or an aisle seat?
(C) Not for another 35 minutes.

中譯 下一班前往機場的巴士是幾點出發？
(A) 每人票價是 25 元。
(B) 您較喜歡靠窗還是靠走道的位子？
(C) 還要再等 35 分鐘。

解析 When 開頭的問句 本題詢問下一班開往機場的公車何時發車。(C) 回答「再過三十五分鐘」，故為正確答案；(B) 的回答僅與題目中的 airport 有所關聯，為陷阱選項。

字彙 aisle seat 靠走道的位子

---

016 澳加

Should we invite Elise to join us?
(A) She's tied up with her project.
(B) To the Tidewater Café.
(C) No. The food was just so-so.

中譯 我們該邀請艾莉絲加入我們嗎？
(A) 她因為自己的專案分身乏術。
(B) 前往潮水咖啡廳。
(C) 不好吃，食物口味普通。

解析 一般問句 本題建議邀請特定人士。(A) 回答她為專案忙得不可開交，間接暗示她無法接受邀請，因此為最適當的答覆。

字彙 be tied up with 忙於　so-so 普通的

---

017 澳英

How much will the new system cost?
(A) We're not sure of the release date.
(B) Between 4 and 5,000 dollars.
(C) It's straight from the manufacturer.

中譯 新系統的要價會是多少？
(A) 我們還不確定上市日期。
(B) 介於四千元和五千元之間。
(C) 是製造商直送。

解析 How much 開頭的問句 本題詢問多少錢。(B) 回答該金額所在的範圍，故為最適當的答覆。

字彙 release date 上市日期　straight 直接的
manufacturer 製造商

---

018 加美

Where should I put this box of pictures?
(A) In the storage cabinet, thanks.
(B) My camera's in the shop.
(C) The frames are expensive.

中譯 我該將這箱照片放在哪裡？
(A) 儲物櫃裡，謝謝。
(B) 我的相機放在店裡。
(C) 相框好貴。

解析 Where 開頭的問句 本題詢問放置照片箱的位置。(A) 回答儲藏櫃，為最適當的答覆；(B) 和 (C) 僅與題目中的 pictures 有所關聯，皆為陷阱選項。

字彙 storage 儲藏

019 美 加

Do you want to meet at my office?
(A) No. I haven't met her yet.
(B) Sounds good. Give me your address.
(C) In case I'm late, start without me.

中譯 你想在我的辦公室碰面嗎？
(A) 沒有，我還沒見到她。
(B) 好主意。給我你的地址。
(C) 萬一我晚到，你們不用等我就先開始吧。

解析 一般問句 本題詢問要不要在自己的辦公室內碰面。(B) 請對方告知地址，以便前往，故為最適當的答覆；(A) 和 (C) 僅與題目中的 meet 有所關聯，皆為陷阱選項。

字彙 in case 萬一

---

020 澳 英

Who decided to buy the new curtains?
(A) The office manager.
(B) Let's ask Mr. Carson for the money.
(C) The decorator will visit our office tomorrow.

中譯 是誰決定買新窗簾？
(A) 辦公室經理。
(B) 我們去向卡爾森先生請款。
(C) 室內設計師明天會來我們的辦公室。

解析 Who 開頭的問句 本題詢問是誰決定的。(A) 表示為辦公室經理，簡短回答出職稱，故為最適當的答覆；(B) 和 (C) 的回答皆與題目詢問的方向有關，務必要了解題意，才能順利避開陷阱選項。

字彙 decorator 室內設計師

---

021 美 澳

Should I invite Bob to the party?
(A) Yes. The party's been canceled.
(B) You should go to bed early.
(C) Sure. It looks like he could use a break.

中譯 我應該邀請鮑勃參加派對嗎？
(A) 對，派對已經取消了。
(B) 你應該早點睡覺。
(C) 當然好。我覺得他需要休息一下。

解析 一般問句 本題詢問是否要邀請特定人士參加派對。(C) 表示肯定，同時提到對方也需要休息一下，故為最符合題意的答覆；(A) 的回答僅與題目中的 party 有所關聯，為陷阱選項。

---

022 英 加

Where is your showroom located?
(A) Next to the bank on Maple Street.
(B) Our airport hotel is convenient.
(C) From 10:00 to 5:00.

中譯 你們的展示中心位於哪裡？
(A) 就在楓葉街上的銀行隔壁。
(B) 我們的機場飯店十分便利。
(C) 從 10 點到 5 點。

解析 Where 開頭的問句 本題詢問展場的位置。(A) 回答位在楓葉街上的銀行旁邊，故為最適當的答覆。

字彙 showroom 展示中心

14

023 美 澳

There isn't any more tea, is there?
(A) There are more participants than expected.
(B) Sorry. We ran out.
(C) I wish you could come.

中譯 已經沒有茶了,對嗎?
(A) 參加者比預期中的多。
(B) 抱歉,已經沒有了。
(C) 我希望你能來。

解析 附加問句 本題以問句確認茶是否都沒有了。(B) 請對方諒解,並且解釋已經用完了,故為最適當的答覆;(A) 的回答僅與「any more」有所關聯,為陷阱選項。

字彙 run out 用盡

---

024 英 美

Why don't we ask for volunteers first?
(A) I doubt anyone will volunteer.
(B) There are no more slots left.
(C) They'll be ready at 10:00.

中譯 我們為什麼不先問問看有沒有人要當志工?
(A) 我懷疑會有人會想當志工。
(B) 已經沒有多餘的時段了。
(C) 他們會在 10 點準備就緒。

解析 Why don't we 開頭的問句 有時選項中會出現重複使用題目中單字的陷阱選項,故意誤導考生;有時則會直接列出明確的答案。本題建議徵求志工,(A) 回答可能不會有人願意,表達反對的立場,為選項中最適當的答覆。

字彙 slot 時段

---

025 加 澳

Are you going to the seminar next week?
(A) Yes. It was a useful one.
(B) No. I'm too busy.
(C) I have an appointment today.

中譯 你會去參加下週的座談會嗎?
(A) 對,我參加過的這場座談會很實用。
(B) 不了,我太忙。
(C) 我今天有約會。

解析 一般問句 本題詢問是否會參加座談會。(B) 回答太忙無法參加,故為選項中最適當的答覆;(A) 的回答僅與 seminar 有所關聯,為陷阱選項。

---

026 澳 英

We don't often get storms like this here.
(A) Let's check with him later.
(B) They're often delayed by weather.
(C) Yes. This one is scary.

中譯 我們這裡不常出現這樣子的暴風雨。
(A) 我們晚點再問他看看。
(B) 通常會因為氣候延遲。
(C) 是的,這場暴風雨很可怕。

解析 直述句 聽到題目句後,務必要理解該句話指出現在遭遇暴風雨的情況。(C) 對於這裡不常出現暴風雨表示同意,並補充說明自己的想法,故為最適當的答覆。選項中出現 this one 這類指示詞時,請務必確認它對應題目句中的哪個單字。

字彙 scary 可怕

027 澳 美

How about switching shifts with
Susan tomorrow?
(A) That's one way to think about it.
(B) She prefers this blue shirt.
(C) Her shift is too late for me.

中譯 明天和蘇珊換班怎麼樣?
(A) 這是一個可能的想法。
(B) 她比較喜歡藍色襯衫。
(C) 她的值班時間對我來說太晚了。

解析 **How about 開頭的問句** 本題以問句建議明天換班一事。(C) 回答她的上班時間對自己來說太晚,表示自己沒辦法接受,故為最適當的答覆;(A) it 所指的對象並不明確。

字彙 switch 交換　shift 輪班

---

028 英 加

Are these 100 brochures going to
be enough or should we order
more?
(A) Let's start with these.
(B) I can't work this new copier.
(C) No. They can't come tomorrow.

中譯 這 100 本手冊夠嗎?還是我們應該多訂?
(A) 我們先用現有的這些。
(B) 我沒辦法操作這台新影印機。
(C) 不用,他們明天不能來。

解析 **選擇疑問句** 本題詢問 100 本手冊是否足夠,還是需要再加購。(A) 表示先使用現有的,故為最適當的答覆;當題目詢問對方的選擇時,較少出現像 (C) 一樣,以 Yes 或 No 來回答的方式。

---

029 美 英

I hope the manager talks to Priscilla
soon.
(A) Whenever she wants.
(B) All of the managers are out.
(C) Why? Is there a problem?

中譯 我希望經理能盡快和普莉希拉談談。
(A) 她想什麼時候都可以。
(B) 所有經理都外出了。
(C) 為什麼?有什麼問題嗎?

解析 **直述句** 本題提到希望經理盡快與普莉希拉談話。(C) 對此表示好奇,並反問有什麼問題,為選項中最適當的答覆;(A) 當中所指的人物和狀況並不明確。

---

030 加 澳

Are they taking the train back?
(A) Yes. We are on the express.
(B) I think they're driving.
(C) No. I haven't heard back from
him.

中譯 他們正要搭火車回來了嗎?
(A) 對,我們在特快車上。
(B) 我想他們是自己開車。
(C) 沒有,我還沒有得到他的回覆。

解析 **一般問句** 本題針對 they 提出問題。(B) 同樣針對 they 回答,為最適當的答覆;(A) 的主詞為 we,不符合題意;題目中並未出現 (C) him 所指的對象。

字彙 express 特快車

14

031 美 加

What made them change their minds?
(A) I don't have any change, sorry.
(B) Our vacation was pleasant.
(C) The new contract terms were attractive.

中譯 是什麼讓他們改變主意？
(A) 抱歉，我沒有零錢。
(B) 我們的假期過得很愉快。
(C) 因為新的合約條件很吸引人。

解析 **What 開頭的問句** What made 開頭的問句詢問的是原因。本題詢問他們為何改變心意。(C) 表示因為新合約的條件更吸引人，為適當的答覆；題目中 change 的意思為「改變」，而 (A) 故意使用同個單字 change，意思為「零錢」，屬於答題陷阱。

字彙 change 改變；零錢　contract terms 合約條件

PART 3 🎧 15

Questions 32-34 refer to the following conversation. 加 美

W ㉜ When we go to our client, the Bradley firm, should we take a company car or the train? They moved recently and now they are out near the airport. No trains go there directly, as far as I know.

M In that case, ㉝ it makes more sense to drive. I'll put in a request for a car. We're going this Friday, right?

W ㉜ Uh, actually, it's next Friday. This Friday is a national holiday.

M Oh, that's right. How could I forget? ㉞ I'm going camping with my family.

女：㉜ 我們去客戶——布萊德利事務所——那裡的時候，應該開公司車或搭火車？他們最近剛遷址，現在位於機場附近。就我所知，沒有火車直達那裡。

男：這樣的話，㉝ 開車會比較合理。我再來申請公司車。我們是這週五要去，對吧？

女：㉜ 呃，其實是下週五。這週五是國定假日。

男：喔，沒錯。我怎麼忘了呢？㉞ 我還要跟家人去露營呢。

字彙 firm 事務所　make sense 合理　put in a request 申請

032

Where are the speakers going next week?
(A) On a business trip
(B) On a camping trip
(C) To a client's office
(D) To a holiday resort

中譯 說話者下週要去哪裡？
(A) 出差　　　　　　(B) 露營
(C) 前往客戶的辦公室　(D) 前往度假勝地

解析 兩人針對前往客戶公司的交通方式進行討論。另外，男子以為這週五要開會，女子告訴他下週五才要開會，由此可以得知說話者下週要去客戶辦公室。

033

How are the speakers going to get to their destination?
(A) By airplane
(B) By bus
(C) By car
(D) By train

中譯 說話者會以何種方式前往目的地？
(A) 搭飛機　　　(B) 搭公車
(C) 開車　　　　(D) 搭火車

解析 男子表示開車去比較好。由此可以得知說話者將開車前往目的地。

232

034

What is mentioned about this Friday?
(A) No company vehicles are available.
(B) **The man will spend time with his family.**
(C) The woman will move to a new place.
(D) There is a company picnic.

中譯 關於本週五，文中提到了什麼？
(A) 沒有公司配車可用。
(B) 男子要陪家人。
(C) 女子要搬新家。
(D) 公司要舉辦野餐活動。

解析 對話最後，男子提到這週五要和家人一起去露營，表示他將花時間陪伴家人。

換句話說 going camping with my family → spend time with his family

Questions 35-37 refer to the following conversation. 英 澳

M Ah, Emily, I was just about to call you about the exhibit tomorrow. We're still going, right?

W Of course. I've been looking forward to it. ㉟ **Pop art is my favorite type of art.** So, should we meet at the gallery or have dinner first?

M ㊱ **Let's have dinner first.** I've been wanting to try the new Greek place, Olympian. It's only a few streets over from the gallery.

W Great. So ㊱ **let's meet in front of Olympian at 6:00.** That should give us enough time to eat and ㊲ **make the artist's introduction at 7:30.**

男：啊，艾蜜莉，我正要打電話問妳明天展覽的事。我們還是要去，對吧？

女：當然，我一直很期待。㉟普普藝術是我最喜歡的藝術類型。那我們要在藝廊碰面還是先吃晚餐？

男：㊱我們先吃晚餐吧。我一直很想試試看新開的希臘餐廳「奧林匹亞」。離藝廊只有幾條街而已。

女：太好了，㊱我們就晚上6點在奧林匹亞門口碰面吧。我們應該有足夠的時間吃飯，㊲且來得及在7點半聽到藝術家的開場致詞。

Actual Test 4

PART 3

🎧 15

035

What does the woman say she likes?
(A) Greek food
(B) **Modern art**
(C) New cafés
(D) Pop music

中譯 女子表示自己有何喜好？
(A) 希臘食物
(B) 現代藝術
(C) 新開的咖啡廳
(D) 流行樂

解析 第一段對話中，女子提到她最喜歡的藝術類型為普普藝術，普普藝術屬於現代藝術，因此答案為 (B)。

036

Where are the speakers planning to meet first?
(A) At a gallery
(B) **At a restaurant**
(C) At an art supply store
(D) At the woman's apartment

中譯 說話者計劃到哪裡碰面？
(A) 藝廊
(B) 餐廳
(C) 藝術用品店
(D) 女子的公寓

解析 第二段對話中，男子提議去吃吃看新開的希臘餐廳，而後從女子的回答，可以得知他們將約在希臘餐廳見面。

037

What will the speakers do tomorrow at 7:30?
(A) Cook dinner
(B) Listen to an artist talk
(C) Participate in an art class
(D) Try a new restaurant

中譯 說話者明天 7:30 會做什麼事？
(A) 煮晚餐
(B) 聽藝術家致詞
(C) 參加藝術課
(D) 到新餐廳嚐鮮

解析 最後一段對話中，女子提到 7 點 30 分將能聽到藝術家本人的致詞，故選 (B)。

換句話說 artist's introduction → artist talk

Questions 38-40 refer to the following conversation. 英 加

M	Hi, I'm calling about a new account that a friend of mine told me about. It's free and uh . . . What's it called?
W	㊳ I think you're talking about our first-time-customer promotion account. ㊴ We've had a lot of calls about that today. I can help you with that over the phone.
M	Well, it's actually for my son. He's in college and I want him to have a local bank account. But he's not here right now.
W	That's okay. ㊵ Please tell him to call us later. The offer is only good until Friday though, so don't delay.
M	Thank you. I'll tell him to call today.

男：嗨，我打來是想問問看朋友跟我說的一種新帳戶。他說是免費的，而且呃……是叫什麼啊？
女：㊳ 我想您說的是首次開戶的促銷帳戶，㊴ 我們今天接到許多詢問此問題的電話。我可以在電話上幫您處理。
男：好的，其實我是要幫兒子開戶。他在讀大學，我想讓他有個當地銀行的帳戶。但他現在人不在這裡。
女：沒關係。㊵ 請轉告他晚點再打給我們。不過此優惠活動僅到週五，所以腳步要加快。
男：謝謝妳。我會叫他今天回電。

字彙 account 帳戶　promotion 促銷　good 有效的

038

What does the man ask the woman about?
(A) A college application
(B) A promotional campaign
(C) His checking account
(D) His son's scholarship

中譯 男子詢問女子什麼問題？
(A) 大學入學申請　(B) 促銷活動
(C) 他的支票帳戶　(D) 他兒子的獎學金

解析 針對男子的提問，女子表示他指的是新客戶的促銷帳戶。由此可以得知男子向女子詢問有關促銷活動一事。

字彙 checking account 支票帳戶　scholarship 獎學金

039 新增題型

Why does the woman say, "We've had a lot of calls about that today"?
(A) Many people have complained that the line is busy.
(B) She has talked with the same customer repeatedly.
(C) She is tired of all the calls.
(D) The new offer is popular.

中譯 女子為何說「我們今天接到許多詢問此問題的電話」？
(A) 許多人抱怨一直忙線中。
(B) 她不斷與同一位顧客說明。
(C) 她對於接聽所有電話感到疲累。
(D) 新優惠十分受歡迎。

解析 女子提到因為該項活動接到很多人的來電，由此可以推測該項活動很受歡迎。

換句話說 promotion → new offer

字彙 busy 忙碌的　repeatedly 重複地

040

What does the woman recommend to the man?
(A) To ask a friend for advice
(B) To come see her again
(C) To call back later
(D) To hurry up

中譯 女子向男子建議什麼？
(A) 尋求朋友的建議
(B) 再來找她一次
(C) 再回撥電話
(D) 加緊腳步

解析 第二段對話中，女子提到活動到週五就結束了，也就是建議對方動作要快。

Questions 41-43 refer to the following conversation. 澳 美

W	Excuse me. ㊶ **Everyone else has already got their bag, but I don't see mine.**
M	I'm sorry about that. ㊶ **It may have gotten put on a different flight.** Can I have your last name and where you're coming from?
W	It's Denison and I just arrived from Atlanta.
M	Okay, Ms. Denison, ㊷ **I see your luggage number and it didn't make it on the flight from Atlanta**, but will be coming on the next flight arriving in about an hour. You can wait here or we can deliver it to your hotel or home.
W	㊸ **Please send it to my hotel. I'm really tired and want to lie down.**

女：不好意思，㊶大家都拿到自己的行李了，但我還沒看到我的行李。
男：我很抱歉，㊶您的行李可能在不同班機上。可以請問告訴我您貴姓以及是從哪裡出發的嗎？
女：我姓丹尼森，我從亞特蘭大出發的。
男：好的，丹尼森小姐，㊷我查到您的行李編號，雖然沒有放上從亞特蘭大出發的這班飛機，但已經在下班飛機上，大約一小時後會抵達。您可在此等候，或是我們可以宅配到您的飯店或府上。
女：㊸請幫我送到飯店。我真的很累，想躺下休息。

字彙 flight 班機

041

Where are the speakers?
(A) At an airport
(B) At a luggage store
(C) At a train station
(D) At a travel agency

中譯 說話者身在何處？
(A) 機場
(B) 行李箱商店
(C) 火車站
(D) 旅行社

解析 第一段對話中，女子表示沒看到自己的行李，而後男子回答她行李有可能在別班飛機上。由這段話可以推測出兩人在機場。

042

What is the problem?
(A) The man forgot to make a reservation.
(B) The man overcharged the woman.
(C) The woman's item did not arrive with her.
(D) The woman's name was spelled wrong.

中譯 出了什麼問題？
(A) 男子忘了訂位。
(B) 男子超收女子的費用。
(C) 女子的物品未隨之抵達。
(D) 女子的名字被拼錯。

解析 第二段對話中，男子提到行李並未送上從亞特蘭大起飛的班機上。由此可以得知女子的行李並未和女子一同抵達。

15

043

Where will the woman probably go next?
(A) To a clinic
(B) To a hotel
(C) To Atlanta
(D) To her home

中譯 女子接下來很有可能去哪裡？
(A) 診所   (B) 飯店
(C) 亞特蘭大   (D) 回家

解析 對話最後，女子表示自己現在很累，只想趕快躺下休息，請對方將行李送至飯店。由此可以推測女子稍後將前往飯店。

Questions 44-46 refer to the following conversation. 美 加

M Angela, ㊹ **have you seen the test version of our new Website?** We need to get everyone's feedback on it by tomorrow when I meet with the designers.

W Oh, yes, I'm just looking at it now. I really like the clean divisions on the side. It makes our product information much easier to see. ㊺ **One thing I would change, though, is the size of the words in the middle. It's much too big.**

M I agree. I will ask the designers to change that. Plus, the logo needs to stand out more.

W ㊻ **Do you want me to come to the meeting with you?**

M ㊻ **I think I can handle it.** I've been working with them for a couple of weeks on this.

男：安琪拉，㊹妳看過我們新網站的測試版了嗎？我們必須在明天和設計師開會之前，先了解大家的意見反饋。

女：喔，有啊，我現在正在瀏覽。我真的很喜歡側邊簡潔的分區，讓我們的產品資訊更清晰易讀。㊺不過，我會想改一個地方，就是中間的文字字級。有點太大了。

男：我同意。我會請設計師改一下。還有，標誌必須更顯眼。

女：㊻你要我跟你一起去開會嗎？

男：㊻我想我可以應付得了。我已經和他們合作處理這件事幾週了。

字彙 division 分區   stand out 顯眼，突出   handle 應付

044

What are the speakers mainly discussing?
(A) A customer order
(B) A feedback form
(C) A new Website
(D) A trial product

中譯 說話者主要在討論什麼？
(A) 顧客的訂單   (B) 意見反饋表
(C) 新網站   (D) 試用品

解析 第一段對話中，男子詢問對方是否看過新網站的測試版本，而後針對網站的設計討論。表示他們主要討論的主題為新網站。

字彙 trial 試用

045

What change does the woman suggest?
(A) Decreasing the font size
(B) Emphasizing the logo
(C) Making the type darker
(D) Modifying the whole design

中譯 女子提議做出什麼改變？
(A) 縮小字級
(B) 強調公司標誌
(C) 字的顏色要深一點
(D) 修改整個設計

解析 女子提到網站中間的字級太大。由此可以得知她建議將字級改小。

字彙 decrease 縮小   emphasize 強調

What does the man mean when he says, "I think I can handle it"?
(A) The man can set up the system by himself.
(B) The man needs no feedback from the woman.
(C) The woman does not have to see the designers.
(D) The woman does not need to give the man a ride.

中譯 男子說「我想我可以應付得了」是什麼意思？
(A) 男子可以自行設定系統。
(B) 男子不需要女子的意見反饋。
(C) 女子不需要去見設計師。
(D) 女子不需要順道接送男子。

解析 女子詢問男子是否要陪他一起去開會，而後男子回答：「I think I can handle it.」，帶有拒絕的意味，表示女子不需要去見設計師。

Questions 47-49 refer to the following conversation. 英 澳 新增題型

M	㊼ Storage Solutions customer care line. How can I help you?
W	Yes, ㊽ I was trying to order some containers on your Website, but I keep getting an error message. It says my credit card is invalid, but I've ordered from you before.
M	I can help you with that. Can I have your name, please?
W	Yes, it's Theresa Gregson.
M	Okay, I see you in our system. It says your credit card is expired.
W	Oh, I must be using my old card. Can I update the information now?
M	㊾ I'm afraid you'll have to do that online. I'll tell you the process if you'd like.

男：㊼ 收納方案公司客服專線您好。請問能幫您什麼忙？
女：是這樣的，㊽ 我試著在你們的網站訂收納箱，但我一直收到錯誤訊息。訊息說我的信用卡失效，但我以前有向你們訂貨過。
男：我可以幫您處理。可以請您告訴我您的大名嗎？
女：好的，我叫泰瑞莎・格瑞格森。
男：好的，我看到系統裡有您的記錄。上面顯示您的信用卡過期了。
女：喔，我一定是用到舊卡。我可以現在更新資料嗎？
男：㊾ 不好意思，您必須在網站上更新。您有需要的話，我可以跟您說明程序。

字彙 invalid 失效的　expire 過期

🎧 15

047

Who most likely is the man?
(A) A credit card company representative
(B) A customer service representative
(C) A new customer
(D) A store clerk

中譯 男子最有可能是誰？
(A) 信用卡公司的代表　(B) 客服代表
(C) 新顧客　　　　　　(D) 商店收銀員

解析 男子在第一句話中提到自己所屬客服單位。

換句話說 customer care line → customer service representative

048

What is the woman's problem?
(A) Her computer is not working.
(B) Her order has not arrived yet.
(C) Her order is incorrect.
(D) Her payment method is not accepted.

中譯 女子遭遇什麼問題？
(A) 電腦故障。　　　　(B) 訂購商品尚未寄達。
(C) 訂單有誤。　　　　(D) 付款方式遭拒。

解析 第一段對話中，女子表示她在網站上訂購收納箱，但一直出現信用卡無效的訊息。由此可以得知女子的問題為她選擇的付款方式不被接受。

049

What might the man do next?
(A) Call the credit card company
(B) Check the woman's purchase record
(C) Explain a procedure
(D) Transfer the woman's call

中譯 男子接下來會怎麼做？
(A) 聯絡信用卡公司 (B) 查看女子的購物記錄
(C) 解說程序 (D) 幫女子轉接電話

解析 最後一段對話中，男子告訴女子得由她親自在網站上操作，並表示可以向她說明更新的程序。由此可以得知男子將向女子說明步驟。

換句話說 tell you the process → explain a procedure

字彙 transfer 轉接

Questions 50-52 refer to the following conversation. 澳 美

W Hi, (50) I'm calling about your grocery delivery service. My neighbor told me about it and I think it would really help me since I just started working full time.	女：嗨，(50) 我打來問一下你們的雜貨配送服務。是我的鄰居告訴我的，我想這對於剛上全職班的我來說大有幫助。
M It is very convenient for working people. Can I first ask where you live? We have different delivery days for different areas.	男：確實會對上班族很方便。我可以先問您住在哪裡嗎？我們不同地區有不同的配送時段。
W I'm in the Rosewood neighborhood. (51) If I could get the delivery on Monday, it would help me a lot.	女：我住在羅斯伍德社區。(51) 如果能在週一收到貨，真的會對我很有幫助。
M I'm afraid we're only delivering on Tuesdays to Rosewood at the moment. (51) But if we get more customers there, we could add another delivery day.	男：不好意思，我們目前只有週二能配送到羅斯伍德。(51) 但如果此區的顧客人數變多，我們就能增加配送日。
W (51) (52) I'll ask my friends around here if they want to join.	女：(51) (52) 我問問看附近的朋友要不要加入。

字彙 grocery 雜貨　delivery 配送　neighborhood 社區　at the moment 目前

050

What are the speakers mainly discussing?
(A) A food delivery service
(B) A neighborhood event
(C) The man's schedule
(D) The woman's new job

中譯 說話者主要在討論什麼？
(A) 食品外送服務 (B) 鄰里事件
(C) 男子的時間表 (D) 女子的新工作

解析 本題的答案出現在女子所述的第一句話當中。她來電詢問食品雜貨的配送服務，後方還談到配送日期，因此答案為(A)。

051

What change would the woman like to see?
(A) A variety of services
(B) A different schedule
(C) Friendlier staff
(D) Lower prices

中譯 女子會希望看到哪項改變？
(A) 多樣化的服務
(B) 不同的時段
(C) 更友善的工作人員
(D) 更低廉的價格

解析 第二段對話中，女子表示希望週一能收到，而後男子回答只能在週二送到女子居住的社區，但是如果能有更多的顧客訂購，也許能增加送貨的天數，由此可知女子希望能在其他天送貨。

052

What does the woman say she will do?
(A) Move to a different area
(B) Change her jobs
(C) Sign up for a service
(D) Talk to her neighbors

中譯 女子表示自己會怎麼做？
(A) 搬到不同區
(B) 換工作
(C) 加入某服務
(D) 找鄰居聊聊

解析 最後一段對話中，女子表示要詢問住在附近的朋友。這表示她將邀請鄰居使用配送服務。

換句話說 ask my friends around here → talk to her neighbors

Questions 53-55 refer to the following conversation. 英 加

M 53 Mr. Stanley, our manufacturer, just called and he said he can't get the part for our new fans for another six weeks.

W Six weeks? 54 The summer will nearly be over by then!

M Don't worry. I talked to Mr. Stanley and explained that our fans are sold out in almost every store and we need to restock them immediately. 55 He's going to check with a different supplier and get back to me by the end of the day.

W Let me know what he says. If it's more bad news, we'll have to start looking for another manufacturer.

男：53 我們的製造商史丹利先生，剛來電說我們新款電扇的零組件必須要六週後才拿得到。

女：六週？ 54 到時候夏季都快結束了！

男：別擔心。我已經和史丹利先生談過，並說明我們的電扇幾乎在每家門市都售罄，必須立即補貨。55 他要再問問不同的供應商，下班前會回覆我。

女：再告訴我他怎麼說。如果有更多壞消息，我們就要開始找另一家製造商。

字彙 part 零組件　restock 補貨

053

What problem are the speakers discussing?
(A) A customer complaint
(B) A financial problem
(C) A product recall
(D) A supply problem

中譯 說話者在討論什麼問題？
(A) 顧客投訴
(B) 財務問題
(C) 產品召回
(D) 供應問題

解析 第一段對話中，男子表示製造商通知他六週內無法拿到新電風扇的零件，這表示零件供應上發生問題。

054 新增題型

What does the woman imply when she says, "The summer will nearly be over by then"?
(A) She is happy that it will be less hotter then.
(B) The company will close after summer.
(C) The product will not be needed then.
(D) The workers will be busier then.

中譯 女子說「到時候夏季都快結束了」是什麼意思？
(A) 她很開心到時候不會那麼熱了。
(B) 該公司夏季之後會停止營業。
(C) 到時候就不需要此產品了。
(D) 到時候工人會更忙。

解析 由第一句話便能得知斷貨的零件為電風扇的零件，因此女子表示到時候夏天都快結束了，便是暗指夏天邁入尾聲，已經不再需要電風扇。

15

055

What will happen at the end of the day?
(A) A manufacturer will call back.
(B) A clearance sale will begin.
(C) The speakers will do an inventory.
(D) The products will be put on the market.

中譯 下班前會發生什麼事？
(A) 製造商會回電。
(B) 出清特賣將開始。
(C) 說話者會進行庫存盤點。
(D) 產品即將上市。

解析 第二段對話中，男子提到製造商史丹利先生表示會向其他供應商確認，並在今天之內回覆。由此可以得知製造商會在今天結束以前回電。

字彙 clearance sale 出清特賣　do an inventory 庫存盤點　put . . . on the market 使……上市

Questions 56-58 refer to the following conversation with three speakers. 美 加 英 新增題型

M1 **⑤⑥ We've experienced a lot of growth at our company in the last six months** and we may need to move offices. I'd like you two to look at properties nearby and report back to me by the end of the month.

W Sure, Mr. Martin. **⑤⑦ I have a realtor friend who could show us some places. I'll set up an appointment with her right away.**

M2 Is there a specific price range we should be looking at?

M1 Well, we pay $3,500 per month for this office. I hope not to pay more than $4,000.

M2 That might be difficult. ⑤⑧ **The rents in this area have really increased since the new station went in.**

W Yes, my friend said the same thing. But we will try to find the best deal.

男1：⑤⑥ 我們公司過去六個月以來成長很多，也許需要遷址。我希望你們兩位去看看附近的處所，月底向我回報。

女：好的，馬丁先生。⑤⑦ 我有房仲業的朋友，可以帶我們看一些地方。我會馬上和她預約時間。

男2：價位的範圍有限制嗎？

男1：我們目前辦公室租金是每月 3,500 元。我希望不會超過 4,000 元。

男2：可能會有點困難。⑤⑧ 此區的租金因為新站點進駐而增加不少。

女：是的，我朋友也是這麼說。但我們會試著找到條件最好的處所。

字彙 realtor 房地產代理　set up an appointment 預約時間　price range 價位範圍　rent 租金

056

What is mentioned about the speakers' company?
(A) It is doing well.
(B) It is hiring new employees.
(C) It is moving to an overseas location.
(D) It is spending more than it takes in.

中譯 關於說話者的公司，文中提到了什麼資訊？
(A) 蓬勃發展。
(B) 聘僱新員工。
(C) 即將搬遷至海外。
(D) 入不敷出。

解析 本篇文章為兩男一女的三人對話。第一段對話中，男 1 提到過去六個月來，公司不斷成長，而後與其他人討論辦公室搬遷一事。由此可以得知公司經營狀況良好。

換句話說 experienced a lot of growth → It is doing well.

057

What does the woman say she will do?
(A) Contact her friend
(B) Look at some contracts
(C) Make a reservation
(D) Visit a new branch office

中譯 女子表示自己會怎麼做？
(A) 聯絡朋友
(B) 查看一些合約
(C) 預約時間
(D) 造訪新的分公司

解析 女子提到自己的朋友從事房仲業，並表示會和她約時間見面。

換句話說 set up an appointment with her → contact her friend

058

What is the reason for the higher rent prices in the area?
(A) Better transportation
(B) Economic growth
(C) Improved safety
(D) New office building construction

中譯 該區租金偏高的原因為何？
(A) 交通條件較佳
(B) 經濟成長
(C) 治安有所改善
(D) 建造新辦公大樓

解析 答案出現在後半段對話男 2 所述的話語中。他提到增建新的車站後，該地區的租金飆漲。由此可以推測交通便利導致該地區的租金上漲。

字彙 improved 有所改善的

Questions 59-61 refer to the following conversation with three speakers. 英 澳 加 新增題型

M	Hi, Ellen. I haven't seen you since you moved to your new place. How are you liking it?
W1	It's great. ㊾ **The only thing is I have to take the train to work now.** I don't really understand the complicated train system and it's always so crowded.
M	Nina, you take the train to work, right? Which direction are you coming from?
W2	Northeast. ㊿ **I take the Yellow Line and transfer at Seven Oaks Station to the Blue Line.**
W1	Oh, I come from the east and I take the Yellow Line, too. I didn't think about changing lines at Seven Oaks.
W2	Oh, yes. It's much easier than going all the way to City Center. The train gets very crowded if you do that.
W1	Thanks for the tip, Nina.
W2	And ㉛ **they just made an app for the trains.** You can look up all the times and see if there are delays. Here, ㉛ **Ellen, I'll show you on my phone.**

男：嗨，艾倫。自從妳搬新家後，我就沒見過妳了。妳喜歡新家嗎？

女1：新家很棒。㊾ 但唯一困擾我的是必須搭火車上班。我不太了解複雜的火車系統，而且一直都很擁擠。

男：妮娜，妳也是搭火車上班，對嗎？妳從哪一個方向過來的？

女2：東北邊。㊿ 我會先搭黃線，然後在七橡木站轉搭藍線。

女1：喔，我從東邊過來，我也是搭黃線。我從沒想過要在七橡木站換線。

女2：喔，對啊，比妳直接一路搭到市中心站還要方便。如果妳那樣搭，火車會很擁擠。

女1：多謝妳的提點，妮娜。

女2：而且 ㉛ 他們最近推出火車 APP。妳可以查詢時刻表，看看有沒有誤點。㉛ 艾倫，我給妳看我手機上的 APP。

字彙 crowded 擁擠的　direction 方向　transfer 轉搭

059

What does Ellen dislike about her new place?
(A) **The access to work**
(B) The crowded station
(C) The color of the house
(D) The size of her room

中譯 艾倫不喜歡新家的哪一點？
(A) 通勤方式　　　　(B) 擁擠的車站
(C) 新家的配色　　　(D) 房間的大小

解析 本篇文章為兩女一男的三人對話。對話主題是名字為艾倫的女1搬新家後的交通問題。第一段對話中，女1提到目前的問題為她必須搭火車上班，交通系統過於複雜，且通勤時間很擁擠。

060

What can be said about Seven Oaks Station?
(A) It is a new station.
(B) It is in the western part of the city.
(C) The women did not know about it.
(D) **Two lines go through it.**

中譯 關於七橡木站，下列何者正確？
(A) 屬於新站點。
(B) 位於該市的西邊。
(C) 女子們不熟悉此站點。
(D) 兩條路線經過此站。

解析 請仔細聆聽提及七橡木站的片段。女2提到她搭乘黃線至七橡木站，再轉搭藍線，由此可以得知有兩條線通過七橡木站。

061

What will Nina do next?
(A) Look for a new place
(B) Check the departure time
(C) **Show Ellen an app**
(D) Take a train

中譯 妮娜接下來會怎麼做？
(A) 找新家　　　　　(B) 查看發車時間
(C) 給艾倫看一個 APP　(D) 搭火車

解析 妮娜為女2。在對話最後，她提到火車的應用程式，並打算拿自己的手機給女1看應用程式。

Questions 62-64 refer to the following conversation. 英 澳 新增題型

M	Hi, Mary Brock? ⑥ **This is Alan Hall from City Life Magazine.** I'm calling to let you know that your catering company has won "The Best in the City" award from our readers.
W	Really? I'm so flattered. ⑥ **We came in second place last year** but, oh, I don't know what to say!
M	Well, congratulations. It seems you've become more popular since last year.
W	I guess so.
M	⑥ ⑥ **I'd like to schedule a time to do an interview with you and possibly take some pictures in your office.**
W	Uh, okay. I'm pretty busy this week. ⑥ **Is next Monday too late?**
M	No, that would be fine. Does 3:00 PM work for you?
W	Sounds great. Thank you, Mr. Hall.

男：嗨，是瑪莉・布羅克嗎？⑥ 我是《都會生活》雜誌的艾倫・霍爾。我打來是想通知您，您的外燴公司被我們讀者評選為「本市最佳外燴公司」。

女：真的嗎？我真是受寵若驚。⑥ 我們去年是第二名，但是，喔，我說不出話了！

男：恭喜您。看來您的公司比去年更受歡迎。

女：我想是的。

男：⑥ ⑥ 我想安排時間訪問您，也可能要拍些您辦公室的照片。

女：呃，好的，不過我這週滿忙的。⑥ 下週一會不會太晚？

男：不會的，下週一可以。下午3點您方便嗎？

女：太好了。謝謝你，霍爾先生。

字彙 catering 外燴　flattered 受寵若驚的　come in second place 排名第二

062

Who most likely is the man?
(A) A caterer
(B) A city official
(C) A grocery store manager
(D) A reporter

中譯 男子最有可能是誰？
(A) 外燴業者　　　　(B) 市府官員
(C) 大賣場經理　　　(D) 記者

解析 第一段對話中，男子表示自己任職於雜誌社，而後他跟女子預約採訪時間，由此可以推測男子為一名記者。

063

What is mentioned about the woman's business?
(A) It almost won the award last year.
(B) It relocated last year.
(C) It remodeled its office this year.
(D) It started this year.

中譯 關於女子公司，文中提及什麼資訊？
(A) 去年差點贏得大獎。
(B) 去年搬遷至新據點。
(C) 今年翻修辦公室。
(D) 今年開始營業。

解析 對於獲獎一事，女子回應去年僅得到第二名。換句話說，去年差點奪冠。

換句話說 came in second place → almost won

字彙 relocate 搬遷

064

What will happen next Monday?
(A) The contest results will be announced.
(B) The magazine issue will be released.
(C) The speakers will meet at the woman's office.
(D) The woman will have a job interview.

中譯 下週一會發生什麼事？
(A) 公布比賽結果。
(B) 發行該期雜誌。
(C) 說話者會在女子的辦公室會面。
(D) 女子要進行工作面試。

解析 後半段對話中，男子表示可能會在女子的辦公室內拍照，而後女子建議約下週一，男子表示同意。由此可以得知下週一對話中的兩人將於女子的辦公室內見面。

🎧15

Questions 65-67 refer to the following conversation and bill. 澳 美

HOTEL SINCLAIR	
1. Room charge	.... $80
🔵65 2. Mini bar	.... $17
3. Room service	.... $12
4. Service charge	.... $8
Total	$117

辛克萊爾飯店	
1. 住房費用	.... 80 元
🔵65 2. 迷你酒吧	.... 17 元
3. 客房服務	.... 12 元
4. 服務費	.... 8 元
總計	117 元

W Hi, I'm ready to check out but I think 🔵65 there's a mistake on my bill. I didn't take anything out of the mini bar.

M Oh, let me check that. Room 343, right? I think I see what happened. 🔵66 Your name is similar to another guest's name. That's why the charges got switched. Does everything else look correct?

女：嗨，我要退房，但我想 🔵65 帳單出錯了。我沒有取用迷你酒吧裡的任何物品。

男：喔，我查一下。您是343號房，對嗎？我大概知道發生什麼事了。🔵66 您的名字和另一位房客很相似，所以費用就登記錯了。那麼其他部分都正確嗎？

W	Um, yeh . . . Wait, what's this service charge?
M	That's something we add for all our guests on the weekend.
W	Oh, I see. Then everything's fine. ⑥⑦ Here's my credit card.

女：嗯，對的……等等，這是什麼服務費？
男：我們週末都會對所有房客加收此費用。
女：喔，原來如此，那就沒有問題了。⑥⑦ 這是我的信用卡。

字彙 bill 帳單　mini bar 飯店房間內放有飲料的小冰箱

065 新增題型

Look at the graphic. How much will be taken off of the bill?
(A) $8
(B) $12
(C) $17
(D) $80

中譯 見圖表。帳單將扣除多少錢？
(A) 8 元　　　　(B) 12 元
(C) 17 元　　　　(D) 80 元

解析 本題為圖表整合題。對話發生在飯店退房時。女子為住客，她提到自己並未使用迷你酒吧，指出帳單金額有誤，而後飯店方面表示弄錯，因此應該扣掉帳單中的 17 元。

066

What does the man say caused the problem?
(A) A cleaning staff mistake
(B) A computer error
(C) A name mix-up
(D) A reservation change

中譯 男子表示是什麼導致該問題？
(A) 清潔人員失誤　　(B) 電腦記錄錯誤
(C) 名字混淆　　　　(D) 訂房異動

解析 第一段對話中，男子表示女子的名字和另一位住客的名字相似，才會不小心弄錯。這表示問題為搞錯名字。

067

What will the man most likely do next?
(A) Call his supervisor
(B) Check something on the computer
(C) Give the woman a key
(D) Process a payment

中譯 男子接下來可能會做什麼？
(A) 打電話給主管　　(B) 查看電腦系統
(C) 將鑰匙交給女子　(D) 處理付款程序

解析 最後一段對話中，女子拿出信用卡，因此男子最有可能做的事為幫她結帳。

字彙 process 處理

Questions 68-70 refer to the following conversation and coupon. 美 加

ABC Furniture

Discount Coupon

⑥⑤ Sofas, Couches	10% OFF!
Dining tables	20% OFF!
Beds	20% OFF!

9791196597504

(Expires July 31)

ABC 家具公司

折價券

⑥⑤ 沙發	九折優惠！
餐桌	八折優惠！
床組	八折優惠！

9791196597504

（7 月 31 日到期）

M	68 This sofa is so comfortable. And it will look great in my new apartment. I'm worried about the price though. 69 Can I use this coupon I found online?
W	69 Sure. And you're in luck! Today only, everything from our Inverness line is an extra 5 percent off!
M	Oh, 69 so you mean this sofa has an additional discount today? Wow, that is lucky. I'll take it.
W	Great. 70 Just come to the counter and we'll get started on your delivery and payment details.

男：	68 這張沙發真舒服，而且會和我的新公寓很搭。但我擔心的是價格。69 我可以使用網上找到的這張折價券嗎？
女：	69 當然可以。而且您很幸運！印威內斯系列的所有商品，只有今天可以再多打九五折！
男：	喔，69 所以妳意思是這張沙發今天還可以再多打折？哇，真的是運氣好。我買了。
女：	太好了。70 請來櫃台，我們將開始處理配送和付款細節。

字彙 be in luck 幸運

068

What does the man mention about the item?
(A) It is his favorite color.
(B) It is suitable for his home.
(C) It is big for his place.
(D) It is within his budget.

中譯 男子針對此商品提出什麼看法？
(A) 是他最喜歡的顏色。
(B) 跟他家的風格很搭。
(C) 對他家來說尺寸太大。
(D) 符合他的預算。

解析 本篇對話發生在家具賣場內。男顧客看上沙發，並表示適合放在新的自家公寓內。

換句話說 look great in my new apartment → suitable

字彙 within budget 符合預算

069 新增題型

Look at the graphic. What discount will the man get on his purchase?
(A) 10%
(B) 15%
(C) 20%
(D) 25%

中譯 見圖表。男子所購商品能打幾折？
(A) 九折
(B) 八五折
(C) 八折
(D) 七五折

解析 本題為圖表整合題。對話中男子詢問是否能使用優惠券，而後女子回答可以，並補充僅限今天還可額外折抵 5%。這表示男子可以使用 10% 優惠加上 5% 優惠，總優惠為 15%。

070

What will the man most likely do next?
(A) Arrange delivery
(B) Check the price online
(C) Look for a different item
(D) Measure the item

中譯 男子接下來可能會做什麼？
(A) 安排配送事宜
(B) 上網查看價格
(C) 尋找不同的品項
(D) 丈量商品的尺寸

解析 對話最後，女子提到要跟男子到櫃台討論送貨和付款事宜。

字彙 arrange 安排　measure 測量

🎧 15

Questions 71-73 refer to the following recorded message. 澳

Thank you for your continued patience. Our customer service representatives are busy helping other customers at this time. Please stay on the line and your call will be answered in the order in which it was received. **71 72 Please make sure you have your frequent flyer number and flight schedule with destinations ready to give to the next available representative. 73 Less heavy call volumes are expected between 8:00 and 9:00 AM and between 5:00 and 6:00 PM.** Or, you can visit our Website at www.skyquik.com to make your reservation online.

感謝您持續地耐心等候。我們的客服人員現正忙於協助其他顧客。請您別掛斷，我們將以來電順序依序接聽。71 72 請確認您準備好飛行常客編號、班機時間與目的地，以便告知下一位可接電話的客服人員。73 客服電話的離峰時段大約是早上 8 點至 9 點，以及下午 5 點至 6 點之間。或者您可至 www.skyquik.com 網站來網上訂位。

字彙 patience 耐心　frequent flyer 飛行常客

071

What type of business is the message for?
(A) A hotel
(B) An airline
(C) An electronics store
(D) An online clothing store

中譯 此訊息針對的行業為何？
(A) 飯店
(B) 航空公司
(C) 電子用品店
(D) 網路服飾店

解析 本文為自動語音回覆系統。當中提到航空會員編號（**frequent flyer number**）和航班時間表（**flight schedule**），表示為航空公司的語音回覆。

072

What are callers asked to have ready?
(A) Their membership number
(B) Their mobile phone number
(C) Their order number
(D) Their passport number

中譯 來電者需準備好什麼資料？
(A) 會員號碼
(B) 手機電話
(C) 訂單編號
(D) 護照號碼

解析 文中要求準備好航空會員編號（**frequent flyer number**）和航班時間表（**flight schedule**）。

073

When is a caller directed to call back for a shorter wait time?
(A) At 10:00 AM
(B) At 5:30 PM
(C) At 7:00 PM
(D) At 8:30 PM

中譯 來電者被指示於何時回撥電話，就可以不用等候多時？
(A) 上午 10:00
(B) 下午 5:30
(C) 晚上 7:00
(D) 晚上 8:30

解析 文中提到上午 8 點至 9 點之間，以及下午 5 點至 6 點之間來電的人數較少（**less heavy call volumes**），因此選項中等待時間較短的時間為下午 5 點 30 分。

Questions 74-76 refer to the following excerpt from a meeting. 美

74 Thank you for inviting me here today to talk about our exciting line of copying equipment. I think you will be impressed with all the functions of these new copiers. I notice that you're using our competitor's machine and that's fine. You might want to think about upgrading to our PaperQ 2000, 75 which copies at twice the speed of the one you have and costs just the same. 76 I'd like to show you a video now. It will give you a very visual idea of what our machine can actually do.

74 感謝大家今天邀請我到此介紹我們令人興奮的影印設備產品系列。我想您會對新影印機的所有功能感到印象深刻。我發現您目前使用的是我們競爭對手的機器,但是沒關係。您也許會想考慮升級成我們的 PaperQ 2000,75 影印速度比您現有機型快兩倍,但費用相同。76 我現在將播放影片給您看。您將清楚看到我們機器的實際功用。

字彙 be impressed with 對……印象深刻　function 功能　visual 視覺的

074

Why is the speaker meeting with the listeners?
(A) To explain how some software works
(B) To find out what they need in a new system
(C) To inform new employees of company policies
(D) To introduce a piece of equipment

中譯 說話者為何與聽話者見面?
(A) 說明某個軟體的運作方式
(B) 了解聽話者對新系統的需求
(C) 告知新進員工公司制度
(D) 介紹一台設備

解析 說話者在開頭提到感謝受邀來此介紹自家的影印機(copying equipment)系列。由此可以得知說話者之所以會與聽者見面,為的是介紹影印機。

075

According to the speaker, what is a benefit of his product over the competitor's?
(A) It is cheaper.
(B) It is faster.
(C) It is higher quality.
(D) It is lighter.

中譯 根據說話者,他的產品勝過競爭對手的優點為何?
(A) 較低價。
(B) 速度較快。
(C) 品質較好。
(D) 重量較輕。

解析 當中強調產品的特色為影印速度,速度比起競爭對手的產品快兩倍(twice the speed),表示其產品的優勢為速度快。

076

What will the listeners do next?
(A) Listen to a presentation
(B) Log into a new system
(C) Use some office equipment
(D) Watch a video

中譯 聽話者接下來會做什麼?
(A) 聆聽簡報
(B) 登入新系統
(C) 使用辦公設備
(D) 觀賞影片

解析 下一步的行動出現在獨白後半段中。當中提到要播放影片給大家看(show you a video),表示聽者接著要收看影片。

Actual Test 4

PART 4

16

Whether you're new to running or an experienced runner, Air Space K running shoes are made with you in mind. **㏐ Thanks to a revolutionary new fabric, they are sturdy enough to last for years,** yet they are the lightest on the market today. You'll feel like you're walking on air. Air Space K shoes are available at Thom's Shoes. Come in soon to get fitted by our shoe specialists. **㏘ We use the latest technology to find out your shoe size and foot shape.** Plenty of free parking and **㏙ mention this ad for a free pair of socks.**

無論您是跑步新手或是資深跑者,我們為您量身打造出 Air Space K 跑步鞋。**㏐** 多虧革命性的新布料,這款鞋不僅可耐用多年,更是市場上最輕薄的布料。穿上它,彷彿漫步在雲端。Air Space K 已於湯瑪斯鞋店販售。即刻前來,我們的跑鞋專員將協助您試穿。**㏘** 我們採用最新科技來評估您的鞋碼與腳型。這裡有許多免費停車位,**㏙** 來店告知您看過此廣告,還可獲得一雙免費襪子。

字彙 revolutionary 革命性的　fabric 布料　sturdy 牢固的　mention 提及

077

What is mentioned about the Air Space K shoes?
(A) They are made for new runners only.
(B) They are only available online.
(C) They are the cheapest on the market.
(D) They use a new type of fabric.

中譯 關於 Air Space K,文中提到了什麼?
(A) 專為新手跑者所設計。
(B) 僅能網上購買。
(C) 是市場上價格最低的鞋款。
(D) 採用新款的布料。

解析 本文為跑步鞋的廣告。說話者提到多虧革命性的新型布料(**thanks to a revolutionary new fabric**),讓鞋子非常耐用,能使用多年。由此可以得知跑步鞋使用了新的布料。

078

What does the store's technology do?
(A) Make custom shoes
(B) Measure foot size
(C) Teach customers how to run
(D) Show customers where to run

中譯 該商店的科技具有什麼功能?
(A) 可量身定製鞋款
(B) 可測量鞋碼
(C) 可教導顧客跑步的方式
(D) 向顧客展示可跑步之處

解析 後半段廣告中介紹了賣場內的最新技術,提到能協助顧客找出鞋子的大小和腳形(**find out your shoe size and foot shape**),也就是指測量腳的尺寸。

079

What does a customer have to do to get a free gift?
(A) Bring in a coupon
(B) Buy two pairs of shoes
(C) Fill out a questionnaire
(D) Say they heard the advertisement

中譯 顧客該怎麼做,才能獲得免費贈禮?
(A) 出示折價券
(B) 買兩雙鞋
(C) 填妥問卷
(D) 說他們聽說過此廣告

解析 廣告最後提到只要提及廣告(**mention this ad**),就免費贈送一雙襪子。這表示如欲收到贈品,顧客需要告知聽過廣告內容。

Attention ladies and gentleman. ⑳ **Those of you waiting for the 8:30 showing of For Once And For All, you may now enter the theater.** Please have your tickets out to give to our staff. Then proceed to Theater 3. ㉑ **For those waiting for the 8:45 showing of Star Games, please do not get in line yet. We will call you in about five minutes.** ㉒ **As part of our public transportation promotional campaign this month, just show your public transportation receipt or card for 10 percent off all of our snacks and drinks.** And please feel free to pick up a copy of *Movie News* on your way out.

先生女士請注意。⑳ 等候觀賞《一勞永逸》8 點 30 分場次的觀眾，您現在已可進場。請拿出電影票，交給我們的人員，然後往第三廳前進。㉑ 等候觀賞《星際遊戲》8 點 45 分場次的觀眾，請先不要排隊，我們大約五分鐘後會再廣播請您入場。㉒ 我們本月有搭配大眾運輸進行促銷活動，只要出示您搭乘大眾運輸的收據或票卡，所有零食及飲品可打九折。離場時，您可自行拿取一本《電影新訊》。

字彙 **proceed** 往前走

080

Where are the listeners?
(A) At a concert venue
(B) At a grocery store
(C) At a movie theater
(D) At a sports venue

中譯 聽話者身在何處？
(A) 音樂廳
(B) 雜貨店
(C) 電影院
(D) 運動比賽場地

解析 本文以廣播通知電影院的觀眾入場。前半段請觀眾進入影廳（**enter the theater**），由此可以推測聽者們正在電影院內。

081

What will happen in five minutes?
(A) A game will begin.
(B) A performer will appear.
(C) Another announcement will be made.
(D) Snacks will be available.

中譯 五分鐘內會發生什麼事？
(A) 比賽將開始。
(B) 表演人員將現身。
(C) 將宣布另一件事。
(D) 將供應零食。

解析 當中提醒觀看 8 點 45 分播映的電影的顧客先不要排隊，五分鐘後會另外廣播通知。由此可以得知五分鐘後會聽到另一則廣播。

082

What will listeners who show a subway card receive?
(A) A copy of a magazine
(B) A food discount
(C) A free gift
(D) A special seat

中譯 出示地鐵卡的聽話者將可獲得什麼？
(A) 雜誌
(B) 食物折價券
(C) 免費贈禮
(D) 特殊座位

解析 配合大眾運輸促銷活動，只要大眾運輸的收據或票卡，就能享有零食和飲料九折的優惠（**10 percent off all of our snacks and drinks**）。這表示聽者出示地鐵票，就能獲得食物的折扣。

16

Questions 83-85 refer to the following talk. 澳

Hello, folks. Welcome to Tony's Café. My name is Brenda and I'll be your server today. In addition to what's on our menu, we have some morning specials on the board over there. I recommend the blueberry pancakes—we're famous for them. Just to let you know, though, ㊻ **we will stop taking breakfast orders in about ten minutes.** ㊼ **If everyone is drinking coffee, I can bring you a carafe that's enough for four. It'll be cheaper than ordering coffee individually.** Let me give you a few minutes to look at our menu and ㊽ **I'll be right back with your water.**

哈囉，大家好。歡迎來到「東尼咖啡廳」。我是布蘭達，今天將由我為您服務。除了菜單上的餐點以外，我們的告示板上還有寫一些晨間特餐。我推薦藍莓鬆餅——這是讓我們打響名號的招牌餐點。不過想讓您知道一下，㊻我們約十分鐘後將停止接受早餐點餐。㊼如果有人想喝咖啡，我可以幫您點一壺四人份的咖啡，價格會比點四杯咖啡還要便宜。我先給您幾分鐘時間瀏覽菜單，㊽待會兒回來幫您送開水。

字彙 **in addition to** 除了……以外　**carafe** 瓶，壺　**individually** 個別地，單一地

083 新增題型

What does the speaker mean when she says, "we will stop taking breakfast orders in about ten minutes"?
(A) The listeners should be in a hurry to leave.
(B) The listeners should decide what they want soon.
(C) The speaker is nearly finished with her shift.
(D) The speaker is running out of breakfast items.

中譯 說話者說「我們約十分鐘後將停止接受早餐點餐」是什麼意思？
(A) 聽話者應趕緊離開。
(B) 聽話者應盡快決定點餐內容。
(C) 說話者快要結束輪班。
(D) 說話者的早餐品項快賣完。

解析 說話者為餐廳的店員。店員表示最後點餐時間還剩十分鐘左右，表示請聽者盡快決定好要點什麼餐點。

084

What does the speaker suggest the listeners do?
(A) Order drinks separately
(B) Pay for their meals individually
(C) Share a common beverage
(D) Try an appetizer

中譯 說話者建議聽話者做什麼事？
(A) 分開點飲料　　(B) 餐點分開結帳
(C) 共享相同的飲品。　(D) 嘗試開胃菜

解析 說話者提到如果每個人都想喝咖啡的話，可以點用一壺咖啡，份量足夠四個人享用，這樣比起分開點更為划算。這表示說話者建議合點飲料後再一起分享，比每個人各點一杯好。

字彙 **separately** 分開地

085

What will the speaker bring the listeners soon?
(A) Coffee
(B) Menus
(C) Silverware
(D) Water

中譯 說話者很快就會為聽話者送上什麼？
(A) 咖啡
(B) 菜單
(C) 銀製餐具
(D) 開水

解析 說話者在獨白最後表示稍後會為聽者送上水。

86 I've been asked to report on the progress of our Website update. **87** We've had to rebuild whole sections, which got hacked, as I mentioned last month. Those are almost complete and the new products section is nearly updated with our new product line. By the middle of next week, we should be able to test a few purchases. **88** My department wants to assure everyone that by Friday of next week we will be up and running again. In addition to recreating the Website, we have installed a stronger firewall so this problem won't occur again. Does anyone have any questions?

86 我應要求報告網站更新的進度。如我上個月提到的，**87** 因為被駭客入侵，我們必須重建所有的區塊。這部分已幾乎完工，新品區幾乎已經更新為我們的新品系列。到下週三或四，我們應能測試一點網購功能。**88** 我們部門希望讓大家放心，在下週五前我們能恢復正常運作。除了重建網站之外，我們也安裝了功能比較強大的防火牆，同樣問題不會再發生。有誰還有任何疑問嗎？

字彙 rebuild 重建　whole 所有的　assure 使……放心　install 安裝　firewall 防火牆

086

Who most likely is giving the report?
(A) A fire official
(B) A product designer
(C) A Web designer
(D) An IT staff member

中譯 提出報告的人最有可能是誰？
(A) 消防官員
(B) 產品設計師
(C) 網頁設計師
(D) 資訊科技部職員

解析 說話者在獨白開頭處提到被要求告知網站更新（**Website update**）進度，表示說話者的職業最有可能為 **IT** 人員。

087

What was the problem?
(A) A fire in the office damaged some equipment.
(B) A product was found to be defective.
(C) A Website had been hacked.
(D) An employee used an unsafe Website.

中譯 出了什麼問題？
(A) 辦公室失火導致部分設備受損。
(B) 發現產品有瑕疵。
(C) 網站被駭客入侵。
(D) 有員工使用不安全的網站。

解析 因為遭駭客入侵（**got hacked**），所以必須更新。文中提到必須重建被駭的部分。

088

When will the problem be fully resolved?
(A) By tomorrow
(B) By the middle of next week
(C) At the end of next week
(D) Next month

中譯 何時能完全解決該問題？
(A) 明天以前
(B) 下週三或四以前
(C) 下週結束前
(D) 下個月

解析 獨白中使用 **be up**（完成）來表達完美解決問題（**fully resolved**），當中提到要到下週五才能重新啟用。

Actual Test 4

PART 4

16

Questions 89-91 refer to the following broadcast. 加

Good afternoon, everyone. This is Marsha Newell reporting live from the new Tech Heaven store downtown. ❽ It's very crowded since the latest device from Nova Electronics, the smart watch, was released today. Representatives of the company say they are producing the watch as fast as they can, but ❾ there are a limited number of watches available at this time. I'm not sure how many are left because, well, ❾ the store opened at 9:00 and it's almost 2:00 now. If you don't make it down here in time, you can order one online, though ❾ I heard there is a waiting list of six weeks.

大家午安。我是瑪莎‧紐威爾,我人在市區新開張的「科技天堂」門市現場直播。❽ 因諾瓦電子公司最新的智慧型手錶於今天上市,這裡擠得水洩不通。該公司的代表表示,他們正在趕製手錶,但 ❾ 現階段的手錶數量仍有限。我不確定剩下多少,❾ 因為此門市是9點開門,現在都快2點了。如果您未及時趕到現場,也可以網上訂購,不過 ❾ 我聽說候補名單已經要等六週。

字彙 latest device 最新裝置

089

What type of item is the speaker reporting on?
(A) A gadget
(B) A laptop computer
(C) A music player
(D) A video camera

中譯 說話者正在報導什麼產品?
(A) 小裝置
(B) 筆記型電腦
(C) 音樂播放器
(D) 攝影機

解析 廣播中提到智慧型手錶於今天上市。

換句話說 smart watch → gadget

字彙 gadget 小裝置

090 新增題型

What does the speaker imply when she says, "the store opened at 9:00 and it's almost 2:00 now"?
(A) The line at the cashier's is getting shorter.
(B) The popular item may be gone by now.
(C) The store clerks are tired already.
(D) The store will be closing soon.

中譯 說話者說「此門市是9點開門,現在都快2點了」是什麼意思?
(A) 結帳的排隊人潮逐漸變少。
(B) 該熱門物品現在可能已售罄。
(C) 店員已經很疲累。
(D) 商店即將關門。

解析 說話者先表示販售的數量有限,然後他又表示不確定現在剩下幾支,接著說出題目列出的句子,即現在已經快要下午兩點,暗示新款智慧手錶可能已經賣光。

091

When can a customer receive their online order?
(A) In three weeks
(B) In six weeks
(C) In about two months
(D) In six months

中譯 網購的顧客可於何時收到商品?
(A) 三週內
(B) 六週內
(C) 大約兩個月內
(D) 六個月內

解析 後半段廣播中,說話者提到等待名單已經排到六週左右。這表示顧客至少要等到六週後才能收到商品。

Questions 92-94 refer to the following telephone message and report. 英

<table>
<tr><td colspan="6">Expense Report</td></tr>
<tr><td colspan="6">Trip purpose: <u>Trade Show</u>　　Department: <u>Sales</u>
Name: <u>Catherine Snow</u>　Manager: <u>Isabelle Perkins</u></td></tr>
<tr><td>Date</td><td>Description</td><td>Air/Transp.</td><td>Hotel</td><td>Meals</td><td>Others</td></tr>
<tr><td>8/20, 23</td><td>RT flight to LA</td><td>$350</td><td></td><td></td><td></td></tr>
<tr><td>8/20-22</td><td>3 nights stay</td><td></td><td>$800</td><td></td><td></td></tr>
<tr><td>8/20-22</td><td>Meals</td><td></td><td></td><td>❽❸
$300</td><td></td></tr>
<tr><td>8/20-22</td><td>Rental car</td><td>$200</td><td></td><td></td><td></td></tr>
</table>

Hello, Catherine. ❾❷ **This is Stuart in the accounting department.** I'm calling about the expense report for the trade show. Your report was fine, but I can't find the receipts for one or more of your meals. ❾❸ **When I add up the receipts you gave me for your meals, the total comes to only $250.** ❾❹ **If you have any more receipts, please drop them by my office.** I'm trying to get all the reports processed by 5:00 today, so I'd appreciate having the receipts as soon as possible. Thank you.

<table>
<tr><td colspan="6" align="center">支出報告</td></tr>
<tr><td colspan="6">出差目的：<u>貿易展</u>　　部門：<u>業務部</u>
姓名：<u>凱瑟琳・史諾</u>　經理：<u>伊莎貝爾・伯金斯</u></td></tr>
<tr><td>日期</td><td>說明</td><td>機票／交通費</td><td>飯店</td><td>餐費</td><td>其他</td></tr>
<tr><td>8/20, 23</td><td>洛杉磯的來回機票</td><td>$350</td><td></td><td></td><td></td></tr>
<tr><td>8/20-22</td><td>住宿三晚</td><td></td><td>$800</td><td></td><td></td></tr>
<tr><td>8/20-22</td><td>餐費</td><td></td><td></td><td>❽❸
$300</td><td></td></tr>
<tr><td>8/20-22</td><td>租車</td><td>$200</td><td></td><td></td><td></td></tr>
</table>

哈囉，凱瑟琳。❾❷ 我是會計部門的斯圖爾特。我打來是想問一下貿易展的支出報告。妳的報告沒有問題，但我找不到妳的幾張餐費收據。❾❸ 我加總妳給我的餐費收據時，總費用只有 250 元。❾❹ 如果妳還有多的收據，麻煩帶來我的辦公室。我希望盡量在今天 5 點前處理完所有報告，所以如果能盡快拿到收據，就太感謝妳了，謝謝。

字彙 accounting department 會計部門　trade show 貿易展　add up 加總

092

Which department does the caller work in?
(A) Accounting
(B) Administration
(C) Personnel
(D) Sales

中譯 來電者在哪一個部門工作？
(A) 會計部　　　　(B) 行政部
(C) 人事部　　　　(D) 業務部

解析 說話者在電話留言開頭便向對方凱瑟琳打招呼，接著報上自己的姓名和所屬會計部門（accounting department）。

 16

093 新增題型

Look at the graphic. For what amount does Catherine have to produce receipts?
(A) $50
(B) $200
(C) $250
(D) $350

中譯 見圖表。凱瑟琳應提出多少金額的收據？
(A) 50 元　　　　(B) 200 元
(C) 250 元　　　　(D) 350 元

解析 留言中段提到凱瑟琳繳交的餐費收據合計為 250 元，但表格中的餐費總額為 300 元，這表示還需繳交 50 元的收據。

094

What is Catherine asked to do soon?
(A) Book the air tickets
(B) Bring a paper to the caller
(C) Change a reservation
(D) Fill out a form

中譯 凱瑟琳被要求盡快進行何事？
(A) 訂機票　　　　(B) 將紙本資料交給來電者
(C) 更改訂位　　　(D) 填寫表格

解析 說話者請對方把收據送至自己的辦公室。

換句話說 receipt → paper

Questions 95-97 refer to the following talk and graph.

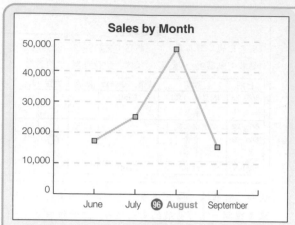

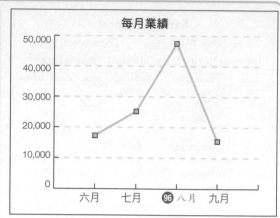

In the meeting today, 95 we're going to go over our recent mobile phone sales numbers and talk a bit about what we want to do in the upcoming months. As you can see on the graph, 96 we had a spike in phone sales corresponding with the blowout sale at all our branches. While the sale was very successful, it was disappointing to see numbers drop so drastically the next month. But, 97 we have a couple of ideas to get more customers into our stores next month to buy, buy, buy. I'll now let Rachel explain what we have in mind.

在今天的會議中，95 我們要討論近期的手機銷售數據，還要談一下未來幾個月要進行的事。大家可從圖表看到，96 由於所有分店的大拍賣活動，我們的手機業績達到尖峰。雖然活動很成功，但下個月的業績卻大幅下跌，讓人非常失望。不過，97 我們已經想出能讓顧客下個月回店大買特買的幾個點子。我現在請瑞秋說明我們的想法。

字彙 **go over** 仔細檢查　**spike** 尖峰　**correspond** 相對應　**blowout sale** 大拍賣　**drastically** 大幅地

095

Where most likely does the speaker work?
(A) At a cable services firm
(B) At a home furnishings company
(C) At a telecommunications company
(D) At a travel agency

中譯 說話者最有可能在哪裡工作？
(A) 有線電視公司
(B) 居家裝潢公司
(C) 電信公司
(D) 旅行社

解析 獨白開頭處提到要來檢視手機銷售數字，最後又談到增加銷售量的方案。這表示說話者任職於電信公司。

096 新增題型

Look at the graphic. When was the sale held?
(A) June
(B) July
(C) August
(D) September

中譯 見圖表。促銷活動於何時舉辦？
(A) 六月
(B) 七月
(C) 八月
(D) 九月

解析 說話者提到在低價拍賣期間的銷售量遽增（**had a spike**），根據表格可以得知八月份的銷售量遽增，為拍賣期間。

097

What will Rachel talk about?
(A) A branch grand opening
(B) A new sales staff member
(C) Some new sales strategies
(D) The disappointing sales numbers

中譯 瑞秋將會討論什麼？
(A) 分公司的盛大開幕活動
(B) 新進的業務人員
(C) 新的銷售策略
(D) 令人失望的業績

解析 後半段獨白中，説話者提到準備了幾個增加銷售量的方案，將由瑞秋來説明（let Rachel explain）。由此可以得知瑞秋將談論的內容為新的銷售策略。

Questions 98-100 refer to the following excerpt from a meeting and flyer. 美

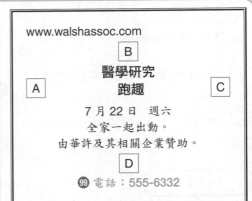

Thanks, everyone, for coming to this last-minute meeting. It won't take long ⑱ because I know you're busy with the quarterly report. As you know, our charity run for medical research is coming up in two weeks. Thanks to Lee's great design work, we have a really colorful and unique flyer this year. I have a question, though, before we take it to the printer. It's about the placement of our Website address. Right now it's in the top left corner, but ⑲ I'm wondering if it would be better near our phone number. ⑳ What do you all think?

謝謝大家來參加此緊急會議。不會占用太多時間，⑱ 因為我知道各位都在忙著準備季報。大家都知道，我們為醫學研究所辦的慈善跑步活動將於兩週後舉行。多虧李的出色設計，我們今年的傳單顏色鮮豔且風格獨特。不過在我們印刷之前，我有個問題，也就是網址的擺放位置。現在是置於左上角，但 ⑲ 我想放在我們的電話號碼旁會不會比較好。⑳ 大家覺得呢？

字彙 last-minute meeting 緊急會議   quarterly 每一季的   placement 擺放

098

Where most likely does the speaker work?
(A) At a print shop
(B) At a sports gym
(C) In a business office
(D) In a shopping mall

中譯 説話者最有可能在哪裡工作？
(A) 印刷店
(B) 健身房
(C) 商務公司
(D) 購物商場

解析 獨白開頭便出現答題線索，説話者表示了解聽者正忙於季報。選項中，在公司辦公室內工作的人，最有可能需要撰寫季報。

099 新增題型

Look at the graphic. Where does the speaker want to put the Web address?
(A) A
(B) B
(C) C
(D) D

中譯 見圖表。說話者想將網址擺放何處？
(A) A
(B) B
(C) C
(D) D

解析 獨白中談到傳單的設計，說話者提出想將電話放在公司網址附近。根據傳單的配置，最有可能將電話放置於 (D)。

100

What will the listeners do next?
(A) Attend an event
(B) Get a flyer printed
(C) Give their opinions
(D) Help the speaker hand out flyers

中譯 聽話者接下來會怎麼做？
(A) 參加活動
(B) 印出傳單
(C) 提出自己的意見
(D) 幫助說話者發傳單

解析 獨白以「**What do you all think?**」作結，表示想詢問聽者們的意見。由此可以得知說話者要求聽者提出他們的看法。

PART 5

101

The express train that the division head took to work was delayed an hour because of mechanical -------.
(A) harm
(B) mistake
(C) revision
(D) trouble

中譯 部門主管上班所搭的那班特快車，因為機械問題而誤點一小時。
(A) 傷害
(B) 錯誤
(C) 修改
(D) 問題

解析 根據題意，火車誤點一小時的原因為機械「問題」最為適當。

字彙 division head 部門主管　revision 修改

102

Long-term testing was required to refine the business risk management process to make it more ------- and consistent.
(A) predict
(B) predictability
(C) predictable
(D) prediction

中譯 長期測試是必要的，它可改進商業風險管理程序，使其更易預期且具有一致性。
(A) 預期
(B) 預期性
(C) 可預期的
(D) 預測

解析 **make it more** 後方適合連接的詞性為形容詞，加上空格後方連接對等連接詞 **and**，其後方連接的是形容詞 **consistent**，表示空格要填入形容詞。

字彙 refine 改善

103

Two poster samples were presented to the team leader, but ------- struck him and the team had to think of something else.
(A) both
(B) each
(C) either
(D) neither

中譯 雖然組長看過海報的兩個版本，但兩者都沒讓他印象深刻，所以小組必須再想出其他點子。
(A) 兩者　　　　　　　(B) 每一個
(C) 不是……就是……　(D) 兩個都沒有

解析 空格後方連接動詞 struck，表示空格為 but 連接的子句的主詞。根據題意，雖然交出了兩個樣本，但是團隊還是得再想其他方案，這表示兩個樣本團隊領導者都不滿意，因此空格適合填入限定詞 neither，表達否定概念。

字彙 present 提交　strike 使……印象深刻

104

The nonprofit organization was fortunate to receive ------- assistance in the amount of $30,000 from the local bank.
(A) educational
(B) informative
(C) monetary
(D) personnel

中譯 此非營利組織有幸獲得當地銀行提供的三萬元金援。
(A) 教育的　　　　　(B) 增長見聞的
(C) 金融的　　　　　(D) 人事

解析 空格用來修飾 assistance，應該填入形容詞，而後方出現金額，選項中與金錢有關的詞彙為 monetary。

字彙 nonprofit 非營利的　fortunate 幸運的
informative 增長見聞的　monetary 金融的

105

Sunshine Security offers free on-site estimates with no ------- to buy for your home or business.
(A) obligate
(B) obligation
(C) oblige
(D) obliged

中譯 陽光保全公司向家庭或企業提供免費的現場報價，且不會強制購買。
(A) 迫使　　　　　(B) 義務
(C) 迫使　　　　　(D) 有義務的

解析 空格前方的 no 為限定詞，表示後方要連接名詞。空格後方的不定詞 to V 用來修飾空格內的名詞。

字彙 on-site 現場的　obligation 義務

106

------- the scheduled staff meeting, the assistant had to print out all the handouts for everyone.
(A) As far as
(B) Except for
(C) Just about
(D) Prior to

中譯 在表定的員工會議前，助理必須先印出所有要給大家的講義。
(A) 就……而言　　　(B) 除了
(C) 大約　　　　　(D) 在……之前

解析 根據題意，助理必須先把資料印好。因此表達「在員工會議『前』完成」最為適當。

字彙 print out 印出　handout 講義

Actual Test 4

PART 5

107

Although he was offered the position of overseas branch manager last week, Ian Lee is ------- considering if he should take the opportunity.
(A) almost
(B) only
(C) still
(D) yet

中譯 雖然伊恩・李上週獲得前往海外分公司擔任經理的機會，但他仍在考慮是否該去。
(A) 幾乎　　(B) 僅有
(C) 仍然　　(D) 卻

解析 根據題意，表達「雖然此人收到了工作提案，但仍在考慮」最為適當。選項中最適合填入空格的單字為 still。yet 的意思為「尚未」，無法搭配現在進行式一起使用。

字彙 overseas branch 海外分公司

108

Owing ------- to the cooler-than-usual summer, the sales of air conditioners have dropped nationwide.
(A) large
(B) largely
(C) largeness
(D) larger

中譯 全國的冷氣銷售量均下滑，很大一部份是因為今年夏季比往年涼快許多。
(A) 巨大的　　(B) 在很大程度上
(C) 巨大　　(D) 較大的

解析 介系詞 owing to 用來表示原因，只有副詞能放在 owing 和 to 之間。

字彙 owing to 由於

109

A voucher ------- to this e-mail in pdf format; please show it to the hotel clerk when you check in.
(A) attached
(B) attaching
(C) is attached
(D) is attaching

中譯 此電子郵件隨附 PDF 格式的折價券；請於入住時向飯店人員出示本券。
(A) 隨附　　(B) 隨附的
(C) 被隨附　　(D) 正在隨附

解析 主詞為電子憑證（A voucher），表達「被附加至電子郵件中」最符合題意。

110

The magazine article succeeded in ------- public attention to the rural agricultural issues.
(A) directing
(B) forcing
(C) promoting
(D) reaching

中譯 此雜誌文章成功地將公眾注意力引導至鄉村農業的議題。
(A) 引導　　(B) 強迫
(C) 推廣　　(D) 觸及

解析 空格連接受詞 public attention，又搭配介系詞 to 一起使用，因此最適合填入 direct，表達「成功引起大眾關注」。

字彙 agricultural 農業的　direct 引導　force 強迫
promote 推廣；升遷　reach 觸及

111

Naomi Boomer rushed to the Fairmont Hotel, ------- she was scheduled to see her client.

(A) when
(B) where
(C) which
(D) who

中譯 娜歐蜜・布墨趕去費爾蒙特飯店，她安排好要在那裡會面客戶。

(A) 何時　　　　　　(B) 何地
(C) 哪一個　　　　　(D) 何者

解析 空格前後方各連接一個子句，因此空格要填入連接詞。空格用來補充說明 the Fairmont Hotel，表示預計在該地點與顧客碰面，因此適合填入關係副詞 where。

字彙 rush 趕緊

112

The administrative manager thought that Central Park would be perfectly ------- for the company's outdoor event.

(A) suit
(B) suitability
(C) suitable
(D) suitably

中譯 行政經理認為中央公園會非常適合舉辦公司的戶外活動。

(A) 適合　　　　　　(B) 合適性
(C) 適合的　　　　　(D) 適合地

解析 空格前方連接 be 動詞和副詞，且句子以介系詞片語結尾，因此空格適合填入形容詞。

113

The most noticeable ------- of the new smartphone series, Xtreme, is a fingerprint sensor to authenticate the user.

(A) fascination
(B) feature
(C) trademark
(D) treasure

中譯 新款智慧型手機 Xtreme 系列最令人注目的特點是，可用指紋感應器驗證使用者身分。

(A) 著迷　　　　　　(B) 特點
(C) 商標　　　　　　(D) 寶藏

解析 空格為 is a fingerprint sensor 的主詞，因此空格要填入名詞。表達「最引人注目的『特色』為指紋辨識」最符合題意。

字彙 noticeable 令人注目的　fingerprint 指紋
authenticate 證實　fascination 著迷　feature 特點
trademark 商標

114

The tour bus will stop at a spot to enjoy a panoramic view of the city ------- at least 20 minutes.

(A) by
(B) for
(C) until
(D) with

中譯 遊覽車將在一個景點停靠至少 20 分鐘，讓大家欣賞此都市的全景。

(A) 藉由　　　　　　(B) 持續
(C) 直到……為止　　(D) 與

解析 空格需要填入與時間有關的介系詞，用來引導後方的 at least 20 minutes。根據題意，適合填入 for，表達「停留二十分鐘的時間」。

字彙 panoramic view 全景

115

The CEO was delighted to hear the news that his firm recorded the ------- sales last quarter.
(A) higher
(B) highest
(C) lower
(D) lowest

中譯 執行長很開心聽到公司於上一季創下最高業績記錄。
(A) 較高的　　　　　(B) 最高的
(C) 較低的　　　　　(D) 最低的

解析 選項由比較級和最高級組成，而空格前方為 the，表示要填入最高級。根據題意，表達「為『最高的』銷售金額感到開心」最為適當。

字彙 delighted 開心的

116

The marketing chief was truly impressed with the new recruit's ------- analysis of the survey results.
(A) considerate
(B) desperate
(C) respectful
(D) thorough

中譯 這名新進人員對市調結果分析得相當完善，這讓行銷主管著實感到印象深刻。
(A) 周到的　　　　　(B) 絕望的
(C) 尊重的　　　　　(D) 完善的

解析 空格要搭配後方的名詞 analysis，且表達令人留下深刻的印象，因此最適合填入形容詞 thorough。

字彙 considerate 周到的　desperate 絕望的
respectful 尊重的　thorough 完善的，徹底的

117

Thanks to the success of its new products, Catty, Inc. was able to reduce its accumulated ------- by 8.5 million dollars last year.
(A) lose
(B) losing
(C) losses
(D) lost

中譯 多虧新品成功，凱提公司去年才能將其累積的虧損打銷 850 萬。
(A) 失去　　　　　(B) 失去
(C) 虧損　　　　　(D) 失去的

解析 該句話的主詞為 Catty, Inc.，空格為動詞 reduce 的受詞，且受到 its accumulated 的修飾，因此要填入名詞「虧損」。

字彙 accumulate 累積　loss 虧損

118

This Website allows anyone who is interested in our city cleaning project ------- its progress.
(A) follow
(B) followed
(C) following
(D) to follow

中譯 此網站能讓有意了解我們城市清掃專案的人追蹤進度。
(A) 追蹤　　　　　(B) 追蹤了
(C) 追蹤　　　　　(D) 追蹤

解析 who . . . project 用來修飾 anyone，因此 allows anyone 後方適合連接不定詞 to V，當作受詞補語使用。

字彙 follow 追蹤

119

As he ------- talked about his colorful career, the lecturer did not realize he had already gone over his time.

(A) confidentially
(B) cooperatively
(C) enormously
(D) passionately

中譯 這名講師熱情地談論著他多采多姿的職涯，沒意識到自己已經超過演講時間。

(A) 機密地　　　　　(B) 合作地
(C) 大量地　　　　　(D) 熱情地

解析 根據題意，講者講到超過時間，因此表達他「熱情地談論」最為適當。

字彙 confidentially 機密地　cooperatively 合作地
enormously 大量地　passionately 熱情地

120

With technology advancing so fast every day, ------- is critical for professionals and job seekers to stay up-to-date in their fields.

(A) it
(B) one
(C) that
(D) there

中譯 隨著科技日新月異，跟上自身領域的最新趨勢對專業人士及求職者是至關重要的。

(A) 它　　　　　　　(B) 一個
(C) 那個　　　　　　(D) 那裡

解析 空格位在句子的主詞位置，後方連接形容詞 critical，適用句型「It is + 形容詞 + 不定詞 to V」，因此答案為 (A)。

字彙 advance 進展

121

In order to fully ------- the vision of our clients, we make every effort to establish a close relationship with them.

(A) realizable
(B) realization
(C) realize
(D) realized

中譯 為了完全實現客戶的願景，我們竭力與客戶建立密切關係。

(A) 可實現的　　　　(B) 實現
(C) 實現　　　　　　(D) 實現過

解析 空格前方為副詞 fully，但是 In order to 後方要連接原形動詞才行。後方的名詞 the vision 則當作原形動詞的受詞使用。

字彙 make every effort 竭力
establish a relationship 建立關係　realize 實現

122

Working for more than 20 years at a charity organization, Tim Davidson gained ------- in fund-raising activities.

(A) commitment
(B) comprehension
(C) expertise
(D) access

中譯 於慈善機構服務超過 20 年，提姆・戴維森在募資活動上獲得了專業知識。

(A) 承諾　　　　　　(B) 理解力
(C) 專業知識　　　　(D) 管道

解析 根據題意，此人在某個領域工作了二十多年，因此他能獲得的東西為該領域的「專業知識」。

字彙 charity organization 慈善機構　fund-raising 募資
comprehension 理解力　expertise 專業知識

123

Everyone seemed exhausted after the long discussion; ------- the supervisor wrapped up the meeting quickly.

(A) accordingly
(B) likewise
(C) meanwhile
(D) nonetheless

中譯 每個人在長時間的討論後均筋疲力盡；主管因此盡速結束會議。

(A) 因此　　　　　(B) 同樣地
(C) 同時　　　　　(D) 然而

解析 空格前方表示大家都已經筋疲力盡，後方連接的子句則表示迅速結束會議。因此前後的狀況最適合使用 accordingly 連接。

字彙 exhausted 筋疲力盡的　accordingly 因而
likewise 同樣地　meanwhile 同時

124

The local bakery is famous for its ------- display of assorted bread and pastries in the window.

(A) appetite
(B) appetizer
(C) appetizing
(D) appetizingly

中譯 這間當地麵包店的馳名之處，在於會將各色麵包和糕點在窗邊展示得相當吸引人。

(A) 胃口　　　　　(B) 開胃菜
(C) 開胃的　　　　(D) 開胃地

解析 空格位在所有格 its 和名詞 display 之間，因此答案為形容詞。

字彙 assorted 綜合的　appetizing 開胃的

125

Please forward us the amount -------, which is indicated on the invoice, by the end of the month.

(A) counted
(B) balanced
(C) owed
(D) refunded

中譯 請於月底前將發票上所示的欠款轉寄給我們。

(A) 已計算的　　　(B) 已結餘的
(C) 已欠的　　　　(D) 已退款的

解析 根據題意，要求支付發票上顯示的金額。選項中，最適合填入 (C)，表達「未付」的金額。

字彙 amount 總額　indicate 指示　balance 使……收支平衡

126

The botanist says that River City Garden benefits ------- from the mild climate of the area.

(A) rich
(B) richer
(C) richly
(D) richness

中譯 此植物學家表示，瑞佛市立花園因該區的溫和氣候而大大受惠。

(A) 豐富的　　　　(B) 較豐富的
(C) 十足地　　　　(D) 豐富

解析 動詞 benefit 為不及物動詞，要搭配後方介系詞 from 一起使用，因此空格適合填入副詞。

字彙 botanist 植物學家　benefit 受惠　richly 十足地

127

The waterfront development project ------- done a week ago, but it is nowhere near completion yet.

(A) had been
(B) **should have been**
(C) was
(D) would be

中譯 濱水區開發專案早該在一週前完成，但至今離完工仍遙遙無期。

(A) 過去曾被　　(B) 早該
(C) 過去被　　　(D) 會被

解析 本題要選出適當的 **be** 動詞時態。根據題意，表示應該要在一週前完成某件事，但尚未完成，因此適合使用的時態為「**should have +** 過去分詞」。

字彙 **nowhere** 無處

128

The division head was really looking forward to reading Molly Shannon's report, but she had not ------- finished yet.

(A) barely
(B) far
(C) **quite**
(D) very

中譯 部門主管十分期待閱讀莫莉・香儂的報告，但她的報告還不算完成。

(A) 幾乎不　　(B) 到很大的程度
(C) 完全　　　(D) 非常

解析 逗點前方表示非常期待閱讀某人的報告，接著使用連接詞 **but** 連接，表示後方子句為預料之外的狀況。(C) 為副詞，用來補充說明，表達尚未完成的程度。

129

The Emerson Group is dedicated to ------- people with limited finances or other special needs.

(A) help
(B) helped
(C) **helping**
(D) helps

中譯 艾莫森集團致力於幫助經濟困頓或有其他特殊需求的人。

(A) 幫助　　　(B) 幫助過
(C) 幫助　　　(D) 幫助

解析 空格前方連接動詞片語 **be dedicated to**，當中的 **to** 為介系詞，因此空格適合填入動名詞 **helping**。

字彙 **be dedicated to** 致力於

130

To enforce the security, Madison Corp. decided to ------- a security guard at each of its three entrances.

(A) layout
(B) moving
(C) premises
(D) **station**

中譯 為了加強安全性，麥迪森企業決定在三個大門都設置一位警衛。

(A) 布置　　　(B) 遷移
(C) 廠區　　　(D) 設置

解析 根據題意，表達目的為加強安全，因此公司決定「設置」保全人員。

字彙 **enforce** 加強　　**premises** 廠區　　**station** 設置

Questions 131-134 refer to the following notice. 通知

Harvey Collins: A Special Cinema Screening
Saturday 15 July

From *West End Lovers* to *All the Beautiful Tomorrows*, Harvey Collins' acting career ------- over five decades.
131.
Now, for the first time, the Creststone Picture House Archives has ------- together highlights from Mr. Collins
132.
award-winning career. Some clips from the collection are never-before-seen outtakes and behind-the-scenes footage while filming in locations all over the world. Films will be introduced by Creststone Archives Officer Kathryn Villa. -------.
133.
Seats are limited at this free event, so book yours soon. Please follow the link below for -------.
134.
https://www.eventbook/harveycollins/creststonearchives. com

哈維・柯林斯：特別電影放映活動
7 月 15 日 週六

　　從《西岸情人》到《美好的明天》，哈維・柯林斯的演藝生涯 ⑬ 已綿延超過五十載。如今，克里斯通影片檔案館首度 ⑬ 集結柯林斯先生獲獎生涯的精彩片段。收集的片段中，有些是他在世界各地拍片時，未公開的剪去鏡頭以及幕後花絮。影片將由克里斯通檔案館的主管凱瑟琳・維拉來做開場介紹。⑬ 她同時會在每部電影結束後，回答觀眾問題。

　　此免費活動的席次有限，因此請盡速訂位。請至以下連結了解 ⑬ 訂位事宜。
https://www.eventbook/harveycollins/creststonearchives.com

字彙 clip 片段　outtake 剪去片段　footage 影片

131
(A) had spanned
(B) is spanned
(C) **spanned**
(D) spans

中譯 (A) 已綿延
(B) 被綿延
(C) 綿延
(D) 綿延

解析 本文為與放映某演員電影的活動有關的公告。span 指的是「橫跨、跨越」一段時間。表達演員的演藝生涯「橫跨」超過五十年，因此填入過去簡單式 (C) 較為適當。

字彙 span 綿延

132
(A) gone
(B) got
(C) moved
(D) **put**

中譯 (A) 消失
(B) 得到
(C) 遷移
(D) 放置

解析 關於特別放映活動，資料庫「集結了」獲獎作品，因此使用 put together 最符合前後文意。

字彙 put together 集結

133 新增題型

(A) She is in charge of all public inquiries about the works.

(B) She will also be taking audience questions after each film.

(C) The Creststone Cinema is undergoing renovation at this time.

(D) There is a $5 charge for each adult, while children are free.

中譯 (A) 她負責大眾對於作品的的所有問題。

(B) 她同時會在每部電影結束後,回答觀眾發問的問題。

(C) 克里斯通電影院此時正在進行翻修。

(D) 每位成人收費 5 元,兒童則免費。

解析 空格前方提到掌管資料庫的官員凱瑟琳 · 維拉,而空格後方則是下一個段落,因此空格補充說明該名女子在活動中負責的內容較為適當。與 (A) 相比,(B) 的內容與活動的關聯性更高,因此空格適合填入 (B)。

字彙 inquiry 發問

134

(A) discounts
(B) lists
(C) purchases
(D) reservations

中譯 (A) 折扣　　　　(B) 清單
(C) 購物　　　　(D) 訂位

解析 文中提到座位數量有限,建議盡快「預約」,後方再附上網址,表示為「預約」用的連結。

Questions 135-138 refer to the following e-mail. 電子郵件

To:	cs@bbluggage.com
From:	matildaikeda@greenmail.com
Subject:	PakTek40
Date:	August 10

To whom it may concern:

I bought your PakTek40 backpack about three weeks ago. I really like all the different pockets and pouches. Since I bike to work, I need a lot of ------- **135.** to carry my stuff. ------- **136.** I tried applying a bit of oil on it, but it won't move at all. I'm not sure ------- **137.** I should send it back to you or take it back to the store where I bought it. Please let me know ------- **138.** to do to resolve this. Thank you.

收件者:	cs@bbluggage.com
寄件者:	matildaikeda@greenmail.com
主旨:	PakTek40
日期:	8 月 10 日

敬啟者:

　　我大約三週前購買你們的 PakTek40 背包。我真的很喜歡各種夾層和內袋。由於我騎單車上班,我需要許多 ❶❸❺ 夾層來收納物品。❶❸❻ 不幸的是,主拉鍊卡住了,我一直修不好。我試著上點潤滑油,但還是完全拉不動。我不確定 ❶❸❼ 是否該寄還給你們,或是拿去我原本購買的商店。請告訴我該做 ❶❸❽ 什麼解決此問題。謝謝您。

字彙 carry 攜帶　apply 塗抹

135

(A) compartments
(B) efforts
(C) parts
(D) alternatives

中譯 (A) 隔間　　　　(B) 努力
(C) 零組件　　　(D) 替代方案

解析 本文為傳送至背包公司的電子郵件。文中提到包包內有各種不同的夾層和內袋,寄件者提到自己需要放置物品的「空間」,因此空格最適合填入 (A),表示包包內的「隔間」。

字彙 compartment 隔間　alternative 替代方案

265

Actual Test 4　PART 6

(A) I discovered yesterday that the small pouch in front has a tear on the bottom.
(B) Just after getting home from the store, I spilled paint on it.
(C) The straps are too short for me to use it on my bicycle.
(D) Unfortunately, the main zipper got stuck and I haven't been able to fix it.

中譯 (A) 我昨天發現前方的小夾袋底部有破損。
(B) 我剛從店面買回家時就把顏料灑到上面。
(C) 背帶太短，我沒辦法掛在單車上。
(D) 不幸的是，主拉鍊卡住了，我一直修不好。

解析 空格後方提到他試過上油，但還是沒辦法拉動。由此可以得知空格內填入與包包拉鍊有問題的相關敘述最符合文意。

字彙 tear 破損　spill 潑灑　strap 掛帶　stuck 卡住的

137

(A) as
(B) if
(C) though
(D) where

中譯 (A) 像……一樣　(B) 是否
(C) 儘管　(D) 哪裡

解析 空格位在兩個子句之間，要填入連接詞。I'm not sure 後方連接的子句中出現 or，表示「不知道是否該寄回公司，還是帶去店家」，因此填入 (B) 最符合文意。

138

(A) how
(B) what
(C) when
(D) whom

中譯 (A) 如何　(B) 何事
(C) 何時　(D) 何者

解析 根據文意，空格後方表達的是「該做什麼事去解決問題」，因此要填入 what。do 後方並未連接受詞，因此空格內不適合填入 how。

PART 6

Questions 139-142 refer to the following article. 文章

Citywide Ferry Service to Launch Soon

The Rockridge ------- will be the first citywide ferry
139.
service to hit the water, with a launch coming in
October. The two other planned routes will begin
early next year. -------. The route includes a stop at
140.
the City Center Terminal on the way from Rockridge
to the ------- stop, Pier 7 in Brantley. Rides will cost
141.
$3.00, but fares won't be integrated with the rest of
the city's transportation, meaning that riders won't
get a ------- transfer from boat to subway.
142.

全市渡輪服務即將開跑

　　洛克瑞志 ⑬ 線即將於今年十月下水服務，它將成為首個全市渡輪服務。其他兩條路線預計將於明年初通航。⑭ 洛克瑞志之所以率先通航，是因為它是本市通勤時間最長的地區。這條路線從洛克瑞志到 ⑭ 終點站白特利 7 號碼頭，中途會在城市中心總站停靠。船票將訂為 3 元，但此交通費無法與其他市立運輸工具合併，也就是乘客無法從輪船 ⑭ 免費轉搭地鐵。

字彙 citywide 全市的　route 路線　integrate 合併

139

(A) bridge
(B) direction
(C) map
(D) route

中譯 (A) 橋樑
(B) 方向
(C) 地圖
(D) 路線

解析 空格後方連接 will be the first citywide ferry service，因此填入渡輪服務有關的名詞「route」較符合文意。

140 新增題型

(A) City officials are hoping to attract tourists to the new park by offering free bus rides from the station.
(B) Rockridge is getting the first service since the area has among the longest commute times in the city.
(C) The city council is expected to vote on the new service's cost and stops at its next monthly meeting.
(D) The ferry was traveling at the usual speed when the accident occurred, according to safety inspectors.

中譯 (A) 市府官員希望藉由提供從車站出發免費接駁的公車，來吸引遊客前往新公園。
(B) 洛克瑞志之所以率先通航，是因為它是本市通勤時間最長的地區。
(C) 市議會預計於下次月會時，針對新服務的成本與站點進行表決。
(D) 根據安全視察人員表示，事故發生時，渡輪的行進速度正常。

解析 本文為針對全市渡輪航線之一的洛克瑞志航線的報導。空格前方提到另外兩條航線則預計於明年初開始；空格後方提到洛克瑞志航線的資訊，因此空格適合填入與洛克瑞志航線有關的說明，選擇 (B) 最符合前後文意。其他選項皆與洛克瑞志航線毫無關聯。

字彙 commute time 通勤時間　inspector 視察人員

141

(A) final
(B) finalized
(C) finalize
(D) finally

中譯 (A) 終點的
(B) 被完結
(C) 完結
(D) 終於

解析 空格前方定冠詞 the，後方連接名詞 stop，意思為「停靠站」，表示空格要填入形容詞。final stop 的意思為「終點站」。

字彙 finalize 完結

142

(A) fast
(B) free
(C) complete
(D) secure

中譯 (A) 快速的
(B) 免費的
(C) 完整的
(D) 安全的

解析 前方提到不會與其他交通資費合併，這表示搭乘渡輪轉乘地鐵的旅客，無法使用「免費」轉車服務。

字彙 complete 完整的

The annual company picnic will be held at Doe Reservoir Beach on Saturday, July 3, starting at 11:00 AM. All employees and their families -------. This year we again plan to ------- volleyball, softball, swimming, and water-skiing (with at least three boats in the water!). -------. The company will provide basic barbecue fare (including vegetarian entrées) and sporting equipment, but all are ------- to bring along their own fun. And don't forget your dessert! Please let Luke Harris know by June 21 how many people you'll be bringing. Looking forward to a wonderful time!

143.
144.
145.
146.

公司的年度野餐將於 7 月 3 日週六早上 11 點，在多伊蓄水海灘舉行。所有員工與其家人都 143 被邀請參加。今年我們再次計劃 144 以排球、壘球、游泳與滑水（至少三艘船！）為特色。145 當然，甜點大賽或許會是一整天下來，最受歡迎的橋段。公司會提供基本的烤肉餐點（包括素食主餐）與運動設備，不過我們仍 146 鼓勵大家自行攜帶娛樂用具。也別忘了帶甜點過來！請於 6 月 21 日前，告知盧克‧哈里斯各位將攜伴人數。期待快樂時光！

143

(A) are invited
(B) invited
(C) inviting
(D) will be inviting

中譯 (A) 被邀約　　(B) 邀約過
(C) 邀約　　(D) 即將邀約

解析 主詞為 **All employees and their families**，空格則為該句話的結尾。**invite** 為及物動詞，要使用被動語態，表達主詞受邀之意。

144

(A) promote
(B) feature
(C) operate
(D) sustain

中譯 (A) 推廣　　(B) 以……為特色
(C) 運作　　(D) 維持

解析 本題要選出適當的動詞，搭配受詞 **volleyball, softball, swimming, and water-skiing** 使用。公司的年度活動應屬於「以前述這些項目為特色」的計畫，因此填入 **(B)** 最符合文意。

字彙 **feature** 以……為特色　**sustain** 維持

145 新增題型

(A) All of us were happy to welcome our newest member, Josh, to the company last week.
(B) If you have any ideas about the ceremony, please let Marie know before next Saturday.
(C) Of course, the dessert contest will likely be the most popular part of the whole day.
(D) Those who have used goods to donate to the charity, you can bring them up till July.

中譯 (A) 大家上週均十分開心迎接新進人員喬許。
(B) 如果大家對儀式有任何想法，請於下週六之前告知瑪莉。
(C) 當然，甜點大賽或許會是一整天下來，最受歡迎的橋段。
(D) 已向慈善團體捐贈二手物品的人，於七月前均能繼續帶東西來。

解析 (A) 和 (D) 的敘述與野餐活動無關。空格前方提到一些特色項目，空格後方又提到公司會提供的東西以及各自要準備的東西。(C) 最適合與其他活動項目連接，且與後半段的「And don't forget your dessert!」相互呼應。

146

(A) encouraged
(B) encouragement
(C) encourager
(D) encourages

中譯 (A) 被鼓勵
(B) 鼓勵
(C) 鼓勵者
(D) 鼓勵

解析 空格位在 be 動詞 are 和不定詞 to V 之間，(B) 和 (C) 皆為單數名詞，得優先排除。be encouraged to 的意思為「被建議、鼓勵……」，最符合前後文意。

PART 7

Questions 147-148 refer to the following memo. 備忘錄

147 After 40 years of service with Parker & Sons, Mr. Howard Trumbo will retire at the end of this month. Mr. Trumbo is known in the industry for his humor and hard work, and has said that he wants to use his golden years to travel and see parts of the globe he has never experienced before. We wish him all the best.

148 Ms. Janet Newsome, who has been selected to fill the seat, is expected to lead the company to a successful future after being our group leader for the last five years. The transition will take a few weeks, as new team members get acquainted with new responsibilities and tasks.

147 服務於「帕克與森斯」公司 40 年後，霍華‧川波先生將於本月月底退休。川波先生以幽默感和工作勤奮聞名業界，並說過希望用自己的黃金歲月四處旅行，欣賞他從未造訪過的世界各處。我們衷心祝福他一切順利。

而獲選接替川波先生職位的 **148** 珍妮特‧紐森小姐，過去五年擔任集團領導人的職務，預計公司在其帶領下，將擁有前途光明的未來。此交接過渡期需要幾週的時間，因為新團隊人員需熟悉新的工作事項。

字彙 transition 過渡期　task 任務

147

What is the purpose of the notice?
(A) To congratulate someone on winning a prize
(B) To give information about merger transition
(C) To inform staff about someone leaving the company
(D) To welcome a new team member to the company

中譯 此通知的目的為何？
(A) 為了恭喜某人贏得獎項
(B) 為了告知合併過渡期的資訊
(C) 為了告知員工有人即將離職
(D) 為了歡迎新進團隊人員加入公司

解析 本文為公司內部備忘錄，告知即將退休的員工和之後要接任的人。主要的內容為川波先生退休一事，因此答案為 (C)。

148

What is true about Ms. Newsome?
(A) She retired a few weeks ago.
(B) She will go on a business trip abroad.
(C) She will transfer to a different office.
(D) She has led a team over years.

中譯 關於紐森小姐，下列何者為真？
(A) 她幾週前剛退休。
(B) 她將去國外出差。
(C) 她將調職到不同分處。
(D) 她已帶領某團隊多年。

解析 紐森小姐為接任川波先生的人，從「after being our group leader for the last five years」可以得知她過去幾年曾領導團隊工作。

字彙 transfer 調職

Questions 149-150 refer to the following text message chain. 簡訊對話 新增題型

BRIAN GRUNSWALD	9:20
I'll be at the station in just a minute. Where is my contact waiting?	

ANITH HEENAN	9:21
⑭⑨ West exit, by the coffee shop. That's the place you suggested.	

BRIAN GRUNSWALD	9:23
That's what I thought, but he's not here. Has he called?	

ANITH HEENAN	9:24
Not that I know of. Which coffee shop are you at?	

BRIAN GRUNSWALD	9:26
Mario's. It's the first one outside the exit gate.	

ANITH HEENAN	9:27
He messaged to say ⑮⓪ he got turned around on the platform. He's on the way now.	

BRIAN GRUNSWALD	9:28
OK. I'll wait right here and look out for him.	

ANITH HEENAN	9:28
He should be there in a few minutes.	

布萊恩・岡斯沃德　9:20
我再一下子就到車站了。我的聯絡人會在哪裡等我？

安妮斯・西納　9:21
⑭⑨西側出口，就在咖啡廳旁邊。那是你提議碰面的地方。

布萊恩・岡斯沃德　9:23
我也是這麼想，但他人不在那裡。他有打電話過去嗎？

安妮斯・西納　9:24
就我所知並沒有。你在哪一家咖啡廳？

布萊恩・岡斯沃德　9:26
馬力歐。這是出口外面的第一家咖啡廳。

安妮斯・西納　9:27
他剛傳簡訊說⑮⓪他在月台上迷路。現在已經往你那邊過去了。

布萊恩・岡斯沃德　9:28
好的。我會在這邊邊等邊看。

安妮斯・西納　9:28
他應該幾分鐘後就會到。

字彙 exit gate 出口　message 傳訊給　get turned around 迷路　look out for 找找看

149

Where will Mr. Grunswald meet his contact?
(A) Beside the exit gate
(B) By a café
(C) Near the station
(D) On the platform

中譯 岡斯沃德先生將在哪裡與他的聯絡人碰面？
(A) 出口旁邊
(B) 咖啡廳
(C) 車站附近
(D) 在月台上

解析 岡斯沃德先生在訊息中問道：「Where is my contact waiting?」，接著西納小姐回答：「West exit, by the coffee shop.」，表示約在咖啡廳旁見面。

At 9:27, what does Ms. Heenan
mean when she says, "he got turned
around on the platform"?
(A) He got confused about the
direction he needed to go.
(B) He started walking around the
platform to look at things.
(C) He wanted to meet at a different
place.
(D) He was walking in a large crowd.

中譯 在9:27時，西納小姐說「他在月台上迷路」是什麼意思？
(A) 他搞錯該走的方向。
(B) 他開始在月台上走來走去看東西。
(C) 他想在不同地方碰面。
(D) 他走在擁擠人群中。

解析 「get turned around」意思是「搞錯方向」，並且後方提到「He's on the way now.」，由此可知岡斯沃德先生要碰面的人應是迷路了。

Questions 151-152 refer to the following memo. 備忘錄

The Conway Accounting Firm is proud to announce a getaway program for all employees! ⑮ We want to show our appreciation for all the hard work you do during the year, and an office party isn't always the best answer, so starting the first week in September, we will be offering complimentary rotating day trips to various parts of the tri-state area.

These day trips will offer everyone a chance to relax, unwind him- or herself after the tough month of hard overtime. We want everyone to be able to enjoy these, so each trip will be within three hours of the office, and ⑯ some of the choices include a day spa, first-class service at a lodge, or the virtual world at VirtuaPlex. There will be over 20 to choose from!

Everyone is eligible to use this program, but the dates are first come, first served; so don't wait too long. Sign up through the company intranet and look for the link marked "Employee Days" to select your day to getaway.

康威會計事務所自豪地宣布，將推出短期旅行畫來慰勞所有員工！⑮ 我們想對大家今年的辛勤表現表達謝意，而舉辦派對並不總是最好的方式。因此，從九月的第一週開始，我們將輪流舉辦前往三州交界景點的免費一日遊行程。

這些一日遊行程能讓每個人都有機會在一個月的辛勤加班後放鬆心情。我們希望每個人都能享受到此福利，因此每一趟行程與公司之間不會超過三小時的交通時間。⑯ 有些行程還包括一日SPA、度假木屋的頂級服務，或是VirtuaPlex主題樂園的虛擬世界。有超過20種行程可以選擇！

每個人均有資格申請此計畫，但先登記的人可先選日期；所以千萬別久候多時。請透過公司內部網站的「員工日」連結，來報名登記你一日遊的日期。

字彙 getaway 短期旅行 complimentary 免費的 rotate 輪流 day trip 一日遊 unwind 使……放鬆 lodge 木屋 virtual 虛擬的

Why is the company offering day trips to the workers?
(A) As a reward for finishing a project
(B) As a thank-you for their effort
(C) As a thank-you for winning a prize
(D) As a year-end bonus for workers

中譯 此公司為何向員工提供一日遊的福利？
(A) 作為完成專案的獎勵
(B) 向員工的努力表達謝意
(C) 向員工贏得大獎一事表達謝意
(D) 作為員工的年終福利

解析 本文為備忘錄，通知公司全體員工的休假計畫。第一段當中便提到舉辦一日遊的理由：「show our appreciation for all the hard work you do during the year」，由此可以得知為的是向努力工作的員工表達感謝之意。

字彙 reward 獎勵

152

What is NOT true about the programs?
(A) They are mainly outdoor activities.
(B) They are offered for free.
(C) They will not take long to travel to.
(D) They will start in early September.

中譯 關於此計畫，下列何者為非？
(A) 主要都是戶外活動。
(B) 公司免費提供。
(C) 交通時間不會很久。
(D) 將於九月初開始進行。

解析 (A) 文中提到「a day spa, first-class service at a lodge, or the virtual world at VirtuaPlex」，與戶外活動相去甚遠；(B) 由「offering complimentary rotating day trips」可以得知為免費的旅遊；(C) 由「within three hours of the office」可以得知一日遊地點在距離不遠的地方；(D)「starting the first week in September」表示於九月初舉行。

Questions 153-154 refer to the following article. 文章

In potentially bad news for their rivals, it is being reported that ⑮ **TES Systems and Holiday Technologies are entering a new business partnership to work together** to increase market share in the very competitive technology market. ⑮ **Combined, the two companies will create one of the largest computer software companies in the world.**

If approved, TES Systems will begin making parts for Holiday in an effort to increase margin by using cost-effective technology. It is reported that ⑮ **TES Systems uses refurbished materials, greatly reducing costs for the manufacturer.** ⑮ **Although both companies are reluctant to use the word "merger," it looks to be the case in this situation.** TES spokesman Greg Harrison said, "This partnership will help both companies increase profits, while benefiting each company with lower production costs."

競爭對手可能要擔心了。報導指出，⑮ TES 系統公司與好樂迪科技公司即將建立嶄新的商業合作關係，以在高度競爭的科技市場裡提升市占率。⑮ 兩家公司一旦合體，其將成為全世界規模最大的電腦軟體公司之一。

合作案經過核准後，TES 系統公司將採用有成本效益的科技，來為好樂迪公司製造零組件，以便增加收益。報導指出，⑮ TES 系統公司運用翻新的材料，大幅降低了製造商的成本。⑮ 雖然兩家公司不願意稱此合作為「合併」，但以目前情勢來看，確實是如此。TES 發言人格瑞格·哈里森表示：「此合作關係將能幫助雙方增加利潤，同時以較低生產成本來達到雙贏局面。」

字彙 margin 成本　cost-effective 有成本效益的　refurbish 翻新　reluctant 不願意的　spokesman 發言人

153

What is the article mainly about?
(A) Company's fiscal condition
(B) A potential merger
(C) Developing new technology
(D) Raising recycling awareness

中譯 此篇文章主要在討論什麼？
(A) 公司的財務狀況
(B) 潛在的合併案
(C) 開發新科技
(D) 提高回收意識

解析 文中提到：「a new business partnership to work together」、「Combined, the two companies will create one of the largest computer software companies」，由此可以得知雖然尚未發生，但是仍先針對兩家公司即將合併一事進行報導。

字彙 fiscal 財務的　awareness 意識

154

How does TES Systems keep costs down?
(A) They have an efficient manufacturing process.
(B) They outsource their manufacturing overseas.
(C) They will cut the costs by half.
(D) They use cheaper materials for their parts.

中譯 TES 系統公司如何降低成本？
(A) 他們擁有效率佳的製造程序。
(B) 他們將製程外包至海外。
(C) 他們將成本減半。
(D) 他們使用價格較低廉的材料來製造零組件。

解析 第二段中提到：「TES Systems uses refurbished materials, greatly reducing costs for the manufacturer」，由此便能確認節省成本的方法。(D) 將 refurbished materials 改寫成 cheaper materials，故為正確答案。

字彙 outsource 外包

Questions 155-157 refer to the following memo. 備忘錄

Attention: All Dream Net Employees

After a few months of negotiation, ⑮ we have made the decision to bring in some new equipment to our office, and we want everyone to get a chance to be introduced to it, as well as learn how to use it. Starting on Monday, you will notice a section of the second floor will be blocked off in preparation of its installation. What is this new equipment? We think you will be very excited to learn that we will now be able to do the highest level Medical 3D printing, right here in the building.

As many of our clients have stated, this new technique is something they are interested in bringing to their network of rehabilitation clinics, and we believe that we can be the number one provider of these services. A number of our clients have stated their preference to use this technology with those they are trying to assist, and with the Wish Foundation, we can help those dreams become a reality. ⑯ Whether it be a 3D printed hand or leg, we can now do our very best to be a part of the team that supports everyone in need.

⑰ Once installed, there will be a few basic training days, and then some more intensive programs for teams working directly with the machines. Questions or any other comments should be sent to Jackie Stevens at extension 49 or e-mail her at: jstevens@dreamnet.com.

所有夢幻之網的員工請注意

經過數月協商後，⑮我們決定為公司增加一些新設備，我們希望每個人都有機會了解及學習操作設備簡介。從週一開始，大家將發現二樓有一個區域會被封住，來為安裝設備做準備。那麼新設備是什麼呢？我想大家一定會非常興奮地得知，我們將能在此大樓裡，使用最高等級的醫學 3D 列印。

如我們許多客戶所述，他們對此新科技十分感興趣，希望能將其引進他們的復健診所。我們相信本公司將可成為此類服務的頭號供應商。我們的許多客戶已表明，他們傾向將此科技用在他們幫助的對象，而在與希望基金會合作的情況下，我們能讓此夢想成真。⑯無論是 3D 列印的手義肢或腳義肢，我們現在能盡自己所能，成為向有需要人士提供協助的一員。

⑰設備安裝完成後，將會有幾天的基本教育訓練，而在工作上需要頻繁操作這些機器的團隊，會要上更進階的課程。如有任何疑問或指教，可直接撥打分機49或傳電子郵件至 jstevens@dreamnet.com 來告知潔姬‧史蒂芬斯。

字彙 get a chance 有機會　block off 封住　state 表示　rehabilitation clinic 復健診所　assist 協助　intensive 密集的

Actual Test 4

PART 7

155

Where will the new equipment be introduced?
(A) At a medical clinic
(B) At a new client's office
(C) At Dream Net's office
(D) At the Wish Foundation's office

中譯 此新設備會引進何處？
(A) 醫療診所 (B) 新客戶的辦公室
(C) 夢幻之網的辦公室 (D) 希望基金會的辦公室

解析 本文為備忘錄，告知公司引進了新設備，先是介紹設備，而後說明往後的計畫。文中提到：「bring in some new equipment to our office」，因此答案為 (C)。

156

What kind of work does the company most likely do?
(A) Aid people with disabilities
(B) Create images with high-tech scanners
(C) Sell office equipment
(D) Use technology to create servers

中譯 此公司最有可能負責何種營運項目？
(A) 幫助身障人士 (B) 以高科技掃描器建立影像
(C) 販售辦公設備 (D) 運用科技來建造伺服器

解析 第二段提到：「Whether it be a 3D printed hand or leg, we can now do our very best to be a part of the team that supports everyone in need.」，由此段話可以推測出該公司從事的工作。該公司使用 3D 印表機製作人工手腳，且本段開頭又提到「復健科診所」，因此答案最有可能為 (A)，為身心障礙人士製作產品。

字彙 disability 身障

157

What will take place next week?
(A) The company will announce a partnership with the Wish Foundation.
(B) The company will discuss new product designs.
(C) The company will join a medical network.
(D) The company will offer training programs.

中譯 下週會發生什麼事？
(A) 公司會宣布與希望基金會的合作案。
(B) 公司會討論新品設計。
(C) 公司會加入醫學網絡。
(D) 公司會提供教育訓練。

解析 第三段說明往後要做的事情。當中提到：「Once installed, there will be a few basic training days, and then some more intensive programs for teams working directly with the machines.」，由此可以得知之後將有培訓課程。

Questions 158-160 refer to the following estimate. 估價單

Ken Brockton's Auto Repair

1928 Ball Road
Culver City, CA 90232
159 August 7

Damage
- Front left fender partially crushed
- Front left headlight and casing
- Bumper has cracks and paint scrapes

肯 · 柏克頓汽車維修公司

90232 加州卡爾弗城包爾路 1928 號
159 8 月 7 日

受損情況
- 左前方擋泥板部分粉碎
- 左前方大燈與外殼
- 保險桿有裂痕、烤漆刮傷

⑯ Repairs
- Repair and smooth front left fender
- Replace headlight
- Fix bumper cracks
- Polish and wax bumper

⑯ Estimated Repair Time	**4 days***
Estimated Cost	**$850.00***

⑯ Insurance Details
- Automobile Insurance (pay for 60 percent)
- Policy # 0323-268-9890

Auto Body Technician	Clark Flynn
Mechanic	Aaron Bernard

Customer
Nicholas Tunney
65 Arrow Lane
Los Angeles, CA 90096
424-555-7404

Please note: Time and costs are subject to change. It is our policy to notify the customer of these changes before action is taken.

---

⑯ 維修項目
- 維修與恢復左前方擋泥板的平整度
- 更換大燈
- 修理保險桿裂痕
- 將保險桿拋光與上蠟

⑯ 預計維修時間	4 天 *
預估費用	850 元 *

⑯ 保險細節
- 汽車保險（理賠 60%）
- 保單編號　0323-268-9890

車體技師	克拉克・費林
機械技工	艾倫・伯納

顧客資料
尼可拉斯・湯尼
90096 加州洛杉磯愛羅大道 65 號
424-555-7404

請注意：維修時間與費用可能會有變動。根據本公司規定，維修前會先通知顧客變動之處。

字彙　fender 擋泥板　crack 裂痕　scrape 刮傷　smooth 使……平滑　polish 磨光
policy 保單　be subject to 易受……的

158

How many automobile parts will be fixed by the service?
(A) 1
(B) 2
(C) 3
(D) 4

中譯　此次服務將修理多少汽車零組件？
(A) 1
(B) 2
(C) 3
(D) 4

解析　本文為汽車維修的估價單。汽車維修項目有四項，包含的零件有「front left fender、front left headlight、bumper」，數量為三樣。

159

When is the soonest the repairs could be finished?
(A) August 9
(B) August 11
(C) August 13
(D) August 15

中譯　維修最快可於何時完成？
(A) 8 月 9 日
(B) 8 月 11 日
(C) 8 月 13 日
(D) 8 月 15 日

解析　維修的時間預計為四天，而該估價單的撰寫日期為 8 月 7 日，因此最快能修好的時間為 8 月 11 日。

160

What is indicated about the cost?
(A) An insurance company will partly cover it.
(B) It is due on August 30.
(C) It is the final amount.
(D) Mr. Tunney should pay $850.

中譯 關於費用，文中指出什麼？
(A) 保險公司會理賠部分金額。
(B) 8 月 30 日是付款截止日。
(C) 此為最終的金額。
(D) 湯尼先生應支付 850 元。

解析 估價單上的價格為 850 元，並提到汽車保險會支付百分之六十，因此 (A) 的敘述正確，表示保險公司會賠償部分金額。

字彙 cover 涵蓋　due 到期的

Questions 161-163 refer to the following e-mail. 電子郵件

To:	Marcus Thorn <thorninyourside@nsm.com>
From:	Anthony Weldon <Mtonyweldon@cwm.com>
Date:	⑯ September 23
Subject:	Cinema Write Magazine subscription

Hello Marcus,

I wanted to get in touch with you and say thank you for subscribing to our magazine for over ten years. It's because of supporters like you that we are able to continue delivering the #1 magazine for screenwriters in the world. —[1]—.

⑯ I noticed that your subscription is ending towards the end of next month, and thought I should see if you are ready to renew it today. ⑯ Since you are in our top-rank subscribers, I am authorized to offer this "for your eyes only" special. —[2]—. With this special, you will receive a 60-percent discount on a two-year subscription, as well as receive commemorative copies of two original scripts used for the best picture winners from the last 50 years.

—[3]—. A chance to meet and interact with some of the hottest screenwriters in the business today! We will be having a Platinum Tier online course for everyone that wishes to attend. Here you can listen to experts, ask questions, and even get advice on how to best sell your script in today's market.

So what do you say, Marcus? Are you ready to continue with us and have the best to be delivered to your door every month? —[4]—.

Regards,
Anthony Weldon

收件人：馬克思・索恩
　　　　<thorninyourside@nsm.com>
寄件人：安東尼・威爾登
　　　　<Mtonyweldon@cwm.com>
主旨：⑯ 9 月 23 日
日期：《電影寫手》雜誌訂閱

哈囉，馬克思：

　　我想與您聯絡，並想對您表達謝意，因為您訂閱我們雜誌超過十年。因為有像您這樣的支持者，我們才能繼續為全球編劇帶來排行第一的雜誌內容。

　　⑯ 我發現到下個月底，您的訂閱就要到期。因此我想了解看看，您是否準備於今日續訂。⑯ 由於您是我們的忠實訂閱者，因此我可以向您提供「僅供您觀看」的特殊訂閱方案。有了此特殊方案，訂閱兩年能享有四折優惠，還能獲得兩份有紀念價值的原創劇本的副本，它們是過去 50 年內曾獲最佳影片獎的影片劇本。

　　⑯ 今天馬上續訂，還會有其他福利。那就是有機會與現今影業最火紅的編劇碰面與互動！我們將為希望參與的每位讀者，提供線上白金級會員課程。您可在此聆聽專家的分享、提問問題，甚至可以得到如何讓自己的劇本於現今市場暢銷的建議。

　　那麼馬克思，您意下如何呢？您準備好續訂，往後每個月均收到內容最棒的雜誌嗎？

謹啟，
安東尼・威爾登

161

When will Mr. Thorn's subscription expire?
(A) At the end of September
(B) At the beginning of October
(C) At the end of October
(D) At the beginning of November

中譯 索恩先生的訂閱何時到期？
(A) 九月底
(B) 十月初
(C) 十月底
(B) 十一月初

解析 本文為雜誌社邀請訂閱用戶延長訂閱的電子郵件。第二段當中提到下個月底就到期，而此封電子郵件的寄件日期為 **9 月 23 日**，表示索恩先生的訂閱時間到十月底到期。

162

Why is Mr. Thorn offered a special program?
(A) He has a top-level membership.
(B) He has donated a large amount of money.
(C) He has worked for the magazine for over ten years.
(D) He introduced the magazine to his friend.

中譯 索恩先生為何能獲得特殊方案？
(A) 因為他是高級會員。
(B) 因為他已捐贈高額款項。
(C) 因為他為該雜誌效力超過十年。
(D) 因為他向朋友介紹該雜誌。

解析 請找出提及特別活動的段落。第二段提到：「**Since you are in our top-rank subscribers, I am authorized to offer this "for your eyes only" special.**」，由此可以得知該活動提供最高等級的訂閱用戶。**(A)** 將 **top-rank subscribers** 改寫成 **top-level membership**，故為正確答案。

163 新增題型

In which of the positions marked [1], [2], [3], or [4] does the following sentence best belong?
"Act today and you will find something else coming to you as well."
(A) [1]
(B) [2]
(C) [3]
(D) [4]

中譯 在標記 [1]、[2]、[3] 和 [4] 的地方，下列這句話最適合放在何處？「今天馬上續訂，還會有其他福利。」
(A) [1]
(B) [2]
(C) [3]
(D) [4]

解析 題目列出的句子表示今天延長訂閱的話，便能獲得額外的優惠，因此適合置於原有優惠與新的優惠活動之間。[3] 前方提到四折優惠一事，後方則提到其他的優惠，包含有機會與人氣編劇見面、提供線上課程等。

Questions 164-167 refer to the following article. 文章

Mayor West and the City Council today announced a plan to resurrect the riverbank area of our fine city. —[1]—. The plan, called the "Banks of Riverdale," 164 will remove many of the older warehouses and buildings and replace them with more family friendly attractions to help visitor experience of downtown Riverdale. There will also be at least two new parks built next to the river with playgrounds, swings, and more for everyone to enjoy. —[2]—.

韋斯特市長和市議會今日宣布，即將為我們這座美麗城市啟動河岸區復興計畫。此這項計畫被稱為「瑞凡戴爾河岸」，164 將拆除許多老舊倉庫和建物，取而代之的是更親子友善的設施，藉此讓遊客體驗瑞凡戴爾的市區風光。河岸旁亦將建造至少兩座新公園，包括遊樂場、盪鞦韆等人人適用的設施。

Actual Test 4

PART 7

More than half of citizens polled said that the downtown area needed ⑯ to be beautified to enhance what many consider to be one of the best cities in the region already. —[3]—. ⑯ Project leaders said that this complete renovation of the area was considered years ago, but could only be funded now, thanks to the successful projects involving the city's sports teams and the revenue they are generating.

According to Mayor West, initial parts of the project will begin this spring, with the areas closest to the sports stadiums being renovated or removed first. From there, ⑯ leaders are hoping new restaurants and shopping areas will catch on with those new and familiar to the area. —[4]—.

超過半數接受民意調查的民眾表示，市區必須加以美化，⑯ 才能讓此區最佳都市的美稱更上一層樓。⑯ 專案領導人表示，雖然多年前已開始考慮對此區進行完善的翻修工程，但一直到現在才得到資助。這都要感謝與市立體育隊相關的成功專案，以及它們帶來的衍生收益。

根據韋斯特市長，今年春季將開啟專案的初步階段，會先從最靠近體育場的區域開始進行翻新或拆除。從那裡開始，⑯ 許多領導人希望新餐廳與購物區能吸引此區的新客與熟客。⑯ 隨著計畫將於接下來幾週定案，我們期待聽到此專案的更多消息。

字彙 resurrect 復興　visitor experience 遊客體驗　enhance 提升　revenue 收益　generate 產生
catch on with 受到……的歡迎

164

How will the city improve the waterfront area?

(A) By building restaurants and tourist sites

(B) By creating an amusement park for kids

(C) By making the river water safer and cleaner

(D) By moving warehouses to another part of the city

中譯 此城市將如何改善河濱區域？
(A) 建造餐廳和觀光景點
(B) 建立兒童樂園
(C) 讓河域更安全、乾淨
(D) 將倉庫遷移至城市的另一區

解析 本文為都市更新計畫的相關報導。文中提到要拆除水岸旁的老舊建築，建造親子友善的景點，看似答案為 (B)，但要注意最後一段提到：「new restaurants and shopping areas will catch on with those new and familiar to the area」，希望新的餐廳和購物區能吸引人潮，這表示有意將水岸打造成觀光景點。

165

What is mentioned about Riverdale?
(A) It is close to a lake.
(B) It is looking for professional sports teams.
(C) It is opening a new stadium soon.
(D) It is seen as one of the top cities in the area.

中譯 關於瑞凡戴爾，文中提到了什麼？
(A) 接近湖邊。
(B) 欲招聘專業體育隊。
(C) 新體育場即將啟動。
(D) 被視為該區頂尖城市之一。

解析 第二段提到：「one of the best cities in the region」，(D) 改寫成 one of the top cities in the area，故為正確答案。

166

Why did the city government decide to proceed with the renovation plan?
(A) The voters in the area agreed it upon after many debates.
(B) Money was finally available for it.
(C) They wanted to upgrade the city before a big sporting event.
(D) They wanted to update the city's look after criticism from the media.

中譯 市政府為何決定進行翻新計畫？
(A) 經過多次辯論後，該區市民終於投票同意。
(B) 終於有可用資金。
(C) 他們想在某運動盛事開賽前，讓該市煥然一新。
(D) 他們想在媒體批判後，讓該市煥然一新。

解析 關於都市計畫的進展，出現在文章第二段中。當中提到雖然多年前就開始討論這項計畫，但到現在才成功籌措資金，同時提到資金來源為體育隊。

字彙 criticism 批判

167 新增題型

In which of the positions marked [1], [2], [3], or [4] does the following sentence best belong?
"We are excited to hear more about this project as the plans become finalized over the next few weeks."
(A) [1]
(B) [2]
(C) [3]
(D) [4]

中譯 在標記 [1]、[2]、[3] 和 [4] 的地方，下列這句話最適合放在何處？「隨著計畫將於接下來幾週定案，我們期待聽到此專案的更多消息。」
(A) [1]
(B) [2]
(C) [3]
(D) [4]

解析 題目列出的句子表示往後會有更多關於該計畫的消息，適合置於後半段報導中。最後一段提到往後的進程，以及對該計畫的期待。若將該句話置於 [4]，表達往後將會聽到更多消息，最符合前後文意。

Questions 168-171 refer to the following notice. 通知

We at Streamline would like to inform all our customers and clients that we are moving to larger offices next month. 168 **We have had such an unbelievable growth in the last few years** thanks to all of you, and we wanted to say thank you for the kind reviews and helping spread the word about us. We at Streamline believe that the customer is the reason that we are here, and we want to make sure that we are doing the best we can to serve you.

Starting on September 1, we will begin our move across town to our new offices located in the Geraldine district. Our offices will be on the corner of 97th and Taft Street, in the Houseman Building, on floors one through five. 169 **Parking for the Houseman offices is in the rear of the building** offering almost one hundred spaces. The first floor will be where most of the day-to-day operations will take place, 170 **our second floor will be for meetings and interviews**, but on floors three through five, we are going to have production studios, where we will have some stages and sets to help create the perfect ideas for your business.

　　流線公司想在此通知所有顧客與客戶，我們將於下個月搬移至空間較大的據點。歸功於各位的支持，169 我們才能在過去幾年來有難以置信的成長。我們亦想感謝各位給予好評，幫我們建立口碑。流線公司相信顧客是成就我們的主因，我們希望確保為各位帶來最棒的服務。

　　從 9 月 1 日起，我們將開始遷移據點至城市另一端的傑洛丹區。新據點將位於第 97 街與塔福特街的街角，那裡有豪斯曼大樓，其一到五樓均為我們的辦公室。169 豪斯曼大樓的停車場位於大樓後方，共有將近一百個停車位。一樓主要規劃為日常營運區，170 二樓是會議訪談區。三樓至五樓則是攝影棚，屆時會設置一些舞台和場景，幫助我們為您的業務創造更多想法。

⑰ As we begin our transition into our new headquarters, we will make sure to have representatives at both the old and new locations, just in case you have questions. You can contact us via our Website at www.streamline.com or by calling 555-2389.

⑰ 在此遷移至新總部的過渡期，我們會確保新、舊據點均有代表留守，以便您有任何問題。各位可上www.streamline.com 網站或撥打 555-2389 聯絡我們。

字彙 unbelievable 難以置信的　spread the word 散佈消息　day-to-day operation 日常營運

168

What is the reason Streamline has decided to change offices?
(A) The business has had much success recently.
(B) The customers asked them to move closer to downtown.
(C) They needed to make room for their new products.
(D) They streamlined their business operations.

中譯 流線公司決定換據點的原因為何？
(A) 公司近期屢創佳績。
(B) 顧客要求他們遷移至離市區較近的地方。
(C) 他們需要可放置新品的空間。
(D) 他們想簡化營運程序。

解析 本文為公司搬遷公告。第一段便提到決定搬遷的原因：「We have had such an unbelievable growth in the last few years」，由此可以推測是因最近在事業上取得極大的成功，所以這家公司決定搬到比較大的據點。

字彙 streamline 簡化

169

Where should people park when visiting the new office?
(A) Behind the building
(B) In front of the building
(C) Next to the building
(D) Underneath the building

中譯 到訪新據點的人該在哪裡停車？
(A) 大樓後方　　(B) 大樓前方
(C) 大樓旁邊　　(D) 大樓地下室

解析 第二段中提到與停車有關的內容：「Parking for the Houseman offices is in the rear of the building offering almost one hundred spaces.」，(A) 將 the rear of the building 改寫成 behind the building，故為正確答案。

170

Which floor will a client visit if they give a presentation?
(A) On the first floor
(B) On the second floor
(C) On the third floor
(D) On the fourth floor

中譯 客戶如果要做簡報，應造訪哪一個樓層？
(A) 一樓　　(B) 二樓
(C) 三樓　　(D) 四樓

解析 第二段最後的各樓層用途中提到：「our second floor will be for meetings and interviews」，表示二樓為開會的地點，因此前來做簡報的客戶要到二樓。

171

Why will some employees stay at the old office?
(A) To answer customers' questions
(B) To clean up old equipment
(C) To complete ongoing projects
(D) To meet some important customers

中譯 為何有些員工會待在舊據點？
(A) 為了回應顧客的問題
(B) 為了清理舊設備
(C) 為了完成進行中的專案
(D) 為了會見重要的顧客

解析 最後一段提到有部門員工留在舊辦公室內，(A) 將 just in case you have questions 改寫成 answer customers' questions，故為正確答案。

Questions 172-175 refer to the following online discussion. 線上討論 新增題型

GREG HUNT	**11:30**
Hello everyone. ⑰ Any news about the exhibition next month?	
TONY PLAYER	**11:31**
I received an e-mail about it yesterday. Didn't you get it?	
JIM JONSON	**11:33**
I got it. Said we were all going to be sharing a room. Is that right?	
GREG HUNT	**11:34**
What? How can we fit four of us in one room? We'll be stuffed in like sardines!	
TONY PLAYER	**11:36**
How do they expect that to work? ⑱ The rooms only have two beds.	
JIM JONSON	**11:37**
That is a problem. I don't want to sleep on the floor for a week either.	
RON BURKE	**11:39**
I'm here now. ⑱ I asked management about the room. They said they would look into it.	
GREG HUNT	**11:39**
Great. OK, let's think about how we will present the products this year.	
TONY PLAYER	**11:40**
I was thinking that we should have some kind of interactive display.	
JIM JONSON	**11:42**
I like that. Then people can try it out as we talk about it.	
RON BURKE	**11:42**
Good plan. ⑲ How about Tony and Jim handle the first presentation?	
TONY PLAYER	**11:44**
OK. I'll work on it this afternoon.	
JIM JONSON	**11:47**
What is the game plan for length of the demo? ⑳ We don't want to go long.	
GREG HUNT	**11:48**
No more than 10 to 15 minutes. We want as many people to see it as possible.	
TONY PLAYER	**11:49**
We should prevent anyone from taking photos at the event as well.	
RON BURKE	**11:50**
Of course. We wouldn't want competitors to "borrow" any ideas from us.	

格瑞格・杭特	**11:30**
哈囉，大家好。⑰ 下個月的展覽有任何消息嗎？	
東尼・佩萊爾	**11:31**
我昨天有收到相關電子郵件。你沒收到嗎？	
吉姆・強森	**11:33**
我有收到。信裡說我們大家要同住一個房間，對嗎？	
格瑞格・杭特	**11:34**
什麼？我們四個人要怎麼住在一間房間？我們會擠得像沙丁魚！	
東尼・佩萊爾	**11:36**
他們怎麼會覺得這樣行得通？⑱ 房裡只有兩張床。	
吉姆・強森	**11:37**
這是個問題。我不想睡在地板上一個禮拜。	
朗恩・柏克	**11:39**
我來了。⑱ 我問過管理部門關於房間的事。他們說會了解看看。	
格瑞格・杭特	**11:39**
太好了。好吧，那我們來想一下，今年該怎麼呈現產品。	
東尼・佩萊爾	**11:40**
我覺得應該要有像是互動式顯示裝置的東西。	
吉姆・強森	**11:42**
我喜歡。觀展者可在我們介紹的時候一邊試用。	
朗恩・柏克	**11:42**
好計畫。⑲ 那麼東尼和吉姆負責第一份簡報怎麼樣？	
東尼・佩萊爾	**11:44**
好的。我今天下午會開始著手。	
吉姆・強森	**11:47**
那麼演示時間長短的策略為何？⑳ 我們不想拖太久。	
格瑞格・杭特	**11:48**
不要超過 10 到 15 分鐘。我們希望盡可能讓更多人看見簡報。	
東尼・佩萊爾	**11:49**
我們也應該要避免任何人在現場拍照。	
朗恩・柏克	**11:50**
那是當然。我們不希望競爭對手「借走」我們任何的點子。	

GREG HUNT	11:51
OK, let's get to work and meet again Friday with how we want to proceed.	

格瑞格・杭特	11:51
好的。我們開始動工吧，週五再開一次會，討論接下來該如何進行。	

字彙 stuffed 擁擠的　interactive 互動式的　game plan 策略　length 長度

172

What is the team preparing for?
(A) A presentation for a client
(B) An industry event
(C) A competition
(D) A sales meeting

中譯 此團隊在準備什麼工作？
(A) 給客戶看的簡報
(B) 產業活動
(C) 一場比賽
(D) 業務會議

解析 杭特先生在 11 點 30 分的訊息中提到「exhibition」，選項改寫成 industry event，因此答案為 (B)。本篇主要在討論如何在下個月舉辦的展示活動中展示產品。

173

Why did Mr. Burke contact management?
(A) To ask about the project
(B) To lower the cost
(C) To request new equipment
(D) To talk about the room size

中譯 柏克先生為何聯絡管理部門？
(A) 詢問專案的事
(B) 為了降低成本
(C) 為了索取新設備
(D) 談談房間大小的事

解析 在柏克先生表示要向管理部門詢問前，他們在討論四個人不適合住在同一個間房間。由此可以推測柏克先生聯絡管理部門，為的是告知房間大小一事，因此答案為 (D)。

174

Who will give the first speech?
(A) Mr. Burke and Mr. Player
(B) Mr. Hunt and Mr. Burke
(C) Mr. Jonson and Mr. Hunt
(D) Mr. Jonson and Mr. Player

中譯 誰會先演說？
(A) 柏克和佩萊爾先生
(B) 杭特和柏克先生
(C) 強森和杭特先生
(D) 強森和佩萊爾先生

解析 柏克先生在 11 點 42 分的訊息中提到：「How about Tony and Jim handle the first presentation?」，接著佩萊爾先生表示同意，因此答案為 (D)。

175 新增題型

At 11:47, what does Mr. Jonson mean when he says, "We don't want to go long"?
(A) He does not like photo sessions.
(B) He expects the event will end early.
(C) He is reluctant to travel far.
(D) He prefers the demo to be short.

中譯 在 11:47 時，強森先生說「我們不想拖太久」的意思為何？
(A) 他不喜歡拍照時段。
(B) 他預期活動能早點結束。
(C) 他不太願意遠行。
(D) 他希望演示能簡短。

解析 強森先生提出「We don't want to go long.」之前，先詢問了展示的時間與策略，這表示他指的是不希望展示時間過長，因此答案為 (D)。

To: Brian Sinclair
From: John Sheridan
Subject: New company policy
Date: July 17

Hi Brian,

Here's the draft for the new company summer shape-up program. I would appreciate some feedback from you on it.

Now that the summer is here, we would like to introduce an exciting new way for employees at Lang & Huston to begin the day. 176 **Starting at 8:00 AM, we will begin a 30-minute warm-up exercise class for everyone to attend.** We are pushing everyone to be as healthy and active as possible this year! We will have a special guest to kick off our first week of morning sessions, but I don't want to 177 **spoil** the surprise.

This will be a great way to stretch both our bodies and minds. After that, we will hold an office meeting to discuss what we can do to improve our daily missions. We want everyone to attend, 178 **so please make sure to be in Meeting Room A by 8:00 AM, starting Monday the 3rd.**

John Sheridan
VP of Personnel
Lang & Huston, Inc.

To: John Sheridan
From: Brian Sinclair
Subject: RE: New company policy
Date: July 17

Hi John,

I am encouraged to read your e-mail about the morning shape-up program; however, I think we may have to make some changes to it. When I read it, I felt as though it was mandatory, and we cannot force anyone to join a workout class at work. How about we offer free classes to anyone that wants to have them? 179 **They would have to be offered at a few different times, since we can't exclude anyone from the opportunity.** 178 **Also, we probably should also remove the special guest mystery.** If you have someone special booked to make everyone excited to join, we should use that to encourage attendance. 180 **And why don't we schedule the sessions on the first and last day of the week, so we can begin and end the week with some team building?**

收件人：布萊恩・辛克萊
寄件者：約翰・雪瑞登
主旨：新公司政策
日期：7 月 17 日

嗨，布萊恩：

　　我附上新的公司夏季改造計畫草稿。如果你能提出一些反饋，我將感激不盡。

　　由於夏季要到了，我們想要介紹一個令人興奮的新作法，讓藍恩與哈士頓公司員工開始每一天。176 從早上 8 點開始，我們會先進行適合大家的 30 分鐘暖身操。希望今年能盡量讓大家維持健康活躍的狀態！我們將請到特別來賓來開啟第一週的晨間運動，但我還不想 177 破壞這個驚喜。

　　這將是一個伸展我們身心的大好機會。接下來，我們會召開辦公室會議，來討論改善日常工作的方法。希望大家都能參加會議，178 因此請記得從 3 號週一開始，早上 8 點到 A 會議室集合。

約翰・雪瑞登
人事部副總
藍恩與休士頓公司

收件人：約翰・雪瑞登
寄件人：布萊恩・辛克萊
主旨：關於：新公司政策
日期：7 月 17 日

嗨，約翰：

　　看到你電子郵件裡提到的晨間改造計畫，我真的深受鼓舞。不過，我覺得可能需要做點更動。我在讀電子郵件時，會覺得這是硬性規定的活動，但我們無法強迫任何人在公司參加健身課程。我們要不要改為向想參加的員工提供免費課程？179 因為我們不能剝奪任何人享有此福利的機會，我們應該安排不同時段的課程。178 此外，我們可能也要取消嘉賓的神秘性。如果你預約特別來賓的目的是想讓大家興奮地加入課程，那就該善用這點來鼓勵大家出席。180 我們何不在每週的第一天和最後一天安排此環節，這樣就能在一週的開始與結束建立團隊向心力？

Brian Sinclair
Sales Manager
Lang & Huston, Inc.

布萊恩・辛克萊
業務經理
藍恩與休士頓公司

字彙 draft 草稿　warm-up exercise 暖身操　kick off 展開　spoil 破壞　mandatory 強制的　exclude 排除
remove 取消

176

What does Mr. Sheridan want employees to do?
(A) Be industry leaders in health services
(B) Be more competitive with each other
(C) Have a better sales record than last year
(D) Have a workout with colleagues

中譯 雪瑞登先生要求員工做什麼事？
(A) 成為保健產業的領導者
(B) 增加同事間的競爭程度
(C) 創造優於去年的業績
(D) 與同事一起健身

解析 第一篇文章為提出公司舉行夏季健身計畫的電子郵件。雪瑞登先生希望員工能以運動作為一天的開始。選項將 a 30-minute warm-up exercise class 改寫成 have a workout，因此答案為 (D)。

字彙 competitive 競爭的

177

In the first e-mail, the word "spoil" in paragraph 2, line 4, is closest in meaning to
(A) assist
(B) create
(C) repair
(D) ruin

中譯 在第一封電子郵件中，第二段第四行的「spoil」與下列何者意思最相近？
(A) 協助
(B) 創建
(C) 修護
(D) 破壞

解析 spoil 出現在「I don't want to spoil the surprise」當中，這句話的意思為我不想「破壞」這項驚喜。選項中意思最為接近的單字為 ruin，表示「毀壞」之意。

字彙 ruin 破壞

178

When does Mr. Sinclair propose revealing a special guest?
(A) As late as possible
(B) At the first session
(C) Next Monday
(D) Sometime before August 3

中譯 辛克萊先生建議何時揭露特別來賓？
(A) 越晚越好
(B) 第一次課程
(C) 下週一
(D) 8 月 3 日之前

解析 第一封由雪瑞登先生傳送的電子郵件中，第二段提到特別嘉賓的內容，表示不願透露驚喜。另外，又提到 8 月 3 日見，表示第一堂課從 8 月 3 日開始。然而，在第二封由辛克萊先生回覆的電子郵件中，他針對特別嘉賓表示：「we probably should also remove the special guest mystery」，建議提前公開。因此選項中最適當的公開時間為開課前 (D)。

字彙 reveal 揭露

179

What does Mr. Sinclair offer to do?
(A) Offer classes for recruits
(B) **Open various times**
(C) Register in advance
(D) Check personal preferences

中譯 辛克萊先生主動提出什麼？
(A) 向新進人員提供課程
(B) 開放不同時段
(C) 事先登記
(D) 了解個人喜好

解析 第二封電子郵件為辛克萊先生針對公司的夏季健身計畫的意見回饋。中間提到：「**They would have to be offered at a few different times, since we can't exclude anyone from the opportunity.**」，建議開放更多的時段供選擇，好讓所有員工都有機會參加。選項將 be offered at a few different times 改寫成 open various times，因此答案為 (B)。

字彙 personal preference 個人喜好

180

Which days does Mr. Sinclair believe would be best for the classes?
(A) On Monday and Tuesday
(B) **On Monday and Friday**
(C) On Thursday and Friday
(D) On Saturday and Sunday

中譯 辛克萊先生認為哪幾天最適合上課？
(A) 週一和週二　　(B) 週一和週五
(C) 週四和週五　　(D) 週六和週日

解析 辛克萊先生在電子郵件後半段提到：「**And why don't we schedule the sessions on the first and last day of the week, so we can begin and end the week with some team building?**」，表示辛克萊先生建議安排在一週的第一天（週一）和最後一天（週五）。

Actual Test 4

PART 7

Questions 181-185 refer to the following order form and e-mail. 訂單 電子郵件

Office Supply Wholesale Order Form

Name: Wolffe Marketing
Address: 66 Order Ave Springfield, IL 62702
Date: ⑱ June 24
Invoice #: C2032
Shipping Address: 2002 Republic Boulevard
Nashville, TN 37201

Item	Qty.	Unit Price	Total Price
Printer paper (case)	⑱ 10	$40.00	$400.00
Office desk 30x48x23	10	$100.00	$1,000.00
Office chairs (black)	10	$60.00	$600.00
Total			$2,000.00
Member Discount*: 10%			$1,800.00 (#OSW23789)
⑱ Tax**: 10%			$180.00
Total Cost			$1,980.00

*Member discount requires membership #
⑱ **No sales tax for orders shipped to KY, TN, MS, or AL

辦公用品批發 訂單

名稱：沃非行銷公司
地址：62702 伊利諾州春田市歐德大道 66 號
日期：⑱ 6 月 24 日
發票編號：C2032
送貨地址：37201 田納西州納許維爾市共和大道 2002 號

品項	數量	單價	總價
印表紙（箱）	⑱ 10	$40.00	$400.00
辦公桌 30x48x23	10	$100.00	$1,000.00
辦公椅 （黑色）	10	$60.00	$600.00
總計			$2,000.00
會員折扣 *：			$1,800.00 (#OSW23789)
⑱ 稅金 **：10%			$180
總費用			$1,980.00

* 需提供會員編號方可享有會員折扣
⑱ ** 肯德基州、田納西州、密西西比州或阿拉巴馬州等訂單無需徵收營業稅

<table>
<tr><td>

To: Customer Service <csr@osw.com>
From: Leila Saldana <leilasaldana@packmail.com>
Subject: Order #OSW23789
Date: ⑱ July 1

</td><td>

收件人：顧客服務部 <csr@osw.com>
寄件人：菜拉・沙丹納
　　　　<leilasaldana@packmail.com>
主旨：訂單 #OSW23789
日期：⑱ 7 月 1 日

</td></tr>
</table>

Attn: Customer Service Department

Our office ordered some new furniture for our new staff (order #2032) from your online store. The order was placed last month.

⑱ Everything arrived fine at our receiving address today, but there are two errors that do need attention. ⑱ The office chairs that we ordered were black, but all ten that we received were red. While these are very nice chairs, we would prefer something a little more suited for our office design. ⑱ Another problem is about the sales tax on the items I have bought. Can I get a price adjustment for that?

We would like to exchange the chairs as soon as possible, as our new employees start at the office on the 12th. ⑱ I would like an authorization label to switch the chairs, as well as reimbursement for the shipping cost for returning them to your warehouse.

Thank you very much for your attention to this issue.

Sincerely,
Leila Saldana
Floor Manager
Wolffe Marketing

顧客服務部請知悉：

　　我們公司從你們的網路商店為新進人員訂購新辦公設備（訂單 #2032）。下訂時間是上個月。

　　⑱ 所有物品今天均完好抵達我們的收貨處，不過有兩項錯誤需要請你們注意一下。⑱ 我們訂購的是黑色辦公椅，但十張辦公椅全部是紅色的。雖然辦公椅的品質很好，我們仍希望樣式能更符合我們辦公室的裝潢。⑱ 另一個問題就是所有訂購物品的營業稅。這個價格是可以調整的嗎？

　　我們希望盡快更換辦公椅，因為新員工 12 號就要來報到了。⑱ 我希望能有可更換辦公椅的許可單，以及補償我們將它們退回貴公司倉庫所支付的運費。

　　十分感謝您處理此問題。

　　誠摯地，
　　菜拉・沙丹納
　　樓層經理
　　沃非行銷公司

字彙 **sales tax** 營業稅　**attn (attention)** 注意　**price adjustment** 調整價格　**authorization** 授權　**reimbursement** 補償

181

<table>
<tr><td>

What can be inferred in the invoice?
(A) The billing and shipping addresses are the same.
(B) A shipping charge has been added.
(C) Each item has the same quantity.
(D) Only office furniture has been ordered.

</td><td>

中譯 從發票可得知什麼訊息？
(A) 帳單地址與送貨地址相同。
(B) 有加上運費。
(C) 每項物品的數量相同。
(D) 只有訂購辦公桌椅。

解析 (A) 帳單地址和送貨地址不同。
(B) 金額並未加上運費。
(C) 訂購物品的數量皆為 10，表示數量相同。
(D) 訂購物品中包含影印紙。

</td></tr>
</table>

182

How long did Wolffe Marketing wait for the supplies?
(A) For a few days
(B) **For about a week**
(C) For a few weeks
(D) For about a month

中譯 沃非行銷公司等了多久才收到貨品？
(A) 幾天
(B) 大約一週
(C) 幾週
(D) 大約一個月

解析 訂購單上的日期為 6 月 24 日，而郵件傳送日為 7 月 1 日，當中還提到今天收到貨，這表示沃非行銷公司訂購完約一週後收到商品。

183

How much will Ms. Saldana get back?
(A) $150
(B) **$180**
(C) $200
(D) $380

中譯 沙丹納小姐能拿回多少退款？
(A) 150 元
(B) 180 元
(C) 200 元
(D) 380 元

解析 沙丹納小姐傳送的電子郵件中提出兩點問題。第一是送錯商品，第二是多加了營業稅。單據上含 10% 的營業稅，送貨地點為田納西州，但是下方備註標明田納西州不用加上營業稅，這表示沙丹納小姐要求拿回 10% 稅金 180 元。

184

What is Ms. Saldana requesting from the supply company?
(A) A discount on their next purchase
(B) Approval to return the order
(C) **An exchange permission form**
(D) Reimbursement for the entire order

中譯 沙丹納小姐向用品公司要求什麼事？
(A) 下次購貨能有折扣
(B) 允許退訂
(C) 換貨許可單
(D) 補償整份訂單的費用

解析 沙丹納小姐在電子郵件中提到想更換送錯的商品，同時要求授權證明並補償運費：「I would like an authorization label to switch the chairs, as well as reimbursement for the shipping cost for returning them to your warehouse.」，選項將 authorization label 改寫成 permission form，因此答案為 (C)。

185

What was the problem with the order?
(A) **The color of an item was wrong.**
(B) The items were shipped to the wrong address.
(C) The number of items was wrong.
(D) The price of the chairs was incorrect.

中譯 此訂單出了什麼問題？
(A) 商品的顏色有誤。
(B) 商品寄送到錯誤的地址。
(C) 商品的數量有誤。
(D) 辦公椅的價格不正確。

解析 電子郵件提出的兩點問題中，其中一項便是送錯成紅色的辦公椅。

Actual Test 4

PART 7

廣告　申請單　網路評價　新增題型

Just moved and need your cable TV and Internet service set up? Having trouble with your cable services? Call Jim the Cable Guy today.
- Low prices
- Convenient service times
- **186** • **Locally owned and operated**

The following packages are available to most customers within the region.

TV + Internet $50/month	Internet only $25/month
- Includes 200 channels and HD for free - Standard speed Internet	- Standard speed Internet - Free installation (online orders only)
TV only $40/month	**189 Deluxe $75/month**
- Includes 200 channels - Extra charge for HD	- Includes 250 channels and HD - High-speed Internet and free installation

您剛搬家且需要安裝有線電視與網路服務嗎？您的有線電視服務是否有問題呢？請今天立刻聯絡吉姆有線電視公司。

* 低價

* 服務時段方便

186 * 當地自營

本區多數顧客均可享有以下套裝服務。

電視節目 + 網路服務 每月 $50	僅有網路 每月 $25
- 包括 200 個頻道，免費觀看高畫質節目 - 標準網速	- 標準網速 - 免安裝費（僅限網路訂單）
僅有電視節目 每月 $40	**189** 尊爵服務 每月 $75 元
- 包括 200 個頻道 - 高畫質節目另外收費	- 包括 250 個頻道與高畫質節目 - 高速網路與免安裝費

Jim the Cable Guy
Service Application

Name: Candace Bauman
Best time of day*: **188** 12:00-1:00 Monday, Wednesday, or Thursday, before noon on weekends
Address: 3801 San Carlos Drive Esposito, California
Phone: 555-2839

Type of residence: Apartment

*We can't guarantee we'll make it at these times, but we **187** strive to match your schedule.

吉姆有線電視公司
服務申請單

姓名：凱蒂絲・鮑曼
最佳安裝時段 *：**188** 週一、週三或週四的 12 點至 1 點，以及週末的中午以前
地址：加州愛斯波西多市聖卡洛斯大道 3801 號
電話：555-2839
住宅類型：公寓

* 我們無法保證能於上述時段抵達，但會 **187** 盡力配合您的行程。

I signed up for Jim's cable service in my new place and the man (not Jim) came to install it today. **190** I was frustrated that he was 30 minutes late. **188** Since I was on my lunch break, I ended up getting back to work late. **190** He also made a lot of noise and broke one of my pictures hanging above the TV. **189** Since I paid top dollar for your service, I expected a much more professional installer. —Candace

我為新家登記了吉姆有線電視的服務，今天有人來安裝（非吉姆本人）。**190** 對於技術員遲到 30 分鐘的情況，我不是很開心。**188** 因為我是在午休時間回家，最後晚回公司。**190** 他安裝時的聲響太大，還弄壞了我掛在電視上的一幅相片。**189** 由於我訂購的是頂級服務，我原本以為會有更專業的安裝技術員前來。——凱蒂絲

字彙 residence 住宅　strive 盡力　frustrated 失望的　end up 最後變成

186

What is mentioned about the owner of Jim the Cable Guy?
(A) He has an engineering degree.
(B) He has owned the business for decades.
(C) He lives in the area.
(D) He recently moved to a new place.

中譯 關於吉姆有線電視公司，文中提及了什麼？
(A) 他具有工程學位。
(B) 他自營此公司數十年的時間。
(C) 他住在該區。
(D) 他最近搬新家。

解析 第一篇文章為有線電視和網路安裝服務的廣告。當中提到：「Locally owned and operated」，表示經營者住在本地。

187

In the application, the word "strive" in line 8 is closest in meaning to
(A) affect
(B) compete
(C) oppose
(D) try

中譯 在申請單中，第八行的「strive」與下列何者意思最相近？
(A) 影響　　　　(B) 競爭
(C) 反對　　　　(D) 試圖

解析 strive 的意思為「努力」，在「we strive to match your schedule」同樣表示「努力」之意。選項中 try 的意思最為接近，表示「試圖、努力」之意。

188

When did an employee of Jim the Cable Guy most likely visit Ms. Bauman's home?
(A) On Monday morning
(B) On Wednesday noon
(C) On Friday noon
(D) On Saturday morning

中譯 吉姆有線電視公司的員工最有可能何時造訪鮑曼小姐的家？
(A) 週一早上　　(B) 週三中午
(C) 週五中午　　(D) 週六早上

解析 申請表上鮑曼小姐標註希望的來訪時間為週一、週三、週四的 12 點至 1 點，以及週末中午之前，而在網路評論中，她提到安裝人員遲到三十分鐘，耽誤她回公司工作的時間。由此可以推測出吉姆有線電視公司的員工可能是在週一、週三或週四的中午到訪。

189

Which package did Ms. Bauman get?
(A) Deluxe
(B) Internet only
(C) TV and Internet
(D) TV only

中譯 鮑曼小姐購買的是哪一種套裝服務？
(A) 尊爵　　　　(B) 僅有網路
(C) 電視節目和網路　(D) 僅有電視節目

解析 鮑曼小姐所寫的評論中提到：「Since I paid top dollar for your service」，表示她選擇的是廣告中最貴的尊爵服務，一個月 75 元，因此答案為 (A)。

190

What did Ms. Bauman complain about?
(A) The behavior of the installer
(B) The cable service price
(C) The quality of her TV picture
(D) The speed of her Internet

中譯 鮑曼小姐抱怨什麼？
(A) 安裝技術員的行為　(B) 有線電視服務的價格
(C) 電視的畫質　　　(D) 網路速度

解析 評論中提到安裝人員遲到三十分鐘，耽誤她回公司的時間。另外，還抱怨他製造很大的噪音、弄壞掛在電視上方的其中一張照片。這些皆是對安裝人員的行為表達不滿；文中並未提及其他選項的敘述。

字彙 behavior 行為

To:	Theodore Slate <tslate@jumbo.com>
From:	Cassandra Holly <cholly@jumbo.com>
Date:	Monday, September 26
Subject:	Pop-up store

Hi Theo,

I was wondering if you could do some research for me? ⑲⑬ I want to put some of our top-selling products in a pop-up store somewhere in town for the week-long vacation starting on October 6. ⑲⓵ We've done well selling our products online, which is good. I'm just not sure how many residents around here know about our products. Could you look around and see if there are any empty storefronts or even outdoor venues where we could set up shop? Thanks.

Cassie

收件人：提爾多・史萊特 <tslate@jumbo.com>
寄件人：卡珊卓・荷莉 <cholly@jumbo.com>
日期：9月26日週一
主旨：快閃店

嗨，提歐：

　　我想問問看，你是不是能幫我搜尋一下資料？⑲⑬ 我想在10月6日起為期一週的假期裡，設立快閃店販售我們的一些暢銷產品。⑲⓵ 我們的產品在網路上賣得很好，這是好現象。我只是不太確定有多少附近居民知道我們的產品。你可以查一下，看看是否還有我們可以設立快閃店的空店面或戶外場地嗎？多謝你。

凱西

To:	Cassandra Holly <cholly@jumbo.com>
From:	Customer Service <cs@steelworks.com> Theodore Slate <tslate@jumbo.com>
Date:	Monday, October 3
Subject:	Pop-up store

Hi Cassandra,

⑲② I'm really excited about your idea to feature our homemade bags in a visible way in Oaktown.
I found several places that might be of interest for the pop-up store. I've attached a list to this message. I'm thinking maybe the first or second would be the best, since they are the biggest and are available now. Although from a traffic standpoint, the last one could be perfect since it's on a busy corner downtown.

Let me know what you think. ⑲④ I can set up appointments with the owners of these places if you'd like to see any of them.

Theo

收件人：卡珊卓・荷莉 <cholly@jumbo.com>
寄件人：顧客服務部 <cs@steelworks.com>；提爾多・史萊特 <tslate@jumbo.com>
日期：10月3日週一
主旨：關於：快閃店

嗨，卡珊卓：

　　⑲② 對於妳想在歐克鎮增加我們手工包曝光率的做法，我感到很興奮。我找到幾個可能適合設立快閃店的地點，並已附上清單。我覺得第一個或第二個地點最適合，因為佔地最廣，且現在就能租用。雖然以交通的角度來看，最後一個最適合，因為地點是在車水馬龍的市區街角。

　　再跟我說妳的想法。⑲④ 如果妳想和這些地點的業主碰面，我可以幫妳預約時間。

提歐

290

Type of Property	Location	Size	Details	場地種類	地點	面積	細節
Storefront	391 Main Street	45 ㎡	Available now	店面	緬因街 391 號	45 平方公尺	現可租用
Mall space	Oaktown – east wing	42 ㎡	Expensive	商場櫃點	歐克鎮東側	42 平方公尺	租金昂貴
Kiosk near station	Greenbay Station exit	31 ㎡	⑲⑤ Security concerns	靠近車站的攤位	綠灣站出口	31 平方公尺	⑲⑤ 治安疑慮
Storefront	208 Redmond Blvd.	40 ㎡	⑲③ Available mid Oct.	店面	瑞蒙德大道 208 號	40 平方公尺	⑲③ 十月中旬可租用

字彙 week-long 為期一週的　storefront 店面　outdoor venue 戶外場地　attach 把……附在電子郵件中
standpoint 角度，觀點　wing 側翼　blvd. (boulevard) 大道

191

Why does Ms. Holly want to have a pop-up store?
(A) She has extra merchandise to sell.
(B) She has just started her business.
(C) She hopes to gain more local customers.
(D) She wants to introduce a new product line.

中譯 荷莉小姐為什麼想設立快閃店？
(A) 她想出售額外商品。
(B) 她剛創業。
(C) 她希望增加更多當地顧客。
(D) 她想推出新產品線。

解析 第一封為荷莉小姐傳送的電子郵件，針對設置快閃店請求協助。當中表示不清楚當地居民是否知道自家的產品。由此可以推測她希望透過快閃店能吸引更多當地顧客前來；文中並未提到其他選項。

192

What type of product does Mr. Slate's company make?
(A) Clothing
(B) Cosmetics
(C) Jewelry
(D) Purses

中譯 史萊特先生的公司製造何種產品？
(A) 服飾
(B) 美妝品
(C) 首飾
(D) 包包

解析 與產品有關的內容出現在第二封電子郵件中「our homemade bags」。選項中關聯性最高的產品為 (D)。

193

Why would the location on the Redmond Boulevard likely not be chosen?
(A) It is not available at the right time.
(B) It is too expensive.
(C) It is too far away.
(D) It is too small.

中譯 瑞蒙德大道的場地為何不太可能被選中？
(A) 時段無法配合。
(B) 租金過高。
(C) 距離太遠。
(D) 空間太小。

解析 第一封電子郵件中，荷莉小姐提到預計 10 月 6 日開設快閃店。而表格中，位在瑞蒙德大道的店家要等到 10 月中旬才能設置，這表示無法在可行的時間開設，因此無法選擇位在瑞蒙德大道的店家。

194

What does Mr. Slate offer to do?
(A) Do more research
(B) Make a list of properties
(C) Make some appointments
(D) Show Ms. Holly some new products

中譯 史萊特先生主動提出什麼？
(A) 搜尋更多資料
(B) 提出場地清單
(C) 幫忙預約
(D) 向荷莉小姐展示新品

解析 請從第二封電子郵件中，找出史萊特先生的建議。郵件最後提到能協助安排跟店面負責人見面。選項將 set up appointments 改寫成 make some appointments，因此答案為 (C)。

195

What is mentioned about the kiosk?
(A) It is close to a mall.
(B) It is downtown.
(C) It is the largest location.
(D) It might not be safe.

中譯 關於攤車，文中提到什麼？
(A) 接近商場。 (B) 位於市區。
(C) 空間最大。 (D) 可能不安全

解析 根據表格，Kiosk near station 的細節列出有安全上問題，這表示有可能不夠安全。

Questions 196-200 refer to the following advertisement, itinerary, and e-mail.

廣告 行程 電子郵件 新增題型

THE BROWN HOTEL
...in the heart of Center Grove

196 The Brown Hotel is one of Center Grove's most well-known landmarks, just off of King Square near the convention center. We feature an in-house coffee shop and a full-service dining room. Here are the specials for the month of September.

198 - Stay two weeknights for the price of one.*

- Groups booking 3 or more double rooms can receive a 20% off discount.**

*Offer does not apply to Mondays if it is a national holiday.
**Not to be combined with any other offer.

伯朗飯店
——位於谷羅夫中心的精華區

196 伯朗飯店是谷羅夫中心最知名的景點之一，地點位於靠近會議中心附近的國王廣場。我們內設咖啡廳與服務完善的用餐區。九月特惠活動如下。

198 - 平日住宿兩晚，一晚免費。*

- 團體預訂三間以上的雙人房，即可獲得八折優惠。**

* 週一如為國定假日，恕不適用優惠活動。
** 不能同時使用其他優惠。

Itinerary for Exhibition in Center Grove
September 23–25

198 Saturday, September 23	
10:00 AM	Arrive in Center Grove
11:00 AM	Set up booth for exhibition
1:00–5:00 PM	Exhibition at Welch Convention Center

到谷羅夫中心參展的行程
9 月 23 日至 25 日

9 月 23 日 198 週六	
上午 10 點	抵達谷羅夫中心
上午 11 點	設立展覽攤位
下午 1 點 –5 點	在威爾奇會議中心展出

(198) **Sunday**, September 24	
10:00 AM	Doors open at exhibition
10:00 AM–4:00 PM	Exhibition
7:00 PM	Dinner with your team
Monday, September 25 (national holiday)	
(199) **09:00 AM**	**Breakfast meeting with Center Grove director**
(197) **11:00 AM**	**Campaign planning with Center Grove team (working lunch)**
3:30 PM	Flight back to Winchester

9 月 24 日 (198) 週日	
上午 10 點	展覽開放入場
上午 10 點–下午 4 點	展覽
晚上 7 點	與自己的團隊共享晚餐
9 月 25 日週一（國定假日）	
(199) 上午 9 點	與谷羅夫中心總監進行早餐會議
(197) 上午 11 點	與谷羅夫中心團隊規劃宣傳活動（工作午餐）
下午 3 點半	搭機返回溫徹斯特

To:	Kate Johnson <kjohnson@mytex.com>
From:	Bradley Dexter <bdexter@mytex.com>
Date:	Monday, September 11
Subject:	Your upcoming trip

Hi Kate,

I understand you're going to the exhibition at Center Grove. I went last year and it was really fun. Our people at the branch office are very nice and they will show you a good time. (199) **Be sure to ask the director to take you to this great breakfast place right on the water called Stanley's.** The omelets are fantastic.

Anyway, I found this advertisement about the Brown Hotel. That's where we stayed last year. It's really convenient to the exhibition venue (200) **and the views of the bay are great, so ask for a bayside room.**

Hope you can get one of the two discounts they're offering this month.

Have a nice trip.

Bradley Dexter

收件人：凱特・強森 <kjohnson@mytex.com>
寄件人：布萊德利・德克斯特 <bdexter@mytex.com>
日期：9 月 11 日 週一
主旨：即將到來的出差

嗨，凱特：

　　我知道妳即將參加谷羅夫中心的展覽。我去年去過，真的很有意思。我們分公司的人員都很親切，他們會讓妳樂在其中。(199) 記得請總監帶妳到史丹利水上餐廳。這是間很棒的早餐店，他們的歐姆蛋超好吃。

　　還有，我找到了這份伯朗飯店的廣告。我們去年就是待在這家飯店。這裡到展場很方便，(200) 而且海灣景色很棒，所以記得要求靠海灣的房型。

　　希望妳能享用到他們這個月兩個優惠的其中之一。

　　祝妳出差愉快。

布萊德利・德克斯特

字彙 **landmark** 景點　**weeknight** 平日晚上　**exhibition venue** 展場

196

What is mentioned about the Brown Hotel?
(A) It has just been renovated.
(B) It is a renowned place.
(C) It offers 24-hour room service.
(D) It serves mostly businesspeople.

中譯 關於伯朗飯店，文中提到什麼？
(A) 剛完成翻新。
(B) 屬於知名景點。
(C) 供應 24 小時的客房服務。
(D) 服務對象大多為商業人士。

解析 第一篇文章為飯店廣告。第一句話寫道：「one of Center Grove's most well-known landmarks」，選項改寫成 a renowned place，因此答案為 (B)；(D) 雖然飯店位置臨近會議中心，但當中並未提到主要住客為商務客。

197

What will Ms. Johnson and her team be doing around noon on Monday?
(A) Discussing a business strategy
(B) Eating out
(C) Taking down the booth
(D) Working at the exhibition

中譯 強森小姐和她的團隊將於週一中午左右做什麼事？
(A) 討論商業策略
(B) 在外用餐
(C) 拆卸攤位
(D) 在展覽值勤

解析 請確認日程表中週一上午的安排。當中列出「Campaign planning with Center Grove team (working lunch)」為活動規劃，等同於討論商業策略，且括號中備註為邊工作邊用餐，因此 (B) 並不正確。

字彙 take down 拆卸

198

Why will the team not be eligible for the hotel's half price discount?
(A) They are not staying long enough.
(B) They are staying at the hotel on the weekend.
(C) They do not have a membership card for the hotel.
(D) They will not book enough rooms.

中譯 團隊為何不符合飯店的半價優惠？
(A) 因為住宿時間不夠久。
(B) 因為是週末入住。
(C) 因為沒有該飯店的會員卡。
(D) 因為訂房數不夠。

解析 飯店廣告中，優惠活動為：「Stay two weeknights for the price of one.」。根據日程表，週六和週日為週末，週一則為國定假日，因此不適用此優惠。

199

When could Ms. Johnson go to Stanley's with her colleagues?
(A) On Saturday lunchtime
(B) On Sunday morning
(C) On Sunday evening
(D) On Monday morning

中譯 強森小姐何時能和同事前往史丹利？
(A) 週六午餐時間
(B) 週日早上
(C) 週日傍晚
(D) 週一早上

解析 德克斯特先生傳給強森小姐的電子郵件中寫道：「Be sure to ask the director to take you to this great breakfast place right on the water called Stanley's.」，當中提到 Stanley，而根據第二篇的日程表，強森小姐與負責人的早餐安排在週一上午。

200

What does Mr. Dexter recommend
doing at the hotel?
(A) Asking for extra pillows
(B) Getting a room on a certain
    side
(C) Going to the music hall
(D) Visiting a gift shop

中譯 德克斯特先生提出何種住宿建議？
(A) 要求多給枕頭
(B) 要求特定位置的房型
(C) 前往音樂廳
(D) 造訪禮品店

解析 電子郵件中，德克斯特先生提到自己入住過飯店的感想，
並建議她要求看得到海灣的房間，換句話說就是推薦她指
定入住的房間。

Actual Test 5

PART 1 ⌢17

001 澳

(A) He's standing on a bench.
(B) He's fishing in a lake.
(C) He's sitting on a bench.
(D) He's walking with a friend.

中譯 (A) 他站在長凳上。
(B) 他在湖邊釣魚。
(C) 他坐在長凳上。
(D) 他和朋友走在一起。

解析 照片中有一名男子坐在戶外的長板凳上看著筆電，因此答案為 (C)「He's sitting on a bench.」；請特別留意，不要誤選成 (A)「standing on a bench」。

---

002 美

(A) They're helping customers with purchases.
(B) They're pouring wine in glasses.
(C) They're putting bottles on shelves.
(D) They're standing behind a cash register.

中譯 (A) 他們在幫顧客處理購買的物品。
(B) 他們將紅酒倒入杯子。
(C) 他們將瓶子放到架上。
(D) 他們站在收銀機後方。

解析 照片中有兩個人站在收銀台後方工作，因此 (D)「They're standing behind a cash register.」為最適當的描述；照片中並未看到與她們互動的客人，因此 (A) 並不正確。

字彙 pour 倒　cash register 收銀機

---

003 澳

(A) Chairs are stacked up by a door.
(B) A man is placing dishes on a table.
(C) People are having meals in a dining room.
(D) Umbrellas are shading café tables.

中譯 (A) 椅子堆放在門邊。
(B) 男子將盤子擺在桌上。
(C) 人們在飯廳用餐。
(D) 咖啡桌有遮陽傘。

解析 照片中看到幾張餐桌和椅子擺放在戶外，大型遮陽傘處於開啟狀態，傘的下方還坐著一些人，因此 (D)「Umbrellas are shading café tables.」為最適當的描述。

字彙 stack up 堆疊　place 置放　shade 遮蔽

004 美

(A) A vehicle is running on the bridge.
(B) **A vehicle is stopped outside.**
(C) Someone is checking under the hood of a vehicle.
(D) Someone is taking a bag out of the vehicle.

中譯 (A) 汽車行駛於橋上。
(B) 汽車停在外頭。
(C) 有人在汽車引擎蓋下檢查東西。
(D) 有人從車裡拿出一個袋子。

解析 照片中車輛停在戶外,開啟的車門旁有一名坐在輪椅上的女子,因此 **(B)**「A vehicle is stopped outside.」為最適當的描述。

字彙 vehicle 車輛　take . . . out 拿出

---

005 加

(A) **Clothing is hung on a rod.**
(B) Chairs are folded by a table.
(C) Purses are lying on the ground.
(D) Women are talking near a building.

中譯 (A) 衣服掛在吊衣桿上。
(B) 桌邊擺放折疊起來的椅子。
(C) 包包平放在地上。
(D) 女子們在建物附近聊天。

解析 照片中有很多衣服被掛在長桿子上擺放在路邊,旁邊有人在看衣服,因此 **(A)**「Clothing is hung on a rod.」為最適當的描述。

字彙 fold 摺疊　lie 平放

---

006 英

(A) The gear shift is attached to the steering wheel.
(B) The glove box is open.
(C) There is no side mirror.
(D) **The steering wheel is on the left side.**

中譯 (A) 排檔桿是裝設在方向盤上。
(B) 雜物箱是開著的。
(C) 沒有側邊後照鏡。
(D) 方向盤位於左側。

解析 本題照片為汽車內部照,方向盤位在左側,因此答案為 **(D)**「The steering wheel is on the left side.」。

字彙 gear shift 排檔桿
glove box (前排座位前面放小物件的) 雜物箱
steering wheel 方向盤

17

007 加 英

Who should I talk to about updating my address?
(A) Landon in Personnel, I think.
(B) The calendars are over there.
(C) I don't have any updates yet.

中譯 我該找誰更新我的地址？
(A) 我想應該是人事部的藍敦。
(B) 月曆在那邊。
(C) 抱歉，我還不知道任何新消息。

解析 **Who 開頭的問句** 本題詢問要找誰更新住址。(A) 告知部門名稱和員工姓名，為適當的答覆，答題關鍵在於聽清楚 **Landon**、**Personnel** 這類的專有名詞；(C) 僅與題目中的 **updating** 有所關聯，為陷阱選項。

字彙 update 為……更新資訊

---

008 美 澳

Could I have a moment of your time?
(A) It's only 4:00.
(B) If only I had known sooner.
(C) Of course. How can I help?

中譯 我可以占用你一點時間嗎？
(A) 現在才 4 點。
(B) 如果我早點知道就好了。
(C) 當然可以。我能幫你什麼忙？

解析 **Could I 開頭的問句** 本題詢問是否能佔用對方一點時間。(C) 反問對方需要什麼幫助，為最適當的答覆，此問答可以當成是商店內顧客與店員間的對話；(A) 僅與題目中的時間有所關聯，為陷阱選項。

---

009 加 美

Where are the markers I bought yesterday?
(A) I think I put them in the supply cabinet.
(B) They were on sale.
(C) At the office equipment store.

中譯 我昨天買的麥克筆在哪裡？
(A) 我想我放在用品櫃了。
(B) 它們在打折。
(C) 在辦公設備商店。

解析 **Where 開頭的問句** 本題詢問麥克筆放在哪裡。(A) 告知在用品櫃內，為適當的答覆；(B) 和 (C) 的回答僅與購買麥克筆有所關聯，屬於陷阱選項。

字彙 marker 麥克筆

---

010 澳 英

He followed up on your questions, didn't he?
(A) He won't be able to pass, I'm afraid.
(B) The doctor isn't in now.
(C) Yes. He answered all my questions.

中譯 他有繼續留意你的問題，對嗎？
(A) 他恐怕無法及格。
(B) 醫生現在不在。
(C) 是的。他回答了我所有的問題。

解析 **附加問句** 本題要找出適合用來回答「確認型問句」的答覆。題目中出現「**followed up on your questions**」，(C) 改寫成「**answered all my questions**」，為最適當的答覆。

011 美 加

How many folders come in a package?
(A) Less than $5.00.
(B) Ten, I guess.
(C) We shouldn't buy them.

中譯 這一包裡有幾個資料夾？
(A) 低於 5 元。
(B) 我猜有 10 個。
(C) 我們不該買這些資料夾。

解析 How many 開頭的問句　本題詢問數量。(B) 告知他所知的個數，故為最適當的答覆。

---

012 澳 英

I don't know which phone number is hers.
(A) She's looking for her phone.
(B) I think it's the top one.
(C) Nobody knows where she is.

中譯 我不知道她的電話號碼是哪一個。
(A) 她在找她的電話。
(B) 我想是最上面那個。
(C) 沒有人知道她在哪裡。

解析 直述句　本題敘述自己正在找特定人士的電話號碼。(B) 告知號碼所在位置，為選項中最適當的答覆；(A) 和 (C) 的回答中出現 she，僅是利用題目句中的 hers，為陷阱選項。

---

013 美 澳

Why are the chairs stacked up in the conference room?
(A) Room A at 3:30.
(B) They're cleaning the carpets tonight.
(C) Because he's too busy right now.

中譯 會議室裡的椅子為什麼疊起來？
(A) 3 點 30 分在 A 會議室。
(B) 因為他們今晚要清理地毯。
(C) 因為他現在太忙。

解析 Why 開頭的問句　本題需要確實理解題意，才能選出答案。題目詢問的是會議室內椅子堆疊起來放在一起的原因。(B) 回答因為今晚要清掃地毯，故為最適當的答覆。

---

014 加 英

Has she gotten back to you about the project yet?
(A) I haven't heard the weather report.
(B) No. They're not coming over.
(C) Yes, and it's going ahead.

中譯 她回覆你專案的事了嗎？
(A) 我還沒聽到氣象報告。
(B) 沒有，他們不過來了。
(C) 有，且專案正持續進行。

解析 一般問句　本題詢問對方是否收到有關專案的答覆。(C) 給予肯定回應，同時告知後續情況，為最適當的答覆；(A) 和 (B) 僅與題目中的「gotten back to you」有所關聯，內容皆答非所問。

字彙 go ahead 進行

18

015 澳 加

Which vehicle is big enough for five people?
(A) I recommend the SUV since you have luggage, too.
(B) Only three days to go.
(C) We charge extra for mileage.

中譯 哪一部車能容納 5 人呢？
(A) 既然你也要載運行李，我推薦運動休旅車。
(B) 只剩下 3 天。
(C) 里程數會另外收費。

解析 **Which 開頭的問句** 本題詢問哪一種車款足以容納五個人。(A) 推薦運動型休旅車，為選項中最適當的答覆。

字彙 mileage 里程數

---

016 美 英

There are no parking spaces left.
(A) Let's try at that other lot.
(B) There's one more space left in the workshop.
(C) We'll have to postpone, I guess.

中譯 已經沒有多餘的停車位了。
(A) 我們試試另一個停車場。
(B) 研習會還剩一個名額。
(C) 我猜我們得延期了。

解析 **直述句** 本題敘述沒有停車位的問題。(A) 提出其他方案，建議改到其他停車場，故為最適當的答覆。parking space 可以改寫成 (parking) lot。

字彙 lot 場地

---

017 英 澳

Can I get two large coffees to go, please?
(A) All of the seats are taken.
(B) Sure. That'll be $5.50.
(C) These are the last batch.

中譯 可以給我外帶兩杯大杯咖啡嗎？
(A) 所有位子都有人坐了。
(B) 好的。總共 5.5 元。
(C) 這些是最後一批了。

解析 **Can I 開頭的問句** 本題為咖啡廳內顧客與店員間的對話，顧客表示要買兩杯咖啡。(B) 告知對方價格，故為最適當的答覆。

字彙 batch 一批，一組

---

018 加 美

When will the president make the announcement?
(A) He's announced our new policy.
(B) The profits were through the roof.
(C) At 3:00, I heard.

中譯 董事長何時會宣布消息？
(A) 他已經宣布了我們的新政策。
(B) 利潤激增。
(C) 我聽說是 3 點。

解析 **When 開頭的問句** 本題詢問未來，預計何時要發表。(C) 回答明確的時間點，故為最適當的答覆；(A) 和 (B) 分別使用現在完成式與過去式回答，時態並不適當。

字彙 be through the roof 激增，飛漲

019 [美][澳]

The theater has a cloakroom, doesn't it?
(A) As far as I know, yes.
(B) It's being torn down.
(C) The new play is fantastic.

中譯　劇院有衣帽間，對嗎？
(A) 就我所知是有的。
(B) 它正在被拆除。
(C) 新劇太好看了。

解析　**附加問句**　本題以問句確認劇院是否有衣帽間，也就是寄物處。**(A)** 使用「As far as I know」，為適當的答覆。題目為確認型問句時，除了用「As far as I know」回答之外，也可以回答「I don't know.」或「I'm not sure.」，三者皆為常見的答案。

字彙　cloakroom 衣帽間

020 [英][加]

Who is the woman next to Mr. Elmore?
(A) He's not coming back today.
(B) I've never seen her before.
(C) She can't make it to the party today.

中譯　艾摩爾先生旁邊的女子是誰？
(A) 他今天不會回來。
(B) 我從來沒看過她。
(C) 她今天沒辦法來參加派對。

解析　**Who 開頭的問句**　本題詢問女子的身份。**(B)** 回答第一次見到這個人，等同於不知道的意思，故為最適當的答覆。

021 [澳][加]

Would you like me to do anything else before I leave?
(A) I'd like to thank you all for being here.
(B) No. That's everything. Thanks.
(C) Whenever you can come is fine.

中譯　我離開前，你需要我再做其他事嗎？
(A) 我想謝謝大家前來捧場。
(B) 沒關係，這樣就可以了，謝謝你。
(C) 你什麼時候來都可以。

解析　**一般問句**　題目表明有幫助對方的意願。**(B)** 回答已經沒有需要幫忙的事，故為最適當的答覆。

022 [澳][英]

The company is opening an office in Singapore.
(A) Oh, that's news to me.
(B) By next fall.
(C) Round trip or one way?

中譯　公司要在新加坡設立分部。
(A) 喔，我第一次聽到這件事。
(B) 明年秋天以前。
(C) 來回票或單程票？

解析　**直述句**　本題指出新加坡開了分公司的消息。**(A)** 回答第一次聽說這個消息，故為最適當的答覆；**(C)** 的回答與交通有關。

字彙　round trip 來回票　one way 單程票

Actual Test 5

PART 2

18

023 加美

Do you think the offer will be accepted?
(A) We don't accept credit cards.
(B) When you have enough time.
(C) No one knows for sure.

中譯 你覺得這個提議會被接受嗎？
(A) 我們不接受信用卡。
(B) 等你有時間的時候。
(C) 沒有人能肯定。

解析 一般問句 本題詢問對方的想法。(C) 表示沒有人能確定，故為最適當的答覆。當題目為詢問對方想法的問句時，「No one knows for sure.」為萬用回答；(A) 僅與題目中的 accept 有所關聯，為陷阱選項。

---

024 澳加

Why isn't this printer working?
(A) We bought a new printer this morning.
(B) It must be out of ink.
(C) Because we sold it.

中譯 這部印表機怎麼無法使用？
(A) 我們今天早上買了新的印表機。
(B) 一定是沒有墨水了。
(C) 因為我們將它賣掉了。

解析 Why 開頭的問句 本題詢問印表機沒辦法用的原因。(B) 表示因為墨水都用完了，故為最適當的答覆。

---

025 英美

Did you buy a laptop computer or tablet?
(A) Neither. I'm still shopping around.
(B) None of the tech people are available.
(C) My work computer is pretty old.

中譯 你買的是筆記型電腦還是平板電腦？
(A) 都不是，我還想再多看看。
(B) 技術人員都沒有空。
(C) 我工作用的電腦相當老舊。

解析 選擇疑問句 本題詢問要買筆電還是平板。(A) 表示尚未決定，為選項中最適當的答覆；(B) 和 (C) 僅和科技產品有所關聯，為陷阱選項。

---

026 美澳

Where do you suggest we stay?
(A) Until at least 5:00 PM.
(B) The hotel near the airport is convenient.
(C) We're all booked, I'm afraid.

中譯 你建議我們在哪裡住宿？
(A) 至少要等到下午 5 點。
(B) 靠近機場的飯店很方便。
(C) 很抱歉，我們都客滿了。

解析 Where 開頭的問句 本題詢問住宿地點。(B) 建議住在機場附近比較方便，故為最適當的答覆；(C) 僅與題目中的 stay 有所關聯，為陷阱選項。

---

027 加英

Feel free to call me with any questions.
(A) Are there any questions?
(B) My number is 555-3892.
(C) Thanks. I'll do that.

中譯 有任何問題，請隨時打給我。
(A) 有任何問題嗎？
(B) 我的電話是 555-3892。
(C) 謝謝你，我會的。

解析 祈使句 本題表示有問題隨時可以聯絡我。(C) 對此表達感謝，並表示自己會的，故為最適當的答覆；(B) 告知自己的電話號碼，答非所問。

028 澳 美

Why don't you join us for dinner tonight?
(A) I'll make a reservation if you like.
(B) Sorry, I already have plans.
(C) We're going to Emma's Café at lunchtime.

中譯 你今晚怎麼不和我們一起吃晚餐？
(A) 如果你想的話，我可以訂位。
(B) 抱歉，我還有事。
(C) 我們要去艾瑪咖啡廳吃午餐。

解析 **Why don't you 開頭的問句** 本題以問句建議對方一起吃晚餐。**(B)** 回答自己已經有約，表示拒絕對方的提議，故為最適當的答覆；**(A)** 為表示可負責訂位，**(C)** 當中提到 **lunchtime**，皆未針對問題回答。

---

029 英 美

Was there an invoice from the supplier?
(A) It should be inside the box.
(B) We need to switch them.
(C) Yes. We paid extra for it.

中譯 供應商有給發票嗎？
(A) 應該在箱子裡。
(B) 我們必須調換一下。
(C) 是的，我們有多付錢。

解析 **一般問句** 本題詢問是否有從供應商那裡收到發票。**(A)** 告知在箱子裡，故為適當答覆。**invoice** 並非購買的商品，因此 **(C)** 的回答並不適當。

---

030 美 加

What do you want to do this weekend?
(A) They're open on Sunday afternoons.
(B) There's not enough time for that.
(C) Whatever you want.

中譯 你這週末想做什麼？
(A) 他們週日下午有營業。
(B) 沒有充足的時間可以這麼做。
(C) 看你囉。

解析 **What 開頭的問句** 本題詢問週末的計畫。**(C)** 把決定權交給對方，為選項中最適當的答覆；**(A)** 當中出現 **Sunday**，僅與題目中的 **weekend** 有所關聯，屬於答題陷阱。

---

031 英 澳

Do you want me to show you the cafeteria?
(A) Aren't you in sales department?
(B) I was given the full tour yesterday, thanks.
(C) Okay. Here's a map.

中譯 你需要我帶你去自助餐廳看看嗎？
(A) 你不是在業務部門嗎？
(B) 昨天已經有人帶我四處認識環境了，謝謝你。
(C) 好的，地圖在這裡。

解析 **一般問句** 本題詢問對方想不想參觀自助餐廳。**(B)** 以「昨天已經都參觀過了」拒絕對方，等同於 **No** 的概念，故為最適當的答覆。

18

Questions 32-34 refer to the following conversation. 澳 英

W	Hi, Jim. I was wondering if I could get your advice on something.
M	Sure, Sarah, come on in. How can I help you?
W	Well, ㉜ **I'm putting together the budget for this year's awards ceremony**, but I'm not really sure how much money we will need.
M	Hmm. ㉝ **When I did it last year**, I ended up having some money left over. The expenses are a lot lower than you think.
W	Oh, that's good because ㉞ **the president asked me to keep the cost down**.

女：嗨，吉姆。我想說妳是不是能給我一點建議。

男：好啊，莎拉，請進。我能幫你什麼忙？

女：是這樣的，㉜ 我在整理今年頒獎典禮的預算，但我不確定我們到底需要多少錢。

男：嗯。㉝ 我去年辦完典禮後，預算還有剩。開銷會比妳想像中的少很多。

女：喔，那太好了，因為 ㉞ 董事長要求我降低成本。

字彙 put together 整理，拼湊　awards ceremony 頒獎典禮　expense 開銷

032

What are the speakers discussing?
(A) A company celebration
(B) An annual salary
(C) A leadership change
(D) A new product's sales

中譯 說話者在討論什麼問題？
(A) 公司慶典事宜　　(B) 年薪
(C) 領導職位異動　　(D) 新品的銷售狀況

解析 在第二段對話中，女子表示她要整理今年頒獎典禮的預算，並請求男子的幫助。

換句話說 awards ceremony → celebration

033

What did the man do last year?
(A) He got promoted.
(B) He moved departments.
(C) He overspent on a project.
(D) He planned an event.

中譯 男子去年做了什麼事？
(A) 獲得升遷。
(B) 調到不同部門。
(C) 他的某專案超出預算。
(D) 他規劃了一項活動。

解析 男子聽完女子的煩惱後，告訴她去年由他負責這項工作。請務必掌握 did it 所指的意思。

字彙 overspend 超支

034

What did the company president tell the woman to do?
(A) Book a larger venue
(B) Make a payment
(C) Increase sales soon
(D) Use less money

中譯 公司董事長要女子做什麼？
(A) 預定空間較大的場地
(B) 付款
(C) 很快增加銷售量
(D) 降低費用

解析 對話最後，女子提到董事長要求她降低費用，表示要求她花少一點錢。

換句話說 keep the cost down → use less money

字彙 overspend 超支

W	Good morning, this is Dr. Allen's office.
M	Hello, ㉟ I'm calling to cancel, well . . . uh, hopefully reschedule my appointment. It's for this morning and I'm just too busy at work. I can't make it.
W	No problem. I can find a time later this afternoon.
M	I'm afraid that's no good, either. I've got meetings until 6:00. If you had a slot tomorrow around 3:00, that would be great. My name is Eric Cameron, by the way.
W	Okay, Mr. Cameron, ㊱ I have you down at 3:00 tomorrow. ㊲ Please don't forget to bring your latest insurance card.

女：早安，這裡是艾倫醫師的診間。

男：哈囉，㉟ 我想打來取消預約……呃，或者可以的話改約其他時間。本來是今天早上，但我工作實在太忙，我來不及過去。

女：沒問題。我可以幫您預約較晚的下午時段。

男：恐怕我也沒辦法到，我要開會到 6 點。如果你們能有明天 3 點左右的時段就好了。對了，我叫艾瑞克・卡麥隆。

女：好的，卡麥隆先生，㊱ 我幫您預約明天 3 點。㊲ 請別忘了攜帶您最新的保險卡。

字彙 slot 時段　insurance card 醫療保險卡

035

What is the purpose of the call?
(A) To cancel an appointment
(B) **To change an appointment**
(C) To confirm an appointment
(D) To make an appointment

中譯 此通電話的目的為何？
(A) 取消預約
(B) 更改預約
(C) 確認預約
(D) 進行預約

解析 男子在對話開頭表示想取消掛號，接著又說想更改看診時間。

換句話說 reschedule → change

036

When will the man go to the woman's office?
(A) This morning
(B) This afternoon
(C) **Tomorrow at 3:00**
(D) Tomorrow at 6:00

中譯 男子何時會前往女子的診療室？
(A) 今天早上
(B) 今天下午
(C) 明天 3 點
(D) 明天 6 點

解析 更改後的時間出現在後半段對話中。女子表示更改成隔天下午 3 點。

037

What does the woman remind the man about?
(A) His annual checkup
(B) His appointment next week
(C) **His insurance information**
(D) His payment from last month

中譯 女子提醒男子什麼事？
(A) 年度檢查
(B) 下週的預約
(C) 他的保險資料
(D) 他上個月的款項

解析 最後一段對話中，女子要求對方記得帶醫療保險卡，等同於請男子攜帶健保相關的資料。

字彙 checkup 健康檢查

Actual Test 5

PART 3

19

Questions 38-40 refer to the following conversation. 澳 美

W Oh, Martin, I heard you are moving to a new apartment closer to the office.

M Yes, Jessica. I found a really great one-bedroom apartment only a couple of stops away on the train from here. One problem, though. ㊳ **I have to sell my couch. It takes up too much space in my new place.**

W That brown leather one? ㊴ **I loved sitting on it at your party a few months ago.** It was so comfortable. I might be interested in it if the price is right.

M Ah, actually, ㊵ **I'm showing it to somebody this afternoon.** He said he was fine with my price.

女：喔，馬丁，我聽說你要搬到離公司比較近的新公寓。

男：對呀，潔西卡。我找到一間很棒的一房一廳的公寓，離這裡只有幾個火車站的距離而已。但我現在有個問題，㊳我得賣掉沙發，因為對我的新公寓來說，太占空間了。

女：是那張棕色皮沙發嗎？㊴幾個月前到你家參加派對時，我覺得很好坐，非常舒適。如果價格不錯的話，我可能有興趣跟你買。

男：啊，其實㊵今天下午會有人來看一下。他說他可以接受我的價格。

字彙 stop 車站　take up 占據

038

Why is the man selling his couch?
(A) He bought a new one.
(B) He is moving overseas.
(C) It is rather old.
(D) It is too big for his new apartment.

中譯 男子為何出售沙發？
(A) 他買了新沙發。
(B) 他要搬到國外。
(C) 沙發很老舊。
(D) 沙發尺寸太大，不適合他的新公寓。

解析 男子表示搬到新家後，沙發佔掉太多空間。

換句話說 takes up too much space → too big

039

What can be said about the woman?
(A) She has been in the man's apartment before.
(B) She is an apartment owner.
(C) She is having a party soon.
(D) She just moved to a new town.

中譯 關於女子，可從文中得知什麼？
(A) 她曾到過男子的公寓。
(B) 她是公寓屋主。
(C) 她很快就要舉辦派對。
(D) 她剛搬到新城鎮。

解析 女子提到幾個月前在男子家開派對時，曾經試坐過沙發，當時的感覺很不錯。由這段話可以推測女子曾去過男子住的公寓。

040 新增題型

What does the man imply when he says, "I'm showing it to somebody this afternoon"?
(A) He does not want the woman to buy his apartment.
(B) He may have found a buyer for the couch.
(C) He thinks someone is interested in his apartment.
(D) He wants to sell the couch quickly.

中譯 男子說「今天下午會有人來看一下」是什麼意思？
(A) 他不希望女子買下他的公寓。
(B) 他可能已經找到沙發的買主。
(C) 他認為有人對他的公寓感興趣。
(D) 他想趕快賣出沙發。

解析 男子在最後提到有人接受他開出的價格，暗指找到願意買沙發的人。

Questions 41-43 refer to the following conversation. 加 英

W Aron, I'm having a hard time deciding who to promote to the assistant manager position. Since Trevor quit suddenly, we've been without an assistant on the evening shift.

M Well, who are your top choices? ㊷ We need someone reliable to keep our grocery store running smoothly during the busy hours.

W ㊶ Either Susan or Mike. They have both been working here for more than three years and they both have good relations with the other employees.

M Hmm, that is tough. ㊸ Why don't you ask them each to write a statement about why they would be a good manager?

女：亞倫，我對於該升遷誰擔任副店長一事感到猶豫不決。由於崔佛突然辭職，我們好一段時間都沒有副店長在輪值晚班。

男：那妳的首推人選有哪些人呢？㊷ 我們需要可以在尖峰時段維持超市順暢運作的可靠人選。

女：㊶ 我覺得要從蘇珊或麥克擇一。他們的年資都超過三年，而且和其他員工的關係都很好。

男：嗯，真的很難選。㊸ 妳何不要求他們寫篇文章，陳述自己勝任副店長的原因呢？

字彙 assistant manager 副店長　shift 輪班　have good relations with 與……的關係良好　statement 說明，陳述

041

What is the woman's difficulty in making a decision?
(A) She has no suitable candidates.
(B) She has pressure from her boss.
(C) She has time pressure.
(D) She has two good choices.

中譯 女子為何難以做決定？
(A) 她沒有合適的人選。
(B) 她的上司對她施壓。
(C) 她有時間的壓力。
(D) 她有兩位好人選。

解析 女子提到候選人有蘇珊和麥克兩位，她正在煩惱要選誰升上副店長。兩人都工作超過三年，並與其他員工互動良好，因此讓她難以下決定。

字彙 pressure 壓力

042

Where do the speakers work?
(A) At a factory
(B) At a clothing store
(C) At a fast food restaurant
(D) At a supermarket

中譯 說話者在哪裡上班？
(A) 工廠
(B) 服飾店
(C) 速食餐廳
(D) 超市

解析 第一段對話中，男子提到需要某個人來負責管理超市。

換句話說 grocery store → supermarket

043

What does the man suggest?
(A) Advertising the position online
(B) Going to different stores to get data
(C) Having a joint interview
(D) Reading an essay from the candidates

中譯 男子提議什麼做法？
(A) 在網路上打徵才廣告
(B) 去不同商店收集資料
(C) 進行聯合面試
(D) 閱讀待選人寫的文章

解析 最後一段對話中，男子建議讓兩名候選人寫下自己適合擔任副店長的原因。這表示他建議檢閱候選人所寫的文章。

19

Questions 44-46 refer to the following conversation. 加 美

W Well, **44 it doesn't look good for our company marathon on Thursday.**

M Oh, no. What is the forecast?

W **44 Rain starting at noon and lasting throughout the day.**

M How about Friday? **46 Maybe we can postpone the marathon to Friday.**

W Let me check the app here on my phone. Uh, it says cloudy in the morning and clear in the afternoon.

M That sounds perfect. Not too hot. **45 I'll post a message on the company intranet** to tell everyone that **46 we're delaying it by a day.**

女：**44** 我們公司週四要舉辦馬拉松，但看起來不太妙。

男：喔，不，氣象預報怎麼說？

女：**44** 從中午開始會下一整天的雨。

男：那週五呢？**46** 也許我們可以將馬拉松延到週五。

女：我查一下我手機的應用程式。呃，上面寫說週五早上是陰天，下午才會轉晴。

男：那太好了。不會太熱。**45** 我會將消息發布在公司的內部網站，通知大家**46** 我們會延後一天。

字彙 forecast 預報　throughout 貫穿　intranet 內部網站

044

What is the problem about the event?
(A) It is largely over budget.
(B) The speakers cannot find the venue.
(C) The weather may be bad.
(D) There are not enough participants.

中譯 此活動出了什麼問題？
(A) 大幅超出預算。
(B) 說話者無法找到場地。
(C) 氣候可能不佳。
(D) 參加人數不夠。

解析 前半段對話中，女子提到公司原訂週四舉辦馬拉松大賽，但當天中午開始就會下雨持續一整天。由此可以得知活動的問題在於天氣狀況不佳。

字彙 largely 大幅地

045

What does the man say he will do?
(A) Call a staff meeting
(B) Inform the media about the event
(C) Post a notice on the staff bulletin board
(D) Put information on an internal network

中譯 男子表示自己會怎麼做？
(A) 召開人員會議
(B) 通知媒體此活動
(C) 在員工布告欄張貼告示
(D) 在公司內部網路張貼資訊

解析 男子在最後提到在公司內網上發文通知，等同於在公司內部上傳資訊之意。

046

When will the event probably be held?
(A) Today
(B) Thursday
(C) Friday
(D) Next Monday

中譯 此活動可能於何時舉辦？
(A) 今天
(B) 週四
(C) 週五
(D) 下週一

解析 由男子所述的最後一句話中，可以確認原訂於週四舉辦的馬拉松活動因天氣因素延後一天。

Questions 47-49 refer to the following conversation. 澳 英

W	Hi, I'd like to make a reservation for Friday, November 24.
M	Yes, ma'am. **㊼ I can help you with that. What type of room do you need?**
W	Just a single, the cheapest you have. I'm actually arriving late and **㊽ leaving early for a conference on Saturday.**
M	I see. Okay, we have a single for $89. Would that be okay?
W	That's great. And I'll also need a shuttle from the airport.
M	I can arrange that for you. **㊾ Let me get your name and phone number first.**

女：嗨，我想訂 11 月 24 日週五的房間。

男：好的，小姐，㊼ 我可以幫您處理。您需要什麼房型？

女：最便宜的單人房就可以了。我其實會晚到，㊽ 週六還要提早退房去參加會議。

男：原來如此。好的，我們有 89 元的單人房。這樣可以嗎？

女：太好了。我還需要機場接駁服務。

男：我可以幫您安排。㊾ 請您先給我大名和電話號碼。

字彙 **arrange** 安排

047

Where does the man most likely work?
(A) At a conference center
(B) At a hotel
(C) At a travel agency
(D) At an airline

中譯 男子最有可能在哪裡上班？
(A) 會議中心
(B) 飯店
(C) 旅行社
(D) 航空公司

解析 本對話情境為女子向男子預訂住宿。由第一句話便能確認答題線索，選項中 **(B)** 飯店為最適當的答案。

048

What is the purpose of the woman's trip?
(A) Wedding
(B) Business
(C) Vacation
(D) Family gathering

中譯 女子此趟旅行的目的為何？
(A) 婚禮
(B) 出差
(C) 度假
(D) 家族聚會

解析 請由女子所述的話推測答案。女子提到她會比較晚入住，且隔天要開會，所以會提早離開。由此可以得知她是商務客。

字彙 **vacation** 度假

049

What will the woman give the man next?
(A) Her contact information
(B) Her credit card number
(C) Her flight information
(D) Her reservation number

中譯 女子接下來會給男子什麼資訊？
(A) 她的聯絡資料
(B) 她的信用卡號
(C) 她的班機資訊
(D) 她的訂房編號

解析 對話最後，男子請女子告知姓名和電話。由此可以推測女子需要告訴男子自己的聯絡資訊，以便男子幫她預訂。

字彙 **contact** 聯絡

Actual Test 5

PART 3

19

Questions 50-52 refer to the following conversation. 澳 美

W Tom, you're going to talk to the president about your idea today, right?
M Uh, you mean, about having a weekly meeting in a different room? Yes, if I get up the courage. He might think that because (50) I just started to work here, I should keep my mouth shut.
W Well, (51) you have my vote. I was thinking the same thing. The old place is just too small.
M Thanks, Tess. Because of you, (52) I'm going to his office right now to talk with him.

女：湯姆，你今天會和董事長談你的點子，對嗎？
男：呃，妳是說在別的會議室召開每週會議的事嗎？會啊，如果我能鼓起勇氣的話。他可能會覺得 (50) 我才剛來這裡上班沒多久，不應該有太多意見。
女：(51) 我投你一票。我也是這麼想的，原有的地方太狹小了。
男：謝謝你，泰絲。因為妳的鼓勵，(52) 我現在要去他辦公室和他討論這件事。

字彙 get up the courage 鼓起勇氣

050

What is mentioned about the man?
(A) He is new at the office.
(B) He wants to be president.
(C) He was assigned a new project.
(D) He would like to help the woman.

中譯 關於男子，文中提到什麼？
(A) 他是此公司的新人。
(B) 他想當董事長。
(C) 他被分配到新專案。
(D) 他想幫助女子。

解析 第一段對話中，男子提到自己剛來這裡工作，由此可以得知他剛來這家公司工作，是公司的新人。

字彙 assign 分配

051 新增題型

What does the woman mean when she says, "you have my vote"?
(A) She hopes the man will run in an election.
(B) She supports the man's idea.
(C) She wants to elect the man to a managerial position.
(D) She will give the man a good review.

中譯 女子說「我投你一票」時是什麼意思？
(A) 她希望男子去參選。
(B) 她支持男子的想法。
(C) 她想選男子擔任管理職位。
(D) 她會給男子好評價。

解析 女子先提到「you have my vote」，接著表示自己也持相同看法。女子説對方已經得到自己的一票，表示女子支持男子的想法。

字彙 run 競選 election 選舉 managerial 管理的

052

Where will the man most likely go next?
(A) To the City Hall
(B) To the president's office
(C) To the voting place
(D) To the woman's office

中譯 男子接下來最可能會去哪裡？
(A) 市政廳
(B) 董事長的辦公室
(C) 投票所
(D) 女子的辦公室

解析 最後一段對話中，男子表示現在要到「他」的辦公室去跟某人説自己的想法，而這裡的「他」指的是對話開頭提到的董事長。

Questions 53-55 refer to the following conversation. 英 加 新增題型

M	Mary, ㊼ **have you looked at the new Internet that was installed over the weekend**?
W	No, not yet, but ㊽ **I have to log in quickly before my meeting at 9:30**. I need a new password, right?
M	Yeah, the IT department sent you a new one by e-mail last week.
W	Honestly, I've been busy since last week and haven't checked my e-mails carefully. I have a big presentation this afternoon and I haven't finished it yet.
M	㊾ **If you need any help or someone to practice with, let me know.** I'm free all morning.
W	Thanks, Dave. I appreciate it. Let me check my password first, then I'll let you know.

男：瑪莉，㊼ 妳看過我們週末安裝的新網路系統了嗎？

女：還沒，但 ㊽ 我9點半開會前要趕快登入系統。我需要新的密碼，對嗎？

男：對，資訊科技部上週已經用電子郵件傳新的密碼給妳了。

女：老實說，我從上週開始一直很忙，還沒仔細收信。我今天下午有場大型報告，我居然還沒完成簡報。

男：㊾ 如果妳需要幫忙或有人和妳練習再跟我說。我早上都沒事。

女：謝謝你，戴維，很感激你的心意。我先查一下我的密碼，看怎麼樣再跟你說。

053

What was changed over the weekend?
(A) **The computer network**
(B) The department spaces
(C) The employees' desks
(D) The office location

中譯 下列何者在週末時發生了變化？
(A) 電腦網絡
(B) 部門空間
(C) 員工的辦公桌
(D) 辦公地點

解析 第一段對話中，男子詢問女子是否有看過週末安裝好的新網路。由此可以得知週末換了網路。

換句話說 Internet → computer network

054

What does the woman say she needs to do?
(A) Finish her report
(B) Find her presentation notes
(C) **Get onto her computer**
(D) Give the man his assignment

中譯 女子表示自己需要做什麼？
(A) 完成報告
(B) 找到簡報筆記
(C) 登入她的電腦
(D) 分配男子工作

解析 女子該做的事出現在第一段對話中。女子提到她得在9點30分開會前登入；(D) 為男子先建議女子可以把工作交給他做。

換句話說 log in → get onto

055

What does the man offer to do for the woman?
(A) Call the IT department
(B) Change her password
(C) **Listen to her speech**
(D) Show her around the office

中譯 男子主動要幫女子做什麼事？
(A) 聯絡資訊科技部
(B) 更換她的密碼
(C) 聽她報告
(D) 帶她認識一下辦公室

解析 最後一段對話中，男子表示自己願意提供協助。在此之前女子提到自己得報告，男子回應自己可以當對方的練習對象，等於男子表示願意聆聽女子報告。

🎧 19

Questions 56-58 refer to the following conversation with three speakers. 加 美 英 新增題型

W	Robert, ㊱ I don't know how we're going to get through all these applications! I never expected so many.
M1	Well, we did advertise in two more places than we usually do. Those Websites are really popular among recent college graduates.
W	You're right. But now, we have too many to sort through with just the two of us.
M1	㊲ Why don't I ask my assistant Tony to help? Oh, there he is. Tony, are you busy now?
M2	Not really. I just finished entering all the data you asked me to.
M1	Good. ㊳ Could you do the initial screening of the applicants? I'll tell you what we're looking for.
M2	Sure, ㊳ I'll start on that right away.

女：羅伯特，㊱我真不曉得該怎麼看完所有求職者的資料！我沒想到有這麼多人應徵。

男1：我們和平常不同，多在兩個管道打廣告。那些都是很受應屆畢業生歡迎的網站。

女：你說得沒錯。但現在資料太多，只有我們兩人是無法整理完的。

男1：㊲我們何不找我的助理東尼來幫忙？喔，他來了。東尼，你現在在忙嗎？

男2：還好。我剛輸入完你要求的資料。

男1：很好。㊳你可以幫忙初步篩選出求職者嗎？我會告訴你我們注重的條件。

男2：好啊，㊳我馬上著手。

字彙 **get through** 做完　**college graduate** 大專院校的畢業生　**sort through** 查看並加以分類整理
enter 輸入　**initial screening** 初步篩選　**applicant** 應徵者，求職者

056

Why is the woman surprised?
(A) Her boss is leaving the company.
(B) Robert was late to the meeting.
(C) The applicants were not qualified.
(D) There are many job candidates.

中譯 女子為何感到驚訝？
(A) 她的上司要離職。　　(B) 羅伯特開會遲到。
(C) 應徵者都不合格。　　(D) 應徵者很多。

解析 本篇文章為兩男一女的三人對話。第一段對話中，女子提到應徵的人實在太多，她不曉得能否看完。選項將對話中的 applications 改寫成 job candidates。

057

What does Robert suggest?
(A) Advertising on more Websites
(B) Asking for some help
(C) Calling some universities
(D) Scheduling interviews soon

中譯 羅伯特提議什麼做法？
(A) 在更多網站上打廣告　(B) 找人幫忙
(C) 連絡一些大專院校　　(D) 儘快安排面試時間

解析 對話中間，男1羅伯特建議請助理東尼幫忙。

058

What will Tony probably do next?
(A) Fill out an application
(B) Enter data into a computer
(C) Interview a candidate
(D) Look through some applicants

中譯 東尼接下來大概會做什麼？
(A) 填寫求職申請表　　(B) 將資料輸入至電腦
(C) 面試應徵者　　　　(D) 瀏覽一些應徵者的資料

解析 最後一段對話中，男1請男2協助第一階段的檢視工作，男2回答他馬上開始進行。這表示東尼之後將瀏覽應徵者的資料。

換句話說 do the initial screening of the applicants →
look through some applicants

字彙 **look through** 瀏覽

W Hi, ❺❾ I'm calling several caterers trying to get an estimate for a dinner at my company. About 35 people. Could you tell me approximately how much the meal would cost?

M It depends what type of food you'd like. For example, chicken is cheaper than beef. If it's casual, we make small finger food. That's even cheaper.

W Oh, ❻⓿ we're going to have a sit down dinner because it's a board meeting. I'm thinking maybe a buffet line.

M Hmm, 35 people, buffet style. Will you be needing beverages, too?

W No, we have wine and other drinks at the office.

M ❻❶ I can put some numbers together and send you an e-mail. Remember, though, that these aren't final costs. I can't give you a real quote until after you pick specific dishes.

女：嗨，❺❾我在打給幾家外燴業者，想了解一下承辦我們公司晚宴的費用估算。大約是 35 人的晚宴。可以請你告訴我大概需要多少費用嗎？

男：需要視您想要的食物類型而定，例如雞肉比牛肉便宜。如果是比較休閒的活動氛圍，我們會做可以一口吃的小份量食物，價格會更低。

女：喔，❻⓿我們是要舉辦圍桌而坐的晚宴，因為是董事會議。我在想是不是能採用自助餐的形式。

男：嗯，35 人，自助餐式。您也需要飲料嗎？

女：不需要，我們辦公室已經有葡萄酒和其他飲品。

男：❻❶我計算一下後，再回傳電子郵件給您。但麻煩您留意一下，這些數字不是最終費用。您還沒挑選特定菜色之前，我沒辦法算出實際報價給您。

字彙 approximately 大約　finger food 可一口吃的食物　sit down dinner 圍桌而坐的晚餐　specific 特定的

059

Who most likely is the man?
(A) A board member
(B) A caterer
(C) A clerical assistant
(D) An organizer

中譯 男子最有可能是什麼身分？
(A) 董事會成員　　(B) 外燴業者
(C) 文書助理　　　(D) 活動主辦單位

解析 女子打電話詢問將晚餐送至公司內的價格，並表示人數約 35 人，而後男子反問活動的類型和餐點要求，由此可以推測男子應為外燴餐飲服務業者。

字彙 organizer 主辦人（單位）

060

What event is the woman calling about?
(A) A birthday party
(B) A retirement party
(C) An awards banquet
(D) An executive gathering

中譯 女子電話上討論的活動為何？
(A) 生日派對　　　(B) 退休派對
(C) 頒獎晚宴　　　(D) 主管聚會

解析 第二段對話中，女子提到為董事會議，表示活動為高層集會。

換句話說 board meeting → executive gathering

字彙 executive 領導階層

061

What will the man send the woman?
(A) A brochure
(B) A menu
(C) A price estimate
(D) A wine list

中譯 男子會向女子傳送什麼？
(A) 手冊　　　　　(B) 菜單
(C) 估價單　　　　(D) 酒單

解析 最後一段對話中，男子提到會以電子郵件傳送報價。

換句話說 numbers → price estimate

Actual Test 5

PART 3

 19

313

Questions 62-64 refer to the following conversation and price list. 美 澳

Rockford Natural History Museum Ticket Prices	
• Regular Exhibits ···················	$18
–with audio tour ··············	$22
• Dinosaur Exhibit ················	$10
⑥ –plus movie················	$14

洛克福德自然歷史博物館 票價	
• 常態展覽 ····························	18 元
- 含語音導覽 ··················	22 元
• 恐龍展 ····························	10 元
⑥ - 外加電影 ··················	14 元

M Hi, ⑥ **I'd like a ticket to the special exhibit on dinosaurs, please.**

W Of course. Would you be interested in watching our special movie about the exhibit? ⑥ **It's not that long and it gives a bit of detail about the exhibit.**

M I see. I think I have time to watch it since it's not very long. Yes, ⑥ **I'd like a ticket with the movie.**

W Here's your ticket. And this is a brochure about our upcoming exhibits and information about becoming a museum member. Members get 10 percent off all tickets.

M Thank you. ⑥ **I'll think about joining.**

男：嗨，⑥ 我想買一張恐龍特展的門票，麻煩妳了。

女：好的。您會有興趣觀賞此特展的特映影片嗎？⑥ 片長不會很長，且會再多介紹一點此展覽。

男：原來如此。我想片長不會很長的話，我有時間觀賞。好，⑥ 那我要加上影片的門票。

女：這是您的門票。這是介紹往後展覽的手冊，還有成為博物館會員的資料。會員購買所有門票均可享有九折優惠。

男：謝謝妳。⑥ 我會考慮要不要加入。

字彙 upcoming 即將到來的

062 新增題型

Look at the graphic. How much did the man pay for his ticket?
(A) $10
(B) $14
(C) $18
(D) $22

中譯 見圖表。男子支付的票價是多少？
(A) 10 元　　　　(B) 14 元
(C) 18 元　　　　(D) 22 元

解析 本題為圖表整合題。男子表示要購買恐龍特展的門票，接著按照女子的建議購買包含觀看影片的門票。根據價格表，包含觀看影片的恐龍特展門票價格為 14 元。

063

What does the woman say about the movie?
(A) It explains the special exhibits.
(B) It has some special effects.
(C) It is very long.
(D) It runs every hour.

中譯 女子對電影有何看法？
(A) 電影講解了此特殊展覽。
(B) 電影運用一些特效。
(C) 片長很久。
(D) 每個小時播放一次。

解析 第一段對話中，女子提到影片長度不長，且會解說展覽的細節。由此段話可以得知影片會針對特展內容進行説明。

064

What does the man say he will do?
(A) Come back to the museum later
(B) Consider the woman's suggestion
(C) Join a museum club
(D) Watch the movie another day

中譯 男子表示自己會做什麼？
(A) 晚一點再過來博物館　　(B) 考慮女子的建議
(C) 加入博物館俱樂部　　　(D) 改天再看電影

解析 後半段對話中，女子提到成為博物館會員能享有的優惠，而後男子表示會考慮看看是否加入。這表示男子願意考慮女子的建議；(C) 男子尚未表示要加入會員，因此該選項並不正確。

Questions 65-67 refer to the following conversation and bookshelf. 英 澳

Mystery	Biography
Science Fiction	67 Horror
History	Fantasy

懸疑類	自傳類
科幻類	67 驚悚類
歷史類	奇幻類

M Excuse me. I'm looking for a book I heard about on the radio. Something with *Hotel* in the title. It's set in 19th century Europe.

W You must be talking about *Hotel Metropole*. 65 It's gotten great reviews! We can hardly keep it on the shelves.

M Yes, that's it! Oh, I hope you still have a copy. 66 If I like it, I'm going to recommend it to my book club.

W I'm sure we do because I stocked them this morning. 67 They're over there next to the science fiction. You see? Below the biographies?

M Ah, yes. Thank you so much.

男：不好意思，我在找我從廣播上聽到的一本書。書名中有「飯店」兩個字，故事背景是 19 世紀的歐洲。

女：您要找的一定是《大都會飯店》。65 它的評價超好！我們幾乎一上架就賣光。

男：對，就是這本！喔，我希望你們還有存貨。66 如果我看完後很喜歡，我要向我的讀書會推薦這本書。

女：我們一定還有貨，因為我今天早上才補貨，67 就放在科幻類書籍的旁邊。看到了嗎？在自傳類書籍下方？

男：啊，看到了。真的很感謝妳。

字彙 be set in 背景設於　stock 儲備，進貨　biography 自傳

065

What does the woman say about the book?
(A) It has gotten mixed reviews.
(B) It is difficult to read.
(C) It is popular.
(D) It is set in Europe.

中譯 女子對此書有何看法？
(A) 此書的評價不一。
(B) 此書很艱澀難懂。
(C) 此書很受歡迎。
(D) 此書故事背景在歐洲。

解析 第一段對話中，女子提到那本書的評價很好，放到書架上馬上就會賣掉，等於表示那本書非常受歡迎。

066

Why does the man want to read the book?
(A) He needs to read it for an assignment.
(B) He wants to see if it is worth recommending.
(C) He read a rare review of the book.
(D) The woman highly recommended it.

中譯 男子為何想閱讀此書？
(A) 他為了交作業而閱讀。
(B) 他想知道是否值得推薦。
(C) 他讀到關於此書罕見的評價。
(D) 女子大力推薦。

解析 第二段對話中，男子表示如果看完喜歡的話，他想要推薦給讀書會的人。這段話表示他想先看看這本是否值得推薦。

067 新增題型

Look at the graphic. What type of book is the man looking for?
(A) Fantasy
(B) History
(C) Horror
(D) Mystery

中譯 見圖表。男子想找哪一類的書籍？
(A) 奇幻類　　　(B) 歷史類
(C) 驚悚類　　　(D) 懸疑類

解析 本題為圖表整合題。女子告知書籍放置位置，提到放在科幻類隔壁，自傳類下方。根據書架位置圖，書本放在「驚悚類」區域。

19

Questions 68-70 refer to the following conversation and list. 加 美

— Inventory List—		
Item No.	Fabric	Amount in Stock
C92	Cotton	18 meters
Ch19	Chiffon	1 meter
⑦ G05	Gauze	10 meters
W83	Wool	7 meters

庫存清單		
品項編號	布料	庫存量
C92	棉質	18 公尺
Ch19	雪紡紗	1 公尺
⑦ G05	薄紗	10 公尺
W83	羊毛	7 公尺

W　Hi, I was hoping to get some fabric for a piece of art I'm working on. It's pretty big, so I'd need a lot of it.

M　❻❽ **What kind of fabric were you looking for?** Wool or cotton or . . . ?

W　I need something very light and almost see-through. I was thinking of chiffon or gauze.

M　I'm looking at the stock information on my computer, and I'm afraid we only have a small amount of chiffon. We could order it from our other stores and that would take, uh, probably about a week.

W　Hmm, ❻❾ **I'd like to finish my piece on the weekend.** I think ⑦ **I'll go with the gauze.**

女：嗨，我目前正在創作一件藝術品，我想找些布料當素材。作品相當大件，所以我需要很多布料。

男：❻❽ 您想找哪一類的布料？羊毛？棉質布料？還是⋯⋯

女：我需要很輕薄、幾乎透明的布料。我想應該是雪紡紗或薄紗。

男：我現在正在查看電腦上的存貨資料，我們恐怕只剩少量的雪紡紗。我們可以從其他門市訂貨，呃，可能需要約一週時間。

女：嗯，❻❾ 我想在這週末完成我的作品。我想 ⑦ 我選薄紗好了。

字彙 **see-through** 透明的　**chiffon** 雪紡紗　**inventory** 存貨

068

Where is this conversation most likely taking place?
(A) At a restaurant
(B) At a clothing store
(C) **At a fabric store**
(D) At an art store

中譯 此對話最有可能發生在哪一個場所？
(A) 餐廳　　　　　(B) 服飾店
(C) 布店　　　　　(D) 美術用品店

解析 對話開頭，女子表示自己正在尋找用在藝術作品上的布料，而後男子詢問她要找什麼材質的布料。由此段對話可以得知對話發生的地點在布店。

069

What does the woman say she is doing this weekend?
(A) Going to a gallery
(B) **Completing a piece of art**
(C) Checking inventory
(D) Working at her company

中譯 女子說她本週末要做什麼？
(A) 去藝廊　　　　(B) 完成一件藝術品
(C) 盤點庫存　　　(D) 在公司上班

解析 男子提到女子想要的布料現場只剩少量，而後女子表示她想在週末完成作品。

換句話說 finish my piece → completing a piece of art

070 新增題型

Look at the graphic. Which fabric will the woman buy?
(A) C92
(B) Ch19
(C) **G05**
(D) W83

中譯 見圖表。女子將購買哪種布料？
(A) C92　　　　　(B) Ch19
(C) G05　　　　　(D) W83

解析 本題為圖表整合題。最後一段對話中，女子表示她要買薄紗，根據存貨清單，薄紗的產品編號為 G05。

Questions 71-73 refer to the following telephone message. 澳

Hello. My name is Melanie Nevins and ❼ I'm planning on attending your winery's grand opening next week. ❼ When I sent in my reservation card, I marked one person, but I'd like to update that to two people. ❼ A friend of mine from California will be in town and I thought he might enjoy seeing our local wine being produced. You can reach me at 555-1871 if you have any questions. Thanks for restoring the old winery and opening it up to the public. I'm looking forward to the event next week.

哈囉，我叫梅蘭妮・尼芬斯，❼ 我打算參加你們釀酒廠下週舉辦的盛大開幕。❼ 我寄出訂位卡時，只有勾選一人，但我想更新為兩人。❼ 我從加州來的朋友會來此城鎮，我想他應該會對我們當地葡萄酒的生產方式感興趣。如有任何疑問，你們可以回撥 555-1871 給我。感謝你們重建舊的釀酒廠，並開放大眾參觀。我很期待下週的活動。

字彙 winery 釀酒廠　produce 生產　restore 重建

071

What event is the speaker attending next week?
(A) A building dedication
(B) A local festival
(C) A restaurant opening
(D) A winery tour

中譯 說話者下週要參加什麼活動？
(A) 落成典禮　　　　(B) 當地慶典
(C) 餐廳開幕典禮　　(D) 釀酒廠之旅

解析 本文為電話留言，告知對方要多增加一名參加者。前半段留言中提到要參加的是酒廠開幕活動（attending your winery's grand opening），由此可以得知說話者下週要去參觀酒廠。

字彙 building dedication 落成典禮

072

Why does the speaker ask the listener to contact her?
(A) To answer a question about the event
(B) To confirm an additional guest
(C) To cancel her attendance
(D) To give directions to the event

中譯 說話者為何請聽話者聯絡她？
(A) 以便回答活動相關問題
(B) 以便確認多加一名來賓
(C) 以便取消出席
(D) 以便指示前往活動的交通路線

解析 說話者的要求與來電目的有關。當中提到當初訂位卡上只標註一人參加，現在想改成兩人參加（update that to two people）。由此可以推測說話者請聽者聯絡自己，為的是確認追加的人數（additional guest）。

073

Who does the speaker mention is coming to visit?
(A) A business contact
(B) A business owner
(C) A friend
(D) A relative

中譯 說話者提到何者會陪同造訪？
(A) 生意夥伴　　　(B) 公司老闆
(C) 朋友　　　　　(D) 親戚

解析 說話者告知追加參加者的理由，並提到朋友來自加州，他應該會喜歡當地生產的葡萄酒。

🎧20

We are so honored tonight to have renowned French Chef Pascal **㉔ here at our community cooking club** to **㉕ show us how to make French food at home**. It really isn't as hard as it looks. **㉖ Chef Pascal has been cooking since he was eight years old**, and as he says in his new book, his mother taught him more about cooking than he ever learned in cooking school. Tonight, he will be making bouillabaisse and ratatouille. These two dishes combined are a simple and satisfying meal the whole family can enjoy. Let's give a warm welcome to Chef Pascal.

我們今晚十分榮幸,能請到法國名廚帕斯柯 ㉔ 來到我們社區的烹飪社,㉕ 向大家示範如何在家也能做出法式料理。其實沒有看起來的那麼困難。㉖ 大廚帕斯柯從八歲就開始接觸烹飪,他的新書裡有說,母親傳授他的烹飪經驗,比他在烹飪學校學到的知識還多。今晚,他將烹煮馬賽魚湯和普羅旺斯燉菜。這兩道菜搭配在一起,就會是簡單又有飽足感的一餐,適合全家享用。我們一起來歡迎大廚帕斯柯。

字彙 renowned 知名的　satisfying 令人滿足的

074

Who most likely are the listeners?
(A) Book club members
(B) Bookstore employees
(C) Community leaders
(D) Cooking club members

中譯 聽話者最有可能是誰?
(A) 讀書會成員
(B) 書店員工
(C) 社區領導人
(D) 烹飪社成員

解析 說話者介紹演講者,並提到:「here at our community cooking club」,由此可以得知聽者為烹飪社成員。

075

According to the speaker, what will Mr. Pascal be doing soon?
(A) Demonstrating a skill
(B) Reading from his book
(C) Signing his book
(D) Taking questions from listeners

中譯 根據說話者,帕斯柯先生很快會進行什麼事?
(A) 示範烹飪技巧
(B) 朗讀他的著作
(C) 在他的著作簽名
(D) 回答聽眾的問題

解析 前半段介紹中,帕斯柯先生將示範如何在家製作法式料理,等同於向烹飪社示範烹飪的技巧;(B) 僅於介紹時提到帕斯柯先生的書;(D) 並未提及是否開放聽者提問。

字彙 demonstrate 展示,示範

076

When did Mr. Pascal's interest in his chosen field start?
(A) After he wrote his first book
(B) In his childhood
(C) When he left France for the first time
(D) While he was in cooking school

中譯 帕斯柯先生何時開始對他選擇的領域產生興趣?
(A) 撰寫第一本書以後
(B) 童年時期
(C) 第一次離開法國時
(D) 他在烹飪學校的時候

解析 介紹中段提到帕斯柯先生從八歲開始做料理,也就是指帕斯柯先生在小時候對料理產生興趣。

Attention passengers. ❼ **We are about to pull into dock at Marina 7.** ❽ **Please line up at the door near the snack bar on the upper deck to exit. Only this exit on the front of the boat will be open.** When you disembark, please make sure to bring all your belongings with you. There is a tourist information center as you step off the ramp, just in front of the fountain. ❼❾ **The staff at the center speak Chinese, Japanese, Korean, and English.** We are happy you chose Sea Star Lines for your journey today. Please come sail with us again.

旅客請注意。❼我們即將停靠在瑪蓮娜 7 號碼頭。❽請在上層甲板的點心吧旁的門口排隊，等候下船。我們僅開放船隻前方的這個出口。您走下斜坡道後，在噴泉前方有一個旅客服務中心。❼❾服務中心的人員會說中文、日文、韓文和英文。很高興您今日的旅程選擇海洋之星航線。歡迎再度與我們航行。

字彙 **pull into** 駛入……後停下　**disembark**（旅途結束後）下交通工具　**ramp** 斜坡道　**fountain** 噴泉　**sail** 航行

077

Where is the announcement being made?
(A) **On a boat**
(B) On a tour bus
(C) On a train
(D) On an airplane

中譯 這段廣播是在哪裡撥放的？
(A) 在船上
(B) 遊覽車上
(C) 火車上
(D) 飛機上

解析 本篇獨白為船上的廣播，告知乘客下船方式。獨白中直接提及 **dock**、**boat** 等相關單字。

078

What is located near the snack bar?
(A) A tourist information counter
(B) Stairs to the exit
(C) The bathrooms
(D) **The only available exit**

中譯 點心吧附近有什麼？
(A) 遊客服務櫃台
(B) 出口樓梯
(C) 廁所
(D) 唯一可用的出口

解析 說話者要求至上層甲板點心吧附近的門排隊，並告知僅開放前方的出口（**Only this exit on the front of the boat will be open.**）。這表示點心吧附近有唯一可用的出口（**the only available exit**）；(B) 廣播中並未提到 **stairs**。

079

Who speaks multiple languages?
(A) Restaurant servers
(B) **Staff at a service center**
(C) The snack bar employees
(D) The crew of the boat

中譯 何者能說多國語言？
(A) 餐廳服務人員
(B) 服務中心的人員
(C) 點心吧員工
(D) 船員

解析 廣播中先告知旅客服務中心的位置，同時提到服務中心的員工通曉中文、日文、韓文和英文，由此可以得知服務中心的員工會說多種語言。

換句話說 tourist information center → service center

Actual Test 5

PART 4

🎧 20

If you have been disappointed with language learning systems in the past, you'll be pleasantly surprised by the newest release from EduLang. **80** *Say Hello!* **is a Web-based language learning program** that helps you become fluent in a foreign language within six weeks. **81 It uses repetition and cool graphics to help you make progress and to keep you coming back.** For one low monthly fee, you can use *Say Hello!* on your mobile phone or PC at home or office. Started by educators in several fields nearly a decade ago, **82 EduLang is the award winning company** that has released some of the most popular educational software in the country.

如果您過去對於語言學習系統感到失望，您將對伊都藍恩最新發行的系統感到驚喜。**80**「說哈囉！」是以網站為中心的語言學習課程，能在六週內幫助您學好流利外語。**81** 這個課程使用重複解說與酷炫圖片，能幫助您有所進步，讓您願意繼續回來上課。只要繳交低廉的月費，就能在手機、家用電腦或辦公室的電腦使用「說哈囉！」。由若干領域的教育人士於將近十年前所創的伊都藍恩，**82** 是一間屢獲殊榮的公司，在國內發行一些最受歡迎的教育軟體。

字彙 foreign language 外語　repetition 重複　make progress 進步

080

What product is being advertised?
(A) A learning app
(B) A book series
(C) A language camp program
(D) A language private lesson

中譯 廣告中的產品為何？
(A) 學習應用程式
(B) 系列叢書
(C) 語言營課程
(D) 語言家教課程

解析 本篇獨白為語言學習應用程式的廣告，請務必掌握產品的名稱為「Say Hello!」。當中介紹它是以網頁為基礎製作的語言學習程式（Web-based language learning program），也就是不需安裝軟體程式，打開瀏覽器即可使用的學習應用程式。

換句話說 Web-based learning program → learning app

081

According to the advertisement, how does *Say Hello!* keep users motivated?
(A) By offering discounts regularly
(B) By offering level-up incentives
(C) By using interesting images
(D) By using popular music

中譯 根據廣告，「說哈囉！」以何種方式保持用戶的學習動力？
(A) 定期提供折扣
(B) 提供晉級獎勵
(C) 使用有趣的影像
(D) 使用流行音樂

解析 雖然廣告中並未直接提到 motivate，但當中表示使用反覆學習和酷炫的圖像幫助學習，達到持之以恆的效果（help you make progress and to keep you coming back）。選項中最適當的答案為使用有趣的圖片。

換句話說 cool graphics → interesting images

字彙 incentive 獎勵

082

What is mentioned about EduLang?
(A) It has received honors.
(B) It is a start-up in the software industry.
(C) It is the most popular company in the industry.
(D) It was started by technology experts.

中譯 關於伊都藍恩，文中提及什麼？
(A) 曾獲得榮譽。
(B) 是軟體產業的新興公司。
(C) 是該產業最熱門的公司。
(D) 由科技專家所創。

解析 廣告開頭提到由伊都藍恩公司推出應用程式，而在後半段廣告中，又介紹該公司曾經得獎（award winning company）。

換句話說 award winning → received honors

字彙 honor 榮譽　start-up 新興小型公司

Questions 83-85 refer to the following telephone message. 澳

Hi, Dominic, ❽ this is Claudia from Personnel. I got all the paperwork on ❽ your new marketing department employee, George Barnes, this morning. Thank you. Um, I noticed that one of the forms is not complete. I'm not sure why that is, but maybe he didn't see that it had a back side. Anyway, ❽ I was hoping to finalize everything later today. Since Payroll needs to add him to the records soon, ❽ could you let him stop by my office to finish up the paperwork? Thanks, Dominic.

嗨，多明尼克，❽ 我是人事部的克勞蒂亞。我今天早上已經拿到 ❽ 你們行銷部新員工喬治‧巴恩斯的所有文件資料，謝謝你。嗯，我發現有一張表格尚未完成。我不確定為什麼會這樣，也許是他沒看到還有背面要寫。總之，❽ 我希望今天晚一點能處理完所有事務，因為工資部門需要儘早把他加進檔案中。❽ 可以請你叫他過來我辦公室填妥文件嗎？謝謝你，多明尼克。

字彙 back side 背面　payroll 工資部門

083

What department does the speaker work in?
(A) Marketing
(B) Payroll
(C) Personnel
(D) Sales

中譯 說話者在哪一個部門工作？
(A) 行銷部
(B) 工資部
(C) 人事部
(D) 業務部

解析 本篇獨白為給多明尼克的留言，說話者表明自己是 Claudia from Personnel。

084 新增題型

What does the speaker mean when she says, "I was hoping to finalize everything later today"?
(A) She wants Dominic to call her soon.
(B) She wants Dominic to hurry up.
(C) She wants help on her final report.
(D) She wants to leave early.

中譯 說話者說「我希望今天晚一點能處理完所有事務」是什麼意思？
(A) 她希望多明尼克儘快打電話給她。
(B) 她希望多明尼克動作快。
(C) 她希望有人幫她完成最終報告。
(D) 她想早點下班。

解析 「I was hoping to finalize everything later today」如同字面上的意思，表示自己想在今天之內完成工作，這表示催促聽者加快速度的意思。

20

085

Who needs to visit the speaker's office today?
(A) Dominic
(B) George
(C) The marketing boss
(D) The payroll director

中譯 何者需要在今天前往說話者的辦公室？
(A) 多明尼克
(B) 喬治
(C) 行銷部主管
(D) 工資部總監

解析 留言最後，要求「他」到自己的辦公室完成工作。此處的「他」指的是行銷部門新進員工喬治‧巴恩斯，說話者於留言開頭提到今天在處理有關他的資料。

Questions 86-88 refer to the following radio broadcast. 美

Good morning and thank you for listening to KWAL. 86 Before we get back to the classical music, I'd like to let everyone know about a fantastic event coming up at the downtown amphitheater. 87 Our local chamber orchestra, The Walden Strings, led by conductor Marshall Young, will be giving free concerts both Saturday afternoon and Sunday evening. These concerts are sponsored by Walden Bank and the local business association. 88 Seating is limited and tickets will be available starting Wednesday morning. 86 Let's return now to a piece by Bach.

早安，謝謝大家收聽 KWAL。86 我們回到古典樂之前，我想先讓大家知道，市區圓形劇場即將舉辦超棒的活動。87 我們當地由馬修‧楊指揮家領軍的室內管弦樂團——沃爾登絃樂，將於週六下午和週日傍晚舉辦免費音樂會。音樂會均由沃爾登銀行和當地商會贊助。88 座位有限，週三早上可開始索取入場券。86 現在我們再回到巴哈的作品。

字彙 chamber orchestra 室內管弦樂團　conductor 指揮家

086

What type of radio program does the speaker host?
(A) Classical music
(B) Local news
(C) Rock and roll
(D) Talk show

中譯 說話者主持的是什麼類型的廣播節目？
(A) 古典樂
(B) 當地新聞
(C) 搖滾樂
(D) 脫口秀

解析 廣播開頭提到古典音樂（classical music），介紹完活動後，又把話題轉回巴哈的作品。這表示說話者正在主持與古典音樂有關的廣播節目。

087

According to the speaker, who is Marshall Young?
(A) A bank employee
(B) A local business leader
(C) An orchestra conductor
(D) A radio station worker

中譯 根據說話者的描述，誰是馬修‧楊？
(A) 銀行員工
(B) 當地企業的領導人
(C) 管弦樂團指揮
(D) 廣播電台員工

解析 廣播中段提到由馬修‧楊指揮（led by conductor Marshall Young,）室內管弦樂團。

088 新增題型

What does the speaker imply when he says, "Seating is limited"?
(A) Listeners are eligible to reserve special tickets.
(B) Listeners can get only front seats.
(C) Listeners can reserve tickets for Wednesday only.
(D) Listeners have to get tickets soon.

中譯 說話者說「座位有限」是什麼意思？
(A) 聽眾有資格預約特殊票券。
(B) 聽眾僅能坐前排座位。
(C) 聽眾僅能預訂週三的票券。
(D) 聽眾必須儘快訂票。

解析 廣播中提到座位數量有限後，並補充週三上午開賣。這暗示座位不多請聽眾盡快購票。

Questions 89-91 refer to the following telephone message. 加

Hi, Marilyn. (89) I'm calling to say a big congratulations on getting Employee of the Year. When I heard the news, I was not surprised in the least. (90) No one deserves this more than you. (91) You've been working so hard on the opening of our new branches in two states, plus training your team leaders. I'd like to treat you to a drink some time this week. Please let me know when you are free. You can ask your husband to join us if you like. See you soon, Marilyn.

嗨，瑪莉蓮。(89) 我打來是想恭喜妳得到年度最佳員工獎。我聽到這個消息時，真的一點都不驚訝，(90) 因為沒有人比妳更適合得到此獎項。(91) 妳非常努力地籌畫在兩個州建立新分公司的事，也很努力在訓練團隊領導人，我想這週找個時間請妳喝一杯。請再跟我說妳什麼時候有空，妳也可以邀請妳先生一起來。瑪莉蓮，期待儘快見到妳。

字彙 in the least 一點都不會

089

What is the main purpose of the call?
(A) To congratulate a colleague
(B) To inform a colleague of an award
(C) To invite a colleague out for dinner
(D) To request help from a colleague

中譯 此通電話的主要目的為何？
(A) 恭喜同事
(B) 告知某同事一個獎項
(C) 邀請同事外出吃晚餐
(D) 請同事幫忙

解析 來電的目的大多會出現在前半段留言中。當中提到打電話來是想恭喜（**say a big congratulations**）對方被選為年度最佳員工，而後還提到對方非常努力工作，這表示為公司同事的祝賀電話。

090 新增題型

What does the speaker mean when she says, "No one deserves this more than you"?
(A) Everyone hoped the listener would win.
(B) No other worker should get the award.
(C) There is no one else on the speaker's team.
(D) We all deserved a better result.

中譯 說話者說「沒有人比妳更適合得到此獎項」是什麼意思？
(A) 大家都希望聽話者能贏得此獎項。
(B) 其他人都不適合得到此獎項。
(C) 說話者的團隊沒有人選。
(D) 我們都應該獲得更棒的成果。

解析 「No one deserves this more than you.」這句話指的是沒有員工比聽者更有資格獲獎。

091

What is mentioned about the speaker's company this year?
(A) It expanded to other places.
(B) It hired many people.
(C) It moved to a new location.
(D) It won an award.

中譯 關於說話者公司今年的狀況，文中提及了什麼？
(A) 拓展至其他地方。　(B) 聘雇許多人。
(C) 已搬遷至新據點。　(D) 贏得獎項。

解析 留言中提到聽者在兩個州開設新的分公司一事付出許多心力，由此可以看出該公司今年開設了新分公司，表示事業上的擴展。

Questions 92-94 refer to the following talk. 英

Welcome everyone to tonight's year-end celebration! After a difficult two years, ㉝ **we've had an amazing turnaround at Stronghold, Inc. this year** and it's all thanks to you. Word has spread within the industry about ㉜ **how we handle data security and protect our customers**, both consumer and corporate, and ㉝ **we're now considered the industry leader.** So, how are we going to thank you all for making this a great year? Well, in addition to raises, ㉞ **we are giving you the opportunity to help grow our company overseas. We are looking for leaders, and that person could be you. If you are interested in heading a new branch, please talk to Ms. Smith in personnel.**

歡迎大家參加今晚的尾牙！熬過這兩年後，㉝ 我們強固公司今年終於時來運轉，一切都要歸功各位。㉜ 我們處理資安問題與保護客戶（包括一般顧客與企業客戶）的做法，如今已成為業界津津樂道的話題，㉝ 我們現在被譽為業界領頭羊。因此，我們該如何感謝各位為今年創下這麼漂亮的成績？除了加薪以外，㉞ 我們還要讓大家有機會協助拓展海外公司。我們想找具領導能力的人，在座的各位都有可能中選。如果大家有意願管理新分公司，請與人事部的史密斯小姐洽談。

字彙 turnaround 好轉　raise 加薪　head 領導

092

What kind of business is Stronghold, Inc.?
(A) Information security
(B) Investment
(C) Law firm
(D) Real estate

中譯 強固公司是什麼類型的公司？
(A) 資安公司　　　　(B) 投資公司
(C) 律師事務所　　　(D) 房地產公司

解析 本文為公司年末慶祝活動上針對公司成長的談話。中間提到：「handle data security and protect our customers」，表示公司從事與數據安全有關的工作，選項中最為相關的為 (A)。

換句話說 data→Information

字彙 law firm 律師事務所

093

Why has this year been good for the company?
(A) They expanded overseas.
(B) They hired experienced employees.
(C) Their reputation increased.
(D) Their sales hit a record high.

中譯 今年對此公司而言為何十分順利？
(A) 因為拓展至海外。
(B) 因為僱用經驗豐富的員工。
(C) 因為聲譽有所提升。
(D) 因為業績創新高。

解析 文中提到因客戶的資安工作做得好，在業界有口皆碑而成了領頭羊：「Word has spread within the industry . . . we're now considered the industry leader.」，由此得知公司聲譽有所提升。

字彙 hit a record high 創新高記錄

094

What is the speaker offering the listeners?
(A) Management positions
(B) Extra security
(C) Larger offices
(D) Year-end bonuses

中譯 說話者主動向聽話者提供什麼？
(A) 管理職位　　　　(B) 額外的安全保障
(C) 較大的辦公室　　(D) 年終獎金

解析 後半段獨白中，提到除了加薪之外，還為聽者提供機會（**opportunity**），同時表示對領導新分公司有興趣的人，請告知人事部門，因此公司提供的是管理職職位。

Questions 95-97 refer to the following excerpt from a meeting and chart. 澳

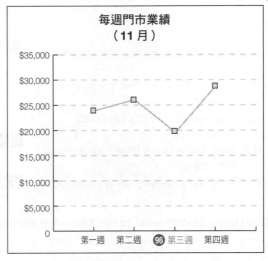

Okay, everyone, we have a lot to talk about, so let's get started. ⑨⑤ **The new store building will be ready soon and we want to have a smooth transition with the least disruption to customers and, of course, sales.** As I was trying to decide when to move, I looked at a sales chart from this time last year. ⑨⑥ **You can see that one week we weren't as busy.** Of course, we don't know that it will be the same this year. But ⑨⑦ **typically sales follow a pattern year to year.**

好的，各位，我們有好多事項要討論，趕緊開始吧。⑨⑤ 新賣場大樓很快就會開張，我們希望在不影響顧客和銷售業績的前提下，儘量安然度過這段期間。我在決定遷址時間的時候，看了一下去年同期的銷售圖表。⑨⑥ 大家可看到有其中一週，我們比較沒有那麼忙碌。當然，我們不曉得今年是否會一樣。但 ⑨⑦ 一般而言，每年的業績模式通常都差不多。

字彙 transition 過渡期　disruption 干擾　typically 一般而言　year to year 年復一年

095

What type of business is the speaker in?
(A) Hospitality
(B) Manufacturing
(C) Retail sales
(D) Construction

中譯 說話者在哪一類型的產業上班？
(A) 飯店餐飲業
(B) 製造業
(C) 零售業
(D) 營造業

解析 說話者提到新的賣場大樓（**new store building**）即將完工，希望能順利搬遷，盡可能減少對顧客和銷售的影響。選項中與賣場、顧客及銷售有關的為零售業。

Look at the graphic. When will the store likely relocate?
(A) The 1st week in November
(B) The 2nd week in November
(C) The 3rd week in November
(D) The 4th week in November

中譯 見圖表。店面最有可能於何時遷址？
(A) 11 月的第一週
(B) 11 月的第二週
(C) 11 月的第三週
(D) 11 月的第四週

解析 前方提到搬遷時，希望盡可能減少對顧客和銷售的影響。根據銷售表，選在銷售量最低的時候搬遷最為適當。說話者提到某一週特別不忙，而表中銷售量最低的一週為 11 月第三週，因此可以推測會在此週搬遷。

097

What does the speaker say about sales?
(A) They are about the same year to year.
(B) They go up during seasonal campaigns.
(C) They have been lower than usual this year.
(D) They vary greatly within a month.

中譯 說話者對業績有何看法？
(A) 每年的業績差不多。
(B) 季節活動期間的業績會攀升。
(C) 今年的業績比平時更低。
(D) 一個月內的變化極大。

解析 說話者提到在一般情況下，每年的銷售量有固定的模式（follow a pattern），等同於表示每年的銷售量差不多。

字彙 about the same 差不多　vary 變化

Questions 98-100 refer to the following announcement and store directory. 美

DIAMOND DEPARTMENT STORE
FLOOR DIRECTORY

99 4th Floor　Women's Wear
3rd Floor　Shoes
2nd Floor　Men's Wear
1st Floor　Cosmetics

鑽石百貨公司
樓層導覽

99 四樓　女裝區
三樓　鞋區
二樓　男裝區
一樓　美妝區

98 Thank you for shopping at Diamond Department Store during our annual sale. We have terrific savings on all floors this week, and today only, we have some extra special savings for women. 99 All women's outerwear, including jackets and coats, are an extra 20 percent off our already low price. You can also find great deals on children's clothing, Men's accessories and shoes for everyone in your family. 100 Don't forget to show your loyalty card when you make your purchases for a chance to win a trip for two to Hawaii in our lottery drawing.

98 感謝您光臨鑽石百貨公司的週年慶活動。我們本週所有樓層均推出大特價活動，另外僅限今日，女裝還有加碼特惠。99 包括外套與大衣等的所有女性外衣，將以已經很便宜的價格再打八折。童裝、男士配件與老少咸宜的鞋款，亦有超棒促銷活動。100 購物時別忘了出示集點卡以參加抽獎，還有機會贏得夏威夷兩人行的大獎。

字彙 terrific 超棒的　savings 省下的錢　outerwear 外衣　lottery drawing 抽獎

098

How often does the store have a sale?
(A) Every quarter
(B) Every six months
(C) Once a month
(D) Once a year

中譯 此百貨多久促銷一次?
(A) 每季
(B) 每六個月
(C) 一個月一次
(D) 一年一次

解析 本篇獨白為百貨公司的廣播通知。當中提到「**annual sale**」,表示為一年一次的優惠活動。

099 新增題型

Look at the graphic. Where can a customer receive an extra discount today?
(A) On the 1st floor
(B) On the 2nd floor
(C) On the 3rd floor
(D) On the 4th floor

中譯 見圖表。顧客今天可至何處獲得額外折扣?
(A) 一樓
(B) 二樓
(C) 三樓
(D) 四樓

解析 本題中的「額外折扣(**extra discount**)」出現在廣播中段「**extra 20 percent off**」。當中提到外套和大衣等所有的女用外衣都額外享有八折的優惠。根據樓層簡介,女性服飾位在百貨公司四樓。

100

What would a customer do for a chance to win a prize?
(A) Fill out a survey
(B) Purchase a minimum amount of goods
(C) Show a coupon
(D) Use their loyalty card

中譯 顧客該怎麼做才有機會贏得大獎?
(A) 填寫問卷
(B) 購物需達最低消費門檻
(C) 出示折價券
(D) 使用集點卡

解析 題目問的 **prize** 指的是百貨公司提供的夏威夷旅遊。廣播中提到在購物時出示集點卡(**show your loyalty card**),就有機會參加夏威夷雙人旅遊的抽獎活動。

PART 5

101

Cosmos House is a leading firm in the industry with a staff of over 200 ------- architects and designers.
(A) advanced
(B) calculated
(C) interested
(D) talented

中譯 「科斯摩斯之家」是業界裡數一數二的公司,共有超過 200 名才華洋溢的建築師與設計師。
(A) 先進的
(B) 計畫好的
(C) 感興趣的
(D) 才華洋溢的

解析 本題要選出適當的形容詞,用來修飾 **architects and designers**。該公司領先業界,其建築師和設計師使用「**talented**」形容最為適當。

字彙 calculated 計畫好的 talented 才華洋溢的

102

Immigration ------- do not permit foreigners to work in the country without the appropriate status.
(A) regulate
(B) regulation
(C) **regulations**
(D) regulatory

中譯 移民法規不允許外國人在沒有適當身分的情況下於本國工作。
(A) 調節 　　(B) 法規
(C) 法規 　　(D) 監管的

解析 空格後方連接動詞,因此空格最適合選出名詞,與前方名詞 immigration 組合成複合名詞。(B) 和 (C) 皆為名詞,但主詞的單複數要與後方的 do 一致,因此選擇 (C) 較為適當。

字彙 immigration 移民　permit 允許　appropriate 恰當的　status 身分　regulation 法規

103

------- on Mr. Gibson's team contributed to the success of the new shoe line.
(A) **Everyone**
(B) Whoever
(C) One another
(D) Each other

中譯 吉布森先生團隊裡的每個人,均對新系列鞋款的成功有所貢獻。
(A) 每個人 　　(B) 無論是誰
(C) 互相 　　(D) 彼此

解析 四個選項皆為代名詞,因此要選出最符合題意的單字。根據題意,表達「團隊裡『每個人』都為新系列鞋款的成功付出貢獻」最為適當。

104

We welcome your ------- to help us continually provide you with first-class service.
(A) motivation
(B) **feedback**
(C) invitation
(D) operation

中譯 我們歡迎您提出意見反饋,來幫助我們持續為您提供頂級服務。
(A) 激勵 　　(B) 意見反饋
(C) 邀約 　　(D) 營運

解析 句中的 you 指的是顧客。根據題意,表達「顧客的『意見反饋』有助於提供頂級的服務」最為適當。

字彙 continually 持續地　motivation 激勵　operation 營運

105

This week only, easybuy.com is offering special discounts on ------- items.
(A) **selected**
(B) selecting
(C) selection
(D) selections

中譯 easybuy.com 將針對精選商品推出本週限定的特價優惠。
(A) 精選的 　　(B) 選取
(C) 選項 　　(D) 選項

解析 空格位在介系詞 on 和名詞 items 之間,表示空格要填入形容詞。(A) 和 (B) 皆為形容詞,根據題意,表達「挑選出來的」商品要用被動語態 selected。

字彙 select 選取,精選

106

------- the software company is
relatively unknown, its new product
could help it become popular.

(A) Although
(B) Despite
(C) In addition
(D) Until

中譯 雖然此軟體公司較鮮為人知，但是他們的新品有助於打響
知名度。

(A) 雖然　　　　　　　　(B) 儘管
(C) 除此之外　　　　　　(D) 直到……為止

解析 空格後方的子句，以及逗點後方的子句中皆有動詞，因此
空格要填入連接詞。選項中，(A) 和 (D) 皆為連接詞，而根
據題意，前後為對比的內容，因此適合填入 Although；(B)
為介系詞，(C) 為副詞片語。

字彙 unknown 不知名的

107

While the delivery fee was
supposed to be $300, the supplier
charged the retailer $100 ------- on
the bill.

(A) above
(B) high
(C) more
(D) up

中譯 運送費應該只要 300 元，但供應商卻對零售商多收 100
元的帳款。

(A) 在……之上　　　　　(B) 高
(C) 更多　　　　　　　　(D) 向上

解析 句首為 While，表示逗點後方要連接相反或對比的內容。根
據題意，可以推測該句話表達的是「運費原為 300 元，但
『多』收了 100 元」。選項中，more 最適合搭配金額 100
元使用。

108

Our customer care line is available
seven days a week, ------- that no
question goes unanswered.

(A) convincing
(B) deciding
(C) ensuring
(D) featuring

中譯 我們的客服專線全年無休，以確保沒有問題會被遺漏。

(A) 說服　　　　　　　　(B) 決定
(C) 確保　　　　　　　　(D) 搭配

解析 根據題意，表達的是「客服專線一週七天皆可使用，為的
是回覆所有問題」，因此空格填入 (C)「確保」最為適當。

字彙 convince 說服

109

------- for the marketing team, the
sales campaign went exceptionally
well and received wide media
coverage.

(A) Fortunate
(B) Fortunately
(C) Fortune
(D) Fortunes

中譯 幸運的是，行銷團隊的銷售活動表異常順利，並受到各大
媒體廣泛報導。

(A) 幸運的　　　　　　　(B) 幸運地
(C) 財富　　　　　　　　(D) 財富

解析 「the sales campaign . . . media coverage」為主要子
句，空格至逗點前為副詞片語，用來修飾主要子句，因
此空格要填入副詞 (B)。

字彙 exceptionally 異常地，特別
coverage 報導

110

Wayfair Company is committed to ------- the latest software at affordable prices.

(A) provide
(B) provided
(C) provision
(D) providing

中譯 威菲爾公司致力於提供平價的最新軟體。
(A) 提供　　　　(B) 提供過
(C) 供給　　　　(D) 提供

解析 **be committed to** 的意思為「致力於……」，當中的 **to** 為介系詞，因此後方連接動詞時，要改成動名詞的形態，才能再連接受詞 the latest software。

字彙 **affordable** 平價的　**provision** 供給

111

According to the specialist, wind turbines generally work ------- better in open, rural areas than mounted on rooftops in cities.

(A) far
(B) further
(C) less
(D) more

中譯 根據專家的說法，一般來說風力發電機在廣闊鄉村區域的效用會遠比裝設於都市建物頂樓來得好。
(A) 很大的程度　(B) 進一步
(C) 較少　　　　(D) 較多

解析 空格用來修飾 **better**，適合填入副詞。所有選項皆為副詞，但只有 **far** 適合修飾比較級 **better**。

字彙 **mount** 裝設

112

If you are a ------- to the digital version of *Movie Times*, you have access to our online archives.

(A) subscribe
(B) subscriber
(C) subscribers
(D) subscription

中譯 如果你是數位版《電影時代》的訂閱者，你可進入我們的線上資料庫。
(A) 訂閱　　　　(B) 訂閱者
(C) 訂閱者　　　(D) 訂閱

解析 空格位在冠詞 **a** 和介系詞 **to** 之間，適合填入名詞。空格前方有冠詞 **a**，因此答案要選單數名詞。根據題意，這裡要選表達「訂閱者」的 **(B)**。

字彙 **archive** 資料庫

113

The division head was having a hard time choosing white ------- light gray for the wallpaper of his new office.

(A) and
(B) but
(C) nor
(D) or

中譯 此部門主管對於新辦公室的壁紙要選白色或淺灰色感到猶豫不決。
(A) 以及　　　　(B) 但是
(C) 都不是　　　(D) 或者

解析 空格前方出現動詞 **choose**，而空格前後分別連接 **white** 和 **light gray**，皆是表示顏色，因此空格最適合填入 **or**，連接前後兩個選項。

114

The CEO always says that conducting ------- research and analysis can minimize the risk of failure.

(A) complicated
(B) redundant
(C) tentative
(D) thorough

中譯 執行長總是主張，徹底研究與分析才能將失敗風險降到最低。

(A) 複雜的　　　　　(B) 累贅的
(C) 試驗性的　　　　(D) 徹底的

解析 根據題意，降低失敗的風險需要的是「徹底的、全面的」研究。

字彙 redundant 累贅的　tentative 試驗性的

115

Mark Tyler worked at Zane Industries in the early years of the company, ------- there were only a few employees.

(A) when
(B) where
(C) which
(D) whose

中譯 馬克‧泰勒在贊恩工業公司初創時於此工作，那時公司只有幾名員工。

(A) 在……的時候　　(B) 何地
(C) 哪一個　　　　　(D) 何者的

解析 空格前後各連接一個子句，且空格引導的是一個結構完整的子句，因此空格要填入關係副詞。逗點前方的「in the early years of the company」表示時間的概念，因此選擇 when 最為適當。

116

Despite her colleagues' enthusiasm about the merger, the news was ------- little interest to Lisa Olsen.

(A) at
(B) in
(C) of
(D) with

中譯 儘管同事均對合併案倍感興趣，但莉莎‧歐森卻對此消息興趣缺缺。

(A) 在……旁　　　　(B) 在……裡面
(C) 含有……的　　　(D) 與

解析 根據題意，莉莎‧歐森對於公司合併一事不怎麼感興趣。空格適合填入介系詞，連接後方名詞 interest，因此可以想到「of + 抽象名詞 = 形容詞」的用法。

字彙 enthusiasm 熱衷

117

Although the job offer was almost too ------- to pass up, Lee Boule was reluctant to commute to a different state.

(A) attracting
(B) attraction
(C) attractive
(D) attractively

中譯 雖然此職缺實在很吸引人，讓人難以放棄，但李‧波爾還是不太願意通勤到別州上班。

(A) 吸引　　　　　　(B) 吸引力
(C) 吸引人的　　　　(D) 吸引人地

解析 「too + 形容詞 + to + 動詞」的用法，其意思為「太（形容詞）……而不能（動詞）……」，因此空格要填入形容詞 (C)。

字彙 pass up 放棄　reluctant 不情願的

118

Please note that the accounting department will only provide ------- for expenses when a receipt is included with the form.
(A) reassessment
(B) reference
(C) **reimbursement**
(D) replica

中譯 請注意，會計部門僅能對附上收據的請款單提供款項補償。
(A) 重新評估　　　(B) 參考
(C) 補償　　　　　(D) 複製品

解析 針對會計部門處理費用的方式，選項中最適當的單字為 reimbursement，意思為「報銷」。

字彙 reassessment 重新評估　reference 參考
reimbursement 報銷，償還　replica 複製品

119

As Amy Lynn ------- the speech every day since last week, her colleagues believe she is ready to deliver it.
(A) could have practiced
(B) had practiced
(C) **has practiced**
(D) practices

中譯 由於艾咪・林恩從上週就開始每天練習演講，她的同事們相信她已經蓄勢待發。
(A) 原本可以練習　　(B) 曾已練習
(C) 一直練習　　　　(D) 練習

解析 本題考的是時態，請先找出表達時間的線索。第一個子句以 since last week 結尾，而主要子句的時態為現在式，因此空格最適合填入現在完成式。

字彙 deliver 發表

120

------- your inquiry about joining our association, we will be more than happy to discuss membership details.
(A) Because
(B) Likewise
(C) **Regarding**
(D) With

中譯 關於您詢問加入我們協會一事，我們將十分樂意與您討論會員資格的細節。
(A) 因為　　　　　(B) 同樣
(C) 關於　　　　　(D) 與

解析 空格至逗點為止為副詞片語，當中沒有動詞，因此請先刪去連接詞 (A)；(B) 為副詞，可以用來修飾整個子句，但是填入後並不符合題意；介系詞 Regarding 最適合搭配空格後方的 inquiry 一起使用，因此答案為 (C)。

字彙 association 協會

121

Milan Properties acquired Colton Tech's former sites, which ------- nearly one million square feet.
(A) gross
(B) net
(C) sum
(D) **total**

中譯 米蘭物業公司收購了柯爾頓科技公司之前的舊址，總面積將近一百萬平方英尺。
(A) 獲得……總收入　(B) 淨賺
(C) 計算……的總和　(D) 合計為

解析 關係代名詞 which 為主詞，因此空格要填入動詞。根據題意，表達「總面積近一百萬平方英尺」最為適當，因此答案要選在此作為及物動詞的 total，意思為「合計為」；動詞 (A) 和 (B) 要搭配金額使用；sum 為及物動詞，意思為「計算……的總和」，不符合題意。

字彙 site 地點，場所　gross 獲得……總收入　net 淨賺
sum 計算……的總和　total 合計為

122

If the administrative manager had ------- his client Ms. Ford on the street, he would have said hello to her.

(A) recognition
(B) recognize
(C) recognized
(D) recognizing

中譯　如果行政經理在街上有認出他的客戶福特小姐，他絕對會和她打招呼。

(A) 認出　　　　　　(B) 認出
(C) 已認出　　　　　(D) 認出

解析　空格位在 if 子句當中，**had** 後方連接空格加上受詞 **his client**，可以看出該句話使用與過去事實相反的假設語氣「**had + 過去分詞**」。另外，主要子句中使用「**would have + 過去分詞**」，也可以由此確認該句話表達與過去事實相反的假設。

字彙　**recognize** 認出

123

If you return the product without a receipt, you will be given a store credit, which can be applied ------- your next purchase.

(A) above
(B) over
(C) through
(D) toward

中譯　如果您在未附上收據的情況下退回產品，我們會折換為抵用金，即可於下次購物使用。

(A) 在……之上　　　(B) 在……之上
(C) 通過　　　　　　(D) 於

解析　根據題意，表達商店抵用金「適用於」下次購物。**apply to** 的意思為「適用於……」，此處以 **toward** 代替 **to** 使用。

字彙　**apply toward** 適用於

124

Sue Ellis became a section chief three years ago and was ------- promoted to sales manager the next year.

(A) chronologically
(B) continually
(C) sincerely
(D) subsequently

中譯　蘇·艾里斯三年前成為課長，隔年又接著被升遷為業務經理。

(A) 按時間順序地　　(B) 持續地
(C) 誠懇地　　　　　(D) 接著

解析　根據題意，蘇·艾里斯三年前成為課長，隔年又升遷為業務經理，因此空格填入副詞 **subsequently**（接著、隨後）最為適當；**chronologically** 表示按時間先後順序；**continually** 表示事件不停發生，皆不符合題意。

字彙　**chronologically** 按時間順序地　　**subsequently** 接著

125

The last chapter of ZDE Steel's corporate history features the company's ------- in the 1980s.

(A) expand
(B) expandable
(C) expander
(D) expansion

中譯　ZDE 鋼鐵企業的歷史最終章，以該公司於 1980 年代的拓展狀況為主。

(A) 拓展　　　　　　(B) 可拓展的
(C) 擴張器　　　　　(D) 拓展

解析　空格前方為定冠詞 **the** 加上所有格 **company's**，空格後方連接介系詞片語，因此空格適合填入名詞。**(C)** 和 **(D)** 皆為名詞，其中 **(D)** 表達公司的「擴展」最符合題意。

字彙　**expansion** 拓展

126

Under the company regulations, factory inspections have to be carried out ------- every two months.
(A) during
(B) once
(C) then
(D) within

中譯 根據公司法規，必須每兩個月執行一次工廠檢查。
(A) 在……期間 　　(B) 一次
(C) 然後 　　(D) 在……之內

解析 該句話的主詞為 factory inspections，動詞為 have to be carried out。動詞使用的是被動語態，因此空格適合填入副詞或介系詞，用來連接後方的 every two months。根據題意，表達「每兩個月一次」最為適當。

127

With the most ------- carry-on luggage, travelers will avoid the inconveniences during the trip.
(A) rigorous
(B) comparable
(C) vigorous
(D) durable

中譯 有了最耐用的隨身行李箱，旅客就能避免旅途中的不便。
(A) 嚴格的 　　(B) 可比較的
(C) 健壯的 　　(D) 耐用的

解析 空格要填入適合搭配後方 carry-on luggage 使用的形容詞。根據題意，選項中只有 durable 意思通順。

字彙 carry-on luggage 隨身行李箱　rigorous 嚴格的
comparable 可比較的　vigorous 健壯的
durable 耐用的

128

The automobile company has announced a recall of over one million cars because their airbags were ------- manufactured.
(A) defect
(B) defective
(C) defectively
(D) defects

中譯 此汽車公司已宣布召回一百多萬輛汽車，因為安全氣囊製造時出現瑕疵。
(A) 瑕疵 　　(B) 有瑕疵的
(C) 有瑕疵地 　　(D) 瑕疵

解析 空格位在動詞 were 和 manufactured 之間，因此只能填入副詞。

字彙 recall 召回　manufacture 製造
defectively 有瑕疵地

129

Some psychological treatments may have more ------- effects than other treatments.
(A) last
(B) lasting
(C) lasted
(D) lastly

中譯 某些心理諮商療程的效果可能比其他療法還要持久。
(A) 上一個的 　　(B) 持久的
(C) 持續 　　(D) 最後

解析 空格位在副詞 more 後方，名詞 effects 前方，因此要填入形容詞。根據題意，表達「特定療程比其他療程的效果更為『持久』」較為適當。

字彙 psychological 心理的　treatment 療程　last 上一個的
lasting 持久的

130

To make an official purchase agreement, a director must hand in ------- from at least two potential vendors.
(A) applications
(B) **estimates**
(C) requirements
(D) comprises

中譯 要簽訂正式的採購合約，主管必須交出至少兩家潛在供應商的估價單。
(A) 申請表　　　　　(B) 估價單
(C) 規定　　　　　　(D) 由……組成

解析 請選出必須繳交（**hand in**）的東西。根據題意，為簽訂採購合約，主管必須交出潛在供應商的某樣東西。選項中，填入 **estimates** 最為適當，意思為「估價單、報價單」。

字彙 purchase agreement 採購合約　vendor 供應商
comprise 由……組成

PART 6

Questions 131-134 refer to the following notice. 通知

Oak Grove Library Presents Business Lunch Hour

On Tuesday, November 7 from 11:30 AM to 12:30 PM, the Oak Grove Library will ------- a free Business Lunch Hour.
131.
Entrepreneurs and small business owners are invited to bring ------- own lunch and meet at the Oak Grove Library
132.
to learn digital skills to help their businesses grow. James Olson, owner of Digital Age, will share ten ways you can boost your visibility online for free. This event is presented in ------- with the Monroe Country Chamber of Commerce.
133.
-------.
134.

歐克葛羅夫圖書館主辦商務午餐聚會

　　11月7日週二的早上11:30到中午12:30，歐克葛羅夫圖書館即將 ⓲ 舉辦免費的商務午餐聚會。我們歡迎創業家與小型企業老闆攜帶 ⓲ 他們自己的午餐，前來歐克葛羅夫圖書館相聚，學習有助於企業成長的數位妙招。數位年代的老闆詹姆斯‧歐森，將免費分享可提升網路曝光率的十種方法。此活動是與孟羅鄉商會 ⓲ 協力舉辦。⓲ 如需了解更多資訊，請撥打 555-2591 聯絡詹姆斯。

字彙 entrepreneur 創業家　boost 提升　visibility 曝光率

131

(A) cater
(B) establish
(C) **host**
(D) plan

中譯 (A) 為……提供外燴　(B) 建立
(C) 舉辦　　　　　　(D) 計劃

解析 主詞為圖書館，後方連接商務午餐會，因此填入 (C) 最符合文意，表示「舉辦」。文中提及明確的時間和活動內容，因此並不適合填入 (D)「計劃」。

字彙 host 舉辦

132

(A) theirs
(B) them
(C) **their**
(D) themselves

中譯 (A) 他們的人事物　(B) 他們
(C) 他們的　　　　(D) 他們自己

解析 主詞為創業家與小企業老闆，因此空格要填入代替他們的代名詞。「**own** + 名詞」前方要使用所有格。

Actual Test 5

PART 6

335

133

(A) collaborate
(B) **collaboration**
(C) collaborative
(D) collaboratively

中譯 (A) 協力   (B) 協力
(C) 協力的   (D) 協力地

解析 空格前後皆為介系詞，表示空格要填入名詞，組合成介系詞片語。「in collaboration with」的意思為「與……合作」。

字彙 in collaboration with 與……合作

134 新增題型

(A) **For more information, call James at 555-2591.**
(B) Participants will be charged a small fee at the door.
(C) The event will be called off in case of rain.
(D) The library will be closed on Monday, November 6.

中譯 (A) 如需了解更多資訊，請撥打 555-2591 聯絡詹姆斯。
(B) 參加者需於進場前繳交小額費用。
(C) 如遇下雨，此活動則將取消。
(D) 圖書館將於 11 月 6 日週一閉館。

解析 本活動為免費參加，因此 (B) 並不正確；(C) 圖書館內舉辦活動，並未提及與戶外有關的內容；(D) 並未有相關說明，因此該選項也不正確；活動說明最後，適合放上索取更多資訊的方式，因此填入 (A) 最為適當。

字彙 call off 取消   in case of rain 如遇下雨

Questions 135-138 refer to the following article. 文章

San Marcos opening new store in Harriston

HARRISTON—Harriston is getting its first San Marcos. The coffee shop chain announced its ------- for a store
135.
in Harriston on Tuesday. It says the store, due to open in February next year, is part of its initiative, which -------
136.
three years ago to invest in more rural communities across the nation. -------. San Marcos also plans to
137.
work with locally-owned businesses to supply products for the store. Harriston officials have said they're excited about the store, believing it will help ------- more foot
138.
traffic to the downtown area.

聖馬克斯於哈里斯頓的新門市即將開張

　　哈里斯頓快訊——哈里斯頓即將迎來第一家聖馬克斯門市。此連鎖咖啡廳於週二宣布即將於哈里斯頓設店的 ⑬ 計畫。該公司表示，預計明年二月開張的此門市是聖馬克斯新計畫的一環，該計畫 ⑯ 始於三年前，目標是在全國各地鄉村進行投資。⑰ 公司主管表示，他們的目標在於為當地年輕人創造就業機會。聖馬克斯亦預計與當地自營事業合作，以他們作為門市產品的供應商。哈里斯頓政府官員表示十分期待門市進駐，並且相信門市能為市區 ⑱ 帶來更多客流量。

字彙 initiative 新計畫   rural community 農業社區   across the nation 全國各地
foot traffic 人流量，踩點量

135

(A) developments
(B) operations
(C) **plans**
(D) promises

中譯 (A) 發展   (B) 營運
(C) 計畫   (D) 承諾

解析 本文為公司開設新門市的報導，提到公司將在哈里斯頓開設分店的「計畫」。

136

(A) began
(B) had begun
(C) have begun
(D) will have begun

中譯 (A) 開始   (B) 曾已開始
(C) 已開始   (D) 早將已開始

解析 本題要選出適當的動詞時態，放在關係代名詞 **which** 的後方。空格後方連接 **three years ago**，表示過去的時間點，因此空格適合填入過去簡單式。

137 新增題型

(A) Company officials say their goal is to create job opportunities for local youth.
(B) San Marcos grows its own beans in several Latin America and African countries.
(C) The investment is expected to be safe for retired couples and young people alike.
(D) Rural communities are usually the last to benefit from economic upturns.

中譯 (A) 公司主管表示，他們的目標在於為當地年輕人創造就業機會。
(B) 聖馬克斯於若干拉丁美洲和非洲國家自種咖啡豆。
(C) 此投資方案預計對退休夫婦與年輕人而言都十分安全。
(D) 農業社區通常是最後受惠於經濟復甦的區塊。

解析 空格前方提到公司打算對鄉村地區進行投資，開設新門市便屬於計畫之一；空格後方則提到與當地企業合作的規畫。(A) 表達公司的目標就是為當地的年輕人創造就業機會，最符合前後文意；(B) 的敘述與此無關；(C) 和 (D) 偏離本篇報導的主題。

字彙 retired 退休的   upturn 好轉

138

(A) bring
(B) keep
(C) offer
(D) occur

中譯 (A) 帶來   (B) 維持
(C) 主動提供   (D) 發生

解析 根據前後文意，表達「能為市區『帶來』更多人潮」最為適當。**bring** 的意思為「帶來、拿來、引起」。

Questions 139-142 refer to the following e-mail. 電子郵件

From:	Henri Saveaux <hsaveaus@visitparis.fr>
To:	Amalia Francis <amaliaf@bloggers.net>
Date:	December 12
Subject:	Permission to reprint

Dear Ms. Francis,

I work for a small publishing company in Paris. We put out an English tourist magazine about France every quarter. We noticed your blog post on toursaroundtheworld.com. It was very ------- written and has some good pictures and maps. -------. Of course, **139.** **140.** we would pay you the ------- rate for contributions to our **141.** magazine. Your writing is so captivating—we're wondering if you'd like to be a regular contributor.

寄件人：亨利・薩沃 <hsaveaus@visitparis.fr>
收件人：亞瑪麗亞・法蘭西斯 <amaliaf@bloggers.net>
日期：12 月 12 日
主旨：轉登文章許可

親愛的法蘭西斯小姐：

    我任職於巴黎的小型出版社。我們每一季都會出版一本介紹法國的英語觀光雜誌。我們在 toursaroundtheworld.com 發現您的部落格文章。內容十分❶³⁹有趣，且具有很棒的照片和地圖。❶⁴⁰我們覺得讀者會很喜歡此篇文章，因此想詢問您可否讓我們刊登於二月號雜誌。當然，我們會依照❶⁴¹行情來支付您投稿雜誌的稿費。您的文筆十分引人入勝，想請問您是否願意定期投稿。再請您回覆是否同意上

Please let us know if you agree to ------- or both offers.
142.
Thank you,
Henri Saveaux

述 ⑫ 任一或全部提案。

謝謝您，

亨利・薩沃

字彙 **publishing company** 出版社　**put out** 出版　**contribution** 投稿；貢獻　**captivating** 引人入勝的

139

(A) entertain
(B) entertaining
(C) entertainingly
(D) entertainment

中譯 (A) 使……娛樂
(B) 娛樂的
(C) 有趣地
(D) 娛樂

解析 空格位在被動語態（**was written**）之間，前方為副詞 **very**，後方為被動型態的動詞 **written**，因此空格要填入副詞。

字彙 **entertainingly** 有趣地

140 新增題型

(A) Each of our issues is focused on a different city around the world, and next time it's Berlin.
(B) Your illustrations were beautiful and we'd like to hang them in our gallery in Paris.
(C) We think our readers would like it and are wondering if we can print it in our February issue.
(D) When you return to Paris, please visit our new office near the River Seine.

中譯 (A) 我們每一期雜誌重點介紹世界各地的不同城市，下一期將介紹柏林。
(B) 您的插畫十分優美，我們希望能在我們巴黎的藝廊展出。
(C) 我們覺得讀者會很喜歡此篇文章，因此想詢問您可否讓我們刊登於二月號雜誌。
(D) 您返回巴黎時，請造訪我們靠近塞納河的新辦公室。

解析 電子郵件寄件人於空格前方表示對方的文章寫得很好，於空格後方提到支付稿費一事，因此空格最適合填入詢問對方「是否能將該文章刊登至雜誌上」的相關敘述。

字彙 **issue** （出版品）一期

141

(A) beneficial
(B) less
(C) reduced
(D) usual

中譯 (A) 有益的　　　　(B) 較少的
(C) 減少的　　　　(D) 慣常的

解析 空格後方連接 **rate**，意思為「費用」，因此要選出適合搭配使用的單字。使用 **usual rate** 最為適當，意思為「一般行情」。

字彙 **reduced** 減少的

142

(A) all
(B) either
(C) many
(D) neither

中譯 (A) 所有的　　　　(B) 兩者選一的
(C) 許多的　　　　(D) 兩者皆非的

解析 前方向收件人提出兩個方案，分別是刊登文章支付對方稿費，以及定期合作刊登文章。該句話請對方告知同意「兩者中的其中一個」方案，或是兩者都同意。

Questions 143-146 refer to the following information. 資訊

Museums Saver Ticket

Buy a museums saver ticket to the Fashion Museum, the Roman Museum, and Torrance Art Gallery and save big on entry prices! ------. You can ------ a saver ticket
143. **144.**
online, at the front desks, or from the Tourist Information Center.

- Adults: £21.50
- Seniors (65 and over) / Students: £18.50
- Children (age 6–16): £11.75
- Groups of more than 20 people: £13.00 each

Season Ticket

------ value for entry for one full year to the Fashion
145.
Museum, the Roman Museum, and Torrance Art Gallery, the season ticket is also available in the same ways as described above. The season ticket is ------ if
146.
you live in the region or even if you just visit Torrance regularly.

- Adults: £30.00
- Seniors (65 and over) / Students: £25.00
- Children (age 6–16): £14.00

博物館優惠票券

　　購買參觀時尚博物館、羅馬博物館與多倫斯藝廊的博物館優惠票券，即可享有超讚的門票折扣！ ❶❹❸ 多倫斯明年還會落成更多博物館。您可至網站、售票櫃檯或遊客資訊中心 ❶❹❹ 購買優惠票券。

- 成人票：21.50 英鎊
- 敬老票（65 歲以上）／學生票：18.50 英鎊
- 兒童票（6–16 歲）：11.75 英鎊
- 20 人以上的團體票：每人 13.00 英鎊

季票

　　可全年參觀時尚博物館、羅馬博物館與多倫斯藝廊的 ❶❹❺ 最超值季票，一樣能以上述管道購得。如果您是此區居民或定期來訪多倫斯的民眾，季票絕對是您的 ❶❹❻ 完美選擇。

- 成人票：30.00 英鎊
- 敬老票（65 歲以上）／學生票：25.00 英鎊
- 兒童票（6–16 歲）：14.00 英鎊

字彙 adult 成人　senior 老人　season ticket 季票　describe 描述　even if 即使

143 新增題型

(A) All of the buildings are unfortunately closed for renovation at this time.

(B) You can buy three tickets to these three locations, all within ten minutes' walk of each other.

(C) There are more museums set to open in the Torrance area next year.

(D) When you visit Torrance by train, please get off at Torrance West Station.

中譯
(A) 可惜的是，所有建物此時均因翻新而關閉。
(B) 您可購買三張門票來參觀這三座博物館，它們之間相隔十分鐘的腳程。
(C) 多倫斯明年還會落成更多博物館。
(D) 您搭火車來訪多倫斯時，請於西多倫斯西站下車。

解析 本文為博物館門票公告，推廣購買一張優惠票券（a museums saver ticket）就能參觀三間博物館。選項中，(C) 提到之後還會擴大優惠範圍，為最適當的選項；(B) 與博物館和門票有關，但是得購買三張票這一點，與文章資訊不符；(A) 和 (D) 與文中資訊毫無關聯。

144

(A) apply
(B) confirm
(C) purchase
(D) reserve

中譯
(A) 申請　　　(B) 確認
(C) 購買　　　(D) 保存

解析 消費者能在網站、售票櫃檯或遊客資訊中心都能從事的行為為「購票」，因此選擇 (C) 最為適當，同時與下方價格有所連結。

Actual Test 5

PART 6

339

145

(A) Accessible
(B) Available
(C) Best
(D) Obvious

中譯 (A) 可取得的   (B) 可購得的
(C) 最佳的   (D) 明顯的

解析 選項中，最適合與名詞 value 搭配使用的形容詞為 (C)，
best value 的意思為「最超值的」。

字彙 accessible 可取得的

146

(A) perfect
(B) perfection
(C) perfectly
(D) perfectness

中譯 (A) 完美的   (B) 完美
(C) 完美地   (D) 完美

解析 空格所在的句子中，主詞為 The season ticket，動詞為
is，空格後方連接 if 開頭的子句，因此空格適合填入形容
詞當主詞補語，因此選擇形容詞 (A) 最為適當。

PART 7

Questions 147-148 refer to the following information. 資訊

In an effort to extend the life of your new Haven sweater, we would like to offer some advice and tips on how to take care of your new favorite top. First, since the material is very delicate, we do not recommend cleaning it in a conventional washer and dryer. ⑭ The tossing and tumbling can cause the cloth to stretch, and after a few washes, it could possibly tear. Please take the sweater to a cleaning professional, such as a dry cleaner, to have it cleaned properly.

We also recommend ⑭ keeping it in a dry, dark box when not wearing it, as it will help keep the colors bright and the materials fresh. Once taken out to wear, a soft felt brush should be used to clean lint or hair from the sweater. If you choose to use something else, it may work fine, but anything with coarse, plastic or metal bristles could cause damage to your top.

為了延長您新購入的哈芬毛衣壽命，我們在此為您最愛的新上衣，提出保養建議與祕訣。首先，由於材質相當脆弱，我們不建議放入傳統洗衣機和烘乾機清潔。⑭ 在筒槽內翻攪會拉長布料，清洗幾次後可能會破損。請將此毛衣送往專業洗衣店，例如乾洗店，以便正確清洗。

我們亦建議您，⑭ 不穿時請置於乾燥的深色收納盒，才能維持色彩的飽和度，讓材質常保如新。取出穿著時，應使用軟毛刷刷除毛衣上的絨毛或毛髮。如果您選用其他類型的毛刷，也許會有不錯的效果，但如果刷毛過硬，或是塑膠、金屬材質的刷毛，都可能會使您的上衣受損。

字彙 delicate 脆弱的   conventional 傳統的   toss and tumble 翻攪   stretch 拉長   tear 破損   lint 絨毛
coarse 粗硬的   bristle 刷毛

147

What could happen if the product is not taken to an experienced cleaner?
(A) It might get wrinkled.
(B) It might rip.
(C) It might shrink.
(D) The color might change.

中譯 如果沒有將產品送專業洗衣店,可能會發生什麼事?
(A) 可能會起皺。　　　(B) 可能會破損。
(C) 可能會縮水。　　　(D) 可能會變色。

解析 本文為毛衣保存方法的資訊。第一段提到:「**Please take the sweater to a cleaning professional**」,此建議前方表示在洗衣機內翻攪可能會導致布料變形,多洗幾次可能還會撕破(**tear**)。選項將 **tear** 改寫成 **rip**,因此答案為 **(B)**。

字彙 **wrinkled** 起皺的　**rip** 破損　**shrink** 縮小

148

According to the information, where should a user keep the product?
(A) In a bright room
(B) In a closet
(C) In a dry, covered container
(D) In a well-ventilated place

中譯 根據上文資訊,使用者應將此產品保存於何處?
(A) 明亮的房間
(B) 衣櫃
(C) 有封蓋的乾燥收納箱
(D) 通風良好的地方

解析 保存方式出現在第二段當中:「**keeping it in a dry, dark box**」,表示要置於乾燥、深色的容器內,因此答案為 **(C)**。

字彙 **ventilate** 使⋯⋯通風

Questions 149-150 refer to the following notice. 通知

149 This is a notice to all employees of Yongwater, Inc. in regard to the new vacation policy that will be implemented on October 1. **150** All employees will be required to inform management at least two weeks prior to their target vacation date. If a time-off request comes up unexpectedly, we will review the need at that time. The updated policy is made to make sure that the company can continue operations without interruption, even if some employees are not available at their regular time. This will also enable the company to fill temporary positions if necessary. Please include the dates and reason for taking time-off and it will be reviewed by the management. Thank you for your cooperation.

149 謹此通知央瓦特公司全體員工,10 月 1 日開始實施的新休假政策一事。**150** 所有員工必須在預計休假日前至少兩週通知管理層。如果臨時要請假,我們屆時會審核其必要性。政策更新是為了確保即使員工在平日上班缺席,公司仍能正常運作,亦能讓公司於必要時請人暫時填補空缺。請記得說明休假日期和原因,管理層將進行審核。感謝大家的配合。

字彙 **in regard to** 關於　**time-off** 請假　**unexpectedly** 意料之外地　**interruption** 干擾

149

What will happen in October?
(A) A new computer system will be introduced.
(B) New rules regarding holiday time will begin.
(C) The company will have temporary workers.
(D) The management will change.

中譯 十月會發生什麼事?
(A) 將引進新的電腦系統。
(B) 將實行新的休假規定。
(C) 公司將請來臨時工。
(D) 管理層會更動。

解析 本文為公司休假規定的通知。第一句話寫道:「**the new vacation policy that will be implemented on October 1**」,由此可以得知將於十月開始實施新的休假規定。

150

When should an employee submit a document?
(A) At the beginning of every month
(B) About half a month before a day off
(C) In two weeks
(D) The next day

中譯 員工應於何時提交文件？
(A) 每個月月初　　　(B) 約於休假日的半個月前
(C) 兩週內　　　　　(D) 隔天

解析 第二句話寫道：「at least two weeks prior to their target vacation date」。選項將 two weeks 改寫成 about half a month，因此答案為 (B)。

Questions 151-152 refer to the following information. 資訊

At Martinez Goods, we are working hard to create the things that we believe you will not want to live without. Therefore, we are proud to announce the Jericho 5000 line of microwaves. Our designers put in many hours of testing, including safety tests, to make sure that these appliances have all the features you need.

⑮ As someone who has purchased Jericho models in the past, we would like to invite you to participate in helping us decide what is important for the newest model of our line. We want to make the best product we can for our loyal customers, and with your help, we think we can. The survey below should only take about 5–7 minutes to complete, ⑮ and as a thank-you, we will send a 10-percent-off coupon for your next purchase on our Website.

馬丁尼茲商品公司致力為您生產不可或缺的產品。因此，我們自豪的預告傑瑞寇5000系列微波爐的到來。我們的設計師花了很多時間進行測試，包含安全測試，確保此系列家電具備全部您所需的功能。

⑮ 因為您曾購買過傑瑞寇型號的微波爐，我們希望邀請您一同決定此系列新機型該具備哪些重要功能。我們希望為忠實顧客製造最棒的產品，在您的協助下，我們一定能達標。以下問卷只要5到7分鐘的時間即可完成。⑮ 為了感謝您的幫忙，我們亦將寄送九折優惠券供您下次網購使用。

字彙 loyal customer 忠實顧客

151

Who does Martinez Goods ask to join the survey?
(A) Any visitors to their Website
(B) Parents of young children
(C) Previous customers
(D) Their designers

中譯 馬丁尼茲商品公司要求何者填寫問卷？
(A) 任何網站造訪者　　(B) 有幼童的家長
(C) 曾消費過的顧客　　(D) 公司的設計師

解析 文中提到隨著新產品的上市，邀請先前購買過系列產品的顧客進行問卷調查。第二段寫道：「As someone who has purchased Jericho models in the past, we would like to invite you to participate in helping us decide what is important for the newest model of our line.」，由此可以得知問卷調查的對象為先前的顧客。

152

What is a responder offered after filling out the survey?
(A) A voucher
(B) A free gift
(C) A link to a special sale
(D) A thank-you e-mail

中譯 填完問卷後，響應者可獲得何物？
(A) 優惠券　　　　　(B) 免費贈禮
(C) 促銷連結　　　　(D) 電子謝函

解析 提供的東西出現在最後一句話中：「we will send a 10-percent-off coupon for your next purchase on our Website」。選項將 coupon 改寫成 voucher，因此答案為 (A)。

字彙 responder 響應者

Questions 153-154 refer to the following text message chain. 簡訊對話 新增題型

Brad Young 1:32 PM	布萊德・楊 下午 1:32
❶⃝153 What did you think of the new human resources proposal Ray sent this morning? It seems like it will fit onto the company vision for the coming year nicely.	❶⃝153 雷今天早上傳來的人資部新提案，妳覺得怎麼樣？內容似乎完美呼應公司明年的願景。
Jessica Imono 1:36 PM	潔西卡・伊莫諾 下午 1:36
I haven't had much time to look it over yet, but from what I've seen, it looks good.	我還沒時間仔細看，不過以我目前所了解的，看起來還不錯。
Brad Young 1:37 PM	布萊德・楊 下午 1:37
I wanted to get your input on something. Did you read the extra section marked "bonus" in the e-mail?	我希望能了解一下妳的看法。妳有讀到電子郵件裡另外標出的「紅利」部分嗎？
Jessica Imono 1:40 PM	潔西卡・伊莫諾 下午 1:40
No, where was it? I didn't see any attachments on the e-mail. Let me check again.	沒有，在哪裡？我的電子郵件裡沒有任何附件。我再確定一下。
Brad Young 1:42 PM	布萊德・楊 下午 1:42
It should either be attached or maybe a link on the bottom on the e-mail. I could forward it to you now.	應該是附件形式，或是電子郵件最下方有連結。我現在可以轉寄給妳。
Jessica Imono 1:43 PM	潔西卡・伊莫諾 下午 1:43
That would be great. ❶⃝154 It's definitely not here.	太好了。❶⃝154 我這裡真的沒看到。
Brad Young 1:44 PM	布萊德・楊 下午 1:44
OK. Check again in a few minutes and then we can talk about it.	好的。妳幾分鐘後收信看看，我們再來討論。

字彙 human resources 人資部　forward 轉寄

153

What is the conversation topic?
(A) A company employee
(B) A company problem
(C) A personnel plan
(D) A missing item

中譯 此對話的主題為何？
(A) 公司員工
(B) 公司問題
(C) 人事計畫
(D) 遺失的物品

解析 本篇文章針對人資部電子郵件中的新提案進行討論。第一封訊息中提到：「human resources proposal」，(C) 改寫成 personnel plan，故為正確答案。

154 新增題型

At 1:43PM, what does Ms. Imono most likely mean when she writes, "It's definitely not here"?
(A) She cannot access a Web page.
(B) She cannot find the information.
(C) The e-mail must be missing.
(D) The information must be posted somewhere else.

中譯 在下午 1:43，伊莫諾小姐回訊「我這裡真的沒看到」，她最有可能是什麼意思？
(A) 她無法存取網頁。
(B) 她找不到相關資訊。
(C) 那封電子郵件肯定不見了。
(D) 此資訊一定是張貼在其他地方。

解析 伊莫諾小姐表示她沒有看到電子郵件中有附件，這表示她找不到附檔的資訊。

To:	Emerson Palmer <emersonp@nextmail.com>
From:	Reginald Teller <representative@dasexpress.com>
Date:	September 28
Subject:	Order #820-00812

Hello Mr. Palmer,

I am writing to you about your order with us for the digital antenna and speaker. ❺ Unfortunately, we had very strong storms near our warehouses this week, which caused some serious damage to our buildings. Therefore, we are unable to immediately ship the items you purchased. It will take 1-2 weeks for the buildings to be repaired and then another few days for order preparation before we anticipate orders resuming.

We have few options that you may choose for your order. ❻ First, approval of a delay will keep your order active, and we will ship it as soon as possible. Next, we can substitute a similar product and have it sent from another warehouse in the country to your location. Lastly, if you would prefer, we can cancel the order for you. ❼ Please let us know which is best for you in the next 48 hours. If we do not receive a response, we will keep the order active. We apologize for any inconvenience this may cause.

Thank you and have a nice day.

Reginald Teller
Service Representative

收件人：艾莫森・帕馬 <emersonp@nextmail.com>
寄件人：瑞吉納德・泰勒 <representative@dasexpress.com>
日期：9 月 28 日
主旨：訂單 #820-00812

哈囉，帕馬先生：

　　我想通知您向我們訂購數位天線與喇叭的訂單事宜。❺ 很不幸地，本週有非常強勁的風暴行經我們倉庫附近，使得建物嚴重受損。因此我們無法立即出貨您所購買的商品。建物需要 1 至 2 週的維修時間，在那之後還要幾天時間準備訂單，才能恢復正常的訂單流程。

　　我們有幾個處理訂單的提議供您選擇。❻ 首先，若您許可延遲出貨，我們會保留訂單，並且儘快出貨。第二，我們可替換為類似產品，並從國內另一個倉庫出貨至府上。最後，如果您想要的話，我們亦可取消訂單。❼ 請您於 48 小時內，回覆我們您希望的處理方式。若我們未收到回覆，將以保留訂單的方式來處理。很抱歉對您造成任何不便。

　　感謝您，祝您有個愉快的一天。

瑞吉納德・泰勒
客服代表

字彙 **resume** 恢復　**active** 在進展中的　**substitute** 替換

155

Why is the shipping delayed?
(A) Due to a delivery problem
(B) Due to inclement weather
(C) Due to mislabeling
(D) Due to a stock shortage

中譯 為何延遲出貨？
(A) 因為運送問題
(B) 因為惡劣氣候
(C) 因為標示錯誤
(D) 因為缺貨

解析 本文為公司寄給顧客的電子郵件，當中提到由於天然災害，導致商品無法如期出貨。選項將無法出貨的原因「very strong storms near our warehouses」改寫成 inclement weather。

字彙 **inclement** 惡劣的　**mislabel** 標示錯誤　**shortage** 缺貨

156

Which option is NOT given to the customer?
(A) An alternate item
(B) The order cancellation
(C) The later shipping of an item
(D) The refund for shipping costs

中譯 下列哪一項不是顧客可以選擇的處理方式？
(A) 替換商品　　　　(B) 取消訂單
(C) 商品延遲出貨　　(D) 退還運費

解析 第二段中為顧客提供幾個選項：
1) ship it as soon as possible → (C)
2) substitute a similar product → (A)
3) cancel the order → (B)
當中並未提到退款一事，因此答案要選 (D)。

字彙 alternate 替代的　cancellation 取消
shipping cost 運費

157

What will happen if Mr. Palmer does not respond in two days?
(A) The order will be canceled.
(B) The order will be charged.
(C) The order will be processed.
(D) The order will be delivered.

中譯 如果帕馬先生未於兩天內回信，會發生什麼事？
(A) 訂單會被取消。　　(B) 訂單會被收費。
(C) 訂單會被處理。　　(D) 訂貨會被配送。

解析 題目的 two days 等同文中的 48 hours，文中提到若帕馬先生未在兩天內回覆，會保留訂單，按照原本的程序受理訂單：「If we do not receive a response, we will keep the order active.」。

Questions 158-160 refer to the following advertisement. 廣告

Fall is almost upon us and now is the best time to get in shape for next year! ⑱ At Gregg's Gym, we offer the most up-to-date techniques in aerobics, cardio, yoga, martial arts, muscle building, and weight loss programs. If you want to shed some pounds before the holidays, or just get some exercise, we have a plan for you.

⑲ Our off-season Body Saver series offer a little something for everyone. You can choose to take only one type of class for the full season, choose a pair of classes for the price of one, or use the mix-and-match system, joining any classes you want during your visit. ⑳ Drop in and take a test drive with any of our qualified instructors and see how you can improve your well-being, and have fun while doing it.

⑱ Gregg's is open 7 days a week, from 6:00 AM to 12:00 AM every day, so we can fit into your schedule at any time you need. ⑱ We are conveniently located at the corner of 17th and Winslow Avenue, right in the heart of the city, and only a two-block walk from the subway.

秋季即將到來，現在就是為明年做好完美體態準備的最佳時機！⑱ 格瑞格健身房提供有氧健身操、有氧運動、瑜珈、武術、肌肉鍛鍊與減重等最新訓練技巧。如果您想在假期前讓體態更加輕盈，或只是想運動一下，我們均有合適的課程。

⑲ 淡季的「體態鍛鍊」系列課程人人皆適用。您可以選擇一整季只上一門課程、選擇花一門課的錢上兩門課，或者是以混搭的方式，在您前來健身房時參加任何課程。⑳ 您可直接前來，試上看看我們任何一位合格教練的課程，了解改善您健康的方式，同時樂在其中。

⑱ 格瑞格健身房全年無休，每天早上 6 點營業至午夜 12 點，能完美配合您的行程。⑱ 我們位於第 17 街與威斯洛大街的交會處，地點便利又位於市中心，離地鐵站僅需步行兩個街區。

字彙 get in shape 恢復體態　cardio 有氧運動　martial art 武術　shed 減去　off-season 淡季
test drive （課程）試聽，試上　conveniently 方便地

158

What is NOT mentioned in the ad?
(A) A type of exercise
(B) Business hours
(C) A location
(D) Requirements

中譯 此廣告未提及什麼？
(A) 運動種類　　　(B) 營業時間
(C) 地點　　　　　(D) 規定

解析 本文為健身房的廣告，宣傳迎接秋天到來的計畫。(A) 出現在第一段當中，列出健身房提供的健身項目；(B) 營業時間出現在第三段開頭；(C) 地點出現在第三段最後；(D) 則未提及。

159

According to the advertisement, what features does Gregg's have?
(A) A lot of staff members
(B) Right next to a station
(C) Open 24 hours a day
(D) Special offers

中譯 根據廣告，格瑞格有什麼特色？
(A) 人員眾多　　　(B) 就在車站旁邊
(C) 24 小時營業　　(D) 課程優惠活動

解析 特色指的是廣告中特別強調的內容。文章第二段中提到健身房提供的優惠項目，包含整季僅選擇上同一門的課程、以一門課的價格上兩門課，或是混搭課程，等來到現場再選擇想上的課。四個選項中，最適當的答案為特別優惠，所以答案要選 (D)；(A) 文中並未提及；(B) 跟 (C) 與廣告內容有出入。

160

How can a person try out a service?
(A) By accompanying a friend
(B) By applying online
(C) By becoming a member at the site
(D) By going directly to the site

中譯 顧客如何能試上課程？
(A) 陪同朋友　　　(B) 線上報名
(C) 現場成為會員　(D) 直接前往現場

解析 第二段中提到：「Drop in and take a test drive」，表示必須親自到場體驗。

Questions 161-163 refer to the following e-mail. 電子郵件

To:	Amelia Hunters <ahunters@sloanefoundation.com>
From:	Rachel Benson <rbenson@nextmail.com>
Date:	October 10
Subject:	Sloane history exhibition

Hi Amelia,

⑯ I wanted to get in touch and see if you wanted to come with us to the Sloane history exhibition this weekend. —[1]—. It's supposed to be one of the best displays of the fall. —[2]—.

The arts director received permission to show everything in the museum's collection about our area's history and ⑯ many things from our foundation will be included. There are so many items that I have wanted to see,

收件人：亞蜜莉亞 • 杭特斯 <ahunters@sloanefoundation.com>
寄件人：瑞秋 • 班森 <rbenson@nextmail.com>
日期：10 月 10 日
主旨：史隆恩歷史展覽

嗨，亞蜜莉亞：

⑯ 我聯絡妳是想問看看，妳這個週末要不要跟我們去參觀史隆恩歷史展覽。這可是秋季最棒的展覽之一。

藝術總監獲得許可，可以展示博物館館藏中有關本地區歷史的所有資料，⑯ 我們基金會的許多資料也包含在其中。有好多展品我早就想看，但過去都存放在保險庫，未開放大眾參觀。⑯ 我甚至聽說，

but were always in the vault and unavailable to the public.
—[3]— I know that you are a big fan of history and wouldn't want to miss a chance to see this.

If you can get back to me before 8:00 tomorrow night, I will be picking up tickets for everyone who wants to go at that time. —[4]—. There will be a group of us, maybe six or so, and ⑯ we will be meeting at the office before heading over.

Rachel

連本市的原創設計圖都會展出。我知道妳很迷歷史，一定不希望錯過這個機會。

如果妳明天晚上八點前能回覆我，到時我可以幫想去的人買票。應該會有六個人左右要一起去，⑯我們會先在辦公室碰面再出發。

瑞秋

字彙 permission 許可　foundation 基金會　vault 保險庫

161

What is the purpose of the e-mail?
(A) To ask Ms. Hunters to an event
(B) To get permission to leave work early
(C) To invite Ms. Hunters to lunch
(D) To respond to an e-mail

中譯 此封電子郵件的目的為何？
(A) 邀請杭特斯小姐參加某活動
(B) 取得提早下班的許可
(C) 邀請杭特斯小姐吃午餐
(D) 回覆電子郵件

解析 本文為邀請對方參觀歷史展覽的電子郵件。第一句寫道：「I wanted to get in touch and see if you wanted to come with us to the Sloane history exhibition this weekend.」，由此可以得知本封電子郵件的目的為詢問對方參加活動的意願。

162

Where does Ms. Benson want to meet Ms. Hunters this weekend?
(A) At the box office
(B) At the city hall
(C) At the foundation office
(D) At the museum

中譯 班森小姐這週末想在哪裡和杭特斯小姐碰面？
(A) 售票亭　　　　　(B) 市政廳
(C) 基金會辦公室　　(D) 博物館

解析 本文邀請對方於週末一同前往的展覽，郵件最後提到見面地點：「we will be meeting at the office」，而第一段中提到：「many things from our foundation will be included」，表示任職於基金會，由此可以得知兩人約在基金會辦公室見面。

163 新增題型

In which of the positions marked [1], [2], [3], or [4] does the following sentence best belong?
"I heard that even the original designs for the city will be shown."
(A) [1]
(B) [2]
(C) [3]
(D) [4]

中譯 在標記 [1]、[2]、[3] 和 [4] 的地方，下列這句話最適合放在何處？「我甚至聽說，連本市的原創設計圖都會展出。」
(A) [1]　　　　　　(B) [2]
(C) [3]　　　　　　(D) [4]

解析 題目列出的句子中出現 even，表示其前方應該會提到展示品相關的內容。[3] 前方提到能看到博物館內的展品，當中包含基金會提供的東西，很多未曾向大眾公開過，因此題目句放在 [3] 最符合前後文意。

To: Amy Loughton
<amyloughton01@parspace.com>
From: Kevin Redd
<kevinredd@beldingnperk.com>
Date: August 25
Subject: Sales Lead Position at Belding&Perk

Hi Amy,

I wanted to thank you for coming to our office last week and speaking with me regarding the Sales Lead position. —[1]—. ⑯ **It was very nice meeting you and hearing your thoughts on what you could bring to our team, and some of the techniques you mentioned that could encourage sales in the coming years.** —[2]—. I would like to offer you the position and wanted you to start with us on the 1st of the month.

We will need you to start off strong and, ⑯ **of course, have introductory meetings, as well as formal meetings with your teams.** As our Sales Lead, we will need you to create goals and set deadlines for all of our teams, have biweekly update meetings with management, and assist in any large sales meetings. —[3]—. I don't want you to get buried during your initial weeks with us, ⑯ **so I will be working closely with you in the first month.**

If you have any questions before or after your start date, please let me know. —[4]—.

⑯ **Kevin Redd**
Sales Manager, Belding & Perk

收件人：艾咪・羅敦
<amyloughton01@parspace.com>
寄件人：凱文・瑞德
<kevinredd@beldingnperk.com>
日期：8 月 25 日
主旨：貝爾丁與波克公司的業務主管職位

嗨，艾咪：

　　我想謝謝妳上週來到我們公司，和我面談業務主管職位的事。⑯ 很開心能認識妳，也很高興聽妳說明自己可為我們團隊做的貢獻，以及一些能促進公司未來業績的技巧。我想錄用妳，希望妳能從這個月 1 日開始上班。

　　我們希望妳一進公司就能擁有穩健根基，⑯ 當然也希望妳參加入職會議，還有與妳的團隊的正式會議。我們希望身為業務主管的妳，能為所有團隊建立目標與制定期限、每兩週與管理階層開會報告進度，並於任何大型業務會議提供協助。⑯ 我知道剛開始好像有很多事要忙，但我們相信妳可以迎頭趕上。我不希望妳上班頭幾個禮拜就被工作壓得喘不過氣，⑯ 所以我會在頭一個月裡和妳密切合作。

　　如果妳在正式上班前或上班後有任何疑問，請告訴我。

⑯ 凱文・瑞德
業務經理　貝爾丁與波克公司

字彙 technique 技能　start off 開始　introductory 介紹的　biweekly 雙週一次的

164

What does Mr. Redd like about the interview with Ms. Loughton?
(A) Her cheerful personality
(B) Her experience in sales
(C) Her management skills
(D) Her sales ideas

中譯 關於與羅敦小姐的面試，瑞德先生喜歡哪一點？
(A) 她討喜的個性
(B) 她的業務經驗
(C) 她的管理技能
(D) 她的銷售點子

解析 本文為寄給面試者的合格通知郵件。第一段提到：「It was very nice meeting you and hearing your thoughts on what you could bring to our team, and some of the techniques you mentioned that could encourage sales in the coming years.」，從瑞德先生的話中可以得知他很喜歡羅敦小姐提出的銷售點子。

165

How will Ms. Loughton get ready for her first week at the company?
(A) She will attend training with other employees.
(B) She will complete assigned tasks.
(C) She will write a speech for her subordinates.
(D) She will have several meetings.

中譯 羅敦小姐會以何種方式為第一週上班做好準備？
(A) 與其他員工一起參加教育訓練。
(B) 完成被分配的任務。
(C) 為向下屬的演講寫講稿。
(D) 參加多場會議。

解析 剛開始的工作內容出現在第二段中：「have introductory meetings, as well as formal meetings with your teams」，當中提到出席入職會議以及團隊會議，由此可以推測羅敦小姐在第一週得參加很多場會議。

166

Who will help Ms. Loughton in September?
(A) Mr. Redd's assistant
(B) Sales team members
(C) The previous Sales Lead
(D) The Sales Manager

中譯 誰會在九月協助羅敦小姐？
(A) 瑞德先生的助理　　(B) 業務團隊人員
(C) 前業務主管　　　　(D) 業務經理

解析 電子郵件的寄件日期為八月，這表示羅敦小姐從九月開始工作。電子郵件最後提到：「I will be working closely with you in the first month」，表示寄件人瑞德先生會提供協助，而他的職位為業務經理。

167 新增題型

In which of the positions marked [1], [2], [3], or [4] does the following sentence best belong?
"I know it sounds like quite a bit of work at first, but we believe that you can keep up."
(A) [1]
(B) [2]
(C) [3]
(D) [4]

中譯 在標記 [1]、[2]、[3] 和 [4] 的地方，下列這句話最適合放在何處？「我知道剛開始好像有很多事要忙，但我們相信妳可以迎頭趕上。」
(A) [1]　　　　　　　(B) [2]
(C) [3]　　　　　　　(D) [4]

解析 題目列出的句子適合放在文中提及羅敦小姐即將接下的工作後方。第二段 [3] 前方提到她之後要負責的工作。

字彙 keep up 趕上

Questions 168-171 refer to the following e-mail. 電子郵件

To:	Jackson Waters <jwaters@noratech.com>
From:	Emily Brewer <eb001@goerslove.com>
Date:	Wednesday, November 1
Subject:	Meeting about our products

Hi Mr. Waters,

I hope you are doing well. ❶❻❽ **I wanted to see if it would be okay to reschedule tomorrow's meeting for the next week.** We want to be able to share with you all of the most up-to-date product information we can, but won't receive the report until this evening. We would like to read and thoroughly go over the report before presenting it to you.

收件人：傑克森・華特斯 <jwaters@noratech.com>
寄件人：艾蜜莉・布魯爾 <eb001@goerslove.com>
日期：11 月 1 日週三
主旨：關於我們產品的會議

嗨，華特斯先生：

希望您一切安好。❶❻❽ 我想問您一下，是否能夠將明天的會議改到下週。我們希望竭盡所能向您分享所有最新產品的資訊，但是我們今晚才能收到相關報告。我們希望能在向您報告之前，徹底詳讀報告內容。❶❻❾ 總的來說，

⑯⑨ Overall, it should take two or three days to read and confirm the product information.

Should we receive the product report earlier, I will, of course, let you know. **⑰⓪ We will have a little extra time to process and work with this information over the weekend, so we will have a demonstration prepared for you during the meeting. ⑰① The beginning of next week should be fine for us.** Would that be okay for you as well?

I look forward to hearing back from you and thank you for working with us on such an important project for both of our companies.

Thank you,
Emily Brewer

我們需要二至三天的時間，才能看完報告與確認產品資訊。

如果我們能夠提早收到產品報告，我一定會通知您。⑰⓪這樣我們週末就能有多一點時間來了解與整理此份資料，並能為您準備一份與您開會用的演示簡報。⑰①我們下週一可以開會。不知您這個時間也方便嗎？

期待收到您的回覆，也感謝您與我們合作這項雙方公司均十分重視的專案。

謝謝您，
艾蜜莉・布魯爾

字彙 thoroughly 徹底地

168

What is the purpose of the e-mail?
(A) To ask for an item description
(B) To ask to delay a meeting time
(C) To extend the meeting time
(D) To give an update on the meeting

中譯 此封電子郵件的目的為何？
(A) 要求商品的介紹　(B) 要求延後會議時間
(C) 延長會議時間　(D) 更新會議資訊

解析 電子郵件開頭寫道：「I wanted to see if it would be okay to reschedule tomorrow's meeting for the next week.」，由此可以得知本文目的為要求將開會時間延期。

169

How much time will the team spend going through the information?
(A) A few hours
(B) A day
(C) A few days
(D) A week

中譯 團隊需要花多少時間仔細了解資料？
(A) 幾小時　　　　(B) 一天
(C) 幾天　　　　　(D) 一週

解析 要求延期的原因為寄件人較晚收到報告，還需要花時間研究。當中提到：「it should take two or three days to read and confirm the product information」，表示需要花幾天研究。

字彙 go through 仔細了解

170

What does Ms. Brewer offer Mr. Waters?
(A) A completed unit
(B) A demo
(C) Printed reports
(D) Support documents

中譯 布魯爾小姐向華特斯先生主動提出什麼？
(A) 完整機組　　　(B) 演示簡報
(C) 書面報告　　　(D) 說明文件

解析 答案出現在第二段中：「we will have a demonstration prepared for you during the meeting」，選項將 demonstration 改寫成 demo，因此答案為 (B)。

171

| What day would Ms. Brewer most likely to meet with Mr. Waters?
(A) On Monday
(B) On Thursday
(C) On Friday
(D) On Saturday | 中譯 布魯爾小姐最有可能在哪一天與華特斯先生開會？
(A) 週一
(B) 週四
(C) 週五
(D) 週六 |

解析 電子郵件第二段最後寫道：「The beginning of next week should be fine for us.」，因此選項中最適當的日子為 (A)。

Questions 172-175 refer to the following online discussion. 線上討論 新增題型

Randal Bunch 11:34 AM Have anyone seen Francis today? I was supposed to speak with him.	藍道・邦奇 上午 11:34 今天有誰看到法蘭西斯嗎？我本來要跟他談話。
Ingrid Colane 11:35 AM ⑫ He got a phone call this morning and said he needed to leave. I think he was heading to a client's office.	英格麗・科藍 上午 11:35 ⑫ 他早上接到一通電話後，就說必須先離開。我想他是去客戶的公司。
Randal Bunch 11:35 AM I see. Does anyone have an update on Kilnesmith?	藍道・邦奇 上午 11:35 原來如此。有人知道克林史密斯客戶的最新進度嗎？
Brian Lagerwood 11:40 AM I think I can assist with that. I was working with Francis on that account. — Ingrid Colane has exited the chat. —	布萊恩・拉格伍德 上午 11:40 我想我能幫忙。我有和法蘭西斯一起處理這個客戶。 ──英格麗・科藍已退出此聊天室──
Randal Bunch 11:41 AM Great, thanks, Brian. I know that Francis has been working with them for quite some time. Do you think they will accept our offer?	藍道・邦奇 上午 11:41 太好了，謝啦，布萊恩。我知道法蘭西斯已經和他們合作一段時間。你覺得他們會接受我們的條件嗎？
Brian Lagerwood 11:41 AM ⑭ Francis and I have met with them multiple times over the last few months. It will come down to us or another company. They should decide by October 13.	布萊恩・拉格伍德 上午 11:41 ⑭ 法蘭西斯跟我過去幾個月已經跟他們會談很多次。他們最終會在我們或另一家公司之間做選擇。他們 10 月 13 日前會做出決定。
Randal Bunch 11:44 AM Hmm, OK. I was hoping to know by September. I need to know if there is anything we can do to encourage them to accept our offer. ⑬ If they don't, it would set our finances back quite a bit for next fiscal year.	藍道・邦奇 上午 11:44 嗯，好吧。我本來希望能在 9 月前知道結果。我需要知道我們是否還能再多做些什麼，來鼓勵他們接受我們的條件。⑬ 如果他們不接受，我們下個會計年度的財務狀況將會受挫。
Brian Lagerwood 11:45 AM Well, I heard that Bromley offered Klinesmith more money, but it was a short-time deal. Ours would be twice as long. ⑮ Should we sweeten the pot?	布萊恩・拉格伍德 上午 11:45 我聽說布朗利向克林史密斯出價更高，但他們的是短期合作案。我們的合作時間是兩倍。⑮ 我們要提高籌碼嗎？

Actual Test 5

PART 7

351

Randal Bunch		**11:46 AM**

Maybe, but let's make sure that we can work with them on this. ⑦ **We can't afford to find another supplier in such a short amount of time.**

Brian Lagerwood		**11:47**

AM I will let you know as soon as I get an update.

藍道・邦奇		上午 11:46

也許吧，但我們要先確保是否能和他們合作。⑦ 我們沒辦法在這麼短的時間內，找到另一家供應商。

布萊恩・拉格伍德		上午 11:47

我有新進度時，會儘快告訴你。

字彙 account 客戶　come down to 最終結果是　sweeten the pot 提高籌碼

172

What does Ms. Colane mention that Francis is doing?
(A) Going on a business trip
(B) **Seeing with a client**
(C) Trying to get a better deal
(D) Visiting a family member

中譯 科藍小姐提到法蘭西斯在做什麼事？
(A) 出差
(B) 見客戶
(C) 試著談到更好的條件
(D) 探訪家人

解析 第一條訊息表示在尋找法蘭西斯，而後於 11 點 35 分的訊息中，科藍小姐回覆：「he was heading to a client's office」，表示法蘭西斯正在跟客戶見面。

173

How does Mr. Bunch describe a deal with Kilnesmith?
(A) Complex
(B) Demanding
(C) **Essential**
(D) Long-lasting

中譯 邦奇先生如何描述與克林史密斯公司談的合作案？
(A) 複雜的　　　　　(B) 要求多的
(C) 十分必要的　　　(D) 持續許久的

解析 邦奇先生為了要談與克林史密斯公司有關的事，所以才要找法蘭西斯。他跟拉格伍德先生談到此事，同時在 11 點 44 分的訊息中提到希望讓克林史密斯接受條件，接著又說：「it would set our finances back quite a bit for next fiscal year」，以能影響財務狀況表達其重要性。

字彙 complex 複雜的　demanding 要求多的
essential 十分必要的

174

What has Mr. Lagerwood been involved with recently?
(A) Looking for a new location for a warehouse
(B) **Meeting with a potential supplier**
(C) Preparing for a business trip
(D) Working on financial details for next year

中譯 拉格伍德先生最近都在幫忙處理什麼事？
(A) 尋找新的倉庫地點
(B) 和潛在供應商開會
(C) 準備出差
(D) 準備明年的詳細財務資料

解析 拉格伍德先生在 11 點 41 分的訊息中提到：「Francis and I have met with them multiple times over the last few months.」，表示最近經常與克林史密斯碰面，而根據邦奇先生 11 點 46 分傳送的訊息內容，表示克林史密斯為他們的潛在供應商，因此答案為 (B)。

字彙 potential 潛在的

At 11:45 AM, what does Mr. Lagerwood most likely mean when he writes, "should we sweeten the pot?"
(A) He wants to know if he should explain why their contract is better.
(B) He wants to know if he should extend the time for them to decide.
(C) He wants to know if he should invite them for a meeting.
(D) He wonders if he should make a better offer.

中譯 在上午 11:45，拉格伍德先生回訊「我們要提高籌碼嗎？」，最有可能是什麼意思？
(A) 他想知道是否應該要解說合約比較好的原因。
(B) 他想知道是否該延長對方的考慮時間。
(C) 他想知道是否該邀請對方開會。
(D) 他思考著是否該提出更優渥的條件。

解析 sweeten the pot 指的是把一項東西變得更好、更有吸引力之意。前方提到希望能順利與克林史密斯進行交易，但別人的提案更好。由此可以得知此話的意思為詢問是否要提出更優渥的條件，來增加成功的可能性。

Questions 176-180 refer to the following program and review. 節目 影評

Shade: The Mark on Banker Hill
Written by Steven Bird
Directed by Lindy Allen

Richard Shade is a tough-talking, hard-boiled detective who knows the city like the back of his hand. He's had the respect of his peers since he was a ⑰ fresh face on his first case. The city is dark and chilling and he feels that today is either his lucky day or maybe the worst day of his life. One of film's iconic crime detectives, Shade works outside the police ⑯ and has many disputes with Maxwell Young, the one cop he trusts. Steven Bird has taken the original film and transformed it for today's audiences, using current technology to create the modern atmosphere that surrounds the story.

We also meet a mysterious woman, Gloria Grey, who believes someone is trying to steal her husband's inheritance, showing up at Shade's office and asking for his help. She lets herself in as Shade naps in his office, and proves to be a woman willing to do anything to get her hands on the money. The streets around Banker Hill are dangerous, but for someone like Richard Shade, it could be murder.

Running Time: 117 minutes

Shade: The Mark on Banker Hill is ⑱ a remake of a classic movie, which tells us the story of a down-on-his-luck detective who is looking for a break. Originally, this was one of a series of films about Shade released in the 1950s and is now considered to be one of the classics of the genre.

《謝德：班克山丘的印記》
編劇：史蒂芬・伯德
導演：林迪・艾倫

李察・謝德是一名說話強勢的冷酷偵探，並且對此城市瞭若指掌。他過去以 ⑰ 新人之姿第一次辦案後，隨即獲得同業的尊敬。城市又暗又冷，他覺得今日如果不是他的幸運日，那就是他人生中最糟糕的一天。謝德是本片代表性的緝凶偵探之一，他不受警察體系的約束，⑯ 並與他信任的警察麥斯威爾・楊產生許多爭執。史蒂芬・伯德運用最新科技將原版電影改編，為現今觀眾營造出整篇故事的現代氛圍。

在劇中我們也可看到一位名叫葛羅莉亞・格瑞的神秘女人，她認為有人想竊取她丈夫的遺產，並因此出現於謝德的辦公室，想尋求他的協助。謝德仍在辦公室小睡一會兒時，她就自行入內。事實證明，她是一位願意為了錢而不擇手段的人。班克山丘的街道危機四伏，但對李察・謝德來說，謀殺案有可能就此而生。

片長：117 分鐘

《謝德：班克山丘的印記》⑱ 翻拍自經典電影，該片描述一名時運不濟的偵探想喘口氣的故事。原本這是一部 1950 年代上映的謝德偵探系列電影，如今已是大眾心目中此類影片的經典作品之一。

⑰ This version of the Shade character has been given a softer side, and the private eye is now more of a fast-thinking joker. ⑱ Stepping into the shoes of Richard Shade is Johnny Baxter, who has been cast historically as a more comedic and musical actor. ⑰ But Baxter comes through with a performance that I believe the classic cast would be proud of. It's definitely a different take on the original, but Baxter handles the scenes like he was born for the role. Marianne Lewis is fantastic in the lead female role and will be seen as an up-and-coming star for sure. ⑱ Since much of the story revolves around these two, it should be noted how well they work off of each other in the film, but there are memorable scenes with the rest of the small cast, too.

Shade is designed to be the first in a new film series for Grand Studios, and ⑱ although this film isn't going to change the way we view crime movies, it is a good way to establish the characters in today's world.

⑰ 在此版本中，謝德這個角色性格較柔和，腦筋動得快、談吐幽默的人物特色也在這名私家偵探身上顯而易見。⑱ 飾演李察・謝德角色的演員，是向來演出喜劇與音樂劇居多的強尼・巴斯特。⑰ 不過我認為當年這部經典電影的原班卡司，一定會對巴斯特的精湛演技感到驕傲。雖然巴斯特的表現方式與原作截然不同，卻能表現得彷彿自己是為這個角色而生。瑪麗安・路易斯擔任女主角的表現令人驚豔，堪稱明日超級巨星。⑱ 由於故事篇幅大多環繞於這兩個角色，大家可留意兩人在片中軋戲精彩畫面，不過其他配角仍有一些值得回味的畫面。

《謝德》是格藍德影業公司打造的新系列電影的首發片，⑱ 雖然本片不會改變我們對犯罪類電影的看法，但可作為在現代背景下建構經典角色的良好範例。

字彙 tough-talking 說話強勢的　hard-boiled 冷酷的，鐵石心腸的
know something like the back of one's hand 對某事瞭若指掌　case 案件　dispute 爭執
inheritance 遺產　let oneself in 自行入內　down-on-one's-luck 時運不濟　private eye 私家偵探
cast 卡司，演員陣容　come through with 設法達成　revolve around 以……中心，環繞於

176

Who is the person that Richard Shade has faith in?
(A) Gloria Grey
(B) Johnny Baxter
(C) Lindy Allen
(D) Maxwell Young

中譯 李察・謝德信任的人是誰？
(A) 葛羅莉亞・格瑞　(B) 強尼・巴斯特
(C) 林迪・艾倫　　(D) 麥斯威爾・楊

解析 兩篇文章分別為電影介紹和評論。李察・謝德為電影的主角，與他信任的人有關的內容出現在第一段當中「Maxwell Young, the one cop he trusts」。

字彙 have faith in 對……信任

177

In the program, the word "fresh" in paragraph 1, line 2 is closest in meaning to
(A) additional
(B) energetic
(C) new
(D) raw

中譯 節目介紹中第一段第二行的「fresh」意思與下列何者最相近？
(A) 新增的　　　　(B) 具有活力的
(C) 新來的　　　　(D) 不假修飾的

解析 單字出現在「he was a fresh face on his first case」當中，fresh face 的意思為「新人、新面孔」，選項中意思最相近的單字為 new。

字彙 raw 不假修飾的

178

What is NOT true about the film?
(A) It's been reproduced.
(B) The director didn't change the original film.
(C) There are two main characters in the film.
(D) It has reflected the today's trend.

中譯 關於影片，下列何者為非？
(A) 屬於翻拍作品。　(B) 導演並未改變原作。
(C) 片中有兩個主角。　(D) 反映現今趨勢。

解析 (A) 評論中第一段第一句：「a remake of a class movie」，提到它是一部改編作品；(B) 文中並未提到沒有改變原作一事；(C) 評論第二段中提到有兩名主角——李察・謝德和瑪麗安・路易斯，以及後面「much of the story revolves around these two」；(D) 評論最後一段提到：「it is a good way to establish the characters in today's world」。

字彙 reproduce 翻拍　reflect 反映

179

What change to the new version does the review focus on?
(A) The lead character
(B) The music
(C) The overall atmosphere
(D) The scenario

中譯 影評著重於新版本的哪些改變？
(A) 主角　　　　　(B) 音樂
(C) 整體氛圍　　　(D) 情境

解析 評論的核心重點出現在中間段落：「This version of the Shade character has been given a softer side」和「Baxter handles the scenes like he was born for the role」，提到主角有別於原作電影的演出。

180

What kind of job is Mr. Baxter usually offered?
(A) Action
(B) Comedy
(C) Drama
(D) Horror

中譯 巴斯特先生通常演出哪類電影？
(A) 動作片　　　　(B) 喜劇片
(C) 劇情片　　　　(D) 恐怖片

解析 演員巴斯特先生飾演李察・謝德一角，文中提到：「Johnny Baxter, who has been cast historically as a more comedic and musical actor」，表示他先前主要擔任喜劇作品中的角色。

Questions 181-185 refer to the following e-mails. 電子郵件

To: Elijah Graham
<elijah2019@inoutbox.com>
From: Tower Hotel
<frontdesk@towerhotelten.com>
Date: September 5
Subject: Confirmation of reservation

Dear Mr. Graham,

⑱ We have received your request to book a room for October 3–12 and can confirm that we have Room 711 ready for you then. ⑱ We can also confirm the wake-up call from October 4–6, at 5:30 AM for the three days.

收件人：伊萊亞・葛拉漢
<elijah2019@inoutbox.com>
寄件人：高塔飯店
<frontdesk@towerhotelten.com>
日期：9月5日
主旨：確認訂房

親愛的葛拉漢先生：

⑱ 我們收到您10月3日至12日訂房需求，想在此向您確認我們可為您在此期間準備711號房。⑱ 我們亦向您確認於10月4日至6日這三天提供早上5:30的晨喚電話服務。

PART 7

355

181 The hotel and the surrounding areas will be very busy during your stay, as the Richmond Harvest Festival will be taking place. The city is expecting around 100,000 people to visit on at least one of the days during the week-long celebration. We appreciate your business and if there is anything we can do to make your stay even better, please do not hesitate to ask.

Service included	Wake-up call **182** Complimentary breakfast Room cleaning
Room 711 at $92/ night (**184** Oct. 3–12, 9 nights)	Total: $828

Thank you for choosing Tower Hotel.

Jason Richards
Hospitality Manager
Tower Hotel, Richmond, Tennessee

To:	Tower Hotel <frontdesk@towerhotelten.com>
From:	Elijah Graham <elijah2019@inoutbox.com>
Date:	September 6
Subject:	Reservation and correction

Dear Mr. Richards,

Thank you for confirming the booking so quickly, but **184** I noticed that there was an error with it. I will be leaving on the 11th, so I will not need the room on the 12th. Can you re-book and confirm the new dates?

Also, I was unaware of the Richmond Harvest Festival, so that may present a problem. **183** I will be in town working with a client and I've requested a wake-up call not to be late. I am now worried that traffic may be difficult during the week. **185** Do you offer shuttle service or hotel buses for your guests? I don't want to be late for my meetings because I have to wait for a public taxi.

Thank you,

Elijah Graham

---

181 您住房期間，我們飯店及周遭地區將十分繁忙，因為屆時正逢李察蒙德豐收嘉年華。為期一週的慶典期間，本市預計至少會有一天湧入將近十萬人共襄盛舉。我們十分感謝您入住，如有能為您提供更佳住宿服務的事項，請您不吝告知。

服務項目包括	晨喚電話 **182** 免費早餐 客房打掃
711 號房 每晚 92 元（**184** 10 月 3 日至 12 日，共 9 夜）	總計：828 元

感謝您選擇高塔飯店。

傑森，李察斯
接待經理
高塔飯店 田納西州李察蒙德市

收件人：	高塔飯店 <frontdesk@towerhotelten.com>
寄件人：	伊萊亞・葛拉漢 <elijah2019@inoutbox.com>
日期：	9 月 6 日
主旨：	訂房與勘誤

親愛的李察斯先生：

謝謝您快速確認訂房事宜，不過我發現資訊有誤。**184** 我 11 號就要退房，所以不需住房到 12 號。可以請您重訂並確認新的住宿時間嗎？

此外，我原本不曉得會有李察蒙德豐收嘉年華，所以可能會有點問題。**183** 我會進城和客戶處理事情，所以我有要求晨喚電話服務以免遲到。我現在擔心當週交通可能會水洩不通。**185** 您們是否有房客可使用的接駁服務或是飯店巴士？我不希望為了等候計程車而參加會議遲到。

謝謝您
伊萊亞・葛拉漢

字彙 **wake-up call** 晨喚電話　**correction** 勘誤　**unaware** 不曉得的

181

When will the festival take place?
(A) At the end of September
(B) At the beginning of October
(C) In mid-October
(D) At the end of October

中譯 嘉年華何時開始？
(A) 九月底 　　　　　(B) 十月初
(C) 十月中 　　　　　(D) 十月底

解析 第一封電子郵件為飯店寄給顧客的預約確認信；第二封電子郵件為顧客欲更改住宿天數和詢問服務項目的回信。請由第一封電子郵件確認與慶典活動有關的內容。當中提到顧客入住期間會碰到舉行李察蒙德豐收嘉年華的時間。顧客於 10 月 3 日入住，因此慶典的舉行時間為十月初。

182

What service will the hotel provide for Mr. Graham?
(A) Refreshments
(B) Laundry
(C) Room service
(D) A free meal

中譯 飯店會為葛拉漢先生提供何種服務？
(A) 飲料 　　　　　(B) 洗衣服務
(C) 客房服務 　　　(D) 免費餐點

解析 請由「Service included」中確認飯店提供的服務。(D) 將 Complimentary breakfast 改寫成 free meal，故為正確答案。

字彙 refreshment 飲料

183

When is Mr. Graham expected to have a meeting?
(A) On October 3−5
(B) On October 4−6
(C) On October 3−11
(C) On October 11−12

中譯 葛拉漢先生預計何時開會？
(A) 10 月 3 日至 5 日
(B) 10 月 4 日至 6 日
(C) 10 月 3 日至 11 日
(D) 10 月 11 日至 12 日

解析 葛拉漢先生是即將入住飯店的旅客。第二封電子郵件中，雖然未提到開會時間，但他向飯店要求晨喚服務，以防止與客戶開會遲到。回到第一封電子郵件，提供晨喚服務的日子為「from October 4 – 6」，由此可以推測會議時間應在 10 月 4 日至 6 日。

184

How many nights is Mr. Graham planning to stay at the hotel?
(A) 6
(B) 7
(C) 8
(D) 9

中譯 葛拉漢先生預計在飯店入住幾夜？
(A) 6 　　　　　(B) 7
(C) 8 　　　　　(D) 9

解析 第一封電子郵件中，飯店向顧客確認預約日期為「Oct. 3–12, 9 nights」，但在第二封電子郵件中，葛拉漢先生回覆：「I will be leaving on the 11th, so I will not need the room on the 12th.」，表示他預計從 10 月 3 日住到 11 日，共八個晚上。

185

What does Mr. Graham ask the hotel about?
(A) A parking space
(B) The festival dates
(C) The room size
(D) Transportation

中譯 葛拉漢先生要求飯店什麼事？
(A) 停車位
(B) 嘉年華日期
(C) 客房大小
(D) 交通工具

解析 詢問的內容出現在第二封電子郵件中。他對於交通狀況表示擔憂，詢問飯店是否有提供接送住客的接駁車。

Questions 186-190 refer to the following e-mails and gift certificate. 電子郵件 禮券 新增題型

To:	Levey Vacuums <leveyvacuums@service.net>
From:	Felix Muncey <fmuncey@indinet.com>
Date:	November 18
Subject:	PowerRave 3000

To whom it may concern,

I have used the Levey PowerRave 3000 vacuum cleaner for nearly ten years. Unfortunately, last month it stopped working suddenly. I tried everything I could think of to get it to start again, but nothing worked. I read the trouble shooting section of the users' manual, with the same result. 189 I even took it to my local repair shop in Indianapolis, but the owner said he couldn't fix it either. 186 As a last resort, I'm contacting you to see if I can send it to your factory for repair. It has served me well all these years and I'd hate to have to replace it.

Thank you in advance for consideration.

Felix Muncey

收件人：李維吸塵器公司 <leveyvacuums@service.net>
寄件人：菲力克斯・蒙西 <fmuncey@indinet.com>
日期：11 月 18 日
主旨：PowerRave 3000

敬啟者：

　　我使用李維 PowerRave 3000 吸塵器已經將近十年的時間。不幸的是，吸塵器於上個月突然故障。我想盡辦法修理它，但都沒有用。我有翻閱使用說明書的疑難排解內容，但結果還是一樣。189 我甚至拿去印第安納波利斯當地的維修店，但老闆說他也修不了。186 我最後不得不聯絡你們，看看我是否能寄回你們的原廠維修。我這幾年來用得很上手，希望不用換掉這支吸塵器。

　　感謝你們考慮處理此問題，我在此先表達謝意。

菲力克斯・蒙西

To:	Felix Muncey <fmuncey@indinet.com>
From:	Levey Vacuums <leveyvacuums@service.net>
Date:	November 19
Subject:	RE: PowerRave 3000

Dear Mr. Muncey,

Thank you for your inquiry. We are sorry to hear that your PowerRave 3000 is no longer functioning. We regret to inform you that this model has been discontinued. However, since you liked the PowerRave so much, we're confident that you'll also like our new model, 188 the Clean Machine XT (retail price: $250).

收件人：菲力克斯・蒙西 <fmuncey@indinet.com>
寄件人：李維吸塵器公司 <leveyvacuums@service.net>
日期：11 月 19 日
主旨：關於：PowerRave 3000

親愛的蒙西先生：

　　感謝您來信詢問。我們對於您的 PowerRave 3000 故障感到遺憾。但很抱歉通知您，此機型已停產。不過，由於您非常喜愛 PowerRave 吸塵器，我們有信心您也會喜歡我們的新機型 188 Clean Machine XT（零售價是 250 元）。

The Clean Machine XT is our newest model cleaner and has many attractive features. ⑱ Its "one-of-a-kind material" means it is much lighter than any other comparable machine on the market, without sacrificing power. Also, the Clean Machine's revolutionary design allows for access into small corners and under furniture.

To honor your loyalty to the Levey vacuum brand, I'd like to offer you a discount on the purchase of the Clean Machine XT. I've attached the coupon to this message, so you can print it out and show it to one of our authorized outlets near you. We hope that we can retain you as a customer for many years to come.

Sincerely,
Marcia Lopez
Customer Care

Clean Machine XT 是我們最新推出的清掃家電，具有許多吸引人的功能。⑱「獨一無二的材質」使其重量比市面上任何一款同類家電還要輕，而且不會耗電。此外，Clean Machine 革命性的設計使其能清理得到小角落和家具底下。

為了感謝您對李維吸塵器品牌的忠誠度，我想向您提供購買 Clean Machine XT 的優惠折扣。我已經將折價券附於此封信件，您可列印出來，並於離您較近的授權店家出示此券。我們希望將來您仍願意成為我們的顧客。

誠摯地，
瑪西亞‧羅培茲
客服部

---

⑲ Date of issue: November 19

Present this coupon (on a mobile device or in paper form) ⑱ to any of the dealers below to receive 20% off the Clean Machine XT.

Al's Vacuums Gary, IN	**Morristown Appliance** Morristown, IN
Flat Irons Appliance Evansville, IN	⑱ **S & B Vacuums** Indianapolis, IN

*Offer not good on any other make or model.
*Not to be combined with any other discounts or deals.
⑲ *Coupon expires six months after date of issue.

⑲ 發券日期：11 月 19 日

請於以下任一經銷商出示本券（可用手機出示或印出本券），⑱ 您購買 Clean Machine XT 即可打八折。

AI 吸塵器專賣店 印第安納州蓋瑞市
莫里斯鎮家電用品店 印第安納州莫里斯鎮
佛萊特艾文思家電用品店 印第安納州艾文斯維爾市
⑱ **S & B 吸塵器專賣店** 印第安納州印第安納波利斯市

* 其他款式或機型不適用本優惠。
* 不能同時與其他折扣或優惠並用。
⑲ *折價券於發券日的六個月後失效。

字彙 trouble shooting 疑難排解 as a last resort 作為最後手段 one-of-a-kind 獨一無二的
sacrifice 犧牲 outlet 專賣店 retain 保有 make 機型

186

What is the purpose of the first e-mail?
(A) To ask about repair shops nearby
(B) To complain about a product
(C) To inquire about factory repair
(D) To request a refund

中譯 第一封電子郵件的目的為何？
(A) 詢問附近是否有維修店
(B) 抱怨某產品
(C) 詢問是否能送原廠維修
(D) 要求退款

解析 第一篇文章為詢問修理故障吸塵器的電子郵件。當中提到他嘗試很多方法，為做最後一次嘗試，想詢問是否能送到原廠修理。

187

What makes the Clean Machine XT unique?
(A) Its power
(B) Its price
(C) Its size
(D) Its weight

中譯 Clean Machine XT 的獨特體現在何處？
(A) 電力
(B) 價格
(C) 尺寸
(D) 重量

解析 Clean Machine XT 為新型號，出現在第二封電子郵件中。第二段中說明產品的特色：「much lighter than any other comparable machine on the market」，由此可以得知 Clean Machine XT 的特色為重量輕巧。

188

How much is the vacuum with the coupon?
(A) $100
(B) $150
(C) $200
(D) $250

中譯 以折價券購買吸塵器的價格是多少？
(A) 100 元
(B) 150 元
(C) 200 元
(D) 250 元

解析 第二封電子郵件中新型號吸塵器的零售價格為 250 元，並表示會提供優惠。根據折價券上的說明，提供八折（20% off）的優惠。250 元打八折後為 200 元。

189

Which retailer is located in the same town as Mr. Muncey?
(A) Al's Vacuums
(B) Morristown Appliance
(C) Flat Irons Appliance
(D) S & B Vacuums

中譯 哪一家零售商位於蒙西先生所居住的城鎮？
(A) Al 吸塵器公司
(B) 莫里斯鎮家電用品店
(C) 佛萊特艾文思家電用品店
(D) S & B 吸塵器專賣店

解析 第一封電子郵件中寫道：「I even took it to my local repair shop in Indianapolis」，表示蒙西先生住在印第安納波利斯。根據折價券，位在印第安納波利的店家為「S & B 吸塵器專賣店」。

190

When will the coupon expire?
(A) On November 30
(B) On December 31
(C) On January 19
(D) On May 19

中譯 折價券何時過期？
(A) 11 月 30 日
(B) 12 月 31 日
(C) 1 月 19 日
(D) 5 月 19 日

解析 折價券的發行日期（date of issue）為 11 月 19 日，最下面寫道：「Coupon expires six months after date of issue.」，表示期限為六個月，所以將於 5 月 19 日到期。

Questions 191-195 refer to the following article, schedule, and e-mail.

文章　行程表　電子郵件　新增題型

Award-winning author Roland Evans has made us wait four long years, but finally, the follow-up to his best-selling smash *Surprise, Surprise!* is here. November 25 is the day to mark on your calendars: the release of *No Surprise Is a Good Surprise* in hardback. ⑲ **Mr. Evans was holed up in his mountain cabin for nearly six months last year finishing the book,** according to his publicist. And it's worth the wait, say all reviewers lucky enough to get an advance copy.

Apparently, *No Surprise Is a Good Surprise* blends all the terrific characters and exciting actions readers loved in *Surprise, Surprise!* The question we're all asking now: is there a movie in the works, bringing these great books to the big screen? On that, Mr. Evans is being suspiciously quiet. We'll just have to see what surprise may await us.

獲獎無數的作家羅蘭德‧艾文斯睽違四年之久,終於推出他的暢銷書《驚喜連連》的續作。在行事曆上的 11 月 25 日做個特別標記,因為這天是《沒有驚喜就是個大驚喜》精裝版的上架日。根據公關的說法,⑲ 艾文斯先生去年有將近六個月的時間,在山中小屋閉關完成此著作。有幸一睹為快的所有書評一致表示本書值得等待。

很顯然,《沒有驚喜就是個大驚喜》結合了《驚喜連連》中廣受讀者喜愛的絕妙角色和刺激動作場景!現在大家都想問:將來是否會有將此系列大作搬上大螢幕的計畫?艾文斯先生對此問題的沉默反應令人懷疑。我們只能看看是否會有任何驚喜等著我們。

Franklin Books Schedule of Events for December

Date	December 4 ⑲ 8:00 PM	December 7 3:00 PM	⑲ December 11 7:00 PM
Author	Lucia Tanak	Elise Pauley	Roland Evans
Type of book	Fantasy	Children's	⑲ Young Adult

Date	December 14 1:00 PM	December 20 8:00 PM
Author	Emil Vargus	Erin Gutierrez
Type of book	History	Science Fiction

富蘭克林書店 12 月活動表

日期	12 月 4 日 ⑲ 晚上 8:00	12 月 7 日 下午 3:00	⑲ 12 月 11 日 晚上 7:00
作家	露西亞‧塔納克	伊利斯‧波利	羅蘭德‧艾文斯
著作類別	奇幻類	童書類	⑲ 青年類

日期	12 月 14 日 下午 1:00	12 月 20 日 晚上 8:00
作家	艾米爾‧凡格斯	艾琳‧古提瑞茲
著作類別	歷史類	科幻類

To:	Johan Klein <jkdemon@fastline.com>	收件人：約翰・凱連 <jkdemon@fastline.com>
From:	Franklin Books <customer@franklinbooks.com>	寄件人：富蘭克林書店 <customer@franklinbooks.com>
Date:	December 21	日期：12 月 21 日
Subject:	Event calendar	主旨：活動行程

Dear Mr. Klein,

Thank you for your message. ⑲ We are sorry your experience at Mr. Evans's event was unsatisfactory. We do mention on our Website that seating is first come, first served as space is limited. If you arrived a bit late, as you indicated, it's not surprising you weren't able to get a seat. As for the long line for signatures, again, we cannot really help the popularity of our guest authors.

⑲ I will pass along your idea to have more than one event for each author. My supervisor takes customer feedback seriously. I hope you will join us again when another of your favorite authors comes to town.

Thank you.

Frannie Poleman
Franklin Books

親愛的凱連先生：

　　感謝您的來信。⑲ 很遺憾您對艾文斯先生的活動感到體驗不佳。由於場地有限，我們的網站有提醒大家座位採先到先入座的方式。如果如您所述，您當天比較晚到場，那麼您找不到位子可坐也就不足為奇。至於簽書活動大排長龍的現象，因為特邀作家人氣火紅，我們對此真的無能為力。

　　⑲ 但我會轉告您的建議，將每位作家的活動場次增加為兩場以上。我的主管非常重視顧客的意見反饋。希望您喜愛的作家下次前來舉辦活動時，您能再度光臨。

謝謝您。

佛蘭妮・波曼
富蘭克林書店

字彙 follow-up 後續　smash 受歡迎的作品　hardback 精裝書　be holed up 躲起來
mountain cabin 山中小屋　publicist 公關，宣傳人員　reviewer 評論家
advance copy 正式發行前的副本　blend 結合　suspiciously 令人懷疑地

191

What is mentioned about Mr. Evans?

(A) He has a shelter in the mountains.
(B) He is making a movie.
(C) He is taking a long vacation.
(D) He wants to quit writing.

中譯 關於艾文斯先生，文中提及了什麼？

(A) 他在山中有隱身的地方。
(B) 他在拍電影。
(C) 他在度長假。
(D) 他想放棄寫作。

解析 由第一篇報導，可以得知艾文斯先生為一名作家。當中提到：「Mr. Evans was holed up in his mountain cabin for nearly six months last year finishing the book」，表示他在山上有住所；(B) 雖然有提到電影，但並未確認由他製作，因此該選項並不適當。

字彙 shelter 遮蔽處　quit 放棄

192

What type of book is *No Surprise Is a Good Surprise*?
(A) Children's
(B) Fantasy
(C) Science Fiction
(D) Young adult

中譯 《沒有驚喜就是個大驚喜》是何種類型的著作？
(A) 童書類　　　　　(B) 奇幻類
(C) 科幻類　　　　　(D) 青年類

解析 書本的類型出現在富蘭克林書店的活動時間表中。羅蘭德・艾文斯的 **Type of book** 那欄寫道：「**Young Adult**」。

193

What can be said of Franklin Books?
(A) It closes at 8:00 PM.
(B) It did not hold morning events in December.
(C) It has a large event space.
(D) It holds an event once a week.

中譯 關於富蘭克林書店，我們可以得知什麼？
(A) 晚上 8 點關門。
(B) 12 月沒有早上的活動。
(C) 具有大型活動空間。
(D) 一週舉辦一次活動。

解析 根據十二月份的活動時間表，所有活動都在中午過後舉辦。

194

When did Mr. Klein likely attend an event at Franklin Books?
(A) On December 4
(B) On December 11
(C) On December 14
(D) On December 20

中譯 凱連先生可能參加過富蘭克林書店在哪一天舉辦的活動？
(A) 12 月 4 日
(B) 12 月 11 日
(C) 12 月 14 日
(D) 12 月 20 日

解析 第三篇文章是電子郵件，寄件人為書店員工，收件人為凱連先生。電子郵件中提到：「**We are sorry your experience at Mr. Evans's event was unsatisfactory.**」，表示凱連先生參加了艾文斯作家的活動。根據時間表，艾文斯作家的活動舉辦日期為 **12 月 11 日**。

195

What does Ms. Poleman promise to do for Mr. Klein?
(A) Call him the next time an author comes
(B) Give his suggestion to her boss
(C) Save him a seat at an event
(D) Send him a discount coupon

中譯 波曼小姐承諾幫凱連先生做什麼事？
(A) 下次有作家舉辦活動時聯繫他
(B) 將他的建議轉告上司
(C) 幫他保留活動座位
(D) 寄送折價券給他

解析 電子郵件後半段寫道：「**I will pass along your idea to have more than one event for each author.**」，表示書店員工波曼小姐承諾會轉達凱連先生的意見，接著又提到主管非常重視顧客的意見。由此段話可以得知波曼小姐承諾會向主管轉達凱連先生的意見。

Actual Test 5

PART 7

From:	Jarvis Sloan <jsloan@allproav.net>
To:	Stephanie Ross <sross@ultrawave.com>
Date:	November 7
Subject:	Presentation equipment

Dear Ms. Ross,

196 Thank you for your e-mail about our line of presentation equipment. I have attached a spec sheet to this e-mail. On the attachment, you will find a brief of features, plus the price ranges. **200** For more details, including color pictures and a helpful video on each of these products, please see our Website at www. allproav.net. You can also set up an account and purchase any item directly from us via our Website.

Please don't hesitate to contact me if I can be of further assistance to you in meeting your company's audio-visual needs.

Sincerely,
Jarvis Sloan
All-Pro Audio-Visual, Inc.
555-2839

寄件人：賈維斯 · 斯隆恩 <jsloan@allproav.net>
收件人：史蒂芬妮 · 羅斯 <sross@ultrawave.com>
日期：11 月 7 日
主旨：簡報設備

親愛的羅斯小姐：

196 感謝您來信詢問我們的簡報設備。我已經在此封電子郵件附上規格表。您可在附檔看到功能簡介與價格範圍。**200** 如需了解更多細節，包括彩色圖片與各款產品清楚的展示影片，請您前往我們的網站：www.allproav.net。您亦可在網站註冊帳戶，直接在上面購買任何商品。

如果您需要我提供更多協助來滿足貴公司的影音需求，請不吝與我聯繫。

誠摯地，
賈維斯 · 斯隆恩
全方位影音公司
555-2839

All-Pro Audio-Visual, Inc. 全方位影音公司

Projectors – portable and in-house
- Choose from 2.5 or 4 GB internal memory
- Wi-Fi connectivity
- USB capability
- Portable models are lightweight for easy travel
- LED lamp never needs replacing
- Price range $299-$495, depending on memory size

Screens
- Portable – easy set up and break down (includes travel case)
- Mounted (permanent) – electric or manual pull-down
198 - 92-120 inches
- Prices range from $99 to $159, depending on size

Smartboards
- Like a giant tablet in your conference room
- **197** Interactive screen makes input from multiple people possible

投影機──攜帶式與室內固定式
* 有 2.5 GB 或 4 GB 內建記憶體的選擇
* 可連接無線網路
* 具 USB 插槽
* 攜帶式機型十分輕盈，適合旅用
* LED 燈不需更換
* 價格視記憶體大小而定，範圍落在 299 元到 495 元之間

螢幕
* 便攜式──易於組裝與拆卸（內含旅用收納包）
* 固定式（永久性）──可電動或手動下拉展開
198 * 92–120 吋
* 價格視螢幕大小而定，範圍落在 99 元至 159 元之間

電子白板
* 形同會議室裡的巨型平板
* **197** 互動式螢幕可供多人同時使用

- Multi-touch screen
- Dry-erase surface for drawing and writing
- Prices range from $559 to $999

The latest in presentation technology, these SMART boards are truly cutting-edge! Though a bit pricey, the collaboration they inspire makes it worth the cost.

* 螢幕具多重觸控的功能
* 表面可乾擦，適用於繪圖和書寫
* 價格範圍落在 559 元至 999 元之間

此智慧白板採用最新簡報科技，堪稱站在時代最前端！雖然價格不斐，其所帶來的協力效益可謂物有所值。

To:	Jarvis Sloan <jsloan@allproav.net>
From:	Stephanie Ross <sross@ultrawave.com>
Date:	November 9
Subject:	RE: Presentation equipment

Dear Mr. Sloan,

Thank you for your quick reply. ⑲ **While I'm interested in having a smartboard, the budget for our new start-up does not allow for this type of purchase right now. Please keep me informed of any reduction in price as you introduce new lines in the future.**

For the moment, ⑱ **I'm interested in the cheapest projector, plus the 92-inch screen.** ⑳ **Please let me know how I can purchase these, as I didn't see that information on the spec sheet.**

Thank you for your help.

Stephanie Ross
Ultra Wave

收件人：賈維斯・斯隆恩
<jsloan@allproav.net>
寄件人：史蒂芬妮・羅斯
<sross@ultrawave.com>
日期：11 月 9 日
主旨：關於：簡報設備

親愛的斯隆恩先生：

謝謝你迅速回信，⑲ 雖然我對智慧白板感興趣，但我們新興公司的預算目前無法購買此類產品。將來貴公司推出新系列產品時，如有降價訊息，再請你隨時通知我。

現階段來說，⑱ 我感興趣的是最低價的投影機和 92 吋的螢幕。⑳ 請告知我購買上述產品的方法，因為我在規格表上沒有看到購買方式的資訊。

感謝你的協助。

史蒂芬妮・羅斯
奧創之浪公司

字彙 **spec sheet** 規格表 **brief** 簡短的 **audio-visual** 影音的 **hesitate** 猶豫 **portable** 可攜帶的 **in-house** 公司內部的 **connectivity** 連線 **capability** 功能 **cutting-edge** 最先進的 **pricey** 價格不斐的 **inspire** 激發 **reduction** 減少

196

Why does Mr. Sloan send the e-mail to Ms. Ross?
(A) To respond to her complaint
(B) To respond to her inquiry
(C) To schedule a meeting time with her
(D) To thank her for her business

中譯 斯隆恩先生為何寄電子郵件給羅斯小姐？
(A) 回應她的申訴信
(B) 回應她的詢問
(C) 與她安排開會時間
(D) 感謝她購貨

解析 由第一封電子郵件的署名，可以得知斯隆恩先生任職於販售簡報設備的「全方位影音公司」；羅斯小姐為詢問產品的人。另外，當中提到：「**Thank you for your e-mail about our line of presentation equipment.**」，表示這封郵件為答覆羅斯小姐問題的回信。

197

According to the information, what is an advantage of a smartboard?
(A) Groups can work together more easily on it.
(B) It can be used as a video screen.
(C) It can be easily carried in a case.
(D) It is cheaper than a projector.

中譯 根據上述資訊，智慧白板的優點為何？
(A) 團隊成員能更輕鬆地同步操作。
(B) 可作為放映螢幕。
(C) 可裝於收納包而方便攜帶。
(D) 比投影機便宜。

解析 請由第二篇文章的 Smartboards 產品介紹中確認產品資訊。當中寫道：「Interactive screen makes input from multiple people possible」，表示互動式電子白板的優點為可供很多人同時輸入。

198

How much will Ms. Ross most likely pay for a screen?
(A) $99
(B) $159
(C) $299
(D) $495

中譯 羅斯小姐最有可能支付多少錢購買螢幕？
(A) 99 元　　　　(B) 159 元
(C) 299 元　　　(D) 495 元

解析 產品資訊當中，螢幕的價格為「Prices range from $99 to $159, depending on size」，表示尺寸最小的螢幕價格為 99 元，最小的螢幕為 92 吋。而在羅斯小姐傳送的電子郵件中寫道：「I'm interested in the cheapest projector, plus the 92-inch screen.」，表示她要支付 99 元。

199

What does Ms. Ross mention about the smartboard?
(A) Her boss does not understand its functions.
(B) Her company cannot afford to buy it.
(C) Her company does not need it.
(D) Her coworkers have never used one before.

中譯 關於智慧白板，羅斯小姐提出什麼？
(A) 她的上司不了解此產品的功能。
(B) 她的公司買不起此產品。
(C) 她的公司不需要此產品。
(D) 她的同事從未使用過此類產品。

解析 羅斯小姐提及電子白板的內容為：「While I'm interested in having a smartboard, the budget for our new start-up does not allow for this type of purchase right now.」，表示她的公司目前沒有足夠的錢購買電子白板。

字彙 afford 買得起

200

What is implied about Ms. Ross?
(A) She did not look at the Website.
(B) She is the head of an established company.
(C) She is new at Mr. Sloan's company.
(D) She will give a presentation to Mr. Sloan.

中譯 關於羅斯小姐，可從文中判斷什麼？
(A) 她沒有去看網站內容。
(B) 她是一家歷史悠久的公司的主管。
(C) 她是斯隆恩先生公司的新進人員。
(D) 她會向斯隆恩先生做簡報。

解析 羅斯小姐傳送的電子郵件中，後半段提到：「Please let me know how I can purchase these, as I didn't see that information on the spec sheet.」。但在第一封電子郵件中，斯隆恩先生表示：「You can also set up an account and purchase any item directly from us via our Website.」，明確告知購買方式。由此可以推測羅斯小姐並未上網查看，所以不清楚購買方式。

Actual Test
解答總表

1. (B)	2. (D)	3. (A)	4. (D)	5. (B)	6. (D)	7. (A)	8. (A)	9. (B)	10. (A)
11. (B)	12. (C)	13. (B)	14. (B)	15. (B)	16. (A)	17. (B)	18. (A)	19. (C)	20. (C)
21. (B)	22. (A)	23. (A)	24. (C)	25. (C)	26. (A)	27. (A)	28. (B)	29. (B)	30. (A)
31. (C)	32. (C)	33. (B)	34. (C)	35. (B)	36. (C)	37. (B)	38. (C)	39. (C)	40. (A)
41. (B)	42. (C)	43. (B)	44. (C)	45. (A)	46. (B)	47. (A)	48. (C)	49. (D)	50. (C)
51. (B)	52. (B)	53. (C)	54. (B)	55. (A)	56. (A)	57. (D)	58. (B)	59. (D)	60. (B)
61. (D)	62. (D)	63. (C)	64. (C)	65. (C)	66. (D)	67. (D)	68. (A)	69. (B)	70. (D)
71. (C)	72. (B)	73. (D)	74. (A)	75. (D)	76. (A)	77. (B)	78. (C)	79. (C)	80. (B)
81. (B)	82. (A)	83. (B)	84. (A)	85. (C)	86. (D)	87. (D)	88. (D)	89. (C)	90. (C)
91. (A)	92. (D)	93. (D)	94. (C)	95. (D)	96. (A)	97. (A)	98. (D)	99. (D)	100. (D)
101. (A)	102. (B)	103. (C)	104. (D)	105. (D)	106. (C)	107. (B)	108. (D)	109. (D)	110. (C)
111. (B)	112. (C)	113. (C)	114. (B)	115. (D)	116. (D)	117. (D)	118. (B)	119. (B)	120. (B)
121. (D)	122. (B)	123. (B)	124. (A)	125. (B)	126. (B)	127. (B)	128. (B)	129. (C)	130. (C)
131. (A)	132. (D)	133. (D)	134. (C)	135. (B)	136. (D)	137. (B)	138. (C)	139. (C)	140. (A)
141. (C)	142. (B)	143. (D)	144. (C)	145. (D)	146. (D)	147. (D)	148. (B)	149. (B)	150. (A)
151. (B)	152. (A)	153. (D)	154. (D)	155. (A)	156. (B)	157. (A)	158. (B)	159. (C)	160. (D)
161. (A)	162. (B)	163. (D)	164. (B)	165. (C)	166. (B)	167. (B)	168. (B)	169. (C)	170. (C)
171. (C)	172. (A)	173. (A)	174. (C)	175. (B)	176. (A)	177. (C)	178. (D)	179. (B)	180. (C)
181. (D)	182. (D)	183. (B)	184. (B)	185. (B)	186. (A)	187. (B)	188. (A)	189. (B)	190. (D)
191. (C)	192. (D)	193. (B)	194. (A)	195. (C)	196. (C)	197. (C)	198. (A)	199. (A)	200. (C)

1. (D)	2. (D)	3. (B)	4. (D)	5. (D)	6. (D)	7. (A)	8. (C)	9. (B)	10. (A)
11. (A)	12. (C)	13. (B)	14. (C)	15. (A)	16. (B)	17. (B)	18. (A)	19. (C)	20. (B)
21. (A)	22. (A)	23. (C)	24. (C)	25. (A)	26. (B)	27. (A)	28. (B)	29. (B)	30. (C)
31. (A)	32. (B)	33. (D)	34. (C)	35. (D)	36. (D)	37. (B)	38. (A)	39. (C)	40. (B)
41. (A)	42. (C)	43. (C)	44. (B)	45. (B)	46. (B)	47. (D)	48. (D)	49. (D)	50. (B)
51. (D)	52. (C)	53. (D)	54. (A)	55. (D)	56. (C)	57. (C)	58. (D)	59. (B)	60. (D)
61. (B)	62. (B)	63. (A)	64. (C)	65. (D)	66. (A)	67. (A)	68. (D)	69. (D)	70. (B)
71. (D)	72. (B)	73. (D)	74. (B)	75. (B)	76. (D)	77. (D)	78. (D)	79. (A)	80. (D)
81. (D)	82. (D)	83. (B)	84. (B)	85. (C)	86. (D)	87. (B)	88. (D)	89. (B)	90. (C)
91. (B)	92. (B)	93. (A)	94. (D)	95. (A)	96. (D)	97. (A)	98. (D)	99. (C)	100. (D)
101. (C)	102. (C)	103. (C)	104. (D)	105. (B)	106. (A)	107. (D)	108. (A)	109. (D)	110. (A)
111. (D)	112. (A)	113. (A)	114. (A)	115. (A)	116. (C)	117. (D)	118. (B)	119. (D)	120. (B)
121. (C)	122. (B)	123. (D)	124. (A)	125. (A)	126. (A)	127. (C)	128. (C)	129. (B)	130. (C)
131. (C)	132. (A)	133. (C)	134. (A)	135. (A)	136. (A)	137. (D)	138. (B)	139. (B)	140. (C)
141. (A)	142. (D)	143. (C)	144. (D)	145. (D)	146. (D)	147. (B)	148. (A)	149. (B)	150. (B)
151. (D)	152. (D)	153. (C)	154. (C)	155. (C)	156. (A)	157. (C)	158. (A)	159. (D)	160. (C)
161. (B)	162. (B)	163. (C)	164. (B)	165. (D)	166. (D)	167. (D)	168. (A)	169. (C)	170. (D)
171. (D)	172. (D)	173. (B)	174. (A)	175. (D)	176. (B)	177. (B)	178. (B)	179. (B)	180. (A)
181. (A)	182. (C)	183. (B)	184. (D)	185. (D)	186. (B)	187. (A)	188. (B)	189. (D)	190. (D)
191. (C)	192. (D)	193. (D)	194. (C)	195. (C)	196. (D)	197. (A)	198. (A)	199. (B)	200. (D)

1. (A)	**2.** (A)	**3.** (B)	**4.** (C)	**5.** (B)	**6.** (D)	**7.** (A)	**8.** (C)	**9.** (C)	**10.** (B)
11. (B)	**12.** (A)	**13.** (B)	**14.** (C)	**15.** (B)	**16.** (A)	**17.** (A)	**18.** (B)	**19.** (C)	**20.** (C)
21. (A)	**22.** (B)	**23.** (A)	**24.** (C)	**25.** (B)	**26.** (A)	**27.** (B)	**28.** (B)	**29.** (C)	**30.** (A)
31. (C)	**32.** (C)	**33.** (C)	**34.** (B)	**35.** (D)	**36.** (B)	**37.** (B)	**38.** (C)	**39.** (A)	**40.** (B)
41. (A)	**42.** (D)	**43.** (B)	**44.** (D)	**45.** (B)	**46.** (C)	**47.** (D)	**48.** (D)	**49.** (D)	**50.** (A)
51. (A)	**52.** (A)	**53.** (A)	**54.** (A)	**55.** (C)	**56.** (D)	**57.** (D)	**58.** (A)	**59.** (B)	**60.** (D)
61. (A)	**62.** (D)	**63.** (B)	**64.** (A)	**65.** (A)	**66.** (D)	**67.** (B)	**68.** (D)	**69.** (D)	**70.** (B)
71. (D)	**72.** (C)	**73.** (D)	**74.** (A)	**75.** (C)	**76.** (C)	**77.** (B)	**78.** (A)	**79.** (A)	**80.** (A)
81. (D)	**82.** (A)	**83.** (D)	**84.** (B)	**85.** (D)	**86.** (D)	**87.** (D)	**88.** (A)	**89.** (A)	**90.** (A)
91. (A)	**92.** (C)	**93.** (B)	**94.** (A)	**95.** (B)	**96.** (C)	**97.** (D)	**98.** (A)	**99.** (A)	**100.** (B)
101. (C)	**102.** (D)	**103.** (A)	**104.** (C)	**105.** (C)	**106.** (D)	**107.** (C)	**108.** (D)	**109.** (D)	**110.** (A)
111. (B)	**112.** (D)	**113.** (D)	**114.** (A)	**115.** (C)	**116.** (B)	**117.** (B)	**118.** (C)	**119.** (D)	**120.** (D)
121. (A)	**122.** (C)	**123.** (C)	**124.** (C)	**125.** (C)	**126.** (D)	**127.** (C)	**128.** (A)	**129.** (A)	**130.** (C)
131. (B)	**132.** (B)	**133.** (A)	**134.** (C)	**135.** (D)	**136.** (A)	**137.** (B)	**138.** (B)	**139.** (A)	**140.** (A)
141. (A)	**142.** (C)	**143.** (A)	**144.** (B)	**145.** (B)	**146.** (A)	**147.** (B)	**148.** (A)	**149.** (B)	**150.** (B)
151. (B)	**152.** (B)	**153.** (A)	**154.** (D)	**155.** (C)	**156.** (C)	**157.** (A)	**158.** (B)	**159.** (C)	**160.** (D)
161. (C)	**162.** (A)	**163.** (C)	**164.** (B)	**165.** (D)	**166.** (D)	**167.** (B)	**168.** (C)	**169.** (B)	**170.** (A)
171. (B)	**172.** (D)	**173.** (C)	**174.** (D)	**175.** (A)	**176.** (A)	**177.** (B)	**178.** (B)	**179.** (A)	**180.** (C)
181. (D)	**182.** (D)	**183.** (A)	**184.** (A)	**185.** (A)	**186.** (D)	**187.** (B)	**188.** (A)	**189.** (B)	**190.** (D)
191. (D)	**192.** (C)	**193.** (C)	**194.** (B)	**195.** (A)	**196.** (D)	**197.** (A)	**198.** (D)	**199.** (A)	**200.** (D)

1. (A)	2. (C)	3. (C)	4. (C)	5. (B)	6. (D)	7. (A)	8. (C)	9. (B)	10. (B)
11. (B)	12. (C)	13. (A)	14. (B)	15. (C)	16. (A)	17. (B)	18. (A)	19. (B)	20. (A)
21. (C)	22. (A)	23. (B)	24. (A)	25. (B)	26. (C)	27. (C)	28. (A)	29. (C)	30. (B)
31. (C)	32. (C)	33. (C)	34. (B)	35. (B)	36. (B)	37. (B)	38. (B)	39. (D)	40. (D)
41. (A)	42. (C)	43. (B)	44. (C)	45. (A)	46. (C)	47. (B)	48. (D)	49. (C)	50. (A)
51. (B)	52. (D)	53. (D)	54. (C)	55. (A)	56. (A)	57. (A)	58. (A)	59. (A)	60. (D)
61. (C)	62. (D)	63. (A)	64. (C)	65. (C)	66. (C)	67. (D)	68. (B)	69. (B)	70. (A)
71. (B)	72. (A)	73. (B)	74. (D)	75. (B)	76. (D)	77. (D)	78. (B)	79. (D)	80. (C)
81. (C)	82. (B)	83. (B)	84. (C)	85. (D)	86. (D)	87. (C)	88. (C)	89. (A)	90. (B)
91. (B)	92. (A)	93. (A)	94. (B)	95. (C)	96. (C)	97. (C)	98. (C)	99. (D)	100. (C)
101. (D)	102. (C)	103. (D)	104. (C)	105. (B)	106. (D)	107. (C)	108. (B)	109. (C)	110. (A)
111. (B)	112. (C)	113. (B)	114. (B)	115. (B)	116. (D)	117. (C)	118. (D)	119. (D)	120. (A)
121. (C)	122. (C)	123. (A)	124. (C)	125. (C)	126. (C)	127. (B)	128. (C)	129. (C)	130. (D)
131. (C)	132. (D)	133. (B)	134. (D)	135. (A)	136. (D)	137. (B)	138. (B)	139. (D)	140. (B)
141. (A)	142. (B)	143. (A)	144. (B)	145. (C)	146. (A)	147. (C)	148. (D)	149. (B)	150. (A)
151. (B)	152. (A)	153. (B)	154. (D)	155. (C)	156. (A)	157. (D)	158. (C)	159. (B)	160. (A)
161. (C)	162. (A)	163. (C)	164. (A)	165. (D)	166. (B)	167. (D)	168. (A)	169. (A)	170. (B)
171. (A)	172. (B)	173. (D)	174. (D)	175. (D)	176. (D)	177. (D)	178. (D)	179. (B)	180. (B)
181. (C)	182. (B)	183. (B)	184. (C)	185. (A)	186. (C)	187. (D)	188. (B)	189. (A)	190. (A)
191. (C)	192. (D)	193. (A)	194. (C)	195. (D)	196. (B)	197. (A)	198. (B)	199. (D)	200. (B)

1. (C)	2. (D)	3. (D)	4. (B)	5. (A)	6. (D)	7. (A)	8. (C)	9. (A)	10. (C)
11. (B)	12. (B)	13. (B)	14. (C)	15. (A)	16. (A)	17. (B)	18. (C)	19. (A)	20. (B)
21. (B)	22. (A)	23. (C)	24. (B)	25. (A)	26. (B)	27. (C)	28. (B)	29. (A)	30. (C)
31. (B)	32. (A)	33. (D)	34. (D)	35. (B)	36. (C)	37. (C)	38. (D)	39. (A)	40. (B)
41. (D)	42. (D)	43. (D)	44. (C)	45. (D)	46. (C)	47. (B)	48. (B)	49. (A)	50. (A)
51. (B)	52. (B)	53. (A)	54. (C)	55. (C)	56. (D)	57. (B)	58. (D)	59. (B)	60. (D)
61. (C)	62. (B)	63. (A)	64. (B)	65. (C)	66. (B)	67. (C)	68. (C)	69. (B)	70. (C)
71. (D)	72. (B)	73. (C)	74. (D)	75. (A)	76. (B)	77. (A)	78. (D)	79. (B)	80. (A)
81. (C)	82. (A)	83. (C)	84. (B)	85. (B)	86. (A)	87. (C)	88. (D)	89. (A)	90. (B)
91. (A)	92. (A)	93. (C)	94. (A)	95. (C)	96. (C)	97. (A)	98. (D)	99. (D)	100. (D)
101. (D)	102. (C)	103. (A)	104. (B)	105. (A)	106. (A)	107. (C)	108. (C)	109. (B)	110. (D)
111. (A)	112. (B)	113. (D)	114. (D)	115. (A)	116. (C)	117. (C)	118. (C)	119. (C)	120. (C)
121. (D)	122. (C)	123. (D)	124. (D)	125. (D)	126. (B)	127. (D)	128. (C)	129. (B)	130. (B)
131. (C)	132. (C)	133. (B)	134. (A)	135. (C)	136. (A)	137. (A)	138. (A)	139. (C)	140. (C)
141. (D)	142. (B)	143. (C)	144. (C)	145. (C)	146. (A)	147. (B)	148. (C)	149. (B)	150. (B)
151. (C)	152. (A)	153. (C)	154. (B)	155. (B)	156. (D)	157. (C)	158. (D)	159. (D)	160. (D)
161. (A)	162. (C)	163. (C)	164. (D)	165. (D)	166. (D)	167. (C)	168. (B)	169. (C)	170. (B)
171. (A)	172. (B)	173. (C)	174. (B)	175. (D)	176. (D)	177. (C)	178. (B)	179. (A)	180. (B)
181. (B)	182. (D)	183. (B)	184. (C)	185. (D)	186. (C)	187. (D)	188. (C)	189. (D)	190. (D)
191. (A)	192. (D)	193. (B)	194. (B)	195. (B)	196. (B)	197. (A)	198. (A)	199. (B)	200. (A)